CHARLOTTE BRONTË

SHIRLEY
THE PROFESSOR

WITH AN INTRODUCTION
BY REBECCA FRASER

EVERYMAN'S LIBRARY
Alfred A. Knopf New York London Toronto
292

THIS IS A BORZOI BOOK
PUBLISHED BY ALFRED A. KNOPF

First included in Everyman's Library, 2008
Introduction Copyright © 2008 by Rebecca Fraser
Bibliography and Chronology Copyright © 2008 by Everyman's Library
Typography by Peter B. Willberg

US website: www.randomhouse.com/everymans

ISBN: 978-0-307-26821-1 (US)
978-1-85715-292-0 (UK)

A CIP catalogue reference for this book is available from the
British Library

Book design by Barbara de Wilde and Carol Devine Carson

Typeset in the UK by AccComputing, North Barrow, Somerset

Printed and bound in Germany by GGP Media GmbH, Pössneck

CHARLOTTE BRONTË

INTRODUCTION

The Professor and *Shirley* have always suffered from being the stable-mates of *Jane Eyre* and *Villette*. In its time *Jane Eyre*'s realism and honesty meant it was widely regarded as a 'dangerous book', while *Villette*, as George Eliot wrote, was 'almost preternatural in its power'. Today *Jane Eyre* is still one of the most popular novels in the English language, while *Villette* maintains its position as an extraordinary portrait of the feminine psyche. Beside such race-horses, *The Professor*, a gentle love story set in a school in Brussels, and *Shirley*, a novel of industrial strife in Yorkshire during the Napoleonic Wars, might look a little humdrum. Yet to those fascinated by the obscure clergyman's daughter who astounded the Victorian establishment, they make essential reading. Their heroines anticipate the revolutionary nature of their more celebrated sisters and the books boldly explore the themes of *Jane Eyre* and *Villette*, particularly the question of how women can find happiness in a society inimical to their needs. Not only are they highly enjoyable – *Shirley* is richly comic, while Mrs Gaskell described Frances Henri as 'the most charming woman [she] ever drew' – they also demonstrate that work-in-progress, the ongoing development of Charlotte Brontë as a writer.

Written in 1846, after the novelist returned from that single visit abroad which was to have such an effect upon her creative powers, *The Professor* was not to be published in her lifetime. Charlotte had spent two years in Brussels, from 1842 to 1844, being taught by a gifted literature professor, M. Constantin Heger. His wife ran the school in the Rue Isabelle where both Charlotte and Emily Brontë boarded as special students. Their aim was to brush up their French so that they might set up a boarding school of their own in their father's parsonage at Haworth, in West Yorkshire. At a time when there were few jobs for women, opening a school for girls seemed a good solution to the problem of earning a living for the highly sensitive Brontës whose means were small. They had tried governessing and detested the social condescension it entailed. Emily, who disliked parting from her natural habitat, loathed the Heger school and left after a year. Charlotte, who had conceived what would become a passionate crush on the charismatic M. Heger, the only gifted teacher she had ever encountered, stayed for another year, inspired by his influence. Then she too left, having become practically ill from the intensity of her feelings. But the school plans were blighted by her brother Branwell's presence at home. Now a disgraced ex-tutor, he was rapidly descending into fatal alcoholism. Matters were further complicated when his adulterous relationship with his employer's wife, Mrs Robinson, forced Charlotte to confront the nature of her own feelings for M. Heger with whom she had attempted to carry on a correspondence, which his wife, at least, felt went beyond the bounds of ordinary friendship.

It has been argued that Charlotte Brontë's famous yearning letters to M. Heger were themselves a form of literary creation. By 1845 when Heger's silence made it obvious there was to be no reply, the effect was to throw Charlotte back onto real artistic endeavour. Once again she began writing a book, but this time she was determined it should be published. Although being a professional writer had been a serious ambition since she was a young girl, it also seemed the only reasonably genteel way of earning a living left to her. Obsessed by literature from a very early age – she had even written to the Poet Laureate Robert Southey for an opinion of her work when she was twenty-one – Charlotte had already written at least ten novels; they were experiments of precocious brilliance in voice and style. Despite being told by Southey that 'literature cannot be the business of a woman's life and it ought not to be', she had never really abandoned her ambition. There is evidence that Charlotte even showed some of her writing to M. Heger. He too appears to have believed that writing was an inappropriate career for the female sex.

An isolated parsonage on the edge of the Yorkshire moors was not a promising situation from which to find a London publisher. Nevertheless the outwardly shy, but inwardly steely Charlotte Brontë had the sort of drive that meant she would not give up. Because she and her sisters believed, as Charlotte

put it, 'that authoresses are likely to be looked on with prejudice', they adopted the noms de plume of Acton, Ellis and
Currer Bell. They were not 'positively masculine' which they
felt would have been dishonest, but they were not feminine
either. By 1846 Charlotte had published her and her sisters'
poems, and hoped to publish *The Professor*, a novel which she
deliberately intended to be satisfyingly realistic. It was to have
the sort of everyday quality which she felt to be lacking in the
current crop of literary offerings. As Charlotte wrote, 'I said
to myself that my hero should work his way through life as
I had seen real living men work theirs – that he should never
get a shilling he had not earned – that no sudden turns should
lift him in a moment to wealth and high station'. And certainly
there are no sudden turns for her hero, the scholarly young
William Crimsworth, born to an uneasy union between an
aristocratic lady and a businessman.

Having rejected his short-tempered aristocratic relations
because he does not want a career in the Church or what would
be in effect an arranged marriage, Crimsworth moves to Yorkshire to work for his cold-hearted manufacturer brother. But
things do not go much better in Yorkshire. Sacked for no fault
of his own from his job as foreign correspondence clerk, he
leaves for Brussels to become a teacher. There he finds happiness at last with a virtuous, sympathetic and impoverished
young lacemaker, Frances Henri, to whom he teaches English.
The character of Frances Henri has more than a hint of Jane
Eyre. The book also includes a first portrait of Charlotte's
Yorkshire friend Mary Taylor's father as the kindly republican,
French-speaking factory owner York Hunsden who reappears
in *Shirley* as Hiram Yorke. It is Mr Hunsden who gets William
Crimsworth to Brussels just as it was Mr Taylor and his family
who encouraged Charlotte to go to there. As York Hunsden's
name suggests, he is a repository of the Yorkshire qualities, for
good or bad, which Charlotte, the child of two transplanted
Celts, found so distinctive.

So far, so everyday. In fact things were not quite as everyday
as they seemed. After reading *Jane Eyre* the critic G. H. Lewes
had told Currer Bell she must watch out for melodrama, and
to 'adhere to the real'. In response she revealed, 'When I first

began to write, so impressed was I with the truth of the principles you advocate, that I determined to take Nature and Truth as my sole guides... I restrained imagination, eschewed romance, repressed excitement; over-bright colouring, too, I avoided, and sought to produce something which should be soft, grave and true.' But this was not strictly accurate. For all Charlotte's later dedication to realism, in fact her first writing, the writing she had practised with her then beloved brother Branwell since her teens, was quite the opposite. Until her late twenties when she left for Brussels, she and Branwell lived in an imaginary, sensual pseudo-Byronic world they invented and wrote about obsessively. As is well known, Charlotte and her siblings were left motherless at the age of six. From then on they ran wild. The four little Brontë sisters briefly attended a harsh and badly run school at Cowan Bridge in Lancashire whose neglect caused two of them to die of tuberculosis. That was the last attempt at formal schooling for Charlotte until she was almost fifteen.

It was not for another six years that she went to school again, Miss Wooler's establishment at Roe Head. But the expense meant it could only last for three terms, though she would return as a teacher a few years later. At Miss Wooler's Charlotte made lifelong friends with ordinary girls of her own age who had nothing of her brother's febrile and excitable nature. In contrast to Branwell they were soothing and kind, offering the timorous Charlotte good sense and simplicity as well as the contacts for subsequent posts as a governess. Nevertheless Charlotte Brontë spent the many years between these short glimpses of normality submerged in the imaginary kingdom known as Angria. A very isolated childhood in the wilds of Yorkshire, the tragic early deaths of her mother and siblings, buried in the churchyard at the end of their garden, and a highly sensitive, artistic nature meant that to her and Branwell the private world books offered was overwhelmingly attractive. Writing and reading became a compulsive way of life which made up for their lack of human contact.

And in the novels about Angria, which grew out of a group of toy soldiers their father brought back as a present one winter's evening, Charlotte and Branwell could be anyone they liked.

Initially very influenced by Sir Walter Scott, later by Byron, they lived and breathed an imaginary existence. From soldiery it moved on to intense amatory intrigue, between their two main protagonists the Duke of Zamorna (Charlotte's) and the Duke of Northangerland (Branwell's), and passionate unortho-dox heroines (Charlotte's). But they also took pleasure in assuming the personas of all the writers and bookmen of the day, details of whose way of life the ambitious pair gleaned from literary journals and magazines such as *Blackwood's*.

By the time Charlotte left for Brussels she had written a great many novels which Mrs Gaskell would deplore (though she did not read most of them) as 'the wildest and most incoherent things . . . They give one the idea of creative power carried to the verge of insanity'. Like many women of her time whose actions were limited by poverty and circumstance, the main part of Charlotte Brontë's life was passed with only her siblings and father for company. In a later age she would have gone to university; in 1837 there were few chances of escape. But by the time she wrote *The Professor* Charlotte's once happy collaboration with Branwell had come to seem like a dangerous addiction. For some time before she left for Brussels Charlotte had been aware that the life of constant 'making out', her other name for describing the imaginary world she and Branwell inhabited, had become dangerous for her sanity.

Her great friend Mary Taylor, the original of Rose Yorke in *Shirley*, would scold her about the imaginary world of which Charlotte had given her a carefully edited version: 'The whole family used to "make out" histories and invent characters and events. I told them they were like potatoes growing in a cellar. She said, sadly, "Yes I know we are!"' but it was almost impos-sible for her to abandon it. Nevertheless it was something that she was determined to do. The well-known piece Charlotte wrote at twenty-three, generally called 'The Farewell to Angria', documents her attempt to break away from the Byronic world. In lyrical prose she describes the need 'to quit for awhile that burning clime where we have sojourned too long – its skies aflame – the glow of sunset is always upon it – the mind would cease from excitement and turn now to a cooler region where the day breaks cold and sober, and the coming day for a time at least is subdued by clouds'.

And yet despite the resolutions which would be the impetus behind *The Professor,* all kinds of signs suggest Charlotte found it very hard to escape the magnates of what would be described as the 'infernal world'. There is evidence that they still filled her mind in Brussels, and she solved the problem of parting from her characters by continuing to scribble away at a manuscript in which the Angrians are simply transported wholesale to Yorkshire. Even the opening of the 'grave and true' *Professor* contains a letter from William Crimsworth to one of the most well-known Angrian characters, a witty man about town, named Charles Townshend.

Living so much in her imaginary world, the most ordinary exchanges assumed extraordinary dimensions for Charlotte. Virginia Woolf's father, Leslie Stephen, was at first perplexed by what he considered to be the prosaic nature of her raw materials. After various sallies in critical essays in which he cuttingly compares Mr Rochester's way of talking to an overwrought lady governess, or grumbles that Rochester is an 'Aeolus of the duckpond', he finally had to surrender and confess his admiration. He concluded, memorably, that 'Miss Brontë's marvellous effects are obtained by the process which enables an "intense and glowing mind" to see everything through its own atmosphere. The ugliest and most trivial objects seem, like objects heated by the sun, to radiate back the glow of passion with which she has regarded them.' And there in a nutshell is the paradox of Charlotte Brontë.

In some way M. Heger was allowed to infiltrate into this imaginary world and become a part of it. Although her return from Brussels and Branwell's behaviour clarified her moral sense it was almost impossible for Charlotte to escape her obsessional nature. Yet that in the end would be the secret of her power. The logical Charlotte accepted that the relationship with M. Heger was over, but the writer Charlotte seems to have found solace by writing a dream of what might have been. Not only was *The Professor* a novel set in a school in Brussels, but the interior and grounds of the real school they were based on, the Pensionnat Heger, were described with minute accuracy.

Charlotte Brontë recreated classroom scenes at the Pensionnat describing the school exactly as it was, making no attempt to disguise it. In *The Professor* she takes her pupil–teacher relationship with M. Heger and gives it a happy ending. Frances Henri, the orphan who triumphs over her circumstances and her rival Mlle Reuter's enmity, winning the love of William Crimsworth in class, is Charlotte: Crimsworth himself is an odd mixture of Charlotte and M. Heger. And Mlle Reuter, with her spying and cold self-interest, is a preview of Madame Beck in *Villette*, the arch-villainess who comes between M. Paul Emanuel and Lucy Snowe. As is well-known, Madame Beck was based on Madame Heger.

Six years later Charlotte would revisit the school in her imagination when her experiences in Brussels were even more accurately reproduced in *Villette*, including the famous passage in St Gudule when the vehemently Protestant Lucy Snow confesses to some secret sin. Before Brussels developers destroyed the Rue Isabelle, Victorian travellers were able to make their way round the Pensionnat Heger with a copy of either *The Professor* or *Villette* in their hands and see the hall paved with black and white marble, glimpse the garden and pear trees which would be so important for the plot of *Villette*. To those who have read *Villette*, the story of the author's relationship with M. Heger is all too easily seen there. For Lucy Snowe read Charlotte Brontë, for M. Paul Emanuel read Constantin Heger. The pupil–teacher relationship which for her at least had so much tenderness in it, was not only the main concern of *The Professor*. It was also to be reworked in *Shirley*, in the passages between the tutor Louis Moore and the heiress Shirley Keeldar.

When *The Professor* was rejected by a large number of publishers, Charlotte began afresh and wrote *Jane Eyre* at white heat. With centrifugal force she whirled up together all her experiences – Angria and the devilish Duke of Zamorna, all the treasured moments in the Pensionnat Heger such as the scent of M. Heger's cigar when he walked in the garden in the evening, big houses like her friend Ellen Nussey's – and began to transmute them into alchemical gold.

Even her third novel *Shirley* could not escape the thrall of Belgium. As Charlotte would admit in *The Professor*, almost laughing at herself: 'Belgium! Name unromantic and unpoetic, yet name that whenever uttered, has in my ear a sound, in my heart an echo such as no other assemblage of syllables, however sweet or classic, can produce.' Never was an apparently light-hearted sentence written which so deeply reflected the truth. Although *Shirley* is entirely set in Yorkshire, Charlotte cannot resist making a little corner of it Belgian. Of the two heroines one, Caroline Helstone, is related to a family of Belgians whose male representatives provide the (Belgian) love-interest, while their sister, Miss Hortense Moore, gives the author a chance to expatiate on Belgian habits and customs.

But although Charlotte still allowed herself these little indulgences, in *Shirley* her most realistic and challenging side is to the fore. For all her romantic obsessional side, Brontë's letters and juvenilia display a sharp intelligence. She found a great deal wanting in the real world particularly when it came to women. Her letters show she had always been a rebel. In both *The Professor* and *Jane Eyre*, she is outspokenly critical of the repressed way of life pronounced proper for middle-class women, and in this she was encouraged by her feminist friend Mary Taylor who would have to emigrate to New Zealand to be allowed to work.

Contemporary attitudes allowed few activities for respectable spinsters like herself and her friends. Their unsatisfying existence was at the heart of the debate about what was known as The Women Question, which had agitated society for some time. By the mid-nineteenth century social and economic change was inexorably drawing women into paid employment, and their need for higher education was one of the issues of the day. At the same time the much promoted theory that women's natural role was a moral influence within the home was a strong influence against liberation. The philosopher John Stuart Mill might decry 'the exaggerated self-abnegation which is the present artificial ideal of feminine character', but it had a terrible grip on England. Engendered by a thousand etiquette books and novels, woman's role as what Coventry Patmore called 'The Angel in the House' had grown into an adamantine tradition. What astounded contemporaries about *Jane Eyre* was the revelatory and extremely realistic depiction of a female character who defended her right to have feelings as strong as any man.

Frances Henri and Jane Eyre both complain about the self-suppression required by social convention. In a particularly vivid passage Jane remarks that 'Nobody knows how many rebellions besides political rebellions ferment in the masses of life which people earth. Women are supposed to be very calm generally: but women feel just as men feel; they need exercise for their faculties, and a field for their efforts as much as their brothers do; they suffer from too rigid a restraint, too absolute a stagnation, precisely as men would suffer . . . It is thoughtless to condemn them, or laugh at them, if they seek to do more or learn more than custom has pronounced necessary for their sex.' But it took the publication of *Jane Eyre* to make Charlotte realize quite how unusual her views were.

Although in 1847 *Jane Eyre* had been a runaway success, a year later it was quite a different matter. The aftermath of the 1848 revolutions on the continent and the coincidental publication of *Wuthering Heights* and *The Tenant of Wildfell Hall* turned critics violently against the honesty and realism of *Jane Eyre*. Derogatory portraits of clergymen such as Mr Brockle-hurst and the fanatical St John Rivers, and Jane's proud and independent spirit, now appeared to challenge the established order in England, where clergymen were supposed to be above reproach and women to toe the (masculine) line. At a time when novels were intended to have an improving moral, the realism of *Wuthering Heights* and *The Tenant of Wildfell Hall* was dismissed as a tendency to purvey a very unpleasant and coarse view of society. By late 1848 newspapers were even warning that ladies should avoid them. Amazingly, *Jane Eyre* became known as a 'naughty' book, which even Charlotte Brontë's biographer and apologist Mrs Gaskell would not allow her daughters to read.

By the time Charlotte completed *Shirley* in 1849, Emily, Anne and Branwell were all dead. *Shirley* is a novel of social protest set in the Yorkshire of 1811 where workers and manufacturers are suffering from the British government's Orders in Council which restricted trade with the continent. Patrick Brontë had been curate at Hartshead when Rawfold's Mill was attacked by Luddites in 1812. This episode, which was well-known as a family story amongst the Brontës, was the inspiration for the attack on Hollow's Mill when the mill-owner Robert Moore defends it against agitators. Perhaps influenced by her favourite novelist Scott, Charlotte sent off for back issues of the *Leeds Mercury* to ensure the novel's historical accuracy, and to present the arguments of both mill-owners and workers even-handedly. The manufacturer Robert Moore must introduce new machinery as he will be ruined without it, yet the effect is to make his workers starve, because they are being thrown out of work. By 1848 the general misery of the 'hungry forties', and the failure of Chartism had turned Charlotte's attention to what she would call 'the warped system of things'.

She wrote to her publisher's reader and confidant William Smith Williams that she saw 'this fact plainly' – that the government must make concessions 'as justice and humanity dictate', and 'mutual kindliness' must be substituted for ill feeling. Like the generation of novelists who produced Condition of England novels, she was affected by reading some of Thomas Carlyle's work that spring. Carlyle's attacks on the factory system, where money was 'the sole nexus between man and man', were inspirational. The appearance of Mrs Gaskell's *Mary Barton* in 1848 while Charlotte was writing *Shirley* made her worry that she had been anticipated in her subject matter. In fact Charlotte had far less of Mrs Gaskell's sympathy and welling indignation for the lives of the working class, or Mrs Gaskell's innovative interest in writing a novel from their point of view. While the situation of men like William Farren who has sold most of his household goods to keep from starving is distressing, Charlotte is less interested in presenting factory conditions than asking for greater understanding on both sides. The novel suggests that though no one can afford to ignore technological change, it must be achieved sensitively.

Halfway through, the novel alters its focus; by the end Charlotte's more vocal demand for change is in the treatment of women. But the second two volumes of *Shirley* were written under such tragic conditions that its modified course is understandable. The work of the three sisters was under attack, and the attacks put Charlotte on her mettle. The claim that *Jane*

Eyre's realism and demands for sexual equality made her a moral Jacobin was met with fire. Caroline Helstone is shown as stifling from a life without purpose, where she is unable to assert herself; it is what Rose Yorke calls 'a long slow death in Briarfield Rectory'. Caroline says that no one in particular is to blame for this state of affairs but she feels 'single women should have more to do – better chances of interesting and profitable occupation than they possess now'. And Charlotte makes Caroline challenge her critics: 'When I speak thus, I have no impression that I displease God by my words; that I am either impious or impatient, irreligious or sacrilegious.'

Contrasted with Caroline is the radical heiress Shirley Keeldar in whose unconventional character and physical daring Charlotte would partly memorialize Emily. Charlotte was so angry about an attack in the *Quarterly Review* which coincided with Emily's death that she had to be dissuaded by her publishers from writing a reply. Instead she satisfied herself by incorporating many of her biting phrases into *Shirley* when Shirley Keeldar's governess Mrs Pryor recounts the cruelty with which she was treated by families she had worked for previously. As a further act of defiance, Charlotte even opened *Shirley* with a disrespectful and amusing portrait of three curates at tea. Her publishers implored her to be careful how she dealt with the Church of England and entreated her not to make the opening words of her new novel a satirical paragraph about the clergy. They would have liked her to write a preface revealing a little more of her own tragic situation to counter the Bells' bad reputation.

But any opposition made Charlotte fiercer. The second edition of *Jane Eyre* carried a fighting Preface where she pointed out 'self-righteousness is not religion', and even though she was now apparently indelibly stigmatized as the enemy of religion she refused to recant and become a hypocrite. Charlotte Brontë felt ever more keenly how important it was to tell the truth, and as she would write piteously to her publishers, now she had nothing left, with her sisters gone, she must have 'her own way in the matter of writing'. Despite all the opprobrium arising from *Jane Eyre* Charlotte Brontë believed she must write truly about human nature or not write at all. As she would tell intimates, it was not with the idea of being elegant and charming that she wrote books. If those were the only terms on which her writing would be tolerated she would 'pass away from the public and trouble it no more'. Not all clergymen were unalloyed saints and there were some clergymen like Mr Helstone who has missed what by nature is his true vocation – 'he should have been a soldier, and circumstances had made him a priest'.

Despite the publishers' fears, reviewers were gentler with *Shirley* than they had been with *Jane Eyre*. Although it was still marred by coarseness, particularly the clergymen's tea party, the *Quarterly Review* was pleased to be able to tell its readers that Shirley enlisted 'the purer sympathies of our nature, instead of appealing to its baser passions'.

In Yorkshire there were reports all over the county of its clergymen being thoroughly entertained by the irreverent portrait of their doings. Charlotte Brontë's future husband, the generally solemn Arthur Bell Nicholls, the original for Mr Macarthey, was even caught roaring with laughter at what by 1850 the whole of clerical Yorkshire knew to be the work of Mr Brontë's talented daughter.

Rebecca Fraser

REBECCA FRASER is the author of *Charlotte Brontë* and *A People's History of Britain*.

SELECT BIBLIOGRAPHY

BIOGRAPHY

ALEXANDER, CHRISTINE, ed., *The Early Writings of Charlotte Brontë*, Blackwell, Oxford, 1983; Prometheus Books, New York, 1983.

BARKER, JULIET, *The Brontës*, Weidenfeld & Nicolson, London, 1994; St Martin's Press, New York, 1994.

BARNARD, ROBERT and LOUISE, *A Brontë Encyclopedia*, Blackwell, Oxford, 2007; Wiley-Blackwell, USA, 2007.

FRASER, REBECCA, *Charlotte Brontë*, Vintage, London, 2003; Pegasus Books, New York, 2008.

GASKELL, ELIZABETH, *The Life of Charlotte Brontë* (1857), Everyman Paperbacks, London, 1997; Oxford University Press, New York, 2002.

GORDON, LYNDALL, *Charlotte Brontë: A Passionate Life*, Chatto and Windus, London, 1994; Norton, New York, 1995.

PETERS, MARGOT, *Unquiet Soul: A Biography of Charlotte Brontë*, Hodder and Stoughton, London, 1975; Doubleday, New York, 1975.

SMITH, MARGARET, ed., *The Letters of Charlotte Brontë: with a selection of letters by family and friends* (3 volumes), Oxford University Press, Oxford and New York, 1995, 2000, 2004.

WINNIFRITH, TOM, ed., *The Poems of Charlotte Brontë: a new annotated and enlarged edition of the Shakespeare Head Brontë*, Blackwell, Oxford and USA, 1984.

CRITICISM

ALLOTT, MIRIAM, ed., *The Brontës: The Critical Heritage*, Routledge and Kegan Paul, London, 1974.

EWBANK INGE-STINA, *Their Proper Sphere: A Study of the Brontë Sisters as Early Victorian Female Novelists*, Edward Arnold, London, 1965; Harvard University Press, Cambridge, MA, 1966.

GILBERT, SANDRA M. and GUBAR, SUSAN, *The Madwoman in the Attic: The Woman Writer and the Nineteenth Century Literary Imagination*, Yale University Press, New Haven, CT, 1979.

GLEN, HEATHER, *Charlotte Brontë: The Imagination in History*, Oxford University Press, Oxford and New York, 2002.

MAYNARD, JOHN, *Charlotte Brontë and Sexuality*, Cambridge University Press, Cambridge and New York, 1984.

MILLER, LUCASTA, *The Brontë Myth*, Jonathan Cape, London, 2001; Alfred A. Knopf, New York, 2003.

MILLETT, KATE, *Sexual Politics*, Doubleday, New York, 1970; Virago, London, 1977.

MOERS, ELLEN, *Literary Women*, Doubleday, New York, 1976; *Women's Press*, London, 1978.

SHOWALTER, ELAINE, *A Literature of their Own: British Women Novelists from Brontë to Lessing*, Princeton University Press, Princeton, NJ, 1977; Virago, London, 1982.

TILLOTSON, KATHLEEN, *Novels of the 1840s*, Oxford University Press, Oxford and New York, 1954.

CHRONOLOGY

DATE	AUTHOR'S LIFE	LITERARY CONTEXT
1790		Ann Radcliffe: *A Sicilian Romance.*
1792		Mary Wollstonecraft: *A Vindication of the Rights of Woman.*
1808		Walter Scott: *Marmion.*
1811		
1812		Byron: *Childe Harold's Pilgrimage,* Cantos I and II.
1815		
1816	Birth of Charlotte, third of the six children of Patrick Brontë, a Yorkshire parson, and his wife Maria.	Coleridge: *Christabel* and *Kubla Khan.* Benjamin Constant: *Adolphe.*
1820	The family moves to Haworth, Charlotte's home for the rest of her life.	
1821	Death of Charlotte's mother.	
1824	The four eldest Brontë girls are sent to Cowan Bridge School.	Goethe: *Wilhelm Meisters Lehrjahre* (1795), trans. Carlyle as *Wilhelm Meister's Apprenticeship.*
1825	Death of Charlotte's two elder sisters. Charlotte and Emily return to Haworth.	
1828		
1829		Balzac: *La Comédie humaine* (17 vols, to 1848).
1830	Charlotte goes for a year to Roe Head School, returning in 1835 as a teacher.	Stendhal: *Le Rouge et le Noir.*
1831		Victor Hugo: *Notre-Dame de Paris.*
1832		George Sand: *Indiana.*
1834		Bulwer Lytton: *The Last Days of Pompeii.*
1837		Dickens: *Oliver Twist.*
1839		Carlyle: *Chartism.* Harriet Martineau: *Deerbrook.*
1839–40	Charlotte takes two successive jobs as a temporary governess.	

First Luddite machine-breaking riots.

Battle of Waterloo.

Death of George III. Prince Regent becomes George IV. Trial of Queen Caroline.

Death of Napoleon.
Death of Byron at Missolonghi.

Duke of Wellington becomes Prime Minister.
Catholic Emancipation Act.

Grey becomes Prime Minister. Death of George IV; accession of William IV. July revolution in France; accession of Louis Philippe.

Great Reform Act.
Robert Peel becomes Prime Minister briefly. Tolpuddle Martyrs. Whigs return to office with Melbourne as Prime Minister (1835–41).
Accession of Queen Victoria.

DATE	AUTHOR'S LIFE	LITERARY CONTEXT
1842	Charlotte and Emily go to Brussels, to the pensionnat run by Monsieur and Madame Heger. Emily leaves after a few months. Charlotte returns as student teacher for a further year.	
1844		Elizabeth Barrett Browning: *Poems*. A. Dumas, *père*: *Les Trois Mousquetaires*.
1845	Branwell Brontë, dismissed from his tutoring job, returns to Haworth dependent on opium and alcohol.	Disraeli: *Sybil*. A. Dumas, *père*: *Le Comte de Monte-Cristo*. Mérimée: *Carmen*.
1846	*Poems by Currer, Ellis and Acton Bell* (Charlotte, Emily and Anne Brontë).	Balzac: *La Cousine Bette*.
1847	*Jane Eyre*.	Thackeray: *Vanity Fair*. Tennyson: *The Princess*. Emily Brontë: *Wuthering Heights*. Anne Brontë: *Agnes Grey*.
1848	Deaths of Branwell and Emily Brontë.	Anne Brontë: *The Tenant of Wildfell Hall*. Dickens: *Dombey and Son*. Mrs Gaskell: *Mary Barton*. George Sand: *François le Champi*; *La Petite Fadette*. Thackeray: *Pendennis* (to 1850).
1849	Death of Anne Brontë. *Shirley*.	Dickens: *David Copperfield*.
1850	Charlotte meets Mrs Gaskell.	Wordsworth: *The Prelude*.
1851		Mrs Oliphant: *Caleb Field*.
1853	*Villette*.	Thackeray: *The Newcomes* (to 1855). Arnold: *Poems*.
1854–6		
1854	Charlotte marries Arthur Nicholls, who had been her father's curate.	George Sand: *Histoire de ma vie*. Mrs Gaskell: *North and South*. Dickens: *Hard Times*.
1855	Death of Charlotte Brontë.	
1857	*The Professor* (Brontë's first but previously unpublished novel).	Mrs Gaskell: *The Life of Charlotte Brontë*. Flaubert: *Madame Bovary*. Trollope: *The Three Clerks*. Mrs Oliphant: *The Athelings*.

CHRONOLOGY

Peel introduces income tax. 'Young England' movement pioneered by Manners, Smythe and Disraeli. Chadwick's report on 'The Sanitary Condition of the Labouring Classes'. Mines Act prohibits employment of women and children underground.

Shaftesbury secures passage of a further Factory Act.

Potato famine in Ireland.

Repeal of the Corn Laws.

Ten Hours Act.

Collapse of Chartist movement. Revolutions in Europe. Louis Philippe flees from France to England, making way for Louis Napoleon. Queen's College, Harley Street, established 'for the education of young ladies generally – of governesses especially'.

Don Pacifico incident.
Louis Napoleon's *coup d'état*. He becomes Emperor Napoleon III the following year.

Crimean War.

Palmerston becomes Prime Minister.
Indian Mutiny.

CONTENTS

SHIRLEY

SHIRLEY
A TALE

CHAPTER I

LEVITICAL

Of late years, an abundant shower of curates has fallen upon the north of England: they lie very thick on the hills; every parish has one or more of them; they are young enough to be very active, and ought to be doing a great deal of good. But not of late years are we about to speak; we are going back to the beginning of this century: late years – present years are dusty, sun-burnt, hot, arid; we will evade the noon, forget it in siesta, pass the mid-day in slumber, and dream of dawn.

If you think, from this prelude, that anything like a romance is preparing for you, reader, you never were more mistaken. Do you anticipate sentiment, and poetry, and reverie? Do you expect passion, and stimulus, and melodrama? Calm your expectations; reduce them to a lowly standard. Something real, cool, and solid, lies before you; something unromantic as Monday morning, when all who have work wake with the consciousness that they must rise and betake themselves thereto. It is not positively affirmed that you shall not have a taste of the exciting, perhaps towards the middle and close of the meal, but it is resolved that the first dish set upon the table shall be one that a Catholic – ay, even an Anglo-Catholic – might eat on Good Friday in Passion Week: it shall be cold lentils and vinegar without oil; it shall be unleavened bread with bitter herbs, and no roast lamb.

Of late years, I say, an abundant shower of curates has fallen upon the north of England: but in eighteen-hundred-eleven-twelve that affluent rain had not descended: curates were scarce then: there was no Pastoral Aid – no Additional Curates' Society

3

to stretch a helping hand to worn-out old rectors and incumbents, and give them the wherewithal to pay a vigorous young colleague from Oxford or Cambridge. The present successors of the apostles, disciples of Dr Pusey and tools of the Propaganda, were at that time being hatched under cradle-blankets, or undergoing regeneration by nursery-baptism in wash-hand-basins. You could not have guessed by looking at any one of them that the Italian-ironed double frills of its net-cap surrounded the brows of a preordained, specially sanctified successor of St Paul, St Peter, or St John; nor could you have foreseen in the folds of its long night-gown the white surplice in which it was hereafter cruelly to exercise the souls of its parishioners, and strangely to nonplus its old-fashioned vicar by flourishing aloft in a pulpit the shirt-like raiment which had never before waved higher than the reading-desk.

Yet even in those days of scarcity there were curates: the precious plant was rare, but it might be found. A certain favoured district in the West Riding of Yorkshire could boast three rods of Aaron blossoming within a circuit of twenty miles. You shall see them, reader. Step into this neat garden-house on the skirts of Whinbury, walk forward into the little parlour – there they are at dinner. Allow me to introduce them to you: – Mr Donne, curate of Whinbury; Mr Malone, curate of Briarfield; Mr Sweeting, curate of Nunnely. These are Mr Donne's lodgings, being the habitation of one John Gale, a small clothier. Mr Donne has kindly invited his brethren to regale with him. You and I will join the party, see what is to be seen, and hear what is to be heard. At present, however, they are only eating; and while they eat we will talk aside.

These gentlemen are in the bloom of youth; they possess all the activity of that interesting age – an activity which their moping old vicars would fain turn into the channel of their pastoral duties, often expressing a wish to see it expended in a diligent superintendence of the schools, and in frequent visits to the sick of their respective parishes. But the youthful Levites feel this to be dull work; they prefer lavishing their energies on a course of proceeding, which, though to other eyes it appear more heavy with ennui, more cursed with monotony, than the toil of the weaver at his loom, seems to yield them an unfailing supply of enjoyment and occupation.

I allude to a rushing backwards and forwards, amongst themselves, to and from their respective lodgings: not a round – but a triangle of visits, which they keep up all the year through, in winter, spring, summer, and autumn. Season and weather make no difference; with unintelligible zeal they dare snow and hail, wind and rain, mire and dust, to go and dine, or drink tea, or sup with each other. What attracts them, it would be difficult to say. It is not friendship; for whenever they meet they quarrel. It is not religion; the thing is never named amongst them: theology they may discuss occasionally, but piety – never. It is not the love of eating and drinking; each might have as good a joint and pudding, tea as potent, and toast as succulent, at his own lodgings, as is served to him at his brother's. Mrs Gale, Mrs Hogg, and Mrs Whipp – their respective landladies – affirm that 'it is just for nought else but to give folk trouble.' By 'folk,' the good ladies of course mean themselves; for indeed they are kept in a continual 'fry' by this system of mutual invasion.

Mr Donne and his guests, as I have said, are at dinner; Mrs Gale waits on them, but a spark of the hot kitchen fire is in her eye. She considers that the privilege of inviting a friend to a meal occasionally, without additional charge (a privilege included in the terms on which she lets her lodgings), has been quite sufficiently exercised of late. The present week is yet but at Thursday, and on Monday, Mr Malone, the curate of Briarfield, came to breakfast and stayed dinner; on Tuesday, Mr Malone and Mr Sweeting of Nunnely, came to tea, remained to supper, occupied the spare bed, and favoured her with their company to breakfast on Wednesday morning; now, on Thursday, they are both here at dinner, and she is almost certain they will stay all night. 'C'en est trop,' she would say, if she could speak French.

Mr Sweeting is mincing the slice of roast-beef on his plate, and complaining that it is very tough; Mr Donne says the beer is flat. Ay! that is the worst of it: if they would only be civil, Mrs Gale wouldn't mind it so much; if they would only seem satisfied with what they get, she wouldn't care, but 'these young parsons is so high and so scornful, they set everybody beneath their "fit;" they treat her with less than civility, just because she doesn't keep a servant, but does the work of the house herself, as her mother did afore her: then they are always speaking against Yorkshire ways and Yorkshire folk,' and by that very token Mrs Gale does not believe one of them to be a real gentleman, or come of gentle kin. 'The old parsons is worth the whole lump of college lads; they know what belangs good manners, and is kind to high and low.'

'More bread!' cries Mr Malone, in a tone which, though prolonged but to utter two syllables, proclaims him at once a native of the land of shamrocks and potatoes. Mrs Gale hates Mr Malone more than either of the other two; but she fears him also, for he is a tall, strongly-built personage, with real Irish legs and arms, and a face as genuinely national: not the Milesian face – not Daniel O'Connell's style, but the high-featured, North-American-Indian sort of visage, which belongs to a certain class of the Irish gentry, and has a petrified and proud look, better suited to the owner of an estate of slaves, than to the landlord of a free peasantry. Mr Malone's father termed himself a gentleman: he was poor and in debt, and besottedly arrogant; and his son was like him.

Mrs Gale offered the loaf.

'Cut it, woman,' said her guest; and the 'woman' cut it accordingly. Had she followed her inclinations, she would have cut the parson also; her Yorkshire soul revolted absolutely from his manner of command.

The curates had good appetites, and though the beef was

'tough,' they ate a great deal of it. They swallowed, too, a tolerable allowance of the 'flat beer,' while a dish of Yorkshire pudding, and two tureens of vegetables, disappeared like leaves before locusts. The cheese, too, received distinguished marks of their attention; and a 'spice-cake,' which followed by way of dessert, vanished like a vision, and was no more found. Its elegy was chanted in the kitchen by Abraham, Mrs Gale's son and heir, a youth of six summers; he had reckoned upon the reversion thereof, and when his mother brought down the empty platter, he lifted up his voice and wept sore.

The curates, meantime, sat and sipped their wine; a liquor of unpretending vintage, moderately enjoyed. Mr Malone, indeed, would much rather have had whisky; but Mr Donne, being an Englishman, did not keep the beverage. While they sipped, they argued; not on politics, nor on philosophy, nor on literature – these topics were now as ever totally without interest for them – not even on theology, practical or doctrinal; but on minute points of ecclesiastical discipline, frivolities which seemed empty as bubbles to all save themselves. Mr Malone, who contrived to secure two glasses of wine, when his brethren contented themselves with one, waxed by degrees hilarious after his fashion; that is, he grew a little insolent, said rude things in a hectoring tone, and laughed clamorously at his own brilliancy.

Each of his companions became in turn his butt. Malone had a stock of jokes at their service, which he was accustomed to serve out regularly on convivial occasions like the present, seldom varying his wit; for which, indeed, there was no necessity, as he never appeared to consider himself monotonous, and did not at all care what others thought. Mr Donne, he favoured with hints about his extreme meagreness, allusions to his turned-up nose, cutting sarcasms on a certain threadbare chocolate surtout, which that gentleman was accustomed to sport whenever it rained, or seemed likely to rain, and criticisms on a choice set of cockney phrases, and modes of pronunciation,

Mr Donne's own property, and certainly deserving of remark for the elegance and finish they communicated to his style.

Mr Sweeting was bantered about his stature – he was a little man, a mere boy in height and breadth compared with the athletic Malone – rallied on his musical accomplishments – he played the flute and sang hymns like a seraph (some young ladies of his parish thought), sneered at as 'the lady's pet,' teased about his mamma and sisters, for whom poor Mr Sweeting had some lingering regard, and of whom he was foolish enough now and then to speak in the presence of the priestly Paddy, from whose anatomy the bowels of natural affection had somehow been omitted.

The victims met these attacks each in his own way: Mr Donne with a stilted self-complacency, and half-sullen phlegm, the sole props of his otherwise somewhat rickety dignity; Mr Sweeting, with the indifference of a light, easy disposition, which never professed to have any dignity to maintain.

When Malone's raillery became rather too offensive, which it soon did, they joined in an attempt to turn the tables on him, by asking him how many boys had shouted 'Irish Peter!' after him, as he came along the road that day (Malone's name was Peter – the Rev. Peter Augustus Malone); requesting to be informed whether it was the mode in Ireland for clergymen to carry loaded pistols in their pockets, and a shilelagh in their hands, when they made pastoral visits; inquiring the signification of such words, as vele, firrum, hellum, storrum (so Mr Malone invariably pronounced veil, firm, helm, storm), and employing such other methods of retaliation as the innate refinement of their minds suggested.

This, of course, would not do. Malone, being neither good-natured nor phlegmatic, was presently in a towering passion. He vociferated, gesticulated; Donne and Sweeting laughed. He reviled them as Saxons and snobs at the very top pitch of his high Celtic voice; they taunted him with being the native of a conquered land. He menaced rebellion in the name of his

'counthry,' vented bitter hatred against English rule; they spoke
of rags, beggary, and pestilence. The little parlour was in an
uproar; you would have thought a duel must follow such viru-
lent abuse; it seemed a wonder that Mr and Mrs Gale did not
take alarm at the noise, and send for a constable to keep the
peace. But they were accustomed to such demonstrations; they
well knew that the curates never dined or took tea together
without a little exercise of the sort, and were quite easy as to
consequences; knowing that these clerical quarrels were as
harmless as they were noisy; that they resulted in nothing; and
that, on whatever terms the curates might part to-night, they
would be sure to meet the best friends in the world to-morrow
morning.

As the worthy pair were sitting by their kitchen fire, listening
to the repeated and sonorous contact of Malone's fist with the
mahogany plane of the parlour table, and to the consequent
start and jingle of decanters and glasses following each assault,
to the mocking laughter of the allied English disputants, and
the stuttering declamation of the isolated Hibernian, – as they
thus sat, a foot was heard on the outer door-step, and the
knocker quivered to a sharp appeal.

Mr Gale went and opened.

'Whom have you up-stairs in the parlour?' asked a voice;
a rather remarkable voice, nasal in tone, abrupt in utterance.

'Oh! Mr Helstone, is it you, sir? I could hardly see you for
the darkness; it is so soon dark now. Will you walk in, sir?'

'I want to know first whether it is worth my while walking
in. Whom have you up-stairs?'

'The curates, sir.'

'What! all of them?'

'Yes, sir.'

'Been dining here?'

'Yes, sir.'

'That will do.'

With these words a person entered, – a middle-aged man,

in black. He walked straight across the kitchen to an inner door, opened it, inclined his head forward, and stood listening. There was something to listen to, for the noise above was just then louder than ever.

'Hey!' he ejaculated to himself; then, turning to Mr Gale, – 'Have you often this sort of work?'

Mr Gale had been a churchwarden, and was indulgent to the clergy.

'They're young, you know, sir, – they're young,' said he, deprecatingly.

'Young! They want caning. Bad boys! – bad boys! and if you were a Dissenter, John Gale, instead of being a good Churchman, they'd do the like; – they'd expose themselves: but I'll –'

By way of finish to this sentence, he passed through the inner door, drew it after him, and mounted the stair. Again he listened a few minutes when he arrived at the upper room. Making entrance without warning, he stood before the curates.

And they were silent; they were transfixed; and so was the invader. He, – a personage short of stature, but straight of port, and bearing on broad shoulders a hawk's head, beak, and eye, the whole surmounted by a Rehoboam, or shovel-hat, which he did not seem to think it necessary to lift or remove before the presence in which he then stood, – *he* folded his arms on his chest and surveyed his young friends – if friends they were – much at his leisure.

'What!' he began, delivering his words in a voice no longer nasal, but deep, – more than deep, – a voice made purposely hollow and cavernous; 'What! has the miracle of Pentecost been renewed? Have the cloven tongues come down again? Where are they? The sound filled the whole house just now. I heard the seventeen languages in full action: – Parthians, and Medes, and Elamites, the dwellers in Mesopotamia, and in Judæa, and Cappadocia, in Pontus and Asia, Phrygia and Pamphylia, in Egypt and in the parts of Libya about Cyrene, strangers of

Rome, Jews and proselytes, Cretes and Arabians, – every one of these must have had its representative in this room two minutes since.'

'I beg your pardon, Mr Helstone,' began Mr Donne; 'take a seat, pray, sir. Have a glass of wine?'

His civilities received no answer: the falcon in the black coat proceeded: –

'What do I talk about the gift of tongues? Gift, indeed! I mistook the chapter, and book, and testament: – Gospel for law, Acts for Genesis, the city of Jerusalem for the plain of Shinar. It was no gift, but the confusion of tongues which has gabbled me deaf as a post. *You*, apostles? What! – you three? Certainly not: – three presumptuous Babylonish masons, – neither more nor less!'

'I assure you, sir, we were only having a little chat together over a glass of wine, after a friendly dinner: – settling the Dissenters.'

'Oh! settling the Dissenters – were you? Was Malone settling the Dissenters? It sounded to me much more like settling his co-apostles. You were quarrelling together; making almost as much noise – you three alone – as Moses Barraclough, the preaching tailor, and all his hearers, are making in the methodist chapel down yonder, where they are in the thick of a revival. I know whose fault it is – it is yours, Malone.'

'Mine! sir?'

'Yours, sir. Donne and Sweeting were quiet before you came, and would be quiet if you were gone. I wish when you crossed the Channel, you had left your Irish habits behind you. Dublin student ways won't do here: the proceedings which might pass unnoticed in a wild bog and mountain district in Connaught will, in a decent English parish, bring disgrace on those who indulge in them, and, what is far worse, on the sacred institution of which they are merely the humble appendages.'

There was a certain dignity in the little elderly gentleman's manner of rebuking these youths; though it was not, perhaps, quite the dignity most appropriate to the occasion. Mr Helstone

– standing straight as a ramrod – looking keen as a kite, presented, despite his clerical hat, black coat, and gaiters, more the air of a veteran officer chiding his subalterns, than of a venerable priest exhorting his sons in the faith. Gospel mildness – apostolic benignity, never seemed to have breathed their influence over that keen brown visage; but firmness had fixed the features, and sagacity had carved her own lines about them.

'I met Supplehough,' he continued, 'plodding through the mud this wet night, going to preach at Milldean opposition shop. As I told you, I heard Barraclough bellowing in the midst of a conventicle like a possessed bull; and I find *you*, gentlemen, tarrying over your half pint of muddy port-wine, and scolding like angry old women. No wonder Supplehough should have dipped sixteen adult converts in a day – which he did a fortnight since; no wonder Barraclough, scamp and hypocrite as he is, should attract all the weaver-girls, in their flowers and ribbons, to witness how much harder are his knuckles than the wooden brim of his tub, as little wonder that *you*, when you are left to yourselves, without your rectors – myself, and Hall, and Boultby – to back you, should too often perform the holy service of our church to bare walls, and read your bit of a dry discourse to the clerk, and the organist, and the beadle. But enough of the subject: I came to see Malone – I have an errand unto thee, O captain!'

'What is it?' inquired Malone, discontentedly; 'there can be no funeral to take at this time of day.'

'Have you any arms about you?'

'Arms, sir? – yes, and legs:' and he advanced the mighty members.

'Bah! weapons, I mean.'

'I have the pistols you gave me yourself; I never part with them: I lay them ready cocked on a chair by my bedside at night. I have my blackthorn.'

'Very good. Will you go to Hollow's-mill?'

'What is stirring at Hollow's-mill?'

'Nothing as yet, nor perhaps will be; but Moore is alone there: he has sent all the workmen he can trust to Stilbro'; there are only two women left about the place. It would be a nice opportunity for any of his well-wishers to pay him a visit, if they knew how straight the path was made before them.'

'I am none of his well-wishers, sir: I don't care for him.'

'Soh! Malone, you are afraid.'

'You know me better than that. If I really thought there was a chance of a row, I would go: but Moore is a strange, shy man, whom I never pretend to understand; and for the sake of his sweet company only, I would not stir a step.'

'But there *is* a chance of a row; if a positive riot does not take place – of which, indeed, I see no signs – yet it is unlikely this night will pass quite tranquilly. You know Moore has resolved to have the new machinery, and he expects two waggon loads of frames and shears from Stilbro' this evening. Scott, the over-looker, and a few picked men, are gone to fetch them.'

'They will bring them in safely and quietly enough, sir.'

'Moore says so, and affirms he wants nobody: some one, however, he must have, if it were only to bear evidence in case anything should happen. I call him very careless. He sits in the counting-house with the shutters unclosed; he goes out here and there after dark, wanders right up the hollow, down Fieldhead-lane, among the plantations, just as if he were the darling of the neighbourhood, or – being, as he is, its detestation – bore a "charmed life" as they say in tale-books. He takes no warning from the fate of Pearson, nor from that of Armitage – shot, one in his own house and the other on the moor.'

'But he should take warning, sir, and use precautions too,' interposed Mr Sweeting; 'and I think he would, if he heard what I heard the other day.'

'What did you hear, Davy?'

'You know Mike Hartley, sir?'

'The Antinomian weaver? Yes.'

'When Mike has been drinking for a few weeks together, he

generally winds up by a visit to Nunnely vicarage, to tell Mr Hall a piece of his mind about his sermons, to denounce the horrible tendency of his doctrine of works, and warn him that he and all his hearers are sitting in outer darkness.'

'Well – that has nothing to do with Moore.'

'Besides being an Antinomian, he is a violent Jacobin and leveller, sir.'

'I know. When he is very drunk, his mind is always running on regicide. Mike is not unacquainted with history, and it is rich to hear him going over the list of tyrants of whom, as he says, "the revenger of blood has obtained satisfaction." The fellow exults strangely in murder done on crowned heads, or on any head for political reasons. I have already heard it hinted that he seems to have a queer hankering after Moore: is that what you allude to, Sweeting?'

'You use the proper term, sir. Mr Hall thinks Mike has no personal hatred of Moore; Mike says he even likes to talk to him, and run after him, but he has a *hankering* that Moore should be made an example of: he was extolling him to Mr Hall the other day as the mill-owner with the most brains in Yorkshire, and for that reason he affirms Moore should be chosen as a sacrifice, an oblation of a sweet savour. Is Mike Hartley in his right mind, do you think, sir?' inquired Sweeting, simply.

'Can't tell, Davy: he may be crazed or he may be only crafty – or, perhaps, a little of both.'

'He talks of seeing visions, sir.'

'Ay! He is a very Ezekiel or Daniel for visions. He came just when I was going to bed, last Friday night, to describe one that had been revealed to him in Nunnely Park that very afternoon.'

'Tell it, sir – what was it?' urged Sweeting.

'Davy, thou hast an enormous organ of Wonder in thy cranium; Malone, you see, has none; neither murders nor visions interest him: see what a big vacant Saph, he looks at this moment.'

'Saph! Who was Saph, sir?'

'I thought you would not know: you may find it out: it is biblical. I know nothing more of him than his name and race; but from a boy upwards, I have always attached a personality to Saph. Depend on it he was honest, heavy, and luckless; he met his end at Gob, by the hand of Sibbechai.'

'But the vision, sir?'

'Davy, thou shalt hear. Donne is biting his nails, and Malone yawning; so I will tell it but to thee. Mike is out of work, like many others, unfortunately; Mr Grame, Sir Philip Nunnely's steward, gave him a job about the priory: according to his account, Mike was busy hedging rather late in the afternoon, but before dark, when he heard what he thought was a band at a distance, bugles, fifes, and the sound of a trumpet; it came from the forest, and he wondered that there should be music there. He looked up: all amongst the trees he saw moving objects, red, like poppies, or white, like May-blossom; the wood was full of them; they poured out and filled the park. He then perceived they were soldiers – thousands and tens of thousands; but they made no more noise than a swarm of midges on a summer evening. They formed in order, he affirmed, and marched, regiment after regiment, across the park; he followed them to Nunnely Common; the music still played soft and distant. On the common he watched them go through a number of evolutions, a man clothed in scarlet stood in the centre and directed them; they extended, he declared, over fifty acres; they were in sight half an hour; then they marched away quite silently: the whole time he heard neither voice nor tread – nothing but the faint music playing a solemn march.'

'Where did they go, sir?'

'Towards Briarfield. Mike followed them; they seemed passing Fieldhead, when a column of smoke, such as might be vomited by a park of artillery, spread noiseless over the fields, the road, the common, and rolled, he said, blue and dim to his very feet. As it cleared away he looked again for the soldiers, but they were vanished; he saw them no more. Mike, like a wise Daniel as he is, not only rehearsed the vision, but gave the interpretation thereof: it signifies, he intimated, bloodshed and civil conflict.'

'Do you credit it, sir?' asked Sweeting.

'Do you, Davy? But come, Malone, why are you not off?'

'I am rather surprised, sir, you did not stay with Moore yourself: you like this kind of thing.'

'So I should have done, had I not unfortunately happened to engage Boultby to sup with me on his way home from the Bible Society meeting at Nunnely. I promised to send you as my substitute; for which, by-the-by, he did not thank me: he would much rather have had me than you, Peter. Should there be any real need of help, I shall join you: the mill-bell will give warning. Meantime, go; unless (turning suddenly to Messrs Sweeting and Donne), – unless Davy Sweeting or Joseph Donne prefers going. What do you say, gentlemen? The commission is an honourable one, not without the seasoning of a little real peril; for the country is in a queer state, as you all know, and Moore and his mill, and his machinery, are held in sufficient odium. There are chivalric sentiments, there is high-beating courage under those waistcoats of yours, I doubt not. Perhaps I am too partial to my favourite, Peter; little David shall be the champion, or spotless Joseph. Malone, you are but a great floundering Saul after all, good only to lend your armour: out with your firearms, fetch your shillelagh; it is there – in the corner.'

With a significant grin, Malone produced his pistols, offering one to each of his brethren. They were not readily seized on: with graceful modesty, each gentleman retired a step from the presented weapon.

'I never touch them: I never did touch anything of the kind,' said Mr Donne.

'I am almost a stranger to Mr Moore,' murmured Sweeting.

'If you never touched a pistol, try the feel of it now, great satrap of Egypt. As to the little minstrel, he probably prefers encountering the Philistines with no other weapon than his flute. Get their hats, Peter; they'll both of 'em go.'

'No, sir; no, Mr Helstone; my mother wouldn't like it,' pleaded Sweeting.

'And I make it a rule never to get mixed up in affairs of the kind,' observed Donne.

Helstone smiled sardonically; Malone laughed a horse-laugh. He then replaced his arms, took his hat and cudgel, and saying that 'he never felt more in tune for a shindy in his life, and that he wished a score of greasy cloth-dressers might beat up Moore's quarters that night,' he made his exit; clearing the stairs at a stride or two, and making the house shake with the bang of the front-door behind him.

CHAPTER II

THE WAGGONS

THE EVENING was pitch-dark: star and moon were quenched in grey rain-clouds – grey they would have been by day, by night they looked sable. Malone was not a man given to close observation of Nature; her changes passed, for the most part, unnoticed by him: he could walk miles on the most varying April day, and never see the beautiful dallying of earth and heaven; never mark when a sunbeam kissed the hill-tops, making them smile clear in green light, or when a shower wept over them, hiding their crests with the low-hanging, dishevelled tresses of a cloud. He did not, therefore, care to contrast the sky as it now appeared – a muffled, streaming vault, all black, save where, towards the east, the furnaces of Stilbro' iron-works threw a tremulous lurid shimmer on the horizon – with the same sky on an unclouded frosty night. He did not trouble himself to ask where the constellations and the planets were gone, or to regret the 'black-blue' serenity of the air-ocean which those white islets stud; and which another ocean, of heavier and denser element, now rolled below and concealed. He just doggedly pursued his way, leaning a little forward as he walked, and wearing his hat on the back of his head, as his Irish manner was. 'Tramp, tramp,' he went along the causeway, where the road boasted the privilege of such an accommodation; 'splash, splash,' through the mire-filled cart-ruts, where the flags were exchanged for soft mud. He looked but for certain landmarks: the spire of Briarfield church; further on, the lights of Redhouse. This was an inn; and when he reached it, the glow of a fire through a half-curtained window, a vision of glasses on a round table, and of revellers on an oaken settle, had nearly drawn aside the curate from his course. He thought longingly of a tumbler of whisky-and-water: in a strange place, he would instantly have realized the dream; but the company assembled in that kitchen were Mr Helstone's own parishioners; they all knew him. He sighed, and passed on.

The high road was now to be quitted, as the remaining distance to Hollow's-mill might be considerably reduced by a short cut across fields. These fields were level and monotonous; Malone took a direct course through them, jumping hedge and wall. He passed but one building here, and that seemed large and hall-like, though irregular: you could see a high gable, then a long front, then a low gable, then a thick, lofty stack of chimneys: there were some trees behind it. It was dark; not a candle shone from any window; it was absolutely still: the rain running from the eaves, and the rather wild, but very low whistle of the wind round the chimneys and through the boughs, were the sole sounds in its neighbourhood.

This building passed, the fields, hitherto flat, declined in a rapid descent: evidently a vale lay below, through which you could hear the water run. One light glimmered in the depth: for that beacon Malone steered.

He came to a little white house – you could see it was white even through this dense darkness – and knocked at the door. A fresh-faced servant opened it; by the candle she held was revealed a narrow passage, terminating in a narrow stair. Two doors covered with crimson baize, a strip of crimson carpet down the steps, contrasted with light-coloured walls and white floor, made the little interior look clean and fresh.

'Mr Moore is at home, I suppose?'

'Yes, sir, but he is not in.'

'Not in! Where is he then?'

'At the mill – in the counting-house.'

Here one of the crimson doors opened.

'Are the waggons come, Sarah?' asked a female voice, and a

female head at the same time was apparent. It might not be the head of a goddess – indeed a screw of curl-paper on each side the temples quite forbade that supposition – but neither was it the head of a Gorgon; yet Malone seemed to take it in the latter light. Big as he was, he shrank bashfully back into the rain at the view thereof; and saying, 'I'll go to him,' hurried in seeming trepidation down a short lane, across an obscure yard, towards a huge black mill.

The work-hours were over; the 'hands' were gone; the machinery was at rest; the mill shut up. Malone walked round it; somewhere in its great sooty flank he found another chink of light; he knocked at another door, using for the purpose the thick end of his shillelagh, with which he beat a rousing tattoo. A key turned; the door unclosed.

'Is it Joe Scott? What news of the waggons, Joe?'

'No, – it's myself. Mr Helstone would send me.'

'Oh! Mr Malone.' The voice in uttering this name had the slightest possible cadence of disappointment. After a moment's pause, it continued, politely, but a little formally: –

'I beg you will come in, Mr Malone. I regret extremely Mr Helstone should have thought it necessary to trouble you so far; there was no necessity: – I told him so; – and on such a night – but walk forwards.'

Through a dark apartment, of aspect undistinguishable, Malone followed the speaker into a light and bright room within: very light and bright indeed it seemed to eyes which for the last hour had been striving to penetrate the double darkness of night and fog; but except for its excellent fire, and for a lamp of elegant design and vivid lustre burning on a table, it was a very plain place. The boarded floor was carpetless; the three or four stiff-backed green-painted chairs seemed once to have furnished the kitchen of some farm-house; a desk of strong, solid formation, the table aforesaid, and some framed sheets on the stone-coloured walls, bearing plans for building, for gardening, designs of machinery, &c., completed the furniture of the place.

Plain as it was, it seemed to satisfy Malone; who, when he had removed and hung up his wet surtout and hat, drew one of the rheumatic-looking chairs to the hearth, and set his knees almost within the bars of the red grate.

'Comfortable quarters you have here, Mr Moore; and all snug to yourself.'

'Yes; but my sister would be glad to see you, if you would prefer stepping into the house.'

'Oh, no! the ladies are best alone. I never was a lady's man. You don't mistake me for my friend Sweeting, do you, Mr Moore?'

'Sweeting! – which of them is that? The gentleman in the chocolate over-coat, or the little gentleman?'

'The little one; – he of Nunnely; – the cavalier of the Misses Sykes, with the whole six of whom he is in love, ha! ha!'

'Better be generally in love with all than specially with one, I should think, in that quarter.'

'But he *is* specially in love with one besides, for when I and Donne urged him to make a choice amongst the fair bevy, he named – which do you think?'

With a queer, quiet smile, Mr Moore replied, 'Dora, of course, or Harriet.'

'Ha! ha! you've an excellent guess; but what made you hit on those two?'

'Because they are the tallest, the handsomest; and Dora, at least, is the stoutest; and as your friend Mr Sweeting is but a little, slight figure, I concluded that, according to a frequent rule in such cases, he preferred his contrast.'

'You are right; Dora it is: but he has no chance, has he, Moore?'

'What has Mr Sweeting, besides his curacy?'

This question seemed to tickle Malone amazingly; he laughed for full three minutes before he answered it.

'What has Sweeting? Why David has his harp, or flute, which come to the same thing. He has a sort of pinchbeck watch; ditto, ring; ditto, eye-glass: that's what he has.'

'How would he propose to keep Miss Sykes in gowns only?'

'Ha! ha! Excellent! I'll ask him that next time I see him. I'll roast him for his presumption: but no doubt he expects old Christopher Sykes would do something handsome. He is rich, is he not? They live in a large house.'

'Sykes carries on an extensive concern.'

'Therefore he must be wealthy, eh?'

'Therefore he must have plenty to do with his wealth; and in these times would be about as likely to think of drawing money from the business to give dowries to his daughters as I should be to dream of pulling down the cottage there, and constructing on its ruins a house as large as Fieldhead.'

'Do you know what I heard, Moore, the other day?'

'No: perhaps that I *was* about to effect some such change. Your Briarfield gossips are capable of saying that or sillier things.'

'That you were going to take Fieldhead on a lease – I thought it looked a dismal place, by-the-by, to-night, as I passed it – and that it was your intention to settle a Miss Sykes there as mistress; to be married, in short, ha! ha! Now, which is it? Dora – I am sure: you said she was the handsomest.'

'I wonder how often it has been settled that I was to be married since I came to Briarfield! They have assigned me every marriageable single woman by turns in the district. Now it was the two Misses Wynns – first the dark, then the light one. Now the red-haired Miss Armitage, then the mature Ann Pearson; at present you throw on my shoulders all the tribe of the Misses Sykes. On what grounds this gossip rests, God knows. I visit nowhere – I seek female society about as assiduously as you do, Mr Malone. If ever I go to Whinbury, it is only to give Sykes or Pearson a call in their counting-house; where our discussions run on other topics than matrimony, and our thoughts are occupied with other things than courtships, establishments, dowries: the cloth we can't sell, the hands we can't employ, the mills we can't run, the perverse course of events generally, which we cannot alter, fill our hearts, I take it, pretty well at present, to the tolerably complete exclusion of such figments as love-making, &c.'

'I go along with you completely, Moore. If there is one notion I hate more than another, it is that of marriage: I mean marriage in the vulgar weak sense, as a mere matter of sentiment; two beggarly fools agreeing to unite their indigence by some fantastic tie of feeling – humbug! But an advantageous connexion, such as can be formed in consonance with dignity of views, and permanency of solid interests, is not so bad – eh?'

'No,' responded Moore, in an absent manner; the subject seemed to have no interest for him: he did not pursue it. After sitting for some time gazing at the fire with a preoccupied air, he suddenly turned his head.

'Hark!' said he: 'did you hear wheels?'

Rising, he went to the window, opened it, and listened. He soon closed it. 'It is only the sound of the wind rising,' he remarked, 'and the rivulet a little swollen, rushing down the hollow. I expected those waggons at six; it is near nine now.'

'Seriously, do you suppose that the putting up of this new machinery will bring you into danger?' inquired Malone. 'Helstone seems to think it will.'

'I only wish the machines – the frames were safe here, and lodged within the walls of this mill. Once put up, I defy the framebreakers: let them only pay me a visit, and take the consequences: my mill is my castle.'

'One despises such low scoundrels,' observed Malone, in a profound vein of reflection. 'I almost wish a party would call upon you to-night; but the road seemed extremely quiet as I came along: I saw nothing astir.'

'You came by the Redhouse?'

'Yes.'

'There would be nothing on that road: it is in the direction of Stilbro' the risk lies.'

'And you think there is risk?'

'What these fellows have done to others, they may do to me. There is only this difference: most of the manufacturers seem paralyzed when they are attacked. Sykes, for instance, when his dressing-shop was set on fire and burned to the ground, when the cloth was torn from his tenters and left in shreds in the field, took no steps to discover or punish the miscreants: he gave up as tamely as a rabbit under the jaws of a ferret. Now I, if I know myself, should stand by my trade, my mill, and my machinery.'

'Helstone says these three are your gods; that the "Orders in Council" are with you another name for the seven deadly sins; that Castlereagh is your Antichrist, and the war-party his legions.'

'Yes; I abhor all these things because they ruin me: they stand in my way: I cannot get on. I cannot execute my plans because of them: I see myself baffled at every turn by their untoward effects.'

'But you are rich and thriving, Moore?'

'I am very rich in cloth, I cannot sell: you should step into my warehouse yonder, and observe how it is piled to the roof with pieces. Roakes and Pearson are in the same condition: America used to be their market, but the Orders in Council have cut that off.'

Malone did not seem prepared to carry on briskly a conversation of this sort; he began to knock the heels of his boots together, and to yawn.

'And then to think,' continued Mr Moore, who seemed too much taken up with the current of his own thoughts to note the symptoms of his guest's *ennui*, – 'to think that these ridiculous gossips of Whinbury and Briarfield will keep pestering one about being married! As if there was nothing to be done in life but to "pay attention," as they say, to some young lady, and then to go to church with her, and then to start on a bridal tour, and then to run through a round of visits, and then, I suppose, to be "having a family." – Oh, que le diable emporte!'

– He broke off the aspiration into which he was launching with a certain energy, and added, more calmly – 'I believe women talk and think only of these things, and they naturally fancy men's minds similarly occupied.'

'Of course – of course,' assented Malone; 'but never mind them.' And he whistled, looked impatiently round, and seemed to feel a great want of something. This time Moore caught, and, it appeared, comprehended his demonstrations.

'Mr Malone,' said he, 'you must require refreshment after your wet walk: I forget hospitality.'

'Not at all,' rejoined Malone; but he looked as if the right nail was at last hit on the head, nevertheless. Moore rose and opened a cupboard.

'It is my fancy,' said he, 'to have every convenience within myself, and not to be dependent on the feminity in the cottage yonder for every mouthful I eat or every drop I drink. I often spend the evening and sup here alone, and sleep with Joe Scott in the mill. Sometimes I am my own watchman; I require little sleep, and it pleases me on a fine night to wander for an hour or two with my musket about the hollow. – Mr Malone, can you cook a mutton-chop?'

'Try me: I've done it hundreds of times at college.'

'There's a dishful, then, and there's the gridiron. Turn them quickly; you know the secret of keeping the juices in?'

'Never fear me – you shall see. Hand a knife and fork, please.'

The curate turned up his coat-cuffs, and applied himself to the cookery with vigour. The manufacturer placed on the table, plates, a loaf of bread, a black bottle, and two tumblers. He then produced a small copper kettle – still from the same well-stored recess, his cupboard – filled it with water from a large stone jar in a corner, set it on the fire beside the hissing gridiron, got lemons, sugar, and a small china punch-bowl; but while he was brewing the punch, a tap at the door called him away.

'Is it you, Sarah?'

'Yes, sir. Will you come to supper, please sir?'

'No; I shall not be in to-night: I shall sleep in the mill. So lock the doors, and tell your mistress to go to bed.' He returned.

'You have your household in proper order,' observed Malone approvingly, as, with his fine face ruddy as the embers over which he bent, he assiduously turned the mutton-chops. 'You are not under petticoat-government, like poor Sweeting; a man – whew! – how the fat spits! – it has burnt my hand – destined to be ruled by women. Now you and I, Moore – there's a fine brown one for you, and full of gravy – you and I will have no grey mares in our stables when we marry.'

'I don't know – I never think about it: if the grey mare is handsome and tractable, why not?'

'The chops are done: is the punch brewed?'

'There is a glassful: taste it. When Joe Scott and his minions return they shall have a share of this, provided they bring home the frames intact.'

Malone waxed very exultant over the supper: he laughed aloud at trifles; made bad jokes and applauded them himself; and, in short, grew unmeaningly noisy. His host, on the contrary, remained quiet as before. It is time, reader, that you should have some idea of the appearance of this same host: I must endeavour to sketch him as he sits at table.

He is what you would probably call, at first view, rather a strange-looking man; for he is thin, dark, sallow; very foreign of aspect, with shadowy hair carelessly streaking his forehead: it appears that he spends but little time at his toilette, or he would arrange it with taste. He seems unconscious that his features are fine, that they have a southern symmetry, clearness, regularity in their chiseling; nor does a spectator become aware of this advantage till he has examined him well, for an anxious countenance, and a hollow, somewhat haggard, outline of face disturb the idea of beauty with one of care. His eyes are large, and grave, and grey; their expression is intent and meditative, rather searching than soft, rather thoughtful than genial. When he parts his lips in a smile, his physiognomy is agreeable: not that it is frank or cheerful even then, but you feel the influence of a certain sedate charm, suggestive, whether truly or delusively, of a considerate, perhaps a kind nature; of feelings that may wear well at home; patient, forbearing, possibly faithful feelings. He is still young – not more than thirty; his stature is tall, his figure slender. His manner of speaking displeases: he has an outlandish accent, which, notwithstanding a studied carelessness of pronunciation and diction, grates on a British, and especially on a Yorkshire ear.

Mr Moore, indeed, was but half a Briton, and scarcely that. He came of a foreign ancestry by the mother's side, and was himself born, and partly reared, on a foreign soil. A hybrid in nature, it is probable he had a hybrid's feeling on many points – patriotism for one; it is likely that he was unapt to attach himself to parties, to sects, even to climes and customs; it is not impossible that he had a tendency to isolate his individual person from any community amidst which his lot might temporarily happen to be thrown, and that he felt it to be his best wisdom to push the interests of Robert Gérard Moore, to the exclusion of philanthropic consideration for general interests: with which he regarded the said Gérard Moore as in a great measure disconnected. Trade was Mr Moore's hereditary calling: the Gérards of Antwerp had been merchants for two centuries back. Once they had been wealthy merchants; but the uncertainties, the involvements of business had come upon them; disastrous speculations had loosened by degrees the foundations of their credit; the house had stood on a tottering base for a dozen years; and at last, in the shock of the French Revolution, it had rushed down a total ruin. In its fall was involved the English and Yorkshire firm of Moore, closely connected with the Antwerp house; and of which one of the partners, resident in Antwerp, Robert Moore, had married Hortense Gérard, with the prospect of his bride inheriting her father Constantine Gérard's share in the business. She inherited, as we have seen, but his share in the liabilities of the firm; and these liabilities, though duly set aside by a composition with creditors, some said her son Robert accepted, in his turn, as a legacy; and that he aspired one day to discharge them, and to rebuild the fallen house of Gérard and Moore on a scale at least equal to its former greatness. It was even supposed that he took bypast circumstances much to heart; and if a childhood passed at the side of a saturnine mother, under foreboding of coming evil, and a manhood drenched and blighted by the pitiless descent of the storm, could painfully impress the mind, *his* probably was impressed in no golden characters.

If, however, he had a great end of restoration in view, it was not in his power to employ great means for its attainment; he was obliged to be content with the day of small things. When he came to Yorkshire, he – whose ancestors had owned warehouses in this seaport, and factories in that inland town, had possessed their town-house and their country-seat – saw no way open to him but to rent a cloth-mill, in an out-of-the-way nook of an out-of-the-way district; to take a cottage adjoining it for his residence, and to add to his possessions, as pasture for his horse, and space for his cloth-tenters, a few acres of the steep rugged land that lined the hollow through which his mill-stream brawled. All this he held at a somewhat high rent (for these war times were hard, and everything was dear), of the trustees of the Fieldhead estate, then the property of a minor.

At the time this history commences, Robert Moore had lived but two years in the district; during which period he had at least proved himself possessed of the quality of activity. The dingy cottage was converted into a neat, tasteful residence. Of part of the rough land he had made garden-ground, which he cultivated with singular, even with Flemish, exactness and care. As to the mill, which was an old structure, and fitted up with old machinery, now become inefficient and out of date, he had from the first evinced the strongest contempt for all its arrangements and appointments: his aim had been to effect a radical reform, which he had executed as fast as his very limited capital would allow; and the narrowness of that capital, and consequent check on his progress, was a restraint which galled his spirit sorely. Moore ever wanted to push on: 'Forward' was the device stamped upon his soul; but poverty curbed him: sometimes (figuratively) he foamed at the mouth when the reins were drawn very tight.

In this state of feeling, it is not to be expected that he would deliberate much as to whether his advance was or was not prejudicial to others. Not being a native, nor for any length of time a resident of the neighbourhood, he did not sufficiently care when the new inventions threw the old work-people out of employ: he never asked himself where those to whom he no longer paid weekly wages found daily bread; and in this negligence he only resembled thousands besides, on whom the starving poor of Yorkshire seemed to have a closer claim.

The period of which I write was an overshadowed one in British history, and especially in the history of the northern provinces. War was then at its height. Europe was all involved therein. England, if not weary, was worn with long resistance: yes, and half her people were weary too, and cried out for peace on any terms. National honour was become a mere empty name, of no value in the eyes of many, because their sight was dim with famine; and for a morsel of meat they would have sold their birthright.

The 'Orders in Council,' provoked by Napoleon's Milan and Berlin decrees, and forbidding neutral powers to trade with France, had, by offending America, cut off the principal market of the Yorkshire woollen trade, and brought it consequently to the verge of ruin. Minor foreign markets were glutted, and would receive no more: the Brazils, Portugal, Sicily, were all overstocked by nearly two years' consumption. At this crisis, certain inventions in machinery were introduced into the staple manufactures of the north, which, greatly reducing the number of hands necessary to be employed, threw thousands out of work, and left them without legitimate means of sustaining life.

A bad harvest supervened. Distress reached its climax. Endurance, overgoaded, stretched the hand of fraternity to sedition. The throes of a sort of moral earthquake were felt heaving under the hills of the northern counties. But, as is usual in such cases, nobody took much notice. When a food-riot broke out in a manufacturing town, when a gig-mill was burnt to the ground, or a manufacturer's house was attacked, the furniture thrown into the streets, and the family forced to flee for their lives, some local measures were or were not taken by the local magistracy; a ringleader was detected, or more frequently suffered to elude detection; newspaper paragraphs were written on the subject, and there the thing stopped. As to the sufferers, whose sole inheritance was labour, and who had lost that inheritance – who could not get work, and consequently could not get wages, and consequently could not get bread – they were left to suffer on; perhaps inevitably left: it would not do to stop the progress of invention, to damage science by discouraging its improvements; the war could not be terminated, efficient relief could not be raised: there was no help then; so the unemployed underwent their destiny – ate the bread and drank the waters of affliction.

Misery generates hate: these sufferers hated the machines which they believed took their bread from them; they hated the buildings which contained those machines; they hated the manufacturers who owned those buildings. In the parish of Briarfield, with which we have at present to do, Hollow's-mill was the place held most abominable; Gérard Moore, in his double character of semi-foreigner and thorough-going progressist, the man most abominated. And it perhaps rather agreed with Moore's temperament than otherwise to be generally hated; especially when he believed the thing for which he was hated a right and an expedient thing; and it was with a sense of warlike excitement he, on this night, sat in his counting-house waiting the arrival of his frame-laden waggons. Malone's coming and company were, it may be, most unwelcome to

him: he would have preferred sitting alone; for he liked a silent,
sombre, unsafe solitude: his watchman's musket would have
been company enough for him; the full-flowing beck in the den
would have delivered continuously the discourse most genial to
his ear.

With the queerest look in the world, had the manufacturer for
some ten minutes been watching the Irish curate, as the latter
made free with the punch; when suddenly that steady grey eye
changed, as if another vision came between it and Malone.
Moore raised his hand.

'Chut!' he said, in his French fashion, as Malone made a
noise with his glass. He listened a moment, then rose, put his
hat on, and went out at the counting-house door.

The night was still, dark, and stagnant; the water yet rushed
on full and fast: its flow almost seemed a flood in the utter
silence. Moore's ear, however, caught another sound – very distant, but yet dissimilar – broken, and rugged: in short, a sound
of heavy wheels crunching a stony road. He returned to the
counting-house and lit a lantern, with which he walked down
the mill-yard, and proceeded to open the gates. The big waggons were coming on; the drayhorses' huge hoofs were heard
splashing in the mud and water. Moore hailed them.

'Hey, Joe Scott! Is all right?'

Probably Joe Scott was yet at too great a distance to hear the
inquiry; he did not answer it.

'Is all right, I say?' again asked Moore, when the elephant-
like leader's nose almost touched his.

Some one jumped out from the foremost waggon into
the road; a voice cried aloud, 'Ay, ay, divil, all's raight! We've
smashed 'em.'

And there was a run. The waggons stood still: they were now
deserted.

'Joe Scott!' No Joe Scott answered, 'Murgatroyd! Pighills!
Sykes!' No reply. Mr Moore lifted his lantern, and looked into

the vehicles; there was neither man nor machinery: they were empty and abandoned.

Now Mr Moore loved his machinery: he had risked the last of his capital on the purchase of these frames and shears which to-night had been expected; speculations most important to his interests depended on the results to be wrought by them: where were they?

The words 'we've smashed 'em!' rung in his ears. How did the catastrophe affect him? By the light of the lantern he held, were his features visible, relaxing to a singular smile: the smile the man of determined spirit wears when he reaches a juncture in his life where this determined spirit is to feel a demand on its strength: when the strain is to be made, and the faculty must bear or break. Yet he remained silent, and even motionless; for at the instant he neither knew what to say nor what to do. He placed the lantern on the ground, and stood with his arms folded, gazing down and reflecting.

An impatient trampling of one of the horses made him presently look up; his eye, in the moment, caught the gleam of something white attached to a part of the harness. Examined by the light of the lantern, this proved to be a folded paper – a billet. It bore no address without; within was the superscription: –

'To the Divil of Hollow's-miln.'

We will not copy the rest of the orthography, which was very peculiar, but translate it into legible English. It ran thus: –

'Your hellish machinery is shivered to smash on Stilbro' Moor, and your men are lying bound hand and foot in a ditch by the roadside. Take this as a warning from men that are starving, and have starving wives and children to go home to when they have done this deed. If you get new machines, or if you otherwise go on as you have done, you shall hear from us again. Beware!'

'Hear from you again? Yes; I'll hear from you again, and you shall hear from me. I'll speak to you directly: on Stilbro' Moor you shall hear from me in a moment.'

Having led the waggons within the gates, he hastened towards the cottage. Opening the door, he spoke a few words quickly, but quietly, to two females who ran to meet him in the passage. He calmed the seeming alarm of one by a brief palliative account of what had taken place; to the other he said, 'Go into the mill, Sarah – there is the key – and ring the mill-bell as loud as you can: afterwards you will get another lantern and help me to light up the front.'

Returning to his horses, he unharnessed, fed, and stabled them with equal speed and care, pausing occasionally, while so occupied, as if to listen for the mill-bell. It clanged out presently, with irregular but loud, and alarming din: the hurried agitated peal seemed more urgent than if the summons had been steadily given by a practised hand. On that still night, at that unusual hour, it was heard a long way round: the guests in the kitchen of the Redhouse were startled by the clangour; and, declaring that 'there must be summat more nor common to do at Hollow's-miln,' they called for lanterns, and hurried to the spot in a body. And scarcely had they thronged into the yard with their gleaming lights, when the tramp of horses was heard, and a little man in a shovel hat, sitting erect on the back of a shaggy pony, 'rode lightly in,' followed by an aid-de-camp mounted on a larger steed.

Mr Moore, meantime, after stabling his dray-horses, had saddled his hackney; and, with the aid of Sarah, the servant, lit up his mill; whose wide and long front now glared one great illumination, throwing a sufficient light on the yard to obviate all fear of confusion arising from obscurity. Already a deep hum of voices became audible. Mr Malone had at length issued from the counting-house, previously taking the precaution to dip his head and face in the stone water-jar; and this precaution, together with the sudden alarm, had nearly restored to him the possession of those senses which the punch had partially scattered. He stood with his hat on the back of his head, and his shillelagh grasped in his dexter fist, answering much at random the questions of the newly-arrived party from the Redhouse. Mr Moore now appeared, and was immediately confronted by the shovel hat and the shaggy pony.

'Well, Moore, what is your business with us? I thought you would want us to-night: me and the hetman here (patting his pony's neck), and Tom and his charger. When I heard your mill-bell, I could sit still no longer, so I left Boultby to finish his supper alone: but where is the enemy? I do not see a mask or a smutted face present; and there is not a pane of glass broken in your windows. Have you had an attack, or do you expect one?'

'Oh, not at all! I have neither had one nor expect one,' answered Moore, coolly. 'I only ordered the bell to be rung because I want two or three neighbours to stay here in the Hollow, while I and a couple or so more go over to Stilbro' Moor.'

'To Stilbro' Moor! What to do? To meet the waggons?'

'The waggons are come home an hour ago.'

'Then all's right. What more would you have?'

'They came home empty; and Joe Scott and Company are left on the moor, and so are the frames. Read that scrawl.'

Mr Helstone received and perused the document of which the contents have before been given.

'Hum! They've only served you as they serve others. But, however, the poor fellows in the ditch will be expecting help with some impatience: this is a wet night for such a berth. I and Tom will go with you; Malone may stay behind and take care of the mill: what is the matter with him? His eyes seem starting out of his head.'

'He has been eating a mutton-chop.'

'Indeed! Peter Augustus, be on your guard. Eat no more mutton-chops to-night. You are left here in command of these premises: an honourable post!'

'Is anybody to stay with me?'

'As many of the present assemblage as choose. My lads, how

many of you will remain here, and how many will go a little way with me and Mr Moore on the Stilbro'-road, to meet some men who have been waylaid and assaulted by frame-breakers?'

The small number of three volunteered to go; the rest preferred staying behind. As Mr Moore mounted his horse, the rector asked him in a low voice, whether he had locked up the mutton-chops, so that Peter Augustus could not get at them? The manufacturer nodded an affirmative, and the rescue-party set out.

CHAPTER III

MR YORKE

CHEERFULNESS, it would appear, is a matter which depends fully as much on the state of things within, as on the state of things without and around us. I make this trite remark, because I happen to know that Messrs Helstone and Moore trotted forth from the mill-yard gates, at the head of their very small company, in the best possible spirits. When a ray from a lantern (the three pedestrians of the party carried each one) fell on Mr Moore's face, you could see an unusual, because a lively, spark dancing in his eyes, and a new-found vivacity mantling on his dark physiognomy; and when the rector's visage was illuminated, his hard features were revealed all agrin and ashine with glee. Yet a drizzling night, a somewhat perilous expedition, you would think were not circumstances calculated to enliven those exposed to the wet and engaged in the adventure. If any member or members of the crew who had been at work on Stilbro' Moor had caught a view of this party, they would have had great pleasure in shooting either of the leaders from behind a wall: and the leaders knew this; and, the fact is, being both men of steely nerves and steady-beating hearts, were elate with the knowledge.

I am aware, reader, and you need not remind me, that it is a dreadful thing for a parson to be warlike: I am aware that he should be a man of peace. I have some faint outline of an idea of what a clergyman's mission is amongst mankind, and I remember distinctly whose servant he is; whose message he delivers, whose example he should follow; yet, with all this, if you are a parson-hater, you need not expect me to go along with you every step of your dismal, downward-tending, un-christian road; you need not expect me to join in your deep anathemas, at once so narrow and so sweeping – in your poison-ous rancour so intense and so absurd, against 'the cloth;' to lift up my eyes and hands with a Supplehough, or to inflate my lungs with a Barraclough, in horror and denunciation of the diabolical rector of Briarfield.

He was not diabolical at all. The evil simply was – he had missed his vocation: he should have been a soldier, and circum-stances had made him a priest. For the rest, he was a conscien-tious, hard-headed, hard-handed, brave, stern, implacable, faithful little man: a man almost without sympathy, ungentle, prejudiced, and rigid; but a man true to principle, – honourable, sagacious, and sincere. It seems to me, reader, that you cannot always cut out men to fit their profession, and that you ought not to curse them because that profession sometimes hangs on them ungracefully: nor will I curse Helstone, clerical Cossack as he was. Yet he *was* cursed, and by many of his own parish-ioners, as by others he was adored: which is the frequent fate of men who show partiality in friendship, and bitterness in enmity; who are equally attached to principles and adherent to prejudices.

Helstone and Moore, being both in excellent spirits, and united for the present in one cause, you would expect that, as they rode side by side, they would converse amicably. Oh, no! These two men, of hard bilious natures both, rarely came into contact but they chafed each other's moods. Their frequent bone of contention was the war. Helstone was a high Tory (there were Tories in those days) and Moore was a bitter Whig – a Whig, at least, as far as opposition to the war-party was con-cerned: that being the question which affected his own interest; and only on that question did he profess any British politics at all. He liked to infuriate Helstone by declaring his belief in the invincibility of Bonaparte; by taunting England and Europe with the impotence of their efforts to withstand him; and by coolly advancing the opinion that it was as well to yield to him soon as late, since he must in the end crush every antagonist, and reign supreme.

Helstone could not bear these sentiments: it was only on the consideration of Moore being a sort of outcast and alien, and having but half measure of British blood to temper the foreign gall which corroded his veins, that he brought himself to listen to them without indulging the wish he felt to cane the speaker. Another thing, too, somewhat allayed his disgust; namely, a fellow-feeling for the dogged tone with which these opinions were asserted, and a respect for the consistency of Moore's crabbed contumacy.

As the party turned into the Stilbro' road, they met what little wind there was; the rain dashed in their faces. Moore had been fretting his companion previously, and now, braced up by the raw breeze, and perhaps irritated by the sharp drizzle, he began to goad him.

'Does your Peninsular news please you still?' he asked.

'What do you mean?' was the surly demand of the Rector.

'I mean have you still faith in that Baal of a Lord Wellington?'

'And what do you mean now?'

'Do you still believe that this wooden-faced and pebble-hearted idol of England has power to send fire down from heaven to consume the French holocaust you want to offer up?'

'I believe Wellington will flog Bonaparte's marshals into the sea, the day it pleases him to lift his arm.'

'But, my dear sir, you can't be serious in what you say. Bonaparte's marshals are great men, who act under the guidance of an omnipotent master-spirit; your Wellington is the most humdrum of common-place martinets, whose slow mechanical movements are further cramped by an ignorant home-government.'

'Wellington is the soul of England. Wellington is the right champion of a good cause; the fit representative of a powerful, a resolute, a sensible, and an honest nation.'

'Your good cause, as far as I understand it, is simply the restoration of that filthy, feeble Ferdinand, to a throne which he disgraced; your fit representative of an honest people is a dull-witted drover, acting for a duller-witted farmer; and against these are arrayed victorious supremacy and invincible genius.'

'Against legitimacy is arrayed usurpation; against modest, single-minded, righteous, and brave resistance to encroachment, is arrayed boastful, double-tongued, selfish, and treacherous ambition to possess. God defend the right!'

'God often defends the powerful.'

'What! I suppose the handful of Israelites standing dry-shod on the Asiatic side of the Red Sea, was more powerful than the host of the Egyptians drawn up on the African side? Were they more numerous? Were they better appointed? Were they more mighty, in a word – eh? Don't speak, or you'll tell a lie, Moore; you know you will. They were a poor over-wrought band of bondsmen. Tyrants had oppressed them through four hundred years; a feeble mixture of women and children diluted their thin ranks; their masters, who roared to follow them through the divided flood, were a set of pampered Ethiops, about as strong and brutal as the lions of Libya. They were armed, horsed, and charioted, the poor Hebrew wanderers were afoot; few of them, it is likely, had better weapons than their shepherds' crooks, or their masons' building-tools; their meek and mighty leader himself had only his rod. But bethink you, Robert Moore, right was with them; the God of battles was on their side. Crime and the lost archangel generalled the ranks of Pharaoh, and which triumphed? We know that well: "The Lord saved Israel that day out of the hand of the Egyptians, and Israel saw the Egyptians dead upon the seashore;" yea, "the depths covered them, they sank to the bottom as a stone." The right hand of the Lord became glorious in power; the right hand of the Lord dashed in pieces the enemy!'

'You are all right; only you forget the true parallel: France is Israel, and Napoleon is Moses. Europe, with her old over-gorged empires and rotten dynasties, is corrupt Egypt; gallant France is the Twelve Tribes, and her fresh and vigorous Usurper the Shepherd of Horeb.'

'I scorn to answer you.'

Moore accordingly answered himself; at least he subjoined to what he had just said an additional observation in a lower voice.

'Oh, in Italy he was as great as any Moses! He was the right thing there; fit to head and organize measures for the regenera-tion of nations. It puzzles me to this day how the conqueror of Lodi should have condescended to become an emperor, a vulgar, stupid humbug; and still more how a people, who had once called themselves republicans, should have sunk again to the grade of mere slaves. I despise France! If England had gone as far on the march of civilisation as France did, she would hardly have retreated so shamelessly.'

'You don't mean to say that besotted imperial France is any worse than bloody republican France?' demanded Helstone, fiercely.

'I mean to say nothing: but I can think what I please, you know, Mr Helstone, both about France and England; and about revolutions, and regicides, and restorations in general; and about the divine right of kings, which you often stickle for in your sermons, and the duty of non-resistance, and the sanity of war, and –'

Mr Moore's sentence was here cut short by the rapid rolling up of a gig, and its sudden stoppage in the middle of the road; both he and the Rector had been too much occupied with their discourse to notice its approach till it was close upon them.

'Nah, maister, did th' waggons hit home?' demanded a voice from the vehicle.

'Can that be Joe Scott?'

'Ay, ay!' returned another voice; for the gig contained two persons, as was seen by the glimmer of its lamp: the men with

the lanterns had now fallen into the rear, or rather the equestrians of the rescue-party had outridden the pedestrians. 'Ay,
Mr Moore, it's Joe Scott. I'm bringing him back to you in a
bonny pickle. I fand him on the top of the moor yonder, him
and three others. What will you give me for restoring him
to you?'

'Why, my thanks, I believe; for I could better have afforded
to lose a better man. That is you, I suppose, Mr Yorke, by your
voice?'

'Ay, lad, it's me. I was coming home from Stilbro' market,
and just as I got to the middle of the moor, and was whipping
on as swift as the wind (for these, they say, are not safe times,
thanks to a bad government!) I heard a groan. I pulled up: some
would have whipt on faster; but I've naught to fear, that I know
of. I don't believe there's a lad in these parts would harm me: at
least I'd give them as good as I got if they offered to do it. I said,
"Is there aught wrong anywhere?" – " 'Deed is there," somebody
says, speaking out of the ground, like. "What's to do? be sharp,
and tell me," I ordered. – "Nobbut four on us ligging in a
ditch," says Joe, as quiet as could be. I tell'd 'em, more shame
to 'em, and bid them get up and move on, or I'd lend them a
lick of the gig-whip; for my notion was, they were all fresh. –
"We'd ha' done that an hour sin'; but we're teed wi' a bit o'
band," says Joe. So in a while I got down and loosed 'em wi'
my penknife; and Scott would ride wi' me, to tell me all how
it happened; and t' others are coming on as fast as their feet
will bring them.'

'Well, I am greatly obliged to you, Mr Yorke.'

'Are you, my lad? you know you're not. However, here are
the rest approaching. And here, by the Lord! is another set with
lights in their pitchers, like the army of Gideon; and as we've
th' parson wi' us, – good-evening, Mr Helstone, – we'se do.'

Mr Helstone returned the salutation of the individual in the
gig very stiffly indeed. That individual proceeded: –

'We're eleven strong men, and there's both horses and chariots amang us. If we could only fall in wi' some of these starved ragamuffins of frame-breakers, we could win a grand victory; we could iv'ry one be a Wellington, – that would please ye, Mr Helstone; and sich paragraphs as we could contrive for t' papers! Briarfield suld be famous: but we'se hev a column and a half i' th' *Stilbro' Courier* ower this job, as it is, I daresay: I'se expect no less.'

'And I'll promise you no less, Mr Yorke, for I'll write the article myself,' returned the Rector.

'To be sure! sartainly! And mind ye recommend weel that them 'at brake t' bits o' frames, and teed Joe Scott's legs wi' band, suld be hung without benefit o' clergy. It's a hanging matter, or suld be; no doubt o' that.'

'If I judged them, I'd give them short shrift!' cried Moore; 'but I mean to let them quite alone this bout, to give them rope enough, certain that in the end they will hang themselves.'

'Let them alone, will ye, Moore? Do you promise that?'

'Promise? No. All I mean to say is, I shall give myself no particular trouble to catch them; but if one falls in my way –'

'You'll snap him up, of course: only you would rather they would do something worse than merely stop a waggon before you reckon with them. Well, we'll say no more on the subject at present. Here we are at my door, gentlemen, and I hope you and the men will step in: you will none of you be the worse of a little refreshment.'

Moore and Helstone opposed this proposition as unnecessary; it was, however, pressed on them so courteously, and the night, besides, was so inclement, and the gleam from the muslin-curtained windows of the house before which they had halted, looked so inviting, that at length they yielded. Mr Yorke, after having alighted from his gig, which he left in charge of a man who issued from an outbuilding on his arrival, led the way in.

It will have been remarked that Mr Yorke varied a little in his phraseology; now he spoke broad Yorkshire, and anon he expressed himself in very pure English. His manner seemed liable to equal alternations; he could be polite and affable, and he could be blunt and rough. His station then you could not easily determine by his speech or demeanour; perhaps the appearance of his residence may decide it.

The men he recommended to take the kitchen way, saying that he would 'see them served wi' summat to taste presently.' The gentlemen were ushered in at the front entrance. They found themselves in a matted hall, lined almost to the ceiling with pictures; through this they were conducted to a large parlour, with a magnificent fire in the grate; the most cheerful of rooms it appeared as a whole, and when you came to examine details, the enlivening effect was not diminished. There was no splendour, but there was taste everywhere, – unusual taste, – the taste, you would have said, of a travelled man, a scholar, and a gentleman. A series of Italian views decked the walls; each of these was a specimen of true art; a connoisseur had selected them: they were genuine and valuable. Even by candlelight, the bright clear skies, the soft distances, with blue air quivering between the eye and the hills, the fresh tints and well massed lights and shadows charmed the view. The subjects were all pastoral, the scenes were all sunny. There was a guitar and some music on a sofa; there were cameos, beautiful miniatures; a set of Grecian-looking vases on the mantelpiece; there were books well arranged in two elegant bookcases.

Mr Yorke bade his guests be seated; he then rang for wine; to the servant who brought it he gave hospitable orders for the refreshment of the men in the kitchen. The Rector remained standing; he seemed not to like his quarters; he would not touch the wine his host offered him.

'E'en as you will,' remarked Mr Yorke. 'I reckon you're thinking of Eastern customs, Mr Helstone, and you'll not eat nor drink under my roof, feared we suld be forced to be friends; but I'm not so particular or superstitious. You might sup the contents of that decanter, and you might give me a bottle of the best in your own cellar, and I'd hold myself free to oppose you at every turn still, – in every vestry-meeting and justice-meeting where we encountered one another.'

'It is just what I should expect of you, Mr Yorke.'

'Does it agree wi' ye now, Mr Helstone, to be riding out after rioters, of a wet night, at your age?'

'It always agrees with me to be doing my duty; and in this case my duty is a thorough pleasure. To hunt down vermin is a noble occupation, – fit for an Archbishop.'

'Fit for ye, at ony rate: but where's t' curate? He's happen gone to visit some poor body in a sick gird, or he's happen hunting down vermin in another direction.'

'He is doing garrison duty at Hollow's-mill.'

'You left him a sup o' wine, I hope, Bob (turning to Mr Moore), to keep his courage up?'

He did not pause for an answer, but continued, quickly – still addressing Moore, who had thrown himself into an old-fashioned chair by the fireside, – 'Move it, Robert! Get up, my lad! That place is mine. Take the sofa, or three other chairs, if you will, but not this; it belangs to me, and nob'dy else.'

'Why are you so particular to that chair, Mr Yorke?' asked Moore, lazily vacating the place, in obedience to orders.

'My father war afore me, and that's all t' answer I sall gie thee; and it's as good a reason as Mr Helstone can give for the main feck o' his notions.'

'Moore, are you ready to go?' inquired the Rector.

'Nay; Robert's not ready; or rather, I'm not ready to part wi' him: he's an ill lad, and wants correcting.'

'Why, sir? What have I done?'

'Made thyself enemies on every hand.'

'What do I care for that? What difference does it make to me whether your Yorkshire louts hate me or like me?'

'Ay, there it is. The lad is a mak' of an alien amang us: his father would never have talked i' that way. Go back to Antwerp, where you were born and bred, mauvaise tête!'

'Mauvaise tête vous-même; je ne fais que mon devoir: quant à vos lourdauds de paysans, je m'en moque!'

'En revanche, mon garçon, nos lourdauds de paysans se moqueront de toi; sois en certain,' replied Yorke, speaking with nearly as pure a French accent as Gérard Moore.

'C'est bon! c'est bon! Et puisque cela m'est égal, que mes amis ne s'en inquiètent pas.'

'Tes amis! Où sont-ils, tes amis?'

'Je fais écho, où sont-ils? et je suis fort aise que l'écho seul y répond. Au diable les amis! Je me souviens encore du moment où mon père et mes oncles Gérard appellèrent autour d'eux leurs amis, et Dieu sait si les amis se sont empressés d'accourir à leur secours! Tenez, M. Yorke, ce mot, ami, m'irrite trop; ne m'en parlez plus.'

'Comme tu voudras.'

And here Mr Yorke held his peace; and while he sits leaning back in his three-cornered, carved oak chair, I will snatch my opportunity to sketch the portrait of this French-speaking Yorkshire gentleman.

CHAPTER IV

MR YORKE (CONTINUED)

A YORKSHIRE GENTLEMAN he was par excellence, in every point. About fifty-five years old, but looking at first sight still older, for his hair was silver white. His forehead was broad, not high; his face fresh and hale; the harshness of the north was seen in his features, as it was heard in his voice; every trait was thoroughly English, not a Norman line anywhere; it was an inelegant, unclassic, unaristocratic mould of visage. Fine people would perhaps have called it vulgar; sensible people would have termed it characteristic; shrewd people would have delighted in it for the pith, sagacity, intelligence – the rude, yet real originality marked in every lineament, latent in every furrow. But it was an indocile, a scornful, and a sarcastic face; the face of a man difficult to lead, and impossible to drive. His stature was rather tall, and he was well-made and wiry, and had a stately integrity of port; there was not a suspicion of the clown about him anywhere.

I did not find it easy to sketch Mr Yorke's person, but it is more difficult to indicate his mind. If you expect to be treated to a Perfection, reader, or even to a benevolent, philanthropic old gentleman in him, you are mistaken. He has spoken with some sense, and with good feeling, to Mr Moore; but you are not thence to conclude that he always spoke and thought justly and kindly.

Mr Yorke, in the first place, was without the organ of Veneration – a great want, and which throws a man wrong on every point where veneration is required. Secondly, he was without the organ of Comparison – a deficiency which strips a man of sympathy; and, thirdly, he had too little of the organs of Benevolence and Ideality, which took the glory and softness from his nature, and for him diminished those divine qualities throughout the universe.

The want of veneration made him intolerant to those above him: kings and nobles and priests, dynasties and parliaments and establishments, with all their doings, most of their enactments, their forms, their rights, their claims, were to him an abomination – all rubbish; he found no use or pleasure in them, and believed it would be clear gain, and no damage to the world, if its high places were razed, and their occupants crushed in the fall. The want of veneration, too, made him dead at heart to the electric delight of admiring what is admirable; it dried up a thousand pure sources of enjoyment; it withered a thousand vivid pleasures. He was not irreligious, though a member of no sect; but his religion could not be that of one who knows how to venerate. He believed in God and heaven; but his God and heaven were those of a man in whom awe, imagination, and tenderness lack.

The weakness of his powers of comparison made him inconsistent; while he professed some excellent general doctrines of mutual toleration and forbearance, he cherished towards certain classes a bigoted antipathy: he spoke of 'parsons' and all who belonged to parsons, of 'lords' and the appendages of lords, with a harshness, sometimes an insolence, as unjust as it was insufferable. He could not place himself in the position of those he vituperated; he could not compare their errors with their temptations, their defects with their disadvantages; he could not realize the effect of such and such circumstances on himself similarly situated, and he would often express the most ferocious and tyrannical wishes regarding those who had acted, as he thought, ferociously and tyrannically. To judge by his threats, he would have employed arbitrary, even cruel, means to advance the cause of freedom and equality. Equality – yes, Mr Yorke talked about equality, but at heart he was a proud man: very friendly to his workpeople, very good to all who were beneath him, and submitted quietly to be beneath him, but haughty as Beelzebub to whomsoever the world deemed (for he deemed no man) his superior. Revolt was in his blood: he could not bear control; his father, his grandfather before him, could not bear it, and his children after him never could.

The want of general benevolence made him very impatient of imbecility, and of all faults which grated on his strong, shrewd nature: it left no check to his cutting sarcasm. As he was not merciful, he would sometimes wound and wound again, without noticing how much he hurt, or caring how deep he thrust.

As to the paucity of ideality in his mind, that can scarcely be called a fault: a fine ear for music, a correct eye for colour and form, left him the quality of taste; and who cares for imagination? Who does not think it a rather dangerous, senseless attribute – akin to weakness – perhaps partaking of frenzy – a disease rather than a gift of the mind?

Probably all think it so, but those who possess – or fancy they possess – it. To hear them speak, you would believe that their hearts would be cold if that elixir did not flow about them; that their eyes would be dim if that flame did not refine their vision; that they would be lonely if this strange companion abandoned them. You would suppose that it imparted some glad hope to spring, some fine charm to summer, some tranquil joy to autumn, some consolation to winter, which you do not feel. All illusion, of course; but the fanatics cling to their dream, and would not give it for gold.

As Mr Yorke did not possess poetic imagination himself, he considered it a most superfluous quality in others. Painters and musicians he could tolerate, and even encourage, because he could relish the results of their art; he could see the charm of a fine picture, and feel the pleasure of good music; but a quiet poet – whatever force struggled, whatever fire glowed, in his breast – if he could not have played the man in the counting-house, or the tradesman in the Piece Hall, might have lived despised, and died scorned, under the eyes of Hiram Yorke.

And as there are many Hiram Yorkes in the world, it is well that the true poet, quiet externally though he may be, has often a truculent spirit under his placidity, and is full of shrewdness in his meekness, and can measure the whole stature of those who look down on him, and correctly ascertain the weight and value of the pursuits they disdain him for not having followed. It is happy that he can have his own bliss, his own society with his great friend and goddess, Nature, quite independent of those who find little pleasure in him, and in whom he finds no pleasure at all. It is just, that while the world and circumstances often turn a dark, cold side to him – and properly, too, because he first turns a dark, cold, careless side to them – he should be able to maintain a festal brightness and cherishing glow in his bosom, which makes all bright and genial for him; while strangers, perhaps, deem his existence a Polar winter never gladdened by a sun. The true poet is not one whit to be pitied; and he is apt to laugh in his sleeve, when any misguided sympathizer whines over his wrongs. Even when utilitarians sit in judgment on him, and pronounce him and his art useless, he hears the sentence with such a hard derision, such a broad, deep, comprehensive, and merciless contempt of the unhappy Pharisees who pronounce it, that he is rather to be chidden than condoled with. These, however, are not Mr Yorke's reflections; and it is with Mr Yorke we have at present to do.

I have told you some of his faults, reader; as to his good points, he was one of the most honourable and capable men in Yorkshire: even those who disliked him were forced to respect him. He was much beloved by the poor, because he was thoroughly kind and very fatherly to them. To his workmen he was considerate and cordial: when he dismissed them from an occupation, he would try to set them on to something else; or, if that was impossible, help them to remove with their families to a district where work might possibly be had. It must also be remarked that if, as sometimes chanced, any individual amongst his 'hands' showed signs of insubordination, Yorke – who, like many who abhor being controlled, knew how to control with vigour – had the secret of crushing rebellion in the germ, of eradicating it like a bad weed, so that it never spread or developed within the sphere of his authority. Such being the happy state of his own affairs, he felt himself at liberty to speak with the utmost severity of those who were differently situated; to ascribe whatever was unpleasant in their position entirely to their own fault, to sever himself from the masters, and advocate freely the cause of the operatives.

Mr Yorke's family was the first and oldest in the district; and he, though not the wealthiest, was one of the most influential men. His education had been good; in his youth, before the French Revolution, he had travelled on the continent: he was an adept in the French and Italian languages. During a two years' sojourn in Italy, he had collected many good paintings and tasteful rarities, with which his residence was now adorned. His manners, when he liked, were those of a finished gentleman of the old school; his conversation, when he was disposed to please, was singularly interesting and original; and if he usually expressed himself in the Yorkshire dialect, it was because he chose to do so, preferring his native Doric to a more refined vocabulary. 'A Yorkshire burr,' he affirmed, 'was as much better than a Cockney's lisp, as a bull's bellow than a ratton's squeak.'

Mr Yorke knew every one, and was known by every one for miles round; yet his intimate acquaintance were very few. Himself thoroughly original, he had no taste for what was ordinary: a racy, rough character, high or low, ever found acceptance with him; a refined, insipid personage, however exalted in station, was his aversion. He would spend an hour any time in talking freely with a shrewd workman of his own, or with some queer, sagacious old woman amongst his cottagers, when he would have grudged a moment to a commonplace fine gentleman, or to the most fashionable and elegant, if frivolous, lady. His preferences on these points he carried to an extreme, forgetting that there may be amiable and even admirable characters amongst those who cannot be original. Yet he made exceptions to his own rule: there was a certain order of mind, plain, ingenuous, neglecting refinement, almost devoid of intellectuality, and quite incapable of appreciating what was intellectual in him; but which, at the same time, never felt disgust at his rudeness, was not easily wounded by his sarcasm, did not closely analyze his sayings, doings, or opinions; with which he was peculiarly at ease, and, consequently, which he peculiarly preferred. He was lord amongst such characters. They, while submitting implicitly to his influence, never acknowledged, because they never reflected on, his superiority; they were quite tractable, therefore, without running the smallest danger of being servile; and their unthinking, easy, artless insensibility was as acceptable, because as convenient to Mr Yorke, as that of the chair he sat on, or of the floor he trod.

It will have been observed that he was not quite uncordial with Mr Moore; he had two or three reasons for entertaining a faint partiality to that gentleman. It may sound odd, but the first of these was that Moore spoke English with a foreign, and French with a perfectly pure accent; and that his dark, thin face, with its fine though rather wasted lines, had a most anti-British and anti-Yorkshire look. These points seem frivolous, unlikely to influence a character like Yorke's; but, the fact is, they recalled old, perhaps pleasurable associations: they brought back his travelling, his youthful days. He had seen, amidst Italian cities and scenes, faces like Moore's; he had heard, in Parisian cafés and theatres, voices like his; he was young then, and when he looked at and listened to the alien, he seemed young again.

Secondly, he had known Moore's father, and had had dealings with him: that was a more substantial, though by no means a more agreeable tie; for, as his firm had been connected with Moore's in business, it had also, in some measure, been implicated in its losses.

Thirdly, he had found Robert himself a sharp man of business. He saw reason to anticipate that he would in the end, by one means or another, make money; and he respected both his resolution and acuteness; perhaps, also, his hardness. A fourth circumstance which drew them together was that of Mr Yorke being one of the guardians of the minor on whose estate Hollow's mill was situated; consequently Moore, in the course of his alterations and improvements, had frequent occasion to consult him.

As to the other guest now present in Mr Yorke's parlour, Mr Helstone, between him and his host there existed a double antipathy: the antipathy of nature and that of circumstances. The free-thinker hated the formalist; the lover of liberty detested the disciplinarian: besides, it was said that in former years they had been rival suitors of the same lady.

Mr Yorke, as a general rule, was, when young, noted for his preference of sprightly and dashing women: a showy shape and air, a lively wit, a ready tongue, chiefly seemed to attract him. He never, however, proposed to any of these brilliant belles, whose society he sought; and all at once he seriously fell in love with, and eagerly wooed a girl who presented a complete contrast to those he had hitherto noticed: a girl with the face of a Madonna; a girl of living marble; stillness personified. No matter that, when he spoke to her, she only answered him in monosyllables; no matter that his sighs seemed unheard, that his glances were unreturned, that she never responded to his opinions, rarely smiled at his jests, paid him no respect and no attention; no matter that she seemed the opposite of everything feminine he had ever, in his whole life, been known to admire: for him Mary Cave was perfect, because somehow, for some reason – no doubt he had a reason – he loved her.

Mr Helstone, at that time curate of Briarfield, loved Mary too; or, at any rate, he fancied her. Several others admired her, for she was beautiful as a monumental angel; but the clergyman was preferred for his office's sake: that office probably investing

him with some of the illusion necessary to allure to the commission of matrimony, and which Miss Cave did not find in any
of the young wool-staplers, her other adorers. Mr Helstone
neither had, nor professed to have, Mr Yorke's absorbing passion
for her: he had known of the humble reverence which seemed
to subdue most of her suitors; he saw her more as she really was
than the rest did; he was, consequently, more master of her
and himself. She accepted him at the first offer, and they were
married.

Nature never intended Mr Helstone to make a very good
husband, especially to a quiet wife. He thought, so long as a
woman was silent, nothing ailed her, and she wanted nothing.
If she did not complain of solitude, solitude, however continued,
could not be irksome to her. If she did not talk and put herself
forward, express a partiality for this, an aversion to that, she had
no partialities or aversions, and it was useless to consult her
tastes. He made no pretence of comprehending women, or comparing them with men: they were a different, probably a very
inferior order of existence; a wife could not be her husband's
companion, much less his confidant, much less his stay. *His*
wife, after a year or two, was of no great importance to him in
any shape; and when she one day, as he thought, suddenly – for
he had scarcely noticed her decline – but as others thought
gradually, took her leave of him and of life, and there was only
a still beautiful-featured mould of clay left, cold and white, in
the conjugal couch, he felt his bereavement – who shall say how
little? Yet, perhaps, more than he seemed to feel it; for he was
not a man from whom grief easily wrung tears.

His dry-eyed and sober mourning scandalized an old housekeeper, and likewise a female attendant, who had waited upon
Mrs Helstone in her sickness; and who, perhaps, had had opportunities of learning more of the deceased lady's nature, of her
capacity for feeling and loving, than her husband knew: they
gossiped together over the corpse, related anecdotes, with
embellishments of her lingering decline, and its real or supposed

cause; in short, they worked each other up to some indignation against the austere little man, who sat examining papers in an adjoining room, unconscious of what opprobium he was the object.

Mrs Helstone was hardly under the sod when rumours began to be rife in the neighbourhood that she had died of a broken heart; these magnified quickly into reports of hard usage, and, finally, details of harsh treatment on the part of her husband: reports grossly untrue, but not the less eagerly received on that account. Mr Yorke heard them, partly believed them. Already, of course, he had no friendly feeling to his successful rival; though himself a married man now, and united to a woman who seemed a complete contrast to Mary Cave in all respects, he could not forget the great disappointment of his life; and when he heard that what would have been so precious to him had been neglected, perhaps abused by another, he conceived for that other a rooted and bitter animosity.

Of the nature and strength of this animosity, Mr Helstone was but half aware: he neither knew how much Yorke had loved Mary Cave, what he had felt on losing her, nor was he conscious of the calumnies concerning his treatment of her, familiar to every ear in the neighbourhood but his own. He believed political and religious differences alone separated him and Mr Yorke; had he known how the case really stood, he would hardly have been induced by any persuasion to cross his former rival's threshold.

Mr Yorke did not resume his lecture of Robert Moore; the conversation erelong recommenced in a more general form, though still in a somewhat disputative tone. The unquiet state of the country, the various depredations lately committed on mill-property in the district, supplied abundant matter for disagreement; especially as each of the three gentlmen present differed more or less in his views on these subjects. Mr Helstone thought the masters aggrieved, the workpeople unreasonable;

he condemned sweepingly the widespread spirit of disaffection against constituted authorities, the growing indisposition to bear with patience evils he regarded as inevitable: the cures he prescribed were vigorous government interference, strict magisterial vigilance; when necessary, prompt military coercion.

Mr Yorke wished to know whether this interference, vigilance and coercion would feed those who were hungry, give work to those who wanted work and whom no man would hire. He scouted the idea of inevitable evils; he said public patience was a camel, on whose back the last atom that could be borne had already been laid, and that resistance was now a duty: the widespread spirit of disaffection against constituted authorities, he regarded as the most promising sign of the times; the masters, he allowed, were truly aggrieved, but their main grievances had been heaped on them by a 'corrupt, base, and bloody' government (these were Mr Yorke's epithets). Madmen like Pitt, demons like Castlereagh, mischievous idiots like Perceval, were the tyrants, the curses of the country, the destroyers of her trade. It was their infatuated perseverance in an unjustifiable, a hopeless, a ruinous war, which had brought the nation to its present pass. It was their monstrously oppressive taxation, it was the infamous 'Orders in Council' – the originators of which deserved impeachment and the scaffold, if ever public men did – that hung a millstone about England's neck.

'But where was the use of talking?' he demanded – 'What chance was there of reason being heard in a land that was king-ridden, priest-ridden, peer-ridden – where a lunatic was the nominal monarch, an unprincipled debauchee the real ruler; where such an insult to common sense as hereditary legislators was tolerated – where such a humbug as a bench of bishops – such an arrogant abuse as a pampered, persecuting established Church was endured and venerated – where a standing army was maintained, and a host of lazy parsons and their pauper families were kept on the fat of the land?'

Mr Helstone, rising up and putting on his shovel-hat,

observed in reply, 'That in the course of his life he had met with two or three instances where sentiments of this sort had been very bravely maintained so long as health, strength, and worldly prosperity had been the allies of him who professed them; but there came a time,' he said, 'to all men, "when the keepers of the house should tremble; when they should be afraid of that which is high, and fear should be in the way;" and that time was the test of the advocate of anarchy and rebellion, the enemy of religion and order. Erenow,' he affirmed, 'he had been called upon to read those prayers our Church has provided for the sick, by the miserable dying-bed of one of her most rancorous foes; he had seen such a one stricken with remorse, solicitous to discover a place for repentance, and unable to find any, though he sought it carefully with tears. He must forewarn Mr Yorke, that blasphemy against God and the king was a deadly sin, and that there was such a thing as "judgment to come." '

Mr Yorke 'believed fully that there was such a thing as judgment to come. If it were otherwise, it would be difficult to imagine how all the scoundrels who seemed triumphant in this world, who broke innocent hearts with impunity, abused unmerited privileges, were a scandal to honourable callings, took the bread out of the mouths of the poor, browbeat the humble, and truckled meanly to the rich and proud – were to be properly paid off, in such coin as they had earned. But,' he added, 'whenever he got low-spirited about such like goings-on, and their seeming success in this mucky lump of a planet, he just reached down t' owd book (pointing to a great Bible in the bookcase), opened it like at a chance, and he was sure to light of a verse blazing wi' a blue brimstone low that set all straight. He knew,' he said, 'where some folk war bound for, just as weel as if an angel wi' great white wings had come in ower t' door-stone and told him.'

'Sir,' said Mr Helstone, collecting all his dignity, 'Sir – the great knowledge of man is to know himself, and the bourne whither his own steps tend.'

'Ay, ay! you'll recollect, Mr Helstone, that Ignorance was carried away from the very gates of heaven, borne through the air, and thrust in at a door in the side of the hill which led down to hell.'

'Nor have I forgotten, Mr Yorke, that Vain-Confidence, not seeing the way before him, fell into a deep pit, which was on purpose there made by the prince of the grounds, to catch vain-glorious fools withal, and was dashed to pieces with his fall.'

'Now,' interposed Mr Moore, who had hitherto sat a silent but amused spectator of this wordy combat, and whose indifference to the party politics of the day, as well as to the gossip of the neighbourhood, made him an impartial, if apa-thetic judge of the merits of such an encounter – 'you have both sufficiently black-balled each other, and proved how cordially you detest each other, and how wicked you think each other. For my part, my hate is still running in such a strong current against the fellows who have broken my frames, that I have none to spare for my private acquaintance, and still less for such a vague thing as a sect or a government: but really, gentlemen, you both seem very bad, by your own showing; worse than ever I suspected you to be. I dare not stay all night with a rebel and blasphemer, like you, Yorke; and I hardly dare ride home with a cruel and tyrannical ecclesiastic, like Mr Helstone.'

'I am going, however, Mr Moore,' said the Rector sternly: 'come with me or not, as you please.'

'Nay, he shall not have the choice – he *shall* go with you,' responded Yorke. 'It's midnight, and past: and I'll have nob'dy staying up i' my house any longer. Ye mun all go.'

He rang the bell.

'Deb,' said he to the servant who answered it, 'clear them folk out o' t' kitchen, and lock t' doors, and be off to bed. Here is your way, gentlemen,' he continued to his guests; and, lighting them through the passage, he fairly put them out at his front-door.

They met their party hurrying out pell-mell by the back way; their horses stood at the gate; they mounted, and rode off – Moore laughing at their abrupt dismissal, Helstone deeply indignant thereat.

CHAPTER V

HOLLOW'S COTTAGE

Moore's good spirits were still with him when he rose next morning. He and Joe Scott had both spent the night in the mill, availing themselves of certain sleeping accommodations producible from recesses in the front and back counting-houses: the master, always an early riser, was up somewhat sooner even than usual; he awoke his man by singing a French song as he made his toilet.

'Ye're not custen dahm, then, maister?' cried Joe.

'Not a stiver, mon garçon – which means, my lad: – get up, and we'll take a turn through the mill before the hands come in, and I'll explain my future plans. We'll have the machinery yet, Joseph: you never heard of Bruce, perhaps?'

'And th' arrand (spider)? Yes, but I hev: I've read th' history o' Scotland, and happen knaw as mich on't as ye; and I understand ye to mean to say ye'll persevere.'

'I do.'

'Is there mony o' your mak' i' your country?' inquired Joe, as he folded up his temporary bed, and put it away.

'In my country! Which is my country?'

'Why, France – isn't it?'

'Not it, indeed! The circumstance of the French having seized Antwerp, where I was born, does not make me a Frenchman.'

'Holland, then?'

'I am not a Dutchman: now you are confounding Antwerp with Amsterdam.'

'Flanders?'

'I scorn the insinuation, Joe! I, a Flamand! Have I a Flemish

59

face? – the clumsy nose standing out – the mean forehead falling back – the pale blue eyes "à fleur de tête?" Am I all body and no legs, like a Flamand? But you don't know what they are like – those Netherlanders. Joe, I'm an Anversois: my mother was an Anversoise, though she came of French lineage, which is the reason I speak French.'

'But your father war Yorkshire, which maks ye a bit Yorkshire too; and onybody may see ye're akin to us, ye're so keen o' making brass, and getting forrards.'

'Joe, you're an impudent dog; but I've always been accustomed to a boorish sort of insolence from my youth up: the "classe ouvrière" – that is, the working people, in Belgium – bear themselves brutally towards their employers; and by *brutally*, Joe, I mean *brutalement* – which, perhaps, when properly translated, should be *roughly*.'

'We allus speak our minds i' this country; and them young parsons and grand folk fro' London is shocked at wer "*incivility*," and we like weel enow to gi'e 'em summat to be shocked at, 'cause it's sport to us to watch 'em turn up the whites o' their een, and spreed out their bits o' hands, like as they're flayed wi' boggards, and then to hear 'em say, nipping off their words short, like – "Dear! dear! Whet seveges! How very corse!"'

'You *are* savages, Joe; you don't suppose you're civilized, do you?'

'Middling, middling, maister. I reckon 'at us manufacturing lads i' th' north is a deal more intelligent, and knaws a deal more nor th' farming folk i' th' south. Trade sharpens wet wits; and them that's mechanics, like me, is forced to think. Ye know, what wi' looking after machinery and sich like, I've getten into that way that when I see an effect, I look straight out for a cause, and I oft lig hold on't to purpose; and then I like reading, and I'm curious to knaw what them that reckons to govern us aims to do for us and wi' us: and there many 'cuter nor me; there's many a one amang them greasy chaps 'at smells o' oil, and amang them dyers wi' blue and black skins, that has a long head, and that can tell what a fooil of a law is, as well as ye or old Yorke, and a deal better not soft uns like Christopher Sykes o' Whinbury, and greet hectoring nowts like yond' Irish Peter, Helstone's curate.'

'You think yourself a clever fellow, I know, Scott.'

'Ay, I'm fairish; I can tell cheese fro' chalk, and I'm varry weel aware that I've improved sich opportunities as I have had, a deal better nor some 'at reckons to be aboon me; but there's thousands i' Yorkshire that's as good as me, and a two-three that's better.'

'You're a great man – you're a sublime fellow; but you're a prig, a conceited noodle with it all, Joe! You need not to think that because you've picked up a little knowledge of practical mathematics, and because you have found some scantling of the elements of chemistry at the bottom of a dyeing vat, that therefore you're a neglected man of science; and you need not to suppose that because the course of trade does not always run smooth, and you, and such as you, are sometimes short of work and of bread, that therefore your class are martyrs, and that the whole form of government under which you live is wrong. And, moreover, you need not for a moment to insinuate that the virtues have taken refuge in cottages and wholly abandoned slated houses. Let me tell you, I particularly abominate that sort of trash, because I know so well that human nature is human nature everywhere, whether under tile or thatch, and that in every specimen of human nature that breathes, vice and virtue are ever found blended, in smaller or greater proportions, and that the proportion is not determined by station. I have seen villains who were rich, and I have seen villains who were poor, and I have seen villains who were neither rich nor poor, but who had realized Agar's wish, and lived in fair and modest competency. The clock is going to strike six: away with you, Joe, and ring the mill-bell.'

It was now the middle of the month of February; by six o'clock, therefore, dawn was just beginning to steal on night, to penetrate with a pale ray its brown obscurity, and give a demi-translucence to its opaque shadows. Pale enough that ray was on this particular morning; no colour tinged the east, no flush warmed it. To see what a heavy lid day slowly lifted, what a wan glance she flung along the hills, you would have thought the sun's fire quenched in last night's floods. The breath of this morning was chill as its aspect; a raw wind stirred the mass of night-cloud, and showed, as it slowly rose – leaving a colourless, silver-gleaming ring all round the horizon – not blue sky, but a stratum of paler vapour beyond. It had ceased to rain, but the earth was sodden, and the pools and rivulets were full.

The mill-windows were alight, the bell still rung loud, and now the little children came running in, in too great a hurry, let us hope, to feel very much nipped by the inclement air; and, indeed, by contrast, perhaps the morning appeared rather favourable to them than otherwise; for they had often come to their work that winter through snow-storms, through heavy rain, through hard frost.

Mr Moore stood at the entrance to watch them pass: he counted them as they went by; to those who came rather late he said a word of reprimand, which was a little more sharply repeated by Joe Scott when the lingerers reached the work-rooms. Neither master nor overlooker spoke savagely; they were not savage men either of them, though it appeared both were rigid, for they fined a delinquent who came considerably too late: Mr Moore made him pay his penny down ere he entered, and informed him that the next repetition of the fault would cost him twopence.

Rules, no doubt, are necessary in such cases, and coarse and cruel masters will make coarse and cruel rules, which, at the time we treat of at least, they used sometimes to enforce tyrannically; but, though I describe imperfect characters (every character in this book will be found to be more or less imperfect, my pen refusing to draw anything in the model line), I have not undertaken to handle degraded or utterly infamous ones.

Child-torturers, slave masters and drivers, I consign to the hands of jailers; the novelist may be excused from sullying his page with the record of their deeds.

Instead, then, of harrowing up my reader's soul, and delighting his organ of Wonder, with effective descriptions of stripes and scourgings, I am happy to be able to inform him that neither Mr Moore nor his overlooker ever struck a child in their mill. Joe had, indeed, once very severely flogged a son of his own for telling a lie and persisting in it; but, like his employer, he was too phlegmatic, too calm, as well as too reasonable a man, to make corporeal chastisement other than the exception to his treatment of the young.

Mr Moore haunted his mill, his mill-yard, his dye-house, and his warehouse, till the sickly dawn strengthened into day. The sun even rose, – at least a white disk, clear, tintless, and almost chill-looking as ice, – peeped over the dark crest of a hill, changed to silver the livid edge of the cloud above it, and looked solemnly down the whole length of the den, or narrow dale, to whose strait bounds we are at present limited. It was eight o'clock; the mill lights were all extinguished; the signal was given for breakfast; the children, released for half an hour from toil, betook themselves to the little tin cans which held their coffee, and to the small baskets which contained their allowance of bread. Let us hope they have enough to eat; it would be a pity were it otherwise.

And now, at last, Mr Moore quitted the mill-yard, and bent his steps to his dwelling-house. It was only a short distance from the factory, but the hedge and high bank on each side of the lane which conducted to it seemed to give it something of the appearance and feeling of seclusion. It was a small, white-washed place, with a green porch over the door; scanty brown stalks showed in the garden soil near this porch, and likewise beneath the windows, – stalks budless and flowerless now, but giving dim prediction of trained and blooming creepers for summer days. A grass plat and borders fronted the cottage;

the borders presented only black mould yet, except where, in sheltered nooks, the first shoots of snowdrop or crocus peeped, green as emerald, from the earth. The spring was late; it had been a severe and prolonged winter; the last deep snow had but just disappeared before yesterday's rains; on the hills, indeed, white remnants of it yet gleamed, flecking the hollows and crowning the peaks: the lawn was not verdant, but bleached, as was the grass on the bank, and under the hedge in the lane. Three trees, gracefully grouped, rose beside the cottage; they were not lofty, but having no rivals near, they looked well and imposing where they grew. Such was Mr Moore's home; a snug nest for content and contemplation, but one within which the wings of action and ambition could not long lie folded.

Its air of modest comfort seemed to possess no particular attraction for its owner; instead of entering the house at once, he fetched a spade from a little shed and began to work in the garden. For about a quarter of an hour he dug on uninterrupted; at length, however, a window opened, and a female voice called to him: –

'Eh, bien! Tu ne déjeûnes pas ce matin?'

The answer and the rest of the conversation was in French, but as this is an English book, I shall translate it into English.

'Is breakfast ready, Hortense?'

'Certainly; it has been ready half an hour.'

'Then I am ready, too: I have a canine hunger.'

He threw down his spade and entered the house: the narrow passage conducted him to a small parlour, where a breakfast of coffee and bread and butter, with the somewhat un-English accompaniment of stewed pears, was spread on the table. Over these viands presided the lady who had spoken from the window. I must describe her before I go any further.

She seemed a little older than Mr Moore, perhaps she was thirty-five, tall, and proportionately stout; she had very black hair, for the present twisted up in curl-papers; a high colour in her cheeks, a small nose, a pair of little black eyes. The lower

part of her face was large in proportion to the upper; her forehead was small and rather corrugated; she had a fretful though
not an ill-natured expression of countenance; there was something in her whole appearance one felt inclined to be half provoked with, and half amused at. The strangest point was her
dress: a stuff petticoat and a striped cotton camisole. The petticoat was short, displaying well a pair of feet and ankles which
left much to be desired in the article of symmetry.

You will think I have depicted a remarkable slattern, reader;
– not at all. Hortense Moore (she was Mr Moore's sister) was a
very orderly, economical person; the petticoat, camisole, and
curl-papers were her morning costume, in which, of forenoons,
she had always been accustomed to 'go her household ways' in
her own country. She did not choose to adopt English fashions
because she was obliged to live in England; she adhered to her
old Belgian modes, quite satisfied that there was a merit in so
doing.

Mademoiselle had an excellent opinion of herself, an opinion
not wholly undeserved, for she possessed some good and sterling
qualities; but she rather over-estimated the kind and degree of
these qualities, and quite left out of the account sundry little
defects which accompanied them. You could never have persuaded her that she was a prejudiced and narrow-minded
person, that she was too susceptible on the subject of her own
dignity and importance, and too apt to take offence about
trifles; yet all this was true. However, where her claims to distinction were not opposed, and where her prejudices were not
offended, she could be kind and friendly enough. To her two
brothers (for there was another Gérard Moore besides Robert),
she was very much attached. As the sole remaining representatives of their decayed family, the persons of both were almost
sacred in her eyes; of Louis, however, she knew less than of
Robert; he had been sent to England when a mere boy, and had
received his education at an English school. His education not
being such as to adapt him for trade, perhaps, too, his natural

bent not inclining him to mercantile pursuits, he had, when
the blight of hereditary prospects rendered it necessary for him
to push his own fortune, adopted the very arduous and very
modest career of a teacher; he had been usher in a school, and
was said now to be tutor in a private family. Hortense, when
she mentioned Louis, described him as having what she called
'des moyens,' but as being too backward and quiet: her praise
of Robert was in a different strain, less qualified; she was very
proud of him; she regarded him as the greatest man in Europe:
all he said and did was remarkable in her eyes, and she expected
others to behold him from the same point of view; nothing
could be more irrational, monstrous. and infamous, than
opposition from any quarter to Robert, unless it were opposition to herself.

Accordingly, as soon as the said Robert was seated at the
breakfast table, and she had helped him to a portion of stewed
pears, and cut him a good-sized Belgian tartine, she began to
pour out a flood of amazement and horror at the transaction of
last night, the destruction of the frames.

'Quelle idée! to destroy them. Quelle action honteuse! On
voyait bien que les ouvriers de ce pays étaient à la fois bêtes et
méchants. C'était absolument comme les domestiques Anglais,
les servantes surtout: rien d'insupportable comme cette Sara,
par exemple!'

'She looks clean and industrious,' Mr Moore remarked.

'Looks! I don't know how she looks; and I do not say that
she is altogether dirty or idle: mais elle est d'une insolence! She
disputed with me a quarter of an hour yesterday about the
cooking of the beef; she said I boiled it to rags, that English
people would never be able to eat such a dish as our bouilli,
that the bouillon was no better than greasy warm water, and as
to the choucroute, she affirms she cannot touch it! That barrel
we have in the cellar – delightfully prepared by my own hands
– she termed a tub of hog-wash, which means food for pigs.
I am harassed with the girl, and yet I cannot part with her lest

I should get a worse. You are in the same position with your workmen, – pauvre cher frère!'

'I am afraid you are not very happy in England, Hortense.'

'It is my duty to be happy where you are, brother; but otherwise, there are certainly a thousand things which make me regret our native town. All the world here appears to me ill-bred (mal-élevé). I find my habits considered ridiculous: if a girl out of your mill chances to come into the kitchen and find me in my jupon and camisole preparing dinner (for you know I cannot trust Sarah to cook a single dish), she sneers. If I accept an invitation out to tea, which I have done once or twice, I perceive I am put quite into the background; I have not that attention paid me which decidedly is my due. Of what an excellent family are the Gérards, as we know, and the Moores also! They have a right to claim a certain respect, and to feel wounded when it is withheld from them. In Antwerp, I was always treated with distinction; here, one would think that when I open my lips in company, I speak English with a ridiculous accent, whereas I am quite assured that I pronounce it perfectly.'

'Hortense, in Antwerp we were known rich; in England we were never known but poor.'

'Precisely, and thus mercenary are mankind. Again, dear brother, last Sunday, if you recollect, was very wet; accordingly, I went to church in my neat black sabots, objects one would not indeed wear in a fashionable city; but which in the country I have ever been accustomed to use for walking in dirty roads. Believe me, as I paced up the aisle, composed and tranquil, as I am always, four ladies, and as many gentlemen, laughed and hid their faces behind their prayer-books.'

'Well, well! don't put on the sabots again. I told you before I thought they were not quite the thing for this country.'

'But, brother, they are not common sabots, such as the peasantry wear. I tell you, they are sabots noirs, très propres, très convenables. At Mons and Leuze – cities not very far removed from the elegant capital of Brussels – it is very seldom that the respectable people wear anything else for walking in winter. Let any one try to wade the mud of the Flemish chaussées in a pair of Paris brodequins, on m'en dirait des nouvelles!'

'Never mind Mons and Leuze, and the Flemish chaussées; do at Rome as the Romans do; and as to the camisole and jupon, I am not quite sure about them either. I never see an English lady dressed in such garments. Ask Caroline Helstone.'

'Caroline! *I* ask Caroline? *I* consult her about my dress? It is *she* who on all points should consult *me*; she is a child.'

'She is eighteen, or at the least seventeen; old enough to know all about gowns, petticoats, and chaussures.'

'Do not spoil Caroline, I entreat you, brother; do not make her of more consequence than she ought to be. At present she is modest and unassuming: let us keep her so.'

'With all my heart. Is she coming this morning?'

'She will come at ten, as usual, to take her French lesson.'

'You don't find that she sneers at you, do you?'

'She does not, she appreciates me better than any one else here; but then she has more intimate opportunities of knowing me: she sees that I have education, intelligence, manner, principles; all, in short, which belongs to a person well born and well bred.'

'Are you at all fond of her?'

'For *fond* – I cannot say: I am not one who is prone to take violent fancies, and, consequently, my friendship is the more to be depended on. I have a regard for her as my relative; her position also inspires interest, and her conduct as my pupil has hitherto been such as rather to enhance than diminish the attachment that springs from other causes.'

'She behaves pretty well at lessons?'

'To *me* she behaves very well; but you are conscious, brother, that I have a manner calculated to repel over-familiarity, to win esteem, and to command respect. Yet, possessed of penetration, I perceive clearly that Caroline is not perfect; that there is much to be desired in her.'

'Give me a last cup of coffee, and while I am drinking it amuse me with an account of her faults.'

'Dear brother, I am happy to see you eat your breakfast with relish, after the fatiguing night you have passed. Caroline, then, is defective; but, with my forming hand and almost motherly care, she may improve. There is about her an occasional something – a reserve, I think – which I do not quite like, because it is not sufficiently girlish and submissive; and there are glimpses of an unsettled hurry in her nature, which put me out. Yet she is usually most tranquil, too dejected and thoughtful indeed sometimes. In time, I doubt not, I shall make her uniformly sedate and decorous, without being unaccountably pensive. I ever disapprove what is not intelligible.'

'I don't understand your account in the least; what do you mean by "unsettled hurries," for instance?'

'An example will, perhaps, be the most satisfactory explanation. I sometimes, you are aware, make her read French poetry by way of practice in pronunciation. She has, in the course of her lessons, gone through much of Corneille and Racine, in a very steady, sober spirit, such as I approve. Occasionally she showed, indeed, a degree of languor in the perusal of those esteemed authors, partaking rather of apathy than sobriety, and apathy is what I cannot tolerate in those who have the benefit of my instructions; besides, one should not be apathetic in studying standard works. The other day I put into her hands a volume of short fugitive pieces. I sent her to the window to learn one by heart, and when I looked up I saw her turning the leaves over impatiently, and curling her lip, absolutely with scorn, as she surveyed the little poems cursorily. I chid her "Ma cousine," said she, "tout cela m'ennuie à la mort.' I told her this was improper language. – "Dieu!" she exclaimed. "Il n'y a donc pas deux lignes de poësie dans toute la littérature française?" I inquired what she meant. She begged my pardon with proper submission. Erelong she was still; I saw her smiling to herself over the book; she began to learn assiduously. In half an hour she came and stood before me, presented the volume, folded her hands, as I always require her to do, and commenced the repetition of that short thing by Chénier, "La Jeune Captive." If you had heard the manner in which she went through this, and in which she uttered a few incoherent comments when she had done, you would have known what I meant by the phrase "unsettled hurry." One would have thought Chénier was more moving than all Racine and all Corneille. You, brother, who have so much sagacity, will discern that this disproportionate preference argues an ill-regulated mind; but she is fortunate in a preceptress. I will give her a system, a method of thought, a set of opinions; I will give her the perfect control and guidance of her feelings.'

'Be sure you do, Hortense: here she comes. That was her shadow passed the window, I believe.'

'Ah! truly. She is too early – half an hour before her time. – My child, what brings you here before I have breakfasted?'

This question was addressed to an individual who now entered the room, a young girl, wrapped in a winter mantle, the folds of which were gathered with some grace round an apparently slender figure.

'I came in haste to see how you were, Hortense, and how Robert was, too. I was sure you would be both grieved by what happened last night. I did not hear till this morning: my uncle told me at breakfast.'

'Ah! it is unspeakable. You sympathize with us? Your uncle sympathizes with us?'

'My uncle is very angry; but he was with Robert, I believe: was he not? Did he not go with you to Stilbro' Moor?'

'Yes: we set out in very martial style, Caroline: but the prisoners we went to rescue met us half-way.'

'Of course, nobody was hurt?'

'Why, no; only Joe Scott's wrists were a little galled with being pinioned too tightly behind his back.'

'You were not there? You were not with the waggons when they were attacked?'

'No: one seldom has the fortune to be present at occurrences at which one would particularly wish to assist.'

'Where are you going this morning? I saw Murgatroyd saddling your horse in the yard.'

'To Whinbury: it is market-day.'

'Mr Yorke is going too: I met him in his gig. Come home with him.'

'Why?'

'Two are better than one, and nobody dislikes Mr Yorke; at least, poor people do not dislike him.'

'Therefore he would be a protection to me, who am hated?'

'Who are *misunderstood*: that, probably, is the word. Shall you be late? – Will he be late, cousin Hortense?'

'It is too probable: he has often much business to transact at Whinbury. Have you brought your exercise-book, child?'

'Yes. What time will you return, Robert?'

'I generally return at seven. Do you wish me to be at home earlier?'

'Try rather to be back by six. It is not absolutely dark at six now; but by seven daylight is quite gone.'

'And what danger is to be apprehended, Caroline, when daylight *is* gone? What peril do you conceive comes as the companion of darkness, for me?'

'I am not sure that I can define my fears; but we all have a certain anxiety at present about our friends. My uncle calls these times dangerous: he says, too, that mill-owners are unpopular.'

'And I one of the most unpopular? Is not that the fact? You are reluctant to speak out plainly, but at heart you think me liable to Pearson's fate, who was shot at – not, indeed, from behind a hedge, but in his own house, through his staircase-window, as he was going to bed.'

'Anne Pearson showed me the bullet in the chamber-door,' remarked Caroline, gravely, as she folded her mantle, and arranged it and her muff on a side-table. 'You know,' she continued, 'there is a hedge all the way along the road from here to Whinbury, and there are the Fieldhead plantations to pass; but you will be back by six – or before?'

'Certainly he will,' affirmed Hortense. 'And now, my child, prepare your lessons for repetition, while I put the pease to soak for the purée at dinner.'

With this direction, she left the room.

'You suspect I have many enemies then, Caroline?' said Mr Moore; 'and, doubtless, you know me to be destitute of friends?'

'Not destitute, Robert. There is your sister, your brother Louis – whom I have never seen – there is Mr Yorke, and there is my uncle; besides, of course, many more.'

Robert smiled. 'You would be puzzled to name your "many more," said he. 'But show me your exercise-book. What extreme pains you take with the writing! My sister, I suppose, exacts this care: she wants to form you in all things after the model of a Flemish school-girl. What life are you destined for, Caroline? What will you do with your French, drawing, and other accomplishments when they are acquired?'

'You may well say, when they are acquired; for, as you are aware, till Hortense began to teach me, I knew precious little. As to the life I am destined for, I cannot tell: I suppose, to keep my uncle's house, till –' she hesitated.

'Till what? Till he dies?'

'No. How harsh to say that! I never think of his dying: he is only fifty-five. But till – in short, till events offer other occupations for me.'

'A remarkably vague prospect! Are you content with it?'

'I used to be, formerly. Children, you know, have little reflection, or rather their reflections run on ideal themes. There are moments *now* when I am not quite satisfied.'

'Why?'

'I am making no money – earning nothing.'

'You come to the point, Lina: you too, then, wish to make money?'

'I do: I should like an occupation; and if I were a boy, it would not be so difficult to find one. I see such an easy, pleasant way of learning a business, and making my way in life.'

'Go on: let us hear what way.'

'I could be apprenticed to your trade – the cloth-trade: I could learn it of you, as we are distant relations. I would do the counting-house work, keep the books, and write the letters, while you went to market. I know you greatly desire to be rich, in order to pay your father's debts; perhaps I could help you to get rich.'

'Help *me*? You should think of yourself.'

'I do think of myself; but must one for ever think only of oneself?'

'Of whom else do I think? Of whom else *dare* I think? The poor ought to have no large sympathies; it is their duty to be narrow.'

'No, Robert –'

'Yes, Caroline. Poverty is necessarily selfish, contracted, grovelling, anxious. Now and then a poor man's heart, when certain beams and dews visit it, may swell like the budding vegetation in yonder garden on this spring-day, may feel ripe to evolve in foliage – perhaps blossom; but he must not encourage the pleasant impulse; he must invoke Prudence to check it, with that frosty breath of hers, which is as nipping as any north wind.'

'No cottage would be happy then.'

'When I speak of poverty, I do not so much mean the natural, habitual poverty of the working-man, as the embarrassed penury of the man in debt; my grub-worm is always a straitened, struggling, care-worn tradesman.'

'Cherish hope, not anxiety. Certain ideas have become too fixed in your mind. It may be presumptuous to say it, but I have the impression that there is something wrong in your notions of the best means of attaining happiness; as there is in –' Second hesitation.

'I am all ear, Caroline.'

'In – (courage! let me speak the truth) – in your manner – mind, I say only *manner* – to these Yorkshire workpeople.'

'You have often wanted to tell me that, have you not?'

'Yes; often – very often.'

'The faults of my manner are, I think, only negative. I am not proud: what has a man in my position to be proud of? I am only taciturn, phlegmatic, and joyless.'

'As if your living cloth-dressers were all machines like your frames and shears: in your own house you seem different.'

'To those of my own house I am no alien, which I am to these English clowns. I might act the benevolent with them, but acting is not my *forte*. I find them irrational, perverse; they hinder me when I long to hurry forward. In treating them justly, I fulfil my whole duty towards them.'

'You don't expect them to love you, of course?'

'Nor wish it.'

'Ah!' said the monitress, shaking her head, and heaving a deep sigh. With this ejaculation, indicative that she perceived a screw to be loose somewhere, but that it was out of her reach to set it right, she bent over her grammar, and sought the rule and exercise for the day.

'I suppose I am not an affectionate man, Caroline; the attachment of a very few suffices me.'

'If you please, Robert, will you mend me a pen or two before you go?'

'First, let me rule your book, for you always contrive to draw the lines aslant... There now... And now for the pens: you like a fine one, I think?'

'Such as you generally make for me and Hortense; not your own broad points.'

'If I were of Louis's calling, I might stay at home and dedicate this morning to you and your studies; whereas I must spend it in Sykes' wool-warehouse.'

'You will be making money.'

'More likely losing it.'

As he finished mending the pens, a horse, saddled and bridled, was brought up to the garden-gate.

'There, Fred is ready for me; I must go. I'll take one look to see what the spring has done in the south border, too, first.'

He quitted the room, and went out into the garden-ground behind the mill. A sweet fringe of young verdure and opening flowers – snowdrop, crocus, even primrose – bloomed in the sunshine under the hot wall of the factory. Moore plucked here and there a blossom and leaf, till he had collected a little bouquet; he returned to the parlour, pilfered a thread of silk from his sister's work-basket, tied the flowers, and laid them on Caroline's desk.

'Now, good-morning.'

'Thank you, Robert; it is pretty; it looks, as it lies there, like sparkles of sunshine and blue sky: good-morning.'

He went to the door – stopped – opened his lips as if to speak – said nothing, and moved on. He passed through the wicket, and mounted his horse: in a second, he had flung himself from the saddle again, transferred the reins to Murgatroyd, and re-entered the cottage.

'I forgot my gloves,' he said, appearing to take something from the side-table; then, as an impromptu thought, he remarked, 'You have no binding engagement at home, perhaps, Caroline?'

'I never have: some children's socks, which Mrs Ramsden has ordered, to knit for the Jew's basket; but they will keep.'

'Jew's basket be – sold! Never was utensil better named. Anything more Jewish than it – its contents, and their prices – cannot be conceived: but I see something, a very tiny curl, at the corners of your lip, which tells me that you know its merits as well as I do. Forget the Jew's basket, then, and spend the day here as a change. Your uncle won't break his heart at your absence?'

She smiled. 'No.'

'The old Cossack! I daresay not,' muttered Moore. 'Then stay and dine with Hortense; she will be glad of your company; I shall return in good time. We will have a little reading in the evening: the moon rises at half-past eight, and I will walk up to the Rectory with you at nine. Do you agree?'

She nodded her head; and her eyes lit up.

Moore lingered yet two minutes: he bent over Caroline's desk and glanced at her grammar, he fingered her pen, he lifted her bouquet and played with it; his horse stamped impatient; Fred Murgatroyd hemmed and coughed at the gate, as if he wondered what in the world his master was doing. 'Good-morning,' again said Moore, and finally vanished.

Hortense, coming in ten minutes after, found, to her surprise, that Caroline had not yet commenced her exercise.

CHAPTER VI

CORIOLANUS

Mademoiselle Moore had that morning a somewhat absent-minded pupil. Caroline forgot, again and again, the explanations which were given to her; however, she still bore with unclouded mood the chidings her inattention brought upon her. Sitting in the sunshine, near the window, she seemed to receive with its warmth a kind influence, which made her both happy and good. Thus disposed, she looked her best, and her best was a pleasing vision.

To her had not been denied the gift of beauty; it was not absolutely necessary to know her in order to like her; she was fair enough to please, even at the first view. Her shape suited her age; it was girlish, light, and pliant; every curve was neat, every limb proportionate: her face was expressive and gentle; her eyes were handsome, and gifted at times with a winning beam that stole into the heart, with a language that spoke softly to the affections. Her mouth was very pretty; she had a delicate skin, and a fine flow of brown hair, which she knew how to arrange with taste; curls became her, and she possessed them in picturesque profusion. Her style of dress announced taste in the wearer; very unobtrusive in fashion, far from costly in material, but suitable in colour to the fair complexion with which it contrasted, and in make to the slight form which it draped. Her present winter garb was of merino, the same soft shade of brown as her hair; the little collar round her neck lay over a pink ribbon, and was fastened with a pink knot: she wore no other decoration.

So much for Caroline Helstone's appearance; as to her

character or intellect, if she had any, they must speak for themselves in due time.

Her connexions are soon explained. She was the child of parents separated soon after her birth, in consequence of disagreement of disposition. Her mother was the half-sister of Mr Moore's father; thus – though there was no mixture of blood – she was, in a distant sense, the cousin of Robert, Louis, and Hortense. Her father was the brother of Mr Helstone – a man of the character friends desire not to recall, after death has once settled all earthly accounts. He had rendered his wife unhappy: the reports which were known to be true concerning him, had given an air of probability to those which were falsely circulated respecting his better-principled brother. Caroline had never known her mother, as she was taken from her in infancy, and had not since seen her; her father died comparatively young, and her uncle, the Rector, had for some years been her sole guardian. He was not, as we are aware, much adapted, either by nature or habits, to have the charge of a young girl: he had taken little trouble about her education; probably, he would have taken none if she, finding herself neglected, had not grown anxious on her own account, and asked, every now and then, for a little attention, and for the means of acquiring such amount of knowledge as could not be dispensed with. Still, she had a depressing feeling that she was inferior, that her attainments were fewer than were usually possessed by girls of her age and station; and very glad was she to avail herself of the kind offer made by her cousin Hortense, soon after the arrival of the latter at Hollow's mill, to teach her French and fine needlework. Mdlle Moore, for her part, delighted in the task, because it gave her importance; she liked to lord it a little over a docile yet quick pupil. She took Caroline precisely at her own estimate, as an irregularly taught, even ignorant girl; and when she found that she made rapid and eager progress, it was to no talent, no application in the scholar, she ascribed the improvement, but entirely to her own superior method of teaching; when she found that Caroline, unskilled in routine, had a knowledge of her own – desultory but varied, the discovery caused her no surprise, for she still imagined that from her conversation had the girl unawares gleaned these treasures: she thought it even when forced to feel that her pupil knew much on subjects whereof she knew little: the idea was not logical, but Hortense had perfect faith in it.

Mademoiselle, who prided herself on possessing 'un esprit positif,' and on entertaining a decided preference for dry studies, kept her young cousin to the same as closely as she could. She worked her unrelentingly at the grammar of the French language, assigning her, as the most improving exercise she could devise, interminable 'analyses logiques.' These 'analyses' were by no means a source of particular pleasure to Caroline; she thought she could have learned French just as well without them, and grudged excessively the time spent in pondering over 'propositions, principales, et incidents;' in deciding the 'incidente determinative' and the 'incidente applicative;' in examining whether the proposition was 'pleine,' 'elliptique,' or 'implicite.' Sometimes she lost herself in the maze, and when so lost, she would, now and then (while Hortense was rummaging her drawers up-stairs, – an unaccountable occupation in which she spent a large portion of each day, arranging, disarranging, rearranging and counter-arranging) – carry her book to Robert in the counting-house, and get the rough place made smooth by his aid. Mr Moore possessed a clear, tranquil brain of his own; almost as soon as he looked at Caroline's little difficulties they seemed to dissolve beneath his eye: in two minutes he would explain all; in two words give the key to the puzzle. She thought if Hortense could only teach like him, how much faster she might learn! Repaying him by an admiring and grateful smile, rather shed at his feet than lifted to his face, she would leave the mill reluctantly to go back to the cottage, and then, while she completed the exercise, or worked out the sum (for Mdlle Moore taught her arithmetic, too,) she would wish nature had made her a boy instead of a girl, that she might ask Robert to let her be his clerk, and sit with him in the counting-house, instead of sitting with Hortense in the parlour.

Occasionally – but this happened very rarely – she spent the evening at Hollow's cottage. Sometimes during these visits, Moore was away, attending a market; sometimes he was gone to Mr Yorke's; often he was engaged with a male visiter in another room; but sometimes, too, he was at home, disengaged, free to talk with Caroline. When this was the case, the evening hours passed on wings of light; they were gone before they were counted. There was no room in England so pleasant as that small parlour when the three cousins occupied it. Hortense, when she was not teaching, or scolding, or cooking, was far from ill-humoured; it was her custom to relax towards evening, and to be kind to her young English kinswoman. There was a means, too, of rendering her delightful, by inducing her to take her guitar and sing and play; she then became quite good-natured; and as she played with skill, and had a well-toned voice, it was not disagreeable to listen to her: it would have been absolutely agreeable, except that her formal and self-important character modulated her strains, as it impressed her manners and moulded her countenance.

Mr Moore, released from the business-yoke, was, if not lively himself, a willing spectator of Caroline's liveliness, a complacent listener to her talk, a ready respondent to her questions. He was something agreeable to sit near, to hover round, to address and look at. Sometimes he was better than this, – almost animated, quite gentle and friendly.

The drawback was, that by the next morning he was sure to be frozen up again; and however much he seemed, in his quiet way, to enjoy these social evenings, he rarely contrived their recurrence. This circumstance puzzled the inexperienced head of his cousin. 'If I had a means of happiness at my command,' she thought, 'I would employ that means often; I would keep it bright with use, and not let it lie for weeks aside, till it gets rusty.'

Yet she was careful not to put in practice her own theory. Much as she liked an evening visit to the cottage, she never paid one unasked. Often, indeed, when pressed by Hortense to come, she would refuse, because Robert did not second, or but slightly seconded the request. This morning was the first time he had ever, of his own unprompted will, given her an invitation; and then he had spoken so kindly, that in hearing him she had received a sense of happiness sufficient to keep her glad for the whole day.

The morning passed as usual. Mademoiselle, ever breathlessly busy, spent it in bustling from kitchen to parlour – now scolding Sarah, now looking over Caroline's exercise or hearing her repetition-lesson. However faultlessly these tasks were achieved, she never commended: it was a maxim with her that praise is inconsistent with a teacher's dignity, and that blame, in more or less unqualified measure, is indispensable to it. She thought incessant reprimand, severe or slight, quite necessary to the maintenance of her authority; and if no possible error was to be found in the lesson, it was the pupil's carriage, or air, or dress, or mien, which required correction.

The usual affray took place about the dinner, which meal, when Sarah at last brought it into the room, she almost flung upon the table, with a look that expressed quite plainly: 'I never dished such stuff i' my life afore; it 's not fit for dogs.' Notwithstanding Sarah's scorn, it was a savoury repast enough. The soup was a sort of purée of dried pease, which Mademoiselle had prepared amidst bitter lamentations that in this desolate country of England no haricot beans were to be had. Then came a dish of meat – nature unknown, but supposed to be miscellaneous – singularly chopped up with crumbs of bread, seasoned uniquely though not unpleasantly, and baked in a mould; a queer, but by no means unpalatable dish. Greens, oddly bruised, formed the accompanying vegetable; and a pâté of fruit, conserved after a receipt devised by Madame Gérard Moore's 'grand'mère,' and from the taste of which it appeared probable that 'mélasse' had been substituted for sugar, completed the dinner.

Caroline had no objection to this Belgian cookery: indeed, she rather liked it for a change, and it was well she did so, for had she evinced any disrelish thereof, such manifestation would have injured her in Mademoiselle's good graces for ever; a positive crime might have been more easily pardoned than a symptom of distaste for the foreign comestibles.

Soon after dinner Caroline coaxed her governess-cousin upstairs to dress: this manœuvre required management. To have hinted that the jupon, camisole, and curl-papers were odious objects, or indeed other than quite meritorious points, would have been a felony. Any premature attempt to urge their disappearance was therefore unwise, and would be likely to issue in the persevering wear of them during the whole day. Carefully avoiding rocks and quicksands, however, the pupil, on pretence of requiring a change of scene, contrived to get the teacher aloft, and, once in the bed-room, she persuaded her that it was not worth while returning thither, and that she might as well make her toilette now; and while Mademoiselle delivered a solemn homily on her own surpassing merit in disregarding all frivolities of fashion, Caroline denuded her of the camisole, invested her with a decent gown, arranged her collar, hair, &c., and made her quite presentable. But Hortense would put the finishing touches herself, and these finishing touches consisted in a thick handkerchief tied round the throat, and a large, servant-like black apron, which spoiled everything. On no account would Mademoiselle have appeared in her own house without the thick handkerchief and the voluminous apron: the first was a positive matter of morality – it was quite improper not to wear a fichu; the second was the ensign of a good housewife – she appeared to think that by means of it she somehow effected a large saving in her brother's income. She had, with her own hands, made and presented to Caroline similar equipments; and the only serious quarrel they had ever had, and which still left a soreness in the elder cousin's soul, had arisen from the refusal of the younger one to accept of and profit by these elegant presents.

'I wear a high dress and a collar,' said Caroline, 'and I should feel suffocated with a handkerchief in addition; and my short aprons do quite as well as that very long one: I would rather make no change.'

Yet Hortense, by dint of perseverance, would probably have compelled her to make a change, had not Mr Moore chanced to overhear a dispute on the subject, and decided that Caroline's little aprons would suffice, and that, in his opinion, as she was still but a child, she might for the present dispense with the fichu, especially as her curls were long, and almost touched her shoulders.

There was no appeal against Robert's opinion, therefore his sister was compelled to yield: but she disapproved entirely of the piquant neatness of Caroline's costume, and the lady-like grace of her appearance: something more solid and homely, she would have considered 'beaucoup plus convenable.'

The afternoon was devoted to sewing. Mademoiselle, like most Belgian ladies, was specially skilful with her needle. She by no means thought it waste of time to devote unnumbered hours to fine embroidery, sight-destroying lace-work, marvellous netting and knitting, and, above all, to most elaborate stocking-mending. She would give a day to the mending of two holes in a stocking any time, and think her 'mission' nobly fulfilled when she had accomplished it. It was another of Caroline's troubles to be condemned to learn this foreign style of darning, which was done stitch by stitch so as exactly to imitate the fabric of the stocking itself; a weariful process, but considered by Hortense Gérard, and by her ancestresses before her for long generations back, as one of the first 'duties of woman.' She herself had had a needle, cotton, and a fearfully torn stocking put into her hand while she yet wore a child's coif on her little black head: her 'hauts faits' in the darning line had been exhibited to company ere she was six years old, and when she first discovered that Caroline was profoundly ignorant of this most essential of attainments, she could have wept with pity over her miserably neglected youth.

No time did she lose in seeking up a hopeless pair of hose, of which the heels were entirely gone, and in setting the ignorant English girl to repair the deficiency: this task had been commenced two years ago, and Caroline had the stockings in her work-bag yet. She did a few rows every day, by way of penance for the expiation of her sins: they were a grievous burden to her; she would much have liked to put them in the fire; and once Mr Moore, who had observed her sitting and sighing over them, had proposed a private incremation in the counting-house, but to this proposal Caroline knew it would have been impolitic to accede – the result could only be a fresh pair of hose, probably in worse condition: she adhered, therefore, to the ills she knew.

All the afternoon the two ladies sat and sewed, till the eyes and fingers, and even the spirits of one of them were weary. The sky since dinner had darkened; it had begun to rain again, to pour fast; secret fears began to steal on Caroline that Robert would be persuaded by Mr Sykes or Mr Yorke to remain at Whinbury till it cleared, and of that there appeared no present chance. Five o'clock struck, and time stole on; still the clouds streamed: a sighing wind whispered in the roof-trees of the cottage; day seemed already closing; the parlour-fire shed on the clear hearth a glow ruddy as at twilight.

'It will not be fair till the moon rises,' pronounced Mademoiselle Moore; 'consequently, I feel assured that my brother will not return till then: indeed, I should be sorry if he did. We will have coffee; it would be vain to wait for him.'

'I am tired – may I leave my work now, cousin?'

'You may, since it grows too dark to see to do it well. Fold it up; put it carefully in your bag; then step into the kitchen, and desire Sarah to bring in the goûter, or tea, as you call it.'

'But it has not yet struck six: he may still come.'

'He will not, I tell you. I can calculate his movements. I understand my brother.'

Suspense is irksome, disappointment bitter. All the world has, some time or other, felt that. Caroline, obedient to orders, passed into the kitchen. Sarah was making a dress for herself at the table.

'You are to bring in coffee,' said the young lady, in a spiritless tone; and then she leaned her arm and head against the kitchen mantelpiece, and hung listlessly over the fire.

'How low you seem, Miss! But it's all because your cousin keeps you so close to work. It's a shame!'

'Nothing of the kind, Sarah,' was the brief reply.

'Oh! but I know it is. You're fit to cry just this minute, for nothing else but because you've sat still the whole day. It would make a kitten dull to be mewed up so.'

'Sarah, does your master often come home early from market when it is wet?'

'Never, hardly; but just to-day, for some reason, he has made a difference.'

'What do you mean?'

'He is come: I am certain I saw Murgatroyd lead his horse into the yard by the back-way, when I went to get some water at the pump five minutes since. He was in the counting-house with Joe Scott, I believe.'

'You are mistaken.'

'What should I be mistaken for? I know his horse surely?'

'But you did not see himself?'

'I heard him speak, though. He was saying something to Joe Scott about having settled all concerning ways and means, and that there would be a new set of frames in the mill before another week passed; and that this time he would get four soldiers from Stilbro' barracks to guard the waggon.'

'Sarah, are you making a gown?'

'Yes: is it a handsome one?'

'Beautiful! Get the coffee ready. I'll finish cutting out that sleeve for you; and I'll give you some trimming for it. I have some narrow satin ribbon of a colour that will just match it.'

'You're very kind, Miss.'

'Be quick, there's a good girl; but first put your master's shoes on the hearth: he will take his boots off when he comes in. I hear him – he is coming.'

'Miss! you're cutting the stuff wrong.'

'So I am; but it is only a snip: there is no harm done.'

The kitchen-door opened; Mr Moore entered, very wet and cold. Caroline half turned from her dressmaking occupation, but renewed it for a moment, as if to gain a minute's time for some purpose. Bent over the dress, her face was hidden; there was an attempt to settle her features and veil their expression, which failed: when she at last met Mr Moore, her countenance beamed.

'We had ceased to expect you: they asserted you would not come,' she said.

'But I promised to return soon: *you* expected me, I suppose?'

'No, Robert: I dared not when it rained so fast. And you are wet and chilled – change everything: if you took cold, I should – we should blame ourselves in some measure.'

'I am not wet through: my riding-coat is water-proof. Dry shoes are all I require. – There ... the fire is pleasant after facing the cold wind and rain for a few miles.'

He stood on the kitchen-hearth; Caroline stood beside him. Mr Moore, while enjoying the genial glow, kept his eyes directed towards the glittering brasses on the shelf above. Chancing for an instant to look down, his glance rested on an uplifted face, flushed, smiling, happy, shaded with silky curls, lit with fine eyes. Sarah was gone into the parlour with the tray: a lecture from her mistress detained her there. Moore placed his hand a moment on his young cousin's shoulder, stooped, and left a kiss on her forehead.

'Oh!' said she, as if the action had unsealed her lips, 'I was miserable when I thought you would not come: I am almost too happy now. Are you happy, Robert? Do you like to come home?'

'I think I do; to-night, at least.'

'Are you certain you are not fretting about your frames, and your business, and the war?'

'Not just now.

'Are you positive you don't feel Hollow's cottage too small for you, and narrow and dismal?'

'At this moment, no.'

'Can you affirm that you are not bitter at heart because rich and great people forget you?'

'No more questions. You are mistaken if you think I am anxious to curry favour with rich and great people. I only want means – a position – a career.'

'Which your own talent and goodness shall win you. You were made to be great – you *shall* be great.'

'I wonder now, if you spoke honestly out of your heart, what receipt you would give me for acquiring this same greatness; but I know it – better than you know it yourself. Would it be efficacious? would it work? Yes – poverty, misery, bankruptcy. Oh! life is not what you think it, Lina!'

'But you are what I think you.'

'I am not.'

'You are better, then?'

'Far worse.'

'No; far better. I know you are good.'

'How do you know it?'

'You look so; and I feel you *are* so.'

'Where do you feel it?'

'In my heart.'

'Ah! you judge me with your heart, Lina; you should judge me with your head.'

'I do; and then I am quite proud of you. Robert, you cannot tell all my thoughts about you.'

Mr Moore's dark face mustered colour; his lips smiled, and yet were compressed; his eyes laughed, and yet he resolutely knit his brow.

'Think meanly of me, Lina,' said he. 'Men, in general, are a sort of scum, very different to anything of which you have an idea; I make no pretension to be better than my fellows.'

'If you did, I should not esteem you so much; it is because you are modest that I have such confidence in your merit.'

'Are you flattering me?' he demanded, turning sharply upon her, and searching her face with an eye of acute penetration.

'No,' she said, softly, laughing at his sudden quickness. She seemed to think it unnecessary to proffer any eager disavowal of the charge.

'You don't care whether I think you flatter me or not?'

'No.'

'You are so secure of your own intentions?'

'I suppose so.'

'What are they, Caroline?'

'Only to ease my mind by expressing for once part of what I think; and then to make you better satisfied with yourself.'

'By assuring me that my kinswoman is my sincere friend?'

'Just so; I am your sincere friend, Robert.'

'And I am – what chance and change shall make me, Lina.'

'Nor my enemy, however?'

The answer was cut short by Sarah and her mistress entering the kitchen together in some commotion. They had been improving the time which Mr Moore and Miss Helstone had spent in dialogue by a short dispute on the subject of 'café au lait,' which Sarah said was the queerest mess she ever saw, and a waste of God's good gifts, as it was 'the nature of coffee to be boiled in water;' and which Mademoiselle affirmed to be 'un breuvage royal,' a thousand times too good for the mean person who objected to it.

The former occupants of the kitchen now withdrew into the

parlour. Before Hortense followed them thither, Caroline had only time again to question, 'Not my enemy, Robert?' And Moore, quaker-like, had replied with another query, 'Could I be?' and then, seating himself at the table, had settled Caroline at his side.

Caroline scarcely heard Mademoiselle's explosion of wrath when she rejoined them; the long declamation about the 'conduite indigne de cette méchante créature,' sounded in her ear as confusedly as the agitated rattling of the china. Robert laughed a little at it, in very subdued sort, and then, politely and calmly entreating his sister to be tranquil, assured her that if it would yield her any satisfaction, she should have her choice of an attendant amongst all the girls in his mill; only he feared they would scarcely suit her, as they were most of them, he was informed, completely ignorant of household work; and pert and self-willed as Sarah was, she was perhaps no worse than the majority of the women of her class.

Mademoiselle admitted the truth of this conjecture: according to her, 'ces paysannes Anglaises étaient tout insupportables.' What would she not give for some 'bonne cuisinière Anversoise,' with the high cap, short petticoat, and decent sabots proper to her class: something better, indeed, than an insolent coquette in a flounced gown, and absolutely without cap! (for Sarah, it appears, did not partake the opinion of St Paul, that 'it is a shame for a woman to go with her head uncovered;' but, holding rather a contrary doctrine, resolutely refused to imprison in linen or muslin the plentiful tresses of her yellow hair, which it was her wont to fasten up smartly with a comb behind, and on Sundays to wear curled in front.)

'Shall I try and get you an Antwerp girl?' asked Mr Moore, who – stern in public – was on the whole very kind in private.

'Merci du cadeau!' was the answer. 'An Antwerp girl would not stay here ten days, sneered at as she would be by all the young coquines in your factory;' then softening, 'You are very good, dear brother – excuse my petulance – but truly, my domestic trials are severe, yet they are probably my destiny; for I recollect that our revered mother experienced similar sufferings, though she had the choice of all the best servants in Antwerp: domestics are in all countries a spoiled and unruly set.'

Mr Moore had also certain reminiscences about the trials of his revered mother. A good mother she had been to him, and he honoured her memory, but he recollected that she kept a hot kitchen of it in Antwerp, just as his faithful sister did here in England. Thus, therefore, he let the subject drop, and when the coffee-service was removed, proceeded to console Hortense by fetching her music-book and guitar; and, having arranged the ribbon of the instrument round her neck with a quiet fraternal kindness he knew to be all-powerful in soothing her most ruffled moods, he asked her to give him some of their mother's favourite songs.

Nothing refines like affection. Family jarring vulgarizes – family union elevates. Hortense, pleased with her brother, and grateful to him, looked, as she touched her guitar, almost graceful, almost handsome; her every-day fretful look was gone for a moment, and was replaced by a 'sourire plein de bonté.' She sang the songs he asked for, with feeling; they reminded her of a parent to which she had been truly attached; they reminded her of her young days. She observed, too, that Caroline listened with naïve interest; this augmented her good-humour; and the exclamation at the close of the song, 'I wish I could sing and play like Hortense!' achieved the business, and rendered her charming for the evening.

It is true, a little lecture to Caroline followed, on the vanity of *wishing*, and the duty of *trying*. 'As Rome,' it was suggested, 'had not been built in a day, so neither had Mademoiselle Gérard Moore's education been completed in a week, or by merely *wishing* to be clever. It was effort that had accomplished that great work: she was ever remarkable for her perseverance, for her industry: her masters had remarked that it was as delightful as it was uncommon to find so much talent united with so much solidity, and so on.' Once on the theme of her own merits, Mademoiselle was fluent.

Cradled at last in blissful self-complacency, she took her knitting and sat down tranquil. Drawn curtains, a clear fire, a softly shining lamp, gave now to the little parlour its best – its evening charm. It is probable that the three there present felt this charm: they all looked happy.

'What shall we do now, Caroline?' asked Mr Moore, returning to his seat beside his cousin.

'What shall we do, Robert?' repeated she playfully. 'You decide.'

'Not play at chess?'

'No.'

'Nor draughts, nor backgammon?'

'No – no; we both hate silent games that only keep one's hands employed, don't we?'

'I believe we do: then, shall we talk scandal?'

'About whom? Are we sufficiently interested in anybody to take pleasure in pulling their character to pieces?'

'A question that comes to the point. For my part – unamiable as it sounds – I must say, no.'

'And I, too. But it is strange – though we want no third – fourth, I mean (she hastily and with contrition glanced at Hortense), living person among us – so selfish we are in our happiness – though we don't want to think of the present existing world, it would be pleasant to go back to the past; to hear people that have slept for generations in graves that are perhaps no longer graves now, but gardens and fields, speak to us and tell us their thoughts, and impart their ideas.'

'Who shall be the speaker? What language shall he utter? French?'

'Your French forefathers don't speak so sweetly, nor so solemnly, nor so impressively as your English ancestors, Robert. To-night you shall be entirely English: you shall read an English book.'

'An old English book?'

'Yes, an old English book, one that you like; and I will choose a part of it that is toned quite in harmony with something in you. It shall waken your nature, fill your mind with music: it shall pass like a skilful hand over your heart, and make its strings sound. Your heart is a lyre, Robert; but the lot of your life has not been a minstrel to sweep it, and it is often silent. Let glorious William come near and touch it; you will see how he will draw the English power and melody out of its chords.'

'I must read Shakspeare?'

'You must have his spirit before you; you must hear his voice with your mind's ear; you must take some of his soul into yours.'

'With a view to making me better; is it to operate like a sermon?'

'It is to stir you; to give you new sensations. It is to make you feel your life strongly, not only your virtues, but your vicious, perverse points.'

'Dieu! que dit-elle?' cried Hortense, who hitherto had been counting stitches in her knitting, and had not much attended to what was said, but whose ear these two strong words caught with a tweak.

'Never mind her, sister: let her talk; now just let her say anything she pleases to-night. She likes to come down hard upon your brother sometimes; it amuses me, so let her alone.'

Caroline, who, mounted on a chair, had been rummaging the book-case, returned with a book.

'Here's Shakspeare,' she said, 'and there's Coriolanus. Now, read, and discover by the feelings the reading will give you at once how low and how high you are.'

'Come then, sit near me, and correct when I mispronounce.'

'I am to be the teacher then, and you my pupil?'

'Ainsi, soit-il!'

'And Shakspeare is our science, since we are going to study?'

'It appears so.'

'And you are not going to be French, and sceptical, and sneering? You are not going to think it a sign of wisdom to refuse to admire?'

'I don't know.'

'If you do, Robert, I'll take Shakspeare away; and I'll shrivel up within myself, and put on my bonnet and go home.'

'Sit down; here I begin.'

'One minute, if you please, brother,' interrupted Mademoiselle, 'when the gentleman of a family reads, the ladies should always sew. Caroline, dear child, take your embroidery; you may get three sprigs done to-night.'

Caroline looked dismayed. 'I can't see by lamp-light; my eyes are tired and I can't do two things well at once. If I sew, I cannot listen; if I listen, I cannot sew.'

'Fi, donc! Quel enfantillage!' began Hortense. Mr Moore, as usual, suavely interposed.

'Permit her to neglect the embroidery for this evening. I wish her whole attention to be fixed on my accent, and to ensure this, she must follow the reading with her eyes; she must look at the book.'

He placed it between them, reposed his arm on the back of Caroline's chair, and thus began to read.

The very first scene in 'Coriolanus' came with smart relish to his intellectual palate, and still as he read he warmed. He delivered the haughty speech of Caius Marcius to the starving citizens with unction; he did not say he thought his irrational pride right, but he seemed to feel it so. Caroline looked up at him with a singular smile.

'There's a vicious point hit already,' she said; 'you sympathize with that proud patrician who does not sympathize with his famished fellow-men, and insults them: there, go on.' He proceeded. The war-like portions did not rouse him much; he said all that was out of date, or should be; the spirit displayed was barbarous, yet the encounter single-handed between Marcius and Tullus Aufidius, he delighted in. As he advanced, he forgot to criticise; it was evident he appreciated the power, the truth of each portion; and, stepping our of the narrow line of private prejudices, began to revel in the large picture of human nature, to feel the reality stamped upon the characters who were speaking from that page before him.

He did not read the comic scenes well, and Caroline, taking the book out of his hand, read these parts for him. From her he seemed to enjoy them, and indeed she gave them with a spirit no one could have expected of her, with a pithy expression with which she seemed gifted on the spot, and for that brief moment only. It may be remarked, in passing, that the general character of her conversation that evening, whether serious or sprightly, grave or gay, was as of something untaught, unstudied, intuitive, fitful; when once gone, no more to be reproduced as it had been, than the glancing ray of the meteor, than the tints of the dew-gem, than the colour or form of the sun-set cloud, than the fleeting and glittering ripple varying the flow of a rivulet.

Coriolanus in glory; Coriolanus in disaster; Coriolanus banished, followed like giant-shades one after the other. Before the vision of the banished man, Moore's spirit seemed to pause. He stood on the hearth of Aufidius's hall, facing the image of greatness fallen, but greater than ever in that low estate. He saw 'the grim appearance,' the dark face 'bearing command in it,' 'the noble vessel with its tackle torn.' With the revenge of Caius Marcius, Moore perfectly sympathized; he was not scandalized by it; and again Caroline whispered, 'There I see another glimpse of brotherhood in error.'

The march on Rome, the mother's supplication, the long resistance, the final yielding of bad passions to good, which ever must be the case in a nature worthy the epithet of noble, the rage of Aufidius at what he considered his ally's weakness, the death of Coriolanus, the final sorrow of his great enemy; all scenes made of condensed truth and strength, came on in succession, and carried with them in their deep, fast flow, the heart and mind of reader and listener.

'Now, have you felt Shakspeare?' asked Caroline, some ten minutes after her cousin had closed the book.

'I think so.'

'And have you felt anything in Coriolanus like you?'

'Perhaps I have.'

'Was he not faulty as well as great?'

Moore nodded. 'And what was his fault? What made him hated by the citizens? What caused him to be banished by his countrymen?'

'What do you think it was?'

'I ask again –

"Whether was it pride,
Which out of daily fortune ever taints
The happy man? whether defect of judgment,
To fail in the disposing of those chances
Which he was lord of? or whether nature,
Not to be other than one thing; not moving
From the casque to the cushion, but commanding peace
Even with the same austerity and garb
As he controlled the war?" '

'Well, answer yourself, Sphynx.'

'It was a spice of all: and you must not be proud to your workpeople; you must not neglect chances of soothing them, and you must not be of an inflexible nature, uttering a request as austerely as if it were a command.'

'That is the moral you tack to the play. What puts such notions into your head?'

'A wish for your good, a care for your safety, dear Robert, and a fear caused by many things which I have heard lately, that you will come to harm.'

'Who tells you these things?'

'I hear my uncle talk about you: he praises your hard spirit, your determined cast of mind, your scorn of low enemies, your resolution not "to truckle to the mob" as he says.'

'And would you have me truckle to them?'

'No, not for the world: I never wish you to lower yourself; but somehow, I cannot help thinking it unjust to include all poor working people under the general and insulting name of "the mob," and continually to think of them and treat them haughtily.'

'You are a little democrat, Caroline: if your uncle knew, what would he say?'

'I rarely talk to my uncle, as you know, and never about such things: he thinks everything but sewing and cooking above women's comprehension, and out of their line.'

'And do you fancy you comprehend the subjects on which you advise me?'

'As far as they concern you, I comprehend them. I know it would be better for you to be loved by your workpeople than to be hated by them, and I am sure that kindness is more likely to win their regard than pride. If you were proud and cold to me and Hortense, should we love you? When you are cold to me, as you are sometimes, can I venture to be affectionate in return?'

'Now, Lina, I've had my lesson both in languages and ethics, with a touch on politics; it is your turn. Hortense tells me you were much taken by a little piece of poetry you learned the other day, a piece by poor André Chénier – "La Jeune Captive;" do you remember it still?'

'I think so.'

'Repeat it, then. Take your time and mind your accent: especially let us have no English u's.'

Caroline, beginning in a low, rather tremulous voice, but gaining courage as she proceeded, repeated the sweet verses of Chénier; the last three stanzas she rehearsed well.

'Mon beau voyage encore est si loin de sa fin!
Je pars, et des ormeaux qui bordent le chemin
     J'ai passé le premiers à peine.

Au banquet de la vie à peine commencé,
Un instant settlement mes lèvres ont pressé
   La coupe en mes mains encore pleine.

'Je ne suis qu'au printemps – je veux voir la moisson;
Et comme le soleil, de saison en saison,
   Je veux achever mon année.
Brillante sur ma tige, et l'honneur du jardin
Je n'ai vu luire encore que les feux du matin,
   Je veux achever ma journée!'

Moore listened at first with his eyes cast down, but soon he furtively raised them: leaning back in his chair, he could watch Caroline without her perceiving where his gaze was fixed. Her cheek had a colour, her eyes a light, her countenance an expression, this evening, which would have made even plain features striking; but there was not the grievous defect of plainness to pardon in her case. The sunshine was not shed on rough barrenness; it fell on soft bloom. Each lineament was turned with grace; the whole aspect was pleasing. At the present moment – animated, interested, touched – she might be called beautiful. Such a face was calculated to awaken not only the calm sentiment of esteem, the distant one of admiration; but some feeling more tender, genial, intimate: friendship, perhaps – affection, interest. When she had finished, she turned to Moore, and met his eye.

'Is that pretty well repeated?' she inquired, smiling like any happy, docile child.

'I really don't know.'

'Why don't you know? Have you not listened?'

'Yes – and looked. You are fond of poetry, Lina?'

'When I meet with *real* poetry, I cannot rest till I have learned it by heart, and so made it partly mine.'

Mr Moore now sat silent for several minutes. It struck nine o'clock: Sarah entered, and said that Mr Helstone's servant was come for Miss Caroline.

'Then the evening is gone already,' she observed; 'and it will be long, I suppose, before I pass another here.'

Hortense had been for some time nodding over her knitting; fallen into a doze now, she made no response to the remark.

'You would have no objection to come here oftener of an evening?' inquired Robert, as he took her folded mantle from the side-table, where it still lay, and carefully wrapped it round her.

'I like to come here; but I have no desire to be intrusive. I am not hinting to be asked: you must understand that.'

'Oh! I understand thee, child. You sometimes lecture me for wishing to be rich, Lina; but if I *were* rich, you should live here always: at any rate, you should live with me wherever my habitation might be.'

'That would be pleasant; and if you were poor – ever so poor – it would still be pleasant. Good-night, Robert.'

'I promised to walk with you up to the Rectory.'

'I know you did; but I thought you had forgotten, and I hardly knew how to remind you, though I wished to do it. But would you like to go? It is a cold night; and, as Fanny is come, there is no necessity –'

'Here is your muff – don't wake Hortense – come.'

The half-mile to the Rectory was soon traversed. They parted in the garden without kiss, scarcely with a pressure of hands: yet Robert sent his cousin in excited and joyously troubled. He had been singularly kind to her that day: not in phrase, compliment, profession; but in manner, in look, and in soft and friendly tones.

For himself, he came home grave, almost morose. As he stood leaning on his own yard-gate, musing in the watery moonlight, all alone – the hushed, dark mill before him, the hill-environed hollow round – he exclaimed, abruptly: –

'This won't do! There's weakness – there's downright ruin in all this. However,' he added, dropping his voice, 'the frenzy is quite temporary. I know it very well: I have had it before. It will be gone to-morrow.'

CHAPTER VII

THE CURATES AT TEA

Caroline Helstone was just eighteen years old; and at eighteen the true narrative of life is yet to be commenced. Before that time, we sit listening to a tale, a marvellous fiction; delightful sometimes, and sad sometimes; almost always unreal. Before that time, our world is heroic; its inhabitants half-divine or semi-demon; its scenes are dream-scenes: darker woods, and stranger hills; brighter skies, more dangerous waters; sweeter flowers, more tempting fruits; wider plains, drearier deserts, sunnier fields than are found in nature, overspread our enchanted globe. What a moon we gaze on before that time! How the trembling of our hearts at her aspect bears witness to its unutterable beauty! As to our sun, it is a burning heaven – the world of gods.

At that time – at eighteen, drawing near the confines of illusive, void dreams, Elf-land lies behind us, the shores of Reality rise in front. These shores are yet distant: they look so blue, soft, gentle, we long to reach them. In sunshine we see a greenness beneath the azure, as of spring meadows; we catch glimpses of silver lines, and imagine the roll of living waters. Could we but reach this land, we think to hunger and thirst no more; whereas many a wilderness, and often the flood of Death, or some stream of sorrow as cold and almost as black as Death, is to be crossed ere true bliss can be tasted. Every joy that life gives must be earned ere it is secured; and how hardly earned, those only know who have wrestled for great prizes. The heart's blood must gem with red beads the brow of the combatant, before the wreath of victory rustles over it.

At eighteen, we are not aware of this. Hope, when she smiles on us, and promises happiness to-morrow, is implicitly believed; – Love, when he comes wandering like a lost angel to our door, is at once admitted, welcomed, embraced: his quiver is not seen; if his arrows penetrate, their wound is like a thrill of new life: there are no fears of poison, none of the barb which no leech's hand can extract: that perilous passion – an agony ever in some of its phases; with many, an agony throughout – is believed to be an unqualified good: in short, at eighteen, the school of Experience is to be entered, and her humbling, crushing, grinding, but yet purifying and invigorating lessons are yet to be learnt.

Alas, Experience! No other mentor has so wasted and frozen a face as yours: none wears a robe so black, none bears a rod so heavy, none with hand so inexorable draws the novice so sternly to his task, and forces him with authority so resistless to its acquirement. It is by your instructions alone that man or woman can ever find a safe track through life's wilds: without it, how they stumble, how they stray! On what forbidden grounds do they intrude, down what dread declivities are they hurled!

Caroline, having been convoyed home by Robert, had no wish to pass what remained of the evening with her uncle; the room in which he sat was very sacred ground to her; she seldom intruded on it, and to-night she kept aloof till the bell rung for prayers. Part of the evening church service was the form of worship observed in Mr Helstone's household: he read it in his usual nasal voice, clear, loud, and monotonous. The rite over, his niece, according to her wont, stepped up to him.

'Good-night, uncle.'

'Hey! You've been gadding abroad all day – visiting, dining out, and what not!'

'Only at the cottage.'

'And have you learnt your lessons?'

'Yes.'

'And made a shirt?'

'Only part of one.'

'Well, that will do: stick to the needle – learn shirt-making and gown-making, and pie-crust-making, and you'll be a clever woman some day. Go to bed now: I'm busy with a pamphlet here.'

Presently the niece was enclosed in her small bed-room; the door bolted, her white dressing-gown assumed, her long hair loosened and falling thick, soft, and wavy to her waist; and as, resting from the task of combing it out, she leaned her cheek on her hand and fixed her eyes on the carpet, before her rose, and close around her drew, the visions we see at eighteen years.

Her thoughts were speaking with her: speaking pleasantly, as it seemed, for she smiled as she listened. She looked pretty, meditating thus: but a brighter thing than she was in that apartment – the spirit of youthful Hope. According to this flattering prophet, she was to know disappointment, to feel chill no more: she had entered on the dawn of a summer day – no false dawn, but the true spring of morning – and her sun would quickly rise. Impossible for her now to suspect that she was the sport of delusion: her expectations seemed warranted, the foundation on which they rested appeared solid.

'When people love, the next step is they marry,' was her argument. 'Now, I love Robert, and I feel sure that Robert loves me: I have thought so many a time before; to-day I *felt* it. When I looked up at him after repeating Chénier's poem, his eyes (what handsome eyes he has!) sent the truth through my heart. Sometimes I am afraid to speak to him, lest I should be too frank, lest I should seem forward: for I have more than once regretted bitterly, overflowing, superfluous words, and feared I had said more than he expected me to say, and that he would disapprove what he might deem my indiscretion; now, to-night, I could have ventured to express any thought, he was so indulgent. How kind he was, as we walked up the lane! He does not flatter or say foolish things; his love-making (friendship, I mean: of course

I don't yet account him my lover, but I hope he will be so some day) is not like what we read of in books – it is far better – original, quiet, manly, sincere. I *do* like him: I would be an excellent wife to him if he did marry me: I would tell him of his faults (for he has a few faults), but I would study his comfort, and cherish him, and do my best to make him happy. Now, I am sure he will not be cold to-morrow: I feel almost certain that to-morrow evening he will either come here, or ask me to go there.'

She recommenced combing her hair, long as a mermaid's; turning her head, as she arranged it, she saw her own face and form in the glass. Such reflections are soberizing to plain people: their own eyes are not enchanted with the image; they are confident then that the eyes of others can see in it no fascination; but the fair must naturally draw other conclusions: the picture is charming, and must charm. Caroline saw a shape, a head, that, daguerreotyped in that attitude and with that expression, would have been lovely: she could not choose but derive from the spectacle confirmation to her hopes: it was then in undiminished gladness she sought her couch.

And in undiminished gladness she rose the next day: as she entered her uncle's breakfast-room, and with soft cheerfulness wished him good-morning, even that little man of bronze himself thought, for an instant, his niece was growing 'a fine girl.' Generally she was quiet and timid with him: very docile, but not communicative; this morning, however, she found many things to say. Slight topics alone might be discussed between them; for with a woman – a girl – Mr Helstone would touch on no other. She had taken an early walk in the garden, and she told him what flowers were beginning to spring there; she inquired when the gardener was to come and trim the borders; she informed him that certain starlings were beginning to build their nests in the church-tower (Briarfield church was close to Briarfield rectory); she wondered the tolling of the bells in the belfry did not scare them.

Mr Helstone opined that 'they were like other fools who had

just paired; insensible to inconvenience just for the moment.'
Caroline, made perhaps a little too courageous by her temporary
good spirits, here hazarded a remark of a kind she had never
before ventured to make on observations dropped by her revered
relative.

'Uncle,' said she, 'whenever you speak of marriage, you speak
of it scornfully: do you think people shouldn't marry?'

'It is decidedly the wisest plan to remain single, especially for
women.'

'Are all marriages unhappy?'

'Millions of marriages are unhappy: if everybody confessed
the truth, perhaps all are more or less so.'

'You are always vexed when you are asked to come and marry
a couple – why?'

'Because one does not like to act as accessory to the commission of a piece of pure folly.'

Mr Helstone spoke so readily, he seemed rather glad of the
opportunity to give his niece a piece of his mind on this point.
Emboldened by the impunity which had hitherto attended her
questions, she went a little further: –

'But why,' said she, 'should it be pure folly? If two people
like each other, why shouldn't they consent to live together?'

'They tire of each other – they tire of each other in a month.
A yokefellow is not a companion; he or she is a fellow-sufferer.'

It was by no means naïve simplicity which inspired Caroline's
next remark: it was a sense of antipathy to such opinions, and
of displeasure at him who held them.

'One would think you had never been married, uncle: one
would think you were an old bachelor.'

'Practically, I am so.'

'But you have been married. Why were you so inconsistent
as to marry?'

'Every man is mad once or twice in his life.'

'So you tired of my aunt, and my aunt of you, and you were
miserable together?'

Mr Helstone pushed out his cynical lip, wrinkled his brown forehead, and gave an inarticulate grunt.

'Did she not suit you? Was she not good-tempered? Did you not get used to her? Were you not sorry when she died?'

'Caroline,' said Mr Helstone, bringing his hand slowly down to within an inch or two of the table, and then smiting it suddenly on the mahogany, 'understand this: it is vulgar and puerile to confound generals with particulars: in every case, there is the rule, and there are the exceptions. Your questions are stupid and babyish. Ring the bell, if you have done breakfast.'

The breakfast was taken away, and that meal over, it was the general custom of uncle and niece to separate, and not to meet again till dinner; but to-day the niece, instead of quitting the room, went to the window-seat, and sat down there. Mr Helstone looked round uneasily once or twice, as if he wished her away, but she was gazing from the window, and did not seem to mind him; so he continued the perusal of his morning paper – a particularly interesting one it chanced to be, as new movements had just taken place in the Peninsula, and certain columns of the journal were rich in long despatches from General Lord Wellington. He little knew, meantime, what thoughts were busy in his niece's mind – thoughts the conversation of the past half-hour had revived, but not generated; tumultuous were they now, as disturbed bees in a hive, but it was years since they had first made their cells in her brain.

She was reviewing his character, his disposition, repeating his sentiments on marriage. Many a time has she reviewed them before, and sounded the gulf between her own mind and his; and then, on the other side of the wide and deep chasm, she had seen, and she now saw, another figure standing beside her uncle's – a strange shape; dim, sinister, scarcely earthly: the half-remembered image of her own father, James Helstone, Matthewson Helstone's brother.

Rumours had reached her ear of what that father's character was; old servants had dropped hints: she knew, too, that he was

not a good man, and that he was never kind to her. She recol-
lected – a dark recollection it was – some weeks that she had
spent with him in a great town somewhere, when she had had
no maid to dress her or take care of her; when she had been
shut up, day and night, in a high garret-room, without a carpet,
with a bare uncurtained bed, and scarcely any other furniture;
when he went out early every morning, and often forgot to
return and give her her dinner during the day, and at night,
when he came back, was like a madman, furious, terrible; or –
still more painful – like an idiot, imbecile, senseless. She knew
she had fallen ill in this place, and that one night when she was
very sick, he had come raving into the room, and said he would
kill her, for she was a burden to him; her screams had brought
aid, and from the moment she was then rescued from him she
had never seen him, except as a dead man in his coffin.

That was her father: also she had a mother; though Mr
Helstone never spoke to her of that mother; though she could
not remember having seen her: but that she was alive she knew.
This mother was then the drunkard's wife: what had *their*
marriage been? Caroline, turning from the lattice whence she
had been watching the starlings (though without seeing them),
in a low voice, and with a sad bitter tone, thus broke the silence
of the room: –

'You term marriage miserable, I suppose, from what you saw
of my father and mother's. If my mother suffered what I suffered
when I was with papa, she must have had a dreadful life.'

Mr Helstone, thus addressed, wheeled about in his chair, and
looked over his spectacles at his niece: he was taken aback.

Her father and mother! What had put it into her head to
mention her father and mother, of whom he had never, during
the twelve years she had lived with him, spoken to her? That
the thoughts were self-matured; that she had any recollections
or speculations about her parents, he could not fancy.

'Your father and mother? Who has been talking to you about
them?'

'Nobody; but I remember something of what papa was, and I pity mamma. Where is she?'

This 'Where is she?' had been on Caroline's lips hundreds of times before; but till now she had never uttered it.

'I hardly know,' returned Mr Helstone; 'I was little acquainted with her. I have not heard from her for years: but wherever she is, she thinks nothing of you; she never inquires about you; I have reason to believe she does not wish to see you. Come, it is schooltime: you go to your cousin at ten, don't you? The clock has struck.'

Perhaps Caroline would have said more; but Fanny coming in, informed her master that the churchwardens wanted to speak to him in the vestry. He hastened to join them, and his niece presently set out for the cottage.

The road from the Rectory to Hollow's mill inclined downwards; she ran, therefore, almost all the way. Exercise, the fresh air, the thought of seeing Robert, at least of being on his premises, in his vicinage, revived her somewhat depressed spirits quickly. Arriving in sight of the white house, and within hearing of the thundering mill and its rushing water-course, the first thing she saw was Moore at his garden-gate. There he stood; in his belted Holland blouse, a light cap covering his head, which undress costume suited him: he was looking down the lane, not in the direction of his cousin's approach. She stopped, withdrawing a little behind a willow, and studied his appearance.

'He has not his peer,' she thought; 'he is as handsome as he is intelligent. What a keen eye he has! What clearly cut, spirited features – thin and serious, but graceful! I do like his face – I do like his aspect – I do like him so much! Better than any of those shuffling curates, for instance, – better than anybody: bonnie Robert!'

She sought 'bonnie Robert's' presence speedily. For his part, when she challenged his sight, I believe he would have passed from before her eyes like a phantom, if he could; but being a tall fact, and no fiction, he was obliged to stand the greeting.

He made it brief: it was cousin-like, brother-like, friend-like, anything but lover-like. The nameless charm of last night had left his manner: he was no longer the same man; or, at any rate, the same heart did not beat in his breast. Rude disappointment! sharp cross! At first the eager girl would not believe in the change, though she saw and felt it. It was difficult to withdraw her hand from his, till he had bestowed at least something like a kind pressure; it was difficult to turn her eyes from his eyes, till his looks had expressed something more and fonder than that cool welcome.

A lover masculine so disappointed can speak and urge explanation; a lover feminine can say nothing: if she did, the result would be shame and anguish, inward remorse for self-treachery. Nature would brand such demonstration as a rebellion against her instincts, and would vindictively repay it afterwards by the thunderbolt of self-contempt smiting suddenly in secret. Take the matter as you find it: ask no questions; utter no remonstrances: it is your best wisdom. You expected bread, and you have got a stone; break your teeth on it, and don't shriek because the nerves are martyrized: do not doubt that your mental stomach – if you have such a thing – is strong as an ostrich's – the stone will digest. You held out your hand for an egg, and fate put into it a scorpion. Show no consternation: close your fingers firmly upon the gift; let it sting through your palm. Never mind: in time, after your hand and arm have swelled and quivered long with torture, the squeezed scorpion will die, and you will have learned the great lesson how to endure without a sob. For the whole remnant of your life, if you survive the test – some, it is said, die under it – you will be stronger, wiser, less sensitive. This you are not aware of, perhaps, at the time, and so cannot borrow courage of that hope. Nature, however, as has been intimated, is an excellent friend in such cases; sealing the lips, interdicting utterance, commanding a placid dissimulation: a dissimulation often wearing an easy and gay mien at first, settling down to sorrow and paleness in time, then passing away and leaving a convenient stoicism, not the less fortifying because it is half-bitter.

Half-bitter! Is that wrong? No – it should be bitter: bitterness is strength – it is a tonic. Sweet mild force following acute suffering, you find nowhere: to talk of it is delusion. There may be apathetic exhaustion after the rack; if energy remains, it will be rather a dangerous energy – deadly when confronted with injustice.

Who has read the ballad of 'Puir Mary Lee?' – that old Scotch ballad, written I know not in what generation nor by what hand. Mary had been ill used – probably in being made to believe that truth which was falsehood: she is not complaining, but she is sitting alone in the snow-storm, and you hear her thoughts. They are not the thoughts of a model-heroine under her circumstances, but they are those of a deeply-feeling, strongly-resentful peasant-girl. Anguish has driven her from the ingle-nook of home, to the white-shrouded and icy hills: crouched under the 'cauld drift,' she recalls every image of horror, – 'the yellow-wymed ask,' 'the hairy adder,' 'the auld moon-bowing tyke,' 'the ghaist at e'en,' 'the sour bullister,' 'the milk on the taed's back:' she hates these, but 'waur she hates Robin-a-Ree!'

> 'Oh! ance I lived happily by yon bonny burn –
>   The warld was in love wi' me;
> But now I maun sit 'neath the cauld drift and mourn,
>   And curse black Robin-a-Ree!
>
> 'Then whudder awa' thou bitter biting blast,
>   And sough through the scrunty tree,
> And smoor me up in the snaw fu' fast,
>   And ne'er let the sun me see!
>
> 'Oh, never melt awa, thou wreath o' snaw,
>   That's sae kind in graving me;
> But hide me frae the scorn and guffaw
>   O' villains like Robin-a-Ree!'

But what has been said in the last page or two is not germane to Caroline Helstone's feelings, or to the state of things between her and Robert Moore. Robert had done her no wrong: he had told her no lie; it was she that was to blame, if any one was: what bitterness her mind distilled should and would be poured on her own head. She had loved without being asked to love, – a natural, sometimes an inevitable chance, but big with misery.

Robert, indeed, had sometimes seemed to be fond of her – but why? Because she had made herself so pleasing to him, he could not, in spite of all his efforts, help testifying a state of feeling his judgment did not approve, nor his will sanction. He was about to withdraw decidedly from intimate communication with her, because he did not choose to have his affections inextricably entangled, nor to be drawn, despite his reason, into a marriage he believed imprudent. Now, what was she to do? – to give way to her feelings, or to vanquish them? To pursue him, or to turn upon herself? If she is weak, she will try the first expedient, – will lose his esteem and win his aversion: if she has sense, she will be her own governor, and resolve to subdue and bring under guidance the disturbed realm of her emotions. She will determine to look on life steadily, as it is; to begin to learn its severe truths seriously, and to study its knotty problems closely, conscientiously.

It appeared she had a little sense, for she quitted Robert quietly, without complaint or question – without the alteration of a muscle or the shedding of a tear – betook herself to her studies under Hortense as usual, and at dinner-time went home without lingering.

When she had dined, and found herself in the Rectory drawing-room alone, having left her uncle over his temperate glass of port wine, the difficulty that occurred to and embarrassed her, was – 'How am I to get through this day?'

Last night she had hoped it would be spent as yesterday was, – that the evening would be again passed with Happiness and

Robert: she had learned her mistake this morning, and yet she could not settle down, convinced that no chance would occur to recall her to Hollow's cottage, or to bring Moore again into her society.

He had walked up after tea, more than once, to pass an hour with her uncle: the door-bell had rung, his voice had been heard in the passage just at twilight, when she little expected such a pleasure; and this had happened twice after he had treated her with peculiar reserve; and, though he rarely talked to her in her uncle's presence, he had looked at her relentingly, as he sat opposite her work-table during his stay: the few words he had spoken to her were comforting; his manner on bidding her good-night was genial. Now, he might come this evening, said False Hope: she almost knew it was False Hope which breathed the whisper, and yet she listened.

She tried to read – her thoughts wandered; she tried to sew – every stitch she put in was an ennui, the occupation was insufferably tedious; she opened her desk, and attempted to write a French composition – she wrote nothing but mistakes.

Suddenly the door-bell sharply rang – her heart leaped – she sprang to the drawing-room door, opened it softly, peeped through the aperture: Fanny was admitting a visiter – a gentleman – a tall man – just the height of Robert. For one second she thought it was Robert – for one second she exulted; but the voice asking for Mr Helstone undeceived her: that voice was an Irish voice, consequently not Moore's but the curate's – Malone's. He was ushered into the dining-room, where, doubtless, he speedily helped his Rector to empty the decanters.

It was a fact to be noted, that at whatever house in Briarfield, Whinbury, or Nunnely, one curate dropped in to a meal – dinner or tea, as the case might be – another presently followed; often two more. Not that they gave each other the rendezvous, but they were usually all on the run at the same time; and when Donne, for instance, sought Malone at his lodgings and found him not, he inquired whither he had posted, and having learned of the landlady his destination, hastened with all speed after him: the same causes operated in the same way with Sweeting. Thus it chanced on that afternoon that Caroline's ears were three times tortured with the ringing of the bell, and the advent of undesired guests: for Donne followed Malone, and Sweeting followed Donne; and more wine was ordered up from the cellar into the dining-room (for though old Helstone chid the inferior priesthood when he found them 'carousing,' as he called it, in their own tents, yet at his hierarchical table he ever liked to treat them to a glass of his best), and through the closed doors Caroline heard their boyish laughter, and the vacant cackle of their voices. Her fear was lest they should stay to tea; for she had no pleasure in making tea for that particular trio. What distinctions people draw! These three were men – young men – educated men, like Moore: yet, for her, how great the difference! Their society was a bore – his a delight.

Not only was she destined to be favoured with their clerical company, but Fortune was at this moment bringing her four other guests – lady-guests, all packed in a pony-phæton now rolling somewhat heavily along the road from Whinbury: an elderly lady, and three of her buxom daughters, were coming to see her 'in a friendly way,' as the custom of that neighbour-hood was. Yes, a fourth time the bell clanged: Fanny brought the present announcement to the drawing-room –

'Mrs Sykes and the three Misses Sykes.'

When Caroline was going to receive company, her habit was to wring her hands very nervously, to flush a little, and come forward hurriedly yet hesitatingly, wishing herself meantime at Jericho. She was, at such crises, sadly deficient in finished manner, though she had once been at school a year. Accordingly, on this occasion, her small white hands sadly maltreated each other, while she stood up, waiting the entrance of Mrs Sykes.

In stalked that lady, a tall bilious gentlewoman, who made an ample and not altogether insincere profession of piety, and was greatly given to hospitality towards the clergy; in sailed her three daughters, a showy trio, being all three well grown, and more or less handsome.

In English country ladies there is this point to be remarked. Whether young or old, pretty or plain, dull or sprightly, they all (or almost all) have a certain expression stamped on their features, which seems to say, 'I know – I do not boast of it – but I *know* that I am the standard of what is proper; let every one therefore whom I approach, or who approaches me, keep a sharp look-out, for wherein they differ from me – be the same in dress, manner, opinion, principle, or practice – therein they are wrong.'

Mrs and Misses Sykes, far from being exceptions to this observation, were pointed illustrations of its truth. Miss Mary – a well-looked, well-meant, and, on the whole, well-dispositioned girl – wore her complacency with some state, though without harshness; Miss Harriet – a beauty – carried it more over-bearingly: she looked high and cold; Miss Hannah, who was conceited, dashing, pushing, flourished hers consciously and openly; the mother evinced it with the gravity proper to her age and religious fame.

The reception was got through somehow. Caroline 'was glad to see them' (an unmitigated fib), hoped they were well, hoped Mrs Sykes's cough was better (Mrs Sykes had had a cough for the last twenty years), hoped the Misses Sykes had left their sisters at home well; to which inquiry, the Misses Sykes, sitting on three chairs opposite the music-stool, whereon Caroline had undesignedly come to anchor, after wavering for some seconds between it and a large arm-chair, into which she at length recol-lected she ought to induct Mrs Sykes: and indeed that lady saved her the trouble by depositing herself therein; the Misses Sykes replied to Caroline by one simultaneous bow, very majestic and mighty awful. A pause followed: this bow was of a character to ensure silence for the next five minutes, and it did. Mrs Sykes then inquired after Mr Helstone, and whether he had had any return of rheumatism, and whether preaching twice on a Sunday fatigued him, and if he was capable of taking a full service now; and on being assured he was, she and all her daughters, combining in chorus, expressed their opinion that he was 'a wonderful man of his years.'

Pause second.

Miss Mary, getting up the steam in her turn, asked whether Caroline had attended the Bible Society Meeting which had been held at Nunnely last Thursday night: the negative answer which truth compelled Caroline to utter – for last Thursday evening she had been sitting at home, reading a novel which Robert had lent her – elicited a simultaneous expression of surprise from the lips of the four ladies.

'We were all there,' said Miss Mary; 'mamma and all of us; we even persuaded papa to go: Hannah would insist upon it; but he fell asleep while Mr Langweilig, the German Moravian minister, was speaking: I felt quite ashamed, he nodded so.'

'And there was Dr Broadbent,' cried Hannah, 'such a beautiful speaker! You couldn't expect it of him, for he is almost a vulgar-looking man.'

'But such a dear man,' interrupted Mary.

'And such a good man, such a useful man,' added her mother.

'Only like a butcher in appearance,' interposed the fair, proud Harriet. 'I couldn't bear to look at him: I listened with my eyes shut.'

Miss Helstone felt her ignorance and incompetency; not having seen Dr Broadbent, she could not give her opinion. Pause third came on. During its continuance, Caroline was feeling at her heart's core what a dreaming fool she was; what an unpractical life she led; how little fitness there was in her for ordinary intercourse with the ordinary world. She was feeling how exclusively she had attached herself to the white cottage in the Hollow; how in the existence of one inmate of that cottage she had pent all her universe: she was sensible that this would not do, and that some day she would be forced to make an alteration: it could not be said that she exactly wished to resemble the ladies before her,

but she wished to become superior to her present self, so as to
feel less scared by their dignity.

The sole means she found of reviving the flagging discourse,
was by asking them if they would all stay to tea; and a cruel
struggle it cost her to perform this piece of civility. Mrs Sykes
had begun – 'We are much obliged to you, but –' when in came
Fanny once more.

'The gentlemen will stay the evening, ma'am,' was the message
she brought from Mr Helstone.

'What gentlemen have you?' now inquired Mrs Sykes. Their
names were specified; she and her daughters interchanged
glances: the curates were not to them what they were to Caroline.
Mr Sweeting was quite a favourite with them; even Mr Malone
rather so, because he was a clergyman. 'Really, since you have
company already, I think we will stay,' remarked Mrs Sykes. 'We
shall be quite a pleasant little party: I always like to meet the
clergy.'

And now Caroline had to usher them up-stairs, to help them
to unshawl, smooth their hair and make themselves smart; to
reconduct them to the drawing-room, to distribute amongst
them books of engravings, or odd things purchased from the
Jew-basket: she was obliged to be a purchaser, though she was
but a slack contributor; and if she had possessed plenty of
money, she would rather, when it was brought to the Rectory
– an awful incubus! – have purchased the whole stock, than
contributed a single pincushion.

It ought perhaps to be explained in passing, for the benefit
of those who are not 'au fait' to the mysteries of the 'Jew-
basket' and 'Missionary-basket,' that these 'meubles' are willow-
repositories, of the capacity of a good-sized family clothes-
basket, dedicated to the purpose of conveying from house to
house a monster collection of pin-cushions, needle-books, card-
racks, work-bags, articles of infantwear, &c. &c. &c., made by
the willing or reluctant hands of the Christian ladies of a parish,
and sold per force to the heathenish gentlemen thereof, at prices

unblushingly exorbitant. The proceeds of such compulsory sales are applied to the conversion of the Jews, the seeking up of the ten missing tribes, or to the regeneration of the interesting coloured population of the globe. Each lady-contributor takes it in her turn to keep the basket a month, to sew for it, and to foist off its contents on a shrinking male public. An exciting time it is when that turn comes round: some active-minded women, with a good trading spirit, like it, and enjoy exceedingly the fun of making hard-handed worsted-spinners cash up, to the tune of four or five hundred per cent. above cost price, for articles quite useless to them; other – feebler souls object to it, and would rather see the prince of darkness himself at their door any morning, than that phantom-basket, brought with 'Mrs Rouse's compliments, and please, ma'am, she says it's your turn now.'

Miss Helstone's duties of hostess performed, more anxiously than cheerily, she betook herself to the kitchen, to hold a brief privy council with Fanny and Eliza about the tea.

'What a lot on 'em!' cried Eliza, who was cook. 'And I put off the baking to-day because I thought there would be bread plenty to fit while morning: we shall never have enow.'

'Are there any tea-cakes?' asked the young mistress.

'Only three and a loaf. I wish these fine folk would stay at home till they're asked: and I want to finish trimming my hat' (bonnet she meant).

'Then,' suggested Caroline, to whom the importance of the emergency gave a certain energy, 'Fanny must run down to Briarfield and buy some muffins and crumpets, and some biscuits: and don't be cross, Eliza, we can't help it now.'

'And which tea-things are we to have?'

'Oh, the best, I suppose: I'll get out the silver service,' and she ran up-stairs, to the plate-closet, and presently brought down tea-pot, cream-ewer, and sugar-basin.

'And mun we have th' urn?'

'Yes; and now get it ready as quickly as you can, for the

sooner we have tea over, the sooner they will go – at least, I hope so. Heigho! I wish they were gone,' she sighed as she returned to the drawing-room. 'Still,' she thought, as she paused at the door ere opening it, 'if Robert would but come even now how bright all would be! How comparatively easy the task of amusing these people, if he were present! There would be an interest in hearing him talk (though he never says much in company) and in talking in his presence: there can be no interest in hearing any of them, or in speaking to them. How they will gabble when the curates come in, and how weary I shall grow with listening to them! But I suppose I am a selfish fool: these are very respectable gentlefolks; I ought no doubt to be proud of their countenance: I don't say they are not as good as I am – far from it – but they are different from me.'

She went in.

Yorkshire people, in those days, took their tea round the table; sitting well into it, with their knees duly introduced under the mahogany. It was essential to have a multitude of plates of bread and butter, varied in sorts and plentiful in quantity: it was thought proper, too, that on the centre-plate should stand a glass dish of marmalade; among the viands was expected to be found a small assortment of cheesecakes and tarts; if there was also a plate of thin slices of pink ham garnished with green parsley, so much the better.

Eliza, the Rector's cook, fortunately knew her business as provider: she had been put out of humour a little at first, when the invaders came so unexpectedly in such strength; but it appeared that she gained her cheerfulness with action, for in due time the tea was spread forth in handsome style; and neither ham, tarts, nor marmalade were wanting among its accompaniments.

The curates, summoned to this bounteous repast, entered joyous; but at once, on seeing the ladies, of whose presence they had not been forewarned, they came to a stand in the door-way. Malone headed the party; he stopped short and fell back, almost capsizing Donne, who was behind him. Donne, staggering three paces in retreat, sent little Sweeting into the arms of old Helstone, who brought up the rear. There was some expostulation, some tittering: Malone was desired to mind what he was about, and urged to push forward; which at last he did, though colouring to the top of his peaked forehead a bluish purple. Helstone, advancing, set the shy curates aside, welcomed all his fair guests, shook hands and passed a jest with each, and seated himself snugly between the lovely Harriet and the dashing Hannah; Miss Mary he requested to move to the seat opposite to him, that he might see her if he couldn't be near her. Perfectly easy and gallant, in his way, were his manners always to young ladies; and most popular was he amongst them: yet, at heart, he neither respected nor liked the sex, and such of them as circumstances had brought into intimate relation with him had ever feared rather than loved him.

The curates were left to shift for themselves. Sweeting, who was the least embarrassed of the three, took refuge beside Mrs Sykes; who, he knew, was almost as fond of him as if he had been her son. Donne, after making his general bow with a grace all his own, and saying in a high pragmatical voice, 'How d'ye do, Miss Helstone?' dropped into a seat at Caroline's elbow: to her unmitigated annoyance, for she had a peculiar antipathy to Donne, on account of his stultified and unmovable self-conceit, and his incurable narrowness of mind. Malone, grinning most unmeaningly, inducted himself into the corresponding seat on the other side: she was thus blessed in a pair of supporters; neither of whom, she knew, would be of any mortal use, whether for keeping up the conversation, handing cups, circulating the muffins, or even lifting the plate from the slop-basin. Little Sweeting, small and boyish as he was, would have been worth twenty of them.

Malone, though a ceaseless talker when there were only men present, was usually tongue-tied in the presence of ladies: three phrases, however, he had ready cut and dried, which he never failed to produce: –

1stly. – 'Have you had a walk to-day, Miss Helstone?'

2dly. – 'Have you seen your cousin, Moore, lately?'

3dly. – 'Does your class at the Sunday-school keep up its number?'

These three questions being put and responded to, between Caroline and Malone reigned silence.

With Donne it was otherwise: he was troublesome, exasperating. He had a stock of small-talk on hand, at once the most trite and perverse that can well be imagined: abuse of the people of Briarfield; of the natives of Yorkshire generally; complaints of the want of high society; of the backward state of civilisation in these districts; murmurings against the disrespectful conduct of the lower orders in the north toward their betters; silly ridicule of the manner of living in these parts, – the want of style, the absence of elegance, as if he, Donne, had been accustomed to very great doings indeed: an insinuation which his somewhat underbred manner and aspect failed to bear out. These strictures he seemed to think must raise him in the estimation of Miss Helstone, or of any other lady who heard him; whereas with her, at least, they brought him to a level below contempt: though sometimes, indeed, they incensed her; for, a Yorkshire girl herself, she hated to hear Yorkshire abused by such a pitiful prater; and when wrought up to a certain pitch, she would turn and say something of which neither the matter nor the manner recommended her to Mr Donne's good-will. She would tell him it was no proof of refinement to be ever scolding others for vulgarity; and no sign of a good pastor to be eternally censuring his flock. She would ask him what he had entered the church for, since he complained there were only cottages to visit, and poor people to preach to? – whether he had been ordained to the ministry merely to wear soft clothing, and sit in kings' houses? These questions were considered by all the curates as, to the last degree, audacious and impious.

Tea was a long time in progress: all the guests gabbled as their hostess had expected they would. Mr Helstone, being in excellent spirits, – when, indeed, was he ever otherwise in society, attractive female society? – it being only with the one lady of his own family that he maintained a grim taciturnity, – kept up a brilliant flow of easy prattle with his right-hand and left-hand neighbours, and even with his *vis-à-vis*, Miss Mary: though as Mary was the most sensible, the least coquettish of the three, to her the elderly widower was the least attentive. At heart, he could not abide sense in women: he liked to see them as silly, as light-headed, as vain, as open to ridicule as possible; because they were then in reality what he held them to be, and wished them to be, – inferior: toys to play with, to amuse a vacant hour and to be thrown away.

Hannah was his favourite. Harriet, though beautiful, egotistical, and self-satisfied, was not quite weak enough for him: she had some genuine self-respect amidst much false pride, and if she did not talk like an oracle, neither would she babble like one crazy: she would not permit herself to be treated quite as a doll, a child, a plaything; she expected to be bent to like a queen.

Hannah, on the contrary, demanded no respect; only flattery: if her admirers only *told* her that she was an angel, she would let them *treat* her like an idiot. So very credulous and frivolous was she; so very silly did she become when besieged with attention, flattered and admired to the proper degree, that there were moments when Helstone actually felt tempted to commit matrimony a second time, and to try the experiment of taking her for his second helpmeet: but, fortunately, the salutary recollection of the ennuis of his first marriage, the impression still left on him of the weight of the millstone he had once worn round his neck, the fixity of his feelings respecting the insufferable evils of conjugal existence, operated as a check to his tenderness, suppressed the sigh heaving his old iron lungs, and restrained him from whispering to Hannah proposals it would have been high fun and great satisfaction to her to hear.

It is probable she would have married him if he had asked her; her parents would have quite approved the match: to them his fifty-five years, his bend-leather heart, could have presented no obstacles; and, as he was a rector, held an excellent living, occupied a good house, and was supposed even to have private property (though in that the world was mistaken: every penny of the £5000 inherited by him from his father had been devoted to the building and endowing of a new church at his native village in Lancashire – for he could show a lordly munificence when he pleased, and, if the end was to his liking, never hesitated about making a grand sacrifice to attain it), – her parents, I say, would have delivered Hannah over to his loving-kindness and his tender mercies without one scruple; and the second Mrs Helstone, inversing the natural order of insect existence, would have fluttered through the honeymoon a bright, admired butterfly, and crawled the rest of her days a sordid, trampled worm.

Little Mr Sweeting, seated between Mrs Sykes and Miss Mary, both of whom were very kind to him, and having a dish of tarts before him, and marmalade and crumpet upon his plate, looked and felt more content than any monarch. He was fond of all the Misses Sykes; they were all fond of him: he thought them magnificent girls, quite proper to mate with one of his inches. If he had a cause of regret at this blissful moment, it was that Miss Dora happened to be absent; Dora being the one whom he secretly hoped one day to call Mrs David Sweeting, with whom he dreamt of taking stately walks, leading her like an empress through the village of Nunnely: and an empress she would have been, if size could make an empress. She was vast, ponderous: seen from behind, she had the air of a very stout lady of forty; but withal she possessed a good face, and no unkindly character.

The meal at last drew to a close: it would have been over long ago, if Mr Donne had not persisted in sitting with his cup half full of cold tea before him, long after the rest had finished, and after he himself had discussed such allowance of viands as he felt competent to swallow – long, indeed, after signs of impatience had been manifested all round the board: till chairs

were pushed back; till the talk flagged; till silence fell. Vainly
did Caroline inquire repeatedly if he would have another cup;
if he would take a little hot tea, as that must be cold, &c.: he
would neither drink it nor leave it. He seemed to think that
this isolated position of his gave him somehow a certain importance: that it was dignified and stately to be the last; that it was
grand to keep all the others waiting. So long did he linger, that
the very urn died: it ceased to hiss. At length, however, the old
Rector himself, who had hitherto been too pleasantly engaged
with Hannah to care for the delay, got impatient.

'For whom are we waiting?' he asked.

'For me, I believe,' returned Donne, complacently; appearing
to think it much to his credit that a party should thus be kept
dependent on his movements.

'Tut!' cried Helstone; then standing up, 'Let us return thanks,'
said he; which he did forthwith, and all quitted the table.
Donne, nothing abashed, still sat ten minutes quite alone,
whereupon Mr Helstone rang the bell for the things to be
removed; the curate at length saw himself forced to empty his
cup, and to relinquish the *rôle* which, he thought, had given
him such a felicitous distinction, drawn upon him such flattering general notice.

And now, in the natural course of events (Caroline, knowing
how it would be, had opened the piano, and produced music-
books in readiness) music was asked for. This was Mr Sweeting's
chance for showing off: he was eager to commence; he undertook, therefore, the arduous task of persuading the young ladies
to favour the company with an air – a song. Con amore, he
went through the whole business of begging, praying, resisting
excuses, explaining away difficulties, and at last succeeded in
persuading Miss Harriet to allow herself to be led to the instrument. Then out came the pieces of his flute (he always carried
them in his pocket, as unfailingly as he carried his handkerchief). They were screwed and arranged; Malone and Donne
meantime herding together, and sneering at him, which the

little man, glancing over his shoulder, saw, but did not heed at all: he was persuaded their sarcasm all arose from envy; they could not accompany the ladies as he could; he was about to enjoy a triumph over them.

The triumph began. Malone, much chagrined at hearing him pipe up in most superior style, determined to earn distinction, too, if possible, and all at once assuming the character of a swain (which character he had endeavoured to enact once or twice before, but in which he had not hitherto met with the success he doubtless opined his merits deserved), approached a sofa on which Miss Helstone was seated, and depositing his great Irish frame near her, tried his hand (or rather tongue) at a fine speech or two, accompanied by grins the most extraordinary and incomprehensible. In the course of his efforts to render himself agreeable, he contrived to possess himself of the two long sofa cushions and a square one; with which, after rolling them about for some time with strange gestures, he managed to erect a sort of barrier between himself and the object of his attentions. Caroline, quite willing that they should be sundered, soon devised an excuse for stepping over to the opposite side of the room, and taking up a position beside Mrs Sykes; of which good lady she entreated some instruction in a new stitch in ornamental knitting, a favour readily granted; and thus Peter Augustus was thrown out.

Very sullenly did his countenance lower when he saw himself abandoned, – left entirely to his own resources, on a large sofa, with the charge of three small cushions on his hands. The fact was, he felt disposed seriously to cultivate acquaintance with Miss Helstone; because he thought, in common with others, that her uncle possessed money, and concluded, that since he had no children, he would probably leave it to his niece. Gérard Moore was better instructed on this point: he had seen the neat church that owed its origin to the Rector's zeal and cash, and more than once, in his inmost soul, had cursed an expensive caprice which crossed his wishes.

The evening seemed long to one person in that room. Caroline at intervals dropped her knitting on her lap, and gave herself up to a sort of brain-lethargy – closing her eyes and depressing her head – caused by what seemed to her the unmeaning hum round her: the inharmonious, tasteless rattle of the piano keys, the squeaking and gasping notes of the flute, the laughter and mirth of her uncle and Hannah and Mary, she could not tell whence originating, for she heard nothing comic or gleeful in their discourse; and, more than all, by the interminable gossip of Mrs Sykes murmured close at her ear; gossip which rang the changes on four subjects: her own health and that of the various members of her family; the Missionary and Jew baskets and their contents; the late meeting at Nunnely, and one which was expected to come off next week at Whinbury.

Tired at length to exhaustion, she embraced the opportunity of Mr Sweeting coming up to speak to Mrs Sykes, to slip quietly out of the apartment, and seek a moment's respite in solitude. She repaired to the dining-room, where the clear but now low remnant of a fire still burnt in the grate. The place was empty and quiet, glasses and decanters were cleared from the table, the chairs were put back in their places, all was orderly. Caroline sank into her uncle's large easy chair, half shut her eyes, and rested herself – rested at least her limbs, her senses, her hearing, her vision – weary with listening to nothing, and gazing on vacancy. As to her mind, that flew directly to the Hollow: it stood on the threshold of the parlour there, then it passed to the counting-house, and wondered which spot was blessed by the presence of Robert. It so happened that neither locality had that honour; for Robert was half a mile away from both, and much nearer to Caroline than her deadened spirit suspected: he was at this moment crossing the churchyard, approaching the Rectory garden-gate: not, however, coming to see his cousin, but intent solely on communicating a brief piece of intelligence to the Rector.

Yes, Caroline; you hear the wire of the bell vibrate: it rings again for the fifth time this afternoon: you start, and you are certain now that this must be him of whom you dream. Why you are so certain you cannot explain to yourself, but you know it. You lean forward, listening eagerly as Fanny opens the door: right! that is *the* voice – low – with the slight foreign accent, but so sweet, as you fancy: you half rise: 'Fanny will tell him Mr Helstone is with company, and then he will go away.' Oh! she cannot let him go: in spite of herself – in spite of her reason she walks half across the room; she stands ready to dart out in case the step should retreat: but he enters the passage. 'Since your master is engaged,' he says, 'just show me into the dining-room; bring me pen and ink: I will write a short note and leave it for him.'

Now, having caught these words, and hearing him advance, Caroline, if there was a door within the dining-room, would glide through it and disappear. She feels caught, hemmed in; she dreads her unexpected presence may annoy him. A second since, she would have flown to him; that second passed, she would flee from him. She cannot; there is no way of escape: the dining-room has but one door, through which now enters her cousin. The look of troubled surprise she expected to see in his face has appeared there, has shocked her, and is gone. She has stammered a sort of apology: –

'I only left the drawing-room a minute for a little quiet.'

There was something so diffident and downcast in the air and tone with which she said this, any one might perceive that some saddening change had lately passed over her prospects, and that the faculty of cheerful self-possession had left her. Mr Moore, probably, remembered how she had formerly been accustomed to meet him with gentle ardour and hopeful confidence; he must have seen how the check of this morning had operated: here was an opportunity for carrying out his new system with effect, if he chose to improve it. Perhaps he found it easier to practise that system in broad daylight, in his mill-yard, amidst busy occupations, than in a quiet parlour, disengaged, at the hour of eventide. Fanny lit the candles, which before had stood unlit on the table, brought writing materials, and left the room: Caroline was about to follow her. Moore, to act consistently, should have let her go; whereas he stood in the doorway, and, holding out his hand, gently kept her back: he did not ask her to stay, but he would not let her go.

'Shall I tell my uncle you are here?' asked she, still in the same subdued voice.

'No: I can say to you all I had to say to him. You will be my messenger?'

'Yes, Robert.'

'Then you may just inform him that I have got a clue to the identity of one, at least, of the men who broke my frames; that he belongs to the same gang who attacked Sykes and Pearson's dressing-shop; and that I hope to have him in custody to-morrow. You can remember that?'

'Oh! yes.' These two monosyllables were uttered in a sadder tone than ever; and, as she said them, she shook her head slightly, and sighed. 'Will you prosecute him?'

'Doubtless.'

'No, Robert.'

'And why no, Caroline?'

'Because it will set all the neighbourhood against you more than ever.'

'That is no reason why I should not do my duty, and defend my property. This fellow is a great scoundrel, and ought to be incapacitated from perpetrating further mischief.'

'But his accomplices will take revenge on you. You do not know how the people of this country bear malice: it is the boast of some of them that they can keep a stone in their pocket seven years, turn it at the end of that time, keep it seven years longer, and hurl it, and hit their mark "at last."'

Moore laughed.

'A most pithy vaunt,' said he; 'one that redounds vastly to the credit of your dear Yorkshire friends. But don't fear for me,

Lina: I am on my guard against these lamb-like compatriots of yours: don't make yourself uneasy about me.'

'How can I help it? You are my cousin. If anything happened –' she stopped.

'Nothing will happen, Lina. To speak in your own language, there is a Providence above all – is there not?'

'Yes, dear Robert. May He guard you!'

'And if prayers have efficacy, yours will benefit me: you pray for me sometimes?'

'Not *sometimes*, Robert: you, and Louis, and Hortense are *always* remembered.'

'So I have often imagined: it has occurred to me, when, weary and vexed, I have myself gone to bed like a heathen, that another had asked forgiveness for my day, and safety for my night. I don't suppose such vicarial piety will avail much; but the petitions come out of a sincere breast, from innocent lips: they should be acceptable as Abel's offering; and doubtless would be, if the object deserved them.'

'Annihilate that doubt: it is groundless.'

'When a man has been brought up only to make money, and lives to make it, and for nothing else, and scarcely breathes any other air than that of mills and markets, it seems odd to utter his name in a prayer, or to mix his idea with anything divine; and very strange it seems, that a good, pure heart should take him in and harbour him, as if he had any claim to that sort of nest. If I could guide that benignant heart, I believe I should counsel it to exclude one who does not profess to have any higher aim in life than that of patching up his broken fortune, and wiping clean from his bourgeois scutcheon the foul stain of bankruptcy.'

The hint, though conveyed thus tenderly and modestly (as Caroline thought), was felt keenly and comprehended clearly.

'Indeed, I only think – or I *will only* think – of you as my cousin,' was the quick answer. 'I am beginning to understand things better than I did, Robert, when you first came to England: better than I did, a week – a day ago. I know it is your duty to try to get on, and that it won't do for you to be romantic; but in future you must not misunderstand me, if I seem friendly. You misunderstood me this morning, did you not?'

'What made you think so?'

'Your look – your manner.'

'But look at me now –'

'Oh! you are different now: at present, I dare speak to you.'

'Yet I am the same, except that I have left the tradesman behind me in the Hollow: your kinsman alone stands before you.'

'My cousin, Robert; not Mr Moore.'

'Not a bit of Mr Moore. Caroline –'

Here the company was heard rising in the other room; the door was opened; the pony-carriage was ordered; shawls and bonnets were demanded; Mr Helstone called for his niece.

'I must go, Robert.'

'Yes, you must go, or they will come in, and find us here; and I, rather than meet all that host in the passage, will take my departure through the window: luckily, it opens like a door. One minute only – put down the candle an instant – goodnight! I kiss you because we are cousins; and, being cousins – one – two – three kisses are allowable. Caroline, good-night!'

CHAPTER VIII

NOAH AND MOSES

THE NEXT DAY, Moore had risen before the sun, and had taken a ride to Whinbury and back ere his sister had made the café au lait, or cut the tartines for his breakfast. What business he transacted there, he kept to himself. Hortense asked no questions: it was not her wont to comment on his movements, nor his to render an account of them. The secrets of business – complicated and often dismal mysteries – were buried in his breast, and never came out of their sepulchre, save now and then to scare Joe Scott, or give a start to some foreign correspondent: indeed, a general habit of reserve on whatever was important seemed bred in his mercantile blood.

Breakfast over, he went to his counting-house. Henry, Joe Scott's boy, brought in the letters and the daily papers; Moore seated himself at his desk, broke the seals of the documents, and glanced them over. They were all short, but not – it seemed – sweet; probably rather sour on the contrary, for as Moore laid down the last, his nostrils emitted a derisive and defiant snuff; and, though he burst into no soliloquy, there was a glance in his eye which seemed to invoke the devil, and lay charges on him to sweep the whole concern to Gehenna. However, having chosen a pen and stripped away the feathered top in a brief spasm of finger-fury – only finger-fury, his face was placid – he dashed off a batch of answers, sealed them, and then went out and walked through the mill: on coming back, he sat down to read his newspaper.

The contents seemed not absorbingly interesting; he more than once laid it across his knee, folded his arms, and gazed into

128

the fire; he occasionally turned his head towards the window; he looked at intervals at his watch: in short, his mind appeared preoccupied. Perhaps he was thinking of the beauty of the weather – for it was a fine and mild morning for the season – and wishing to be out in the fields enjoying it. The door of his counting-house stood wide open, the breeze and sunshine entered freely; but the first visitant brought no spring perfume on its wings, only an occasional sulphur-puff from the soot-thick colum of smoke rushing sable from the gaunt mill-chimney.

A dark blue apparition (that of Joe Scott, fresh from a dyeing vat) appeared momentarily at the open door, uttered the words 'He's comed, sir,' and vanished.

Mr Moore raised not his eyes from the paper. A large man, broad-shouldered and massive-limbed, clad in fustian garments and grey-worsted stockings, entered, who was received with a nod, and desired to take a seat; which he did, making the remark – as he removed his hat (a very bad one), stowed it away under his chair, and wiped his forehead with a spotted cotton handker-chief extracted from the hat-crown – that it was 'raight dahn warm for Febewerry.' Mr Moore assented: at least he uttered some slight sound, which, though inarticulate, might pass for an assent. The visiter now carefully deposited in the corner beside him an official-looking staff which he bore in his hand; this done, he whistled, probably by way of appearing at his ease.

'You have what is necessary, I suppose,' said Mr Moore.

'Ay! ay! all 's raight.'

He renewed his whistling, Mr Moore his reading: the paper apparently had become more interesting. Presently, however, he turned to his cupboard, which was within reach of his long arm, opened it without rising, took out a black bottle – the same he had produced for Malone's benefit – a tumbler, and a jug, placed them on the table, and said to his guest, –

'Help yourself; there's water in that jar in the corner.'

'I dunnut knaw that there's mich need, for all a body is dry (thirsty) in a morning,' said the fustian gentleman, rising and doing as requested.

'Will you tak' naught yourseln, Mr Moore?' he inquired, as with skilled hand he mixed a portion, and having tested it by a deep draught, sank back satisfied and bland in his seat. Moore – chary of words – replied by a negative movement and murmur.

'Yah'd as good,' continued his visiter; 'it 'uld set ye up, wald a sup o' this stuff. Uncommon good Hollands! ye get it fro' furrin' parts, I 'se think?'

'Ay!'

'Tak' my advice, and try a glass on 't; them lads 'at 's coming 'll keep ye talking, nob'dy knows how long: ye'll need propping.'

'Have you seen Mr Sykes this morning?' inquired Moore.

'I seed him a hauf an hour – nay – happen a quarter of an hour sin', just afore I set off: he said he aimed to come here, and I sudn't wonder but ye 'll have old Helstone too; I seed 'em saddling his little nag as I passed at back o' t' Rectory.

The speaker was a true prophet, for the trot of a little nag's hoofs were, five minutes after, heard in the yard; it stopped, and a well-known nasal voice cried aloud – 'Boy (probably addressing Harry Scott, who usually hung about the premises from nine a.m. to five p.m.), take my horse and lead him into the stable.'

Helstone came in marching nimbly and erect, looking browner, keener, and livelier than usual.

'Beautiful morning, Moore: how do, my boy? Ha! Whom have we here (turning to the personage with the staff)? Sugden! What! you're going to work directly? On my word, you lose no time: but I come to ask explanations: your message was delivered to me; are you sure you are on the right scent? How do you mean to set about the business? Have you got a warrant?'

'Sugden has.'

'Then you are going to seek him now? I'll accompany you.'

'You will be spared that trouble, sir; he is coming to seek me. I'm just now sitting in state, waiting his arrival.'

'And who is it? One of my parishioners?'

Joe Scott had entered unobserved; he now stood, a most sinister phantom, half his person being dyed of the deepest tint of indigo, leaning on the desk. His master's answer to the Rector's question was a smile; Joe took the word; putting on a quiet but pawky look, he said, –

'It's a friend of yours, Mr Helstone; a gentleman you often speak of.'

'Indeed! His name, Joe? – You look well this morning.'

'Only the Rev. Moses Barraclough: t' tub orator you call him sometimes, I think.'

'Ah!' said the Rector, taking out his snuff-box, and administering to himself a very long pinch – 'Ah! couldn't have supposed it. Why, the pious man never was a workman of yours, Moore? He's a tailor by trade.'

'And so much the worse grudge I owe him, for interfering, and setting my discarded men against me.'

'And Moses was actually present at the battle of Stilbro' Moor? He went there – wooden leg and all?'

'Ay, sir,' said Joe; 'he went there on horseback, that his leg mightn't be noticed: he was the captain and wore a mask; the rest only had their faces blacked.'

'And how was he found out?'

'I'll tell you, sir,' said Joe: 't' maister 's not so fond of talking; I've no objections. He courted Sarah, Mr Moore's sarvant lass, and so it seems she would have nothing to say to him; she either didn't like his wooden leg, or she 'd some notion about his being a hypocrite. Happen (for women is queer hands – we may say that amang werseln when there none of 'em nigh) she'd have encouraged him, in spite of his leg and his deceit – just to pass time like; I've known some on 'em do as mich, and some o' t' bonniest and mimmest-looking too – ay! I've seen clean, trim young things, that looked as denty and pure as daisies, and wi' time a body fun' 'em out to be nowt but stinging, venomed nettles.'

'Joe's a sensible fellow,' interjected Helstone.

'Howsiver, Sarah had another string to her bow: Fred Murga-troyd, one of our lads, is for her, and as women judge men by their faces – and Fred has a middling face, while Moses is none so handsome, as we all knaw – the lass took on wi' Fred A two-three months sin', Murgatroyd and Moses chanced to meet one Sunday night; they'd both come lurking about these premises wi' the notion of counselling Sarah to tak' a bit of a walk wi' them; they fell out, had a tussel, and Fred was worsted: for he's young and small, and Barraclough, for all he has only one leg, is almost as strong as Sugden there; indeed, anybody that hears him roaring at a revival or a love-feast, may be sure he's no weakling.'

'Joe, you're insupportable,' here broke in Mr Moore. 'You spin out your explanation as Moses spins out his sermons. The long and short of it is, Murgatroyd was jealous of Barraclough; and last night, as he and a friend took shelter in a barn from a shower, they heard and saw Moses conferring with some associates within. From their discourse, it was plain he had been the leader, not only at Stilbro' Moor, but in the attack on Sykes's property: moreover they planned a deputation to wait on me this morning, which the tailor is to head, and which, in the most religious and peaceful spirit, is to entreat me to put the accursed thing out of my tent. I rode over to Whinbury this morning, got a constable and a warrant, and I am now waiting to give my friend the reception he deserves: here, meantime, comes Sykes: Mr Helstone, you must spirit him up; he feels timid at the thoughts of prosecuting.'

A gig was heard to roll into the yard: Mr Sykes entered; a tall stout man of about fifty, comely of feature, but feeble of physiognomy: he looked anxious.

'Have they been? Are they gone? Have you got him? Is it over?' he asked.

'Not yet,' returned Moore with phlegm. 'We are waiting for them.'

'They'll not come; it's near noon: better give it up; it will excite bad feeling – make a stir – cause perhaps fatal consequences.'

'*You* need not appear,' said Moore. 'I shall meet them in the yard when they come; *you* can stay here.'

'But my name must be seen in the law proceedings: a wife and family, Mr Moore – a wife and family make a man cautious.'

Moore looked disgusted. 'Give way, if you please,' said he; 'leave me to myself; I have no objection to act alone: only be assured you will not find safety in submission; your partner, Pearson, gave way, and conceded, and forbore – well, that did not prevent them from attempting to shoot him in his own house.'

'My dear sir, take a little wine and water,' recommended Mr Helstone. The wine and water was Hollands and water, as Mr Sykes discovered when he had compounded and swallowed a brimming tumbler thereof: it transfigured him in two minutes, brought the colour back to his face, and made him at least *word*-valiant. He now announced that he hoped he was above being trampled on by the common people; he was determined to endure the insolence of the working-classes no longer; he had considered of it and made up his mind to go all lengths; if money and spirit could put down these rioters, they should be put down; Mr Moore might do as he liked, but *he* – Christie Sykes – would spend his last penny in law before he would be beaten: he'd settle them, or he'd see.

'Take another glass,' urged Moore.

Mr Sykes didn't mind if he did; this was a cold morning (Sugden had found it a warm one); it was necessary to be careful at this season of the year – it was proper to take something to keep the damp out; he had a little cough already (here he coughed in attestation of the fact); something of this sort (lifting the black bottle) was excellent taken medicinally (he poured the physic into his tumbler); he didn't make a practice of drinking spirits in a morning, but occasionally it really was prudent to take precautions.

'Quite prudent, and take them by all means,' urged the host.

Mr Sykes now addressed Mr Helstone, who stood on the hearth, his shovel-hat on his head, watching him significantly with his little keen eyes.

'You, sir, as a clergyman,' said he, 'may feel it disagreeable to be present amidst scenes of hurry and flurry, and, I may say, peril: I dare say your nerves won't stand it; you're a man of peace, sir, but we manufacturers, living in the world and always in turmoil, get quite belligerent. Really there's an ardour excited by the thoughts of danger that makes my heart pant. When Mrs Sykes is afraid of the house being attacked and broke open – as she is every night – I get quite excited. I couldn't describe to you, sir, my feelings: really, if anybody was to come – thieves or anything – I believe I should enjoy it, such is my spirit.'

The hardest of laughs, though brief and low, and by no means insulting, was the response of the Rector. Moore would have pressed upon the heroic mill-owner a third tumbler, but the clergyman, who never transgressed, nor would suffer others in his presence to transgress the bounds of decorum, checked him.

'Enough is as good as a feast, is it not, Mr Sykes?' he said, and Mr Sykes assented; and then sat and watched Joe Scott remove the bottle at a sign from Helstone, with a self-satisfied simper on his lips, and a regretful glisten in his eye. Moore looked as if he should have liked to fool him to the top of his bent. What would a certain young kinswoman of his have said, could she have seen her dear, good, great Robert – her Coriolanus – just now? Would she have acknowledged in that mischievous sardonic visage the same face to which she had looked up with such love, which had bent over her with such gentleness last night? Was that the man who had spent so quiet an evening with his sister and his cousin – so suave to one, so tender to the other – reading Shakspeare and listening to Chénier?

Yes, it was the same man, only seen on a different side; a side Caroline had not yet fairly beheld, though perhaps she had enough sagacity faintly to suspect its existence. Well, Caroline had, doubtless, her defective side too: she was human, she must then have been very imperfect, and had she seen Moore on his very worst side, she would probably have said this to herself and excused him. Love can excuse anything except Meanness; but Meanness kills Love, cripples even Natural Affection: without Esteem, True Love cannot exist. Moore with all his faults might be esteemed; for he had no moral scrofula in his mind, no hopeless polluting taint, such, for instance, as that of falsehood; neither was he the slave of his appetites; the active life to which he had been born and bred had given him something else to do than to join the futile chase of the pleasure-hunter: he was a man undegraded, the disciple of Reason, *not* the votary of Sense. The same might be said of old Helstone: neither of these two would look, think, or speak a lie; for neither of them had the wretched black bottle, which had just been put away, any charms; both might boast a valid claim to the proud title of 'lord of the creation,' for no animal vice was lord of them: they looked and were superior beings to poor Sykes.

A sort of gathering and trampling sound was heard in the yard, and then a pause. Moore walked to the window, Helstone followed; both stood on one side, the tall junior behind the under-sized senior, looking forth carefully, so that they might not be visible from without, their sole comment on what they saw was a cynical smile flashed into each other's stern eyes.

A flourishing oratical cough was now heard, followed by the interjection, 'Whisht!' designed, as it seemed, to still the hum of several voices. Moore opened his casement an inch or two to admit sound more freely.

'Joseph Scott,' began a snuffling voice – Scott was standing sentinel at the counting-house door – 'might we inquire if your master be within, and is to be spoken to?'

'He's within, ay!' said Joe, nonchalantly.

'Would you, then, if *you* please (emphasis on "you"), have the goodness to tell *him* that twelve gentlemen wants to see him.'

'He'd happen ax what for,' suggested Joe. 'I mught as weel tell him that at t' same time.'

'For a purpose,' was the answer. Joe entered.

'Please, sir, there's twelve gentlemen wants to see ye "for a purpose."'

'Good, Joe; I'm their man. Sugden, come when I whistle.'

Moore went out, chuckling drily. He advanced into the yard, one hand in his pocket, the other in his waistcoat, his cap brim over his eyes, shading in some measure their deep dancing ray of scorn. Twelve men waited in the yard, some in their shirt-sleeves, some in blue aprons: two figured conspicuously in the van of the party. One, a little dapper strutting man, with a turned-up nose; the other, a broad-shouldered fellow, distinguished no less by his demure face and cat-like, trustless eyes, than by a wooden leg and stout crutch: there was a kind of leer about his lips, he seemed laughing in his sleeve at some person or thing, his whole air was anything but that of a true man.

'Good-morning, Mr Barraclough,' said Moore debonnairly, for him.

'Peace be unto you!' was the answer: Mr Barraclough entirely closing his naturally half-shut eyes as he delivered it.

'I'm obliged to you: peace is an excellent thing; there's nothing I more wish for myself; but that is not all you have to say to me, I suppose? I imagine peace is not your purpose?'

'As to our purpose,' began Barraclough, 'it's one that may sound strange, and perhaps foolish to ears like yours, for the childer of this world is wiser in their generation than the childer of light.'

'To the point, if you please, and let me hear what it is.'

'Ye 'se hear, sir; if I cannot get it off, there's eleven behint can help me. It is a grand purpose, and (changing his voice from a half-sneer to a whine) it's the Looard's own purpose, and that's better.'

'Do you want a subscription to a new Ranter's chapel, Mr

Barraclough? Unless your errand be something of that sort, I cannot see what you have to do with it.'

'I hadn't that duty on my mind, sir; but as Providence has led ye to mention the subject, I'll make it i' my way to tak' ony trifle ye may have to spare; the smallest contribution will be acceptable.'

With that he doffed his hat, and held it out as a begging-box; a brazen grin at the same time crossing his countenance.

'If I gave you sixpence, you would drink it.'

Barraclough uplifted the palms of his hands and the whites of his eyes, evincing in the gesture a mere burlesque of hypocrisy.

'You seem a fine fellow,' said Moore, quite coolly and drily; 'you don't care for showing me that you are a double-dyed hypocrite, that your trade is fraud: you expect indeed to make me laugh at the cleverness with which you play your coarsely farcical part, while at the same time you think you are deceiving the men behind you.'

Moses' countenance lowered; he saw he had gone too far: he was going to answer, when the second leader, impatient of being hitherto kept in the background, stepped forward. This man did not look like a traitor, though he had an exceedingly self-confident and conceited air.

'Mr Moore,' commenced he, speaking also in his throat and nose, and enunciating each word very slowly, as if with a view to giving his audience time to appreciate fully the uncommon elegance of the phraseology; 'it might, perhaps, justly be said that reason rather than peace is our purpose. We come, in the first place, to request you to hear reason, and should *you* refuse, it is my duty to warn *you*, in very decided terms, that measures will be had resort to (he meant recourse), which will probably terminate in – in bringing *you* to a sense of the unwisdom, of the – the foolishness, which seems to guide and guard your perceedings as a tradesman in this – this manufacturing part of the country. Hem! . . . sir, I would beg to allude that as a furriner, coming from a distant coast, another quarter and hemisphere of this globe, thrown, as I may say, a perfect outcast on these shores – the cliffs of Albion – you have not that understanding of huz and wer ways which might conduce to the benefit of the working-classes. If, to come at once to partic'lars, you'd consider to give up this here miln, and go without further protractions straight home to where you belong, it 'ud happen be as well. I can see naught ageean such a plan. What hev ye to say tull 't, lads?' turning round to the other members of the deputation, who responded unanimously, 'Hear! hear!'

'Brayvo, Noah o' Tim's!' murmured Joe Scott, who stood behind Mr Moore. 'Moses'll niver beat that – Cliffs o' Albion, and t' other hemisphere! my certy! Did ye come fro' th' Antarctic Zone, maister? Moses is dished.'

Moses, however, refused to be dished; he thought he would try again. Casting a somewhat ireful glance at 'Noah o' Tim's,' he launched out in his turn: and now he spoke in a serious tone, relinquishing the sarcasm which he found had not answered.

'Or iver you set up the pole o' your tent amang us, Mr Moore, we lived i' peace and quietness; yea, I may say, in all loving-kindness. I am not myself an aged person as yet, but I can remember as far back as maybe some twenty year, when hand-labour were encouraged and respected, and no mischief-maker had ventured to introduce these here machines, which is so pernicious. Now, I'm not a cloth-dresser myself, but by trade a tailor; howsiver, my heart is of a softish natur': I'm a very feeling man, and when I see my brethren oppressed like my great name-sake of old, I stand up for 'em; for which intent, I this day speak with you face to face, and advises you to part wi' your infernal machinery, and tak' on more hands.'

'What if I don't follow your advice, Mr Barraclough?'

'The Looard pardon you! The Looard soften your heart, sir!'

'Are you in connexion with the Wesleyans now, Mr Barraclough?'

'Praise God! Bless His Name! I'm a joined Methody!'

'Which in no respect prevents you from being at the same

time a drunkard and a swindler. I saw you one night a week ago laid dead-drunk by the roadside, as I returned from Stilbro' market; and while you preach peace, you make it the business of your life to stir up dissention. You no more sympathize with the poor who are in distress, than you sympathize with me: you incite them to outrage for bad purposes of your own; so does the individual called Noah o' Tim's. You two are restless, meddling, impudent scoundrels, whose chief motive-principle is a selfish ambition, as dangerous as it is puerile. The persons behind you are some of them honest though misguided men; but you two I count altogether bad.'

Barraclough was going to speak.

'Silence! You have had your say, and now I will have mine. As to being dictated to by you, or any Jack, Jem, or Jonathan on earth, I shall not suffer it for a moment. You desire me to quit the country; you request me to part with my machinery; in case I refuse, you threaten me. I *do* refuse – point-blank! Here I stay; and by this mill I stand; and into it will I convey the best machinery inventors can furnish. What will you do? The utmost you *can* do – and this you will never *dare* to do – is to burn down my mill, destroy its contents, and shoot me. What then? Suppose that building was a ruin and I was a corpse, what then? – you lads behind these two scamps, would that stop invention or exhaust science? – Not for the fraction of a second of time! Another and better gig-mill would rise on the ruins of this, and perhaps a more enterprising owner come in my place. Hear me! – I'll make my cloth as I please, and according to the best lights I have. In its manufacture I will employ what means I choose. Whoever, after hearing this, shall dare to inter-fere with me, may just take the consequences. An example shall prove I'm in earnest.'

He whistled shrill and loud. Sugden, his staff and warrant, came on to the scene.

Moore turned sharply to Barraclough: 'You were at Stilbro',' said he; 'I have proof of that. You were on the moor, – you wore a mask, – you knocked down one of my men with your own hand, – you! a preacher of the Gospel! Sugden, arrest him!'

Moses was captured. There was a cry and a rush to rescue, but the right hand which all this while had lain hidden in Moore's breast, reappearing, held out a pistol.

'Both barrels are loaded,' said he. 'I'm quite determined! – keep off!'

Stepping backwards, facing the foe as he went, he guarded his prey to the counting-house. He ordered Joe Scott to pass in with Sugden and the prisoner, and to bolt the door inside. For himself, he walked backwards and forwards along the front of the mill, looking meditatively on the ground, his hand hanging carelessly by his side, but still holding the pistol. The eleven remaining deputies watched him some time, talking under their breath to each other: at length one of them approached. This man looked very different from either of the two who had previously spoken: he was hard-favoured, but modest, and manly-looking.

'I've not much faith i' Moses Barraclough,' said he; 'and I would speak a word to you myseln, Mr Moore. It's out o' no ill-will that I'm here, for my part; it's just to mak' a effort to get things straightened, for they're sorely a crooked. Ye see we're ill off, – varry ill off: wer families is poor and pined. We're thrown out o' work wi' these frames: we can get nought to do: we can earn nought. What is to be done? Mun we say, wisht! and lig us down and dee? Nay: I've no grand words at my tongue's end, Mr Moore, but I feel that it would be a low principle for a reasonable man to starve to death like a dumb cratur': – I will n't do 't. I'm not for shedding blood: I'd neither kill a man nor hurt a man; and I'm not for pulling down mills and breaking machines: for, as ye say, that way o' going on 'll niver stop invention; but I'll talk, – I'll mak' as big a din as ever I can. Invention may be all tight, but I know it isn't right for poor folks to starve. Them that governs mun find a way to help us: they mun mak' fresh orderations. Ye'll say that's hard to do: –

so mich louder mun we shout out then, for so much slacker will t' Parliament-men be to set on to a tough job.'

'Worry the Parliament-men as much as you please,' said Moore; 'but to worry the mill-owners is absurd; and I, for one, won't stand it.'

'Ye're a raight hard 'un!' returned the workman. 'Will n't ye gie us a bit o' time? – Will n't ye consent to mak' your changes rather more slowly?'

'Am I the whole body of clothiers in Yorkshire? Answer me that!'

'Ye're yourseln.'

'And only myself; and if I stopped by the way an instant, while others are rushing on, I should be trodden down. If I did as you wish me to do, I should be bankrupt in a month: and would my bankruptcy put bread into your hungry children's mouths? William Farren, neither to your dictation, nor to that of any other, will I submit. Talk to me no more about machinery; I will have my own way. I shall get new frames in to-morrow: – If you broke these, I would still get more. *I'll never give in.*'

Here the mill-bell rang twelve o'clock: it was the dinner hour. Moore abruptly turned from the deputation and re-entered his counting-house.

His last words had left a bad, harsh impression: he, at least, had 'failed in the disposing of a chance he was lord of.' By speaking kindly to William Farren, – who was a very honest man, without envy or hatred of those more happily circumstanced than himself; thinking it no hardship and no injustice to be forced to live by labour; disposed to be honourably content if he could but get work to do, – Moore might have made a friend. It seemed wonderful how he could turn from such a man without a conciliatory or a sympathizing expression. The poor fellow's face looked haggard with want: he had the aspect of a man who had not known what it was to live in comfort and plenty for weeks, perhaps months past; and yet there was no ferocity, no malignity in his countenance: it was worn, dejected, austere, but still patient. How could Moore leave him thus, with the words 'I'll never give in,' and not a whisper of good-will, or hope, or aid?

Farren, as he went home to his cottage, – once, in better times, a decent, clean, pleasant place, but now, though still clean, very dreary, because so poor – asked himself this question. He concluded that the foreign mill-owner was a selfish, an unfeeling, and, he thought, too, a foolish man. It appeared to him that emigration, had he only the means to emigrate, would be prefer-able to service under such a master. He felt much cast down, – almost hopeless.

On his entrance, his wife served out, in orderly sort, such dinner as she had to give him and the bairns: it was only por-ridge, and too little of that. Some of the younger children asked for more when they had done their portion – an application which disturbed William much: while his wife quieted them as well as she could, he left his seat, and went to the door. He whistled a cheery stave, which did not, however, prevent a broad drop or two (much more like the 'first of a thunder-shower' than those which oozed from the wound of the gladiator) from gathering on the lids of his grey eyes, and plashing thence to the threshold. He cleared his vision with his sleeve, and the melting mood over, a very stern one followed.

He still stood brooding in silence, when a gentleman in black came up – a clergyman, it might be seen at once; but neither Helstone, nor Malone, nor Donne, nor Sweeting. He might be forty years old; he was plain-looking, dark-complexioned, and already rather grey-haired. He stooped a little in walking. His countenance, as he came on, wore an abstracted and somewhat doleful air; but, in approaching Farren, he looked up, and then a hearty expression illuminated the preoccupied, serious face.

'Is it you, William? How are you?' he asked.

'Middling, Mr Hall: how are *ye*? Will ye step in and rest ye?'

Mr Hall, whose name the reader has seen mentioned before,

(and who, indeed, was vicar of Nunnely, of which parish Farren was a native, and from whence he had removed but three years ago to reside in Briarfield, for the convenience of being near Hollow's mill, where he had obtained work) entered the cottage, and, having greeted the goodwife and the children, sat down. He proceeded to talk very cheerfully about the length of time that had elapsed since the family quitted his parish, the changes which had occurred since; he answered questions touching his sister Margaret, who was inquired after with much interest; he asked questions in his turn, and at last, glancing hastily and anxiously round through his spectacles (he wore spectacles, for he was short-sighted) at the bare room, and at the meagre and wan faces of the circle about him – for the children had come round his knee, and the father and mother stood before him – he said, abruptly, –

'And how are you all? How do you get on?'

Mr Hall, be it remarked, though an accomplished scholar, not only spoke with a strong northern accent, but, on occasion, used freely north-country expressions.

'We get on poorly,' said William: 'we're all out of work. I've selled most o' t' household stuff, as ye may see; and what we're to do next, God knows.'

'Has Mr Moore turned you off?'

'He has turned us off; and I've sich an opinion of him now, that I think, if he'd tak' me on again to-morrow, I wouldn't work for him.'

'It is not like you to say so, William.'

'I know it isn't; but I'm getting different to mysel': I feel I am changing. I wad n't heed, if t' bairns and t' wife had enough to live on; but they're pinched – they're pined –'

'Well, my lad, and so are you; I see you are. These are grievous times; I see suffering wherever I turn. William, sit down; Grace, sit down; let us talk it over.'

And in order the better to talk it over, Mr Hall lifted the least of the children on to his knee, and placed his hand on the head of the next least; but when the small things began to chatter to him, he bid them 'Whisht!' and, fixing his eyes on the grate, he regarded the handful of embers which burnt there very gravely.

'Sad times!' he said, 'and they last long. It is the will of God: His will be done! but He tries us to the utmost.'

Again he reflected.

'You've no money, William, and you've nothing you could sell to raise a small sum?'

'No; I've selled t' chest o' drawers, and t' clock, and t' bit of a mahogany stand, and t' wife's bonny tea-tray and set o' cheeney 'at she brought for a portion when we were wed.'

'And if somebody lent you a pound or two, could you make any good use of it? Could you get into a new way of doing something?'

Farren did not answer; but his wife said quickly, 'Ay, I'm sure he could, sir; he's a very contriving chap, is our William. If he'd two or three pounds, he could begin selling stuff.'

'Could you, William?'

'Please God,' returned William, deliberately, 'I could buy groceries, and bits o' tapes, and thread, and what I thought would sell, and I could begin hawking at first.'

'And you know, sir,' interposed Grace, 'you're sure William would neither drink, nor idle, nor waste in any way. He's my husband, and I shouldn't praise him; but I *will* say, there's not a soberer, honester man i' England nor he is.'

'Well, I'll speak to one or two friends, and I think I can promise to let him have £5 in a day or two: as a loan, ye mind, not a gift: he must pay it back.'

'I understand, sir: I'm quite agreeable to that.'

'Meantime, there's a few shillings for you, Grace, just to keep the pot boiling till custom comes. Now, bairns, stand up in a row and say your catechism, while your mother goes and buys some dinner: for you've not had much to-day, I'll be bound. You begin, Ben. What is your name?'

Mr Hall stayed till Grace came back; then he hastily took his leave, shaking hands with both Farren and his wife: just at the door, he said to them a few brief but very earnest words of religious consolation and exhortation: with a mutual 'God bless you, sir!' 'God bless you, my friends!' they separated.

CHAPTER IX

BRIARMAINS

MESSRS HELSTONE and Sykes began to be extremely jocose and congratulatory with Mr Moore when he returned to them after dismissing the deputation; he was so quiet, however, under their compliments upon his firmess, &c., and wore a countenance so like a still, dark day, equally beamless and breezeless, that the Rector, after glancing shrewdly into his eyes, buttoned up his felicitations with his coat, and said to Sykes, whose senses were not acute enough to enable him to discover unassisted where his presence and conversation were a nuisance: –

'Come, sir; your road and mine lie partly together: had we not better bear each other company? We'll bid Moore good-morning, and leave him to the happy fancies he seems disposed to indulge.'

'And where is Sugden?' demanded Moore, looking up.

'Ah, ha!' cried Helstone. 'I've not been quite idle while you were busy. I've been helping you a little: I flatter myself, not injudiciously. I thought it better not to lose time; so, while you were parleying with that down-looking gentleman – Farren, I think his name is – I opened this back window, shouted to Murgatroyd, who was in the stable, to bring Mr Sykes's gig round; then I smuggled Sugden and brother Moses – wooden leg and all – through the aperture, and saw them mount the gig (always with our good friend Sykes's permission, of course). Sugden took the reins – he drives like Jehu, and in another quarter of an hour, Barraclough will be safe in Stilbro' jail.'

'Very good: thank you,' said Moore, 'and good-morning,

gentlemen,' he added, and so politely conducted them to the door and saw them clear of his premises.

He was a taciturn, serious man the rest of the day: he did not even bandy a repartee with Joe Scott; who, for his part, said to his master only just what was absolutely necessary to the progress of business, but looked at him a good deal out of the corners of his eyes, frequently came to poke the counting-house fire for him, and once, as he was locking up for the day (the mill was then working short time, owing to the slackness of trade), observed that it was a grand evening, and he 'could wish Mr Moore to tak' a bit of a walk up th' Hollow; it would do him good.'

At this recommendation, Mr Moore burst into a short laugh, and after demanding of Joe what all this solicitude meant, and whether he took him for a woman or a child, seized the keys from his hand, and shoved him by the shoulders out of his presence. He called him back, however, ere he had reached the yard-gate.

'Joe, do you know those Farrens? They are not well off, I suppose?'

'They cannot be well off, sir, when they've not had work as a three month. Ye'd see yoursel' 'at William's sorely changed, – fair pared: they've selled most o' t' stuff out o' th' house.'

'He was not a bad workman?'

'Ye never had a better, sir, sin' ye began trade.'

'And decent people – the whole family?'

'Niver dacenter: th' wife's a raight cant body, and as clean –! ye mught eat your porridge off th' house floor: they're sorely comed down. I wish William could get a job as gardener or summat i' that way; he understands gardening weel. He once lived wi' a Scotchman that tached him the mysteries o' that craft, as they say.'

'Now, then, you can go, Joe; you need not stand there staring at me.'

'Ye've no orders to give, sir?'

'None, but for you to take yourself off.'

Which Joe did accordingly.

Spring evenings are often cold and raw, and though this had been a fine day, warm even in the morning and meridian sunshine, the air chilled at sunset, the ground crisped, and ere dusk a hoar frost was insidiously stealing over growing grass and unfolding bud. It whitened the pavement in front of Briarmains (Mr Yorke's residence), and made silent havoc among the tender plants in his garden, and on the mossy level of his lawn. As to that great tree, strong-trunked and broad-armed, which guarded the gable nearest the road, it seemed to defy a spring-night frost to harm its still bare boughs; and so did the leafless grove of walnut-trees rising tall behind the house.

In the dusk of the moonless if starry night, lights from windows shone vividly: this was no dark or lonely scene, nor even a silent one. Briarmains stood near the highway; it was rather an old place, and had been built ere that highway was cut, and when a lane winding up through fields was the only path conducting to it. Briarfield lay scarce a mile off; its hum was heard, its glare distinctly seen. Briar-chapel, a large, new, raw, Wesleyan place of worship, rose but a hundred yards distant; and, as there was even now a prayer-meeting being held within its walls, the illumination of its windows cast a bright reflection on the road, while a hymn of a most extraordinary description, such as a very Quaker might feel himself moved by the spirit to dance to, roused cheerily all the echoes of the vicinage. The words were distinctly audible by snatches: here is a quotation or two from different strains; for the singers passed jauntily from hymn to hymn and from tune to tune, with an ease and buoyancy all their own.

> 'Oh! who can explain
>   This struggle for life,
> This travail and pain,

This trembling and strife?
Plague, earthquake, and famine,
   And tumult and war,
The wonderful coming
   Of Jesus declare!

'For every fight
   Is dreadful and loud, –
The warrior's delight
   Is slaughter and blood;
His foes overturning,
   Till all shall expire, –
And this is with burning,
   And fuel, and fire!'

Here followed an interval of clamorous prayer, accompanied
by fearful groans. A shout of 'I've found liberty!' 'Doad o' Bill's
has fun' liberty!' rung from the chapel, and out all the assembly
broke again.

'What a mercy is this!
   What a heaven of bliss!
How unspeakably happy am I!
   Gather'd into the fold,
   With thy people enroll'd,
With thy people to live and to die!

'Oh, the goodness of God
   In employing a clod
His tribute of glory to raise;
   His standard to bear,
   And with triumph declare
His unspeakable riches of grace!

'Oh, the fathomless love,
   That has deign'd to approve
And prosper the work of my hands;

With my pastoral crook,
    I went over the brook,
And behold I am spread into bands!

'Who, I ask in amaze,
    Hath begotten me these?
And inquire from what quarter they came;
    My full heart it replies,
    They are born from the skies,
And gives glory to God and the Lamb!'

The stanza which followed this, after another and longer
interregnum of shouts, yells, ejaculations, frantic cries, agonized
groans, seemed to cap the climax of noise and zeal.

'Sleeping on the brink of sin,
    Tophet gaped to take us in;
Mercy to our rescue flew, –
    Broke the snare, and brought us through.

'Here, as in a lion's den,
    Undevour'd we still remain;
Pass secure the watery flood,
    Hanging on the arm of God.

'Here' –

(Terrible, most distracting to the ear was the strained shout
in which the last stanza was given).

'Here we raise our voices higher,
        Shout in the refiner's fire;
    Clap our hands amidst the flame,
        Glory give to Jesus' name!'

The roof of the chapel did *not* fly off; which speaks volumes
in praise of its solid slating.

But if Briar-chapel seemed alive, so also did Briarmains:
though certainly the mansion appeared to enjoy a quieter phase

of existence than the temple; some of its windows too were a-glow: the lower casements opened upon the lawn, curtains concealed the interior, and partly obscured the ray of the candles which lit it, but they did not entirely muffle the sound of voice and laughter. We are privileged to enter that front-door, and to penetrate to the domestic sanctum.

It is not the presence of company which makes Mr Yorke's habitation lively, for there is none within it save his own family, and they are assembled in that farthest room to the right, the back-parlour.

This is the usual sitting-room of an evening. Those windows would be seen by daylight to be of brilliantly-stained glass – purple and amber the predominant hues, glittering round a gravely tinted medallion in the centre of each, representing the suave head of William Shakspeare, and the serene one of John Milton. Some Canadian views hang on the walls – green forest and blue water-scenery – and in the midst of them blazes a night-eruption of Vesuvius; very ardently it glows, contrasted with the cool foam and azure of cataracts, and the dusky depths of woods.

The fire illuminating this room, reader, is such as, if you be a southern, you do not often see burning on the hearth of a private apartment; it is a clear, hot, coal fire, heaped high in the ample chimney. Mr Yorke *will* have such fires even in warm summer weather: he sits beside it with a book in his hand, a little round stand at his elbow supporting a candle – but he is not reading, he is watching his children. Opposite to him sits his lady – a personage whom I might describe minutely, but I feel no vocation to the task. I see her, though, very plainly before me: a large woman of the gravest aspect, care on her front and on her shoulders – but not overwhelming, inevitable care – rather the sort of voluntary, exemplary cloud and burden people ever carry who deem it their duty to be gloomy. Ah, well-a-day! Mrs Yorke had that notion, and grave as Saturn she was, morning, noon, and night; and hard things she thought of any unhappy wight – especially of the female sex – who dared in her presence to show the light of a gay heart on a sunny countenance. In her estimation, to be mirthful was to be profane; to be cheerful was to be frivolous: she drew no distinctions. Yet she was a very good wife, a very careful mother, looked after her children unceasingly, was sincerely attached to her husband; only, the worst of it was, if she could have had her will, she would not have permitted him to have any friend in the world beside herself: all his relations were insupportable to her, and she kept them at arm's length.

Mr Yorke and she agreed perfectly well; yet he was naturally a social, hospitable man – an advocate for family unity – and in his youth, as has been said, he liked none but lively cheerful women. Why he chose her – how they contrived to suit each other, is a problem puzzling enough, but which might soon be solved if one had time to go into the analysis of the case. Suffice it here to say, that Yorke had a shadowy as well as a sunny side to his character, and that his shadowy side found sympathy and affinity in the whole of his wife's uniformly overcast nature. For the rest, she was a strong-minded woman; never said a weak or a trite thing; took stern, democratic views of society, and rather cynical ones of human nature; considered herself perfect and safe, and the rest of the world all wrong. Her main fault was a brooding, eternal, immitigable suspicion of all men, things, creeds, and parties: this suspicion was a mist before her eyes, a false guide in her path, wherever she looked, wherever she turned.

It may be supposed that the children of such a pair were not likely to turn out quite ordinary, common-place beings; and they were not. You see six of them, reader: the youngest is a baby on the mother's knee; it is all her own yet – and that one she has not yet begun to doubt, suspect, condemn; it derives its sustenance from her, it hangs on her, it clings to her, it loves her above everything else in the world: she is sure of that, because, as it lives by her, it cannot be otherwise, therefore she loves it.

The two next are girls, Rose and Jessy; they are both now at their father's knee; they seldom go near their mother, except when obliged to do so. Rose, the elder, is twelve years old; she is like her father, – the most like him of the whole group, – but it is a granite head copied in ivory; all is softened in colour and line. Yorke himself has a harsh face; his daughter's is not harsh, neither is it quite pretty; it is simple, – childlike in feature; the round cheeks bloom: as to the grey eyes, they are otherwise than childlike, – a serious soul lights them, – a young soul yet, but it will mature, if the body lives; and neither father nor mother have a spirit to compare with it. Partaking of the essence of each, it will one day be better than either, – stronger, much purer, more aspiring. Rose is a still, sometimes a stubborn girl now: her mother wants to make of her such a woman as she is herself, – a woman of dark and dreary duties, – and Rose has a mind full-set, thick-sown with the germs of ideas her mother never knew. It is agony to her often to have these ideas trampled on and repressed. She has never rebelled yet; but if hard driven, she will rebel one day, and then it will be once for all. Rose loves her father: her father does not rule her with a rod of iron; he is good to her. He sometimes fears she will not live, so bright are the sparks of intelligence which, at moments, flash from her glance, and gleam in her language. This idea makes him often sadly tender to her.

He has no idea that little Jessy will die young, she is so gay and chattering, arch – original even now; passionate when provoked, but most affectionate if caressed; by turns gentle and rattling; exacting yet generous; fearless – of her mother for instance, whose irrationally hard and strict rule she has often defied – yet reliant on any who will help her. Jessy, with her little piquant face, engaging prattle, and winning ways, is made to be a pet; and her father's pet she accordingly is. It is odd that the doll should resemble her mother feature by feature, as Rose resembles her father, and yet the physiognomy – how different!

Mr Yorke, if a magic mirror were now held before you, and

if therein were shown you your two daughters as they will be twenty years from this night, what would you think? The magic mirror is here: you shall learn their destinies – and first that of your little life, Jessy.

Do you know this place? No, you never saw it; but you recognise the nature of these trees, this foliage, – the cypress, the willow, the yew. Stone crosses like these are not unfamiliar to you, nor are these dim garlands of everlasting flowers. Here is the place; green sod and a grey marble headstone – Jessy sleeps below. She lived through an April day; much loved was she, much loving. She often, in her brief life, shed tears, she had frequent sorrows; she smiled between, gladdening whatever saw her. Her death was tranquil and happy in Rose's guardian arms, for Rose had been her stay and defence through many trials: the dying and the watching English girls were at that hour alone in a foreign country, and the soil of that country gave Jessy a grave.

Now, behold Rose, two years later. The crosses and garlands looked strange, but the hills and woods of this landscape look still stranger. This, indeed, is far from England; remote must be the shores which wear that wild, luxuriant aspect. This is some virgin solitude: unknown birds flutter round the skirts of that forest; no European river this, on whose banks Rose sits thinking. The little, quiet Yorkshire girl is a lonely emigrant in some region of the southern hemisphere. Will she ever come back?

The three eldest of the family are all boys: Matthew, Mark, and Martin. They are seated together in that corner, engaged in some game. Observe their three heads: much alike at a first glance; at a second, different; at a third, contrasted. Dark-haired, dark-eyed, red-cheeked, are the whole trio; small English features they all possess; all own a blended resemblance to sire and mother, and yet a distinctive physiognomy, mark of a separate character, belongs to each.

I shall not say much about Matthew, the first-born of the

house; though it is impossible to avoid gazing at him long, and conjecturing what qualities that visage hides or indicates. He is no plain-looking boy: that jet-black hair, white brow, high-coloured cheek, those quick, dark eyes, are good points in their way. How is it that, look as long as you will, there is but one object in the room, and that the most sinister, to which Matthew's face seems to bear an affinity, and of which, ever and anon, it reminds you strangely – the eruption of Vesuvius. Flame and shadow seem the component parts of that lad's soul: no daylight in it, and no sunshine, and no pure, cool moonbeam ever shone there. He has an English frame, but, apparently, not an English mind: you would say, an Italian stiletto in a sheath of British workmanship. He is crossed in the game – look at his scowl. Mr Yorke sees it, and what does he say? In a low voice, he pleads: 'Mark and Martin, don't anger your brother.' And this is ever the tone adopted by both parents. Theoretically, they decry partiality; no rights of primogeniture are to be allowed in that house; but Matthew is never to be vexed, never to be opposed: they avert provocation from him as assiduously as they would avert fire from a barrel of gunpowder. 'Concede, conciliate,' is their motto wherever he is concerned. The republicans are fast making a tyrant of their own flesh and blood. This the younger scions know and feel, and at heart they all rebel against the injustice: they cannot read their parents' motives; they only see the difference of treatment. The dragon's teeth are already sown amongst Mr Yorke's young olive-branches: discord will one day be the harvest.

Mark is a bonnie-looking boy, the most regular-featured of the family; he is exceedingly calm; his smile is shrewd; he can say the driest, most cutting things in the quietest of tones. Despite his tranquillity, a somewhat heavy brow speaks temper, and reminds you that the smoothest waters are not always the safest. Besides, he is too still, unmoved, phlegmatic, to be happy. Life will never have much joy in it for Mark: by the time he is five-and-twenty, he will wonder why people ever laugh, and think all fools who seem merry. Poetry will not exist for Mark, either in literature or in life; its best effusions will sound to him mere rant and jargon: enthusiasm will be his aversion and contempt. Mark will have no youth: while he looks juvenile and blooming, he will be already middle-aged in mind. His body is now fourteen years of age, but his soul is already thirty.

Martin, the youngest of the three, owns another nature. Life may, or may not, be brief for him; but it will certainly be brilliant: he will pass through all its illusions, half believe in them, wholly enjoy them, then outlive them. That boy is not handsome – not so handsome as either of his brothers: he is plain; there is a husk upon him, a dry shell, and he will wear it till he is near twenty; then he will put it off: about that period, he will make himself handsome. He will wear uncouth manners till that age, perhaps homely garments; but the chrysalis will retain the power of transfiguring itself into the butterfly, and such transfiguration will, in due season, take place. For a space, he will be vain, probably a downright puppy, eager for pleasure, and desirous of admiration; athirst, too, for knowledge. He will want all that the world can give him, both of enjoyment and lore; he will, perhaps, take deep draughts at each fount. That thirst satisfied – what next? I know not. Martin might be a remarkable man: whether he will or not, the seer is powerless to predict: on that subject, there has been no open vision.

Take Mr Yorke's family in the aggregate, there is as much mental power in those six young heads, as much originality, as much activity and vigour of brain, as – divided amongst half a dozen common-place broods – would give to each rather more than an average amount of sense and capacity. Mr Yorke knows this and is proud of his race. Yorkshire has such families here and there amongst her hills and wolds – peculiar, racy, vigorous; of good blood and strong brain; turbulent somewhat in the pride of their strength, and intractable in the force of their native powers; wanting polish, wanting consideration, wanting docility, but sound, spirited, and true-bred as the eagle on the cliff or the steed in the steppe.

A low tap is heard at the parlour door; the boys have been making such a noise over their game, and little Jessy, besides, has been singing so sweet a Scotch song to her father – who delights in Scotch and Italian songs, and has taught his musical little daughter some of the best – that the ring at the outer door was not observed.

'Come in,' says Mrs Yorke, in that conscientiously con-strained and solemnized voice of hers, which ever modulates itself to a funeral dreariness of tone, though the subject it is exercised upon be but to give orders for the making of a pudding in the kitchen, to bid the boys hang up their caps in the hall, or to call the girls to their sewing: 'Come in!' And in came Robert Moore.

Moore's habitual gravity, as well as his abstemiousness (for the case of spirit-decanters is never ordered up when he pays an evening visit), has so far recommended him to Mrs Yorke, that she has not yet made him the subject of private animadversions with her husband: she has not yet found out that he is hampered by a secret intrigue which prevents him from marrying, or that he is a wolf in sheep's clothing; discoveries which she made at an early date after marriage concerning most of her husband's bachelor friends, and excluded them from her board accord-ingly: which part of her conduct, indeed, might be said to have its just and sensible, as well as its harsh side.

'Well, is it you?' she says to Mr Moore, as he comes up to her and gives his hand. 'What are you roving about at this time of night for? You should be at home.'

'Can a single man be said to have a home, madam?' he asks.

'Pooh!' says Mrs Yorke, who despises conventional smooth-ness quite as much as her husband does, and practices it as little, and whose plain speaking, on all occasions, is carried to a point calculated, sometimes, to awaken admiration, but oftener alarm – 'Pooh! you need not talk nonsense to me; a single man can have a home if he likes. Pray, does not your sister make a home for you?'

'Not she,' joined in Mr Yorke. 'Hortense is an honest lass; but when I was Robert's age, I had five or six sisters, all as decent and proper as she is; but you see, Hesther, for all that, it did not hinder me from looking out for a wife.'

'And sorely he has repented marrying me,' added Mrs Yorke, who liked occasionally to crack a dry jest against matrimony, even though it should be at her own expense. 'He has repented it in sackcloth and ashes, Robert Moore, as you may well believe when you see his punishment (here she pointed to her children). Who would burden themselves with such a set of great, rough lads as those, if they could help it? It is not only bringing them into the world, though that is bad enough, but they are all to feed, to clothe, to rear, to settle in life. Young sir, when you feel tempted to marry, think of our four sons and two daughters, and look twice before you leap.'

'I am not tempted now, at any rate: I think these are not times for marrying or giving in marriage.'

A lugubrious sentiment of this sort was sure to obtain Mrs Yorke's approbation: she nodded and groaned acquiescence; but in a minute she said: –

'I make little account of the wisdom of a Solomon of your age; it will be upset by the first fancy that crosses you. Meantime, sit down, sir: you can talk, I suppose, as well sitting as standing?'

This was her way of inviting her guest to take a chair; he had no sooner obeyed her, than little Jessy jumped from her father's knee, and ran into Mr Moore's arms, which were very promptly held out to receive her.

'You talk of marrying him,' said she to her mother, quite indignantly, as she was lifted lightly to his knee, 'and he is married now, or as good: he promised that I should be his wife last summer, the first time he saw me in my new white frock and blue sash. Didn't he, father?' (These children were not

accustomed to say papa and mamma; their mother would allow
no such 'namby-pamby.')

'Ay, my little lassie, he promised; I'll bear witness. But make
him say it over again now, Jessy: such as he are only false loons.'

'He is not false: he is too bonnie to be false,' said Jessy,
looking up to her tall sweetheart with the fullest confidence in
his faith.

'Bonnie!' cried Mr Yorke; 'that's the reason that he should
be, and proof that he is – a scoundrel.'

'But he looks too sorrowful to be false,' here interposed a
quiet voice from behind the father's chair. 'If he were always
laughing, I should think he forgot promises soon, but Mr
Moore never laughs.'

'Your sentimental buck is the greatest cheat of all, Rose,'
remarked Mr Yorke.

'He's not sentimental,' said Rose.

Mr Moore turned to her with a little surprise, smiling at the
same time.

'How do you know I am not sentimental, Rose?'

'Because I heard a lady say you were not.'

'Voilà, qui devient intéressant!' exclaimed Mr Yorke, hitching
his chair nearer the fire. 'A lady! That has quite a romantic
twang: we must guess who it is. Rosy, whisper the name low to
your father: don't let *him* hear.'

'Rose, don't be too forward to talk,' here interrupted Mrs
Yorke, in her usual kill-joy fashion; 'nor Jessy either: it becomes
all children, especially girls, to be silent in the presence of their
elders.'

'Why have we tongues, then?' asked Jessy, pertly; while Rose
only looked at her mother with an expression that seemed to
say, she should take that maxim in, and think it over at her
leisure. After two minutes' grave deliberation, she asked, –

'And why especially girls, mother?'

'Firstly, because I say so; and, secondly, because discretion
and reserve is a girl's best wisdom.'

'My dear madam,' observed Moore, 'what you say is excellent: it reminds me, indeed, of my dear sister's observations; but really it is not applicable to these little ones. Let Rose and Jessy talk to me freely, or my chief pleasure in coming here is gone. I like their prattle: it does me good.'

'Does it not?' asked Jessy. 'More good than if the rough lads came round you: you call them rough, mother, yourself.'

'Yes, mignonne, a thousand times more good: I have rough lads enough about me all day long, poulet.'

'There are plenty of people,' continued she, 'who take notice of the boys: all my uncles and aunts seem to think their nephews better than their nieces; and when gentlemen come here to dine, it is always Matthew, and Mark, and Martin, that are talked to, and never Rose and me. Mr Moore is *our* friend, and we'll keep him: but mind, Rose, he's not so much your friend as he is mine: he is my *particular acquaintance*; remember that!' And she held up her small hand with an admonitory gesture.

Rose was quite accustomed to be admonished by that small hand; her will daily bent itself to that of the impetuous little Jessy: she was guided – overruled by Jessy in a thousand things. On all occasions of show and pleasure, Jessy took the lead, and Rose fell quietly into the background; whereas, when the disagreeables of life – its work and privations were in question, Rose instinctively took upon her, in addition to her own share, what she could of her sister's. Jessy had already settled it in her mind that she, when she was old enough, was to be married; Rose, she decided, must be an old maid, to live with her, look after her children, keep her house. This state of things is not uncommon between two sisters, where one is plain and the other pretty; but in this case, if there *was* a difference in external appearance, Rose had the advantage: her face was more regular-featured than that of the piquant little Jessy. Jessy, however, was destined to possess, along with sprightly intelligence and vivacious feeling, the gift of fascination, the power to charm when, where, and whom she would. Rose was to have a fine, generous soul, a noble intellect profoundly cultivated, a heart as true as steel, but the manner to attract was not to be hers.

'Now, Rose, tell me the name of this lady who denied that I was sentimental,' urged Mr Moore.

Rose had no idea of tantalization, or she would have held him a while in doubt; she answered briefly: –

'I can't: I don't know her name.'

'Describe her to me: what was she like? Where did you see her?'

'When Jessy and I went to spend the day at Whinbury with Kate and Susan Pearson, who were just come home from school, there was a party at Mrs Pearson's, and some grown-up ladies were sitting in a corner of the drawing-room talking about you.'

'Did you know none of them?'

'Hannah, and Harriet, and Dora, and Mary Sykes.'

'Good. Were they abusing me, Rosy?'

'Some of them were: they called you a misanthrope: I remember the word – I looked for it in the dictionary when I came home: it means a man-hater.'

'What besides?'

'Hannah Sykes said you were a solemn puppy.'

'Better!' cried Mr Yorke, laughing. 'Oh! excellent! Hannah – that's the one with the red hair: a fine girl, but half-witted.'

'She has wit enough for me, it appears,' said Moore. 'A solemn puppy, indeed! Well, Rose, go on.'

'Miss Pearson said she believed there was a good deal of affectation about you, and that with your dark hair and pale face, you looked to her like some sort of a sentimental noodle.'

Again Mr Yorke laughed: Mrs Yorke even joined in this time. 'You see in what esteem you are held behind your back,' said she; 'yet I believe *that* Miss Pearson would like to catch you: she set her cap at you when you first came into the country, old as she is.'

'And who contradicted her, Rosy?' inquired Moore.

'A lady whom I don't know, because she never visits here,

though I see her every Sunday at church; she sits in the pew near the pulpit. I generally look at her, instead of looking at my prayer-book; for she is like a picture in our dining-room, that woman with the dove in her hand: at least she has eyes like it, and a nose too, a straight nose, that makes all her face look, somehow, what I call clear.'

'And you don't know her!' exclaimed Jessy, in a tone of exceeding surprise. 'That's so like Rose. Mr Moore, I often wonder in what sort of a world my sister lives; I am sure she does not live all her time in this: one is continually finding out that she is quite ignorant of some little matter which everybody else knows. To think of her going solemnly to church every Sunday, and looking all service-time at one particular person, and never so much as asking that person name! She means Caroline Helstone, the Rector's niece: I remember all about it. Miss Helstone was quite angry with Anne Pearson: she said, "Robert Moore is neither affected nor sentimental; you mistake his character utterly, or rather not one of you here knows anything about it." Now, shall I tell you what she is like? I can tell what people are like, and how they are dressed, better than Rose can.'

'Let us hear.'

'She is nice; she is fair; she has a pretty white slender throat; she has long curls, not stiff ones, they hang loose and soft, their colour is brown but not dark; she speaks quietly, with a clear tone; she never makes a bustle in moving; she often wears a grey silk dress; she is neat all over: her gowns, and her shoes, and her gloves always fit her. She is what I call a lady, and when I am as tall as she is, I mean to be like her. Shall I suit you if I am? Will you really marry me?'

Moore stroked Jessy's hair: for a minute he seemed as if he would draw her nearer to him, but instead he put her a little farther off.

'Oh! you won't have me? You push me away.'

'Why, Jessy, you care nothing about me: you never come to see me now at the Hollow.'

'Because you don't ask me.'

Hereupon Mr Moore gave both the little girls an invitation to pay him a visit next day, promising, that as he was going to Stilbro' in the morning, he would buy them each a present, of what nature he would not then declare, but they must come and see. Jessy was about to reply, when one of the boys unexpectedly broke in.

'I know that Miss Helstone you have all been palavering about: she's an ugly girl. I hate her! I hate all womenites. I wonder what they were made for.'

'Martin!' said his father – for Martin it was – the lad only answered by turning his cynical young face, half-arch, half-truculent, towards the paternal chair. 'Martin, my lad, thou'rt a swaggering whelp, now; thou wilt some day be an outrageous puppy: but stick to those sentiments of thine. See, I'll write down the words now i' my pocket-book. (The senior took out a morocco-covered book, and deliberately wrote therein). Ten years hence, Martin, if thou and I be both alive at that day, I'll remind thee of that speech.'

'I'll say the same then: I mean always to hate women; they're such dolls: they do nothing but dress themselves finely, and go swimming about to be admired. I'll never marry: I'll be a bachelor.'

'Stick to it! stick to it! Hesther (addressing his wife) I was like him when I was his age, a regular misogamist; and, behold! by the time I was three-and-twenty, – being then a tourist in France and Italy, and the Lord knows where! – I curled my hair every night before I went to bed, and wore a ring i' my ear, and would have worn one i' my nose if it had been the fashion – and all that I might make mysel' pleasing and charming to the ladies. Martin will do the like.'

'Will I? Never! I've more sense. What a Guy you were, father! As to dressing, I make this vow: I'll never dress more finely than as you see me at present. Mr Moore, I'm clad in blue cloth from top to toe, and they laugh at me, and call me sailor at the grammar-school. I laugh louder at them, and say they are all magpies and parrots, with their coats one colour, and their waistcoats another, and their trousers a third. I'll always wear blue cloth, and nothing but blue cloth: it is beneath a human being's dignity to dress himself in parti-coloured garments.'

'Ten years hence, Martin, no tailor's shop will have choice of colours varied enough for thy exacting taste; no perfumer's stores essences exquisite enough for thy fastidious senses.'

Martin looked disdain, but vouchsafed no further reply. Meantime Mark, who for some minutes had been rummaging amongst a pile of books on a side-table, took the word. He spoke in a peculiarly slow, quiet voice, and with an expression of still irony in his face not easy to describe.

'Mr Moore,' said he, 'you think perhaps it was a compliment on Miss Caroline Helstone's part to say you were not senti-mental. I thought you appeared confused when my sisters told you the words, as if you felt flattered: you turned red, just like a certain vain little lad at our school, who always thinks proper to blush when he gets a rise in the class. For your benefit, Mr Moore, I've been looking up the word "sentimental" in the dictionary, and I find it to mean "tinctured with sentiment." On examining further, sentiment is explained to be, thought, idea, notion. A sentimental man, then, is one who has thoughts, ideas, notions; an unsentimental man is one destitute of thought, idea, or notion.'

And Mark stopped: he did not smile, he did not look round for admiration: he had said his say, and was silent.

'Ma foi! mon ami,' observed Mr Moore to Yorke; 'ce sont vraiment des enfants terribles, que les vôtres!'

Rose, who had been listening attentively to Mark's speech, replied to him: –

'There are different kinds of thoughts, ideas, and notions,' said she, 'good and bad: sentimental must refer to the bad, or Miss Helstone must have taken it in that sense, for she was not blaming Mr Moore; she was defending him.'

'That's my kind little advocate!' said Moore, taking Rose's hand.

'She was defending him,' repeated Rose, 'as I should have done had I been in her place, for the other ladies seemed to speak spitefully.'

'Ladies always do speak spitefully,' observed Martin; 'it is the nature of womenites to be spiteful.'

Matthew now, for the first time, opened his lips: –

'What a fool Martin is, to be always gabbling about what he does not understand.'

'It is my privilege, as a freeman, to gabble on whatever subject I like,' responded Martin.

'You use it, or rather abuse it, to such an extent,' rejoined the elder brother, 'that you prove you ought to have been a slave.'

'A slave! a slave! That to a Yorke, and from a Yorke! This fellow,' he added, standing up at the table, and pointing across it to Matthew, – 'this fellow forgets, what every cottier in Briarfield knows, that all born of our house have that arched instep under which water can flow – proof that there has not been a slave of the blood for three hundred years.'

'Mountebank!' said Matthew.

'Lads, be silent!' exclaimed Mr Yorke. 'Martin, you are a mischief-maker: there would have been no disturbance, but for you.'

'Indeed! Is that correct? Did I begin, or did Matthew? Had I spoken to him when he accused me of gabbling like a fool?'

'A presumptuous fool!' repeated Matthew.

Here Mrs Yorke commenced rocking herself – rather a portentous movement with her, as it was occasionally followed, especially when Matthew was worsted in a conflict, by a fit of hysterics.

'I don't see why I should bear insolence from Matthew Yorke, or what right he has to use bad language to me,' observed Martin.

'He has no right, my lad; but forgive your brother until seventy and seven times,' said Mr Yorke soothingly.

'Always alike, and theory and practice always adverse!' murmured Martin as he turned to leave the room.

'Where art thou going, my son?' asked the father.

'Somewhere where I shall be safe from insult: if in this house I can find any such place.'

Matthew laughed very insolently: Martin threw a strange look at him, and trembled through all his slight lad's frame, but he restrained himself.

'I suppose there is no objection to my withdrawing?' he inquired.

'No; go, my lad: but remember not to bear malice.'

Martin went, and Matthew sent another insolent laugh after him. Rose, lifting her fair head from Moore's shoulder, against which, for a moment, it had been resting, said, as she directed a steady gaze to Matthew – 'Martin is grieved, and you are glad; but I would rather be Martin than you: I dislike your nature.'

Here Mr Moore, by way of averting, or at least escaping, a scene – which a sob from Mrs Yorke warned him was likely to come on – rose, and putting Jessy off his knee, he kissed her and Rose; reminding them, at the same time, to be sure and come to the Hollow in good time to-morrow afternoon: then, having taken leave of his hostess, he said to Mr Yorke – 'May I speak a word with you?' and was followed by him from the room. Their brief conference took place in the hall.

'Have you employment for a good workman?' asked Moore.

'A nonsense question in these times, when you know that every master has many good workmen to whom he cannot give full employment.'

'You must oblige me by taking on this man, if possible.'

'My lad, I can take on no more hands to oblige all England.'

'It does not signify; I must find him a place somewhere.'

'Who is he?'

'William Farren.'

'I know William; a right-down honest man is William.'

'He has been out of work three months; he has a large family:

we are sure they cannot live without wages: he was one of a deputation of cloth-dressers who came to me this morning to complain and threaten. William did not threaten: he only asked me to give them rather more time, – to make my changes more slowly. You know I cannot do that: straitened on all sides as I am, I have nothing for it but to push on. I thought it would be idle to palaver long with them. I sent them away, after arresting a rascal amongst them, whom I hope to transport – a fellow who preaches at the chapel yonder sometimes.'

'Not Moses Barraclough?'

'Yes.'

'Ah! you've arrested him? Good! Then out of a scoundrel you're going to make a martyr: you've done a wise thing.'

'I've done a right thing. Well, the short and the long of it is, I'm determined to get Farren a place, and I reckon on you to give him one.'

'This is cool, however!' exclaimed Mr Yorke. 'What right have you to reckon on me to provide for your dismissed work-men? What do I know about your Farrens and your Williams? I've heard he's an honest man; but am I to support all the honest men in Yorkshire? You may say that would be no great charge to undertake; but great or little I'll none of it.'

'Come, Mr Yorke, what can you find for him to do?'

'*I* find! You'll make me use language I'm not accustomed to use. I wish you would go home – here is the door – set off.'

Moore sat down on one of the hall chairs.

'You can't give him work in your mill – good – but you have land: find him some occupation on your land, Mr Yorke.'

'Bob, I thought you cared nothing about our "lourdauds de paysans:" I don't understand this change.'

'I do: the fellow spoke to me nothing but truth and sense. I answered him just as roughly as I did the rest, who jabbered mere gibberish. I couldn't make distinctions there and then: his appearance told what he had gone through lately clearer than his words: but where is the use of explaining? Let him have work.'

'Let him have it yourself. If you are so very much in earnest, strain a point.'

'If there was a point left in my affairs to strain, I would strain it till it cracked again; but I received letters this morning which show me pretty nearly where I stand, and it is not far off the end of the plank. My foreign market, at any rate, is gorged. If there is no change – if there dawns no prospect of peace – if the Orders in Council are not, at least, suspended, so as to open our way in the West – I do not know where I am to turn. I see no more light than if I were sealed in a rock; so that for me to pretend to offer a man a livelihood would be to do a dishonest thing.'

'Come, let us take a turn on the front: it is a starlight night,' said Mr Yorke.

They passed out, closing the front-door after them, and, side by side, paced the frost-white pavement to and fro.

'Settle about Farren at once,' urged Mr Moore. 'You have large fruit-gardens at Yorke Mills: he is a good gardener: give him work there.'

'Well, so be it. I'll send for him to-morrow, and we'll see. And now, my lad, you're concerned about the condition of your affairs?'

'Yes: a second failure – which I may delay, but which, at this moment, I see no way finally to avert – would blight the name of Moore completely; and you are aware I had fine intentions of paying off every debt, and re-establishing the old firm on its former basis.'

'You want capital – that's all you want.'

'Yes; but you might as well say that breath is all a dead man wants to live.'

'I know – I know capital is not to be had for the asking; and if you were a married man, and had a family, like me, I should think your case pretty nigh desperate; but the young and un-encumbered have chances peculiar to themselves. I hear gossip now and then about your being on the eve of marriage with this miss and that; but I suppose it is none of it true?'

'You may well suppose that: I think I am not in a position to be dreaming of marriage. Marriage! I cannot bear the word: it sounds so silly and utopian. I have settled it decidedly that marriage and love are superfluities, intended only for the rich, who live at ease, and have no need to take thought for the morrow; or desperations, the last and reckless joy of the deeply wretched, who never hope to rise out of the slough of their utter poverty.'

'I should not think so if I were circumstanced as you are: I should think I could very likely get a wife with a few thousands, who would suit both me and my affairs.'

'I wonder where?'

'Would you try, if you had a chance?'

'I don't know: it depends on – in short, it depends on many things.'

'Would you take an old woman?'

'I'd rather break stones on the road.'

'So would I. Would you take an ugly one?'

'Bah! I hate ugliness and delight in beauty: my eyes and heart, Yorke, take pleasure in a sweet, young, fair face, as they are repelled by a grim, rugged, meagre one: soft delicate lines and hues please – harsh ones prejudice me. I won't have an ugly wife.'

'Not if she were rich?'

'Not if she were dressed in gems. I could not love – I could not fancy – I could not endure her. My taste must have satisfaction, or disgust would break out in despotism – or worse – freeze to utter iciness.'

'What, Bob, if you married an honest, good-natured, and wealthy lass, though a little hard-favoured, couldn't you put up with the high cheek-bones, the rather wide mouth, and reddish hair?'

'I'll never try, I tell you. Grace at least I *will* have, and youth and symmetry – yes, and what I call beauty.'

'And poverty, and a nursery full of bairns you can neither

clothe nor feed, and very soon an anxious faded mother – and then bankruptcy, discredit – a life-long struggle.'

'Let me alone, Yorke.'

'If you are romantic, Robert, and especially if you are already in love, it is of no use talking.'

'I am not romantic. I am stript of romance as bare as the white tenters in that field are of cloth.'

'Always use such figures of speech, lad; I can understand them: and there is no love-affair to disturb your judgment?'

'I thought I had said enough on that subject before. Love for me? Stuff!'

'Well, then; if you are sound both in heart and head, there is no reason why you should not profit by a good chance if it offers: therefore, wait and see.'

'You are quite oracular, Yorke.'

'I think I am a bit i' that line. I promise ye naught and I advise ye naught; but I bid ye keep your heart up, and be guided by circumstances.'

'My namesake the physician's almanack could not speak more guardedly.'

'In the mean time, I care naught about ye, Robert Moore: ye are nothing akin to me or mine, and whether ye lose or find a fortune it makes no difference to me. Go home, now: it has stricken ten. Miss Hortense will be wondering where ye are.'

CHAPTER X

OLD MAIDS

Time wore on, and spring matured. The surface of England began to look pleasant: her fields grew green, her hills fresh, her gardens blooming; but at heart she was no better: still her poor were wretched, still their employers were harassed: commerce, in some of its branches, seemed threatened with paralysis, for the war continued; England's blood was shed and her wealth lavished: all, it seemed, to attain most inadequate ends. Some tidings there were indeed occasionally of successes in the Peninsula, but these came in slowly; long intervals occurred between, in which no note was heard but the insolent self-felicitations of Bonaparte on his continued triumphs. Those who suffered from the results of the war felt this tedious, and – as they thought – hopeless, struggle against what their fears or their interests taught them to regard as an invincible power, most insufferable: they demanded peace on any terms: men like Yorke and Moore – and there were thousands whom the war placed where it placed them, shuddering on the verge of bankruptcy – insisted on peace with the energy of desperation.

They held meetings; they made speeches; they got up petitions to extort this boon: on what terms it was made, they cared not.

All men, taken singly, are more or less selfish; and taken in bodies they are intensely so. The British merchant is no exception to this rule: the mercantile classes illustrate it strikingly. These classes certainly think too exclusively of making money: they are too oblivious of every national consideration but that of extending England's (*i.e.* their own) commerce. Chivalrous feeling, disinterestedness, pride in honour, is too dead in their hearts. A land ruled by them alone would too often make ignominious submission – not at all from the motives Christ teaches, but rather from those Mammon instils. During the late war, the tradesmen of England would have endured buffets from the French on the right cheek and on the left; their cloak they would have given to Napoleon, and then have politely offered him their coat also, nor would they have withheld their waistcoat if urged: they would have prayed permission only to retain their one other garment, for the sake of the purse in its pocket. Not one spark of spirit, not one symptom of resistance would they have shown till the hand of the Corsican bandit had grasped that beloved purse; *then*, perhaps, transfigured at once into British bull-dogs, they would have sprung at the robber's throat, and there they would have fastened, and there hung – inveterate, insatiable, till the treasure had been restored. Tradesmen, when they speak against war, always profess to hate it because it is a bloody and barbarous proceeding: you would think, to hear them talk, that they are peculiarly civilized – especially gentle and kindly of disposition to their fellow-men. This is not the case. Many of them are extremely narrow and cold-hearted, have no good feeling for any class but their own, are distant – even hostile to all others; call them useless; seem to question their right to exist; seem to grudge them the very air they breathe, and to think the circumstance of their eating, drinking, and living in decent houses, quite unjustifiable. They do not know what others do in the way of helping, pleasing, or teaching their race; they will not trouble themselves to inquire: whoever is not in trade is accused of eating the bread of idleness, of passing a useless existence. Long may it be ere England really becomes a nation of shopkeepers!

We have already said that Moore was no self-sacrificing patriot, and we have also explained what circumstances rendered him specially prone to confine his attention and efforts to the furtherance of his individual interest; accordingly, when he felt himself urged a second time to the brink of ruin, none struggled harder than he against the influences which would have thrust him over. What he *could* do towards stirring agitation in the north against the war, he did, and he instigated others whose money and connexions gave them more power than he possessed. Sometimes, by flashes, he felt there was little reason in the demands his party made on Government: when he heard of all Europe threatened by Bonaparte, and of all Europe arming to resist him; when he saw Russia menaced, and beheld Russia rising, incensed and stern, to defend her frozen soil, her wild provinces of serfs, her dark native despotism, from the tread, the yoke, the tyranny of a foreign victor, he knew that England, a free realm, could not *then* depute her sons to make concessions and propose terms to the unjust, grasping French leader. When news came from time to time of the movements of that MAN then representing England in the Peninsula; of his advance from success to success – that advance so deliberate but so un-swerving, so circumspect but so certain, so 'unhasting' but so 'unresting;' when he read Lord Wellington's own despatches in the columns of the newspapers, documents written by Modesty to the dictation of Truth – Moore confessed at heart that a power was with the troops of Britain, of that vigilant, enduring, genuine, unostentatious sort, which must win victory to the side it led, in the end. In the end! but that end, he thought, was yet far off; and meantime he, Moore, as an individual, would be crushed, his hopes ground to dust: it was himself he had to care for, his hopes he had to pursue, and he would fulfil his destiny.

He fulfilled it so vigorously that erelong he came to a decisive rupture with his old Tory friend the Rector. They quarrelled at a public meeting, and afterwards exchanged some pungent letters in the newspapers. Mr Helstone denounced Moore as a Jacobin, ceased to see him, would not even speak to him when they met: he intimated also to his niece, very distinctly, that her communications with Hollow's cottage must for the present cease; she must give up taking French lessons. The language, he

observed, was a bad and frivolous one at the best, and most of
the works it boasted were bad and frivolous, highly injurious in
their tendency to weak female minds. He wondered (he
remarked parenthetically) what noodle first made it the fashion
to teach women French: nothing was more improper for them;
it was like feeding a rickety child on chalk and water-gruel:
Caroline must give it up, and give up her cousins too: they were
dangerous people.

Mr Helstone quite expected opposition to this order: he
expected tears. Seldom did he trouble himself about Caroline's
movements, but a vague idea possessed him that she was fond
of going to Hollow's cottage: also he suspected that she liked
Robert Moore's occasional presence at the Rectory. The Cossack
had perceived that whereas if Malone stepped in of an evening
to make himself sociable and charming, by pinching the ears of
an aged black cat, which usually shared with Miss Helstone's
feet the accommodation of her footstool, or by borrowing a
fowlingpiece, and banging away at a tool-shed door in the
garden while enough of daylight remained to show that conspicuous mark – keeping the passage and sitting-room doors
meantime uncomfortably open, for the convenience of running
in and out to announce his failures and successes with noisy
brusquerie – he had observed that under such entertaining circumstances, Caroline had a trick of disappearing, tripping
noiselessly up-stairs, and remaining invisible till called down to
supper. On the other hand, when Robert Moore was the guest,
though he elicited no vivacities from the cat, did nothing to it,
indeed, beyond occasionally coaxing it from the stool to his
knee, and there letting it purr, climb to his shoulder and rub
its head against his cheek; though there was no ear-splitting
cracking off of firearms, no diffusion of sulphurous gunpowder
perfume, no noise, no boasting during his stay, that still
Caroline sat in the room, and seemed to find wondrous content
in the stitching of Jew-basket pincushions, and the knitting of
Missionary-basket socks.

She was very quiet, and Robert paid her little attention, scarcely ever addressing his discourse to her; but Mr Helstone, not being one of those elderly gentlemen who are easily blinded, on the contrary, finding himself on all occasions extremely wide-awake, had watched them when they bade each other good-night: he had just seen their eyes meet once – only once. Some natures would have taken pleasure in the glance then surprised, because there was no harm and some delight in it. It was by no means a glance of mutual intelligence, for mutual love-secrets existed not between them: there was nothing then of craft and concealment to offend; only Mr Moore's eyes, look-ing into Caroline's, felt they were clear and gentle, and Caroline's eyes encountering Mr Moore's, confessed they were manly and searching: each acknowledged the charm in his or her own way. Moore smiled slightly, and Caroline coloured as slightly. Mr Helstone could, on the spot, have rated them both: they annoyed him; why? – impossible to say. If you had asked him what Moore merited at that moment, he would have said 'a horsewhip;' if you had inquired into Caroline's deserts, he would have adjudged her a box on the ear; if you had further demanded the reason of such chastisements, he would have stormed against flirtation and love-making, and vowed he would have no such folly going on under his roof.

These private considerations, combined with political reasons, fixed his resolution of separating the cousins. He announced his will to Caroline one evening, as she was sitting at work near the drawing-room window: her face was turned towards him, and the light fell full upon it. It had struck him a few minutes before that she was looking paler and quieter than she used to look; it had not escaped him either that Robert Moore's name had never, for some three weeks past, dropped from her lips; nor during the same space of time had that personage made his appearance at the Rectory. Some suspicion of clandestine meetings haunted his mind; having but an indifferent opinion of women, he always suspected them: he thought they needed

constant watching. It was in a tone drily significant he desired
her to cease her daily visits to the Hollow; he expected a start,
a look of deprecation: the start he saw, but it was a very slight
one; no look whatever was directed to him.

'Do you hear me?' he asked.

'Yes, uncle.'

'Of course, you mean to attend to what I say.'

'Yes, certainly.'

'And there must be no letter-scribbling to your cousin
Hortense: no intercourse whatever. I do not approve of the
principles of the family; they are Jacobinical.'

'Very well,' said Caroline quietly. She acquiesced then:
there was no vexed flushing of the face, no gathering tears: the
shadowy thoughtfulness which had covered her features ere Mr
Helstone spoke remained undisturbed: she was obedient.

Yes, perfectly; because the mandate coincided with her own
previous judgment; because it was now become pain to her to go
to Hollow's cottage; nothing met her there but disappointment:
hope and love had quitted that little tenement, for Robert
seemed to have deserted its precincts. Whenever she asked after
him – which she very seldom did, since the mere utterance of
his name made her face grow hot – the answer was, he was from
home, or he was quite taken up with business: Hortense feared
he was killing himself by application: he scarcely ever took a
meal in the house; he lived in the counting-house.

At church only Caroline had the chance of seeing him, and
there she rarely looked at him: it was both too much pain and too
much pleasure to look: it excited too much emotion; and that it
was all wasted emotion, she had learned well to comprehend.

Once, on a dark, wet Sunday, when there were few people at
church, and when especially certain ladies were absent, of whose
observant faculties and tomahawk tongues Caroline stood in
awe, she had allowed her eye to seek Robert's pew, and to rest
a while on its occupant. He was there alone: Hortense had been
kept at home by prudent considerations relative to the rain and

a new spring 'chapeau.' During the sermon, he sat with folded arms and eyes cast down, looking very sad and abstracted. When depressed, the very hue of his face seemed more dusk than when he smiled, and to-day cheek and forehead wore their most tintless and sober olive. By instinct Caroline knew, as she examined that clouded countenance, that his thoughts were running in no familiar or kindly channel; that they were far away, not merely from her, but from all which she could comprehend, or in which she could sympathize. Nothing that they had ever talked of together was now in his mind: he was wrapt from her by interests and responsibilities in which it was deemed such as she could have no part.

Caroline meditated in her own way on the subject; speculated on his feelings, on his life, on his fears, on his fate; mused over the mystery of 'business,' tried to comprehend more about it than had ever been told her – to understand its perplexities, liabilities, duties, exactions; endeavoured to realize the state of mind of a 'man of business,' to enter into it, feel what he would feel, aspire to what he would aspire. Her earnest wish was to see things as they were, and not to be romantic. By dint of effort she contrived to get a glimpse of the light of truth here and there, and hoped that scant ray might suffice to guide her.

'Different, indeed,' she concluded, 'is Robert's mental condition to mine: I think only of him; he has no room, no leisure to think of me. The feeling called love is and has been for two years the predominant emotion of my heart; always there, always awake, always astir: quite other feelings absorb his reflections, and govern his faculties. He is rising now, going to leave the church, for service is over. Will he turn his head towards this pew? – no – not once – he has not one look for me: that is hard: a kind glance would have made me happy till to-morrow: I have not got it; he would not give it; he is gone. Strange that grief should now almost choke me, because another human being's eye has failed to greet mine.'

That Sunday evening, Mr Malone coming, as usual, to pass it with his Rector, Caroline withdrew after tea to her chamber. Fanny, knowing her habits, had lit her a cheerful little fire, as the weather was so gusty and chill. Closeted there, silent and solitary, what could she do but think? She noiselessly paced too and fro the carpeted floor; her head drooped, her hands folded: it was irksome to sit: the current of reflection ran rapidly through her mind: to-night she was mutely excited.

Mute was the room, – mute the house. The double-door of the study muffled the voices of the gentlemen: the servants were quiet in the kitchen, engaged with books their young mistress had lent them; books which she had told them were 'fit for Sunday reading.' And she herself had another of the same sort open on the table, but she could not read it: its theology was incomprehensible to her, and her own mind was too busy, teeming, wandering, to listen to the language of another mind.

Then, too, her imagination was full of pictures: images of Moore; scenes where he and she had been together; winter fireside sketches; a glowing landscape of a hot summer afternoon passed with him in the bosom of Nunnely wood: divine vignettes of mild spring or mellow autumn moments, when she had sat at his side in Hollow's copse, listening to the call of the May cuckoo, or sharing the September treasure of nuts and ripe blackberries – a wild dessert which it was her morning's pleasure to collect in a little basket, and cover with green leaves and fresh blossoms, and her afternoon's delight to administer to Moore, berry by berry, and nut by nut, like a bird feeding its fledgling.

Robert's features and form were with her; the sound of his voice was quite distinct in her ear; his few caresses seemed renewed. But these joys being hollow, were, erelong, crushed in: the pictures faded, the voice failed, the visionary clasp melted chill from her hand, and where the warm seal of lips had made impress on her forehead, it felt now as if a sleety rain-drop had fallen. She returned from an enchanted region to the real world:

SHIRLEY

SHIRLEY

for Nunnely wood in June, she saw her narrow chamber; for the songs of birds in alleys, she heard the rain on her casement; for the sigh of the south wind, came the sob of the mournful east; and for Moore's manly companionship, she had the thin illusion of her own dim shadow on the wall. Turning from the pale phantom which reflected herself in its outline, and her reverie in the drooped attitude of its dim head and colourless tresses, she sat down – inaction would suit the frame of mind into which she was now declining – she said to herself: –

'I have to live, perhaps, till seventy years. As far as I know, I have good health: half a century of existence may lie before me. How am I to occupy it? What am I to do to fill the interval of time which spreads between me and the grave?'

She reflected.

'I shall not be married, it appears,' she continued. 'I suppose, as Robert does not care for me, I shall never have a husband to love, nor little children to take care of. Till lately I had reckoned securely on the duties and affections of wife and mother to occupy my existence. I considered, somehow, as a matter of course, that I was growing up to the ordinary destiny, and never troubled myself to seek any other; but now, I perceive plainly, I may have been mistaken. Probably I shall be an old maid. I shall live to see Robert married to some one else, some rich lady: I shall never marry. What was I created for, I wonder? Where is my place in the world?'

She mused again.

'Ah! I see,' she pursued presently; 'that is the question which most old maids are puzzled to solve: other people solve it for them by saying, "Your place is to do good to others, to be helpful whenever help is wanted." That is right its some measure, and a very convenient doctrine for the people who hold it; but I perceive that certain sets of human beings are very apt to maintain that other sets should give up their lives to them and their service, and then they requite them by praise: they call them devoted and virtuous. Is this enough? Is it to live? Is there not a terrible hollowness, mockery, want, craving, in that existence which is given away to others, for want of something of your own to bestow it on? I suspect there is. Does virtue lie in abnegation of self? I do not believe it. Undue humility makes tyranny; weak concession creates selfishness. The Romish religion especially teaches renunciation of self, submission to others, and nowhere are found so many grasping tyrants as in the ranks of the Romish priesthood. Each human being has his share of rights. I suspect it would conduce to the happiness and welfare of all, if each knew his allotment, and held to it as tenaciously as the martyr to his creed. Queer thoughts these, that surge in my mind: are they right thoughts? I am not certain.

'Well, life is short at the best: seventy years, they say, pass like a vapour, like a dream when one awaketh; and every path trod by human feet terminates in one bourne – the grave: the little chink in the surface of this great globe – the furrow where the mighty husbandman with the scythe deposits the seed he has shaken from the ripe stem; and there it falls, decays, and thence it springs again, when the world has rolled round a few times more. So much for the body: the soul meantime wings its long flight upward, folds its wings on the brink of the sea of fire and glass, and gazing down through the burning clearness, finds there mirrored the vision of the Christian's triple Godhead: the Sovereign Father; the Mediating Son; the Creator Spirit. Such words, at least, have been chosen to express what is inexpressible: to describe what baffles description. The soul's real hereafter, who shall guess?'

Her fire was decayed to its last cinder; Malone had departed; and now the study-bell rang for prayers.

The next day Caroline had to spend altogether alone, her uncle being gone to dine with his friend Dr Boultby, vicar of Whinbury. The whole time she was talking inwardly in the same strain: looking forwards, asking what she was to do with life. Fanny, as she passed in and out of the room occasionally, intent on housemaid errands, perceived that her young mistress sat very still. She was always in the same place, always bent industriously over a piece of work: she did not lift her head to speak to Fanny, as her custom was; and when the latter remarked that the day was fine, and she ought to take a walk, she only said – 'It is cold.'

'You are very diligent at that sewing, Miss Caroline,' continued the girl, approaching her little table.

'I am tired of it, Fanny.'

'Then why do you go on with it? Put it down: read, or do something to amuse you.'

'It is solitary in this house, Fanny: don't you think so?'

'I don't find it so, Miss. Me and Eliza are company for one another; but you are quite too still – you should visit more. Now, be persuaded; go up stairs and dress yourself smart, and go and take tea, in a friendly way, with Miss Mann or Miss Ainley: I am certain either of those ladies would be delighted to see you.'

'But their houses are dismal: they are both old maids. I am certain old maids are a very unhappy race.'

'Not they, Miss: they can't be unhappy; they take such care of themselves. They are all selfish.'

'Miss Ainley is not selfish, Fanny: she is always doing good. How devotedly kind she was to her stepmother, as long as the old lady lived; and now when she is quite alone in the world, without brother or sister, or any one to care for her, how charitable she is to the poor, as far as her means permit! Still nobody thinks much of her, or has pleasure in going to see her: and how gentlemen always sneer at her!'

'They shouldn't, Miss; I believe she is a good woman: but gentlemen think only of ladies' looks.'

'I'll go and see her,' exclaimed Caroline, starting up: 'and if she asks me to stay to tea, I'll stay. How wrong it is to neglect people because they are not pretty, and young, and merry! And I will certainly call to see Miss Mann, too: she may not be amiable; but what has made her unamiable? What has life been to her?'

Fanny helped Miss Helstone to put away her work, and afterwards assisted her to dress.

'*You* 'll not be an old maid, Miss Caroline,' she said, as she tied the sash of her brown-silk frock, having previously smoothed her soft, full, and shining curls; 'there are no signs of an old maid about you.'

Caroline looked at the little mirror before her, and she thought there were some signs. She could see that she was altered within the last month; that the hues of her complexion were paler, her eyes changed – a wan shade seemed to circle them, her countenance was dejected: she was not, in short, so pretty or so fresh as she used to be. She distantly hinted this to Fanny, from whom she got no direct answer, only a remark that people did vary in their looks; but that at her age a little falling away signified nothing, – she would soon come round again, and be plumper and rosier than ever. Having given this assurance, Fanny showed singular zeal in wrapping her up in warm shawls and handkerchiefs, till Caroline, nearly smothered with the weight, was fain to resist further additions.

She paid her visits: first to Miss Mann, for this was the most difficult point: Miss Mann was certainly not quite a lovable person. Till now, Caroline had always unhesitatingly declared she disliked her, and more than once she had joined her cousin Robert in laughing at some of her peculiarities. Moore was not habitually given to sarcasm, especially on anything humbler or weaker than himself; but he had once or twice happened to be in the room when Miss Mann had made a call on his sister, and after listening to her conversation and viewing her features for a time, he had gone out into the garden where his little cousin was tending some of his favourite flowers, and while standing near and watching her, he had amused himself with comparing fair youth – delicate and attractive – with shrivelled eld, livid and loveless, and in jestingly repeating to a smiling girl the vinegar discourse of a cankered old maid. Once on such an occasion, Caroline had said to him, looking up from the luxuriant creeper she was binding to its frame, –

'Ah! Robert, you do not like old maids. I, too, should come under the lash of your sarcasm, if I were an old maid.'

'You an old maid!' he had replied. 'A piquant notion suggested by lips of that tint and form. I can fancy you, though, at forty, quietly dressed, pale and sunk, but still with that straight nose, white forehead, and those soft eyes. I suppose, too, you will keep your voice, which has another "timbre" than that hard, deep organ of Miss Mann's. Courage, Cary! – even at fifty you will not be repulsive.'

'Miss Mann did not make herself, or tune her voice, Robert.'

'Nature made her in the mood in which she makes her briars and thorns; whereas for the creation of some women, she reserves the May morning hours, when with light and dew she woos the primrose from the turf, and the lily from the wood-moss.'

Ushered into Miss Mann's little parlour, Caroline found her, as she always found her, surrounded by perfect neatness, cleanliness, and comfort; (after all, is it not a virtue in old maids that solitude rarely makes them negligent or disorderly?) no dust on her polished furniture, none on her carpet, fresh flowers in the vase on her table, a bright fire in the grate. She herself sat primly and somewhat grimly-tidy in a cushioned rocking-chair, her hands busied with some knitting: this was her favourite work, as it required the least exertion. She scarcely rose as Caroline entered; to avoid excitement was one of Miss Mann's aims in life: she had been composing herself ever since she came down in the morning, and had just attained a certain lethargic state of tranquillity when the visiter's knock at the door startled her, and undid her day's work. She was scarcely pleased, therefore, to see Miss Helstone: she received her with reserve, bade her be seated with austerity, and when she had got her placed opposite, she fixed her with her eye.

This was no ordinary doom – to be fixed with Miss Mann's eye. Robert Moore had undergone it once, and had never forgotten the circumstance.

He considered it quite equal to anything Medusa could do: he professed to doubt whether, since that infliction, his flesh had been quite what it was before, – whether there was not something stony in its texture. The gaze had had such an effect on him as to drive him promptly from the apartment and house; it had even sent him straightway up to the Rectory, where he had appeared in Caroline's presence with a very queer face, and amazed her by demanding a cousinly salute on the spot, to rectify a damage that had been done him.

Certainly Miss Mann had a formidable eye for one of the softer sex: it was prominent, and showed a great deal of the white, and looked as steadily, as unwinkingly, at you as if it were a steel ball soldered in her head; and when, while looking, she began to talk in an indescribably dry monotonous tone – a tone without vibration or inflection – you felt as if a graven image of some bad spirit were addressing you. But it was all a figment of fancy, a matter of surface. Miss Mann's goblin-grimness scarcely went deeper than the angel-sweetness of hundreds of beauties. She was a perfectly honest, conscientious woman, who had performed duties in her day from whose severe anguish many a human Peri, gazelle-eyed, silken-tressed, and silver-tongued, would have shrunk appalled: she had passed alone through protracted scenes of suffering, exercised rigid self-denial, made large sacrifices of time, money, health, for those who had repaid her only by ingratitude, and now her main – almost her sole – fault was, that she was censorious.

Censorious she certainly was. Caroline had not sat five minutes ere her hostess, still keeping her under the spell of that dread and Gorgon gaze, began flaying alive certain of the families in the neighbourhood. She went to work at this business in a singularly cool, deliberate manner, like some surgeon practising with his scalpel on a lifeless subject: she made few distinctions; she allowed scarcely any one to be good; she dissected impartially almost all her acquaintance. If her auditress ventured now and then to put in a palliative word, she set it aside with a certain disdain. Still, though thus pitiless in moral anatomy, she was no scandal-monger: she never disseminated really malignant or dangerous reports: it was not her heart so much as her temper that was wrong.

Caroline made this discovery for the first time to-day; and, moved thereby to regret divers unjust judgments she had more than once passed on the crabbed old maid, she began to talk to her softly, not in sympathizing words, but with a sympathizing voice. The loneliness of her condition struck her visiter in a new light; as did also the character of her ugliness, – a bloodless pallor of complexion, and deeply worn lines of feature. The girl pitied the solitary and afflicted woman; her looks told what she felt: a sweet countenance is never so sweet as when the moved heart animates it with compassionate tenderness. Miss Mann, seeing such a countenance raised to her, was touched in her turn: she acknowledged her sense of the interest thus unexpec- tedly shown in her, who usually met with only coldness and ridicule, by replying to her candidly. Communicative on her own affairs she usually was not, because no one cared to listen to her; but to-day she became so, and her confidant shed tears as she heard her speak: for she told of cruel, slow-wasting, obstinate sufferings. Well might she be corpse-like; well might she look grim, and never smile; well might she wish to avoid excitement, to gain and retain composure! Caroline, when she knew all, acknowledged that Miss Mann was rather to be admired for fortitude than blamed for moroseness. Reader! when you behold an aspect for whose constant gloom and frown you cannot account, whose unvarying cloud exasperates you by its apparent causelessness, be sure that there is a canker somewhere, and a canker not the less deeply corroding because concealed.

Miss Mann felt that she was understood partly, and wished to be understood further; for however old, plain, humble, desolate, afflicted we may be, so long as our hearts preserve the feeblest spark of life, they preserve also, shivering near that pale ember, a starved, ghostly longing for appreciation and affection. To this extenuated spectre, perhaps, a crumb is not thrown once a-year; but when ahungered and athirst to famine – when all humanity has forgotten the dying tenant of a decaying house – Divine Mercy remembers the mourner, and a shower of manna falls for lips that earthly nutriment is to pass no more. Biblical promises, heard first in health, but then unheeded, come whispering to the couch of sickness: it is felt that a pitying God watches what all mankind have forsaken; the tender compassion of Jesus is recalled and relied on: the faded eye, gazing beyond Time, sees a Home, a Friend, a Refuge in Eternity.

Miss Mann, drawn on by the still attention of her listener, proceeded to allude to circumstances in her past life. She spoke like one who tells the truth – simply, and with a certain reserve: she did not boast, nor did she exaggerate. Caroline found that the old maid had been a most devoted daughter and sister, an unwearied watcher by lingering deathbeds; that to prolonged and unrelaxing attendance on the sick the malady that now poisoned her own life owed its origin; that to one wretched relative she had been a support and succour in the depths of self-earned degradation, and that it was still her hand which kept him from utter destitution. Miss Helstone stayed the whole evening, omitting to pay her other intended visit; and when she left Miss Mann, it was with the determination to try in future to excuse her faults, never again to make light of her peculiarities or to laugh at her plainness; and, above all things, not to neglect her, but to come once a-week, and to offer her, from one human heart at least, the homage of affection and respect: she felt she could now sincerely give her a small tribute of each feeling.

Caroline, on her return, told Fanny she was very glad she had gone out, as she felt much better for the visit. The next day she failed not to seek Miss Ainley. This lady was in narrower circumstances than Miss Mann, and her dwelling was more humble: it was, however, if possible, yet more exquisitely clean; though the decayed gentlewoman could not afford to keep a servant, but waited on herself, and had only the occasional assistance of a little girl who lived in a cottage near.

Not only was Miss Ainley poorer, but she was even plainer than the other old maid. In her first youth she must have been ugly; now, at the age of fifty, she was very ugly. At first sight, all but peculiarly well-disciplined minds were apt to turn from her with annoyance: to conceive against her a prejudice, simply on the ground of her unattractive look. Then she was prim in dress and manner: she looked, spoke, and moved the complete old maid.

Her welcome to Caroline was formal, even in its kindness – for it was kind; but Miss Helstone excused this. She knew something of the benevolence of the heart which beat under that starched kerchief; all the neighbourhood – at least all the female neighbourhood – knew something of it: no one spoke against Miss Ainley except lively young gentlemen, and inconsiderate old ones, who declared her hideous.

Caroline was soon at home in that tiny parlour; a kind hand took from her her shawl and bonnet, and installed her in the most comfortable seat near the fire. The young and the antiquated woman were presently deep in kindly conversation, and soon Caroline became aware of the power a most serene, unselfish, and benignant mind could exercise over those to whom it was developed. She talked never of herself – always of others. Their faults she passed over; her theme was their wants, which she sought to supply; their sufferings, which she longed to alleviate. She was religious – a professor of religion – what some would call 'a saint,' and she referred to religion often in sanctioned phrase – in phrase which those who possess a perception of the ridiculous, without owning the power of exactly testing and truly judging character, would certainly have esteemed a proper subject for satire – a matter for mimicry and laughter. They would have been hugely mistaken for their pains. Sincerity is never ludicrous; it is always respectable. Whether truth – be it religious or moral truth – speak eloquently and in well-chosen language or not, its voice should be heard with reverence. Let those who cannot nicely, and with certainty, discern the difference between the tones of hypocrisy and those of sincerity, never presume to laugh at all, lest they should have the miserable misfortune to laugh in the wrong place, and commit impiety when they think they are achieving wit.

Not from Miss Ainley's own lips did Caroline hear of her good works; but she knew much of them nevertheless: her beneficence was the familiar topic of the poor in Briarfield. They were not works of almsgiving: the old maid was too poor to give much, though she straitened herself to privation that she might contribute her mite when needful: they were the works of a Sister of Charity, far more difficult to perform than those of a Lady Bountiful. She would watch by any sickbed: she seemed to fear no disease; she would nurse the poorest whom none else would nurse: she was serene, humble, kind, and equable through everything.

For this goodness she got but little reward in this life. Many of the poor became so accustomed to her services that they hardly thanked her for them: the rich heard them mentioned with wonder, but were silent, from a sense of shame at the difference between her sacrifices and their own. Many ladies, however, respected her deeply: they could not help it; one gentleman – one only – gave her his friendship and perfect confidence: this was Mr Hall, the vicar of Nunnely. He said, and said truly, that her life came nearer the life of Christ, than that of any other human being he had ever met with. You must not think, reader, that in sketching Miss Ainley's character, I depict a figment of imagination – no – we seek the originals of such portraits in real life only.

Miss Helstone studied well the mind and heart now revealed to her. She found no high intellect to admire: the old maid was merely sensible; but she discovered so much goodness, so much usefulness, so much mildness, patience, truth, that she bent her own mind before Miss Ainley's in reverence. What was her love of nature, what was her sense of beauty, what were her more varied and fervent emotions, what was her deeper power of thought, what her wider capacity to comprehend, compared to the practical excellence of this good woman? Momently, they seemed only beautiful forms of selfish delight; mentally, she trod them under foot.

It is true, she still felt with pain that the life which made Miss Ainley happy could not make her happy: pure and active as it was, in her heart she deemed it deeply dreary because it was so loveless – to her ideas, so forlorn. Yet, doubtless, she reflected, it needed only habit to make it practicable and agreeable to any one: it was despicable, she felt, to pine sentimentally, to cherish secret griefs, vain memories; to be inert, to waste youth in aching languor, to grow old doing nothing.

'I will bestir myself,' was her resolution, 'and try to be wise if I cannot be good.'

She proceeded to make inquiry of Miss Ainley, if she could help her in anything. Miss Ainley, glad of an assistant, told her that she could, and indicated some poor families in Briarfield that it was desirable she should visit; giving her likewise, at her further request, some work to do for certain poor women who had many children, and who were unskilled in using the needle for themselves.

Caroline went home, laid her plans, and took a resolve not to swerve from them. She allotted a certain portion of her time for her various studies, and a certain portion for doing anything Miss Ainley might direct her to do; the remainder was to be spent in exercise; not a moment was to be left for the indulgence of such fevered thoughts as had poisoned last Sunday evening.

To do her justice, she executed her plans conscientiously, perseveringly. It was very hard work at first – it was even hard work to the end, but it helped her to stem and keep down anguish: it forced her to be employed; it forbade her to brood; and gleams of satisfaction chequered her grey life here and there when she found she had done good, imparted pleasure, or allayed suffering.

Yet I must speak truth; these efforts brought her neither health of body nor continued peace of mind: with them all, she wasted, grew more joyless and more wan; with them all, her memory kept harping on the name of Robert Moore: an elegy over the past still rung constantly in her ear; a funereal inward cry haunted and harassed her: the heaviness of a broken spirit, and of pining and palsifying faculties, settled slow on her buoyant youth. Winter seemed conquering her spring: the mind's soil and its treasures were freezing gradually to barren stagnation.

CHAPTER XI

FIELDHEAD

Yet Caroline refused tamely to succumb: she had native strength in her girl's heart, and she used it. Men and women never struggle so hard as when they struggle alone, without witness, counsellor, or confidant; unencouraged, unadvised, and unpitied.

Miss Helstone was in this position. Her sufferings were her only spur; and being very real and sharp, they roused her spirit keenly. Bent on victory over a mortal pain, she did her best to quell it. Never had she been seen so busy, so studious, and, above all, so active. She took walks in all weathers – long walks in solitary directions. Day by day she came back in the evening, pale and wearied-looking, yet seemingly not fatigued; for still, as soon as she had thrown off her bonnet and shawl, she would, instead of resting, begin to pace her apartment: sometimes she would not sit down till she was literally faint. She said she did this to tire herself well, that she might sleep soundly at night. But if that was her aim it was unattained, for at night, when others slumbered, she was tossing on her pillow, or sitting at the foot of her couch in the darkness, forgetful apparently of the necessity of seeking repose. Often, unhappy girl! she was crying – crying in a sort of intolerable despair; which, when it rushed over her, smote down her strength, and reduced her to childlike helplessness.

When thus prostrate, temptations besieged her: weak suggestions whispered in her weary heart to write to Robert, and say that she was unhappy because she was forbidden to see him and Hortense, and that she feared he would withdraw his friendship (not love) from her, and forget her entirely, and begging him to remember her, and sometimes to write to her. One or two such letters she actually indited, but she never sent them: shame and good sense forbade.

At last the life she led reached the point when it seemed she could bear it no longer; that she must seek and find a change somehow, or her heart and head would fail under the pressure which strained them. She longed to leave Briarfield, to go to some very distant place. She longed for something else: the deep, secret, anxious yearning to discover and know her mother strengthened daily; but with the desire was coupled a doubt, a dread – if she knew her, could she love her? There was cause for hesitation, for apprehension on this point: never in her life had she heard that mother praised: whoever mentioned her, mentioned her coolly. Her uncle seemed to regard his sister-in-law with a sort of tacit antipathy; an old servant, who had lived with Mrs James Helstone for a short time after her marriage, whenever she referred to her former mistress, spoke with chilling reserve: sometimes she called her 'queer,' sometimes she said she did not understand her. These expressions were ice to the daughter's heart; they suggested the conclusion that it was perhaps better never to know her parent, than to know her and not like her.

But one project could she frame whose execution seemed likely to bring her a hope of relief; it was to take a situation, to be a governess – she could do nothing else. A little incident brought her to the point, when she found courage to break her design to her uncle.

Her long and late walks lay always, as has been said, on lonely roads; but in whatever direction she had rambled, whether along the drear skirts of Stilbro' Moor, or over the sunny stretch of Nunnely Common, her homeward path was still so contrived as to lead her near the Hollow. She rarely descended the den, but she visited its brink at twilight almost as regularly as the stars rose over the hillcrests. Her resting-place was at a certain stile under a certain old thorn: thence she could look down on the cottage, the mill, the dewy garden-ground, the still, deep dam; thence was visible the well-known counting-house window, from whose panes at a fixed hour shot, suddenly bright, the ray of the well-known lamp. Her errand was to watch for this ray: her reward to catch it, sometimes sparkling bright in clear air, sometimes shimmering dim through mist, and anon flashing broken between slant lines of rain – for she came in all weathers.

There were nights when it failed to appear: she knew then that Robert was from home, and went away doubly sad; whereas its kindling rendered her elate, as though she saw in it the promise of some indefinite hope. If, while she gazed, a shadow bent between the light and lattice, her heart leaped – that eclipse was Robert: she had seen him. She would return home comforted, carrying in her mind a clearer vision of his aspect, a distincter recollection of his voice, his smile, his bearing; and, blent with these impressions, was often a sweet persuasion that, if she could get near him, his heart might welcome her presence yet: that at this moment he might be willing to extend his hand and draw her to him and shelter her at his side as he used to do. That night, though she might weep as usual, she would fancy her tears less scalding; the pillow they watered seemed a little softer; the temples pressed to that pillow ached less.

The shortest path from the Hollow to the Rectory wound near a certain mansion, the same under whose lone walls Malone passed on that night-journey mentioned in an early chapter of this work – the old and tenantless dwelling yclept Fieldhead. Tenantless by the proprietor it had been for ten years, but it was no ruin: Mr Yorke had seen it kept in good repair, and an old gardener and his wife had lived in it, cultivated the grounds, and maintained the house in habitable condition.

If Fieldhead had few other merits as a building, it might at least be termed picturesque: its irregular architecture, and the grey and mossy colouring communicated by time, gave it a just claim to this epithet. The old latticed windows, the stone porch, the walls, the roof, the chimney-stacks, were rich in crayon touches and sepia lights and shades. The trees behind were fine, bold, and spreading; the cedar on the lawn in front was grand, and the granite urns on the garden wall, the fretted arch of the gateway, were, for an artist, as the very desire of the eye.

One mild May evening, Caroline passing near about moonrise, and feeling, though weary, unwilling yet to go home, where there was only the bed of thorns and the night of grief to anticipate, sat down on the mossy ground near the gate, and gazed through towards cedar and mansion. It was a still night – calm, dewy, cloudless: the gables, turned to the west, reflected the clear amber of the horizon they faced; the oaks behind were black; the cedar was blacker; under its dense, raven boughs a glimpse of sky opened gravely blue: it was full of the moon, which looked solemnly and mildly down on Caroline from beneath that sombre canopy.

She felt this night and prospect mournfully lovely. She wished she could be happy: she wished she could know inward peace: she wondered Providence had no pity on her, and would not help or console her. Recollections of happy trysts of lovers, commemorated in old ballads, returned on her mind: she thought such tryst in such scene would be blissful. Where now was Robert? she asked: not at the Hollow: she had watched for his lamp long, and had not seen it. She questioned within herself whether she and Moore were ever destined to meet and speak again. Suddenly the door within the stone porch of the Hall opened, and two men came out; one elderly and white-headed, the other young, dark-haired, and tall. They passed across the lawn, out through a portal in the garden wall: Caroline saw them cross the road, pass the stile, descend the fields; she saw them disappear. Robert Moore had passed before her with his friend Mr Yorke: neither had seen her.

The apparition had been transient – scarce seen ere gone; but its electric passage left her veins kindled, her soul insurgent.

It found her despairing: it left her desperate – two different states.

'Oh! had he but been alone! Had he but seen me!' was her cry, 'he would have said something; he would have given me his hand. He *does*, he *must* love me a little: he would have shown some token of affection: in his eye, on his lips, I should have read comfort: but the chance is lost. The wind – the cloud's shadow does not pass more silently, more emptily than he. I have been mocked, and Heaven is cruel!'

Thus, in the utter sickness of longing and disappointment, she went home.

The next morning at breakfast, where she appeared white-cheeked and miserable-looking as one who had seen a ghost, she inquired of Mr Helstone, –

'Have you any objection, uncle, to my inquiring for a situation in a family?'

Her uncle, ignorant as the table supporting his coffee-cup of all his niece had undergone and was undergoing, scarcely believed his ears.

'What whim now?' he asked. 'Are you bewitched? What can you mean?'

'I am not well, and need a change,' she said.

He examined her. He discovered she had *experienced* a change, at any rate. Without his being aware of it, the rose had dwindled and faded to a mere snow drop: bloom had vanished, flesh wasted; she sat before him drooping, colourless, and thin. But for the soft expression of her brown eyes, the delicate lines of her features, and the flowing abundance of her hair, she would no longer have possessed a claim to the epithet – pretty.

'What on earth is the matter with you?' he asked. 'What is wrong? How are you ailing?'

No answer, only the brown eyes filled, the faintly-tinted lips trembled.

'Look out for a situation, indeed! For what situation are you fit? What have you been doing with yourself? You are not well.'

'I should be well if I went from home.'

'These women are incomprehensible. They have the strangest knack of startling you with unpleasant surprises. To-day you see them bouncing, buxom, red as cherries, and round as apples; to-morrow they exhibit themselves effete as dead weeds, blanched and broken down. And the reason of it all? that's the puzzle. She has her meals, her liberty, a good house to live in, and good clothes to wear, as usual: a while since that sufficed to keep her handsome and cheery, and there she sits now a poor, little, pale, puling chit enough. Provoking! Then comes the question, what is to be done? I suppose I must send for advice. Will you have a doctor, child?'

'No, uncle; I don't want one: a doctor could do me no good. I merely want change of air and scene.'

'Well, if that be the caprice, it shall be gratified. You shall go to a watering-place. I don't mind the expense: Fanny shall accompany you.'

'But, uncle, some day I must do something for myself: I have no fortune. I had better begin now.'

'While I live, you shall not turn out as a governess, Caroline. I will not have it said that my niece is a governess.'

'But the later in life one makes a change of that sort, uncle, the more difficult and painful it is. I should wish to get accustomed to the yoke before any habits of ease and independence are formed.'

'I beg you will not harass me, Caroline. I mean to provide for you. I have always meant to provide for you: I will purchase an annuity. Bless me! I am but fifty-five; my health and constitution are excellent: there is plenty of time to save and take measures. Don't make yourself anxious respecting the future: is that what frets you?'

'No, uncle; but I long for a change.'

He laughed. 'There speaks the woman!' cried he, 'the very woman! A change! a change! Always fantastical and whimsical! Well, it's in her sex.'

'But it is not fantasy and whim, uncle.'

'What is it then?'

'Necessity, I think. I feel weaker than formerly, I believe I should have more to do.'

'Admirable! She feels weak, and *therefore* she should be set to hard labour – "clair comme le jour" – as Moore – confound Moore! You shall go to Cliff-bridge; and there are two guineas to buy a new frock. Come, Cary, never fear; we'll find balm in Gilead.'

'Uncle, I wish you were less generous, and more –'

'More what?'

Sympathizing was the word on Caroline's lips, but it was not uttered: she checked herself in time: her uncle would indeed have laughed if that namby-pamby word had escaped her. Finding her silent, he said, –

'The fact is, you don't know precisely what you want.'

'Only to be a governess.'

'Pooh! mere nonsense! I'll not hear of governessing. Don't mention it again. It is rather too feminine a fancy. I have finished breakfast, ring the bell: put all crotchets out of your head, and run away and amuse yourself.'

'What with? My doll?' asked Caroline to herself as she quitted the room.

A week or two passed; her bodily and mental health neither grew worse nor better. She was now precisely in that state, when, if her constitution had contained the seeds of consumption, decline, or slow fever, those diseases would have been rapidly developed, and would soon have carried her quietly from the world. People never die of love or grief alone; though some die of inherent maladies, which the tortures of those passions prematurely force into destructive action. The sound by nature undergo these tortures, and are racked, shaken, shattered: their beauty and bloom perish, but life remains untouched. They are brought to a certain point of dilapidation; they are reduced to pallor, debility, and emaciation. People think, as they see them gliding languidly about, that they will soon withdraw to sick-beds, perish there, and cease from among the healthy and happy. This does not happen: they live on; and though they cannot regain youth and gaity, they may regain strength and serenity. The blossom which the March wind nips, but fails to sweep away, may survive to hang a withered apple on the tree late into autumn: having braved the last frosts of spring, it may also brave the first of winter.

Every one noticed the change in Miss Helstone's appearance, and most people said she was going to die. She never thought so herself: she felt in no dying case; she had neither pain nor sickness. Her appetite was diminished; she knew the reason: it was because she wept so much at night. Her strength was lessened; she could account for it; sleep was coy and hard to be won; dreams were distressing and baleful. In the far future she still seemed to anticipate a time when this passage of misery should be got over, and when she should once more be calm, though perhaps never again happy.

Meanwhile her uncle urged her to visit; to comply with the frequent invitations of their acquaintance: this she evaded doing; she could not be cheerful in company: she felt she was observed there with more curiosity than sympathy. Old ladies were always offering her their advice, recommending this or that nostrum; young ladies looked at her in a way she under-stood, and from which she shrank. Their eyes said they knew she had been 'disappointed,' as custom phrases it: by whom, they were not certain.

Commonplace young ladies can be quite as hard as common-place young gentlemen, – quite as worldly and selfish. Those who suffer should always avoid them; grief and calamity they despise: they seem to regard them as the judgments of God on the lowly. With them to 'love' is merely to contrive a scheme for achieving a good match: to be 'disappointed' is to have their scheme seen through and frustrated. They think the feelings and projects of others on the subject of love, similar to their own, and judge them accordingly.

All this Caroline knew, partly by instinct, partly by observation: she regulated her conduct by her knowledge, keeping her pale face and wasted figure as much out of sight as she could. Living thus in complete seclusion, she ceased to receive intelligence of the little transactions of the neighbourhood.

One morning her uncle came into the parlour, where she sat endeavouring to find some pleasure in painting a little group of wild flowers, gathered under a hedge at the top of the Hollow fields, and said to her in his abrupt manner: –

'Come, child, you are always stooping over palette, or book, or sampler: leave that tinting work. By-the-by, do you put your pencil to your lips when you paint?'

'Sometimes, uncle, when I forget.'

'Then it is that which is poisoning you. The paints are deleterious, child: there is white lead, and red lead, and verdigris, and gamboge, and twenty other poisons in those colour cakes. Lock them up! lock them up! Get your bonnet on: I want you to make a call with me.'

'With *you*, uncle?'

This question was asked in a tone of surprise. She was not accustomed to make calls with her uncle: she never rode or walked out with him on any occasion.

'Quick! quick! I am always busy, you know: I have no time to lose.'

She hurriedly gathered up her materials, asking, meantime, where they were going.

'To Fieldhead.'

'Fieldhead! What, to see old James Booth, the gardener? Is he ill?'

'We are going to see Miss Shirley Keeldar.'

'Miss Keeldar! Is she come to Yorkshire! Is she at Fieldhead?'

'She is. She has been there a week. I met her at a party last night: – that party to which you would not go. I was pleased with her: I choose that you shall make her acquaintance: it will do you good.'

'She is now come of age, I suppose?'

'She is come of age, and will reside for a time on her property. I lectured her on the subject: I showed her her duty: she is not intractable: she is rather a fine girl; she will teach you what it is to have a sprightly spirit: nothing lackadaisical about *her*.'

'I don't think she will want to see me, or to have me intro-duced to her. What good can I do her? How can I amuse her?'

'Pshaw! Put your bonnet on.'

'Is she proud, uncle?'

'Don't know. You hardly imagine she would show her pride to me, I suppose? A chit like that would scarcely presume to give herself airs with the Rector of her parish, however rich she might be.'

'No, – but how did she behave to other people?'

'Didn't observe. She holds her head high, and probably can be saucy enough where she dare, – she wouldn't be a woman otherwise. There, – away now for your bonnet at once!'

Not naturally very confident, a failure of physical strength and a depression of spirits had not tended to increase Caroline's presence of mind and ease of manner, or to give her additional courage to face strangers, and she quailed, in spite of self-remon-strance, as she and her uncle walked up the broad, paved approach leading from the gateway of Fieldhead to its porch. She followed Mr Helstone reluctantly through that porch into the sombre old vestibule beyond.

Very sombre it was; long, vast, and dark: one latticed window lit it but dimly; the wide old chimney contained now no fire, for the present warm weather needed it not; it was filled instead with willow-boughs. The gallery on high, opposite the entrance, was seen but in outline, so shadowy became this hall towards its ceiling; carved stags' heads, with real antlers, looked down grotesquely from the walls. This was neither a grand nor a comfortable house: within as without it was antique, rambling, and incommodious. A property of a thousand a-year belonged to it; which property had descended, for lack of male heirs, on a female. There were mercantile families in the district boasting twice the income, but the Keeldars, by virtue of their antiquity, and their distinction of lords of the manor, took the precedence of all.

Mr and Miss Helstone were ushered into a parlour: of course, as was to be expected in such a gothic old barrack, this parlour was lined with oak: fine dark, glossy panels compassed the walls gloomily and grandly. Very handsome, reader, these shining, brown panels are: very mellow in colouring and tasteful in effect, but – if you know what a 'Spring-clean' is – very execrable and inhuman. Whoever, having the bowels of humanity, has seen servants scrubbing at these polished wooden walls with bees-waxed cloths on a warm May day, must allow that they are 'tolerable and not to be endured;' and I cannot but secretly applaud the benevolent barbarian who had painted another and larger apartment of Fieldhead – the drawing-room to-wit, formerly also an oak-room – of a delicate pinky white; thereby earning for himself the character of a Hun, but mightily enhancing the cheerfulness of that portion of his abode, and saving future housemaids a world of toil.

The brown-panelled parlour was furnished all in old style, and with real old furniture. On each side of the high mantel-piece stood two antique chairs of oak, solid as sylvan thrones, and in one of these sat a lady. But if this were Miss Keeldar, she must have come of age at least some twenty years ago: she was of matronly form, and though she wore no cap, and possessed hair of quite an undimmed auburn, shading small and naturally young-looking features, she had no youthful aspect, nor apparently the wish to assume it. You could have wished her attire of a newer fashion: in a well-cut, well-made gown, hers would have been no uncomely presence. It puzzled you to guess why a garment of handsome materials should be arranged in such scanty folds, and devised after such an obsolete mode: you felt disposed to set down the wearer as somewhat eccentric at once.

This lady received the visiters with a mixture of ceremony and diffidence quite English: no middle-aged matron who was not an Englishwoman *could* evince precisely the same manner; a manner so uncertain of herself, of her own merits, of her power to please; and yet so anxious to be proper, and, if possible, rather agreeable than otherwise. In the present instance, however, more embarrassment was shown than is usual even with diffident Englishwomen: Miss Helstone felt this, sympathized with the stranger, and knowing by experience what was good for the timid, took a seat quietly near her, and began to talk to her with a gentle ease, communicated for the moment by the presence of one less self-possessed than herself.

She and this lady would, if alone, have at once got on extremely well together. The lady had the clearest voice imaginable: infinitely softer and more tuneful than could have been reasonably expected from forty years, and a form decidedly inclined to embonpoint. This voice Caroline liked; it atoned for the formal, if correct, accent and language: the lady would soon have discovered she liked it and her, and in ten minutes they would have been friends. But Mr Helstone stood on the rug looking at them both; looking especially at the strange lady with his sarcastic, keen eye, that clearly expressed impatience of her chilly ceremony, and annoyance at her want of aplomb. His hard gaze and rasping voice discomfited the lady more and more; she tried, however, to get up little speeches about the weather, the aspect of the country, &c., but the impracticable Mr Helstone presently found himself somewhat deaf: whatever she said, he affected not to hear distinctly, and she was obliged to go over each elaborately constructed nothing twice. The effort soon became too much for her; she was just rising in a perplexed flutter, nervously murmuring that she knew not what detained Miss Keeldar – that she would go and look for her, when Miss Keeldar saved her the trouble by appearing: it was to be presumed at least that she who now came in through a glass-door from the garden owned that name.

There is real grace in ease of manner, and so old Helstone felt when an erect, slight girl walked up to him, retaining with her left hand her little silk apron full of flowers, and, giving him her right hand, said pleasantly: –

'I knew you would come to see me, though you *do* think Mr Yorke has made me a Jacobin. Good-morning.'

'But we'll not have you a Jacobin,' returned he. 'No, Miss Shirley, they shall not steal the flower of my parish from me: now that you are amongst us, you shall be my pupil in politics and religion: I'll teach you sound doctrine on both points.'

'Mrs Pryor has anticipated you,' she replied, turning to the elder lady. 'Mrs Pryor, you know, was my governess, and is still my friend; and of all the high and rigid Tories, she is queen; of all the staunch churchwomen, she is chief. I have been well drilled both in theology and history, I assure you, Mr Helstone.'

The Rector immediately bowed very low to Mrs Pryor, and expressed himself obliged to her.

The ex-governess disclaimed skill either in political or religious controversy, explained that she thought such matters little adapted for female minds, but avowed herself in general terms the advocate of order and loyalty, and, of course, truly attached to the Establishment. She added, she was ever averse to change under any circumstances; and something scarcely audible about the extreme danger of being too ready to take up new ideas, closed her sentence.

'Miss Keeldar thinks as you think, I hope, madam.'

'Difference of age and difference of temperament occasion difference of sentiment,' was the reply. 'It can scarcely be expected that the eager and young should hold the opinions of the cool and middle-aged.'

'Oh! oh! we are independent: we think for ourselves!' cried Mr Helstone. 'We are a little Jacobin, for anything I know: a little free-thinker, in good earnest. Let us have a confession of faith on the spot.'

And he took the heiress's two hands – causing her to let fall her whole cargo of flowers – and seated her by him on the sofa.

'Say your creed,' he ordered.

'The Apostles' Creed?'

'Yes.'

She said it like a child.

'Now for St Athanasius's: that's the test!'

'Let me gather up my flowers: here is Tartar coming, he will tread upon them.'

Tartar was a rather large, strong, and fierce-looking dog, very ugly, being of a breed between mastiff and bull-dog, who at this moment entered through the glass door, and posting directly to the rug, snuffed the fresh flowers scattered there. He seemed to scorn them as food; but probably thinking their velvety petals might be convenient as litter, he was turning round preparatory to depositing his tawny bulk upon them, when Miss Helstone and Miss Keeldar simultaneously stooped to the rescue.

'Thank you,' said the heiress, as she again held out her little apron for Caroline to heap the blossoms into it. 'Is this your daughter, Mr Helstone?' she asked.

'My niece, Caroline.'

Miss Keeldar shook hands with her, and then looked at her. Caroline also looked at her hostess.

Shirley Keeldar (she had no Christian name but Shirley: her parents, who had wished to have a son, finding that, after eight years of marriage, Providence had granted them only a daughter, bestowed on her the same masculine family cognomen they would have bestowed on a boy, if with a boy they had been blessed) – Shirley Keeldar was no ugly heiress: she was agreeable to the eye. Her height and shape were not unlike Miss Helstone's: perhaps in stature she might have the advantage by an inch or two; she was gracefully made, and her face, too, possessed a charm as well described by the word grace as any other. It was pale naturally, but intelligent, and of varied expression. She was not a blonde, like Caroline: clear and dark were the characteristics of her aspect as to colour: her face and brow were clear, her eyes of the darkest grey: no green lights in them, – transparent, pure, neutral grey; and her hair of the darkest brown. Her features were distinguished; by which I do not mean that they were high, bony, and Roman, being indeed rather small and slightly marked than otherwise; but only that they were, to use a few French words, 'fins, gracieux, spirituels:' mobile they were and speaking; but their changes were not to be understood, nor their language interpreted all at once. She examined Caroline seriously, inclining her head a little to one side, with a thoughtful air.

'You see she is only a feeble chick,' observed Mr Helstone.

'She looks young – younger than I. How old are you?' she inquired, in a manner that would have been patronizing if it had not been extremely solemn and simple.

'Eighteen years and six months.'

'And I am twenty-one.'

She said no more; she had now placed her flowers on the table, and was busied in arranging them.

'And St Athanasius's creed?' urged the Rector; 'you believe it all – don't you?'

'I can't remember it quite all. I will give you a nosegay, Mr Helstone, when I have given your niece one.'

She had selected a little bouquet of one brilliant and two or three delicate flowers, relieved by a spray of dark verdure: she tied it with silk from her workbox, and placed it on Caroline's lap; and then she put her hands behind her, and stood, bending slightly towards her guest, still regarding her, in the attitude and with something of the aspect of a grave but gallant little cavalier. This temporary expression of face was aided by the style in which she wore her hair, parted on one temple and brushed in a glossy sweep above the forehead, whence it fell in curls that looked natural, so free were their wavy undulations.

'Are you tired with your walk?' she inquired.

'No – not in the least; it is but a short distance – but a mile.'

'You look pale. Is she always so pale?' she asked, turning to the Rector.

'She used to be as rosy as the reddest of your flowers.'

'Why is she altered? What has made her pale? Has she been ill?'

'She tells me she wants a change.'

'She ought to have one: you ought to give her one: you should send her to the seacoast.'

'I will, ere summer is over. Meantime, I intend her to make acquaintance with you, if you have no objection.'

'I am sure Miss Keeldar will have no objection,' here observed Mrs Pryor. 'I think I may take it upon me to say that Miss Helstone's frequent presence at Fieldhead will be esteemed a favour.'

'You speak my sentiments precisely, ma'am,' said Shirley, 'and I thank you for anticipating me. Let me tell you,' she continued, turning again to Caroline, 'that you also ought to thank my governess; it is not every one she would welcome as she has welcomed you: you are distinguished more than you think. This morning, as soon as you are gone, I shall ask Mrs Pryor's opinion of you. I am apt to rely on her judgment of character, for hitherto I have found it wondrous accurate. Already I foresee a favourable answer to my inquiries: do I not guess rightly, Mrs Pryor?'

'My dear – you said but now you would ask my opinion when Miss Helstone was gone; I am scarcely likely to give it in her presence.'

'No – and perhaps it will be long enough before I obtain it. I am sometimes sadly tantalized, Mr Helstone, by Mrs Pryor's extreme caution: her judgments ought to be correct when they come, for they are often as tardy of delivery as a lord-chancellor's: on some people's characters I cannot get her to pronounce sentence, entreat as I may.'

Mrs Pryor here smiled.

'Yes,' said her pupil, 'I know what that smile means: you are thinking of my gentleman-tenant. Do you know Mr Moore of the Hollow?' she asked Mr Helstone.

'Ay! ay! your tenant – so he is: you have seen a good deal of him, no doubt, since you came?'

'I have been obliged to see him: there was business to transact. Business! Really the word makes me conscious I am indeed no longer a girl, but quite a woman and something more. I am an esquire: Shirley Keeldar, Esquire, ought to be my style and title. They gave me a man's name; I hold a man's position: it is enough to inspire me with a touch of manhood; and when I see such people as that stately Anglo-Belgian – that Gérard Moore before me, gravely talking to me of business, really I feel quite gentlemanlike. You must choose me for your churchwarden, Mr Helstone, the next time you elect new ones: they ought to make me a magistrate and a captain of yeomanry: Tony Lumpkin's mother was a colonel, and his aunt a justice of the peace – why shouldn't I be?'

'With all my heart. If you choose to get up a requisition on the subject, I promise to head the list of signatures with my name. But you were speaking of Moore?'

'Ah! yes. I find it a little difficult to understand Mr Moore – to know what to think of him: whether to like him or not. He seems a tenant of whom any proprietor might be proud – and proud of him I am, in that sense – but as a neighbour, what is he? Again and again I have entreated Mrs Pryor to say what she thinks of him, but she still evades returning a direct answer. I hope you will be less oracular, Mr Helstone, and pronounce at once: do you like him?'

'Not at all, just now: his name is entirely blotted from my good books.'

'What is the matter? What has he done?'

'My uncle and he disagree on politics,' interposed the low voice of Caroline. She had better not have spoken just then:

having scarcely joined in the conversation before, it was not apropos to do it now: she felt this, with nervous acuteness, as soon as she had spoken, and coloured to the eyes.

'What are Moore's politics?' inquired Shirley.

'Those of a tradesman,' returned the Rector; 'narrow, selfish, and unpatriotic. The man is eternally writing and speaking against the continuance of the war: I have no patience with him.'

'The war hurts his trade. I remember he remarked that only yesterday. But what other objection have you to him?'

'That is enough.'

'He looks the gentleman, in my sense of the term,' pursued Shirley, 'and it pleases me to think he is such.'

Caroline rent the Tyrian petals of the one brilliant flower in her bouquet, and answered in distinct tones – 'Decidedly he is.' Shirley, hearing this courageous affirmation, flashed an arch, searching glance at the speaker from her deep, expressive eyes.

'*You* are his friend, at any rate,' she said; 'you defend him in his absence.'

'I am both his friend and his relative,' was the prompt reply. 'Robert Moore is my cousin.'

'Oh, then, you can tell me all about him. Just give me a sketch of his character.'

Insuperable embarrassment seized Caroline when this demand was made: she could not, and did not attempt to comply with it. Her silence was immediately covered by Mrs Pryor, who proceeded to address sundry questions to Mr Helstone regarding a family or two in the neighbourhood, with whose connexions in the south she said she was acquainted. Shirley soon withdrew her gaze from Miss Helstone's face. She did not renew her interrogations, but returning to her flowers, proceeded to choose a nosegay for the Rector. She presented it to him as he took leave, and received the homage of a salute on the hand in return.

'Be sure you wear it for my sake,' said she.

'Next my heart, of course,' responded Helstone. 'Mrs Pryor,

take care of this future magistrate, this churchwarden in perspective, this captain of yeomanry, this young squire of Briar-field, in a word: don't let him exert himself too much: don't let him break his neck in hunting: especially, let him mind how he rides down that dangerous hill near the Hollow.'

'I like a descent,' said Shirley – 'I like to clear it rapidly; and especially I like that romantic Hollow, with all my heart.'

'Romantic – with a mill in it?'

'Romantic with a mill in it. The old mill and the white cottage are each admirable in its way.'

'And the counting-house, Mr Keeldar?'

'The counting-house is better than my bloom-coloured drawing-room: I adore the counting-house.'

'And the trade? The cloth – the greasy wool – the polluting dyeing-vats?'

'The trade is to be thoroughly respected.'

'And the tradesman is a hero? Good!'

'I am glad to hear you say so: I thought the tradesman looked heroic.'

Mischief, spirit, and glee sparkled all over her face as she thus bandied words with the old Cossack, who almost equally enjoyed the tilt.

'Captain Keeldar, you have no mercantile blood in your veins: why are you so fond of trade?'

'Because I am a mill-owner, of course. Half my income comes from the works in that Hollow.'

'Don't enter into partnership, that's all.'

'You've put it into my head! you've put it into my head!' she exclaimed, with a joyous laugh. 'It will never get out: thank you.' And waving her hand, white as a lily and fine as a fairy's, she vanished within the porch, while the Rector and his niece passed out through the arched gateway.

CHAPTER XII

SHIRLEY AND CAROLINE

Shirley showed she had been sincere in saying she should be glad of Caroline's society, by frequently seeking it: and, indeed, if she had not sought it, she would not have had it; for Miss Helstone was slow to make fresh acquaintance. She was always held back by the idea that people could not want her, – that she could not amuse them; and a brilliant, happy, youthful creature, like the heiress of Fieldhead, seemed to her too completely independent of society so uninteresting as hers, ever to find it really welcome.

Shirley might be brilliant, and probably happy likewise, but no one is independent of genial society; and though in about a month she had made the acquaintance of most of the families round, and was on quite free and easy terms with all the Misses Sykes, and all the Misses Pearson, and the two superlative Misses Wynne of Walden Hall; yet, it appeared, she found none amongst them very genial: she fraternized with none of them, to use her own words. If she had had the bliss to be really Shirley Keeldar, Esq., Lord of the Manor of Briarfield, there was not a single fair one in this and the two neighbouring parishes, whom she should have felt disposed to request to become Mrs Keeldar, lady of the manor. This declaration she made to Mrs Pryor, who received it very quietly, as she did most of her pupil's off-hand speeches, responding, –

'My dear, do not allow that habit of alluding to yourself as a gentleman to be confirmed: it is a strange one. Those who do not know you, hearing you speak thus, would think you affected masculine manners.'

Shirley never laughed at her former governess: even the little formalities and harmless peculiarities of that lady were respectable in her eyes: had it been otherwise, she would have proved herself a weak character at once: for it is only the weak who make a butt of quiet worth; therefore she took her remonstrance in silence. She stood quietly near the window, looking at the grand cedar on her lawn, watching a bird on one of its lower boughs. Presently she began to chirrup to the bird: soon her chirrup grew clearer; erelong she was whistling; the whistle struck into a tune, and very sweetly and deftly it was executed.

'My dear!' expostulated Mrs Pryor.

'Was I whistling?' said Shirley; 'I forgot. I beg your pardon, ma'am. I had resolved to take care not to whistle before you.'

'But, Miss Keeldar, where did you learn to whistle? You must have got the habit since you came down into Yorkshire. I never knew you guilty of it before.'

'Oh! I learned to whistle a long while ago.'

'Who taught you?'

'No one: I took it up by listening, and I had laid it down again; but lately yesterday evening, as I was coming up our lane, I heard a gentleman whistling that very tune in the field on the other side of the hedge, and that reminded me.'

'What gentleman was it?'

'We have only one gentleman in this region, ma'am, and that is Mr Moore; at least he is the only gentleman who is not grey-haired: my two venerable favourites, Mr Helstone and Mr Yorke, it is true, are fine old beaux; infinitely better than any of the stupid young ones.'

Mrs Pryor was silent.

'You do not like Mr Helstone, ma'am?'

'My dear, Mr Helstone's office secures him from criticism.'

'You generally contrive to leave the room when he is announced.'

'Do you walk out this morning, my dear?'

'Yes, I shall go to the Rectory, and seek and find Caroline

Helstone, and make her take some exercise: she shall have a breezy walk over Nunnely Common.'

'If you go in that direction, my dear, have the goodness to remind Miss Helstone to wrap up well, as there is a fresh wind, and she appears to me to require care.'

'You shall be minutely obeyed, Mrs Pryor: meantime, will you not accompany us yourself?'

'No, my love; I should be a restraint upon you: I am stout, and cannot walk so quickly as you would wish to do.'

Shirley easily persuaded Caroline to go with her: and when they were fairly out on the quiet road, traversing the extensive and solitary sweep of Nunnely Common, she as easily drew her into conversation. The first feelings of diffidence overcome, Caroline soon felt glad to talk with Miss Keeldar. The very first interchange of slight observations sufficed to give each an idea of what the other was. Shirley said she liked the green sweep of the common turf, and, better still, the heath on its ridges, for the heath reminded her of moors: she had seen moors when she was travelling on the borders near Scotland. She remembered particularly a district traversed one long afternoon, on a sultry but sunless day in summer: they journeyed from noon till sunset, over what seemed a boundless waste of deep heath, and nothing had they seen but wild sheep; nothing heard but the cries of wild birds.

'I know how the heath would look on such a day,' said Caroline; 'purple-black: a deeper shade of the sky-tint, and that would be livid.'

'Yes – quite livid, with brassy edges to the clouds, and here and there a white gleam, more ghastly than the lurid tinge, which, as you looked at it, you momentarily expected would kindle into blinding lightning.'

'Did it thunder?'

'It muttered distant peals, but the storm did not break till evening, after we had reached our inn: that inn being an isolated house at the foot of a range of mountains.'

'Did you watch the clouds come down over the mountains?'

'I did: I stood at the window an hour watching them. The hills seemed rolled in a sullen mist, and when the rain fell in whitening sheets, suddenly they were blotted from the prospect: they were washed from the world.'

'I have seen such storms in hilly districts in Yorkshire; and at their riotous climax, while the sky was all cataract, the earth all flood, I have remembered the Deluge.'

'It is singularly reviving after such hurricanes to feel calm return, and from the opening clouds to receive a consolatory gleam, softly testifying that the sun is not quenched.'

'Miss Keeldar, just stand still now, and look down at Nunnely dale and wood.'

They both halted on the green brow of the Common: they looked down on the deep valley robed in May raiment; on varied meads, some pearled with daisies, and some golden with king-cups: to-day all this young verdure smiled clear in sunlight; transparent emerald and amber gleams played over it. On Nunnwood – the sole remnant of antique British forest in a region whose lowlands were once all sylvan chase, as its high-lands were breast-deep heather – slept the shadow of a cloud; the distant hills were dappled, the horizon was shaded and tinted like mother-of-pearl; silvery blues, soft purples, evanescent greens and rose-shades, all melting into fleeces of white cloud, pure as azury snow, allured the eye as with a remote glimpse of heaven's foundations. The air blowing on the brow was fresh, and sweet, and bracing.

'Our England is a bonnie island,' said Shirley, 'and Yorkshire is one of her bonniest nooks.'

'You are a Yorkshire girl too?'

'I am – Yorkshire in blood and birth. Five generations of my race sleep under the aisles of Briarfield Church: I drew my first breath in the old black hall behind us.'

Hereupon Caroline presented her hand, which was accord-ingly taken and shaken. 'We are compatriots,' said she.

'Yes,' agreed Shirley, with a grave nod.

'And that,' asked Miss Keeldar, pointing to the forest, – 'that is Nunnwood?'

'It is.'

'Were you ever there?'

'Many a time.'

'In the heart of it?'

'Yes.'

'What is it like?'

'It is like an encampment of forest sons of Anak. The trees are huge and old. When you stand at their roots, the summits seem in another region: the trunks remain still and firm as pillars, while the boughs sway to every breeze. In the deepest calm their leaves are never quite hushed, and in high wind a flood rushes – a sea thunders above you.'

'Was it not one of Robin Hood's haunts?'

'Yes, and there are mementos of him still existing. To penetrate into Nunnwood, Miss Keeldar, is to go far back into the dim days of eld. Can you see a break in the forest, about the centre?'

'Yes, distinctly.'

'That break is a dell; a deep, hollow cup, lined with turf as green and short as the sod of this Common: the very oldest of the trees, gnarled mighty oaks, crowd about the brink of this dell: in the bottom lie the ruins of a nunnery.'

'We will go – you and I alone, Caroline – to that wood, early some fine summer morning, and spend a long day there. We can take pencils and sketch-books, and any interesting reading-book we like; and of course we shall take something to eat. I have two little baskets, in which Mrs Gill, my housekeeper, might pack our provisions, and we could each carry our own. It would not tire you too much to walk so far?'

'Oh, no; especially if we rested the whole day in the wood, and I know all the pleasantest spots: I know where we could get nuts in nutting time; I know where wild strawberries abound; I know certain lonely, quite untrodden glades, carpeted with strange mosses, some yellow as if gilded, some a sober grey, some gem-green. I know groups of trees that ravish the eye with their perfect, picture-like effects: rude oak, delicate birch, glossy beech, clustered in contrast; and ash trees stately as Saul, standing isolated, and superannuated wood-giants clad in bright shrouds of ivy. Miss Keeldar, I could guide you.'

'You would be dull with me alone?'

'I should not. I think we should suit: and what third person is there whose presence would not spoil our pleasure?'

'Indeed, I know of none about our own ages – no lady at least, and as to gentlemen –'

'An excursion becomes quite a different thing when there are gentlemen of the party,' interrupted Caroline.

'I agree with you – quite a different thing to what we were proposing.'

'We were going simply to see the old trees, the old ruins; to pass a day in old times, surrounded by olden silence, and above all by quietude.'

'You are right; and the presence of gentlemen dispels the last charm, I think. If they are of the wrong sort, like your Malones, and your young Sykes, and Wynnes, irritation takes the place of serenity. If they are of the right sort, there is still a change – I can hardly tell what change, one easy to feel, difficult to describe.'

'We forget Nature, imprimis.'

'And then Nature forgets us; covers her vast, calm brow with a dim veil, conceals her face, and withdraws the peaceful joy with which, if we had been content to worship her only, she would have filled our hearts.'

'What does she give us instead?'

'More elation and more anxiety: an excitement that steals the hours away fast, and a trouble that ruffles their course.'

'Our power of being happy lies a good deal in ourselves, I believe,' remarked Caroline, sagely. 'I have gone to Nunnwood with a large party, all the curates and some other gentry of these parts, together with sundry ladies; and I found the affair insufferably tedious and absurd: and I have gone quite alone, or accompanied but by Fanny, who sat in the woodman's hut and sewed, or talked to the goodwife, while I roamed about and made sketches, or read; and I have enjoyed much happiness of a quiet kind all day long. But that was when I was young – two years ago.'

'Did you ever go with your cousin, Robert Moore?'

'Yes; once.'

'What sort of a companion is he on these occasions?'

'A cousin, you know, is different to a stranger.'

'I am aware of that; but cousins, if they are stupid, are still more insupportable than strangers, because you cannot so easily keep them at a distance. But your cousin is not stupid?'

'No; but –'

'Well?'

'If the company of fools irritates, as you say, the society of clever men leaves its own peculiar pain also. Where the goodness or talent of your friend is beyond and above all doubt, your own worthiness to be his associate often becomes a matter of question.'

'Oh! there I cannot follow you: that crotchet is not one I should choose to entertain for an instant. I consider myself not unworthy to be the associate of the best of them – of gentlemen, I mean: though that is saying a great deal. Where they are good, they are very good, I believe. Your uncle, by-the-by, is not a bad specimen of the elderly gentleman: I am always glad to see his brown, keen, sensible old face, either in my own house or any other. Are you fond of him? Is he kind to you? Now, speak the truth.'

'He has brought me up from childhood, I doubt not, precisely as he would have brought up his own daughter, if he had had one; and that is kindness; but I am not fond of him: I would rather be out of his presence than in it.'

'Strange! when he has the art of making himself so agreeable.'

'Yes, in company; but he is stern and silent at home. As he puts away his cane and shovel-hat in the Rectory-hall, so he locks his liveliness in his book-case and study-desk: the knitted brow and brief word for the fireside; the smile, the jest, the witty sally, for society.'

'Is he tyrannical?'

'Not in the least: he is neither tyrannical nor hypocritical: he is simply a man who is rather liberal than good-natured, rather brilliant than genial, rather scrupulously equitable than truly just, – if you can understand such superfine distinctions?'

'Oh! yes: good-nature implies indulgence, which he has not; geniality, warmth of heart, which he does not own; and genuine justice is the offspring of sympathy and considerateness, of which, I can well conceive, my bronzed old friend is quite innocent.'

'I often wonder, Shirley, whether most men resemble my uncle in their domestic relations; whether it is necessary to be new and unfamiliar to them, in order to seem agreeable or estimable in their eyes; and whether it is impossible to their natures to retain a constant interest and affection for those they see every day.'

'I don't know: I can't clear up your doubts. I ponder over similar ones myself sometimes. But, to tell you a secret, if I were convinced that they are necessarily and universally different from us – fickle, soon petrifying, unsympathizing – I would never marry. I should not like to find out that what I loved did not love me, that it was weary of me, and that whatever effort I might make to please would hereafter be worse than useless, since it was inevitably in its nature to change and become indifferent. That discovery once made, what should I long for? To go away – to remove from a presence where my society gave no pleasure.'

'But you could not, if you were married.'

'No, I could not, – there it is. I could never be my own

mistress more. A terrible thought! – it suffocates me! Nothing irks me like the idea of being a burden and a bore, – an inevitable burden, – a ceaseless bore! Now, when I feel my company superfluous, I can comfortably fold my independence round me like a mantle, and drop my pride like a veil, and withdraw to solitude. If married, that could not be.'

'I wonder we don't all make up our minds to remain single,' said Caroline: 'we should if we listened to the wisdom of experience. My uncle always speaks of marriage as a burden; and I believe whenever he hears of a man being married, he invariably regards him as a fool, or, at any rate, as doing a foolish thing.'

'But, Caroline, men are not all like your uncle: surely not – I hope not.'

She paused and mused.

'I suppose we each find an exception in the one we love, till we *are* married,' suggested Caroline.

'I suppose so: and this exception we believe to be of sterling materials; we fancy it like ourselves; we imagine a sense of harmony. We think his voice gives the softest, truest promise of a heart that will never harden against us: we read in his eyes that faithful feeling – affection. I don't think we should trust to what they call passion at all, Caroline. I believe it is a mere fire of dry sticks, blazing up and vanishing: but we watch him, and see him kind to animals, to little children, to poor people. He is kind to us likewise – good – considerate: he does not flatter women, but he is patient with them, and he seems to be easy in their presence, and to find their company genial. He likes them not only for vain and selfish reasons, but as *we* like him – because we like him. Then we observe that he is just – that he always speaks the truth – that he is conscientious. We feel joy and peace when he comes into a room: we feel sadness and trouble when he leaves it. We know that this man has been a kind son, that he is a kind brother: will any one dare to tell me that he will not be a kind husband?'

'My uncle would affirm it unhesitatingly. "He will be sick of you in a month," he would say.'

'Mrs Pryor would seriously intimate the same.'

'Mrs Yorke and Miss Mann would darkly suggest ditto.'

'If they are true oracles, it is good never to fall in love.'

'Very good, if you can avoid it.'

'I choose to doubt their truth.'

'I am afraid that proves you are already caught.'

'Not I: but if I were, do you know what soothsayers I would consult?'

'Let me hear.'

'Neither man nor woman, elderly nor young: – the little Irish beggar that comes barefoot to my door; the mouse that steals out of the cranny in the wainscot; the bird that in frost and snow pecks at my window for a crumb; the dog that licks my hand and sits beside my knee.'

'Did you ever see any one who was kind to such things?'

'Did you ever see any one whom such things seemed instinctively to follow, like, rely on?'

'We have a black cat and an old dog at the Rectory. I know somebody to whose knee that black cat loves to climb; against whose shoulder and cheek it likes to purr. The old dog always comes out of his kennel and wags his tail, and whines affection-ately when somebody passes.'

'And what does that somebody do?'

'He quietly strokes the cat, and lets her sit while he con-veniently can, and when he must disturb her by rising, he puts her softly down, and never flings her from him roughly; he always whistles to the dog and gives him a caress.'

'Does he? It is not Robert?'

'But it is Robert.'

'Handsome fellow!' said Shirley, with enthusiasm: her eyes sparkled.

'Is he not handsome? Has he not fine eyes and well-cut features, and a clear, princely forehead?'

'He has all that, Caroline. Bless him! he is both graceful and good.'

'I was sure you would see that he was: when I first looked at your face I knew you would.'

'I was well inclined to him before I saw him. I liked him when I did see him: I admire him now. There is charm in beauty for itself, Caroline; when it is blent with goodness, there is a powerful charm.'

'When mind is added, Shirley?'

'Who can resist it?'

'Remember my uncle, Mesdames Pryor, Yorke, and Mann.'

'Remember the croaking of the frogs of Egypt! He is a noble being. I tell you when they *are* good, they are the lords of the creation, – they are the sons of God. Moulded in their Maker's image, the minutest spark of His spirit lifts them almost above mortality. Indisputably, a great, good, handsome man is the first of created things.'

'Above us?'

'I would scorn to contend for empire with him, – I would scorn it. Shall my left hand dispute for precedence with my right? – shall my heart quarrel with my pulse? – shall my veins be jealous of the blood which fills them?'

'Men and women, husbands and wives quarrel horribly, Shirley.'

'Poor things! – poor, fallen, degenerate things! God made them for another lot – for other feelings.'

'But are we men's equals, or are we not?'

'Nothing ever charms me more than when I meet my superior – one who makes me sincerely feel that he is my superior.'

'Did you ever meet him?'

'I should be glad to see him any day: the higher above me, so much the better: it degrades to stoop – it is glorious to look up. What frets me is, that when I try to esteem, I am baffled: when religiously inclined, there are but false gods to adore. I disdain to be a Pagan.'

'Miss Keeldar, will you come in? We are here at the Rectory gates.'

'Not to-day; but to-morrow I shall fetch you to spend the evening with me. Caroline Helstone – if you really are what at present to me you seem – you and I will suit. I have never in my whole life been able to talk to a young lady as I have talked to you this morning. Kiss me – and good-bye.'

Mrs Pryor seemed as well-disposed to cultivate Caroline's acquaintance as Shirley. She, who went nowhere else, called on an early day at the Rectory. She came in the afternoon, when the Rector happened to be out. It was rather a close day; the heat of the weather had flushed her, and she seemed fluttered, too, by the circumstance of entering a strange house; for it appeared her habits were most retiring and secluded. When Miss Helstone went to her in the dining-room, she found her seated on the sofa, trembling, fanning herself with her handker-chief, and seeming to contend with a nervous discomposure that threatened to become hysterical.

Caroline marvelled somewhat at this unusual want of self-command in a lady of her years, and also at the lack of real strength in one who appeared almost robust: for Mrs Pryor hastened to allege the fatigue of her walk, the heat of the sun, &c., as reasons for her temporary indisposition; and still as, with more hurry than coherence, she again and again enumer-ated these causes of exhaustion, Caroline gently sought to relieve her by opening her shawl and removing her bonnet. Attentions of this sort, Mrs Pryor would not have accepted from every one: in general, she recoiled from touch or close approach, with a mixture of embarrassment and coldness far from flattering to those who offered her aid: to Miss Helstone's little light hand, however, she yielded tractably, and seemed soothed by its contact. In a few minutes she ceased to tremble, and grew quiet and tranquil.

Her usual manner being resumed, she proceeded to talk of

ordinary topics. In a miscellaneous company, Mrs Pryor rarely opened her lips; or, if obliged to speak, she spoke under restraint, and consequently not well; in dialogue, she was a good converser: her language, always a little formal, was well chosen; her sentiments were just; her information was varied and correct. Caroline felt it pleasant to listen to her: more pleasant than she could have anticipated.

On the wall opposite the sofa where they sat, hung three pictures: the centre one, above the mantelpiece, that of a lady; the two others, male portraits.

'That is a beautiful face,' said Mrs Pryor, interrupting a brief pause which had followed half an hour's animated conversation: 'the features may be termed perfect; no statuary's chisel could improve them: it is a portrait from the life, I presume?'

'It is a portrait of Mrs Helstone.'

'Of Mrs Matthewson Helstone? Of your uncle's wife?'

'It is, and is said to be a good likeness: before her marriage, she was accounted the beauty of the district.'

'I should say she merited the distinction: what accuracy in all the lineaments! It is, however, a passive face: the original could not have been, what is generally termed, "a woman of spirit."'

'I believe she was a remarkably still, silent person.'

'One would scarcely have expected, my dear, that your uncle's choice should have fallen on a partner of that description. Is he not fond of being amused by lively chat?'

'In company he is; but he always says he could never do with a talking wife: he must have quiet at home. You go out to gossip, he affirms; you come home to read and reflect.'

'Mrs Matthewson lived but a few years after her marriage, I think I have heard?'

'About five years.'

'Well, my dear,' pursued Mrs Pryor, rising to go, 'I trust it is understood that you will frequently come to Fieldhead: I hope you will. You must feel lonely here, having no female relative in the house: you must necessarily pass much of your time in solitude.'

'I am inured to it: I have grown up by myself. May I arrange your shawl for you?'

Mrs Pryor submitted to be assisted.

'Should you chance to require help in your studies,' she said, 'you may command me.'

Caroline expressed her sense of such kindness.

'I hope to have frequent conversations with you. I should wish to be of use to you.'

Again Miss Helstone returned thanks. She thought what a kind heart was hidden under her visiter's seeming chilliness. Observing that Mrs Pryor again glanced with an air of interest towards the portraits, as she walked down the room, Caroline casually explained: –

'The likeness that hangs near the window, you will see, is my uncle, taken twenty years ago; the other, to the left of the mantelpiece, is his brother James, my father.'

'They resemble each other in some measure,' said Mrs Pryor; 'yet a difference of character may be traced in the different mould of the brow and mouth.'

'What difference?' inquired Caroline, accompanying her to the door. 'James Helstone – that is, my father – is generally considered the best-looking of the two: strangers, I remark, always exclaim, What a handsome man! Do you think his picture handsome, Mrs Pryor?'

'It is much softer or finer featured than that of your uncle.'

'But where or what is the difference of character to which you alluded? Tell me: I wish to see if you guess right.'

'My dear, your uncle is a man of principle: his forehead and his lips are firm, and his eye is steady.'

'Well, and the other? Do not be afraid of offending me: I always like the truth.'

'Do you like the truth? It is well for you: adhere to that preference – never swerve thence. The other, my dear, if he had been living now, would probably have furnished little support to his daughter. It is, however, a graceful head – taken in youth, I should think. My dear (turning abruptly), you acknowledge an inestimate value in principle?'

'I am sure no character can have true worth without it.'

'You feel what you say? You have considered the subject?'

'Often. Circumstances early forced it upon my attention.'

'The lesson was not lost, then, though it came so prematurely. I suppose the soil is not light nor stony, otherwise seed falling in that season never would have borne fruit. My dear, do not stand in the air of the door, you will take cold: good-afternoon.'

Miss Helstone's new acquaintance soon became of value to her: their society was acknowledged a privilege. She found she would have been in error indeed to have let slip this chance of relief – to have neglected to avail herself of this happy change: a turn was thereby given to her thoughts; a new channel was opened for them, which, diverting a few of them at least from the one direction in which all had hitherto tended, abated the impetuosity of their rush, and lessened the force of their pressure on one worn-down point.

Soon she was content to spend whole days at Fieldhead, doing by turns whatever Shirley or Mrs Pryor wished her to do: and now one would claim her, now the other. Nothing could be less demonstrative than the friendship of the elder lady; but also nothing could be more vigilant, assiduous, untiring. I have intimated that she was a peculiar personage; and in nothing was her peculiarity more shown than in the nature of the interest she evinced for Caroline. She watched all her movements: she seemed as if she would have guarded all her steps: it gave her pleasure to be applied to by Miss Helstone for advice and assistance; she yielded her aid, when asked, with such quiet yet obvious enjoyment, that Caroline erelong took delight in depending on her.

Shirley Keeldar's complete docility with Mrs Pryor had at

first surprised Miss Helstone, and not less the fact of the reserved ex-governess being so much at home and at ease in the residence of her young pupil, where she filled with such quiet independency a very dependent post; but she soon found that it needed but to know both ladies to comprehend fully the enigma. Every one, it seemed to her, must like, must love, must prize Mrs Pryor when they knew her. No matter that she perseveringly wore old-fashioned gowns; that her speech was formal, and her manner cool; that she had twenty little ways such as nobody else had – she was still such a stay, such a counsellor, so truthful, so kind in her way, that, in Caroline's idea, none once accustomed to her presence could easily afford to dispense with it.

As to dependency or humiliation, Caroline did not feel it in her intercourse with Shirley, and why should Mrs Pryor? The heiress was rich – very rich – compared with her new friend: one possessed a clear thousand a-year – the other not a penny; and yet there was a safe sense of equality experienced in her society, never known in that of the ordinary Briarfield and Whinbury gentry.

The reason was, Shirley's head ran on other things than money and position. She was glad to be independent as to property: by fits she was even elated at the notion of being lady of the manor, and having tenants and an estate: she was especially tickled with an agreeable complacency when reminded of 'all that property' down in the Hollow, 'comprising an excellent cloth-mill, dyehouse, warehouse, together with the messuage, gardens, and outbuildings, termed Hollow's cottage;' but her exultation being quite undisguised was singularly inoffensive; and, for her serious thoughts, they tended elsewhere. To admire the great, reverence the good, and be joyous with the genial, was very much the bent of Shirley's soul: she mused therefore on the means of following this bent far oftener than she pondered on her social superiority.

In Caroline, Miss Keeldar had first taken an interest because she was quiet, retiring, looked delicate, and seemed as if she needed some one to take care of her. Her predilection increased greatly when she discovered that her own way of thinking and talking was understood and responded to by this new acquaintance. She had hardly expected it. Miss Helstone, she fancied, had too pretty a face, manners and voice too soft, to be anything out of the common way in mind and attainments; and she very much wondered to see the gentle features light up archly to the reveillé of a dry sally or two risked by herself; and more did she wonder to discover the self-won knowledge treasured, and the untaught speculations working in that girl-ish, curl-veiled head. Caroline's instinct of taste, too, was like her own: such books as Miss Keeldar had read with the most pleasure, were Miss Helstone's delight also. They held many aversions too in common, and could have the comfort of laugh-ing together over works of false sentimentality and pompous pretension.

Few, Shirley conceived, men or women have the right taste in poetry: the right sense for discriminating between what is real and what is false. She had again and again heard very clever people pronounce this or that passage, in this or that versifier, altogether admirable, which, when she read, her soul refused to acknowledge as anything but cant, flourish, and tinsel, or at the best, elaborate wordiness; curious, clever, learned perhaps; haply even tinged with the fascinating hues of fancy, but, God knows, as different from real poetry as the gorgeous and massy vase of mosaic is from the little cup of pure metal; or, to give the reader a choice of similes, as the milliner's artificial wreath is from the fresh-gathered lily of the field.

Caroline, she found, felt the value of the true ore, and knew the deception of the flashy dross. The minds of the two girls being toned in harmony, often chimed very sweetly together.

One evening, they chanced to be alone in the oak-parlour. They had passed a long wet day together without ennui; it was now on the edge of dark; candles were not yet brought in; both, as twilight deepened, grew meditative and silent. A western

wind roared high round the hall, driving wild clouds and
stormy rain up from the far-remote ocean: all was tempest
outside the antique lattices, all deep peace within. Shirley sat
at the window, watching the rack in heaven, the mist on earth,
listening to certain notes of the gale that plained like restless
spirits – notes which, had she not been so young, gay, and
healthy, would have swept her trembling nerves like some
omen, some anticipatory dirge: in this her prime of existence
and bloom of beauty, they but subdued vivacity to pensiveness.
Snatches of sweet ballads haunted her ear; now and then she
sang a stanza: her accents obeyed the fitful impulse of the wind;
they swelled as its gusts rushed on, and died as they wandered
away. Caroline, withdrawn to the farthest and darkest end of
the room, her figure just discernible by the ruby shine of the
flameless fire, was pacing to and fro, murmuring to herself
fragments of well-remembered poetry. She spoke very low, but
Shirley heard her; and while singing softly, she listened. This
was the strain: –

> 'Obscurest night involved the sky,
>   The Atlantic billows roar'd,
> When such a destined wretch as I,
>   Washed headlong from on board,
> Of friends, of hope, of all bereft,
> His floating home for ever left.'

Here the fragment stopped; because Shirley's song, erewhile
somewhat full and thrilling, had become delicately faint.
'Go on,' said she.
'Then you go on, too. I was only repeating, "The Castaway." '
'I know: if you can remember it all, say it all.'
And as it was nearly dark, and, after all, Miss Keeldar was no
formidable auditor, Caroline went through it. She went through
it as she should have gone through it. The wild sea, the drowning mariner, the reluctant ship swept on in the storm, you heard
were realized by her; and more vividly was realized the heart of

the poet, who did not weep for the 'The Castaway,' but who, in an hour of tearless anguish, traced a semblance to his own God-abandoned misery in the fate of that man-forsaken sailor, and cried from the depths where he struggled: –

> 'No voice divine the storm allayed,
>   No light propitious shone,
> When, snatch'd from all effectual aid,
>   We perish'd – each alone!
> But I – beneath a rougher sea,
> And whelm'd in deeper gulfs than he.'

'I hope William Cowper is safe and calm in heaven now,' said Caroline.

'Do you pity what he suffered on earth?' asked Miss Keeldar.

'Pity him, Shirley? What can I do else? He was nearly broken-hearted when he wrote that poem, and it almost breaks one's heart to read it. But he found relief in writing it – I know he did; and that gift of poetry – the most divine bestowed on man – was, I believe, granted to allay emotions when their strength threatens harm. It seems to me, Shirley, that nobody should write poetry to exhibit intellect or attainment. Who cares for that sort of poetry? Who cares for learning – who cares for fine words in poetry? And who does not care for feeling – real feeling – however simply, even rudely expressed?'

'It seems you care for it, at all events: and certainly, in hearing that poem, one discovers that Cowper was under an impulse strong as that of the wind which drove the ship – an impulse which, while it would not suffer him to stop to add ornament to a single stanza, filled him with force to achieve the whole with consummate perfection. You managed to recite it with a steady voice, Caroline: I wonder thereat.'

'Cowper's hand did not tremble in writing the lines: why should my voice falter in repeating them? Depend on it, Shirley, no tear blistered the manuscript of "The Castaway," I hear in it no sob of sorrow, only the cry of despair; but, that cry uttered,

I believe the deadly spasm passed from his heart; that he wept abundantly, and was comforted.'

Shirley resumed her ballad minstrelsy. Stopping short, she remarked erelong:

'One could have loved Cowper, if it were only for the sake of having the privilege of comforting him.'

'You never would have loved Cowper,' rejoined Caroline promptly: 'he was not made to be loved by woman.'

'What do you mean?'

'What I say. I know there is a kind of natures in the world – and very noble, elevated natures, too – whom love never comes near. You might have sought Cowper with the intention of loving him; and you would have looked at him, pitied him, and left him: forced away by a sense of the impossible, the incongruous, as the crew were borne from their drowning comrade by "the furious blast." '

'You may be right. Who told you this?'

'And what I say of Cowper, I should say of Rousseau. Was Rousseau ever loved? He loved passionately; but was his passion ever returned? I am certain, never. And if there were any female Cowpers and Rousseaus, I should assert the same of them.'

'Who told you this, I ask? Did Moore?'

'Why should anybody have told me? Have I not an instinct? Can I not divine by analogy? Moore never talked to me either about Cowper, or Rousseau, or love. The voice we hear in solitude told me all I know on these subjects.'

'Do you like characters of the Rousseau order, Caroline?'

'Not at all, as a whole. I sympathize intensely with certain qualities they possess: certain divine sparks in their nature dazzle my eyes, and make my soul glow. Then, again, I scorn them. They are made of clay and gold. The refuse and the ore make a mass of weakness: taken altogether, I feel them unnatural, unhealthy, repulsive.'

'I dare say I should be more tolerant of a Rousseau than you would, Cary: submissive and contemplative yourself, you like the stern and the practical. By-the-way, you must miss that Cousin Robert of yours very much, now that you and he never meet?'

'I do.'

'And he must miss you?'

'That he does not.'

'I cannot imagine,' pursued Shirley, who had lately got a habit of introducing Moore's name into the conversation, even when it seemed to have no business there, – 'I cannot imagine but that he was fond of you, since he took so much notice of you, talked to you, and taught you so much.'

'He never was fond of me: he never professed to be fond of me. He took pains to prove that he only just tolerated me.'

Caroline, determined not to err on the flattering side in estimating her cousin's regard for her, always now habitually thought of it and mentioned it in the most scanty measure. She had her own reasons for being less sanguine than ever in hopeful views of the future: less indulgent to pleasurable retrospections of the past.

'Of course, then,' observed Miss Keeldar, 'you only just tolerated him, in return?'

'Shirley, men and women are so different: they are in such a different position. Women have so few things to think about – men so many: you may have a friendship for a man, while he is almost indifferent to you. Much of what cheers your life may be dependent on him, while not a feeling or interest of moment in his eyes may have reference to you. Robert used to be in the habit of going to London, sometimes for a week or a fortnight together; well, while he was away, I found his absence a void: there was something wanting; Briarfield was duller. Of course, I had my usual occupations; still I missed him. As I sat by myself in the evenings, I used to feel a strange certainty of conviction I cannot describe: that if a magician or a genius had, at that moment, offered me Prince Ali's tube (you remember it in the Arabian Nights?), and if, with its aid, I had been enabled to

take a view of Robert – to see where he was, how occupied –
I should have learned, in a startling manner, the width of
the chasm which gaped between such as he and such as I.
I knew that, however my thoughts might adhere to him, his
were effectually sundered from me.'

'Caroline,' demanded Miss Keeldar, abruptly, 'don't you wish
you had a profession – a trade?'

'I wish it fifty times a-day. As it is, I often wonder what
I came into the world for. I long to have something absorbing
and compulsory to fill my head and hands, and to occupy my
thoughts.'

'Can labour alone make a human being happy?'

'No; but it can give varieties of pain, and prevent us from
breaking our hearts with a single tyrant master-torture. Besides,
successful labour has its recompense; a vacant, weary, lonely,
hopeless life has none.'

'But hard labour and learned professions, they say, make
women masculine, coarse, unwomanly.'

'And what does it signify, whether unmarried and never-to-
be-married women are unattractive and inelegant, or not? –
provided only they are decent, decorous, and neat, it is enough.
The utmost which ought to be required of old maids, in the
way of appearance, is that they should not absolutely offend
men's eyes as they pass them in the street; for the rest, they
should be allowed, without too much scorn, to be as absorbed,
grave, plain-looking, and plain-dressed as they please.'

'You might be an old maid yourself, Caroline, you speak so
earnestly.'

'I shall be one: it is my destiny. I will never marry a Malone
or a Sykes – and no one else will ever marry me.'

Here fell a long pause: Shirley broke it. Again the name by
which she seemed bewitched was almost the first on her lips.

'Lina – did not Moore call you Lina sometimes?'

'Yes: it is sometimes used as the abbreviation of Caroline in
his native country.'

'Well, Lina, do you remember my one day noticing an in-equality in your hair – a curl wanting on that right side – and your telling me that it was Robert's fault, as he had once cut therefrom a long lock?'

'Yes.'

'If he is, and always was, as indifferent to you as you say, why did he steal your hair?'

'I don't know – yes, I do: it was my doing, not his. Everything of that sort always was my doing. He was going from home, to London, as usual; and the night before he went, I had found in his sister's work-box a lock of black hair – a short, round curl: Hortense told me it was her brother's and a keepsake. He was sitting near the table; I looked at his head – he has plenty of hair; on the temples were many such round curls. I thought he could spare me one: knew I should like to have it, and I asked for it. He said, on condition that he might have his choice of a tress from my head; so he got one of my long locks of hair, and I got one of his short ones. I keep his, but, I dare say, he has lost mine. It was my doing, and one of those silly deeds it distresses the heart and sets the face on fire to think of: one of those small but sharp recollections that return, lacerating your self-respect like tiny penknives, and forcing from your lips, as you sit alone, sudden, insane-sounding interjections.'

'Caroline!'

'I *do* think myself a fool, Shirley, in some respects: I *do* despise myself. But I said I would not make you my confessor; for you cannot reciprocate foible for foible: you are not weak. How steadily you watch me now! turn aside your clear, strong, she-eagle eye: it is an insult to fix it on me thus.'

'What a study of character you are! Weak, certainly; but not in the sense you think. – Come in!'

This was said in answer to a tap at the door. Miss Keeldar happened to be near it at the moment, Caroline at the other end of the room: she saw a note put into Shirley's hands, and heard the words –

'From Mr Moore, ma'am.'

'Bring candles,' said Miss Keeldar.

Caroline sat expectant.

'A communication on business,' said the heiress; but when candles were brought, she neither opened nor read it. The Rector's Fanny was presently announced, and the Rector's niece went home.

CHAPTER XIII

FURTHER COMMUNICATIONS ON
BUSINESS

In Shirley's nature prevailed at times an easy indolence: there were periods when she took delight in perfect vacancy of hand and eye – moments when her thoughts, her simple existence, the fact of the world being around – and heaven above her, seemed to yield her such fulness of happiness, that she did not need to lift a finger to increase the joy. Often, after an active morning, she would spend a sunny afternoon in lying stirless on the turf, at the foot of some tree of friendly umbrage: no society did she need but that of Caroline, and it sufficed if she were within call; no spectacle did she ask but that of the deep blue sky, and such cloudlets as sailed afar and aloft across its span; no sound but that of the bee's hum, the leaf's whisper. Her sole book in such hours was the dim chronicle of memory, or the sibyl page of anticipation; from her young eyes fell on each volume a glorious light to read by; round her lips at moments played a smile which revealed glimpses of the tale or prophecy: it was not sad, not dark. Fate had been benign to the blissful dreamer, and promised to favour her yet again. In her past were sweet passages; in her future rosy hopes.

Yet one day when Caroline drew near to rouse her, thinking she had lain long enough, behold, as she looked down, Shirley's cheek was wet as if with dew: those fine eyes of hers shone humid and brimming.

'Shirley, why do *you* cry?' asked Caroline, involuntarily laying stress on *you*.

Miss Keeldar smiled, and turned her picturesque head

234

towards the questioner. 'Because it pleases me mightily to cry,' she said; 'my heart is both sad and glad: but why, you good, patient child – why do you not bear me company? I only weep tears, delightful and soon wiped away: you might weep gall, if you choose.'

'Why should I weep gall?'

'Mateless, solitary bird!' was the only answer.

'And are not you, too, mateless, Shirley?'

'At heart – no.'

'Oh! who nestles there, Shirley?'

But Shirley only laughed gaily at this question, and alertly started up. 'I have dreamed,' she said: 'a mere day-dream; certainly bright, probably baseless!'

Miss Helstone was by this time free enough from illusions: she took a sufficiently grave view of the future, and fancied she knew pretty well how her own destiny and that of some others were tending. Yet old associations retained their influence over her, and it was these, and the power of habit, which still frequently drew her of an evening to the field-stile and the old thorn overlooking the Hollow.

One night, the night after the incident of the note, she had been at her usual post, watching for her beacon – watching vainly; that evening no lamp was lit. She waited till the rising of certain constellations warned her of lateness, and signed her away. In passing Fieldhead, on her return, its moonlight beauty attracted her glance, and stayed her step an instant. Tree and hall rose peaceful under the night sky and clear full orb; pearly paleness gilded the building; mellow brown gloom bosomed it round; shadows of deep green brooded above its oak-wreathed roof. The broad pavement in front shone pale also; it gleamed as if some spell had transformed the dark granite to glistering Parian: on the silvery space slept two sable shadows, thrown sharply defined from two human figures. These figures when first seen were motionless and mute; presently they moved in harmonious step, and spoke low in harmonious key. Earnest was the gaze that scrutinized them as they emerged from behind the trunk of the cedar. 'Is it Mrs Pryor and Shirley?'

Certainly it is Shirley. Who else has a shape so lithe, and proud, and graceful? And her face, too, is visible: her countenance careless and pensive, and musing and mirthful, and mocking and tender. Not fearing the dew, she has not covered her head; her curls are free: they veil her neck and caress her shoulder with their tendril rings. An ornament of gold gleams through the half-closed folds of the scarf she has wrapped across her bust, and a large bright gem glitters on the white hand which confines it. Yes, that is Shirley.

Her companion then is, of course, Mrs Pryor?

Yes, if Mrs Pryor owns six feet of stature, and if she has changed her decent widow's weeds for masculine disguise. The figure walking at Miss Keeldar's side is a man – a tall, young, stately man – it is her tenant, Robert Moore.

The pair speak softly, their words are not distinguishable: to remain a moment to gaze is not to be an eavesdropper; and as the moon shines so clearly and their countenances are so distinctly apparent, who can resist the attraction of such interest? Caroline it seems cannot, for she lingers.

There was a time when, on summer nights, Moore had been wont to walk with his cousin, as he was now walking with the heiress. Often had she gone up the Hollow with him after sunset, to scent the freshness of the earth, where a growth of fragrant herbage carpeted a certain narrow terrace, edging a deep ravine, from whose rifted gloom was heard a sound like the spirit of the lonely watercourse, moaning amongst its wet stones, and between its weedy banks, and under its dark bower of alders.

'But I used to be closer to him,' thought Caroline: 'he felt no obligation to treat me with homage; I needed only kindness. He used to hold my hand: he does not touch hers. And yet Shirley is not proud where she loves. There is no haughtiness in her aspect now, only a little in her port; what is natural to and inseparable from her: what she retains in her most careless as in her most guarded moments. Robert must think as I think, that he is at this instant looking down on a fine face; and he must think it with a man's brain, not with mine. She has such generous, yet soft fire in her eyes. She smiles – what makes her smile so sweet? I saw that Robert felt its beauty, and he must have felt it with his man's heart, not with my dim woman's perceptions. They look to me like two great happy spirits: yonder silvered pavement reminds me of that white shore we believe to be beyond the death-flood: they have reached it, they walked there united. And what am I – standing here in shadow, shrinking into concealment, my mind darker than my hiding-place? I am one of this world, no spirit – a poor, doomed mortal, who asks, in ignorance and hopelessness, wherefore she was born, to what end she lives; whose mind for ever runs on the question, how she shall at last encounter, and by whom be sustained through death?

'This is the worst passage I have come to yet: still I was quite prepared for it. I gave Robert up, and gave him up to Shirley, the first day I heard she was come: the first moment I saw her – rich, youthful, and lovely. She has him now: he is her lover; she is his darling: she will be far more his darling yet when they are married: the more Robert knows of Shirley, the more his soul will cleave to her. They will both be happy, and I do not grudge them their bliss; but I groan under my own misery: some of my suffering is very acute. Truly, I ought not to have been born: they should have smothered me at the first cry.'

Here, Shirley stepping aside to gather a dewy flower, she and her companion turned into a path that lay nearer the gate: some of their conversation became audible. Caroline would not stay to listen: she passed away noiselessly, and the moonlight kissed the wall which her shadow had dimmed. The reader is privileged to remain, and try what he can make of the discourse.

'I cannot conceive why Nature did not give you a bulldog's head, for you have all a bulldog's tenacity,' said Shirley.

'Not a flattering idea: am I so ignoble?'

'And something also you have of the same animal's silent ways of going about its work: you give no warning; you come noiselessly behind, seize fast, and hold on.'

'This is guess-work; you have witnessed no such feat on my part: in your presence I have been no bulldog.'

'Your very silence indicates your race. How little you talk in general, yet how deeply you scheme! You are far-seeing; you are calculating.'

'I know the ways of these people. I have gathered information of their intentions. My note last night informed you that Barraclough's trial had ended in his conviction and sentence to transportation: his associates will plot vengeance. I shall lay my plans so as to counteract, or, at least, be prepared for theirs; that is all. Having now given you as clear an explanation as I can, am I to understand that for what I propose doing I have your approbation?'

'I shall stand by you so long as you remain on the defensive. Yes.'

'Good! Without any aid – even opposed or disapproved by you – I believe I should have acted precisely as I now intend to act; but in another spirit. I now feel satisfied. On the whole, I relish the position.'

'I dare say you do; that is evident: you relish the work which lies before you still better than you would relish the execution of a government order for army-cloth.'

'I certainly feel it congenial.'

'So would old Helstone. It is true there is a shade of difference in your motives: many shades, perhaps. Shall I speak to Mr Helstone? I will, if you like.'

'Act as you please: your judgment, Miss Keeldar, will guide you accurately. I could rely on it myself, in a more difficult crisis; but I should inform you, Mr Helstone is somewhat prejudiced against me at present.'

'I am aware, I have heard all about your differences: depend upon it they will melt away; he cannot resist the temptation of an alliance under present circumstances.'

'I should be glad to have him: he is of true metal.'

'I think so also.'

'An old blade, and rusted somewhat; but the edge and temper still excellent.'

'Well, you shall have him, Mr Moore: that is, if I can win him.'

'Whom can you not win?'

'Perhaps not the Rector; but I will make the effort.'

'Effort! He will yield for a word – a smile.'

'By no means. It will cost me several cups of tea, some toast and cake, and an ample measure of remonstrances, expostulations, and persuasions. It grows rather chill.'

'I perceive you shiver. Am I acting wrongly to detain you here? Yet it is so calm: I even feel it warm; and society such as yours is a pleasure to me so rare. – If you were wrapped in a thicker shawl –'

'I might stay longer, and forget how late it is, which would chagrin Mrs Pryor. We keep early and regular hours at Field-head, Mr Moore; and so, I am sure, does your sister at the cottage.'

'Yes; but Hortense and I have an understanding the most convenient in the world, that we shall each do as we please.'

'How do you please to do?'

'Three nights in the week I sleep in the mill: but I require little rest; and when it is moonlight and mild, I often haunt the Hollow till daybreak.'

'When I was a very little girl, Mr Moore, my nurse used to tell me tales of fairies being seen in that Hollow. That was before my father built the mill, when it was a perfectly solitary ravine: you will be falling under enchantment.'

'I fear it is done,' said Moore, in a low voice.

'But there are worse things than fairies to be guarded against,' pursued Miss Keeldar.

'Things more perilous,' he subjoined.

'Far more so. For instance, how would you like to meet Michael Hartley, that mad Calvinist and Jacobin weaver? They say he is addicted to poaching, and often goes abroad at night with his gun.'

'I have already had the luck to meet him. We held a long argument together one night. A strange little incident it was: I liked it.'

'Liked it? I admire your taste! Michael is not sane. Where did you meet him?'

'In the deepest, shadiest spot in the glen, where the water runs low, under brushwood. We sat down near that plank bridge. It was moonlight, but clouded, and very windy. We had a talk.'

'On politics?'

'And religion. I think the moon was at the full, and Michael was as near crazed as possible: he uttered strange blasphemy in his Antinomian fashion.'

'Excuse me, but I think you must have been nearly as mad as he, to sit listening to him.'

'There is a wild interest in his ravings. The man would be half a poet, if he were not wholly a maniac; and perhaps a prophet, if he were not a profligate. He solemnly informed me that hell was fore-ordained my inevitable portion; that he read the mark of the beast on my brow; that I had been an outcast from the beginning. God's vengeance, he said, was preparing for me, and affirmed that in a vision of the night he had beheld the manner and the instrument of my doom. I wanted to know further, but he left me with these words, "The end is not yet."'

'Have you ever seen him since?'

'About a month afterwards, in returning from market, I encountered him and Moses Barraclough both in an advanced stage of inebriation: they were praying in frantic sort at the roadside. They accosted me as Satan, bid me avaunt, and clamoured to be delivered from temptation. Again, but a few days ago,

Michael took the trouble of appearing at the counting-house door, hatless, in his shirt-sleeves, – his coat and castor having been detained at the public-house in pledge: he delivered himself of the comfortable message that he could wish Mr Moore to set his house in order, as his soul was likely shortly to be required of him.'

'Do you make light of these things?'

'The poor man had been drinking for weeks, and was in a state bordering on delirium tremens.'

'What then? He is the more likely to attempt the fulfilment of his own prophecies.'

'It would not do to permit incidents of this sort to affect one's nerves.'

'Mr Moore, go home!'

'So soon?'

'Pass straight down the fields, not round by the lane and plantations.'

'It is early yet.'

'It is late: for my part I am going in. Will you promise me not to wander in the Hollow to-night?'

'If you wish it.'

'I do wish it. May I ask whether you consider life valueless?'

'By no means: on the contrary, of late I regard my life as invaluable.'

'Of late?'

'Existence is neither aimless nor hopeless to me now; and it was both three months ago. I was then drowning, and rather wished the operation over. All at once a hand was stretched to me, – such a delicate hand, I scarcely dared trust it: – its strength, however, has rescued me from ruin.'

'Are you really rescued?'

'For the time: your assistance has given me another chance.'

'Live to make the best of it. Don't offer yourself as a target to Michael Hartley, and good-night!'

*

Miss Helstone was under a promise to spend the evening of the next day at Fieldhead: she kept her promise. Some gloomy hours had she spent in the interval. Most of the time had been passed shut up in her own apartment; only issuing from it, indeed, to join her uncle at meals, and anticipating inquiries from Fanny by telling her that she was busy altering a dress, and preferred sewing upstairs, to avoid interruption.

She did sew: she plied her needle continuously, ceaselessly; but her brain worked faster than her fingers. Again, and more intensely than ever, she desired a fixed occupation, – no matter how onerous, how irksome. Her uncle must be once more entreated, but first she would consult Mrs Pryor. Her head laboured to frame projects as diligently as her hands to plait and stitch the thin texture of the muslin summer dress spread on the little white couch at the foot of which she sat. Now and then, while thus doubly occupied, a tear would fill her eyes and fall on her busy hands; but this sign of emotion was rare, and quickly effaced: the sharp pang passed, the dimness cleared from her vision; she would re-thread her needle, re-arrange tuck and trimming, and work on.

Late in the afternoon she dressed herself: she reached Fieldhead, and appeared in the oak parlour just as tea was brought in. Shirley asked her why she came so late.

'Because I have been making my dress,' said she. 'These fine sunny days began to make me ashamed of my winter merino; so I have furbished up a lighter garment.'

'In which you look as I like to see you,' said Shirley. 'You are a lady-like little person, Caroline: is she not, Mrs Pryor?'

Mrs Pryor never paid compliments, and seldom indulged in remarks, favourable or otherwise, on personal appearance. On the present occasion she only swept Caroline's curls from her cheek as she took a seat near her, caressed the oval outline, and observed, –

'You get somewhat thin, my love, and somewhat pale. Do

you sleep well? Your eyes have a languid look;' and she gazed at her anxiously.

'I sometimes dream melancholy dreams,' answered Caroline; 'and if I lie awake for an hour or two in the night, I am continually thinking of the Rectory as a dreary old place. You know it is very near the churchyard: the back part of the house is extremely ancient, and it is said that the out-kitchens there were once enclosed in the churchyard, and that there are graves under them. I rather long to leave the Rectory.'

'My dear! You are surely not superstitious?'

'No, Mrs Pryor; but I think I grow what is called nervous. I see things under a darker aspect than I used to do. I have fears I never used to have – not of ghosts, but of omens and disastrous events; and I have an inexpressible weight on my mind which I would give the world to shake off, and I cannot do it.'

'Strange!' cried Shirley. 'I never feel so.' Mrs Pryor said nothing.

'Fine weather, pleasant days, pleasant scenes are powerless to give me pleasure,' continued Caroline. 'Calm evenings are not calm to me: moonlight, which I used to think mild, now only looks mournful. Is this weakness of mind, Mrs Pryor, or what is it? I cannot help it: I often struggle against it: I reason; but reason and effort make no difference.'

'You should take more exercise,' said Mrs Pryor.

'Exercise! I exercise sufficiently: I exercise till I am ready to drop.'

'My dear, you should go from home.'

'Mrs Pryor, I should like to go from home, but not on any purposeless excursion or visit. I wish to be a governess as you have been. It would oblige me greatly if you would speak to my uncle on the subject.'

'Nonsense!' broke in Shirley. 'What an idea! Be a governess! Better be a slave at once. Where is the necessity of it? Why should you dream of such a painful step?'

'My dear,' said Mrs Pryor, 'you are very young to be a governess, and not sufficiently robust: the duties a governess undertakes are often severe.'

'And I believe I want severe duties to occupy me.'

'Occupy you!' cried Shirley. 'When are you idle? I never saw a more industrious girl than you: you are always at work. Come,' she continued, – 'come and sit by my side, and take some tea to refresh you. You don't care much for my friendship, then, that you wish to leave me?'

'Indeed I do, Shirley; and I don't wish to leave you. I shall never find another friend so dear.'

At which words Miss Keeldar put her hand into Caroline's with an impulsively affectionate movement, which was well seconded by the expression of her face.

'If you think so, you had better make much of me,' she said, 'and not run away from me. I hate to part with those to whom I am become attached. Mrs Pryor there sometimes talks of leaving me, and says I might make a more advantageous connexion than herself. I should as soon think of exchanging an old-fashioned mother for something modish and stylish. As for you – why I began to flatter myself we were thoroughly friends; that you liked Shirley almost as well as Shirley likes you: and she does not stint her regard.'

'I *do* like Shirley: I like her more and more every day; but that does not make me strong or happy.'

'And would it make you strong or happy to go and live as a dependant amongst utter strangers? It would not; and the experiment must not be tried. I tell you it would fail: it is not in your nature to bear the desolate life governesses generally lead: you would fall ill: I won't hear of it.'

And Miss Keeldar paused, having uttered this prohibition very decidedly. Soon she recommenced, still looking somewhat 'courroucée:' –

'Why, it is my daily pleasure now to look out for the little cottage bonnet and the silk scarf glancing through the trees in the lane, and to know that my quiet, shrewd, thoughtful companion and monitress is coming back to me: that I shall have her sitting in the room to look at, to talk to, or to let alone, as she and I please. This may be a selfish sort of language – I know it is; but it is the language which naturally rises to my lips; therefore I utter it.'

'I would write to you, Shirley.'

'And what are letters? Only a sort of pis-aller. Drink some tea, Caroline: eat something – you eat nothing; laugh and be cheerful, and stay at home.'

Miss Helstone shook her head and sighed. She felt what difficulty she would have to persuade any one to assist or sanction her in making that change in her life which she believed desirable. Might she only follow her own judgment, she thought she should be able to find, perhaps a harsh, but an effectual cure for her sufferings. But this judgment, founded on circumstances she could fully explain to none, least of all to Shirley, seemed, in all eyes but her own, incomprehensible and fantastic, and was opposed accordingly.

There really was no present pecuniary need for her to leave a comfortable home and 'take a situation;' and there was every probability that her uncle might in some way permanently provide for her. So her friends thought, and, as far as their lights enabled them to see, they reasoned correctly: but of Caroline's strange sufferings, which she desired so eagerly to overcome or escape, they had no idea, – of her racked nights and dismal days, no suspicion. It was at once impossible and hopeless to explain: to wait and endure was her only plan. Many that want food and clothing have cheerier lives and brighter prospects than she had; many, harassed by poverty, are in a strait less afflictive.

'Now, is your mind quieted?' inquired Shirley. 'Will you consent to stay at home?'

'I shall not leave it against the approbation of my friends,' was the reply; 'but I think in time they will be obliged to think as I do.'

During this conversation Mrs Pryor looked far from easy. Her extreme habitual reserve would rarely permit her to talk freely, or to interrogate others closely. She could think a multitude of questions she never ventured to put; give advice in her mind which her tongue never delivered. Had she been alone with Caroline, she might possibly have said something to the point: Miss Keeldar's presence, accustomed as she was to it, sealed her lips. Now, as on a thousand other occasions, inexplicable nervous scruples kept her back from interfering. She merely showed her concern for Miss Helstone in an indirect way, by asking her if the fire made her too warm, placing a screen between her chair and the hearth, closing a window whence she imagined a draught proceeded, and often and restlessly glancing at her. Shirley resumed, –

'Having destroyed your plan,' she said, 'which I hope I have done, I shall construct a new one of my own. Every summer I make an excursion. This season I propose spending two months either at the Scotch lochs or the English lakes: that is, I shall go there, provided you consent to accompany me: if you refuse, I shall not stir a foot.'

'You are very good, Shirley.'

'I would be very good, if you would let me: I have every disposition to be good. It is my misfortune and habit, I know, to think of myself paramount to anybody else: but who is not like me in that respect? However, when Captain Keeldar is made comfortable, accommodated with all he wants, including a sensible genial comrade, it gives him a thorough pleasure to devote his spare efforts to making that comrade happy. And should we not be happy, Caroline, in the Highlands? We will go to the Highlands. We will, if you can bear a sea-voyage, go to the Isles, – the Hebrides, the Shetland, the Orkney Islands. Would you not like that? I see you would: Mrs Pryor, I call you to witness; her face is all sunshine at the bare mention of it.'

'I should like it much,' returned Caroline; to whom, indeed, the notion of such a tour was not only pleasant, but gloriously reviving. Shirley rubbed her hands.

'Come, I can bestow a benefit,' she exclaimed. 'I can do a good deed with my cash. My thousand a-year is not merely a matter of dirty bank-notes and jaundiced guineas (let me speak respectfully of both though, for I adore them); but, it may be, health to the drooping, strength to the weak, consolation to the sad. I was determined to make something of it better than a fine old house to live in, than satin gowns to wear; better than deference from acquaintance, and homage from the poor. Here is to begin. This summer – Caroline, Mrs Pryor, and I go out into the North Atlantic, beyond the Shetland – perhaps to the Faroe Isles. We will see seals in Suderoe, and, doubtless, mermaids in Stromoe. Caroline is laughing, Mrs Pryor: I made her laugh; *I* have done her good.'

'I shall like to go, Shirley,' again said Miss Helstone. 'I long to hear the sound of waves – ocean-waves, and to see them as I have imagined them in dreams, like tossing banks of green light, strewed with vanishing and reappearing wreaths of foam, whiter than lilies. I shall delight to pass the shores of those lone rock-islets where the sea-birds live and breed unmolested. We shall be on the track of the old Scandinavians – of the Norsemen: we shall almost see the shores of Norway. This is a very vague delight that I feel, communicated by your proposal, but it *is* a delight.'

'Will you think of Fitful-Head now, when you lie awake at night; of gulls shrieking round it, and waves tumbling in upon it, rather than of the graves under the Rectory back-kitchen?'

'I will try; and instead of musing about remnants of shrouds, and fragments of coffins, and human bones and mould, I will fancy seals lying in the sunshine on solitary shores, where neither fisherman nor hunter ever come: of rock-crevices full of pearly eggs bedded in seaweed; of unscared birds covering white sands in happy flocks.'

'And what will become of that inexpressible weight you said you had on your mind?'

'I will try to forget it in speculation on the sway of the whole Great Deep above a herd of whales rushing through the livid and liquid thunder down from the frozen zone: a hundred of them, perhaps, wallowing, flashing, rolling in the wake of a patriarch bull, huge enough to have been spawned before the Flood: such a creature as poor Smart had in his mind when he said, –

> "Strong against tides, the enormous whale
> Emerges as he goes." '

'I hope our bark will meet with no such shoal, or herd, as you term it, Caroline: (I suppose you fancy the sea-mammoths pasturing about the bases of the "everlasting hills," devouring strange provender in the vast valleys through and above which sea-billows roll). I should not like to be capsized by the patriarch bull.'

'I suppose you expect to see mermaids, Shirley?'

'One of them at any rate: I do not bargain for less: and she is to appear in some such fashion as this. I am to be walking by myself on deck, rather late of an August evening, watching and being watched by a full harvest-moon: something is to rise white on the surface of the sea, over which that moon mounts silent, and hangs glorious: the object glitters and sinks. It rises again. I think I hear it cry with an articulate voice: I call you up from the cabin: I show you an image, fair as alabaster, emerging from the dim wave. We both see the long hair, the lifted and foam-white arm, the oval mirror brilliant as a star. It glides nearer: a human face is plainly visible; a face in the style of yours, whose straight, pure (excuse the word, it is appropriate), – whose straight, pure lineaments, paleness does not disfigure. It looks at us, but not with your eyes. I see a preternatural lure in its wily glance: it beckons. Were we men, we should spring at the sign, the cold billow would be dared for the sake of the colder enchantress; being women, we stand safe, though not dreadless. She comprehends our unmoved gaze; she feels herself powerless;

anger crosses her front; she cannot charm, but she will appal us: she rises high, and glides, all revealed, on the dark wave-ridge. Temptress-terror! monstrous likeness of ourselves! Are you not glad, Caroline, when at last, and with a wild shriek, she dives?'

'But, Shirley, she is not like us: we are neither temptresses, nor terrors, nor monsters.'

'Some of our kind, it is said, are all three. There are men who ascribe to "woman," in general, such attributes.'

'My dears,' here interrupted Mrs Pryor, 'does it not strike you that your conversation for the last ten minutes has been rather fanciful?'

'But there is no harm in our fancies: is there ma'am?'

'We are aware that mermaids do not exist: why speak of them as if they did? How can you find interest in speaking of a nonentity?'

'I don't know,' said Shirley.

'My dear, I think there is an arrival. I heard a step in the lane, while you were talking; and is not that the garden-gate which creaks?'

Shirley stepped to the window.

'Yes, there is some one,' said she, turning quietly away; and, as she resumed her seat, a sensitive flush animated her face, while a trembling ray at once kindled and softened her eye. She raised her hand to her chin, cast her gaze down, and seemed to think as she waited.

The servant announced Mr Moore, and Shirley turned round when Mr Moore appeared at the door. His figure seemed very tall as he entered, and stood in contrast with the three ladies, none of whom could boast a stature much beyond the average. He was looking well, better than he had been known to look for the past twelve months: a sort of renewed youth glowed in his eye and colour, and an invigorated hope and settled purpose sustained his bearing: firmness his countenance still indicated, but not austerity: it looked as cheerful as it was earnest.

'I am just returned from Stilbro,' he said to Miss Keeldar, as he greeted her; 'and I thought I would call to impart to you the result of my mission.'

'You did right not to keep me in suspense,' she said; 'and your visit is well-timed. Sit down: we have not finished tea. Are you English enough to relish tea; or do you faithfully adhere to coffee?'

Moore accepted tea.

'I am learning to be a naturalized Englishman,' said he; 'my foreign habits are leaving me one by one.'

And now he paid his respects to Mrs Pryor, and paid them well, with a grave modesty that became his age, compared with hers. Then he looked at Caroline – not, however, for the first time – his glance had fallen upon her before: he bent towards her as she sat, gave her his hand, and asked her how she was. The light from the window did not fall upon Miss Helstone, her back was turned towards it: a quiet though rather low reply, a still demeanour, and the friendly protection of early twilight, kept out of view each traitorous symptom. None could affirm that she had trembled or blushed, that her heart had quaked, or her nerves thrilled: none could prove emotion: a greeting showing less effusion was never interchanged. Moore took the empty chair near her, opposite Miss Keeldar. He had placed himself well: his neighbour, screened by the very closeness of his vicinage from his scrutiny, and sheltered further by the dusk which deepened each moment, soon regained, not merely *seeming*, but *real* mastery of the feelings which had started into insurrection at the first announcement of his name.

He addressed his conversation to Miss Keeldar.

'I went to the barracks,' he said, 'and had an interview with Colonel Ryde: he approved my plans, and promised the aid I wanted: indeed, he offered a more numerous force than I require – half a dozen will suffice. I don't intend to be swamped by red-coats: they are needed for appearance rather than anything else; my main reliance is on my own civilians.'

'And on their captain,' interposed Shirley.

'What, Captain Keeldar?' inquired Moore, slightly smiling, and not lifting his eyes: the tone of raillery in which he said this was very respectful and suppressed.

'No,' returned Shirley, answering the smile; 'Captain Gérard Moore, who trusts much to the prowess of his own right arm, I believe.'

'Furnished with his counting-house ruler,' added Moore. Resuming his usual gravity, he went on: 'I received by this evening's post a note from the Home-Secretary in answer to mine: it appears they are uneasy at the state of matters here in the north; they especially condemn the supineness and pusillanimity of the mill-owners; they say, as I have always said, that inaction, under present circumstances, is criminal, and that cowardice is cruelty, since both can only encourage disorder, and lead finally to sanguinary outbreaks. There is the note: I brought it for your perusal; and there is a batch of newspapers, containing further accounts of proceedings in Nottingham, Manchester, and elsewhere.'

He produced letters and journals, and laid them before Miss Keeldar. While she perused them, he took his tea quietly; but, though his tongue was still, his observant faculties seemed by no means off duty. Mrs Pryor, sitting in the background, did not come within the range of his glance, but the two younger ladies had the full benefit thereof.

Miss Keeldar, placed directly opposite, was seen without effort: she was the object his eyes, when lifted, naturally met first; and, as what remained of daylight – the gilding of the west – was upon her, her shape rose in relief from the dark panelling behind. Shirley's clear cheek was tinted yet with the colour which had risen into it a few minutes since: the dark lashes of her eyes looking down as she read, the dusk yet delicate line of her eyebrows, the almost sable gloss of her curls, made her heightened complexion look fine as the bloom of a red wild-flower, by contrast. There was natural grace in her attitude, and there was artistic effect in the ample and shining folds of her silk dress – an attire simply fashioned, but almost splendid from the shifting brightness of its dye, warp and woof being of tints deep and changing as the hue on a pheasant's neck. A glancing bracelet on her arm produced the contrast of gold and ivory: there was something brilliant in the whole picture. It is to be supposed that Moore thought so, as his eye dwelt long on it, but he seldom permitted his feelings or his opinions to exhibit themselves in his face: his temperament boasted a certain amount of phlegm, and he preferred an undemonstrative, not ungentle, but serious aspect, to any other.

He could not, by looking straight before him, see Caroline, as she was close at his side; it was necessary, therefore, to manœuvre a little to get her well within the range of his observation: he leaned back in his chair, and looked down on her. In Miss Helstone, neither he nor any one else could discover brilliancy. Sitting in the shade, without flowers or ornaments, her attire the modest muslin dress, colourless but for its narrow stripe of pale azure, her complexion unflushed, unexcited, the very brownness of her hair and eyes invisible by this faint light, she was, compared with the heiress, as a graceful pencil-sketch compared with a vivid painting. Since Robert had seen her last, a great change had been wrought in her; whether he perceived it, might not be ascertained: he said nothing to that effect.

'How is Hortense?' asked Caroline, softly.

'Very well; but she complains of being unemployed: she misses you.'

'Tell her that I miss her, and that I write and read a portion of French every day.'

'She will ask if you sent your love: she is always particular on that point. You know she likes attention.'

'My best love – my very best; and say to her, that whenever she has time to write me a little note, I shall be glad to hear from her.'

'What if I forget? I am not the surest messenger of compliments.'

'No, don't forget, Robert: it is no compliment – it is in good earnest.'

'And must therefore be delivered punctually?'

'If you please.'

'Hortense will be ready to shed tears. She is tender-hearted on the subject of her pupil; yet she reproaches you sometimes for obeying your uncle's injunctions too literally. Affection, like love, will be unjust now and then.'

And Caroline made no answer to this observation; for indeed her heart was troubled, and to her eyes she would have raised her handkerchief, if she had dared. If she had dared, too, she would have declared how the very flowers in the garden of Hollow's cottage were dear to her; how the little parlour of that house was her earthly paradise; how she longed to return to it, as much almost as the First Woman, in her exile, must have longed to revisit Eden. Not daring, however, to say these things, she held her peace: she sat quiet at Robert's side, waiting for him to say something more. It was long since this proximity had been hers – long since his voice had addressed her: could she, with any show of probability, even of possibility, have imagined that the meeting gave him pleasure, to her it would have given deep bliss. Yet, even in doubt that it pleased – in dread that it might annoy him – she received the boon of the meeting as an imprisoned bird would the admission of sunshine to its cage: it was of no use arguing – contending against the sense of present happiness: to be near Robert was to be revived.

Miss Keeldar laid down the papers.

'And are you glad or sad for all these menacing tidings?' she inquired of her tenant.

'Not precisely either; but I certainly am instructed. I see that our only plan is to be firm. I see that efficient preparation and a resolute attitude are the best means of averting bloodshed.'

He then inquired if she had observed some particular

paragraph, to which she replied in the negative, and he rose to show it to her: he continued the conversation standing before her. From the tenor of what he said, it appeared evident that they both apprehended disturbances in the neighbourhood of Briarfield, though in what form they expected them to break out was not specified. Neither Caroline nor Mrs Pryor asked questions: the subject did not appear to be regarded as one ripe for free discussion; therefore the lady and her tenant were suffered to keep details to themselves, unimportuned by the curiosity of their listeners.

Miss Keeldar, in speaking to Mr Moore, took a tone at once animated and dignified, confidential and self-respecting. When, however, the candles were brought in, and the fire was stirred up, and the fulness of light thus produced rendered the expression of her countenance legible, you could see that she was all interest, life, and earnestness: there was nothing coquettish in her demeanour: whatever she felt for Moore, she felt it seriously. And serious, too, were his feelings, and settled were his views, apparently; for he made no petty effort to attract, dazzle, or impress. He contrived, notwithstanding, to command a little; because the deeper voice, however mildly modulated, the somewhat harder mind, now and then, though involuntarily and unintentionally, bore down by some peremptory phrase or tone the mellow accents and susceptible, if high, nature of Shirley. Miss Keeldar looked happy in conversing with him, and her joy seemed twofold, – a joy of the past and present, of memory and of hope.

What I have just said are Caroline's ideas of the pair: she felt what has just been described. In thus feeling, she tried not to suffer; but suffered sharply, nevertheless. She suffered, indeed, miserably: a few minutes before, her famished heart had tasted a drop and crumb of nourishment that, if freely given, would have brought back abundance of life where life was failing; but the generous feast was snatched from her, spread before another, and she remained but a bystander at the banquet.

The clock struck nine: it was Caroline's time for going home: she gathered up her work, put the embroidery, the scissors, the thimble into her bag: she bade Mrs Pryor a quiet good-night, receiving from that lady a warmer pressure of the hand than usual: she stepped up to Miss Keeldar.

'Good-night, Shirley!'

Shirley started up. 'What! – so soon? Are you going already?'

'It is past nine.'

'I never heard the clock. You will come again to-morrow; and you will be happy to-night, will you not? Remember our plans.'

'Yes,' said Caroline; 'I have not forgotten.'

Her mind misgave her that neither those plans nor any other could permanently restore her mental tranquillity. She turned to Robert, who stood close behind her: as he looked up, the light of the candles on the mantelpiece fell full on her face: all its paleness, all its change, all its forlorn meaning were clearly revealed. Robert had good eyes, and might have seen it, if he would: whether he did see it, nothing indicated.

'Good-night!' she said, shaking like a leaf, offering her thin hand hastily, anxious to part from him quickly.

'You are going home?' he asked, not touching her hand.

'Yes.'

'Is Fanny coming for you?'

'Yes.'

'I may as well accompany you a step of the way: not up to the Rectory, though, lest my old friend, Helstone, should shoot me from the window.'

He laughed and took his hat. Caroline spoke of unnecessary trouble: he told her to put on her bonnet and shawl. She was quickly ready, and they were soon both in the open air. Moore drew her hand under his arm, just in his old manner, – that manner which she ever felt to be so kind.

'You may run on, Fanny,' he said to the housemaid; 'we shall overtake you:' and when the girl had got a little in advance, he enclosed Caroline's hand in his, and said he was glad to find she was a familiar guest at Fieldhead: he hoped her intimacy with Miss Keeldar would continue; such society would be both pleasant and improving.

Caroline replied that she liked Shirley.

'And there is no doubt the liking is mutual,' said Moore: 'if she professes friendship, be certain she is sincere: she cannot feign; she scorns hypocrisy. And, Caroline, are we never to see you at Hollow's cottage again?'

'I suppose not, unless my uncle should change his mind.'

'Are you much alone now?'

'Yes; a good deal. I have little pleasure in any society but Miss Keeldar's.'

'Have you been quite well lately?'

'Quite.'

'You must take care of yourself. Be sure not to neglect exercise. Do you know I fancied you somewhat altered; – a little fallen away, and pale. Is your uncle kind to you?'

'Yes; he is just as he always is.'

'Not too tender, that is to say; not too protective and attentive. And what ails you, then? – tell me, Lina.'

'Nothing, Robert.' but her voice faltered.

'That is to say, nothing that you will tell me: I am not to be taken into confidence. Separation is then quite to estrange us, is it?'

'I do not know: sometimes I almost fear it is.'

'But it ought not to have that effect. "Should auld acquaintance be forgot, and days o' lang syne?"'

'Robert, I don't forget.'

'It is two months, I should think, Caroline, since you were at the cottage.'

'Since I was *within* it – yes.'

'Have you ever passed that way in your walk?'

'I have come to the top of the fields sometimes of an evening, and looked down. Once I saw Hortense in the garden watering her flowers, and I know at what time you light your lamp in the counting-house: I have waited for it to shine out now and then; and I have seen you bend between it and the window: I knew it was you – I could almost trace the outline of your form.'

'I wonder I never encountered you: I occasionally walk to the top of the Hollow's fields after sunset.'

'I know you do: I had almost spoken to you one night, you passed so near me.'

'Did I? I passed near you, and did not see you! Was I alone?'

'I saw you twice, and neither time were you alone.'

'Who was my companion? Probably nothing but Joe Scott, or my own shadow by moonlight.'

'No; neither Joe Scott nor your shadow, Robert. The first time you were with Mr Yorke; and the second time what you call your shadow was a shape with a white forehead and dark curls, and a sparkling necklace round its neck; but I only just got a glimpse of you and that fairy shadow: I did not wait to hear you converse.'

'It appears you walk invisible. I noticed a ring on your hand this evening; can it be the ring of Gyges? Henceforth, when sitting in the counting-house by myself, perhaps at dead of night, I shall permit myself to imagine that Caroline may be leaning over my shoulder reading with me from the same book, or sitting at my side engaged in her own particular task, and now and then raising her unseen eyes to my face to read there my thoughts.'

'You need fear no such infliction: I do not come near you: I only stand afar off, watching what may become of you.'

'When I walk out along the hedgerows in the evening after the mill is shut – or at night, when I take the watchman's place – I shall fancy the flutter of every little bird over its nest, the rustle of every leaf, a movement made by you; tree-shadows will take your shape; in the white sprays of hawthorn, I shall imagine glimpses of you. Lina, you will haunt me.'

'I will never be where you would not wish me to be, nor see nor hear what you would wish unseen and unheard.'

'I shall see you in my very mill in broad daylight: indeed, I have seen you there once. But a week ago, I was standing at the top of one of my long rooms, girls were working at the other end, and amongst half a dozen of them, moving to and fro, I seemed to see a figure resembling yours. It was some effect of doubtful light or shade, or of dazzling sunbeam. I walked up to this group; what I sought had glided away: I found myself between two buxom lasses in pinafores.'

'I shall not follow you into your mill, Robert, unless you call me there.'

'Nor is that the only occasion on which imagination has played me a trick. One night, when I came home late from market, I walked into the cottage parlour thinking to find Hortense; but instead of her, I thought I found you. There was no candle in the room: my sister had taken the light up-stairs with her; the window-blind was not drawn, and broad moon-beams poured through the panes: there you were, Lina, at the casement, shrinking a little to one side in an attitude not unusual with you. You were dressed in white, as I have seen you dressed at an evening party. For half a second, your fresh, living face seemed turned towards me, looking at me; for half a second, my idea was to go and take your hand, to chide you for your long absence, and welcome your present visit. Two steps forward broke the spell: the drapery of the dress changed outline; the tints of the complexion dissolved, and were formless: positively, as I reached the spot, there was nothing left but the sweep of a white muslin curtain, and a balsam plant in a flower-plot, covered with a flush of bloom – "sic transit," et cetera.'

'It was not my wraith, then? I almost thought it was.'

'No; only gauze, crockery, and pink blossom; a sample of earthly illusions.'

'I wonder you have time for such illusions, occupied as your mind must be.'

'So do I. But I find in myself, Lina, two natures; one for the world and business, and one for home and leisure. Gérard Moore is a hard dog, brought up to mill and market: the person you call your cousin Robert is sometimes a dreamer, who lives elsewhere than in Cloth-hall and counting-house.'

'Your two natures agree with you: I think you are looking in good spirits and health: you have quite lost that harassed air which it often pained one to see in your face a few months ago.'

'Do you observe that? Certainly, I am disentangled of some difficulties: I have got clear of some shoals, and have more sea-room.'

'And, with a fair wind, you may now hope to make a prosperous voyage?'

'I may *hope* it – yes – but hope is deceptive: there is no controlling wind or wave: gusts and swells perpetually trouble the mariner's course; he dare not dismiss from his mind the expectation of tempest.'

'But you are ready for a breeze – you are a good seaman – an able commander: you are a skilful pilot, Robert; you will weather the storm.'

'My kinswoman always thinks the best of me, but I will take her words for a propitious omen: I will consider that in meeting her to-night, I have met with one of those birds whose appearance is to the sailor the harbinger of good-luck.'

'A poor harbinger of good-luck is she who can do nothing – who has no power. I feel my incapacity: it is of no use saying I have the will to serve you, when I cannot prove it; yet I have that will. I wish you success; I wish you high fortune and true happiness.'

'When did you ever wish me anything else? What is Fanny waiting for – I told her to walk on? Oh! we have reached the churchyard; then, we are to part here, I suppose: we might have sat a few minutes in the church-porch, if the girl had not been with us. It is so fine a night, so summer-mild and still, I have no particular wish to return yet to the Hollow.'

'But we cannot sit in the porch now, Robert.'

Caroline said this because Moore was turning her round towards it.

'Perhaps not, but tell Fanny to go in; say we are coming: a few minutes will make no difference.'

The church-clock struck ten.

'My uncle will be coming out to take his usual sentinel round, and he always surveys the church and churchyard.'

'And if he does? If it were not for Fanny, who knows we are here, I should find pleasure in dodging and eluding him. We could be under the east window when he is at the porch; as he came round to the north side, we could wheel off to the south; we might at a pinch hide behind some of the monuments: that tall erection of the Wynnes would screen us completely.'

'Robert, what good spirits you have! Go – go!' added Caroline hastily, 'I hear the front door –'

'I don't want to go; on the contrary, I want to stay.'

'You know my uncle will be terribly angry: he forbade me to see you because you are a Jacobin.'

'A queer Jacobin!'

'Go, Robert, he is coming; I hear him cough.'

'Diable! It is strange – what a pertinacious wish I feel to stay!'

'You remember what he did to Fanny's –' began Caroline, and stopped abruptly short. Sweetheart was the word that ought to have followed, but she could not utter it; it seemed calculated to suggest ideas she had no intention to suggest; ideas delusive and disturbing. Moore was less scrupulous; 'Fanny's sweetheart?' he said at once. 'He gave him a shower-bath under the pump – did he not? He'd do as much for me, I daresay, with pleasure. I should like to provoke the old Turk – not however against *you*: but he would make a distinction between a cousin and a lover, would he not?'

'Oh! he would not think of you in that way, of course not; his quarrel with you is entirely political; yet I should not like the breach to be widened, and he is so testy. Here he is at the garden-gate – for your own sake and mine, Robert, go!'

The beseeching words were aided by a beseeching gesture and a more beseeching look. Moore covered her clasped hands an instant with his, answered her upward by a downward gaze, said 'Good-night!' and went.

Caroline was in a moment at the kitchen-door behind Fanny; the shadow of the shovel-hat at that very instant fell on a moon-lit tomb; the Rector emerged, erect as a cane, from his garden, and proceeded in slow march, his hands behind him, down the cemetery. Moore was almost caught: he had to 'dodge' after all, to coast round the church, and finally to bend his tall form behind the Wynnes' ambitious monument. There he was forced to hide full ten minutes, kneeling with one knee on the turf, his hat off, his curls bare to the dew, his dark eye shining, and his lips parted with inward laughter at his position; for the Rector meantime stood coolly star-gazing, and taking snuff within three feet of him.

It happened, however, that Mr Helstone had no suspicion whatever on his mind; for being usually but vaguely informed of his niece's movements, not thinking it worth while to follow them closely, he was not aware that she had been out at all that day, and imagined her then occupied with book or work in her chamber: where, indeed, she was by this time; though not absorbed in the tranquil employment he ascribed to her, but standing at her window with fast-throbbing heart, peeping anxiously from behind the blind, watching for her uncle to re-enter and her cousin to escape; and at last she was gratified: she heard Mr Helstone come in; she saw Robert stride the tombs and vault the wall; she then went down to prayers. When she returned to her chamber, it was to meet the memory of Robert. Slumber's visitation was long averted: long she sat at her lattice, long gazed down on the old garden and older church, on the tombs laid out all grey and calm, and clear in moonlight. She followed the steps of the night, on its pathway of stars, far into the 'wee sma' hours ayont the twal':' she was with Moore, in spirit, the whole time: she was at his side: she heard his voice:

she gave her hand into his hand; it rested warm in his fingers. When the church-clock struck, when any other sound stirred, when a little mouse familiar to her chamber, an intruder for which she would never permit Fanny to lay a trap, came rattling amongst the links of her locket-chain, her one ring, and another trinket or two, on the toilette-table, to nibble a bit of biscuit laid ready for it, she looked up, recalled momentarily to the real. Then she said half aloud, as if deprecating the accusation of some unseen and unheard monitor, –

'I am not cherishing love-dreams: I am only thinking because I cannot sleep: of course, I know he will marry Shirley.'

With returning silence, with the lull of the chime, and the retreat of her small untamed and unknown protégé, she still resumed the dream, nestling to the vision's side, – listening to, conversing with it. It paled at last: as dawn approached, the setting stars and breaking day dimmed the creation of Fancy: the wakened song of birds hushed her whispers. The tale full of fire, quick with interest, borne away by the morning wind, became a vague murmur. The shape that, seen in a moonbeam, lived, had a pulse, had movement, wore health's glow and youth's freshness, turned cold and ghostly grey, confronted with the red of sunrise. It wasted. She was left solitary at last: she crept to her couch, chill and dejected.

CHAPTER XIV

SHIRLEY SEEKS TO BE SAVED BY WORKS

'OF COURSE, I know he will marry Shirley,' were her first words when she rose in the morning. 'And he ought to marry her: she can help him,' she added firmly. 'But I shall be forgotten when they are married,' was the cruel succeeding thought. 'Oh! I shall be wholly forgotten! And what – *what* shall I do when Robert is taken quite from me? Where shall I turn? *My* Robert! I wish I could justly call him mine: but I am poverty and incapacity; Shirley is wealth and power: and she is beauty too, and love – I cannot deny it. This is no sordid suit: she loves him – not with inferior feelings: she loves, or will love, as he must feel proud to be loved. Not a valid objection can be made. Let them be married then: but afterwards I shall be nothing to him. As for being his sister, and all that stuff, I despise it. I will either be all or nothing to a man like Robert: no feeble shuffling, or false cant, is endurable. Once let that pair be united, and I will certainly leave them. As for lingering about, playing the hypocrite, and pretending to calm sentiments of friendship, when my soul will be wrung with other feelings, I shall not descend to such degradation. As little could I fill the place of their mutual friend as that of their deadly foe: as little could I stand between them as trample over them. Robert is a first-rate man – in my eyes: I *have* loved, *do* love, and *must* love him. I would be his wife, if I could; as I cannot, I must go where I shall never see him. There is but one alternative – to cleave to him as if I were a part of him, or to be sundered from him wide as the two poles of a sphere. Sunder me then, Providence. Part us speedily.'

Some such aspirations as these were again working in her mind late in the afternoon, when the apparition of one of the personages haunting her thoughts passed the parlour window. Miss Keeldar sauntered slowly by: her gait, her countenance wearing that mixture of wistfulness and carelessness which, when quiescent, was the wonted cast of her look, and character of her bearing. When animated, the carelessness quite vanished, the wistfulness became blent with a genial gaiety, seasoning the laugh, the smile, the glance, with an unique flavour of sentiment, so that mirth from her never resembled 'the crackling of thorns under a pot.'

'What do you mean by not coming to see me this afternoon, as you promised?' was her address to Caroline as she entered the room.

'I was not in the humour,' replied Miss Helstone, very truly.

Shirley had already fixed on her a penetrating eye.

'No,' she said; 'I see you are not in the humour for loving me: you are in one of your sunless, inclement moods, when one feels a fellow-creature's presence is not welcome to you. You have such moods: are you aware of it?'

'Do you mean to stay long, Shirley?'

'Yes: I am come to have my tea, and must have it before I go. I shall take the liberty then of removing my bonnet, without being asked.'

And this she did, and then stood on the rug with her hands behind her.

'A pretty expression you have in your countenance,' she went on, still gazing keenly, though not inimically, rather indeed pityingly at Caroline. 'Wonderfully self-supported you look, you solitude-seeking, wounded deer. Are you afraid Shirley will worry you, if she discovers that you are hurt, and that you bleed?'

'I never do fear Shirley.'

'But sometimes you dislike her: often you avoid her. Shirley can feel when she is slighted and shunned. If you had not walked home in the company you did last night, you would have been a different girl to-day. What time did you reach the Rectory?'

'By ten.'

'Humph! You took three-quarters of an hour to walk a mile. Was it you, or Moore, who lingered so?'

'Shirley, you talk nonsense.'

'*He* talked nonsense – that I doubt not; or he looked it, which is a thousand times worse: I see the reflection of his eyes on your forehead at this moment. I feel disposed to call him out, if I could only get a trustworthy second: I feel desperately irritated: I felt so last night, and have felt it all day.

'You don't ask me why,' she proceeded, after a pause, 'you little, silent, over-modest thing; and you don't deserve that I should pour out my secrets into your lap without an invitation. Upon my word, I could have found it in my heart to have dogged Moore yesterday evening with dire intent: I have pistols, and can use them.'

'Stuff, Shirley! Which would you have shot – me or Robert?'

'Neither, perhaps – perhaps myself – more likely a bat or a tree-bough. He is a puppy – your cousin: a quiet, serious, sensible, judicious, ambitious puppy. I see him standing before me, talking his half-stern, half-gentle talk, bearing me down (as I am very conscious he does) with his fixity of purpose, &c.; and then – I have no patience with him!'

Miss Keeldar started off on a rapid walk through the room, repeating energetically that she had no patience with men in general, and with her tenant in particular.

'You are mistaken,' urged Caroline, in some anxiety: 'Robert is no puppy or male flirt; I can vouch for that.'

'*You* vouch for it! Do you think I'll take your word on the subject? There is no one's testimony I would not credit sooner than yours. To advance Moore's fortune, you would cut off your right hand.'

'But not tell lies; and if I speak the truth, I must assure you that he was just civil to me last night – that was all.'

'I never asked what he was – I can guess: I saw him from the window take your hand in his long fingers, just as he went out at my gate.'

'That is nothing. I am not a stranger, you know: I am an old acquaintance, and his cousin.'

'I feel indignant; and that is the long and short of the matter,' responded Miss Keeldar. 'All my comfort,' she added presently, 'is broken up by his manœuvres. He keeps intruding between you and me: without him we should be good friends; but that six feet of puppyhood makes a perpetually recurring eclipse of our friendship. Again and again he crosses and obscures the disk I want always to see clear: ever and anon he renders me to you a mere bore and nuisance.'

'No, Shirley; no.'

'He does. You did not want my society this afternoon, and I feel it hard: you are naturally somewhat reserved, but I am a social personage, who cannot live alone. If we were but left unmolested, I have that regard for you that I could bear you in my presence for ever, and not for the fraction of a second do I ever wish to be rid of you. You cannot say as much respecting me.'

'Shirley, I can say anything you wish: Shirley, I like you.'

'You will wish me at Jericho to-morrow, Lina.'

'I shall not. I am every day growing more accustomed to – fonder of you. You know I am too English to get up a vehement friendship all at once; but you are so much better than common – you are so different to everyday young ladies – I esteem you – I value you: you are never a burden to me – never. Do you believe what I say?'

'Partly,' replied Miss Keeldar, smiling rather incredulously; 'but you are a peculiar personage: quiet as you look, there is both a force and a depth somewhere within, not easily reached or appreciated: then you certainly are not happy.'

'And unhappy people are rarely good – is that what you mean?'

'Not at all: I mean rather that unhappy people are often preoccupied, and not in the mood for discoursing with companions of my nature. Moreover, there is a sort of unhappiness which not only depresses, but corrodes – and that, I fear, is your portion. Will pity do you any good, Lina? If it will, take some from Shirley: she offers largely, and warrants the article genuine.'

'Shirley, I never had a sister – you never had a sister; but it flashes on me at this moment how sisters feel towards each other. Affection twined with their life, which no shocks of feeling can uproot, which little quarrels only trample an instant that it may spring more freshly when the pressure is removed; affection that no passion can ultimately outrival, with which even love itself cannot do more than compete in force and truth. Love hurts us so, Shirley: it is so tormenting, so racking, and it burns away our strength with its flame; in affection is no pain and no fire, only sustenance and balm. I am supported and soothed when you – that is, *you only* – are near, Shirley. Do you believe me now?'

'I am always easy of belief when the creed pleases me. We really are friends then, Lina, in spite of the black eclipse?'

'We really are,' returned the other, drawing Shirley towards her, and making her sit down, 'chance what may.'

'Come, then, we will talk of something else than the Troubler.' But at this moment the Rector came in, and the 'something else' of which Miss Keeldar was about to talk was not again alluded to till the moment of her departure; she then delayed a few minutes in the passage to say –

'Caroline, I wish to tell you that I have a great weight on my mind: my conscience is quite uneasy, as if I had committed, or was going to commit, a crime. It is not my *private* conscience, you must understand, but my landed-proprietor and lord-of-the-manor conscience. I have got into the clutch of an eagle with iron talons. I have fallen under a stern influence, which I scarcely approve, but cannot resist. Something will be done erelong, I fear, which it by no means pleases me to think of. To ease my mind, and to prevent harm as far as I can, I mean to enter on a series of good works. Don't be surprised, therefore, if you see me all at once turn outrageously charitable. I have no idea how to begin, but you must give me some advice: we will talk more on the subject to-morrow; and just ask that excellent person, Miss Ainley, to step up to Fieldhead: I have some notion of putting myself under her tuition – won't she have a precious pupil? Drop a hint to her, Lina, that, though a well-meaning, I am rather a neglected character, and then she will feel less scandalized at my ignorance about clothing societies, and such things.'

On the morrow, Caroline found Shirley sitting gravely at her desk, with an account-book, a bundle of bank-notes, and a well-filled purse before her. She was looking mighty serious, but a little puzzled. She said she had been 'casting an eye' over the weekly expenditure in housekeeping at the Hall, trying to find out where she could retrench; that she had also just given audience to Mrs Gill, the cook, and had sent that person away with a notion that her (Shirley's) brain was certainly crazed. 'I have lectured her on the duty of being careful,' said she, 'in a way quite new to her. So eloquent was I on the text of economy, that I surprised myself; for, you see, it is altogether a fresh idea: I never thought, much less spoke, on the subject till lately. But it is all theory; for when I came to the practical part I could retrench nothing. I had not firmness to take off a single pound of butter, or to prosecute to any clear result an inquest into the destiny of either dripping, lard, bread, cold meat, or other kitchen perquisite whatever. I know we never get up illuminations at Fieldhead, but I could not ask the meaning of sundry quite unaccountable pounds of candles: we do not wash for the parish, yet I viewed in silence items of soap and bleaching powder calculated to satisfy the solicitude of the most anxious inquirer after our position in reference to those articles: carnivorous I am not, nor is Mrs Pryor, nor is Mrs Gill herself, yet

I only hemmed and opened my eyes a little wide when I saw butchers' bills whose figure seemed to prove that fact – falsehood, I mean. Caroline, you may laugh at me, but you can't change me. I am a poltroon on certain points – I feel it. There is a base alloy of moral cowardice in my composition. I blushed and hung my head before Mrs Gill, when she ought to have been faltering confessions to me. I found it impossible to get up the spirit even to hint, much less to prove, to her that she was a cheat. I have no calm dignity – no true courage about me.'

'Shirley, what fit of self-injustice is this? My uncle, who is not given to speak well of women, says there are not ten thousand men in England as genuinely fearless as you.'

'I am fearless, physically: I am never nervous about danger. I was not startled from self-possession when Mr Wynne's great red bull rose with a bellow before my face, as I was crossing the cowslip-lea alone, stooped his begrimed, sullen head, and made a run at me; but I was afraid of seeing Mrs Gill brought to shame and confusion of face. You have twice – ten times my strength of mind on certain subjects, Caroline: you, whom no persuasions can induce to pass a bull, however quiet he looks, would have firmly shown my housekeeper she had done wrong; then you would have gently and wisely admonished her; and at last, I daresay, provided she had seemed penitent, you would have very sweetly forgiven her. Of this conduct I am incapable. However, in spite of exaggerated imposition, I still find we live within our means: I have money in hand, and I really must do some good with it. The Briarfield poor are badly off: they must be helped. What ought I to do, think you, Lina? Had I not better distribute the cash at once?'

'No, indeed, Shirley; you will not manage properly. I have often noticed that your only notion of charity is to give shillings and half-crowns in a careless, freehanded sort of way, which is liable to continual abuse. You must have a prime minister, or you will get yourself into a series of scrapes. You suggested Miss Ainley yourself: to Miss Ainley I will apply; and, meantime, promise to keep quiet, and not begin throwing away your money. What a great deal you have, Shirley! – you must feel very rich with all that?'

'Yes; I feel of consequence. It is not an immense sum, but I feel responsible for its disposal; and really this responsibility weighs on my mind more heavily than I could have expected. They say that there are some families almost starving to death in Briarfield: some of my own cottagers are in wretched circumstances: I must and will help them.'

'Some people say we shouldn't give alms to the poor. Shirley.'

'They are great fools for their pains. For those who are not hungry, it is easy to palaver about the degradation of charity, and so on; but they forget the brevity of life, as well as its bitterness. We have none of us long to live: let us help each other through seasons of want and woe, as well as we can, without heeding in the least the scruples of vain philosophy.'

'But you do help others, Shirley: you give a great deal as it is.'

'Not enough: I must give more, or, I tell you, my brother's blood will some day be crying to Heaven against me. For, after all, if political incendiaries come here to kindle conflagration in the neighbourhood, and my property is attacked, I shall defend it like a tigress – I know I shall. Let me listen to Mercy as long as she is near me: her voice once drowned by the shout of ruffian defiance, and I shall be full of impulses to resist and quell. If once the poor gather and rise in the form of the snob, I shall turn against them as an aristocrat: if they bully me, I must defy; if they attack, I must resist, – and I will.'

'You talk like Robert.'

'I feel like Robert, only more fierily. Let them meddle with Robert, or Robert's mill, or Robert's interests, and I shall hate them. At present I am no patrician, nor do I regard the poor round me as plebeians; but if once they violently wrong me or mine, and then presume to dictate to us, I shall quite forget pity for their wretchedness and respect for their poverty, in scorn of their ignorance and wrath at their insolence.'

'Shirley – how your eyes flash!'

'Because my soul burns. Would you, any more than me, let Robert be borne down by numbers?'

'If I had your power to aid Robert, I would use it as you mean to use it. If I could be such a friend to him as you can be, I would stand by him as you mean to stand by him – till death.'

'And now, Lina, though your eyes don't flash, they glow. You drop your lids; but I saw a kindled spark. However, it is not yet come to fighting. What I want to do is to *prevent* mischief. I cannot forget, either day or night, that these imbittered feelings of the poor against the rich have been generated in suffering: they would neither hate nor envy us if they did not deem us so much happier than themselves. To allay this suffering, and thereby lessen this hate, let me, out of my abundance, give abundantly; and that the donation may go farther, let it be made wisely. To that intent, we must introduce some clear, calm, practical sense into our councils: so go, and fetch Miss Ainley.'

Without another word, Caroline put on her bonnet and departed. It may, perhaps, appear strange that neither she nor Shirley thought of consulting Mrs Pryor on their scheme; but they were wise in abstaining. To have consulted her – and this they knew by instinct – would only have been to involve her in painful embarrassment. She was far better informed, better read, a deeper thinker than Miss Ainley, but of administrative energy, of executive activity, she had none. She would subscribe her own modest mite to a charitable object willingly, – secret almsgiving suited her; but in public plans, on a large scale, she could take no part: as to originating them, that was out of the question. This Shirley knew, and therefore she did not trouble Mrs Pryor by unavailing conferences, which could only remind her of her own deficiencies, and do no good.

It was a bright day for Miss Ainley, when she was summoned to Fieldhead to deliberate on projects so congenial to her; when she was seated with all honour and deference at a table with paper, pen, ink and – what was best of all – cash before her, and requested to draw up a regular plan for administering relief to the destitute poor of Briarfield. She, who knew them all, had studied their wants, had again and again felt in what way they might best be succoured, could the means of succour only be found, was fully competent to the undertaking, and a meek exultation gladdened her kind heart as she felt herself able to answer clearly and promptly the eager questions put by the two young girls; as she showed them in her answers how much and what serviceable knowledge she had acquired of the condition of her fellow-creatures round her.

Shirley placed at her disposal £300, and at sight of the money Miss Ainley's eyes filled with joyful tears; for she already saw the hungry fed, the naked clothed, the sick comforted thereby. She quickly drew up a simple, sensible plan for its expenditure; and she assured them brighter times would now come round, for she doubted not the lady of Fieldhead's example would be followed by others: she should try to get additional sub-scriptions, and to form a fund; but first she must consult the clergy: yes, on that point, she was peremptory: Mr Helstone, Dr Boultby, Mr Hall, *must* be consulted – (for not only must Briarfield be relieved, but Whinbury and Nunnely) – it would, she averred, be presumption in her to take a single step un-authorized by them.

The clergy were sacred beings in Miss Ainley's eyes: no matter what might be the insignificance of the individual, his station made him holy. The very curates – who, in their trivial arro-gance, were hardly worthy to tie her patten-strings, or carry her cotton umbrella, or check woollen-shawl – she, in her pure, sincere enthusiasm, looked upon as sucking saints. No matter how clearly their little vices and enormous absurdities were pointed out to her, she could not see them: she was blind to ecclesiastical defects: the white surplice covered a multitude of sins.

Shirley, knowing this harmless infatuation on the part of her recently chosen prime minister, stipulated expressly that the curates were to have no voice in the disposal of the money; that their meddling fingers were not to be inserted into the pie. The rectors, of course, must be paramount, and they might be trusted: they had some experience, some sagacity, and Mr Hall, at least, had sympathy and loving-kindness for his fellow-men; but as for the youth under them, they must be set aside, kept down, and taught that subordination and silence best became their years and capacity.

It was with some horror Miss Ainley heard this language: Caroline, however, interposing with a mild word or two in praise of Mr Sweeting, calmed her again. Sweeting was, indeed, her own favourite: she endeavoured to respect Messrs Malone and Donne; but the slices of spunge-cake, and glasses of cowslip or primrose wine, she had at different times administered to Sweeting, when he came to see her in her little cottage, were ever offered with sentiments of truly motherly regard. The same innocuous collation she had once presented to Malone; but that personage evinced such open scorn of the offering, she had never ventured to renew it. To Donne she always served the treat, and was happy to see his approbation of it proved beyond a doubt, by the fact of his usually eating two pieces of cake, and putting a third in his pocket.

Indefatigable in her exertions where good was to be done, Miss Ainley would immediately have set out on a walk often miles round to the three rectors, in order to show her plan, and humbly solicit their approval: but Miss Keeldar interdicted this, and proposed as an amendment, to collect the clergy in a small select reunion that evening at Fieldhead. Miss Ainley was to meet them, and the plan was to be discussed in full privy council.

Shirley managed to get the senior priesthood together accordingly; and before the old maid's arrival she had, further, talked all the gentlemen into the most charming mood imaginable.

She herself had taken in hand Dr Boultby and Mr Helstone. The first was a stubborn old Welshman, hot, opinionated, and obstinate, but withal a man who did a great deal of good, though not without making some noise about it: the latter, we know. She had rather a friendly feeling for both; especially for old Helstone; and it cost her no trouble to be quite delightful to them. She took them round the garden; she gathered them flowers; she was like a kind daughter to them. Mr Hall she left to Caroline – or rather, it was to Caroline's care Mr Hall consigned himself.

He generally sought Caroline in every party where she and he happened to be. He was not in general a lady's man, though all ladies liked him: something of a book-worm he was, near-sighted, spectacled, now and then abstracted. To old ladies he was kind as a son. To men of every occupation and grade he was acceptable: the truth, simplicity, frankness of his manners, the nobleness of his integrity, the reality and elevation of his piety, won him friends in every grade: his poor clerk and sexton delighted in him; the noble patron of his living esteemed him highly. It was only with young, handsome, fashionable, and stylish ladies he felt a little shy: being himself a plain man – plain in aspect, plain in manners, plain in speech – he seemed to fear their dash, elegance, and airs. But Miss Helstone had neither dash nor airs, and her native elegance was of a very quiet order – quiet as the beauty of a ground-loving hedge-flower. He was a fluent, cheerful, agreeable talker. Caroline could talk, too, in a *tête-à-tête*: she liked Mr Hall to come and take the seat next her in a party, and thus secure her from Peter Augustus Malone, Joseph Donne, or John Sykes; and Mr Hall never failed to avail himself of this privilege when he possibly could. Such preference shown by a single gentleman to a single lady would certainly, in ordinary cases, have set in motion the tongues of the gossips; but Cyril Hall was forty-five years old, slightly bald, and slightly grey, and nobody ever said or thought he was likely to be married to Miss Helstone. Nor did he think so himself: he was wedded already to his books and his parish: his kind sister Margaret, spectacled and learned like himself, made him happy in his single state; he considered it too late to change. Besides, he had known Caroline as a pretty little girl: she had sat on his knee many a time; he had bought her toys and given her books; he felt that her friendship for him was mixed with a sort of filial respect; he could not have brought himself to attempt to give another colour to her sentiments, and his serene mind could glass a fair image without feeling its depths troubled by the reflection.

When Miss Ainley arrived, she was made kindly welcome by every one: Mrs Pryor and Margaret Hall made room for her on the sofa between them; and when the three were seated, they formed a trio which the gay and thoughtless would have scorned, indeed, as quite worthless and unattractive – a middle-aged widow and two plain spectacled old maids – yet which had its own quiet value, as many a suffering and friendless human being knew.

Shirley opened the business and showed the plan.

'I know the hand which drew up that,' said Mr Hall, glancing at Miss Ainley, and smiling benignantly: his approbation was won at once. Boultby heard and deliberated with bent brow and protruded under lip: his consent he considered too weighty to be given in a hurry. Helstone glanced sharply round with an alert, suspicious expression, as if he apprehended that female craft was at work, and that something in petticoats was some-how trying underhand to acquire too much influence, and make itself of too much importance. Shirley caught and compre-hended the expression: –

'This scheme is nothing,' said she, carelessly; 'it is only an outline – a mere suggestion; you, gentlemen, are requested to draw up rules of your own.'

And she directly fetched her writing-case, smiling queerly to herself as she bent over the table where it stood: she produced a sheet of paper, a new pen, drew an arm-chair to the table, and presenting her hand to old Helstone, begged permission to instal him in it. For a minute he was a little stiff, and stood wrinkling his copper-coloured forehead strangely. At last he muttered: –

'Well – you are neither my wife nor my daughter, so I'll be led for once; but mind – I know I *am* led: your little female manœuvres don't blind me.'

'Oh!' said Shirley, dipping the pen in the ink, and putting it into his hand, 'you must regard me as Captain Keeldar to-day. This is quite a gentleman's affair – yours and mine entirely, Doctor (so she had dubbed the Rector). The ladies there are only to be our aides-de-camp, and at their peril they speak, till we have settled the whole business.'

He smiled a little grimly, and began to write. He soon interrupted himself to ask questions, and consult his brethren, disdainfully lifting his glance over the curly heads of the two girls, and the demure caps of the elder ladies, to meet the winking glasses and grey pates of the priests. In the discussion which ensued, all three gentlemen, to their infinite credit, showed a thorough acquaintance with the poor of their parishes, – an even minute knowledge of their separate wants. Each rector knew where clothing was needed, where food would be most acceptable, where money could be bestowed with a probability of it being judiciously laid out. Wherever their memories fell short, Miss Ainley or Miss Hall, if applied to, could help them out; but both ladies took care not to speak unless spoken to. Neither of them wanted to be foremost, but each sincerely desired to be useful, and useful the clergy consented to make them: with which boon they were content.

Shirley stood behind the rectors, leaning over their shoulders now and then to glance at the rules drawn up, and the list of cases making out, listening to all they said, and still at intervals smiling her queer smile – a smile not ill-natured, but significant: too significant to be generally thought amiable. Men rarely like such of their fellows as read their inward nature too clearly and truly. It is good for women, especially, to be endowed with a soft blindness: to have mild, dim eyes, that never penetrate below the surface of things – that take all for what it seems: thousands, knowing this, keep their eyelids drooped, on system; but the most downcast glance has its loophole, through which it can, on occasion, take its sentinel-survey of life. I remember once seeing a pair of blue eyes, that were usually thought sleepy, secretly on the alert, and I knew by their expression – an expression which chilled my blood, it was in that quarter so wondrously unexpected – that for years they had been accustomed to silent soul-reading. The world called the owner of these blue eyes 'bonne petite femme' (she was not an Englishwoman): I learned her nature afterwards – got it off by heart – studied it in its farthest, most hidden recesses – she was the finest, deepest, subtlest schemer in Europe.

When all was at length settled to Miss Keeldar's mind, and the clergy had entered so fully into the spirit of her plans as to head the subscription-list with their signatures for £50 each, she ordered supper to be served; having previously directed Mrs Gill to exercise her utmost skill in the preparation of this repast. Mr Hall was no bonvivant: he was naturally an abstemious man, indifferent to luxury; but Boultby and Helstone both liked good cookery; the recherché supper consequently put them into excellent humour: they did justice to it, though in a gentlemanly way – not in the mode Mr Donne would have done, had he been present. A glass of fine wine was likewise tasted, with discerning though most decorous relish. Captain Keeldar was complimented on his taste; the compliment charmed him: it had been his aim to gratify and satisfy his priestly guests: he had succeeded, and was radiant with glee.

CHAPTER XV

MR DONNE'S EXODUS

THE NEXT DAY Shirley expressed to Caroline how delighted she felt that the little party had gone off so well.

'I rather like to entertain a circle of gentlemen,' said she: 'it is amusing to observe how they enjoy a judiciously concocted repast. For ourselves, you see, these choice wines and these scientific dishes are of no importance to us; but gentlemen seem to retain something of the naïveté of children about food, and one likes to please them: that is, when they show the becoming, decent self-government of our admirable rectors. I watch Moore sometimes, to try and discover how he can be pleased; but he has not that child's simplicity about him. Did you ever find out his accessible point, Caroline? You have seen more of him than I.'

'It is not, at any rate, that of my uncle and Dr Boultby,' returned Caroline, smiling. She always felt a sort of shy pleasure in following Miss Keeldar's lead respecting the discussion of her cousin's character: left to herself, she would never have touched on the subject; but when invited, the temptation of talking about him of whom she was ever thinking was irresistible. 'But,' she added, 'I really don't know what it is; for I never watched Robert in my life but my scrutiny was presently baffled by finding he was watching me.'

'There it is!' exclaimed Shirley: 'you can't fix your eyes on him but his presently flash on you. He is never off his guard: he won't give you an advantage: even when he does not look at you, his thoughts seem to be busy amongst your own thoughts, tracing your words and actions to their source, contemplating

278

your motives at his ease. Oh! I know that sort of character, or something in the same style: it is one that piques me singularly – how does it affect you?'

This question was a specimen of one of Shirley's sharp, sudden turns: Caroline used to be fluttered by them at first, but she had now got into the way of parrying these home-thrusts like a little quakeress.

'Pique you? In what way does it pique you?' she said.

'Here he comes!' suddenly exclaimed Shirley, breaking off, starting up and running to the window. 'Here comes a diversion. I never told you of a superb conquest I have made lately – made at those parties to which I can never persuade you to accompany me; and the thing has been done without effort or intention on my part: that I aver. There is the bell – and, by all that's delicious! there are two of them. Do they never hunt, then, except in couples? You may have one, Lina, and you may take your choice: I hope I am generous enough. Listen to Tartar!'

The black-muzzled, tawny dog, a glimpse of which was seen in the chapter which first introduced its mistress to the reader, here gave tongue in the hall, amidst whose hollow space the deep bark resounded formidably. A growl, more terrible than the bark – menacing as muttered thunder – succeeded.

'Listen!' again cried Shirley, laughing. 'You would think that the prelude to a bloody onslaught: they will be frightened: they don't know old Tartar as I do: they are not aware his uproars are all sound and fury, signifying nothing.'

Some bustle was heard. 'Down, sir! – down!' exclaimed a high-toned, imperious voice, and then came a crack of a cane or whip. Immediately there was a yell – a scutter – a run – a positive tumult.

'Oh! Malone! Malone!'

'Down! down! down!' cried the high voice.

'He really is worrying them!' exclaimed Shirley. 'They have struck him: a blow is what he is not used to, and will not take.'

Out she ran: a gentleman was fleeing up the oak staircase, making for refuge in the gallery or chambers in hot haste; another was backing fast to the stair-foot, wildly flourishing a knotty stick, at the same time reiterating, 'Down! down! down!' while the tawny dog bayed, bellowed, howled at him, and a group of servants came bundling from the kitchen. The dog made a spring; the second gentleman turned tail and rushed after his comrade: the first was already safe in a bed-room: he held the door against his fellow; – nothing so merciless as terror; – but the other fugitive struggled hard: the door was about to yield to his strength.

'Gentlemen,' was uttered in Miss Keeldar's silvery but vibrating tones, 'spare my locks, if you please. Calm yourselves! – come down! Look at Tartar, – he won't harm a cat.'

She was caressing the said Tartar: he lay crouched at her feet, his fore-paws stretched out, his tail still in threatening agitation, his nostrils snorting, his bulldog eyes conscious of a dull fire. He was an honest, phlegmatic, stupid, but stubborn canine character: he loved his mistress, and John – the man who fed him, – but was mostly indifferent to the rest of the world: quiet enough he was, unless struck or threatened with a stick, and that put a demon into him at once.

'Mr Malone, how do you do!' continued Shirley, lifting up her mirth-lit face to the gallery. 'That is not the way to the oak-parlour: that is Mrs Pryor's apartment. Request your friend Mr Donne to evacuate: I shall have the greatest pleasure in receiving him in a lower room.'

'Ha! ha!' cried Malone, in hollow laughter, quitting the door, and leaning over the massive balustrade. 'Really that animal alarmed Donne. He is a little timid,' he proceeded, stiffening himself, and walking trimly to the stair-head. 'I thought it better to follow, in order to reassure him.'

'It appears you did: well, come down, if you please. John' (turning to her man-servant), 'go up-stairs and liberate Mr Donne. Take care, Mr Malone, the stairs are slippery.'

In truth they were; being of polished oak. The caution came a little late for Malone: he had slipped already in his stately descent, and was only saved from falling by a clutch at the banisters, which made the whole structure creak again.

Tartar seemed to think the visiter's descent effected with unwarranted éclat, and accordingly he growled once more. Malone, however, was no coward: the spring of the dog had taken him by surprise; but he passed him now in suppressed fury rather than fear: if a look could have strangled Tartar, he would have breathed no more. Forgetting politeness, in his sullen rage, Malone pushed into the parlour before Miss Keeldar. He glanced at Miss Helstone; he could scarcely bring himself to bend to her. He glared on both the ladies: he looked as if, had either of them been his wife, he would have made a glorious husband at the moment: in each hand he seemed as if he would have liked to clutch one and gripe her to death.

However, Shirley took pity: she ceased to laugh; and Caroline was too true a lady to smile even at any one under mortification. Tartar was dismissed; Peter Augustus was soothed: for Shirley had looks and tones that might soothe a very bull: he had sense to feel that, since he could not challenge the owner of the dog, he had better be civil; and civil he tried to be; and his attempts being well received, he grew presently *very* civil and quite himself again. He had come, indeed, for the express purpose of making himself charming and fascinating: rough portents had met him on his first admission to Fieldhead; but that passage got over, charming and fascinating he resolved to be. Like March, having come in like a lion, he purposed to go out like a lamb.

For the sake of air, as it appeared, or perhaps for that of ready exit in case of some new emergency arising, he took his seat – not on the sofa, where Miss Keeldar offered him enthronization, nor yet near the fireside, to which Caroline, by a friendly sign, gently invited him, – but on a chair close to the door. Being no longer sullen or furious, he grew, after his fashion, constrained and embarrassed. He talked to the ladies by fits and starts, choosing for topics whatever was most intensely commonplace: he sighed deeply, significantly, at the close of every sentence; he sighed in each pause; he sighed ere he opened his mouth. At last, finding it desirable to add ease to his other charms, he drew forth to aid him an ample silk pocket-handkerchief. This was to be the graceful toy with which his unoccupied hands were to trifle. He went to work with a certain energy: he folded the red and yellow square cornerwise; he whipped it open with a waft: again he folded it in narrower compass: he made of it a handsome band. To what purpose would he proceed to apply the ligature? Would he wrap it about his throat – his head? Should it be a comforter or a turban? Neither. Peter Augustus had an inventive – an original genius: he was about to show the ladies graces of action possessing at least the charm of novelty. He sat on the chair with his athletic Irish legs crossed, and these legs, in that attitude, he circled with the bandana and bound firmly together. It was evident he felt this device to be worth an encore: he repeated it more than once. The second performance sent Shirley to the window to laugh her silent but irrepressible laugh unseen: it turned Caroline's head aside, that her long curls might screen the smile mantling on her features. Miss Helstone, indeed, was amused by more than one point in Peter's demeanour: she was edified at the complete though abrupt diversion of his homage from herself to the heiress: the £5000 he supposed her likely one day to inherit, were not to be weighed in the balance against Miss Keeldar's estate and hall. He took no pains to conceal his calculations and tactics: he pretended to no gradual change of views; he wheeled about at once: the pursuit of the lesser fortune was openly relinquished for that of the greater. On what grounds he expected to succeed in his chase, himself best knew: certainly not by skilful management.

From the length of time that elapsed, it appeared that John had some difficulty in persuading Mr Donne to descend. At length, however, that gentleman appeared: nor, as he presented himself at the oak-parlour door, did he seem in the slightest degree ashamed or confused – not a whit. Donne, indeed, was of that coldly phlegmatic, immovably complacent, densely self-satisfied nature which is insensible to shame. He had never blushed in his life: no humiliation could abash him: his nerves were not capable of sensation enough to stir his life, and make colour mount to his cheek: he had no fire in his blood, and no modesty in his soul: he was a frontless, arrogant, decorous slip of the commonplace; conceited, inane, insipid: and this gentleman had a notion of wooing Miss Keeldar! He knew no more, however, how to set about the business than if he had been an image carved in wood: he had no idea of a taste to be pleased, a heart to be reached in courtship: his notion was, when he should have formally visited her a few times, to write a letter proposing marriage; then he calculated she would accept him for love of his office, then they would be married, then he should be master of Fieldhead, and he should live very comfortably, have servants at his command, eat and drink of the best, and be a great man. You would not have suspected his intentions when he addressed his intended bride in an impertinent injured tone: –

'A very dangerous dog that, Miss Keeldar. I wonder you should keep such an animal.'

'Do you, Mr Donne? Perhaps you will wonder more when I tell you I am very fond of him.'

'I should say you are not serious in the assertion. Can't fancy a lady fond of that brute – 'tis so ugly – a mere carter's dog – pray hang him.'

'Hang what I am fond of?'

'And purchase in his stead some sweetly pooty pug or poodle: something appropriate to the fair sex: ladies generally like lap-dogs.'

'Perhaps I am an exception.'

'Oh! you can't be, you know. All ladies are alike in those matters: that is universally allowed.'

'Tartar frightened you terribly, Mr Donne. I hope you won't take any harm.'

'That I shall, no doubt. He gave me a turn I shall not soon forget. When I *sor* him (such was Mr Donne's pronunciation) about to spring, I thought I should have fainted.'

'Perhaps you did faint in the bed-room – you were a long time there?'

'No; I bore up that I might hold the door fast: I was determined not to let any one enter: I thought I would keep a barrier between me and the enemy.'

'But what if your friend Mr Malone had been worried?'

'Malone must take care of himself. Your man persuaded me to come out at last by saying the dog was chained up in his kennel: if I had not been assured of this, I would have remained all day in the chamber. But what is that? I declare the man has told a falsehood! The dog is there!'

And indeed Tartar walked past the glass-door opening to the garden, stiff, tawny, and black-muzzled as ever. He still seemed in bad humour; he was growling again, and whistling a half-strangled whistle, being an inheritance from the bulldog side of his ancestry.

'There are other visitors coming,' observed Shirley, with that provoking coolness which the owners of formidable-looking dogs are apt to show while their animals are all bristle and bay. Tartar sprang down the pavement towards the gate, bellowing 'avec explosion.' His mistress quietly opened the glass-door, and stepped out chirruping to him. His bellow was already silence, and he was lifting up his huge, blunt, stupid head to the new callers to be patted.

'What – Tartar, Tartar!' said a cheery, rather boyish voice: 'don't you know us? Good-morning, old boy!'

And little Mr Sweeting, whose conscious good-nature made him comparatively fearless of man, woman, child, or brute, came through the gate, caressing the guardian. His vicar, Mr Hall, followed: he had no fear of Tartar either, and Tartar had no ill-will to him: he snuffed both the gentlemen round, and then, as if concluding that they were harmless, and might be allowed to pass, he withdrew to the sunny front of the hall, leaving the archway free. Mr Sweeting followed, and would have played with him, but Tartar took no notice of his caresses: it was only his mistress's hand whose touch gave him pleasure; to all others he showed himself obstinately insensible.

Shirley advanced to meet Messrs Hall and Sweeting, shaking hands with them cordially: they were come to tell her of certain successes they had achieved that morning in applications for subscriptions to the fund. Mr Hall's eyes beamed benignantly through his spectacles: his plain face looked positively hand-some with goodness, and when Caroline, seeing who was come, ran out to meet him, and put both her hands into his, he gazed down on her with a gentle, serene, affectionate expression, that gave him the aspect of a smiling Melancthon.

Instead of re-entering the house, they strayed through the garden, the ladies walking one on each side of Mr Hall. It was a breezy sunny day; the air freshened the girls' cheeks, and gracefully dishevelled their ringlets: both of them looked pretty, – one, gay: Mr Hall spoke oftenest to his brilliant companion, looked most frequently at the quiet one. Miss Keeldar gathered handfuls of the profusely blooming flowers, whose perfume filled the enclosure; she gave some to Caroline, telling her to choose a nosegay for Mr Hall; and with her lap filled with delicate and splendid blossoms, Caroline sat down on the steps of a summer-house: the Vicar stood near her, leaning on his cane.

Shirley, who could not be inhospitable, now called out the neglected pair in the oak-parlour: she convoyed Donne past his dread enemy Tartar, who, with his nose on his fore-paws, lay snoring under the meridian sun. Donne was not grateful: he never *was* grateful for kindness and attention; but he was glad of the safeguard. Miss Keeldar, desirous of being impartial, offered the curates flowers: they accepted them with native awkwardness. Malone seemed specially at a loss, when a bouquet filled one hand, while his shillelagh occupied the other. Donne's 'Thank you!' was rich to hear: it was the most fatuous and arrogant of sounds, implying that he considered this offering an homage to his merits, and an attempt on the part of the heiress to ingratiate herself into his priceless affections. Sweeting alone received the posy like a smart, sensible, little man, as he was; putting it gallantly and nattily into his button-hole.

As a reward for his good manners, Miss Keeldar beckoning him apart, gave him some commission, which made his eyes sparkle with glee. Away he flew, round by the courtyard to the kitchen: no need to give him directions; he was always at home everywhere. Erelong he re-appeared, carrying a round table, which he placed under the cedar; then he collected six garden-chairs from various nooks and bowers in the grounds, and placed them in a circle. The parlour-maid – Miss Keeldar kept no footman – came out, bearing a napkin-covered tray. Sweeting's nimble fingers aided in disposing glasses, plates, knives and forks: he assisted her too in setting forth a neat luncheon, consisting of cold chicken, ham, and tarts.

This sort of impromptu regale, it was Shirley's delight to offer any chance guests; and nothing pleased her better than to have an alert, obliging little friend, like Sweeting, to run about her hand, cheerily receive and briskly execute her hospitable hints. David and she were on the best terms in the world; and his devotion to the heiress was quite disinterested, since it prejudiced in nothing his faithful allegiance to the magnificent Dora Sykes.

The repast turned out a very merry one. Donne and Malone, indeed, contributed but little to its vivacity, the chief part they played in it being what concerned the knife, fork, and wine-glass; but where four such natures as Mr Hall, David Sweeting, Shirley, and Caroline, were assembled in health and amity, on a green lawn, under a sunny sky, amidst a wilderness of flowers, there could not be ungenial dulness.

In the course of conversation, Mr Hall reminded the ladies that Whitsuntide was approaching, when the grand United Sunday-School tea-drinking and procession of the three parishes of Briarfield, Whinbury, and Nunnely were to take place. Caroline he knew would be at her post as teacher, he said, and he hoped Miss Keeldar would not be wanting: he hoped she would make her first public appearance amongst them at that time. Shirley was not the person to miss an occasion of this sort: she liked festive excitement, a gathering of happiness, a concentration and combination of pleasant details, a throng of glad faces, a muster of elated hearts: she told Mr Hall they might count on her with security: she did not know what she would have to do, but they might dispose of her as they pleased.

'And,' said Caroline, 'you will promise to come to my table, and to sit near me, Mr Hall?'

'I shall not fail, Deo volente,' said he. 'I have occupied the place on her right hand at these monster tea-drinkings for the last six years,' he proceeded, turning to Miss Keeldar. 'They made her a Sunday-school teacher when she was a little girl of twelve: she is not particularly self-confident by nature, as you may have observed; and the first time she had to "take a tray," as the phrase is, and make tea in public, there was some piteous trembling and flushing. I observed the speechless panic, the cups shaking in the little hand, and the over-flowing teapot filled too full from the urn. I came to her aid, took a seat near her, managed the urn and the slop-basin, and in fact made the tea for her like any old woman.'

'I was very grateful to you,' interposed Caroline.

'You were: you told me so with an earnest sincerity that repaid me well; inasmuch as it was not like the majority of little ladies of twelve, whom you may help and caress for ever without their evincing any quicker sense of the kindness done and meant than if they were made of wax and wood, instead of flesh and nerves. She kept close to me, Miss Keeldar, the rest of the evening, walking with me over the grounds where the children were playing; she followed me into the vestry when all were summoned into church: she would, I believe, have mounted with me to the pulpit, had I not taken the previous precaution of conducting her to the Rectory-pew.'

'And he has been my friend ever since,' said Caroline.

'And always sat at her table, near her tray, and handed the cups, – that is the extent of my services. The next thing I do for her will be to marry her some day to some curate or mill-owner: but mind, Caroline, I shall inquire about the bride-groom's character, and if he is not a gentleman likely to render happy the little girl who walked with me hand in hand over Nunnely Common, I will not officiate: so take care.'

'The caution is useless: I am not going to be married. I shall live single like your sister Margaret, Mr Hall.'

'Very well – you might do worse – Margaret is not unhappy: she has her books for a pleasure, and her brother for a care, and is content. If ever you want a home; if the day should come when Briarfield Rectory is yours no longer, come to Nunnely Vicarage. Should the old maid and bachelor be still living, they will make you tenderly welcome.'

'There are your flowers. Now,' said Caroline, who had kept the nosegay she had selected for him till this moment, '*you* don't care for a bouquet, but you must give it to Margaret: only – to be sentimental for once – keep that little forget-me-not, which is a wild-flower I gathered from the grass; and – to be still more sentimental – let me take two or three of the blue blossoms and put them in my souvenir.'

And she took out a small book with enamelled cover and silver clasp, wherein, having opened it, she inserted the flowers, writing round them in pencil – 'To be kept for the sake of the Rev. Cyril Hall, my friend. May – 18–.'

The Rev. Cyril Hall, on his part also, placed a sprig in safety between the leaves of a pocket Testament: he only wrote on the margin – 'Caroline.'

'Now,' said he, smiling, 'I trust we are romantic enough.

Miss Keeldar,' he continued (the curates, by-the-by, during this conversation, were too much occupied with their own jokes to notice what passed at the other end of the table), 'I hope you are laughing at this trait of "*exaltation*" in the old grey-headed Vicar; but, the fact is, I am so used to comply with the requests of this young friend of yours, I don't know how to refuse her when she tells me to do anything. You would say it is not much in my way to traffic with flowers and forget-me-nots; but, you see, when requested to be sentimental, I am obedient.'

'He is naturally rather sentimental,' remarked Caroline: 'Margaret told me so, and I know what pleases him.'

'That you should be good and happy? Yes; that is one of my greatest pleasures. May God long preserve to you the blessings of peace and innocence! By which phrase, I mean *comparative* innocence; for in His sight, I am well aware *none* are pure. What, to our human perceptions, looks spotless as we fancy angels, is to Him but frailty, needing the blood of His Son to cleanse, and the strength of His Spirit to sustain. Let us each and all cherish humility – I, as you, my young friends; and we may well do it when we look into our own hearts, and see there temptations, inconsistencies, propensities, even we blush to recognise. And it is not youth, nor good looks, nor grace, nor any gentle outside charm which makes either beauty or good-ness in God's eyes. Young ladies, when your mirror or men's tongues flatter you, remember that, in the sight of her Maker, Mary Anne Ainley – a woman whom neither glass nor lips have ever panegyrized – is fairer and better than either of you. She is, indeed,' he added, after a pause – 'she is, indeed. You young things – wrapt up in yourselves and in earthly hopes – scarcely live as Christ lived: perhaps you cannot do it yet, while existence is so sweet and earth so smiling to you; it would be too much to expect: she, with meek heart and due reverence, treads close in her Redeemer's steps.'

Here the harsh voice of Donne broke in on the mild tones of Mr Hall: –

'Ahem!' he began, clearing his throat evidently for a speech of some importance. 'Ahem! Miss Keeldar, your attention an instant, if you please.'

'Well,' said Shirley, nonchalantly. 'What is it? I listen: all of me is ear that is not eye.'

'I hope part of you is hand also,' returned Donne, in his vulgarly presumptuous and familiar style, 'and part purse: it is to the hand and purse I propose to appeal. I came here this morning with a view to beg of you' –

'You should have gone to Mrs Gill: she is my almoner.'

'To beg of you a subscription to a school. I and Dr Boultby intend to erect one in the hamlet of Ecclefigg which is under our vicarage of Whinbury. The Baptists have got possession of it: they have a chapel there, and we want to dispute the ground.'

'But I have nothing to do with Ecclefigg: I possess no property there.'

'What does that signify? You're a Churchwoman, ain't you?'

'Admirable creature!' muttered Shirley, under her breath: 'exquisite address: fine style! What raptures he excites in me!' then, aloud, 'I am a Churchwoman, certainly.'

'Then you can't refuse to contribute in this case. The population of Ecclefigg are a parcel of brutes – we want to civilize them.'

'Who is to be the missionary?'

'Myself, probably.'

'You won't fail through lack of sympathy with your flock.'

'I hope not – I expect success; but we must have money. There is the paper – pray give a handsome sum.'

When asked for money, Shirley rarely held back. She put down her name for £5: after the £300 she had lately given, and the many smaller sums she was giving constantly, it was as much as she could at present afford. Donne looked at it, declared the subscription 'shabby,' and clamorously demanded more. Miss Keeldar flushed up with some indignation and more astonishment.

'At present, I shall give no more,' said she.

'Not give more! Why, I expected you to head the list with a cool hundred. With your property, you should never put down a signature for less.'

She was silent.

'In the south,' went on Donne, 'a lady with a thousand a-year would be ashamed to give five pounds for a public object.'

Shirley, so rarely haughty, looked so now. Her slight frame became nerved; her distinguished face quickened with scorn.

'Strange remarks!' said she: 'most inconsiderate! Reproach in return for bounty is misplaced.'

'Bounty! Do you call five pounds bounty?'

'I do: and bounty which, had I not given it to Dr Boultby's intended school, of the erection of which I approve, and in no sort to his curate, who seems ill-advised in his manner of applying for – or rather extorting subscriptions, – bounty, I repeat, which, but for this consideration, I should instantly reclaim.'

Donne was thick-skinned: he did not feel all or half that the tone, air, glance of the speaker expressed: he knew not on what ground he stood.

'Wretched place – this Yorkshire,' he went on. 'I could never have formed an idea*r* of the country had I not seen it; and the people – rich and poor – what a set! How *corse* and uncultivated! They would be scouted in the south.'

Shirley leaned forwards on the table, her nostrils dilating a little, her taper fingers interlaced and compressing each other hard.

'The rich,' pursued the infatuated and unconscious Donne, 'are a parcel of misers – never living as persons with their incomes ought to live: you scarsley – (you must excuse Mr Donne's pro-nunciation, reader; it was very choice; he considered it genteel, and prided himself on his southern accent; northern ears received with singular sensations his utterance of certain words); you scarsley ever see a fam'ly where a propa carriage or a reg'la butla is kep; and as to the poor – just look at them when they come crowding about the church-doors on the occasion of a marriage or a funeral, clattering in clogs; the men in their shirt-sleeves and wool-combers' aprons, the women in mob-caps and bed-gowns. They pos'tively deserve that one should turn a mad cow in amongst them to rout their rabble-ranks – he! he! What fun it would be!'

'There, – you have reached the climax,' said Shirley, quietly. 'You have reached the climax,' she repeated, turning her glowing glance towards him. 'You cannot go beyond it, and,' she added with emphasis, 'you *shall* not, in my house.'

Up she rose: nobody could control her now, for she was exasperated; straight she walked to her garden-gates, wide she flung them open.

'Walk through,' she said austerely, 'and pretty quickly, and set foot on this pavement no more.'

Donne was astounded. He had thought all the time he was showing himself off to high advantage, as a lofty-souled person of the first 'ton;' he imagined he was producing a crushing impression. Had he not expressed disdain of everything in York-shire? What more conclusive proof could be given that he was better than anything there? And yet here was he about to be turned like a dog out of a Yorkshire garden! Where, under such circumstances, was the 'concatenation accordingly?'

'Rid me of you instantly – instantly!' reiterated Shirley, as he lingered.

'Madam – a clergyman! Turn out a clergyman?'

'Off! Were you an archbishop: you have proved yourself no gentleman, and must go. Quick!'

She was quite resolved: there was no trifling with her: besides, Tartar was again rising; he perceived symptoms of a commotion: he manifested a disposition to join in; there was evidently noth-ing for it but to go, and Donne made his Exodus; the heiress sweeping him a deep curtsy as she closed the gates on him.

'How dare the pompous priest abuse his flock? How dare the

lisping cockney revile Yorkshire?' was her sole observation on the circumstance, as she returned to the table.

Erelong, the little party broke up: Miss Keeldar's ruffled and darkened brow, curled lip, and incensed eye, gave no invitation to further social enjoyment.

CHAPTER XVI

WHITSUNTIDE

THE FUND prospered. By dint of Miss Keeldar's example, the three rectors' vigorous exertions, and the efficient though quiet aid of their spinster and spectacled lieutenants, Mary Ann Ainley and Margaret Hall, a handsome sum was raised; and this being judiciously managed, served for the present greatly to alleviate the distress of the unemployed poor. The neighbourhood seemed to grow calmer: for a fortnight past no cloth had been destroyed; no outrage on mill or mansion had been committed in the three parishes. Shirley was sanguine that the evil she wished to avert was almost escaped; that the threatened storm was passing over: with the approach of summer she felt certain that trade would improve – it always did; and then this weary war could not last for ever; peace must return one day: with peace what an impulse would be given to commerce!

Such was the usual tenor of her observations to her tenant, Gérard Moore, whenever she met him where they could converse, and Moore would listen very quietly – too quietly to satisfy her. She would then by her impatient glance demand something more from him – some explanation, or at least some additional remark. Smiling in his way, with that expression which gave a remarkable cast of sweetness to his mouth, while his brow remained grave, he would answer to the effect, that himself, too, trusted in the finite nature of the war; that it was indeed on that ground the anchor of his hopes was fixed: thereon his speculations depended. 'For you are aware,' he would continue, 'that I now work Hollow's mill entirely on speculation:

I sell nothing; there is no market for my goods. I manufacture for a future day: I make myself ready to take advantage of the first opening that shall occur. Three months ago this was impossible to me; I had exhausted both credit and capital: you well know who came to my rescue; from what hand I received the loan which saved me. It is on the strength of that loan I am enabled to continue the bold game which, a while since, I feared I should never play more. Total ruin I know will follow loss, and I am aware that gain is doubtful, but I am quite cheerful: so long as I can be active, so long as I can strive, so long, in short, as my hands are not tied, it is impossible for me to be depressed. One year, nay, but six months of the reign of the olive, and I am safe; for, as you say, peace will give an impulse to commerce. In this you are right; but as to the restored tranquillity of the neighbourhood – as to the permanent good effect of your charitable fund – I doubt. Eleemosynary relief never yet tranquillized the working-classes – it never made them grateful; it is not in human nature that it should. I suppose, were all things ordered aright, they ought not to be in a position to need that humiliating relief; and this they feel: we should feel it were we so placed. Besides, to whom should they be grateful? To you – to the clergy perhaps, but not to us mill-owners. They hate us worse than ever. Then, the disaffected here are in correspondence with the disaffected elsewhere: Nottingham is one of their head-quarters, Manchester another, Birmingham a third. The subalterns receive orders from their chiefs; they are in a good state of discipline: no blow is struck without mature deliberation. In sultry weather, you have seen the sky threaten thunder day by day, and yet night after night the clouds have cleared, and the sun has set quietly; but the danger was not gone, it was only delayed: the long-threatening storm is sure to break at last. There is analogy between the moral and physical atmosphere.'

'Well, Mr Moore' (so these conferences always ended), 'take care of yourself. If you think that I have ever done you any good, reward me by promising to take care of yourself.'

'I do: I will take close and watchful care. I wish to live, not to die: the future opens like Eden before me; and still, when I look deep into the shades of my paradise, I see a vision, that I like better than seraph or cherub, glide across remote vistas.'

'Do you? Pray, what vision?'

'I see –'

The maid came bustling in with the tea-things.

The early part of that May, as we have seen, was fine, the middle was wet; but in the last week, at change of moon, it cleared again. A fresh wind swept off the silver-white, deep-piled rain-clouds, bearing them, mass on mass, to the eastern horizon; on whose verge they dwindled, and behind whose rim they disappeared, leaving the vault behind all pure blue space, ready for the reign of the summer sun. That sun rose broad on Whitsuntide: the gathering of the schools was signalized by splendid weather.

Whit-Tuesday was the great day, in preparation for which the two large schoolrooms of Briarfield, built by the present rector, chiefly at his own expense, were cleaned our, white-washed, repainted, and decorated with flowers and evergreens – some from the Rectory-garden, two cart-loads from Field-head, and a wheelbarrowful from the more stingy domain of De Walden, the residence of Mr Wynne. In these schoolrooms twenty tables, each calculated to accommodate twenty guests, were laid out, surrounded with benches, and covered with white cloths: above them were suspended at least some twenty cages, containing as many canaries, according to a fancy of the district, specially cherished by Mr Helstone's clerk, who delighted in the piercing song of these birds, and knew that amidst confusion of tongues they always caroled loudest. These tables, be it understood, were not spread for the twelve hundred scholars to be assembled from the three parishes, but only for the patrons and teachers of the schools: the children's feast was to be spread in the open air. At one o'clock the troops were to come in; at two they were to be marshalled; till four they were to parade the parish; then came the feast, and afterwards the meeting, with music and speechifying in the church.

Why Briarfield was chosen for the point of rendezvous – the scene of the fête – should be explained. It was not because it was the largest or most populous parish – Whinbury far outdid it in that respect; nor because it was the oldest – antique as were the hoary Church and Rectory, Nunnely's low-roofed Temple and mossy Parsonage, buried both in coëval oaks, outstanding sentinels of Nunwood, were older still: it was simply because Mr Helstone willed it so, and Mr Helstone's will was stronger than that of Boultby or Hall; the former *could* not, the latter *would* not, dispute a point of precedence with their resolute and imperious brother: they let him lead and rule.

This notable anniversary had always hitherto been a trying day to Caroline Helstone, because it dragged her perforce into public, compelling her to face all that was wealthy, respectable, influential in the neighbourhood; in whose presence, but for the kind countenance of Mr Hall, she would have appeared unsupported. Obliged to be conspicuous: obliged to walk at the head of her regiment, as the Rector's niece, and first teacher of the first class; obliged to make tea at the first table for a mixed multitude of ladies and gentlemen; and to do all this without the countenance of mother, aunt, or other chaperon – she, meantime, being a nervous person, who mortally feared publicity – it will be comprehended that, under these circumstances, she trembled at the approach of Whitsuntide.

But this year Shirley was to be with her, and that changed the aspect of the trial singularly – it changed it utterly: it was a trial no longer – it was almost an enjoyment. Miss Keeldar was better in her single self than a host of ordinary friends. Quite self-possessed, and always spirited and easy; conscious of her social importance, yet never presuming upon it, it would be enough to give one courage only to look at her. The only fear was, lest the heiress should not be punctual to tryst: she often had a careless way of lingering behind time, and Caroline knew her uncle would not wait a second for any one: at the moment of the church-clock tolling two, the bells would clash out and the march begin. She must look after Shirley, then, in this matter, or her expected companion would fail her.

Whit-Tuesday saw her rise almost with the sun. She, Fanny, and Eliza were busy the whole morning arranging the Rectory-parlours in first-rate company order, and setting out a collation of cooling refreshments – wine, fruit, cakes – on the dining-room sideboard. Then she had to dress in her freshest and fairest attire of white muslin; the perfect fineness of the day and the solemnity of the occasion warranted, and even exacted, such costume. Her new sash – a birthday-present from Margaret Hall, which she had reason to believe Cyril himself had bought, and in return for which she had indeed given him a set of cambric-bands in a handsome case – was tied by the dexterous fingers of Fanny, who took no little pleasure in arraying her fair young mistress for the occasion; her simple bonnet had been trimmed to correspond with her sash; her pretty but inexpensive scarf of white crape suited her dress. When ready, she formed a picture, not bright enough to dazzle, but fair enough to interest; not brilliantly striking, but very delicately pleasing; a picture in which sweetness of tint, purity of air, and grace of mien, atoned for the absence of rich colouring and magnificent contour. What her brown eye and clear forehead showed of her mind, was in keeping with her dress and face – modest, gentle, and, though pensive, harmonious. It appeared that neither lamb nor dove need fear her, but would welcome rather, in her look of simplicity and softness, a sympathy with their own natures, or with the natures we ascribe to them.

After all, she was an imperfect, faulty human being: fair enough of form, hue, and array; but, as Cyril Hall said, neither so good nor so great as the withered Miss Ainley, now putting on her best black gown and Quaker-drab shawl and bonnet in her own narrow cottage-chamber.

Away Caroline went, across some very sequestered fields and

through some quite hidden lanes, to Fieldhead. She glided quickly under the green hedges and across the greener leas. There was no dust – no moisture – to soil the hem of her stainless garment, or to damp her slender sandal: after the late rains all was clean, and under the present glowing sun all was dry: she walked fearlessly, then, on daisy and turf, and through thick plantations; she reached Fieldhead, and penetrated to Miss Keeldar's dressing-room.

It was well she had come, or Shirley would have been too late. Instead of making ready with all speed, she lay stretched on a couch, absorbed in reading: Mrs Pryor stood near, vainly urging her to rise and dress. Caroline wasted no words: she immediately took the book from her, and, with her own hands, commenced the business of disrobing and re-robing her. Shirley, indolent with the heat, and gay with her youth and pleasurable nature, wanted to talk, laugh, and linger; but Caroline, intent on being in time, persevered in dressing her as fast as fingers could fasten strings or insert pins. At length, as she united a final row of hooks and eyes, she found leisure to chide her, saying, she was very naughty to be so unpunctual; that she looked even now the picture of incorrigible carelessness: and so Shirley did – but a very lovely picture of that tiresome quality.

She presented quite a contrast to Caroline: there was style in every fold of her dress and every line of her figure: the rich silk suited her better than a simpler costume; the deep-embroidered scarf became her; she wore it negligently, but gracefully; the wreath on her bonnet crowned her well: the attention to fashion, the tasteful appliance of ornament in each portion of her dress, were quite in place with her: all this suited her, like the frank light in her eyes, the rallying smile about her lips, like her shaft-straight carriage and lightsome step. Caroline took her hand when she was dressed, hurried her downstairs, out of doors, and thus they sped through the fields, laughing as they went, and looking very much like a snow-white dove and gem-tinted bird-of-paradise joined in social flight.

Thanks to Miss Helstone's promptitude, they arrived in good time. While yet trees hid the church, they heard the bell tolling a measured but urgent summons for all to assemble; the trooping in of numbers, the trampling of many steps, and murmuring of many voices were likewise audible. From a rising-ground they presently saw, on the Whinbury-road, the Whinbury-school approaching: it numbered five hundred souls. The Rector and Curate, Boultby and Donne, headed it: the former, looming large in full canonicals, walking, as became a beneficed priest, under the canopy of a shovel-hat, with the dignity of an ample corporation, the embellishment of the squarest and vastest of black coats, and the support of the stoutest of gold-headed canes. As the Doctor walked, he now and then slightly flourished his cane, and inclined his shovel-hat with a dogmatical wag towards his aide-de-camp. That aide-de-camp – Donne, to wit – narrow as the line of his shape was compared to the broad bulk of his principal, contrived, notwithstanding, to look every inch a curate: all about him was pragmatical and self-complacent, from his turned-up nose and elevated chin to his clerical black gaiters, his somewhat short, strapless trousers, and his square-toed shoes.

Walk on, Mr Donne! You have undergone scrutiny. You think you look well – whether the white and purple figures watching you from yonder hill think so, is another question.

These figures come running down when the regiment has marched by: the churchyard is full of children and teachers, all in their very best holiday attire: and – distressed as is the district, bad as are the times – it is wonderful to see how respectably – how handsomely even – they have contrived to clothe themselves. That British love of decency will work miracles: the poverty which reduces an Irish girl to rags is impotent to rob the English girl of the neat wardrobe she knows necessary to her self-respect. Besides, the lady of the manor – that Shirley, now gazing with pleasure on this well-dressed and happy-looking crowd – has really done them good: her seasonable bounty consoled many a poor family against the coming holiday, and supplied many a child with a new frock or bonnet for the occasion; she knows it, and is elate with the consciousness: glad that her money, example, and influence have really – substantially – benefited those around her. She cannot be charitable like Miss Ainley – it is not in her nature: it relieves her to feel that there is another way of being charitable, practicable for other characters, and under other circumstances.

Caroline, too, is pleased; for she also has done good in her small way; robbed herself of more than one dress, ribbon, or collar she could ill spare, to aid in fitting out the scholars of her class; and, as she could not give money, she has followed Miss Ainley's example, in giving her time and her industry to sew for the children.

Nor only is the churchyard full, but the Rectory-garden is also thronged: pairs and parties of ladies and gentlemen are seen walking amongst the waving lilacs and laburnums. The house also is occupied: at the wide-open parlour-windows, gay groups are standing. These are the patrons and teachers, who are to swell the procession. In the parson's croft, behind the Rectory, are the musicians of the three parish bands, with their instruments. Fanny and Eliza, in the smartest of caps and gowns, and the whitest of aprons, move amongst them, serving out quarts of ale; whereof a stock was brewed very sound and strong some weeks since, by the Rector's orders, and under his special superintendence. Whatever he had a hand in, must be managed handsomely: 'shabby doings,' of any description, were not endured under his sanction: from the erection of a public building, a church, school, or courthouse, to the cooking of a dinner, he still advocated the lordly, liberal, and effective. Miss Keeldar was like him in this respect, and they mutually approved each other's arrangements.

Caroline and Shirley were soon in the midst of the company; the former met them very easily for her: instead of sitting down in a retired corner, or stealing away to her own room till the procession should be marshalled, according to her wont, she moved through the three parlours, conversed and smiled, absolutely spoke once or twice she was spoken to, and, in short, seemed a new creature. It was Shirley's presence which thus transformed her: the view of Miss Keeldar's air and manner did her a world of good. Shirley had no fear of her kind; no tendency to shrink from, to avoid it. All human beings, men, women, or children, whom low breeding or coarse presumption did not render positively offensive, were welcome enough to her: some much more so than others, of course; but, generally speaking, till a man had indisputably proved himself bad and a nuisance, Shirley was willing to think him good and an acquisition, and to treat him accordingly. This disposition made her a general favourite, for it robbed her very raillery of its sting, and gave her serious or smiling conversation a happy charm: nor did it diminish the value of her intimate friendship, which was a distinct thing from this social benevolence, depending, indeed, on quite a different part of her character. Miss Helstone was the choice of her affection and intellect; the Misses Pearson, Sykes, Wynne, &c., &c., only the profiters by her good-nature and vivacity.

Donne happened to come into the drawing-room while Shirley, sitting on the sofa, formed the centre of a tolerably wide circle. She had already forgotten her exasperation against him, and she bowed and smiled good-humouredly. The disposition of the man was then seen. He knew neither how to decline the advance with dignity, as one whose just pride has been wounded, nor how to meet it with frankness, as one who is glad to forget and forgive; his punishment had impressed him with no sense of shame, and he did not experience that feeling on encountering his chastiser: he was not vigorous enough in evil to be actively malignant, – he merely passed by sheepishly with a rated, scowling look. Nothing could ever again reconcile him to his enemy; while no passion of resentment, for even sharper and more ignominious inflictions, could his lymphatic nature know.

'He was not worth a scene!' said Shirley to Caroline. 'What a fool I was! To revenge on poor Donne his silly spite at Yorkshire, is something like crushing a gnat for attacking the hide of a rhinoceros. Had I been a gentleman, I believe I should have helped him off the premises by dint of physical force: I am glad now I only employed the moral weapon. But he must come near me no more: I don't like him: he irritates me: there is not even amusement to be had out of him: Malone is better sport.'

It seemed as if Malone wished to justify the preference; for the words were scarcely out of the speaker's mouth, when Peter Augustus came up, all in 'grande tenue,' gloved and scented, with his hair oiled and brushed to perfection, and bearing in one hand a huge bunch of cabbage-roses, five or six in full blow: these he presented to the heiress with a grace to which the most cunning pencil could do but defective justice. And who, after this, could dare to say that Peter was not a lady's man? He had gathered and he had given flowers: he had offered a sentimental – a poetic tribute at the shrine of Love or Mammon. Hercules holding the distaff was but a faint type of Peter bearing the roses. He must have thought this himself, for he seemed amazed at what he had done: he backed without a word; he was going away with a husky chuckle of self-felicitation; then he be-thought himself to stop and turn, to ascertain by ocular testi-mony that he really had presented a bouquet: yes – there were the six red cabbages on the purple satin lap, a very white hand, with some gold rings on the fingers, slightly holding them together, and streaming ringlets, half-hiding a laughing face, drooped over them: only *half*-hiding: Peter saw the laugh – it was unmistakable – he was made a joke of – his gallantry, his chivalry were the subject of a jest for a petticoat – for two petticoats – Miss Helstone too was smiling. Moreover, he felt he was seen through, and Peter grew black as a thunder-cloud. When Shirley looked up, a fell eye was fastened on her: Malone, at least, had energy enough to hate: she saw it in his glances.

'Peter *is* worth a scene, and shall have it, if he likes, one day,' she whispered to her friend.

And now – solemn and sombre as to their colour, though bland enough as to their faces – appeared at the dining-room door the three rectors: they had hitherto been busy in the church, and were now coming to take some little refreshment for the body, ere the march commenced. The large morocco-covered easy chair had been left vacant for Dr Boultby; he was put into it, and Caroline, obeying the instigations of Shirley, who told her now was the time to play the hostess, hastened to hand to her uncle's vast, revered, and, on the whole, worthy friend, a glass of wine and a plate of macaroons. Boultby's churchwardens, patrons of the Sunday-school both, as he insisted on their being, were already beside him; Mrs Sykes and the other ladies of his congregation were on his right hand and on his left, expressing their hopes that he was not fatigued, their fears that the day would be too warm for him. Mrs Boultby, who held an opinion that when her lord dropped asleep after a good dinner his face became as the face of an angel, was bending over him, tenderly wiping some perspiration, real or imaginary, from his brow: Boultby, in short, was in his glory, and in a round sound 'voix de poitrine,' he rumbled out thanks for attentions, and assurances of his tolerable health. Of Caroline he took no manner of notice as she came near, save to accept what she offered: he did not see her, he never did see her: he hardly knew that such a person existed. He saw the macaroons, however, and being fond of sweets, possessed himself of a small handful thereof. The wine, Mrs Boultby insisted on mingling with hot water, and qualifying with sugar and nutmeg.

Mr Hall stood near an open window, breathing the fresh air and scent of flowers, and talking like a brother to Miss Ainley. To him Caroline turned her attention with pleasure. 'What should she bring him? He must not help himself – he must be served by her;' and she provided herself with a little salver, that she might offer him variety. Margaret Hall joined them; so did

Miss Keeldar: the four ladies stood round their favourite pastor: they also had an idea that they looked on the face of an earthly angel: Cyril Hall was their pope, infallible to them as Dr Thomas Boultby to his admirers. A throng, too, enclosed the Rector of Briarfield: twenty or more pressed round him; and no parson was ever more potent in a circle than old Helstone. The curates herding together after their manner, made a constellation of three lesser planets: divers young ladies watched them afar off, but ventured not nigh.

Mr Helstone produced his watch. 'Ten minutes to two,' he announced aloud. 'Time for all to fall into line. Come.' He seized his shovel-hat and marched away; all rose and followed en masse.

The twelve hundred children were drawn up in three bodies of four hundred souls each: in the rear of each regiment was stationed a band; between every twenty there was an interval, wherein Helstone posted the teachers in pairs: to the van of the armies he summoned: –

'Grace Boultby and Mary Sykes lead out Whinbury.'

'Margaret Hall and Mary Ann Ainley conduct Nunnely.'

'Caroline Helstone and Shirley Keeldar head Briarfield.'

Then again he gave command: –

'Mr Donne to Whinbury; Mr Sweeting to Nunnely; Mr Malone to Briarfield.'

And these gentlemen stepped up before the lady-generals.

The rectors passed to the full front – the parish clerks fell to the extreme rear; Helstone lifted his shovel-hat; in an instant out dashed the eight bells in the tower, loud swelled the sounding bands, flute spoke and clarion answered, deep rolled the drums, and away they marched.

The broad white road unrolled before the long procession, the sun and sky surveyed it cloudless, the wind tossed the tree-boughs above it, and the twelve hundred children, and one hundred and forty adults, of which it was composed, trod on in time and tune, with gay faces and glad hearts. It was a joyous scene, and a scene to do good: it was a day of happiness for rich and poor; the work, first of God, and then of the clergy. Let England's priests have their due: they are a faulty set in some respects, being only of common flesh and blood, like us all; but the land would be badly off without them: Britain would miss her church, if that church fell. God save it! God also reform it!

CHAPTER XVII

THE SCHOOL-FEAST

NOT ON COMBAT bent, nor of foemen in search, was this priest-led and woman-officered company: yet their music played martial tunes, and – to judge by the eyes and carriage of some, Miss Keeldar, for instance – these sounds awoke, if not a martial, yet a longing spirit. Old Helstone, turning by chance, looked into her face, and he laughed, and she laughed at him.

'There is no battle in prospect,' he said; 'our country does not want us to fight for it: no foe or tyrant is questioning or threatening our liberty: there is nothing to be done: we are only taking a walk. Keep your hand on the reins, captain, and slack the fire of that spirit: it is not wanted; the more's the pity.'

'Take your own advice, Doctor,' was Shirley's response. To Caroline, she murmured, 'I'll borrow of imagination what reality will not give me. We are not soldiers – bloodshed is not my desire; or if we are, we are soldiers of the Cross. Time has rolled back some hundreds of years, and we are bound on a pilgrimage to Palestine. But no, – that is too visionary. I need a sterner dream: we are Lowlanders of Scotland, following a covenanting captain up into the hills to hold a meeting out of the reach of persecuting troopers. We know that battle may follow prayer; and, as we believe that in the worst issue of battle, heaven must be our reward, we are ready and willing to redden the peat-moss with our blood. That music stirs my soul; it wakens all my life; it makes my heart beat: not with its temperate daily pulse, but with a new, thrilling vigour. I almost long for danger; for a faith – a land – or, at least, a lover to defend.'

'Look, Shirley!' interrupted Caroline. 'What is that red speck above Stilbro' Brow? You have keener sight than I; just turn your eagle eye to it.'

Miss Keeldar looked. 'I see,' she said: then added, presently, 'there is a line of red. They are soldiers – cavalry soldiers,' she subjoined quickly: 'they ride fast; there are six of them: they will pass us: no – they have turned off to the right: they saw our procession, and avoid it by making a circuit. Where are they going?'

'Perhaps they are only exercising their horses.'

'Perhaps so. We see them no more now.'

Mr Helstone here spoke.

'We shall pass through Royd-lane, to reach Nunnely Common by a short cut,' said he.

And into the straits of Royd-lane they accordingly defiled. It was very narrow, – so narrow that only two could walk abreast without falling into the ditch which ran along each side. They had gained the middle of it, when excitement became obvious in the clerical commanders: Boultby's spectacles and Helstone's Rehoboam were agitated: the curates nudged each other: Mr Hall turned to the ladies and smiled.

'What is the matter?' was the demand.

He pointed with his staff to the end of the lane before them. Lo and behold! another, – an opposition procession was there entering, headed also by men in black, and followed also, as they could now hear, by music.

'Is it our double?' asked Shirley: 'our manifold wraith? Here is a card turned up.'

'If you wanted a battle, you are likely to get one, – at least of looks,' whispered Caroline, laughing.

'They shall not pass us!' cried the curates, unanimously: 'we'll not give way!'

'Give way!' retorted Helstone, sternly, turning round; 'who talks of giving way? You, boys, mind what you are about: the ladies, I know, will be firm; I can trust them. There is not a churchwoman here but will stand her ground against these folks, for the honour of the Establishment. What does Miss Keeldar say?'

'She asks what is it?'

'The Dissenting and Methodist schools, the Baptists, Independents, and Wesleyans, joined in unholy alliance, and turning purposely into this lane with the intention of obstructing our march and driving us back.'

'Bad manners!' said Shirley; 'and I hate bad manners. Of course, they must have a lesson.'

'A lesson in politeness,' suggested Mr Hall, who was ever for peace: 'not an example of rudeness.'

Old Helstone moved on. Quickening his step, he marched some yards in advance of his company. He had nearly reached the other sable leaders, when he who appeared to act as the hostile commander-in-chief – a large, greasy man, with black hair combed flat on his forehead – called a halt. The procession paused: he drew forth a hymn-book, gave our a verse, set a tune, and they all struck up the most dolorous of canticles.

Helstone signed to his bands: they clashed our with all the power of brass. He desired them to play 'Rule, Britannia,' and ordered the children to join in vocally, which they did with enthusiastic spirit. The enemy was sung and stormed down; his psalm quelled: as far as noise went, he was conquered.

'Now, follow me!' exclaimed Helstone; 'not at a run, but at a firm, smart pace. Be steady, every child and woman of you: – keep together: – hold on by each other's skirts, if necessary.'

And he strode on with such a determined and deliberate gait, and was, besides, so well seconded by his scholars and teachers – who did exactly as he told them, neither running nor faltering, but marching with cool, solid impetus; the curates, too, being compelled to do the same, as they were between two fires, – Helstone and Miss Keeldar, – both of whom watched any deviation with lynx-eyed vigilance, and were ready, the one with his cane, the other with her parasol, to rebuke the slightest

breach of orders, the least independent or irregular demonstration, – that the body of Dissenters were first amazed, then
alarmed, then borne down and pressed back, and at last forced
to turn tail and leave the outlet from Royd-lane free. Boultby
suffered in the onslaught, but Helstone and Malone, between
them, held him up, and brought him through the business,
whole in limb, though sorely tried in wind.

The fat Dissenter who had given out the hymn was left sitting
in the ditch. He was a spirit-merchant by trade, a leader of the
Non-conformists, and, it was said, drank more water in that
one afternoon than he had swallowed for a twelvemonth before.
Mr Hall had taken care of Caroline, and Caroline of him: he
and Miss Ainley made their own quiet comments to each other
afterwards on the incident. Miss Keeldar and Mr Helstone
shook hands heartily when they had fairly got the whole party
though the lane. The curates began to exult, but Mr Helstone
presently put the curb on their innocent spirits: he remarked
that they never had sense to know what to say, and had better
hold their tongues; and he reminded them that the business
was none of their managing.

About half-past three the procession turned back, and at four
once more regained the starting-place. Long lines of benches
were arranged in the close-shorn fields round the school: there
the children were seated, and huge baskets, covered up with
white cloths, and great smoking tin vessels were brought out. Ere
the distribution of good things commenced, a brief grace was
pronounced by Mr Hall, and sung by the children: their young
voices sounded melodious, even touching, in the open air. Large
currant buns, and hot, well-sweetened tea, were then administered in the proper spirit of liberality: no stinting was permitted
on this day, at least; the rule for each child's allowance being that
it was to have about twice as much as it could possibly eat, thus
leaving a reserve to be carried home for such as age, sickness, or
other impediment, prevented from coming to the feast. Buns
and beer circulated, meantime, amongst the musicians and

church-singers: afterwards the benches were removed, and they were left to unbend their spirits in licensed play.

A bell summoned the teachers, patrons, and patronesses to the schoolroom; Miss Keeldar, Miss Helstone, and many other ladies were already there, glancing over the arrangement of their separate trays and tables. Most of the female servants of the neighbourhood, together with the clerks', the singers', and the musicians' wives, had been pressed into the service of the day as waiters: each vied with the other in smartness and daintiness of dress, and many handsome forms were seen amongst the younger ones. About half a score were cutting bread and butter; another half-score supplying hot water, brought from the coppers of the Rector's kitchen. The profusion of flowers and evergreens decorating the white walls, the show of silver teapots and bright porcelain on the tables, the active figures, blithe faces, gay dresses flitting about everywhere, formed altogether a refreshing and lively spectacle. Everybody talked, not very loudly, but merrily, and the canary birds sang shrill in their high-hung cages.

Caroline, as the Rector's niece, took her place at one of the three first tables; Mrs Boultby and Margaret Hall officiated at the others. At these tables the élite of the company were to be entertained; strict rules of equality not being more in fashion at Briarfield than elsewhere. Miss Helstone removed her bonnet and scarf, that she might be less oppressed with the heat; her long curls, falling on her neck, served almost in place of a veil, and for the rest, her muslin dress was fashioned modestly as a nun's robe, enabling her thus to dispense with the encumbrance of a shawl.

The room was filling: Mr Hall had taken his post beside Caroline, who now, as she re-arranged the cups and spoons before her, whispered to him in a low voice remarks on the events of the day. He looked a little grave about what had taken place in Royd-lane, and she tried to smile him out of his seriousness. Miss Keeldar sat near; for a wonder, neither laughing nor talking; on the contrary, very still, and gazing round her vigilantly: she seemed afraid lest some intruder should take a seat she apparently wished to reserve next her own; ever and anon she spread her satin dress over an undue portion of the bench, or laid her gloves or her embroidered handkerchief upon it. Caroline noticed this manège at last, and asked her what friend she expected. Shirley bent towards her, almost touched her ear with her rosy lips, and whispered with a musical softness that often characterized her tones, when what she said tended even remotely to stir some sweet secret source of feeling in her heart: –

'I expect Mr Moore: I saw him last night, and I made him promise to come with his sister, and to sit at our table: he won't fail me, I feel certain, but I apprehend his coming too late, and being separated from us. Here is a fresh batch arriving; every place will be taken: provoking!'

In fact Mr Wynne the magistrate, his wife, his son, and his two daughters, now entered in high state. They were Briarfield gentry: of course their place was at the first table, and being conducted thither, they filled up the whole remaining space. For Miss Keeldar's comfort, Mr Sam Wynne inducted himself into the very vacancy she had kept for Moore, planting himself solidly on her gown, her gloves, and her handkerchief. Mr Sam was one of the objects of her aversion; and the more so because he showed serious symptoms of an aim at her hand. The old gentleman, too, had publicly declared that the Fieldhead estate and the De Walden estate were delightfully *conta-gious* – a malapropism which rumour had not failed to repeat to Shirley.

Caroline's ears yet rung with that thrilling whisper, 'I expect Mr Moore,' her heart yet beat and her cheek yet glowed with it, when a note from the organ pealed above the confused hum of the place. Dr Boultby, Mr Helstone, and Mr Hall rose, so did all present, and grace was sung to the accompaniment of the music; and then tea began. She was kept too busy with her office for a while to have leisure for looking round, but the last cup being filled, she threw a restless glance over the room. There were some ladies and several gentlemen standing about yet unaccommodated with seats: amidst a group she recognised her spinster friend, Miss Mann, whom the fine weather had tempted, or some urgent friend had persuaded, to leave her drear solitude for one hour of social enjoyment. Miss Mann looked tired of standing: a lady in a yellow bonnet brought her a chair. Caroline knew well that 'chapeau en satin jaune;' she knew the black hair, and the kindly, though rather opinionated and froward-looking face under it; she knew that 'robe de soie noire;' she knew even that 'schal gris de lin;' she knew, in short, Hortense Moore, and she wanted to jump up and run to her and kiss her – to give her one embrace for her own sake, and two for her brother's. She half rose, indeed, with a smothered exclamation, and perhaps – for the impulse was very strong – she would have run across the room, and actually saluted her, but a hand replaced her in her seat, and a voice behind her whispered: –

'Wait till after tea, Lina, and then I'll bring her to you.'

And when she *could* look up she did, and there was Robert himself close behind, smiling at her eagerness, looking better than she had ever seen him look – looking, indeed, to her partial eyes, so very handsome, that she dared not trust herself to hazard a second glance; for his image struck on her vision with painful brightness, and pictured itself on her memory as vividly as if there daguerreotyped by a pencil of keen lightning.

He moved on, and spoke to Miss Keeldar. Shirley, irritated by some unwelcome attentions from Sam Wynne, and by the fact of that gentleman being still seated on her gloves and handkerchief – and probably, also, by Moore's want of punctuality – was by no means in good humour. She first shrugged her shoulder at him, and then she said a bitter word or two about his 'insupportable tardiness.' Moore neither apologized nor retorted: he stood near her quietly, as if waiting to see whether she would recover her temper; which she did in little more than three minutes, indicating the change by offering him her hand. Moore took it with a smile, half-corrective, half-grateful: the slightest possible shake of the head delicately marked the former quality; it is probable a gentle pressure indicated the latter.

'You may sit where you can now, Mr Moore,' said Shirley, also smiling: 'you see there is not an inch of room for you here; but I discern plenty of space at Mrs Boultby's table, between Miss Armitage and Miss Birtwhistle; go: John Sykes will be your vis-à-vis, and you will sit with your back towards us.'

Moore, however, preferred lingering about where he was: he now and then took a turn down the long room, pausing in his walk to interchange greetings with other gentlemen in his own placeless predicament; but still he came back to the magnet, Shirley, bringing with him, each time he returned, observations it was necessary to whisper in her ear.

Meantime, poor Sam Wynne looked far from comfortable: his fair neighbour, judging from her movements, appeared in a mood the most unquiet and unaccommodating: she would not sit still two seconds: she was hot; she fanned herself; complained of want of air and space. She remarked, that, in her opinion, when people had finished their tea they ought to leave the tables, and announced distinctly that she expected to faint if the present state of things continued. Mr Sam offered to accompany her into the open air; just the way to give her her death of cold, she alleged: in short, his post became untenable; and having swallowed his quantum of tea, he judged it expedient to evacuate.

Moore should have been at hand, whereas he was quite at the other extremity of the room, deep in conference with Christopher Sykes. A large corn-factor, Timothy Ramsden, Esq., happened to be nearer, and feeling himself tired of standing, he advanced to fill the vacant seat. Shirley's expedients did not fail her: a sweep of her scarf upset her teacup, its contents were shared between the bench and her own satin dress. Of course, it became necessary to call a waiter to remedy the mischief: Mr Ramsden, a stout, puffy gentleman, as large in person as he was in property, held aloof from the consequent commotion. Shirley, usually almost culpably indifferent to slight accidents affecting dress, &c., now made a commotion that might have become the most delicate and nervous of her sex: Mr Ramsden opened his mouth, withdrew slowly, and, as Miss Keeldar again intimated her intention to 'give way' and swoon on the spot, he turned on his heel, and beat a heavy retreat.

Moore at last returned: calmly surveying the bustle, and somewhat quizzically scanning Shirley's enigmatical-looking countenance, he remarked, that in truth this was the hottest end of the room; that he found a climate there calculated to agree with none but cool temperaments like his own; and, putting the waiters, the napkins, the satin robe, the whole turmoil, in short, to one side, he installed himself where destiny evidently decreed he should sit. Shirley subsided; her features altered their lines: the raised knit brow and inexplicable curve of the mouth became straight again: wilfulness and roguery gave place to other expressions; and all the angular movements with which she had vexed the soul of Sam Wynne were conjured to rest as by a charm. Still no gracious glance was cast on Moore: on the contrary, he was accused of giving her a world of trouble, and roundly charged with being the cause of depriving her of the esteem of Mr Ramsden, and the invaluable friendship of Mr Samuel Wynne.

'Wouldn't have offended either gentleman for the world,' she averred: 'I have always been accustomed to treat both with the most respectful consideration, and there, owing to you, how they have been used! I shall not be happy till I have made it up: I never am happy till I am friends with my neighbours; so to-morrow I must make a pilgrimage to Royd corn-mill, soothe the miller, and praise the grain; and next day I must call at De Walden – where I hate to go – and carry in my reticule half an oat-cake to give to Mr Sam's favourite pointers.'

'You know the surest path to the heart of each swain, I doubt not,' said Moore, quietly. He looked very content to have at last secured his present place; but he made no fine speech expressive of gratification, and offered no apology for the trouble he had given. His phlegm became him wonderfully: it made him look handsomer, he was so composed: it made his vicinage pleasant, it was so peace-restoring. You would not have thought, to look at him, that he was a poor, struggling man seated beside a rich woman; the calm of equality stilled his aspect: perhaps that calm, too, reigned in his soul. Now and then, from the way in which he looked down on Miss Keeldar as he addressed her, you would have fancied his station towered above hers as much as his stature did. Almost stern lights sometimes crossed his brow and gleamed in his eyes: their conversation had become animated, though it was confined to a low key; she was urging him with questions – evidently, he refused to her curiosity all the gratification it demanded. She sought his eye once with hers: you read, in its soft yet eager expression, that it solicited clearer replies. Moore smiled pleasantly, but his lips continued sealed. Then she was piqued and turned away, but he recalled her attention in two minutes: he seemed making promises, which he soothed her into accepting, in lieu of information.

It appeared that the heat of the room did not suit Miss Helstone: she grew paler and paler as the process of tea-making was protracted. The moment thanks were returned, she quitted the table, and hastened to follow her cousin Hortense, who, with Miss Mann, had already sought the open air. Robert Moore had risen when she did – perhaps he meant to speak to her; but there was yet a parting word to exchange with Miss Keeldar, and while it was being uttered, Caroline had vanished.

Hortense received her former pupil with a demeanour of more dignity than warmth: she had been seriously offended by Mr Helstone's proceedings, and had all along considered Caroline to blame, in obeying her uncle too literally.

'You are a very great stranger,' she said, austerely, as her pupil held and pressed her hand. The pupil knew her too well to remonstrate or complain of coldness; she let the punctilious whim pass, sure that her natural *bonté* (I use this French word, because it expresses just what I mean; neither goodness nor good nature, but something between the two) would presently get the upper-hand. It did: Hortense had no sooner examined her face well, and observed the change its somewhat wasted features betrayed, than her mien softened. Kissing her on both cheeks, she asked anxiously after her health: Caroline answered gaily. It would, however, have been her lot to undergo a long cross-examination, followed by an endless lecture on this head, had not Miss Mann called off the attention of the questioner by requesting to be conducted home. The poor invalid was already fatigued: her weariness made her cross – too cross almost to speak to Caroline; and besides, that young person's white dress and lively look were displeasing in the eyes of Miss Mann: the everyday garb of brown stuff or grey gingham, and the everyday air of melancholy, suited the solitary spinster better: she would hardly know her young friend to-night, and quitted her with a cool nod. Hortense having promised to accompany her home, they departed together.

Caroline now looked round for Shirley. She saw the rainbow scarf and purple dress in the centre of a throng of ladies, all well known to herself, but all of the order whom she system-atically avoided whenever avoidance was possible. Shyer at some moments than at others, she felt just now no courage at all to join this company: she could not, however, stand alone where all others went in pairs or parties, so she approached a group of her own scholars, great girls, or rather young women, who were standing watching some hundreds of the younger children playing at blind-man's-buff.

Miss Helstone knew these girls liked her, yet she was shy even with them out of school: they were not more in awe of her than she of them: she drew near them now, rather to find protection in their company than to patronize them with her presence. By some instinct they knew her weakness, and with natural politeness they respected it. Her knowledge commanded their esteem when she taught them; her gentleness attracted their regard; and because she was what they considered wise and good when *on* duty, they kindly overlooked her evident timidity when off: they did not take advantage of it. Peasant girls as they were, they had too much of her own English sensibility to be guilty of the coarse error: they stood round her still, civil, friendly, receiving her slight smiles, and rather hurried efforts to converse, with a good feeling and good breeding: the last quality being the result of the first, which soon set her at her ease.

Mr Sam Wynne coming up with great haste, to insist on the elder girls joining in the game as well as the younger ones, Caroline was again left alone. She was meditating a quiet retreat to the house, when Shirley, perceiving from afar her isolation, hastened to her side.

'Let us go to the top of the fields,' she said: 'I know you don't like crowds, Caroline.'

'But it will be depriving you of a pleasure, Shirley, to take you from all these fine people, who court your society so assiduously, and to whom you can, without art or effort, make yourself so pleasant.'

'Not quite without effort: I am already tired of the exertion: it is but insipid, barren work, talking and laughing with the good gentlefolks of Briarfield. I have been looking out for your white dress for the last ten minutes: I like to watch those I love in a crowd, and to compare them with others: I have thus compared you. You resemble none of the rest, Lina: there are some prettier faces than yours here; you are not a model-beauty like Harriet Sykes, for instance; beside her, your person appears almost insignificant; but you look agreeable – you look reflective – you look what I call interesting.'

'Hush, Shirley! You flatter me.'

'I don't wonder that your scholars like you.'

'Nonsense, Shirley: talk of something else.'

'We will talk of Moore, then, and we will watch him: I see him even now.'

'Where?' And as Caroline asked the question, she looked not over the fields, but into Miss Keeldar's eyes, as was her wont whenever Shirley mentioned any object she descried afar. Her friend had quicker vision than herself; and Caroline seemed to think that the secret of her eagle acuteness might be read in her dark grey irids: or rather, perhaps, she only sought guidance by the direction of those discriminating and brilliant spheres.

'There is Moore,' said Shirley, pointing right across the wide field where a thousand children were playing, and now nearly a thousand adult spectators walking about. 'There – can you miss the tall stature and straight port? He looks amidst the set that surround him like Eliab amongst humbler shepherds – like Saul in a war-council: and a war-council it is, if I am not mistaken.'

'Why so, Shirley?' asked Caroline, whose eye had at last caught the object it sought. 'Robert is just now speaking to my uncle, and they are shaking hands; they are then reconciled.'

'Reconciled not without good reason, depend on it: making common cause against some common foe. And why, think you, are Messrs Wynne and Sykes, and Armitage and Ramsden, gathered in such a close circle round them? And why is Malone beckoned to join them? Where *he* is summoned, be sure a strong arm is needed.'

Shirley, as she watched, grew restless: her eyes flashed.

'They won't trust me,' she said: 'that is always the way when it comes to the point.'

'What about?'

'Cannot you feel? There is some mystery afloat: some event is expected; some preparation is to be made, I am certain: I saw it all in Mr Moore's manner this evening: he was excited, yet hard.'

'Hard to *you*, Shirley!'

'Yes, to *me*. He often is hard to me. We seldom converse

tête-à-tête, but I am made to feel that the basis of his character is not of eider down.'

'Yet he seemed to talk to you softly.'

'Did he not? Very gentle tones and quiet manner; yet the man is peremptory and secret: his secrecy vexes me.'

'Yes – Robert is secret.'

'Which he has scarcely a right to be with me; especially as he commenced by giving me his confidence. Having done nothing to forfeit that confidence, it ought not to be withdrawn: but I suppose I am not considered iron-souled enough to be trusted in a crisis.'

'He fears, probably, to occasion you uneasiness.'

'An unnecessary precaution: I am of elastic materials, not soon crushed; he ought to know that: but the man is proud: he has his faults, say what you will, Lina. Observe how engaged that group appear: they do not know we are watching them.'

'If we keep on the alert, Shirley, we shall perhaps find the clue to their secret.'

'There will be some unusual movements erelong – perhaps to-morrow – possibly to-night. But my eyes and ears are wide open: Mr Moore, you shall be under surveillance. Be you vigilant also, Lina.'

'I will: Robert is going, I saw him turn – I believe he noticed us – they are shaking hands.'

'Shaking hands, with emphasis,' added Shirley; 'as if they were ratifying some solemn league and covenant.'

They saw Robert quit the group, pass through a gate, and disappear. 'And he has not bid us good-bye,' murmured Caroline.

Scarcely had the words escaped her lips, when she tried by a smile to deny the confession of disappointment they seemed to imply. An unbidden suffusion for one moment both softened and brightened her eyes.

'Oh, that is soon remedied!' exclaimed Shirley. 'We'll *make* him bid us good-bye.'

'*Make* him! That is not the same thing,' was the answer.

'It *shall* be the same thing.'

'But he is gone: you can't overtake him.'

'I know a shorter way than that he has taken: we will intercept him.'

'But, Shirley, I would rather not go.'

Caroline said this as Miss Keeldar seized her arm, and hurried her down the fields. It was vain to contend: nothing was so wilful as Shirley, when she took a whim into her head: Caroline found herself our of sight of the crowd almost before she was aware, and ushered into a narrow shady spot, embowered above with hawthorns, and enamelled under foot with daisies. She took no notice of the evening sun chequering the turf, nor was she sensible of the pure incense exhaling at this hour from tree and plant; she only heard the wicker opening at one end, and knew Robert was approaching. The long sprays of the haw-thorns, shooting out before them, served as a screen; they saw him before he observed them. At a glance Caroline perceived that his social hilarity was gone: he had left it behind him in the joy-echoing fields round the school; what remained now was his dark, quiet, business countenance. As Shirley had said, a certain hardness characterized his air, while his eye was excited, but austere. So much the worse-timed was the present freak of Shirley's: if he had looked disposed for holiday mirth, it would not have mattered much, but now –

'I told you not to come,' said Caroline, somewhat bitterly, to her friend. She seemed truly perturbed: to be intruded on Robert thus, against her will and his expectation, and when he evidently would rather not be delayed, keenly annoyed her. It did not annoy Miss Keeldar in the least: she stepped forward and faced her tenant, barring his way: –

'You omitted to bid us good-bye,' she said.

'Omitted to bid you good-bye! Where did you come from? Are you fairies? I left two like you, one in purple and one in white, standing at the top of a bank, four fields off, but a minute ago.'

'You left us there and find us here. We have been watching you; and shall watch you still: you must be questioned one day, but not now: at present, all you have to do is to say good-night, and then pass.'

Moore glanced from one to the other, without unbending his aspect. 'Days of fête have their privileges, and so have days of hazard,' observed he, gravely.

'Come – don't moralize: say good-night, and pass,' urged Shirley.

'Must I say good-night to you, Miss Keeldar?'

'Yes, and to Caroline likewise. It is nothing new, I hope: you have bid us both good-night before.'

He took her hand, held it in one of his, and covered it with the other: he looked down at her gravely, kindly, yet commandingly. The heiress could not make this man her subject: in his gaze on her bright face there was no servility, hardly homage; but there was interest and affection, heightened by another feeling: something in his tone when he spoke, as well as in his words, marked that last sentiment to be gratitude.

'Your debtor bids you good-night! – May you rest safely and serenely till morning!'

'And you, Mr Moore, – what are you going to do? What have you been saying to Mr Helstone, with whom I saw you shake hands? Why did all those gentlemen gather round you? Put away reserve for once: be frank with me.'

'Who can resist you? I will be frank: to-morrow, if there is anything to relate, you shall hear it.'

'Just now,' pleaded Shirley: 'don't procrastinate.'

'But I could only tell half a tale; and my time is limited, – I have not a moment to spare: hereafter I will make amends for delay by candour.'

'But are you going home?'

'Yes.'

'Not to leave it any more to-night?'

'Certainly not. At present, farewell to both of you!'

He would have taken Caroline's hand and joined it in the same clasp in which he held Shirley's, but somehow it was not ready for him; she had withdrawn a few steps apart: her answer to Moore's adieu was only a slight bend of the head, and a gentle, serious smile. He sought no more cordial token: again he said 'Farewell!' and quitted them both.

'There! – it is over!' said Shirley, when he was gone. 'We have made him bid us good-night, and yet not lost ground in his esteem, I think, Cary.'

'I hope not,' was the brief reply.

'I consider you very timid and undemonstrative,' remarked Miss Keeldar. 'Why did you not give Moore your hand when he offered you his? He is your cousin: you like him. Are you ashamed to let him perceive your affection?'

'He perceives all of it that interests him: no need to make a display of feeling.'

'You are laconic: you would be stoical if you could. Is love, in your eyes, a crime, Caroline?'

'Love, a crime! No, Shirley: – love is a divine virtue; but why drag that word into the conversation? it is singularly irrelevant!'

'Good!' pronounced Shirley.

The two girls paced the green lane in silence. Caroline first resumed.

'Obtrusiveness is a crime; forwardness is a crime; and both disgust: but love! – no purest angel need blush to love! And when I see or hear either man or woman couple shame with love, I know their minds are coarse, their associations debased. Many who think themselves refined ladies and gentlemen, and on whose lips the word "vulgarity" is for ever hovering, cannot mention "love" without betraying their own innate and imbecile degradation: it is a low feeling in their estimation, connected only with low ideas for them.'

'You describe three-fourths of the world, Caroline.'

'They are cold – they are cowardly – they are stupid on the subject, Shirley? They never loved – they never were loved!'

'Thou art right, Lina! And in their dense ignorance they blaspheme living fire, seraph-brought from a divine altar.'

'They confound it with sparks mounting from Tophet!'

The sudden and joyous clash of bells here stopped the dialogue by summoning all to the church.

CHAPTER XVIII

WHICH THE GENTEEL READER IS RECOMMENDED TO SKIP, LOW PERSONS BEING HERE INTRODUCED

THE EVENING was still and warm; close and sultry it even promised to become. Round the descending sun the clouds glowed purple: summer tints, rather Indian than English, suffused the horizon, and cast rosy reflections on hill-side, house-front, tree-bole; on winding road, and undulating pasture-ground. The two girls came down from the fields slowly: by the time they reached the churchyard the bells were hushed; the multitudes were gathered into the church: the whole scene was solitary.

'How pleasant and calm it is!' said Caroline.

'And how hot it will be in the church!' responded Shirley; 'and what a dreary long speech Dr Boultby will make! and how the curates will hammer over their prepared orations! For my part, I would rather not enter.'

'But my uncle will be angry, if he observes our absence.'

'I will bear the brunt of his wrath: he will not devour me. I shall be sorry to miss his pungent speech. I know it will be all sense for the Church, and all causticity for Schism: he'll not forget the battle of Royd-lane. I shall be sorry also to deprive you of Mr Hall's sincere friendly homily, with all its racy Yorkshireisms; but here I must stay. The grey church and greyer tombs look divine with this crimson gleam on them. Nature is now at her evening prayers: she is kneeling before those red hills. I see her prostrate on the great steps of her altar, praying for a fair night for mariners at sea, for travellers in deserts, for lambs on moors, and unfledged birds in woods. Caroline, I see her! and I will tell you what she is like: she is like what Eve was when she and Adam stood alone on earth.'

'And that is not Milton's Eve, Shirley.'

'Milton's Eve! Milton's Eve! I repeat. No, by the pure Mother of God, she is not! Cary, we are alone: we may speak what we think. Milton was great; but was he good? His brain was right; how was his heart? He saw heaven: he looked down on hell. He saw Satan, and Sin his daughter, and Death their horrible offspring. Angels serried before him their battalions: the long lines of adamantine shields flashed back on his blind eyeballs the unutterable splendour of heaven. Devils gathered their legions in his sight: their dim, discrowned, and tarnished armies passed rank and file before him. Milton tried to see the first woman; but, Cary, he saw her not.'

'You are bold to say so, Shirley.'

'Not more bold than faithful. It was his cook that he saw; or it was Mrs Gill, as I have seen her, making custards, in the heat of summer, in the cool dairy, with rose-trees and nasturtiums about the latticed window, preparing a cold collation for the rectors, – preserves, and "dulcet creams" – puzzled "what choice to choose for delicacy best; what order so contrived as not to mix tastes, not well-joined, inelegant; but bring taste after taste, upheld with kindliest change."'

'All very well too, Shirley.'

'I would beg to remind him that the first men of the earth were Titans, and that Eve was their mother: from her sprang Saturn, Hyperion, Oceanus; she bore Prometheus –'

'Pagan that you are! what does that signify?'

'I say, there were giants on the earth in those days: giants that strove to scale heaven. The first woman's breast that heaved with life on this world yielded the daring which could contend with Omnipotence: the strength which could bear a thousand years of bondage, – the vitality which could feed that vulture death through uncounted ages, – the unexhausted life and uncorrupted excellence, sisters to immortality, which, after millenniums of crimes, struggles, and woes, could conceive and bring forth a Messiah. The first woman was heaven-born: vast was the heart whence gushed the well-spring of the blood of nations; and grand the undegenerate head where rested the consort-crown of creation.'

'She coveted an apple, and was cheated by a snake: but you have got such a hash of Scripture and mythology into your head that there is no making any sense of you. You have not yet told me what you saw kneeling on those hills.'

'I saw – I now see – a woman-Titan: her robe of blue air spreads to the outskirts of the heath, where yonder flock is grazing; a veil white as an avalanche sweeps from her head to her feet, and arabesques of lightning flame on its borders. Under her breast I see her zone, purple like that horizon: through its blush shines the star of evening. Her steady eyes I cannot picture; they are clear – they are deep as lakes – they are lifted and full of worship – they tremble with the softness of love and the lustre of prayer. Her forehead has the expanse of a cloud, and is paler than the early moon, risen long before dark gathers: she reclines her bosom on the ridge of Stilbro' Moor; her mighty hands are joined beneath it. So kneeling, face to face she speaks with God. That Eve is Jehovah's daughter, as Adam was his son.'

'She is very vague and visionary! Come, Shirley, we ought to go into church.'

'Caroline, I will not: will stay out here with my mother Eve, in these days called Nature. I love her – undying, mighty being! Heaven may have faded from her brow when she fell in paradise; but all that is glorious on earth shines there still. She is taking me to her bosom, and showing me her heart. Hush, Caroline! you will see her and feel as I do, if we are both silent.'

'I will humour your whim; but you will begin talking again, ere ten minutes are over.'

Miss Keeldar, on whom the soft excitement of the warm

summer evening seemed working with unwonted power, leaned against an upright headstone: she fixed her eyes on the deep-burning west, and sank into a pleasurable trance. Caroline, going a little apart, paced to and fro beneath the Rectory garden-wall, dreaming, too, in her way. Shirley had mentioned the word 'mother:' that word suggested to Caroline's imagination not the mighty and mystical parent of Shirley's visions, but a gentle human form – the form she ascribed to her own mother; unknown, unloved, but not unlonged-for.

'Oh, that the day would come when she would remember her child! Oh, that I might know her, and knowing, love her!'

Such was her aspiration.

The longing of her childhood filled her soul again. The desire which many a night had kept her awake in her crib, and which fear of its fallacy had of late years almost extinguished, relit suddenly, and glowed warm in her heart: that her mother might come some happy day, and send for her to her presence – look upon her fondly with loving eyes, and say to her tenderly, in a sweet voice: –

'Caroline, my child. I have a home for you: you shall live with me. All the love you have needed, and not tasted, from infancy, I have saved for you carefully. Come! it shall cherish you now.'

A noise on the road roused Caroline from her filial hopes, and Shirley from her Titan visions. They listened, and heard the tramp of horses: they looked, and saw a glitter through the trees: they caught through the foliage glimpses of martial scarlet; helm shone, plume waved. Silent and orderly, six soldiers rode softly by.

'The same we saw this afternoon,' whispered Shirley: 'they have been halting somewhere till now. They wish to be as little noticed as possible, and are seeking their rendezvous at this quiet hour, while the people are at church. Did I not say we should see unusual things erelong?'

Scarcely were sight and sound of the soldiers lost, when

another and somewhat different disturbance broke the night-hush – a child's impatient scream. They looked: a man issued from the church, carrying in his arms an infant – a robust, ruddy little boy, of some two years old – roaring with all the power of his lungs; he had probably just awaked from a church-sleep: two little girls, of nine and ten followed. The influence of the fresh air, and the attraction of some flowers gathered from a grave, soon quieted the child; the man sat down with him, dandling him on his knee as tenderly as any woman; the two little girls took their places one on each side.

'Good-evening, William,' said Shirley, after due scrutiny of the man. He had seen her before, and apparently was waiting to be recognised; he now took off his hat, and grinned a smile of pleasure. He was a rough-headed, hard featured personage, not old, but very weather-beaten; his attire was decent and clean, that of his children singularly neat; it was our old friend, Farren. The young ladies approached him.

'You are not going into the church?' he inquired, gazing at them complacently, yet with a mixture of bashfulness in his look: a sentiment not by any means the result of awe of their station, but only of appreciation of their elegance and youth. Before gentlemen – such as Moore or Helstone, for instance – William was often a little dogged; with proud or insolent ladies, too, he was quite unmanageable, sometimes very resentful; but he was most sensible of, most tractable to, good-humour and civility. His nature – a stubborn one – was repelled by inflexibility in other natures; for which reason, he had never been able to like his former master, Moore; and, unconscious of that gentleman's good opinion of himself, and of the service he had secretly rendered him in recommending him as gardener to Mr Yorke, and by this means to other families in the neighbourhood, he continued to harbour a grudge against his austerity. Latterly, he had often worked at Fieldhead; Miss Keeldar's frank, hospitable manners were perfectly charming to him. Caroline he had known from her childhood: unconsciously, she was his ideal of a lady. Her gentle mien, step, gestures, her grace of person and attire, moved some artist-fibres about his peasant heart: he had a pleasure in looking at her, as he had in examining rare flowers, or in seeing pleasant landscapes. Both the ladies liked William: it was their delight to lend him books, to give him plants; and they preferred his conversation far before that of many coarse, hard, pretentious people, immeasurably higher in station.

'Who was speaking, William, when you came out?' asked Shirley.

'A gentleman ye set a deal of store on, Miss Shirley – Mr Donne.'

'You look knowing, William. How did you find out my regard for Mr Donne?'

'Ay, Miss Shirley, there's a gleg light i' your een sometimes which betrays you. You look raight down scornful sometimes, when Mr Donne is by.'

'Do you like him yourself, William?'

'Me? I'm stalled o' t' curates, and so is t' wife: they've no manners; they talk to poor folk fair as if they thought they were beneath them. They're allus magnifying their office: it is a pity but their office could magnify them; but it does nought o' t' soart. I fair hate pride.'

'But you are proud in your own way yourself,' interposed Caroline: 'you are what you call house-proud; you like to have everything handsome about you: sometimes you look as if you were almost too proud to take your wages. When you were out of work, you were too proud to get anything on credit; but for your children, I believe you would rather have starved than gone to the shops without money; and when I wanted to give you something, what a difficulty I had in making you take it!'

'It is partly true, Miss Caroline: ony day I'd rather give than take, especially from sich as ye. Look at t' difference between us: ye're a little, young, slender lass, and I'm a great strong man: I'm rather more nor twice your age. It is not *my* part then,

I think, to tak' fro' *ye* – to be under obligations (as they say) to *ye*; and that day ye came to our house, and called me to t' door, and offered me five shillings, which I doubt ye could ill spare, – for ye've no fortin', I know, – that day I war fair a rebel – a radical – an insurrectionist; and *ye* made me so. I thought it shameful that, willing and able as I was to work, I suld be i' such a condition that a young cratur about the age o' my own eldest lass suld think it needful to come and offer me her bit o' brass.'

'I suppose you were angry with me, William?'

'I almost was, in a way; but I forgave ye varry soon: ye meant well. Ay, I *am* proud, and so are *ye*; but your pride and mine is t' raight mak' – what we call i' Yorkshire "clean pride," – such as Mr Malone and Mr Donne knows nought about: theirs is mucky pride. Now, I shall teach my lasses to be as proud as Miss Shirley there, and my lads to be as proud as myseln; but I dare ony o' 'em to be like t' curates: I'd lick little Michael, if I seed him show any signs o' that feeling.'

'What is the difference, William?'

'Ye know t' difference weel enew, but ye want me to get a gate o' talking. Mr Malone and Mr Donne is almost too proud to do aught for theirsel'n; *we* are almost too proud to let any-body do aught for us. T' curates can hardly bide to speak a civil word to them they think beneath them; *we* can hardly bide to tak' an uncivil word fro' them that thinks themsel'n aboon us.'

'Now, William, be humble enough to tell me truly how you are getting on in the world? Are you well off?'

'Miss Shirley – I am varry well off. Since I got into t' garden-ing line, wi' Mr Yorke's help, and since Mr Hall (another o' t' raight sort) helped my wife to set up a bit of a shop, I've nought to complain of. My family has plenty to eat and plenty to wear: my pride makes me find means to save an odd pound now and then against rainy days; for I think I'd die afore I'd come to t' parish: and me and mine is content; but th' neighbours is poor yet: I see a great deal of distress.'

'And, consequently, there is still discontent, I suppose?' inquired Miss Keeldar.

'*Consequently* – ye say right – *consequently*. In course, starving folk cannot be satisfied or settled folk. The country's not in a safe condition; – I'll say so mich!'

'But what can be done? What more can I do, for instance?'

'Do? – ye can do naught mich, poor young lass! Ye've gi'en your brass: ye've done well. If ye could transport your tenant, Mr Moore, to Botany Bay, ye'd happen do better. Folks hate him.'

'William, for shame!' exclaimed Caroline, warmly. 'If folks *do* hate him, it is to their disgrace, not his. Mr Moore himself hates nobody; he only wants to do his duty, and maintain his rights: you are wrong to talk so!'

'I talk as I think. He has a cold, unfeeling heart, yond' Moore.'

'But,' interposed Shirley, 'supposing Moore was driven from the country, and his mill razed to the ground, would people have more work?'

'They'd have less. I know that, and they know that; and there is many an honest lad driven desperate by the certainty that whichever way he turns, he cannot better himself, and there is dishonest men plenty to guide them to the devil: scoundrels that reckons to be the "people's friends," and that knows naught about the people, and is as insincere as Lucifer. I've lived aboon forty year in the world, and I believe that "the people" will never have any true friends but their-sel'n, and them two or three good folk i' different stations, that is friends to all the world. Human natur', taking it i' th' lump, is naught but selfishness. It is but excessive few; it is but just an exception here and there, now and then, sich as ye two young 'uns and me, that being in a different sphere, can understand t' one t' other, and be friends wi'out slavishness o' one hand, or pride o' t' other. Them that reckons to be friends to a lower class than their own fro' political motives is never to be trusted: they

always try to make their inferiors tools. For my own part, I will
neither be patronized nor misled for no man pleasure. I've had
overtures made to me lately that I saw were treacherous, and
I flung 'em back i' the faces o' them that offered 'em.'

'You won't tell us what overtures?'

'I will not: it would do no good; it would mak' no difference:
them they concerned can look after theirsel'n.'

'Ay, we'se look after wersel'n,' said another voice. Joe Scott
had sauntered forth from the church to get a breath of fresh air,
and there he stood.

'I'll warrant *ye*, Joe,' observed William, smiling.

'And I'll warrant my maister,' was the answer. 'Young ladies,'
continued Joe, assuming a lordly air, 'ye'd better go into th'
house.'

'I wonder what for?' inquired Shirley, to whom the overlooker's somewhat pragmatical manners were familiar, and who
was often at war with him; for Joe, holding supercilious
theories about women in general, resented greatly, in his secret
soul, the fact of his master and his master's mill being, in a
manner, under petticoat government, and had felt as wormwood and gall, certain business-visits of the heiress to the
Hollow's counting-house.

'Because there is naught agate that fits women to be
consarned in.'

'Indeed! There is prayer and preaching agate in that church;
are we not concerned in that?'

'Ye have been present neither at the prayer nor preaching,
ma'am, if I have observed aright. What I alluded to was politics:
William Farren, here, was touching on that subject, if I'm not
mista'en.'

'Well, what then? Politics are our habitual study, Joe. Do you
know I see a newspaper every day, and two of a Sunday?'

'I should think you'll read the marriages, probably, Miss, and
the murders, and the accidents, and sich like?'

'I read the leading articles, Joe, and the foreign intelligence, and I look over the market prices: in short, I read just what gentlemen read.'

Joe looked as if he thought this talk was like the chattering of a pie. He replied to it, by a disdainful silence.

'Joe,' continued Miss Keeldar, 'I never yet could ascertain properly, whether you are a Whig or a Tory: pray which party has the honour of your alliance?'

'It is rayther difficult to explain where you are sure not to be understood,' was Joe's haughty response; 'but, as to being a Tory, I'd as soon be an old woman, or a young one, which is a more flimsier article still. It is the Tories that carries on the war and ruins trade; and, if I be of any party – though political parties is all nonsense – I'm of that which is most favourable to peace, and, by consequence, to the mercantile interests of this here land.'

'So am I, Joe,' replied Shirley, who had rather a pleasure in teazing the overlooker, by persisting in talking on subjects with which he opined she – as a woman – had no right to meddle: 'partly, at least, I have rather a leaning to the agricultural interest, too; as good reason is, seeing that I don't desire England to be under the feet of France, and that if a share of my income comes from Hollow's mill, a larger share comes from the landed estate around it. It would not do to take any measures injurious to the farmers, Joe, I think?'

'The dews at this hour is unwholesome for females,' observed Joe.

'If you make that remark out of interest in me, I have merely to assure you that I am impervious to cold. I should not mind taking my turn to watch the mill one of these summer nights, armed with your musket, Joe.'

Joe Scott's chin was always rather prominent: he poked it out, at this speech, some inches further than usual.

'But – to go back to my sheep,' she proceeded – 'clothier and mill-owner as I am, besides farmer, I cannot get out of my head a certain idea that we manufacturers and persons of business are sometimes a little – a *very little* selfish and short-sighted in our views, and rather *too* regardless of human suffering, rather heartless in our pursuit of gain: don't you agree with me, Joe?'

'I cannot argue, where I cannot be comprehended,' was again the answer.

'Man of mystery! Your master will argue with me sometimes, Joe: he is not so stiff as you are.'

'May be not: we've all our own ways.'

'Joe, do you seriously think all the wisdom in the world is lodged in male skulls?'

'I think that women are a kittle and a froward generation; and I've a great respect for the doctrines delivered in the second chapter of St Paul's first Epistle to Timothy.'

'What doctrines, Joe?'

'Let the woman learn in silence, with all subjection. I suffer not a woman to teach, nor to usurp authority over the man; but to be in silence. For Adam was first formed, then Eve.'

'What has that to do with the business?' interjected Shirley: 'that smacks of rights of primogeniture. I'll bring it up to Mr Yorke the first time he inveighs against those rights.'

'And,' continued Joe Scott, 'Adam was not deceived; but the woman, being deceived, was in the transgression.'

'More shame to Adam to sin with his eyes open!' cried Miss Keeldar. 'To confess the honest truth, Joe, I never was easy in my mind concerning that chapter: it puzzles me.'

'It is very plain, Miss: he that runs may read.'

'He may read it in his own fashion,' remarked Caroline, now joining in the dialogue for the first time. 'You allow the right of private judgment, I suppose, Joe?'

'My certy, that I do! I allow and claim it for every line of the holy Book.'

'Women may exercise it as well as men?'

'Nay: women is to take their husbands' opinion, both in politics and religion: it's wholesomest for them.'

'Oh! oh!' exclaimed both Shirley and Caroline.

'To be sure; no doubt on 't,' persisted the stubborn overlooker.

'Consider yourself groaned down, and cried shame over, for such a stupid observation,' said Miss Keeldar. 'You might as well say, men are to take the opinions of their priests without examination. Of what value would a religion so adopted be? It would be mere blind, besotted superstition.'

'And what is *your* reading, Miss Helstone, o' these words o' St Paul's?'

'Hem! I – I account for them in this way: he wrote that chapter for a particular congregation of Christians, under peculiar circumstances; and besides, I dare say, if I could read the original Greek, I should find that many of the words have been wrongly translated, perhaps misapprehended altogether. It would be possible, I doubt not, with a little ingenuity, to give the passage quite a contrary turn; to make it say, "Let the woman speak out whenever she sees fit to make an objection;" – "it is permitted to a woman to teach and to exercise authority as much as may be. Man, meantime, cannot do better than hold his peace," and so on.'

'That will n't wash, Miss.'

'I dare say it will. My notions are dyed in faster colours than yours, Joe. Mr Scott, you are a thoroughly dogmatical person, and always were: I like William better than you.'

'Joe is well enough in his own house,' said Shirley: 'I have seen him as quiet as a lamb at home. There is not a better nor a kinder husband in Briarfield. He does not dogmatize to his wife.'

'My wife is a hard-working, plain woman: time and trouble has ta'en all the conceit out of her; but that is not the case with you, young Misses. And then you reckon to have so much knowledge; and i' my thoughts it's only a superficial sort o' vanities you're acquainted with. I can tell – happen a year sin' – one day Miss Caroline coming into our counting-house when I war packing up summut behind t' great desk, and she didn't see me, and she brought a slate wi a sum on it to t' maister: it were only a bit of a sum in practice, that our Harry would have settled i' two minutes. She couldn't do it; Mr Moore had to show her how; and when he did show her, she couldn't understand him.'

'Nonsense, Joe!'

'Nay, it's no nonsense: and Miss Shirley, there, reckons to hearken to t' maister when he's talking ower trade, so attentive like, as if she followed him word for word, and all war as clear as a lady's looking-glass to her een; and all t' while she's peeping and peeping out o' t' window to see if t' mare stands quiet; and then looking at a bit of a splash on her riding-skirt; and then glancing glegly round at wer counting-house cobwebs and dust, and thinking what mucky folk we are, and what a grand ride she'll have just i' now ower Nunnely-common. She hears no more o' Mr Moore's talk nor if he spake Hebrew.'

'Joe, you are a real slanderer. I would give you your answer, only the people are coming out of church: we must leave you. Man of prejudice, good-bye: William, good-bye. Children, come up to Fieldhead to-morrow, and you shall choose what you like best out of Mrs Gill's store-room.'

CHAPTER XIX

A SUMMER NIGHT

THE HOUR was now that of dusk. A clear air favoured the kindling of the stars.

'There will be just light enough to show me the way home,' said Miss Keeldar, as she prepared to take leave of Caroline at the Rectory garden-door.

'You must not go alone, Shirley. Fanny shall accompany you.'

'That she shall not. Of what need I be afraid in my own parish? I would walk from Fieldhead to the church any fine mid-summer night, three hours later than this, for the mere pleasure of seeing the stars, and the chance of meeting a fairy.'

'But just wait till the crowd is cleared away.'

'Agreed. There are the five Misses Armitage streaming by. Here comes Mrs Sykes's phaeton, Mr Wynne's close carriage, Mrs Birtwhistle's car: I don't wish to go through the ceremony of bidding them all good-bye, so we will step into the garden and take shelter amongst the laburnums for an instant.'

The rectors, their curates and their churchwardens, now issued from the church-porch. There was a great confabulation, shaking of hands, congratulation on speeches, recommendation to be careful of the night air, &c. By degrees the throng dispersed; the carriages drove off. Miss Keeldar was just emerging from her flowery refuge, when Mr Helstone entered the garden and met her.

'Oh! I want you!' he said: 'I was afraid you were already gone. Caroline, come here!'

Caroline came, expecting, as Shirley did, a lecture on not

having been visible at church. Other subjects, however, occupied the Rector's mind.

'I shall not sleep at home to-night,' he continued. 'I have just met with an old friend, and promised to accompany him. I shall return probably about noon to-morrow. Thomas, the clerk, is engaged, and I cannot get him to sleep in the house, as I usually do when I am absent for a night; now –'

'Now,' interrupted Shirley, 'you want me as a gentleman – the first gentleman in Briarfield, in short, to supply your place, be master of the Rectory, and guardian of your niece and maids while you are away?'

'Exactly, captain: I thought the post would suit you. Will you favour Caroline so far as to be her guest for one night? Will you stay here instead of going back to Fieldhead?'

'And what will Mrs Pryor do? She expects me home.'

'I will send her word. Come, make up your mind to stay. It grows late; the dew falls heavily: you and Caroline will enjoy each other's society I doubt not.'

'I promise you then to stay with Caroline,' replied Shirley. 'As you say, we shall enjoy each other's society: we will not be separated to-night. Now, rejoin your old friend, and fear nothing for us.'

'If there should chance to be any disturbance in the night, captain – if you should hear the picking of a lock, the cutting out of a pane of glass, a stealthy tread of steps about the house (and I need not fear to tell *you*, who bear a well-tempered, mettlesome heart under your girl's ribbon-sash, that such little incidents are very possible in the present time), what would you do?'

'Don't know – faint, perhaps – fall down, and have to be picked up again. But, doctor, if you assign me the post of honour, you must give me arms. What weapons are there in your stronghold?'

'You could not wield a sword?'

'No; I could manage the carving-knife better.'

'You will find a good one in the dining-room side-board: a lady's knife, light to handle, and as sharp-pointed as a poniard.'

'It will suit Caroline; but you must give me a brace of pistols: I know you have pistols.'

'I have two pairs; one pair I can place at your disposal. You will find them suspended over the mantelpiece of my study in cloth cases.'

'Loaded?'

'Yes, but not on the cock. Cock them before you go to bed. It is paying you a great compliment, captain, to lend you these: were you one of the awkward squad you should not have them.'

'I will take care. You need delay no longer, Mr Helstone: you may go now. He is gracious to me to lend me his pistols,' she remarked, as the Rector passed out at the garden-gate. 'But come, Lina,' she continued; 'let us go in and have some supper: I was too much vexed at tea with the vicinage of Mr Sam Wynne to be able to eat, and now I am really hungry.'

Entering the house, they repaired to the darkened dining-room, through the open windows of which apartment stole the evening air, bearing the perfume of flowers from the garden, the very distant sound of far-retreating steps from the road, and a soft, vague murmur, whose origin Caroline explained by the remark, uttered as she stood listening at the casement:

'Shirley, I hear the beck in the Hollow.'

Then she rung the bell, asked for a candle and some bread and milk – Miss Keeldar's usual supper and her own. Fanny, when she brought in the tray, would have closed the windows and the shutters, but was requested to desist for the present: the twilight was too calm, its breath too balmy to be yet excluded. They took their meal in silence: Caroline rose once, to remove to the window-sill a glass of flowers which stood on the side-board; the exhalation from the blossoms being somewhat too powerful for the sultry room: in returning, she half opened a drawer, and took from it something that glittered clear and keen in her hand.

'You assigned this to me, then, Shirley – did you? It is bright, keen-edged, finely-tapered: it is dangerous-looking. I never yet felt the impulse which could move me to direct this against a fellow-creature. It is difficult to fancy what circumstances could nerve my arm to strike home with this long knife.'

'I should hate to do it,' replied Shirley; 'but I think I could do it, if goaded by certain exigencies which I can imagine.' And Miss Keeldar quietly sipped her glass of new milk, looking somewhat thoughtful, and a little pale: though, indeed, when did she not look pale? She was never florid.

The milk sipped and the bread eaten, Fanny was again summoned: she and Eliza were recommended to go to bed, which they were quite willing to do, being weary of the day's exertions, of much cutting of currant-buns, and filling of urns and teapots, and running backwards and forwards with trays. Erelong the maids' chamber-door was heard to close; Caroline took a candle, and went quietly all over the house, seeing that every window was fast and every door barred. She did not even evade the haunted back-kitchen, nor the vault-like cellars. These visited, she returned.

'There is neither spirit nor flesh in the house at present,' she said, 'which should not be there. It is now near eleven o'clock, fully bedtime, yet I would rather sit up a little longer, if you do not object, Shirley. Here,' she continued, 'I have brought the brace of pistols from my uncle's study: you may examine them at your leisure.'

She placed them on the table before her friend.

'Why would you rather sit up longer?' asked Miss Keeldar, taking up the firearms, examining them, and again laying them down.

'Because I have a strange, excited feeling in my heart.'

'So have I.'

'Is this state of sleeplessness and restlessness caused by something electrical in the air, I wonder?'

'No: the sky is clear, the stars numberless; it is a fine night.'

'But very still. I hear the water fret over its stony bed in Hollow's Copse as distinctly as if it ran below the churchyard-wall.'

'I am glad it is so still a night: a moaning wind or rushing rain would vex me to fever just now.'

'Why, Shirley?'

'Because it would baffle my efforts to listen.'

'Do you listen towards the Hollow?'

'Yes; it is the only quarter whence we can hear a sound just now.'

'The only one, Shirley.'

They both sat near the window, and both leaned their arms on the sill and both inclined their heads towards the open lattice. They saw each other's young faces by the starlight, and that dim, June twilight which does not wholly fade from the west till dawn begins to break in the east.

'Mr Helstone thinks we have no idea which way he is gone,' murmured Miss Keeldar, 'nor on what errand, nor with what expectations, nor how prepared; but I guess much – do not you?'

'I guess something.'

'All those gentlemen – your cousin Moore included – think that you and I are now asleep in our beds, unconscious.'

'Caring nothing about them – hoping and fearing nothing for them,' added Caroline.

Both kept silence for full half an hour. The night was silent, too; only the church-clock measured its course by quarters. Some words were interchanged about the chill of the air: they wrapped their scarves closer round them, resumed their bonnets which they had removed, and again watched.

Towards midnight, the teasing, monotonous bark of the house-dog disturbed the quietude of their vigil. Caroline rose, and made her way noiselessly through the dark passages to the kitchen, intending to appease him with a piece of bread: she succeeded. On returning to the dining-room, she found it all dark, Miss Keeldar having extinguished the candle: the outline of her shape was visible near the still open window, leaning out. Miss Helstone asked no questions: she stole to her side. The dog recommenced barking furiously; suddenly he stopped, and seemed to listen. The occupants of the dining-room listened too, and not merely now to the flow of the mill-stream: there was a nearer, though a muffled sound on the road below the churchyard; a measured, beating, approaching sound; a dull tramp of marching feet.

It drew near. Those who listened, by degrees comprehended its extent. It was not the tread of two, nor of a dozen, nor of a score of men: it was the tread of hundreds. They could see nothing: the high shrubs of the garden formed a leafy screen between them and the road. To hear, however, was not enough; and this they felt as the troop trod forwards, and seemed actually passing the Rectory. They felt it more when a human voice – though that voice spoke but one word – broke the hush of the night.

'Halt!'

A halt followed! the march was arrested. Then came a low conference, of which no word was distinguishable from the dining-room.

'We *must* hear this,' said Shirley.

She turned, took her pistols from the table, silently passed out though the middle window of the dining-room, which was, in fact, a glass door, stole down the walk to the garden-wall, and stood listening under the lilacs. Caroline would not have quitted the house had she been alone, but where Shirley went she would go. She glanced at the weapon on the side-board, but left it behind her, and presently stood at her friend's side. They dared not look over the wall, for fear of being seen: they were obliged to crouch behind it: they heard these words: –

'It looks a rambling old building. Who lives in it besides the damned parson?'

'Only three women: his niece and two servants.'

'Do you know where they sleep?'

'The lasses behind: the niece in a front room.'

'And Helstone?'

'Yonder is his chamber. He uses burning a light; but I see none now.'

'Where would you get in?'

'If I were ordered to do his job – and he desarves it – I'd try yond' long window: it opens to the dining-room: I could grope my way up-stairs, and I know his chamber.'

'How would you manage about the women folk?'

'Let 'em alone, except they shrieked, and then I'd soon quieten 'em. I could wish to find the old chap asleep: if he waked, he'd be dangerous.'

'Has he arms?'

'Fire-arms, allus, – and allus loadened.'

'Then you're a fool to stop us here; a shot would give the alarm: Moore would be on us before we could turn round. We should miss our main object.'

'You might go on, I tell you. I'd engage Helstone alone.'

A pause. One of the party dropped some weapon which rang on the stone causeway: at this sound the Rectory dog barked again furiously – fiercely.

'That spoils all!' said the voice; 'he'll awake: a noise like that might rouse the dead. You did not say there was a dog. Damn you! Forward!'

Forward they went, – tramp, tramp, – with mustering, manifold, slow-filing tread. They were gone.

Shirley stood erect; looked over the wall, along the road.

'Not a soul remains,' she said.

She stood and mused. 'Thank God!' was the next observation.

Caroline repeated the ejaculation, not in so steady a tone: she was trembling much; her heart was beating fast and thick; her face was cold; her forehead damp.

'Thank God for us!' she reiterated; 'but what will happen elsewhere? They have passed us by that they may make sure of others.'

'They have done well,' returned Shirley, with composure:

'the others will defend themselves, – they can do it, – they are prepared for them: with us it is otherwise. My finger was on the trigger of this pistol. I was quite ready to give that man, if he had entered, such a greeting as he little calculated on; but behind him followed three hundred: I have neither three hundred hands nor three hundred weapons. I could not have effectually protected either you, myself, or the two poor women asleep under that roof; therefore I again earnestly thank God for insult and peril escaped.'

After a second pause, she continued: 'What is it my duty and wisdom to do next? Not to stay here inactive, I am glad to say, but of course to walk over to the Hollow.'

'To the Hollow, Shirley?'

'To the Hollow. Will you go with me?'

'Where those men are gone?'

'They have taken the highway: we should not encounter them: the road over the fields is as safe, silent, and solitary as a path through the air would be. Will you go?'

'Yes,' was the answer, given mechanically, not because the speaker wished, or was prepared to go; or, indeed, was otherwise than scared at the prospect of going, but because she felt she could not abandon Shirley.

'Then we must fasten up these windows, and leave all as secure as we can behind us. Do you know what we are going for, Cary?'

'Yes – no – because you wish it.'

'Is that all? And are you so obedient to a mere caprice of mine? What a docile wife you would make to a stern husband. The moon's face is not whiter than yours at this moment; and the aspen at the gate does not tremble more than your busy fingers; and so tractable and terror-struck, and dismayed and devoted, you would follow me into the thick of real danger! Cary, let me give your fidelity a motive: we are going for Moore's sake; to see if we can be of use to him: to make an effort to warn him of what is coming.'

'To be sure! I am a blind, weak fool, and you are acute and sensible, Shirley! I will go with you! I will gladly go with you!'

'I do not doubt it. You would die blindly and meekly for me, but you would intelligently and gladly die for Moore: but in truth there is no question of death to-night, – we run no risk at all.'

Caroline rapidly closed shutter and lattice. 'Do not fear that I shall not have breath to run as fast as you can possibly run, Shirley. Take my hand: let us go straight across the fields.'

'But you cannot climb walls?'

'Tonight I can.'

'You are afraid of hedges, and the beck which we shall be forced to cross?'

'I can cross it.'

They started: they ran. Many a wall checked but did not baffle them. Shirley was surefooted and agile: she could spring like a deer when she chose. Caroline, more timid, and less dexterous, fell once or twice, and bruised herself; but she rose again directly, saying she was not hurt. A quickset hedge bounded the last field: they lost time in seeking a gap in it: the aperture, when found, was narrow, but they worked their way through: the long hair, the tender skin, the silks and the muslins suffered; but what was chiefly regretted was the impediment this difficulty had caused to speed. On the other side they met the beck, flowing deep in a rough bed: at this point a narrow plank formed the only bridge across it. Shirley had trodden the plank successfully and fearlessly many a time before: Caroline had never yet dared to risk the transit.

'I will carry you across,' said Miss Keeldar: 'you are light, and I am not weak: let me try.'

'If I fall in, you may fish me out,' was the answer, as a grateful squeeze compressed her hand. Caroline, without pausing, trod forward on the trembling plank as if it were a continuation of the firm turf: Shirley, who followed, did not cross it more resolutely or safely. In their present humour, on their present errand, a strong and foaming channel would have been a barrier to neither. At the moment they were above the control either of fire or water: all Stilbro' Moor, alight and aglow with bonfires, would not have stopped them, nor would Calder or Aire thundering in flood. Yet one sound made them pause. Scarce had they set foot on the solid opposite bank, when a shot split the air from the north. One second lapsed. Further off, burst a like note in the south. Within the space of three minutes, similar signals boomed in the east and west.

'I thought we were dead at the first explosion,' observed Shirley, drawing a long breath. 'I felt myself hit in the temples, and I concluded your heart was pierced; but the reiterated voice was an explanation: those are signals – it is their way – the attack must be near. We should have had wings: our feet have not borne us swiftly enough.'

A portion of the copse was now to clear: when they emerged from it, the mill lay just below them: they could look down upon the buildings, the yard; they could see the road beyond. And the first glance in that direction told Shirley she was right in her conjecture: they were already too late to give warning: it had taken more time than they calculated on to overcome the various obstacles which embarrassed the short cut across the fields.

The road, which should have been white, was dark with a moving mass: the rioters were assembled in front of the closed yard gates, and a single figure stood within, apparently addressing them: the mill itself was perfectly black and still; there was neither life, light, nor motion around it.

'Surely he is prepared: surely that is not Moore meeting them alone!' whispered Shirley.

'It is – we must go to him! I *will* go to him.'

'*That* you will not.'

'Why did I come, then? I came only for him. I shall join him.'

'Fortunately, it is out of your power: there is no entrance to the yard.'

'There *is* a small entrance at the back, besides the gates in front: it opens by a secret method which I know – I will try it.'

'Not with my leave.'

Miss Keelder clasped her round the waist with both arms and held her back. 'Not one step shall you stir,' she went on authoritatively. 'At this moment, Moore would be both shocked and embarrassed, if he saw either you or me. Men never want women near them in time of real danger.'

'I would not trouble – I would help him,' was the reply.

'How? By inspiring him with heroism? Pooh! These are not the days of chivalry: it is not a tilt at a tournament we are going to behold, but a struggle about money, and food, and life.'

'It is natural that I should be at his side.'

'As queen of his heart? His mill is his lady-love, Cary! Backed by his factory and his frames, he has all the encouragement he wants or can know. It is not for love or beauty, but for ledger and broad-cloth, he is going to break a spear. Don't be sentimental; Robert is not so.'

'I *could* help him – I *will* seek him.'

'Off then – I let you go – seek Moore: you'll not find him.'

She loosened her hold. Caroline sped like levelled shaft from bent bow; after her rang a jesting, gibing laugh. 'Look well there is no mistake!' was the warning given.

But there *was* a mistake. Miss Helstone paused, hesitated, gazed. The figure had suddenly retreated from the gate, and was running back hastily to the mill.

'Make haste, Lina!' cried Shirley: 'meet him before he enters.'

Caroline slowly returned. 'It is not Robert,' she said: 'it has neither his height, form, nor bearing.'

'I saw it was not Robert when I let you go. How could you imagine it? It is a shabby little figure of a private soldier: they had posted him as sentinel. He is safe in the mill now: I saw the door open and admit him. My mind grows easier; Robert is prepared: our warning would have been superfluous, and now I am thankful we came too late to give it: it has saved us the trouble of a scene. How fine to have entered the counting-house "toute éperdue," and to have found oneself in presence

of Messrs Armitage and Ramsden smoking, Malone swaggering, your uncle sneering, Mr Sykes sipping a cordial, and Moore
himself in his cold man-of-business vein: I am glad we missed
it all.'

'I wonder if there are many in the mill, Shirley?'

'Plenty to defend it. The soldiers we have twice seen to-
day were going there, no doubt, and the group we noticed
surrounding your cousin in the fields will be with him.'

'What are they doing now, Shirley? What is that noise?'

'Hatchets and crow-bars against the yard-gates: they are
forcing them. Are you afraid?'

'No; but my heart throbs fast; I have a difficulty in standing:
I will sit down. Do you feel unmoved?'

'Hardly that – but I am glad I came: we shall see what trans-
pires with our own eyes: we are here on the spot, and none
know it. Instead of amazing the curate, the clothier, and the
corn-dealer with a romantic rush on the stage, we stand alone
with the friendly night, its mute stars, and these whispering
trees, whose report our friends will not come to gather.'

'Shirley – Shirley, the gates are down! That crash was like the
felling of great trees. Now they are pouring through. They will
break down the mill-doors as they have broken the gate: what
can Robert do against so many? Would to God I were a little
nearer him – could hear him speak – could speak to him! With
my will – my longing to serve him – I could not be a useless
burden in his way: I could be turned to some account.'

'They come on!' cried Shirley. 'How steadily they march in!
There is discipline in their ranks – I will not say there is courage:
hundreds against tens are no proof of that quality; but' (she
dropped her voice) 'there is suffering and desperation enough
amongst them – these goads will urge them forwards.'

'Forwards against Robert – and they hate him. Shirley, is
there much danger they will win the day?'

'We shall see. Moore and Helstone are of "earth's first blood"
– no bunglers – no cravens –'

A crash – smash – shiver – stopped their whispers. A simulta-neously-hurled volley of stones had saluted the broad front of the mill, with all its windows; and now every pane of every lattice lay in shattered and pounded fragments. A yell followed this demonstration – a rioters' yell – a North-of-England – a Yorkshire – a West-Riding – a West-Riding-clothing-district-of-Yorkshire rioters' yell. You never heard that sound, perhaps, reader? So much the better for your ears – perhaps for your heart; since, if it rends the air in hate to yourself, or to the men or principles you approve, the interests to which you wish well, Wrath wakens to the cry of Hate: the Lion shakes his mane, and rises to the howl of the Hyena: Caste stands up, ireful, against Caste; and the indignant, wronged spirit of the Middle Rank bears down in zeal and scorn on the famished and furious mass of the Operative Class. It is difficult to be tolerant – difficult to be just – in such moments.

Caroline rose; Shirley put her arm round her: they stood together as still as the straight stems of two trees. That yell was a long one, and when it ceased, the night was yet full of the swaying and murmuring of a crowd.

'What next?' was the question of the listeners. Nothing came yet. The mill remained mute as a mausoleum.

'He *cannot* be alone!' whispered Caroline.

'I would stake all I have, that he is as little alone as he is alarmed,' responded Shirley.

Shots were discharged by the rioters. Had the defenders waited for this signal? It seemed so. The hitherto inert and passive mill woke: fire flashed from its empty window-frames; a volley of musketry pealed sharp through the Hollow.

'Moore speaks at last!' said Shirley, 'and he seems to have the gift of tongues; that was not a single voice.'

'He has been forbearing; no one can accuse him of rashness,' alleged Caroline: 'their discharge preceded his; they broke his gates and his windows; they fired at his garrison before he repelled them.'

What was going on now? It seemed difficult in the darkness, to distinguish, but something terrible, a still-renewing tumult, was obvious; fierce attacks, desperate repulses; the mill-yard, the mill itself, was full of battle-movement: there was scarcely any cessation now of the discharge of firearms; and there was struggling, rushing, trampling, and shouting between. The aim of the assailants seemed to be to enter the mill, that of the defendants to beat them off. They heard the rebel leader cry, 'To the back, lads!' They heard a voice retort, 'Come round, we will meet you!'

'To the counting-house!' was the order again.

'Welcome! – We shall have you there!' was the response. And accordingly, the fiercest blaze that had yet glowed, the loudest rattle that had yet been heard, burst from the counting-house front, when the mass of rioters rushed up to it.

The voice that had spoken was Moore's own voice. They could tell by its tones that his soul was now warm with the conflict: they could guess that the fighting animal was roused in every one of those men there struggling together, and was for the time quite paramount above the rational human being. Both the girls felt their faces glow and their pulses throb: both knew they would do no good by rushing down into the mêlée: they desired neither to deal nor to receive blows; but they could not have run away – Caroline no more than Shirley; they could not have fainted; they could not have taken their eyes from the dim, terrible scene – from the mass of cloud, of smoke – the musket-lightning – for the world.

'How and when would it end?' was the demand throbbing in their throbbing pulses. 'Would a juncture arise in which they could be useful?' was what they waited to see; for, though Shirley put off their too-late arrival with a jest, and was ever ready to satirize her own or any other person's enthusiasm, she would have given a farm of her best land for a chance of rendering good service.

The chance was not vouchsafed her; the looked-for juncture

never came: it was not likely. Moore had expected this attack for days, perhaps weeks: he was prepared for it at every point. He had fortified and garrisoned his mill, which in itself was a strong building: he was a cool, brave man: he stood to the defence with unflinching firmness; those who were with him caught his spirit, and copied his demeanour. The rioters had never been so met before. At other mills they had attacked, they had found no resistance; an organized, resolute defence was what they never dreamed of encountering. When their leaders saw the steady fire kept up from the mill, witnessed the composure and determination of its owner, heard themselves coolly defied and invited on to death, and beheld their men falling wounded round them, they felt that nothing was to be done here. In haste, they mustered their forces, drew them away from the building: a roll was called over, in which the men answered to figures instead of names: they dispersed wide over the fields, leaving silence and ruin behind them. The attack, from its commencement to its termination, had not occupied an hour.

Day was by this time approaching: the west was dim, the east beginning to gleam. It would have seemed that the girls who had watched this conflict would now wish to hasten to the victors, on whose side all their interest had been enlisted; but they only very cautiously approached the now battered mill, and, when suddenly a number of soldiers and gentlemen appeared at the great door opening into the yard, they quickly stepped aside into a shed, the deposit of old iron and timber, whence they could see without being seen.

It was no cheering spectacle: these premises were now a mere blot of desolation on the fresh front of the summer-dawn. All the copse up the Hollow was shady and dewy, the hill at its head was green; but just here in the centre of the sweet glen, Discord, broken loose in the night from control, had beaten the ground with his stamping hoofs, and left it waste and pulverized. The mill yawned all ruinous with unglazed frames; the yard was thickly bestrewn with stones and brick-bats, and, close under the mill, with the glittering fragments of the shattered windows; muskets and other weapons lay here and there; more than one deep crimson stain was visible on the gravel: a human body lay quiet on its face near the gates; and five or six wounded men writhed and moaned in the bloody dust.

Miss Keeldar's countenance changed at this view: it was the after-taste of the battle, death and pain replacing excitement and exertion: it was the blackness the bright fire leaves when its blaze is sunk, its warmth failed, and its glow faded.

'This is what I wished to prevent,' she said, in a voice whose cadence betrayed the altered impulse of her heart.

'But you could not prevent it; you did your best; it was in vain,' said Caroline, comfortingly. 'Don't grieve, Shirley.'

'I am sorry for those poor fellows,' was the answer, while the spark in her glance dissolved to dew. 'Are any within the mill hurt, I wonder? Is that your uncle?'

'It is, and there is Mr Malone, and, oh Shirley! There is Robert!'

'Well,' (resuming her former tone,) 'don't squeeze your fingers quite into my hand: I see, there is nothing wonderful in that. We knew he, at least, was here, whoever might be absent.'

'He is coming here toward us, Shirley!'

'Towards the pump, that is to say, for the purpose of washing his hands and his forehead, which has got a scratch, I perceive.'

'He bleeds, Shirley: don't hold me; I must go.'

'Not a step.'

'He is hurt, Shirley!'

'Fiddlestick!'

'But I *must* go to him: I wish to go so much: I cannot bear to be restrained.'

'What for?'

'To speak to him, to ask how he is, and what I can do for him?'

'To teaze and annoy him; to make a spectacle of yourself and him before those soldiers, Mr Malone, your uncle, et cetera.

Would he like it, think you? Would you like to remember it a week hence?'

'Am I always to be curbed and kept down?' demanded Caroline, a little passionately.

'For his sake, yes. And still more for your own. I tell you, if you showed yourself now, you would repent it an hour hence, and so would Robert.'

'You think he would not like it, Shirley?'

'Far less than he would like our stopping him to say good-night, which you were so sore about.'

'But that was all play; there was no danger.'

'And this is serious work: he must be unmolested.'

'I only wish to go to him because he is my cousin, – you understand?'

'I quite understand. But now, watch him. He has bathed his forehead, and the blood has ceased trickling; his hurt is really a mere graze: I can see it from hence: he is going to look after the wounded men.'

Accordingly Mr Moore and Mr Helstone went round the yard, examining each prostrate form. They then gave directions to have the wounded taken up and carried into the mill. This duty being performed, Joe Scott was ordered to saddle his master's horse, and Mr Helstone's pony, and the two gentlemen rode away full gallop, to seek surgical aid in different directions.

Caroline was not yet pacified.

'Shirley, Shirley, I should have liked to speak one word to him before he went,' she murmured, while the tears gathered glittering in her eyes.

'Why do you cry, Lina?' asked Miss Keeldar a little sternly. 'You ought to be glad instead of sorry. Robert has escaped any serious harm; he is victorious; he has been cool and brave in combat; he is now considerate in triumph: is this a time – are these causes for weeping?'

'You do not know what I have in my heart,' pleaded the other: 'what pain, what distraction; nor whence it arises. I can understand that you should exult in Robert's greatness and goodness; so do I, in one sense, but, in another, I feel *so* miserable. I am too far removed from him: I used to be nearer. Let me alone, Shirley: do let me cry a few minutes; it relieves me.'

Miss Keeldar, feeling her tremble in every limb, ceased to expostulate with her: she went out of the shed, and left her to weep in peace. It was the best plan: in a few minutes Caroline rejoined her, much calmer: she said with her natural, docile, gentle manner –

'Come, Shirley, we will go home now. I promise not to try to see Robert again till he asks for me. I never will try to push myself on him. I thank you for restraining me just now.'

'I did it with a good intention,' returned Miss Keeldar.

'Now, dear Lina,' she continued; 'let us turn our faces to the cool morning breeze, and walk very quietly back to the Rectory. We will steal in as we stole out: none shall know where we have been, or what we have seen to-night: neither taunt nor misconstruction can consequently molest us. To-morrow, we will see Robert, and be of good cheer; but I will say no more, lest I should begin to cry too. I seem hard towards you, but I am not so.'

CHAPTER XX

TO-MORROW

THE TWO girls met no living soul on their way back to the Rectory: they let themselves in noiselessly; they stole upstairs unheard: the breaking morning gave them what light they needed. Shirley sought her couch immediately; and, though the room was strange – for she had never slept at the Rectory before – and though the recent scene was one unparalleled for excitement and terror by any it had hitherto been her lot to witness, yet, scarce was her head laid on the pillow, ere a deep, refreshing sleep closed her eyes, and calmed her senses.

Perfect health was Shirley's enviable portion; though warm-hearted and sympathetic, she was not nervous: powerful emotions could rouse and sway, without exhausting, her spirit: the tempest troubled and shook her while it lasted; but it left her elasticity unbent, and her freshness quite unblighted. As every day brought her stimulating emotion, so every night yielded her recreating rest. Caroline now watched her sleeping, and read the serenity of her mind in the beauty of her happy countenance.

For herself, being of a different temperament, she could not sleep. The common-place excitement of the tea-drinking and school-gathering, would alone have sufficed to make her restless all night: the effect of the terrible drama which had just been enacted before her eyes was not likely to quit her for days. It was vain even to try to retain a recumbent posture: she sat up by Shirley's side, counting the slow minutes, and watching the June sun mount the heavens.

Life wastes fast in such vigils as Caroline had of late but too often kept; vigils during which the mind, – having no pleasant food to nourish it – no manna of hope – no hived-honey of joyous memories – tries to live on the meagre diet of wishes, and failing to derive thence either delight or support, and feeling itself ready to perish with craving want, turns to philosophy, to resolution, to resignation; calls on all these gods for aid, calls vainly, – is unheard, unhelped, and languishes.

Caroline was a Christian; therefore in trouble she framed many a prayer after the Christian creed; preferred it with deep earnestness; begged for patience, strength, relief. This world, however, we all know, is the scene of trial and probation; and, for any favourable result her petitions had yet wrought, it seemed to her that they were unheard and unaccepted. She believed, sometimes, that God had turned his face from her. At moments she was a Calvinist, and, sinking into the gulf of religious despair, she saw darkening over her the doom of reprobation.

Most people have had a period or periods in their lives when they have felt thus forsaken; when, having long hoped against hope, and still seen the day of fruition deferred, their hearts have truly sickened within them. This is a terrible hour, but it is often that darkest point which precedes the rise of day; that turn of the year when the icy January wind carries over the waste at once the dirge of departing winter, and the prophecy of coming spring. The perishing birds, however, cannot thus understand the blast before which they shiver; and as little can the suffering soul recognise, in the climax of its affliction, the dawn of its deliverance. Yet, let whoever grieves still cling fast to love and faith in God: God will never deceive, never finally desert him. 'Whom He loveth, He chasteneth.' These words are true, and should not be forgotten.

The household was astir at last: the servants were up; the shutters were opened below. Caroline, as she quitted the couch, which had been but a thorny one to her, felt that revival of spirits which the return of day, of action, gives to all but the wholly despairing or actually dying: she dressed herself, as usual, carefully, trying so to arrange her hair and attire that nothing of the forlornness she felt at heart should be visible externally: she looked as fresh as Shirley when both were dressed, only that Miss Keeldar's eyes were lively, and Miss Helstone's languid.

'To-day, I shall have much to say to Moore,' were Shirley's first words; and you could see in her face that life was full of interest, expectation, and occupation for her. 'He will have to undergo cross-examination,' she added: 'I daresay he thinks he has outwitted me cleverly. And this is the way men deal with women; still concealing danger from them: thinking, I suppose, to spare them pain. They imagined we little knew where they were to-night: we *know* they little conjectured where we were. Men, I believe, fancy women's minds something like those of children. Now, that is a mistake.'

This was said as she stood at the glass, training her naturally waved hair into curls, by twining it round her fingers. She took up the theme again five minutes after, as Caroline fastened her dress and clasped her girdle.

'If men could see us as we really are, they would be a little amazed; but the cleverest, the acutest men are often under an illusion about women: they do not read them in a true light: they misapprehend them, both for good and evil: their good woman is a queer thing, half doll, half angel; their bad woman almost always a fiend. Then to hear them fall into ecstasies with each other's creations, worshipping the heroine of such a poem – novel – drama, thinking it fine – divine! Fine and divine it may be, but often quite artificial – false as the rose in my best bonnet there. If I spoke all I think on this point; if I gave my real opinion of some first-rate female characters in first-rate works, where should I be? Dead under a cairn of avenging stones in half an hour.'

'Shirley, you chatter so, I can't fasten you: be still. And after all, authors' heroines are almost as good as authoress's heroes.'

'Not at all: women read men more truly than men read

women. I'll prove that in a magazine paper some day when I've time; only it will never be inserted: it will be "declined with thanks," and left for me at the publisher's.'

'To be sure: you could not write cleverly enough; you don't know enough; you are not learned, Shirley.'

'God knows, I can't contradict you, Cary: I'm as ignorant as a stone. There's one comfort, however, you are not much better.'

They descended to breakfast.

'I wonder how Mrs Pryor and Hortense Moore have passed the night,' said Caroline, as she made the coffee. 'Selfish being that I am! I never thought of either of them till just now: they will have heard all the tumult, Fieldhead and the Cottage are so near; and Hortense is timid in such matters: so no doubt is Mrs Pryor.'

'Take my word for it, Lina, Moore will have contrived to get his sister out of the way: she went home with Miss Mann; he will have quartered her there for the night. As to Mrs Pryor, I own I am uneasy about her; but in another half-hour we will be with her.'

By this time the news of what had happened at the Hollow was spread all over the neighbourhood. Fanny, who had been to Fieldhead to fetch the milk, returned in panting haste, with tidings that there had been a battle in the night at Mr Moore's mill, and that some said twenty men were killed. Eliza, during Fanny's absence, had been apprized by the butcher's boy that the Mill was burnt to the ground. Both women rushed into the parlour to announce these terrible facts to the ladies, terminating their clear and accurate narrative by the assertion that they were sure master must have been in it all: he and Thomas, the clerk, they were confident, must have gone last night to join Mr Moore and the soldiers: Mr Malone, too, had not been heard of at his lodgings since yesterday afternoon; and Joe Scott's wife and family were in the greatest distress, wondering what had become of their head.

Scarcely was this information imparted when a knock at the

kitchen-door announced the Fieldhead errand-boy, arrived in hot haste, bearing a billet from Mrs Pryor. It was hurriedly written, and urged Miss Keeldar to return directly, as the neighbourhood and the house seemed likely to be all in confusion, and orders would have to be given which the mistress of the hall alone could regulate. In a postscript it was entreated that Miss Helstone might not be left alone at the Rectory: she had better, it was suggested, accompany Miss Keeldar.

'There are not two opinions on that head,' said Shirley, as she tied on her own bonnet, and then ran to fetch Caroline's.

'But what will Fanny and Eliza do? And if my uncle returns?'

'Your uncle will not return yet; he has other fish to fry; he will be galloping backwards and forwards from Briarfield to Stilbro' all day, rousing the magistrates in the courthouse, and the officers at the barracks; and Fanny and Eliza can have in Joe Scott's and the clerk's wives to bear them company. Besides, of course, there is no real danger to be apprehended now: weeks will elapse before the rioters can again rally, or plan any other attempt; and I am much mistaken if Moore and Mr Helstone will not take advantage of last night's outbreak to quell them altogether: they will frighten the authorities of Stilbro' into energetic measures. I only hope they will not be too severe – not pursue the discomfited too relentlessly.'

'Robert will not be cruel: we saw that last night,' said Caroline.

'But he will be hard,' retorted Shirley; 'and so will your uncle.'

As they hurried along the meadow and plantation-path to Fieldhead, they saw the distant highway already alive with an unwonted flow of equestrians and pedestrians, tending in the direction of the usually solitary Hollow. On reaching the hall, they found the backyard gates open, and the court and kitchen seemed crowded with excited milk-fetchers – men, women, and children, whom Mrs Gill, the housekeeper, appeared vainly persuading to take their milk-cans and depart. (It *is*, or *was*, by-the-by, the custom in the north of England for the cottagers on a country squire's estate to receive their supplies of milk and butter from the dairy of the Manor-House, on whose pastures a herd of milch kine was usually fed for the convenience of the neighbourhood. Miss Keeldar owned such a herd – all deep-dewlapped, Craven cows, reared on the sweet herbage and clear waters of bonnie Airedale; and very proud she was of their sleek aspect and high condition.) Seeing now the state of matters, and that it was desirable to effect a clearance of the premises, Shirley stepped in amongst the gossipping groups. She bade them good-morning with a certain frank, tranquil ease – the natural characteristic of her manner when she addressed num-bers; especially if those numbers belonged to the working-class: she was cooler amongst her equals, and rather proud to those above her. She then asked them if they had all got their milk measured out, and understanding that they had, she further observed that she 'wondered what they were waiting for, then.'

'We're just talking a bit over this battle there has been at your mill, Mistress,' replied a man.

'Talking a bit! Just like you!' said Shirley. 'It is a queer thing all the world is so fond of *talking* over events: you *talk* if any-body dies suddenly; you *talk* if a fire breaks out; you *talk* if a mill-owner fails; you *talk* if he's murdered. What good does your talking do?'

There is nothing the lower orders like better than a little downright good-humoured rating. Flattery they scorn very much: honest abuse they enjoy. They call it speaking plainly, and take a sincere delight in being the objects thereof. The homely harshness of Miss Keeldar's salutation won her the ear of the whole throng in a second.

'We're no war nor some 'at is aboon us; are we?' asked a man, smiling.

'Nor a whit better: you that should be models of industry are just as gossip-loving as the idle. Fine, rich people that have nothing to do, may be partly excused for trifling their time away: you who have to earn your bread with the sweat of your brow are quite inexcusable.'

'That's queer, Mistress: suld we never have a holiday because we work hard?'

'*Never*,' was the prompt answer; 'unless,' added the 'mistress' with a smile that half-belied the severity of her speech, 'unless you knew how to make a better use of it than to get together over rum and tea, if you are women – or over beer and pipes, if you are men, and *talk* scandal at your neighbour's expense. Come, friends,' she added, changing at once from bluntness to courtesy, 'oblige me by taking your cans and going home. I expect several persons to call to-day, and it will be inconvenient to have the avenues to the house crowded.'

Yorkshire people are as yielding to persuasion as they are stubborn against compulsion: the yard was clear in five minutes.

'Thank you, and good-bye to you, friends,' said Shirley, as she closed the gates on a quiet court.

Now, let me hear the most refined of Cockneys presume to find fault with Yorkshire manners! Taken as they ought to be, the majority of the lads and lasses of the West-Riding are gentlemen and ladies, every inch of them: it is only against the weak affectation and futile pomposity of a would-be aristocrat they turn mutinous.

Entering by the back-way, the young ladies passed through the kitchen (or *house*, as the inner kitchen is called) to the hall. Mrs Pryor came running down the oak staircase to meet them. She was all unnerved: her naturally sanguine complexion was pale; her usually placid, though timid, blue eye was wandering, unsettled, alarmed. She did not, however, break out into any exclamations, or hurried narrative of what had happened. Her predominant feeling had been in the course of the night, and was now this morning, a sense of dissatisfaction with herself that she could not feel firmer, cooler, more equal to the demands of the occasion.

'You are aware,' she began with a trembling voice, and yet the most conscientious anxiety to avoid exaggeration in what she was about to say, – 'that a body of rioters has attacked Mr

Moore's mill to-night: we heard the firing and confusion very plainly here: we none of us slept: it was a sad night: the house has been in great bustle all the morning with people coming and going: the servants have applied to me for orders and directions, which I really did not feel warranted in giving. Mr Moore has, I believe, sent up for refreshments for the soldiers and others engaged in the defence; for some conveniences also for the wounded. I could not undertake the responsibility of giving orders or taking measures. I fear delay may have been injurious in some instances; but this is not my house: you were absent, my dear Miss Keeldar – what could I do?'

'Were no refreshments sent?' asked Shirley, while her coun- tenance, hitherto so clear, propitious, and quiet, even while she was rating the milk-fetchers, suddenly turned dark and warm.

'I think not, my dear.'

'And nothing for the wounded? no linen – no wine – no bedding?'

'I think not. I cannot tell what Mrs Gill did; but it seemed impossible to me, at the moment, to venture to dispose of your property by sending supplies to soldiers – provisions for a com- pany of soldiers sounds formidable: how many there are I did not ask; but I could not think of allowing them to pillage the house, as it were. I intended to do what was right; yet I did not see the case quite clearly, I own.'

'It lies in a nutshell, notwithstanding. These soldiers have risked their lives in defence of my property – I suppose they have a right to my gratitude: the wounded are our fellow-creatures – I suppose we should aid them. Mrs Gill!'

She turned, and called in a voice more clear than soft. It rung through the thick oak of the hall and kitchen doors more effectually than a bell's summons. Mrs Gill, who was deep in bread-making, came with hands and apron in culinary case, not having dared to stop to rub the dough from the one, or to shake the flour from the other. Her mistress had never called a servant in that voice, save once before, and that was when she had seen from the window Tartar in full tug with two carriers' dogs, each of them a match for him in size, if not in courage, and their masters standing by, encouraging their animals, while hers was unbefriended: then, indeed, she had summoned John as if the Day of Judgment were at hand: nor had she waited for the said John's coming, but had walked out into the lane bonnetless; and after informing the carriers that she held them far less of men than the three brutes whirling and worrying in the dust before them, had put her hands round the thick neck of the largest of the curs and given her whole strength to the essay of choking it from Tartar's torn and bleeding eye, just above and below which organ the vengeful fangs were inserted. Five or six men were presently on the spot to help her, but she never thanked one of them: 'They might have come before, if their will had been good,' she said. She had not a word for anybody during the rest of the day; but sat near the hall fire till evening watching and tending Tartar, who lay all gory, stiff, and swelled, on a mat at her feet. She wept furtively over him sometimes, and murmured the softest words of pity and endearment, in tones whose music the old, scarred, canine warrior acknowledged by licking her hand or her sandal alternately with his own red wounds. As to John, his lady turned a cold shoulder on him for a week afterwards.

Mrs Gill, remembering this little episode, came 'all of a tremble,' as she said herself. In a firm, brief voice, Miss Keeldar proceeded to put questions and give orders. That at such a time Fieldhead should have evinced the inhospitality of a miser's hovel, stung her haughty spirit to the quick; and the revolt of its pride was seen in the heaving of her heart; stirred stormily under the lace and silk which veiled it.

'How long is it since that message came from the mill?'

'Not an hour yet, ma'am,' answered the housekeeper, soothingly.

'Not an hour! You might almost as well have said not a day. They will have applied elsewhere by this time. Send a man instantly down to tell them that everything this house contains is at Mr Moore's, Mr Helstone's, and the soldiers' service. Do that first!'

While the order was being executed, Shirley moved away from her friends, and stood at the hall-window, silent, un-approachable. When Mrs Gill came back, she turned: the purple flush which painful excitement kindles on a pale cheek, glowed on hers: the spark which displeasure lights in a dark eye fired her glance.

'Let the contents of the larder and the wine-cellar be brought up, put into the hay-carts, and driven down to the Hollow. If there does not happen to be much bread or much meat in the house, go to the butcher and baker, and desire them to send what they have: but I will see for myself.'

She moved off.

'All will be right soon: she will get over it in an hour,' whispered Caroline to Mrs Pryor. 'Go up-stairs, dear madam,' she added, affectionately, 'and try to be as calm and easy as you can. The truth is, Shirley will blame herself more than you before the day is over.'

By dint of a few more gentle assurances and persuasions, Miss Helstone contrived to soothe the agitated lady. Having accom-panied her to her apartment, and promised to rejoin her there when things were settled, Caroline left her to see, as she said, 'if she could be useful.' She presently found that she could be very useful; for the retinue of servants at Fieldhead was by no means numerous, and just now their mistress found plenty of occupa-tion for all the hands at her command, and for her own also. The delicate good-nature and dexterous activity which Caroline brought to the aid of the housekeeper and maids, – all somewhat scared by their lady's unwonted mood – did a world of good at once: it helped the assistants and appeased the directress. A chance glance and smile from Caroline moved Shirley to an answering smile directly. The former was carrying a heavy basket up the cellar-stairs.

'This is a shame!' cried Shirley, running to her. 'It will strain your arm.'

She took it from her, and herself bore it out into the yard. The cloud of temper was dispelled when she came back; the flash in her eye was melted; the shade on her forehead vanished: she resumed her usual cheerful and cordial manner to those about her, tempering her revived spirits with a little of the softness of shame at her previous unjust anger.

She was still superintending the lading of the cart, when a gentleman entered the yard and approached her ere she was aware of his presence.

'I hope I see Miss Keeldar well this morning?' he said, examining with rather significant scrutiny her still flushed face.

She gave him a look, and then again bent to her employment, without reply. A pleasant enough smile played on her lips, but she hid it. The gentleman repeated his salutation, stooping, that it might reach her ear with more facility.

'Well enough, if she be good enough,' was the answer; 'and so is Mr Moore too, I dare say. To speak truth, I am not anxious about him; some slight mischance would be only his just due: his conduct has been – we will say *strange*, just now, till we have time to characterize it by a more exact epithet. Meantime, may I ask what brings him here?'

'Mr Helstone and I have just received your message, that everything at Fieldhead was at our service. We judged, by the unlimited wording of the gracious intimation, that you would be giving yourself too much trouble: I perceive, our conjecture was correct. We are not a regiment, remember: only about half a dozen soldiers, and as many civilians. Allow me to retrench something from these too abundant supplies.'

Miss Keeldar blushed, while she laughed at her own over-eager generosity, and most disproportionate calculations. Moore laughed too – very quietly, though; and as quietly, he ordered basket after basket to be taken from the cart, and remanded vessel after vessel to the cellar.

'The Rector must hear of this,' he said: 'he will make a good story of it. What an excellent army contractor Miss Keeldar would have been!' again he laughed, adding – 'It is precisely as I conjectured.'

'You ought to be thankful,' said Shirley, 'and not mock me. What could I do? How could I gauge your appetites, or number your band? For aught I knew, there might have been fifty of you at least to victual. You told me nothing; and then, an application to provision soldiers naturally suggests large ideas.'

'It appears so,' remarked Moore, levelling another of his keen, quiet glances at the discomfited Shirley. 'Now,' he continued, addressing the carter, 'I think you may take what remains to the Hollow. Your load will be somewhat lighter than the one Miss Keeldar destined you to carry.'

As the vehicle rumbled out of the yard, Shirley, rallying her spirits, demanded what had become of the wounded.

'There was not a single man hurt on our side,' was the answer.

'You were hurt yourself, on the temples,' interposed a quick, low voice – that of Caroline, who, having withdrawn within the shade of the door, and behind the large person of Mrs Gill, had till now escaped Moore's notice: when she spoke, his eye searched the obscurity of her retreat.

'Are you much hurt?' she inquired.

'As you might scratch your finger with a needle in sewing.'

'Lift your hair, and let us see.'

He took his hat off, and did as he was bid, disclosing only a narrow slip of court-plaster. Caroline indicated, by a slight movement of the head, that she was satisfied, and disappeared within the clear obscure of the interior.

'How did she know I was hurt?' asked Moore.

'By rumour, no doubt. But it is too good in her to trouble herself about you. For my part, it was of your victims I was thinking when I inquired after the wounded: what damage have your opponents sustained?'

'One of the rioters, or victims, as you call them, was killed, and six were hurt.'

'What have you done with them?'

'What you will perfectly approve. Medical aid was procured immediately; and as soon as we can get a couple of covered waggons, and some clean straw, they will be removed to Stilbro'.'

'Straw! you must have beds and bedding. I will send my waggon directly, properly furnished; and Mr Yorke, I am sure, will send his.'

'You guess correctly: he has volunteered already; and Mrs Yorke – who, like you, seems disposed to regard the rioters as martyrs, and me, and especially Mr Helstone, as murderers – is at this moment, I believe, most assiduously engaged in fitting it up with feather-beds, pillows, bolsters, blankets, &c. The *victims* lack no attentions – I promise you. Mr Hall – your favourite parson – has been with them ever since six o'clock, exhorting them, praying with them, and even waiting on them like any nurse; and Caroline's good friend, Miss Ainley, that *very* plain old maid, sent in a stock of lint and linen, something in the proportion of another lady's allowance of beef and wine.'

'That will do. Where is your sister?'

'Well cared for. I had her securely domiciled with Miss Mann. This very morning, the two set out for Wormwood Wells (a noted watering-place), and will stay there some weeks.'

'So Mr Helstone domiciled me at the Rectory! Mighty clever you gentlemen think you are! I make you heartily welcome to the idea, and hope its savour, as you chew the cud of reflection upon it, gives you pleasure. Acute and astute, why are you not also omniscient? How is it that events transpire, under your very noses, of which you have no suspicion? It should be so, otherwise the exquisite gratification of out-manœuvring you would be unknown. Ah! friend, you may search my countenance, but you cannot read it.'

Moore, indeed, looked as if he could not.

'You think me a dangerous specimen of my sex. Don't you, now?'

'A peculiar one, at least.'

'But Caroline – is she peculiar?'

'In her way – yes.'

'Her way! What is her way?'

'You know her as well as I do.'

'And knowing her I assert that she is neither eccentric nor difficult of control: is she?'

'That depends –'

'However, there is nothing masculine about *her*?'

'Why lay such emphasis on *her*? Do you consider her a contrast, in that respect, to yourself?'

'You do, no doubt: but that does not signify. Caroline is neither masculine, nor of what they call the spirited order of women.'

'I have seen her flash out.'

'So have I – but not with manly fire: it was a short, vivid, trembling glow, that shot up, shone, vanished –'

'And left her scared at her own daring. You describe others besides Caroline.'

'The point I wish to establish is, that Miss Helstone, though gentle, tractable, and candid enough, is still perfectly capable of defying even Mr Moore's penetration.'

'What have you and she been doing?' asked Moore, suddenly. 'Have you had any breakfast?'

'What is your mutual mystery?'

'If you are hungry, Mrs Gill will give you something to eat here. Step into the oak-parlour, and ring the bell – you will be served as if at an inn; or, if you like better, go back to the Hollow.'

'The alternative is not open to me: I *must* go back. Good-morning: the first leisure I have, I will see you again.'

CHAPTER XX1

MRS PRYOR

WHILE SHIRLEY was talking with Moore, Caroline rejoined Mrs Pryor up-stairs. She found that lady deeply depressed. She would not say that Miss Keeldar's hastiness had hurt her feelings; but it was evident an inward wound galled her. To any but a congenial nature, she would have seemed insensible to the quiet, tender attentions by which Miss Helstone sought to impart solace; but Caroline knew that, unmoved or slightly moved as she looked, she felt, valued, and was healed by them.

'I am deficient in self-confidence and decision,' she said at last. 'I always have been deficient in those qualities: yet I think Miss Keeldar should have known my character well enough by this time, to be aware that I always feel an even painful solicitude to do right, to act for the best. The unusual nature of the demand on my judgment puzzled me, especially following the alarms of the night. I could not venture to act promptly for another: but I trust no serious harm will result from my lapse of firmness.'

A gentle knock was here heard at the door: it was half-opened.

'Caroline, come here,' said a low voice.

Miss Helstone went out: there stood Shirley in the gallery, looking contrite, ashamed, sorry as any repentant child.

'How is Mrs Pryor?' she asked.

'Rather out of spirits,' said Caroline.

'I have behaved very shamefully, very ungenerously, very ungratefully to her,' said Shirley. 'How insolent in me to turn on her thus, for what after all was no fault, only an excess of conscientiousness on her part. But I regret my error most sincerely: tell her so, and ask if she will forgive me.'

Caroline discharged the errand with heartfelt pleasure. Mrs Pryor rose, came to the door: she did not like scenes; she dreaded them as all timid people do: she said falteringly –

'Come in, my dear.'

Shirley did come in with some impetuosity: she threw her arms round her governess, and while she kissed her heartily, she said –

'You know you *must* forgive me, Mrs Pryor. I could not get on at all if there was a misunderstanding between you and me.'

'I have nothing to forgive,' was the reply. 'We will pass it over now if you please. The final result of the incident is, that it proves more plainly than ever how unequal I am to certain crises.'

And that was the painful feeling which *would* remain on Mrs Pryor's mind: no effort of Shirley's or Caroline's could efface it thence: she could forgive her offending pupil, not her innocent self.

Miss Keeldar, doomed to be in constant request during the morning, was presently summoned down-stairs again. The Rector called first: a lively welcome and livelier reprimand were at his service; he expected both, and, being in high spirits, took them in equally good part.

In the course of his brief visit, he quite forgot to ask after his niece: the riot, the rioters, the mill, the magistrates, the heiress, absorbed all his thoughts to the exclusion of family ties. He alluded to the part himself and curate had taken in the defence of the Hollow.

'The vials of pharisaical wrath will be emptied on our heads, for our share in this business,' he said; 'but I defy every calumniator. I was there only to support the law, to play my part as a man and a Briton; which characters I deem quite compatible with those of the priest and Levite, in their highest sense. Your tenant, Moore,' he went on, 'has won my approbation. A cooler commander I would not wish to see, nor a more determined. Besides, the man has shown sound judgment and good sense; first, in being thoroughly prepared for the event which has taken place, and subsequently, when his well-concerted plans had secured him success, in knowing how to use without abusing his victory. Some of the magistrates are now well frightened, and, like all cowards, show a tendency to be cruel; Moore restrains them with admirable prudence. He has hitherto been very unpopular in the neighbourhood; but, mark my words, the tide of opinion will now take a turn in his favour: people will find out that they have not appreciated him, and will hasten to remedy their error; and he, when he perceives the public disposed to acknowledge his merits, will show a more gracious mien than that with which he has hitherto favoured us.'

Mr Helstone was about to add to this speech some half-jesting, half-serious warnings to Miss Keeldar, on the subject of her rumoured partiality for her talented tenant, when a ring at the door, announcing another caller, checked his raillery; and as that other caller appeared in the form of a white-haired, elderly gentleman, with a rather truculent countenance and disdainful eye – in short, our old acquaintance, and the Rector's old enemy, Mr Yorke, the priest and Levite seized his hat, and with the briefest of adieux to Miss Keeldar, and the sternest of nods to her guest, took an abrupt leave.

Mr Yorke was in no mild mood, and in no measured terms did he express his opinion on the transaction of the night: Moore, the magistrates, the soldiers, the mob-leaders, each and all came in for a share of his invectives; but he reserved his strongest epithets – and real, racy Yorkshire Doric adjectives they were – for the benefit of the fighting parsons, the 'sanguinary, demoniac' rector and curate. According to him, the cup of ecclesiastical guilt was now full indeed.

'The Church,' he said, 'was in a bonnie pickle now: it was time it came down when parsons took to swaggering amang soldiers, blazing away wi' bullet and gunpowder, taking the lives of far honester men than themselves.'

'What would Moore have done, if nobody had helped him?' asked Shirley.

'Drunk as he'd brewed – eaten as he'd baked.'

'Which means, you would have left him by himself to face that mob. Good. He has plenty of courage; but the greatest amount of gallantry that ever garrisoned one human breast could scarce avail against two hundred.'

'He had the soldiers; those poor slaves who hire out their own blood and spill other folks for money.'

'You abuse soldiers almost as much as you abuse clergymen. All who wear red coats are national refuse in your eyes, and all who wear black are national swindlers. Mr Moore, according to you, did wrong to get military aid, and he did still worse to accept of any other aid. Your way of talking amounts to this: – he should have abandoned his mill and his life to the rage of a set of misguided madmen, and Mr Helstone and every other gentleman in the parish should have looked on, and seen the building razed and its owner slaughtered, and never stirred a finger to save either.'

'If Moore had behaved to his men from the beginning as a master ought to behave, they never would have entertained their present feelings towards him.'

'Easy for you to talk,' exclaimed Miss Keeldar, who was beginning to wax warm in her tenant's cause: 'you, whose family have lived at Briarmains for six generations, to whose person the people have been accustomed for fifty years, who know all their ways, prejudices, and preferences. Easy, indeed, for *you* to act so as to avoid offending them; but Mr Moore came a stranger into the district: he came here poor and friendless, with nothing but his own energies to back him; nothing but his honour, his talent, and his industry to make his way for him. A monstrous crime indeed that, under such circumstances, he could not popularize his naturally grave, quiet manners, all at once: could not be jocular, and free, and cordial with a strange peasantry, as you are with your fellow-townsmen! An unpardonable transgression, that when he introduced improvements he did not go about the business in quite the most politic way; did not graduate his changes as delicately as a rich capitalist might have done! For errors of this sort is he to be the victim of mob-outrage? Is he to be denied even the privilege of defending himself? Are those who have the hearts of men in their breasts (and Mr Helstone – say what you will of him – has such a heart) to be reviled like malefactors because they stand by him – because they venture to espouse the cause of one against two hundred?'

'Come – come now – be cool,' said Mr Yorke, smiling at the earnestness with which Shirley multiplied her rapid questions.

'Cool! Must I listen coolly to downright nonsense – to dangerous nonsense? No. I like you very well, Mr Yorke, as you know; but I thoroughly dislike some of your principles. All that cant – excuse me, but I repeat the word – all that *cant* about soldiers and parsons is most offensive in my ears. All ridiculous, irrational crying up of one class, whether the same be aristocrat or democrat – all howling down of another class, whether clerical or military – all exacting injustice to individuals, whether monarch or mendicant – is really sickening to me: all arraying of ranks against ranks, all party hatreds, all tyrannies disguised as liberties, I reject and wash my hands of. *You* think you are a philanthropist; *you* think you are an advocate of liberty; but I will tell you this – Mr Hall, the parson of Nunnely, is a better friend both of man and freedom, than Hiram Yorke, the Reformer of Briarfield.'

From a man, Mr Yorke would not have borne this language very patiently, nor would he have endured it from some women; but he accounted Shirley both honest and pretty, and her plainspoken ire amused him: besides he took a secret pleasure in hearing her defend her tenant, for we have already intimated he had Robert Moore's interest very much at heart: moreover, if he wished to avenge himself for her severity, he knew the means lay in his power: a word, he believed, would suffice to tame and silence her, to cover her frank forehead with the rosy shadow of shame, and veil the glow of her eye under down-drooped lid and lash.

'What more hast thou to say?' he inquired, as she paused, rather it appeared to take breath, than because her subject or her zeal was exhausted.

'Say, Mr Yorke?' was the answer, the speaker meantime walking fast from wall to wall of the oak – parlour. 'Say? I have a great deal to say, if I could get it out in lucid order, which I never *can* do. I have to say that your views, and those of most extreme politicians are such as none but men in an irresponsible position *can* advocate; that they are purely opposition views, meant only to be talked about, and never intended to be acted on. Make you prime minister of England to-morrow, and you would have to abandon them. You abuse Moore for defending his mill: had you been in Moore's place you could not with honour or sense have acted otherwise than he acted. You abuse Mr Helstone for everything he does: Mr Helstone has his faults: he sometimes does wrong, but oftener right. Were you ordained vicar of Briarfield, you would find it no easy task to sustain all the active schemes for the benefit of the parish planned and persevered in by your predecessor. I wonder people cannot judge more fairly of each other and themselves. When I hear Messrs Malone and Donne chatter about the authority of the Church, the dignity and claims of the priesthood, the deference due to them as clergymen; when I hear the outbreaks of their small spite against Dissenters; when I witness their silly narrow jealousies and assumptions; when their palaver about forms, and traditions, and superstitions, is sounding in my ear; when I behold their insolent carriage to the poor, their often base servility to the rich, I think the Establishment is indeed in a poor way, and both she and her sons appear in the utmost need of reformation. Turning away distressed from minster-tower and village-spire – ay, as distressed as a churchwarden who feels the exigence of whitewash, and has not wherewithal to purchase lime – I recall your senseless sarcasms on the "fat bishops," the "pampered parsons, old mother church," &c. I remember your strictures on all who differ from you, your sweeping condemnation of classes

and individuals, without the slightest allowance made for circumstances or temptations; and then, Mr Yorke, doubt clutches
my inmost heart as to whether men exist clement, reasonable,
and just enough to be intrusted with the task of reform. I don't
believe *you* are of the number.'

'You have an ill opinion of me, Miss Shirley: you never told
me so much of your mind before.'

'I never had an opening; but I have sat on Jessy's stool by your
chair in the back-parlour at Briarmains, for evenings together,
listening excitedly to your talk, half-admiring what you said,
and half-rebelling against it. I think you a fine old Yorkshire-
man, sir: I am proud to have been born in the same county and
parish as yourself – truthful, upright, independent you are, as
a rock based below seas; but also you are harsh, rude, narrow,
and merciless.'

'Not to the poor, lass – nor to the meek of the earth – only
to the proud and high-minded.'

'And what right have you, sir, to make such distinctions?
A prouder – a higher-minded man than yourself does not exist.
You find it easy to speak comfortably to your inferiors – you
are too haughty, too ambitious, too jealous to be civil to those
above you. But you are all alike. Helstone also is proud and
prejudiced. Moore, though juster and more considerate than
either you or the Rector, is still haughty, stern, and, in a public
sense, selfish. It is well there are such men as Mr Hall to be
found occasionally: men of large and kind hearts, who can love
their whole race, who can forgive others for being richer, more
prosperous, or more powerful than they are. Such men may
have less originality, less force of character than you, but they
are better friends to mankind.'

'And when is it to be?' said Mr Yorke, now rising.

'When is what to be?'

'The wedding.'

'Whose wedding?'

'Only that of Robert Gérard Moore, Esq. of Hollow's Cottage, with Miss Keeldar, daughter and heiress of the late Charles Cave Keeldar of Fieldhead Hall.'

Shirley gazed at the questioner with rising colour; but the light in her eye was not faltering: it shone steadily – yes – it burned deeply.

'That is your revenge,' she said, slowly: then added; 'Would it be a bad match, unworthy of the late Charles Cave Keeldar's representative?'

'My lass, Moore is a gentleman: his blood is pure and ancient as mine or thine.'

'And we two set store by ancient blood? We have family pride, though one of us at least is a Republican?'

Yorke bowed as he stood before her. His lips were mute, but his eye confessed the impeachment. Yes – he had family pride – you saw it in his whole bearing.

'Moore *is* a gentleman,' echoed Shirley, lifting her head with glad grace. She checked herself – words seemed crowding to her tongue, she would not give them utterance; but her look spoke much at the moment: what – Yorke tried to read, but could not – the language was there – visible, but untranslatable – a poem – a fervid lyric in an unknown tongue. It was not a plain story, however – no simple gush of feeling – no ordinary love-confession – that was obvious; it was something other, deeper, more intricate than he guessed at: he felt his revenge had not struck home; he felt that Shirley triumphed – she held him at fault, baffled, puzzled; *she* enjoyed the moment – not *he*.

'And if Moore is a gentleman, you *can* be only a lady, therefore –'

'Therefore there would be no inequality in our union?'

'None.'

'Thank you for your approbation. Will you give me away when I relinquish the name of Keeldar for that of Moore?'

Mr Yorke instead of replying, gazed at her much puzzled. He could not divine what her look signified; whether she spoke in earnest or in jest: there was purpose and feeling, banter and scoff playing, mingled, on her mobile lineaments.

'I don't understand thee,' he said, turning away.

She laughed: 'Take courage, sir; you are not singular in your ignorance: but I suppose if Moore understands me that will do – will it not?'

'Moore may settle his own matters henceforward for me; I'll neither meddle nor make with them further.'

A new thought crossed her: her countenance changed magically: with a sudden darkening of the eye, and austere fixing of the features, she demanded, –

'Have you been asked to interfere? Are you questioning me as another's proxy?'

'The Lord save us! Whoever weds thee must look about him! Keep all your questions for Robert; I'll answer no more on 'em. Good-day, lassie!'

The day being fine, or at least fair – for soft clouds curtained the sun, and a dim but not chill or waterish haze slept blue on the hills – Caroline, while Shirley was engaged with her callers, had persuaded Mrs Pryor to assume her bonnet and summer shawl, and to take a walk with her up towards the narrow end of the Hollow.

Here, the opposing sides of the glen approaching each other, and becoming clothed with brushwood and stunted oaks, formed a wooded ravine; at the bottom of which ran the mill-stream, in broken unquiet course, struggling with many stones, chafing against rugged banks, fretting with gnarled tree-roots, foaming, gurgling, battling as it went. Here, when you had wandered half a mile from the mill, you found a sense of deep solitude: found it in the shade of unmolested trees; received it in the singing of many birds, for which that shade made a home. This was no trodden way: the freshness of the woodflowers attested that foot of man seldom pressed them: the abounding wild-roses looked as if they budded, bloomed, and faded under the watch of solitude, as in a sultan's harem. Here you saw the sweet azure of blue-bells, and recognised in pearl-white blossoms, spangling the grass, an humble type of some star-lit spot in space.

Mrs Pryor liked a quiet walk: she ever shunned highroads, and sought byways and lonely lanes: one companion she preferred to total solitude, for in solitude she was nervous: a vague fear of annoying encounters broke the enjoyment of quite lonely rambles; but she feared nothing with Caroline: when once she got away from human habitations, and entered the still demesne of Nature, accompanied by this one youthful friend, a propitious change seemed to steal over her mind and beam in her coun-tenance. When with Caroline – and Caroline only – her heart, you would have said, shook off a burden, her brow put aside a veil, her spirits too escaped from a restraint: with her she was cheerful; with her, at times, she was tender: to her she would impart her knowledge, reveal glimpses of her experience, give her opportunities for guessing what life she had lived, what cultivation her mind had received, of what calibre was her intelligence, how and where her feelings were vulnerable.

To-day, for instance, as they walked along, Mrs Pryor talked to her companion about the various birds singing in the trees, discriminated their species, and said something about their habits and peculiarities. English natural history seemed familiar to her. All the wild flowers round their path were recognised by her: tiny plants springing near stones and peeping out of chinks in old walls – plants such as Caroline had scarcely noticed before – received a name and an intimation of their properties: it appeared that she had minutely studied the botany of English fields and woods. Having reached the head of the ravine, they sat down together on a ledge of grey and mossy rock jutting from the base of a steep green hill, which towered above them: she looked round her, and spoke of the neighbourhood as she had once before seen it long ago. She alluded to its changes, and compared its aspect with that of other parts of England;

revealing in quiet, unconscious touches of description, a sense of the picturesque, an appreciation of the beautiful or common-place, a power of comparing the wild with the cultured, the grand with the tame, that gave to her discourse a graphic charm as pleasant as it was unpretending.

The sort of reverent pleasure with which Caroline listened – so sincere, so quiet, yet so evident, stirred the elder lady's faculties to gentle animation. Rarely, probably, had she, with her chill, repellent outside – her diffident mien and incom-municative habits, known what it was to excite in one whom she herself could love, feelings of earnest affection and admiring esteem. Delightful, doubtless, was the consciousness that a young girl towards whom it seemed – judging by the moved expression of her eyes and features – her heart turned with almost a fond impulse, looked up to her as an instructor, and clung to her as a friend. With a somewhat more marked accent of interest than she often permitted herself to use, she said, as she bent towards her youthful companion, and put aside from her forehead a pale brown curl which had strayed from the confining comb, –

'I do hope this sweet air blowing from the hill will do you good, my dear Caroline: I wish I could see something more of colour in these cheeks – but perhaps you were never florid?'

'I had red cheeks once,' returned Miss Helstone, smiling. 'I remember a year – two years ago, when I used to look in the glass, I saw a different face there to what I see now – rounder and rosier. But when we are young,' added the girl of eighteen, 'our minds are careless and our lives easy.'

'Do you' – continued Mrs Pryor, mastering by an effort that tyrant timidity which made it difficult for her, even under present circumstances, to attempt the scrutiny of another's heart, – 'Do you, at your age, fret yourself with cares for the future? Believe me, you had better not: let the morrow take thought for the things of itself.'

'True, dear madam: it is not over the future I pine. The evil of the day is sometimes oppressive – *too* oppressive, and I long to escape it.'

'That is – the evil of the day – that is – your uncle perhaps is not – you find it difficult to understand – he does not appreciate –'

Mrs Pryor could not complete her broken sentences: she could not manage to put the question whether Mr Helstone was too harsh with his niece, but Caroline comprehended.

'Oh, that is nothing,' she replied; 'my uncle and I get on very well: we never quarrel – I don't call him harsh – he never scolds me. Sometimes I wish somebody in the world loved me; but I cannot say that I particularly wish him to have more affection for me than he has. As a child, I should perhaps have felt the want of attention, only the servants were very kind to me; but when people are long indifferent to us, we grow indifferent to their indifference. It is my uncle's way not to care for women and girls – unless they be ladies that he meets in company: he could not alter, and I have no wish that he should alter, as far as I am concerned. I believe it would merely annoy and frighten me were he to be affectionate towards me now. But you know, Mrs Pryor, it is scarcely *living* to measure time as I do at the Rectory. The hours pass, and I get them over somehow, but I do not *live*. I endure existence, but I rarely enjoy it. Since Miss Keeldar and you came, I have been – I was going to say – happier, but that would be untrue.' She paused.

'How, untrue? You are fond of Miss Keeldar, are you not, my dear?'

'Very fond of Shirley: I both like and admire her: but I am painfully circumstanced: for a reason I cannot explain, I want to go away from this place, and to forget it.'

'You told me before you wished to be a governess; but, my dear, if you remember, I did not encourage the idea. I have been a governess myself a great part of my life. In Miss Keeldar's acquaintance, I esteem myself most fortunate: her talents and her really sweet disposition have rendered my office easy to me; but when I was young, before I married, my trials were severe, poignant. I should not like a – . I should not like you to endure similar ones. It was my lot to enter a family of considerable pretensions to good birth and mental superiority, and the members of which also believed that "on them was perceptible" an unusual endowment of the "Christian graces": that all their hearts were regenerate, and their spirits in a peculiar state of discipline. I was early given to understand, that "as I was not their equal," so I could not expect "to have their sympathy." It was in no sort concealed from me that I was held a "burden and a restraint in society." The gentlemen, I found, regarded me as a "tabooed woman," to whom "they were interdicted from granting the usual privileges of the sex," and yet who "annoyed them by frequently crossing their path." The ladies too made it plain that they thought me "a bore." The servants, it was signified, "detested me": *why*, I could never clearly comprehend. My pupils, I was told, "however much they might love me, and how deep soever the interest I might take in them, could not be my friends." It was intimated, that I must "live alone, and never transgress the invisible but rigid line which established the difference between me and my employers." My life in this house was sedentary, solitary, constrained, joyless, toilsome. The dreadful crushing of the animal spirits, the ever prevailing sense of friendlessness and homelessness consequent on this state of things, began erelong to produce mortal effects on my constitution – I sickened. The lady of the house told me coolly I was the victim of "wounded vanity." She hinted, that if I did not make an effort to quell my "ungodly discontent," to cease "murmuring against God's appointment," and to cultivate the profound humility befitting my station, my mind would very likely "go to pieces" on the rock that wrecked most of my sisterhood – morbid self-esteem; and that I should die an inmate of a lunatic asylum.

'I said nothing to Mrs Hardman; it would have been useless;

but to her eldest daughter I one day dropped a few observations, which were answered thus: –

'There were hardships, she allowed, in the position of a governess: "doubtless they had their trials; but," she averred, with a manner it makes me smile now to recall – "but it must be so. *She* (Miss H.) had neither view, hope, nor *wish* to see these things remedied; for, in the inherent constitution of English habits, feelings, and prejudices, there was no possibility that they should be. Governesses," she observed, "must ever be kept in a sort of isolation: it is the only means of maintaining that distance which the reserve of English manners and the decorum of English families exact."

'I remember I sighed as Miss Hardman quitted my bedside: she caught the sound, and turning, said severely, –

' "I fear, Miss Grey, you have inherited in fullest measure the worst sin of our fallen nature – the sin of pride. You are proud. and therefore you are ungrateful too. Mamma pays you a handsome salary; and, if you had average sense, you would thankfully put up with much that is fatiguing to do and irksome to bear, since it is so well made worth your while."

'Miss Hardman, my love, was a very strong-minded young lady, of most distinguished talents: the aristocracy are decidedly a very superior class, you know – both physically and morally and mentally – as a high Tory I acknowledge that – I could not describe the dignity of her voice and mien as she addressed me thus: still, I fear, she was selfish, my dear. I would never wish to speak ill of my superiors in rank; but I think she was a little selfish.

'I remember,' continued Mrs Pryor, after a pause, 'another of Miss H.'s observations, which she would utter with quite a grand air. "WE," she would say, – "WE need the imprudences, extravagances, mistakes, and crimes of a certain number of fathers to sow the seed from which WE reap the harvest of governesses. The daughters of trades-people, however well educated, must necessarily be under-bred, and as such unfit to be inmates of OUR dwellings, or guardians of OUR children's minds and persons. WE shall ever prefer to place those about OUR offspring, who have been born and bred with somewhat of the same refinement as OURSELVES." '

'Miss Hardman must have thought herself something better than her fellow-creatures, ma'am, since she held that their calamities, and even crimes, were necessary to minister to her convenience. You say she was religious: her religion must have been that of the Pharisee, who thanked God that he was not as other men are, nor even as that publican.'

'My dear, we will not discuss the point: I should be the last person to wish to instil into your mind any feeling of dissatisfaction with your lot in life, or any sentiment of envy or insubordination towards your superiors. Implicit submission to authorities, scrupulous deference to our betters (under which term I, of course, include the higher classes of society) are, in my opinion, indispensable to the wellbeing of every community. All I mean to say, my dear, is, that you had better not attempt to be a governess, as the duties of the position would be too severe for your constitution. Not one word of disrespect would I breathe towards either Mrs or Miss Hardman; only, recalling my own experience, I cannot but feel that, were you to fall under auspices such as theirs, you would contend a while courageously with your doom; then you would pine and grow too weak for your work: you would come home – if you still had a home – broken down. Those languishing years would follow, of which none but the invalid and her immediate friends feel the heart-sickness and know the burden: consumption or decline would close the chapter. Such is the history of many a life: I would not have it yours. My dear, we will now walk about a little, if you please.'

They both rose and slowly paced a green natural terrace bordering the chasm.

'My dear,' erelong again began Mrs Pryor, a sort of timid, embarrassed abruptness marking her manner as she spoke, 'the young, especially those to whom nature has been favourable – often – frequently – anticipate – look forward to – to marriage as the end, the goal of their hopes.'

And she stopped. Caroline came to her relief with promptitude, showing a great deal more self-possession and courage than herself on the formidable topic now broached.

'They do; and naturally,' she replied, with a calm emphasis that startled Mrs Pryor. 'They look forward to marriage with some one they love as the brightest, – the only bright destiny that can await them. Are they wrong?'

'Oh, my dear!' exclaimed Mrs Pryor, clasping her hands: and again she paused. Caroline turned a searching, an eager eye on the face of her friend: that face was much agitated. 'My dear,' she murmured, 'life is an illusion.'

'But not love! Love is real: the most real, the most lasting, – the sweetest and yet the bitterest thing we know.'

'My dear – it is very bitter. It is said to be strong – strong as death! Most of the cheats of existence are strong. As to their sweetness – nothing is so transitory: its date is a moment, – the twinkling of an eye: the sting remains for ever: it may perish with the dawn of eternity, but it tortures through time into its deepest night.'

'Yes, it tortures through time,' agreed Caroline, 'except when it is mutual love.'

'Mutual love! My dear, romances are pernicious. You do not read them, I hope?'

'Sometimes – whenever I can get them, indeed; but romance-writers might know nothing of love, judging by the way in which they treat of it.'

'Nothing whatever, my dear!' assented Mrs Pryor, eagerly; 'nor of marriage; and the false pictures they give of those subjects cannot be too strongly condemned. They are not like reality: they show you only the green tempting surface of the marsh, and give not one faithful or truthful hint of the slough underneath.'

'But it is not always slough,' objected Caroline: 'there are happy marriages. Where affection is reciprocal and sincere, and minds are harmonious, marriage *must* be happy.'

'It is never wholly happy. Two people can never literally be as one: there is, perhaps, a possibility of content under peculiar circumstances, such as are seldom combined; but it is as well not to run the risk: you may make fatal mistakes. Be satisfied, my dear: let all the single be satisfied with their freedom.'

'You echo my uncle's words!' exclaimed Caroline, in a tone of dismay: 'you speak like Mrs Yorke, in her most gloomy moments: – like Miss Mann, when she is most sourly and hypochondriacally disposed. This is terrible!'

'No, it is only true. Oh, child! you have only lived the pleasant morning time of life: the hot, weary noon, the sad evening, the sunless night, are yet to come for you! Mr Helstone, you say, talks as I talk; and I wonder how Mrs Matthewson Helstone would have talked had she been living. She died! she died!'

'And, alas! my own mother and father . . .' exclaimed Caroline, struck by a sombre recollection.

'What of them?'

'Did I never tell you that they were separated?'

'I have heard it.'

'They must then have been very miserable.'

'You see all *facts* go to prove what I say.'

'In this case there ought to be no such thing as marriage.'

'There ought, my dear, were it only to prove that this life is a mere state of probation, wherein neither rest nor recompense is to be vouchsafed.'

'But your own marriage, Mrs Pryor?'

Mrs Pryor shrunk and shuddered as if a rude finger had pressed a naked nerve: Caroline felt she had touched what would not bear the slightest contact.

'My marriage was unhappy,' said the lady, summoning courage at last; 'but yet –' she hesitated.

'But yet,' suggested Caroline, 'not immitigably wretched?'

'Not in its results, at least. No,' she added, in a softer tone;

'God mingles something of the balm of mercy even in vials of the most corrosive woe. He can so turn events, that from the very same blind, rash act whence sprang the curse of half our life, may flow the blessing of the remainder. Then, I am of a peculiar disposition, I own that: far from facile, without address, in some points eccentric. I ought never to have married: mine is not the nature easily to find a duplicate, or likely to assimilate with a contrast. I was quite aware of my own ineligibility; and if I had not been so miserable as a governess, I never should have married; and then –'

Caroline's eyes asked her to proceed: they entreated her to break the thick cloud of despair, which her previous words had seemed to spread over life.

'And then, my dear, Mr –, that is, the gentleman I married, was, perhaps, rather an exceptional than an average character. I hope, at least, the experience of few has been such as mine was, or that few have felt their sufferings as I felt mine. They nearly shook my mind: relief was so hopeless, redress so un-attainable: but, my dear, I do not wish to dishearten, I only wish to warn you, and to prove that the single should not be too anxious to change their state, as they may change for the worse.'

'Thank you, my dear madam, I quite understand your kind intentions; but there is no fear of my falling into the error to which you allude. I, at least, have no thoughts of marriage, and, for that reason, I want to make myself a position by some other means.'

'My dear, listen to me. On what I am going to say, I have carefully deliberated; having, indeed, revolved the subject in my thoughts ever since you first mentioned your wish to obtain a situation. You know I at present reside with Miss Keeldar in the capacity of companion: should she marry (and that she *will* marry erelong, many circumstances induce me to conclude), I shall cease to be necessary to her in that capacity. I must tell you that I possess a small independency, arising partly from my own savings, and partly from a legacy left me some years since; whenever I leave Fieldhead, I shall take a house of my own: I could not endure to live in solitude: I have no relations whom I care to invite to close intimacy; for, as you must have observed, and as I have already avowed, my habits and tastes have their peculiarities: to you, my dear, I need not say I am attached; with you I am happier than I have ever been with any living thing' (this was said with marked emphasis). 'Your society I should esteem a very dear privilege – an inestimable privilege, a comfort, a blessing. You shall come to me then. Caroline, do you refuse me? I hope you can love me?'

And with these two abrupt questions she stopped.

'Indeed, I *do* love you,' was the reply. 'I should like to live with you: but you are too kind.'

'All I have,' went on Mrs Pryor, 'I would leave to you: you should be provided for, but never again say I am too kind. You pierce my heart, child!'

'But, my dear madam – this generosity – I have no claim –'

'Hush! you must not talk about it: there are some things we cannot bear to hear. Oh! it is late to begin, but I may yet live a few years: I can never wipe out the past, but perhaps a brief space in the future may yet be mine!'

Mrs Pryor seemed deeply agitated: large tears trembled in her eyes and rolled down her cheeks. Caroline kissed her, in her gentle caressing way, saying softly –

'I love you dearly. Don't cry.'

But the lady's whole frame seemed shaken: she sat down, bent her head to her knee, and wept aloud. Nothing could console her till the inward storm had had its way. At last the agony subsided of itself.

'Poor thing!' she murmured, returning Caroline's kiss: 'poor lonely lamb! But come,' she added abruptly; 'come, we must go home.'

For a short distance Mrs Pryor walked very fast: by degrees, however, she calmed down to her wonted manner, fell into her

usual characteristic pace, – a peculiar one like all her movements, – and by the time they reached Fieldhead, she had
re-entered into herself: the outside was, as usual, still and shy.

CHAPTER XXII

TWO LIVES

Only half of Moore's activity and resolution had been seen in his defence of the mill: he showed the other half (and a terrible half it was) in the indefatigable, the relentless assiduity with which he pursued the leaders of the riot. The mob, the mere followers, he let alone: perhaps an innate sense of justice told him that men misled by false counsel, goaded by privations, are not fit objects of vengeance, and that he who would visit an even violent act on the bent head of suffering, is a tyrant, not a judge. At all events, though he knew many of the number, having recognised them during the latter part of the attack when day began to dawn, he let them daily pass him on street and road without notice or threat.

The leaders he did not know. They were strangers: emissaries from the large towns. Most of these were not members of the operative class: they were chiefly 'downdraughts,' bankrupts, men always in debt and often in drink – men who had nothing to lose, and much – in the way of character, cash, and cleanliness – to gain. These persons Moore hunted like any sleuth-hound; and well he liked the occupation: its excitement was of a kind pleasant to his nature: he liked it better than making cloth.

His horse must have hated these times, for it was ridden both hard and often: he almost lived on the road, and the fresh air was as welcome to his lungs as the policeman's quest to his mood: he preferred it to the steam of dye-houses. The magistrates of the district must have dreaded him: they were slow, timid men; he liked both to frighten and to rouse them. He liked to force them to betray a certain fear, which made them alike falter in resolve and recoil in action – the fear, simply, of assassination. This, indeed, was the dread which had hitherto hampered every manufacturer and almost every public man in the district. Helstone alone had ever repelled it. The old Cossack knew well he might be shot: he knew there was risk; but such death had for his nerves no terrors: it would have been his chosen – might he have had a choice.

Moore likewise knew his danger: the result was an unquench-able scorn of the quarter whence such danger was to be appre-hended. The consciousness that he hunted assassins was the spur in his high-mettled temper's flank. As for fear, he was too proud – too hard-nurtured – (if you will) – too phlegmatic a man to fear. Many a time he rode belated over moors, moonlit or moonless as the case might be, with feelings far more elate, faculties far better refreshed, than when safety and stagnation environed him in the counting-house. Four was the number of the leaders to be accounted for: two, in the course of a fortnight, were brought to bay near Stilbro'; the remaining two it was necessary to seek further off: their haunts were supposed to lie near Birmingham.

Meantime, the clothier did not neglect his battered mill: its reparation was esteemed a light task; carpenters' and glaziers' work alone being needed. The rioters not having succeeded in effecting an entrance, his grim, metal darlings – the machines – had escaped damage.

Whether, during this busy life – whether, while stern justice and exacting business claimed his energies and harassed his thoughts – he now and then gave one moment, dedicated one effort, to keep alive gentler fires than those which smoulder in the fane of Nemesis, it was not easy to discover. He seldom went near Fieldhead; if he did, his visits were brief: if he called at the Rectory, it was only to hold conferences with the Rector in his study. He maintained his rigid course very steadily. Mean-time, the history of the year continued troubled: there was no lull in the tempest of war; her long hurricane still swept the

Continent. There was not the faintest sign of serene weather: no opening amid 'the clouds of battle-dust and smoke;' no fall of pure dews genial to the olive; no cessation of the red rain which nourishes the baleful and glorious laurel. Meantime, Ruin had her sappers and miners at work under Moore's feet, and whether he rode or walked – whether he only crossed his counting-house hearth, or galloped over sullen Rushedge – he was aware of a hollow echo, and felt the ground shake to his tread.

While the summer thus passed with Moore, how did it lapse with Shirley and Caroline? Let us first visit the heiress. How does she look? Like a love-lorn maiden, pale and pining for a neglectful swain? Does she sit the day long bent over some sedentary task? Has she for ever a book in her hand, or sewing on her knee, and eyes only for that, and words for nothing, and thoughts unspoken?

By no means. Shirley is all right. If her wistful cast of physiognomy is not gone, no more is her careless smile. She keeps her dark old manor-house light and bright with her cheery presence: the gallery, and the low-ceiled chambers that open into it, have learned lively echoes from her voice: the dim entrance-hall, with its one window, has grown pleasantly accustomed to the frequent rustle of a silk dress, as its wearer sweeps across from room to room, now carrying flowers to the barbarous peach-bloom salon, now entering the dining-room to open its casements and let in the scent of mignonette and sweetbriar, anon bringing plants from the staircase-window to place in the sun at the open porch-door.

She takes her sewing occasionally: but, by some fatality, she is doomed never to sit steadily at it for above five minutes at a time: her thimble is scarcely fitted on, her needle scarce threaded, when a sudden thought calls her up-stairs: perhaps she goes to seek some just-then-remembered old ivory-backed needle-book, or older china-topped workbox, quite unneeded, but which seems at the moment indispensable; perhaps to arrange her hair, or a drawer which she recollects to have seen that morning in a state of curious confusion; perhaps only to take a peep from a particular window at a particular view, whence Briarfield Church and Rectory are visible, pleasantly bowered in trees. She has scarcely returned, and again taken up the slip of cambric, or square of half-wrought canvass, when Tartar's bold scrape and strangled whistle are heard at the porch-door, and she must run to open it for him; it is a hot day; he comes in panting; she must convoy him to the kitchen, and see with her own eyes that his water-bowl is replenished. Through the open kitchen-door the court is visible, all sunny and gay, and peopled with turkeys and their poults, peahens and their chicks, pearl-flecked Guinea fowls, and a bright variety of pure white, and purple-necked, and blue and cinnamon-plumed pigeons. Irresistible spectacle to Shirley! She runs to the pantry for a roll, and she stands on the door-step scattering crumbs: around her throng her eager, plump, happy, feathered vassals. John is about the stables, and John must be talked to, and her mare looked at. She is still petting and patting it, when the cows come in to be milked: this is important; Shirley must stay and take a review of them all. There are perhaps some little calves, some little new-yeaned lambs – it may be twins, whose mothers have rejected them: Miss Keeldar must be introduced to them by John – must permit herself the treat of feeding them with her own hand, under the direction of her careful foreman. Meantime, John moots doubtful questions about the farming of certain 'crofts,' and 'ings,' and 'holms,' and his mistress is necessitated to fetch her garden-hat – a gipsy-straw – and accompany him, over stile and along hedgerow, to hear the conclusion of the whole agricultural matter on the spot, and with the said 'crofts,' 'ings,' and 'holms' under her eye. Bright afternoon thus wears into soft evening, and she comes home to a late tea, and after tea she never sews.

After tea Shirley reads, and she is just about as tenacious of her book as she is lax of her needle. Her study is the rug, her seat a foot-stool, or perhaps only the carpet at Mrs Pryor's feet – there she always learned her lessons when a child, and old habits have a strong power over her. The tawny and lion-like bulk of Tartar is ever stretched beside her; his negro muzzle laid on his forepaws, straight, strong, and shapely as the limbs of an Alpine wolf. One hand of the mistress generally reposes on the loving serf's rude head, because if she takes it away he groans and is discontented. Shirley's mind is given to her book; she lifts not her eyes; she neither stirs nor speaks: unless, indeed, it be to return a brief respectful answer to Mrs Pryor, who addresses deprecatory phrases to her now and then.

'My dear, you had better not have that great dog so near you: he is crushing the border of your dress.'

'Oh, it is only muslin: I can put a clean one on to-morrow.'

'My dear, I wish you could acquire the habit of sitting to a table when you read.'

'I will try, ma'am, some time; but it is so comfortable to do as one has always been accustomed to do.'

'My dear, let me beg of you to put that book down: you are trying your eyes by the doubtful firelight.'

'No, ma'am, not at all: my eyes are never tired.'

At last, however, a pale light falls on the page from the window: she looks, the moon is up; she closes the volume, rises, and walks through the room. Her book has perhaps been a good one; it has refreshed, refilled, rewarmed her heart; it has set her brain astir, furnished her mind with pictures. The still parlour, the clean hearth, the window opening on the twilight sky, and showing its 'sweet regent,' new throned and glorious, suffice to make earth an Eden, life a poem, for Shirley. A still, deep, inborn delight glows in her young veins; unmingled – untroubled; not to be reached or ravished by human agency, because by no human agency bestowed: the pure gift of God to His creature, the free dower of Nature to her child. This joy gives her experience of a genii-life. Buoyant, by green steps, by glad hills, all verdure and light, she reaches a station scarcely

lower than that whence angels looked down on the dreamer of
Beth-el, and her eye seeks, and her soul possesses, the vision of
life as she wishes it. No – not as she wishes it; she has not time
to wish: the swift glory spreads out, sweeping and kindling,
and multiplies its splendours faster than Thought can effect his
combinations, faster than Aspiration can utter her longings.
Shirley says nothing while the trance is upon her – she is quite
mute; but if Mrs Pryor speaks to her now, she goes out quietly,
and continues her walk up-stairs in the dim gallery.

If Shirley were not an indolent, a reckless, an ignorant being,
she would take a pen at such moments; or at least while the
recollection of such moments was yet fresh on her spirit: she
would seize, she would fix the apparition, tell the vision
revealed. Had she a little more of the organ of Acquisitiveness
in her head – a little more of the love of property in her nature,
she would take a good-sized sheet of paper and write plainly
out, in her own queer but clear and legible hand, the story that
has been narrated, the song that has been sung to her, and thus
possess what she was enabled to create. But indolent she is,
reckless she is, and most ignorant, for she does not know her
dreams are rare – her feelings peculiar: she does not know, has
never known, and will die without knowing, the full value of
that spring whose bright fresh bubbling in her heart keeps it
green.

Shirley takes life easily: is not that fact written in her eye? In
her good-tempered moments, is it not as full of lazy softness as
in her brief fits of anger it is fulgent with quick-flashing fire?
Her nature is in her eye: so long as she is calm, indolence,
indulgence, humour, and tenderness possess that large grey
sphere: incense her, – a red ray pierces the dew, – it quickens
instantly to flame.

Ere the month of July was passed, Miss Keeldar would probably have started with Caroline on that northern tour they had
planned; but just at that epoch an invasion befell Fieldhead:
a genteel foraging party besieged Shirley in her castle, and

compelled her to surrender at discretion. An uncle, an aunt, and two cousins from the south, a Mr, Mrs, and two Misses Sympson, of Sympson Grove, —shire, came down upon her in state. The laws of hospitality obliged her to give in, which she did with a facility which somewhat surprised Caroline, who knew her to be prompt in action and fertile in expedient, where a victory was to be gained for her will. Miss Helstone even asked her how it was she submitted so readily? – she answered, old feelings had their power: she had passed two years of her early youth at Sympson Grove.

'How did she like her relatives?'

She had nothing in common with them, she replied: little Harry Sympson, indeed, the sole son of the family, was very unlike his sisters, and of him she had formerly been fond; but he was not coming to Yorkshire: at least, not yet.

The next Sunday the Fieldhead pew in Briarfield church appeared peopled with a prim, trim, fidgety, elderly gentleman, who shifted his spectacles and changed his position every three minutes; a patient, placid-looking elderly lady, in brown satin, and two pattern young ladies, in pattern attire, with pattern deportment. Shirley had the air of a black swan, or a white crow, in the midst of this party; and very forlorn was her aspect. Having brought her into respectable society, we will leave her there a while, and look after Miss Helstone.

Separated from Miss Keeldar for the present, as she could not seek her in the midst of her fine relatives; scared away from Fieldhead by the visiting commotion which the new arrivals occasioned in the neighbourhood, Caroline was limited once more to the grey Rectory; the solitary morning walk in remote bypaths; the long, lonely afternoon sitting in a quiet parlour which the sun forsook at noon, or in the garden alcove where it shone bright, yet sad, on the ripening red currants trained over the trellis, and on the fair monthly roses entwined between, and through them fell chequered on Caroline sitting in her white summer dress, still as a garden statue. There she read old books, taken from her uncle's library: the Greek and Latin were of no use to her; and its collection of light literature was chiefly contained on a shelf which had belonged to her aunt Mary: some venerable Lady's Magazines, that had once performed a sea-voyage with their owner, and undergone a storm, and whose pages were stained with salt water; some mad Methodist Magazines, full of miracles and apparitions, of preternatural warnings, ominous dreams, and frenzied fanaticism; the equally mad Letters of Mrs Elizabeth Rowe from the Dead to the Living, a few old English Classics: – from these faded flowers Caroline had in her childhood extracted the honey, – they were tasteless to her now. By way of change, and also of doing good, she would sew: make garments for the poor, according to good Miss Ainley's direction. Sometimes, as she felt and saw her tears fall slowly on her work, she would wonder how the excellent woman who had cut it out and arranged it for her, managed to be so equably serene in *her* solitude.

'I never find Miss Ainley oppressed with despondency, or lost in grief,' she thought; 'yet her cottage is a still, dim little place, and she is without a bright hope or near friend in the world. I remember, though, she told me once, she had tutored her thoughts to tend upwards to Heaven. She allowed there was, and ever had been, little enjoyment in this world for her; and she looks, I suppose, to the bliss of the world to come. So do nuns – with their close cell, their iron lamp, their robe strait as a shroud, their bed narrow as a coffin. She says, often, she has no fear of death – no dread of the grave: no more, doubtless, had St Simeon Stylites, lifted up terrible on his wild column in the wilderness: no more has the Hindoo votary stretched on his couch of iron spikes. Both these having violated nature, their natural likings and antipathies are reversed: they grow altogether morbid. I do fear death as yet, but I believe it is because I am young: poor Miss Ainley would cling closer to life, if life had more charms for her. God surely did not create us, and cause us to live, with the sole end of wishing always to die. I believe, in my heart, we were intended to prize life and enjoy it, so long as we retain it. Existence never was originally meant to be that useless, blank, pale, slow-trailing thing it often becomes to many, and is becoming to me, among the rest.

'Nobody,' she went on – 'nobody in particular is to blame, that I can see, for the state in which things are; and I cannot tell, however much I puzzle over it, how they are to be altered for the better; but I feel there is something wrong somewhere. I believe single women should have more to do – better chances of interesting and profitable occupation than they possess now. And when I speak thus, I have no impression that I displease God by my words; that I am either impious or impatient, irreligious or sacrilegious. My consolation is, indeed, that God hears many a groan, and compassionates much grief which man stops his ears against, or frowns on with impotent contempt. I say *impotent*, for I observe that to such grievances as society cannot readily cure, it usually forbids utterance, on pain of its scorn: this scorn being only a sort of tinselled cloak to its deformed weakness. People hate to be reminded of ills they are unable or unwilling to remedy: such reminder, in forcing on them a sense of their own incapacity, or a more painful sense of an obligation to make some unpleasant effort, troubles their ease and shakes their self-complacency. Old maids, like the houseless and unemployed poor, should not ask for a place and an occupation in the world: the demand disturbs the happy and rich: it disturbs parents. Look at the numerous families of girls in this neighbourhood: the Armitages, the Birtwhistles, the Sykes. The brothers of these girls are every one in business or in professions; they have something to do: their sisters have no earthly employment, but household work and sewing; no earthly pleasure, but an unprofitable visiting; and no hope, in all their life to come, of anything better. This stagnant state of things makes them decline in health: they are never well; and their minds and views shrink to wondrous narrowness. The great wish – the sole aim of every one of them is to be married, but the majority will never marry: they will die as they now live. They scheme, they plot, they dress to ensnare husbands. The gentlemen turn them into ridicule: they don't want them; they hold them very cheap: they say – I have heard them say it with sneering laughs many a time – the matrimonial market is over-stocked. Fathers say so likewise, and are angry with their daughters when they observe their manœuvres: they order them to stay at home. What do they expect them to do at home? If you ask, – they would answer, sew and cook. They expect them to do this, and this only, contentedly, regularly, uncomplainingly all their lives long, as if they had no germs of faculties for anything else: a doctrine as reasonable to hold, as it would be that the fathers have no faculties but for eating what their daughters cook, or for wearing what they sew. Could men live so themselves? Would they not be very weary? And, when there came no relief to their weariness, but only reproaches at its slightest manifestation, would not their weariness ferment in time to frenzy? Lucretia, spinning at midnight in the midst of her maidens, and Solomon's virtuous woman, are often quoted as patterns of what "the sex" (as they say) ought to be. I don't know: Lucretia, I daresay, was a most worthy sort of person, much like my cousin Hortense Moore; but she kept her servants up very late. I should not have liked to be amongst the number of the maidens. Hortense would just work me and Sarah in that fashion, if she could, and neither of us would bear it. The "virtuous woman," again, had her household up in the very middle of the night; she "got breakfast over" (as Mrs Sykes says) before one o'clock a.m.; but *she* had something more to do than spin and give out portions: she was a manufacturer – she made fine linen and sold it: she was an agriculturist – she bought estates and planted vineyards. *That* woman was a manager: she was what the matrons hereabouts call "a clever woman." On the whole, I like her a good deal better than Lucretia; but I don't believe either Mr Armitage or Mr Sykes could have got the advantage of her in a bargain: yet, I like her. "Strength and honour were her clothing: the heart of her husband safely trusted in her. She opened her mouth with wisdom; in her tongue was the law of kindness: her children rose up and called her blessed; her husband also praised her." King of Israel! your model of a woman is a worthy model! But are we, in these days, brought up to be like her? Men of Yorkshire! do your daughters reach this royal standard? Can they reach it? Can you help them to reach it? Can you give them a field in which their faculties may be exercised and grow? Men of England! look at your poor girls, many of them fading around you, dropping off in consumption or decline; or, what is worse, degenerating to sour old maids, – envious, backbiting, wretched, because life is a desert to them; or, what is worst of all, reduced to strive, by scarce modest coquetry and debasing artifice, to gain that position and consideration by marriage, which to celibacy is denied. Fathers! cannot you alter these things? Perhaps not all at once; but consider the matter well when it is brought before you, receive it as a theme worthy of thought: do not dismiss it with an idle jest or an unmanly insult. You would wish to be proud of your daughters and not to blush for them – then seek for them an interest and an occupation which shall raise them above the flirt, the manœuvrer, the mischief-making tale-bearer. Keep your girls' minds narrow and fettered – they will still be a plague and a care, sometimes a disgrace to you: cultivate them – give them scope and work – they will be your gayest companions in health; your tenderest nurses in sickness; your most faithful prop in age.'

CHAPTER XXIII

AN EVENING OUT

ONE FINE summer day that Caroline had spent entirely alone (her uncle being at Whinbury), and whose long, bright, noiseless, breezeless, cloudless hours (how many they seemed since sunrise!) had been to her as desolate as if they had gone over her head in the shadowless and trackless wastes of Zahara, instead of in the blooming garden of an English home, she was sitting in the alcove, – her task of work on her knee, her fingers assiduously plying the needle, her eyes following and regulating their movements, her brain working restlessly, – when Fanny came to the door, looked round over the lawn and borders, and not seeing her whom she sought, called out – 'Miss Caroline!'

A low voice answered – 'Fanny!' It issued from the alcove, and thither Fanny hastened – a note in her hand, which she delivered to fingers that hardly seemed to have nerve to hold it. Miss Helstone did not ask whence it came, and she did not look at it: she let it drop amongst the folds of her work.

'Joe Scott's son, Harry, brought it,' said Fanny.

The girl was no enchantress, and knew no magic-spell, yet what she said took almost magical effect on her young mistress: she lifted her head with the quick motion of revived sensation; she shot – not a languid, but a life-like, questioning glance at Fanny.

'Harry Scott! Who sent him?'

'He came from the Hollow.'

The dropped note was snatched up eagerly – the seal was broken: it was read in two seconds. An affectionate billet from Hortense, informing her young cousin that she was returned from Wormwood Wells; that she was alone to-day, as Robert was gone to Whinbury market; that nothing would give her greater pleasure than to have Caroline's company to tea; and – the good lady added – she was sure such a change would be most acceptable and beneficial to Caroline, who must be sadly at a loss both for safe guidance and improving society since the misunderstanding between Robert and Mr Helstone had occasioned a separation from her 'meilleure amie, Hortense Gérard Moore.' In a postscript, she was urged to put on her bonnet and run down directly.

Caroline did not need the injunction: glad was she to lay by the child's brown holland slip she was trimming with braid for the Jew's basket, to hasten up-stairs, cover her curls with her straw bonnet, and throw round her shoulders the black silk scarf, whose simple drapery suited as well her shape as its dark hue set off the purity of her dress and the fairness of her face; glad was she to escape for a few hours the solitude, the sadness, the nightmare of her life; glad to run down the green lane sloping to the Hollow, to scent the fragrance of hedge-flowers sweeter than the perfume of moss-rose or lily. True, she knew Robert was not at the cottage; but it was delight to go where he had lately been: so long, so totally separated from him, merely to see his home, to enter the room where he had that morning sat, felt like a reunion. As such it revived her; and then Illusion was again following her in Peri-mask: the soft agitation of wings caressed her cheek, and the air, breathing from the blue summer sky, bore a voice which whispered – 'Robert may come home while you are in his house; and then, at least, you may look in his face – at least you may give him your hand: perhaps, for a minute, you may sit beside him.'

'Silence!' was her austere response: but she loved the comforter and the consolation.

Miss Moore probably caught from the window the gleam and flutter of Caroline's white attire through the branchy garden-shrubs, for she advanced from the cottage-porch to meet her.

Straight, unbending, phlegmatic as usual, she came on: no haste or ecstacy was ever permitted to disorder the dignity of *her* movements; but she smiled, well pleased to mark the delight of her pupil, to feel her kiss, and the gentle, genial strain of her embrace. She led her tenderly in – half-deceived and wholly flattered. Half deceived! had it not been so, she would in all probability have put her to the wicket, and shut her out. Had she known clearly to whose account the chief share of this child-like joy was to be placed, Hortense would most likely have felt both shocked and incensed. Sisters do not like young ladies to fall in love with their brothers: it seems, if not presumptuous, silly, weak, a delusion, an absurd mistake. *They* do not love these gentlemen – whatever sisterly affection they may cherish towards them – and that others should, repels them with a sense of crude romance. The first movement, in short, excited by such discovery (as with many parents on finding their children to be in love), is one of mixed impatience and contempt. Reason – if they be rational people – corrects the false feeling in time; but if they be irrational, it is never corrected, and the daughter or sister-in-law is disliked to the end.

'You would expect to find me alone, from what I said in my note,' observed Miss Moore, as she conducted Caroline towards the parlour; 'but it was written this morning: since dinner, company has come in.'

And, opening the door, she made visible an ample spread of crimson skirts overflowing the elbow-chair at the fireside, and above them, presiding with dignity, a cap more awful than a crown. That cap had never come to the cottage under a bonnet: no, it had been brought in a vast bag, or rather a middle-sized balloon of black silk, held wide with whalebone. The screed, or frill of the cap, stood a quarter of a yard broad round the face of the wearer: the ribbon, flourishing in puffs and bows about the head, was of the sort called love-ribbon: there was a good deal of it, – I may say, a very great deal. Mrs Yorke wore the cap – it became her: she wore the gown also – it suited her no less.

That great lady was come in a friendly way to take tea with Miss Moore. It was almost as great and as rare a favour as if the Queen were to go uninvited to share pot-luck with one of her subjects: a higher mark of distinction she could not show, – she who, in general, scorned visiting and tea-drinking, and held cheap, and stigmatized as 'gossips,' every maid and matron of the vicinage.

There was no mistake, however; Miss Moore *was* a favourite with her: she had evinced the fact more than once; evinced it by stopping to speak to her in the churchyard on Sundays; by inviting her, almost hospitably, to come to Briarmains; evinced it to-day by the grand condescension of a personal visit. Her reasons for the preference, as assigned by herself, were, that Miss Moore was a woman of steady deportment, without the least levity of conversation or carriage; also, that, being a foreigner, she must feel the want of a friend to countenance her. She might have added, that her plain aspect, homely precise dress, and phlegmatic unattractive manner were, to her, so many additional recommendations. It is certain, at least, that ladies remarkable for the opposite qualities of beauty, lively bearing, and elegant taste in attire, were not often favoured with her approbation. Whatever gentlemen are apt to admire in women, Mrs Yorke condemned; and what they overlook or despise, she patronized.

Caroline advanced to the mighty matron with some sense of diffidence: she knew little of Mrs Yorke; and, as a parson's niece, was doubtful what sort of a reception she might get. She got a very cool one, and was glad to hide her discomfiture by turning away to take off her bonnet. Nor, upon sitting down, was she displeased to be immediately accosted by a little personage in a blue frock and sash, who started up like some fairy from the side of the great dame's chair, where she had been sitting on a foot-stool, screened from view by the folds of the wide red gown, and running to Miss Helstone, unceremoniously threw her arms round her neck and demanded a kiss.

'My mother is not civil to you,' said the petitioner, as she received and repaid a smiling salute; 'and Rose, there, takes no notice of you: it is their way. If, instead of you, a white angel, with a crown of stars, had come into the room, mother would nod stiffly, and Rose never lift her head at all; but I will be your friend: I have always liked you!'

'Jessie, curb that tongue of yours, and repress your forwardness!' said Mrs Yorke.

'But, mother, you are so frozen!' expostulated Jessie. 'Miss Helstone has never done you any harm: why can't you be kind to her? You sit so stiff, and look so cold, and speak so dry: what for? That's just the fashion in which you treat Miss Shirley Keeldar, and every other young lady who comes to our house. And Rose, there, is such an aut – aut – I have forgotten the word, but it means a machine in the shape of a human being. However, between you, you will drive every soul away from Briarmains, – Martin often says so!'

'I am an automaton? Good! Let me alone then,' said Rose, speaking from a corner where she was sitting on the carpet at the foot of a bookcase, with a volume spread open on her knee. 'Miss Helstone – how do you do?' she added, directing a brief glance to the person addressed, and then again casting down her grey, remarkable eyes on the book, and returning to the study of its pages.

Caroline stole a quiet gaze towards her, dwelling on her young, absorbed countenance, and observing a certain unconscious movement of the mouth as she read, – a movement full of character. Caroline had tact, and she had fine instinct: she felt that Rose Yorke was a peculiar child, – one of the unique: she knew how to treat her. Approaching quietly, she knelt on the carpet at her side, and looked over her little shoulder at her book. It was a romance of Mrs Radcliffe's – 'The Italian.'

Caroline read on with her, making no remark: presently Rose showed her the attention of asking, ere she turned a leaf, –

'Are you ready?'

Caroline only nodded.

'Do you like it?' inquired Rose, erelong.

'Long since, when I read it as a child, I was wonderfully taken with it.'

'Why?'

'It seemed to open with such promise, – such foreboding of a most strange tale to be unfolded.'

'And in reading it, you feel as if you were far away from England, – really in Italy – under another sort of sky, – that blue sky of the south which travellers describe.'

'You are sensible of that, Rose?'

'It makes me long to travel, Miss Helstone.'

'When you are a woman, perhaps, you maybe able to gratify your wish.'

'I mean to make a way to do so, if one is not made for me. I cannot live always in Briarfield. The whole world is not very large compared with creation: I must see the outside of our own round planet at least.'

'How much of its outside?'

'First this hemisphere where we live; then the other. I am resolved that my life shall be a life: not a black trance like the toad's, buried in marble; nor a long, slow death like yours in Briarfield Rectory.'

'Like mine! What can you mean, child?'

'Might you not as well be tediously dying, as for ever shut up in that glebe-house – a place that, when I pass it, always reminds me of a windowed grave? I never see any movement about the door: I never hear a sound from the wall: I believe smoke never issues from the chimneys. What do you do there?'

'I sew, I read, I learn lessons.'

'Are you happy?'

'Should I be happier wandering alone in strange countries, as you wish to do?'

'Much happier, even if you did nothing but wander. Remember, however, that I shall have an object in view: but if you only went on and on, like some enchanted lady in a fairy tale, you might be happier than now. In a day's wandering, you would pass many a hill, wood, and water-course, each perpetually altering in aspect as the sun shone out or was overcast; as the weather was wet or fair, dark or bright. Nothing changes in Briarfield Rectory: the plaster of the parlour-ceilings, the paper on the walls, the curtains, carpets, chairs, are still the same.'

'Is change necessary to happiness?'

'Yes.'

'It is synonymous with it?'

'I don't know; but I feel monotony and death to be almost the same.'

Here Jessie spoke.

'Isn't she mad?' she asked.

'But, Rose,' pursued Caroline, 'I fear a wanderer's life, for me at least, would end like that tale you are reading, – in disappointment, vanity, and vexation of spirit.'

'Does "The Italian" so end?'

'I thought so when I read it.'

'Better to try all things and find all empty, than to try nothing and leave your life a blank. To do this is to commit the sin of him who buried his talent in a napkin – despicable sluggard!'

'Rose,' observed Mrs Yorke, 'solid satisfaction is only to be realized by doing one's duty.'

'Right, mother! And if my Master has given me ten talents, my duty is to trade with them, and make them ten talents more. Not in the dust of household drawers shall the coin be interred. I will *not* deposit it in a broken-spouted tea-pot, and shut it up in a china-closet among tea-things. I will not commit it to your work-table to be smothered in piles of woollen hose. I will not prison it in the linen-press to find shrouds among the sheets: and least of all, mother – (she got up from the floor) – least of all will I hide it in a tureen of cold potatoes, to be ranged with bread, butter, pastry, and ham on the shelves of the larder.'

She stopped – then went on: –

'Mother, the Lord who gave each of us our talents will come home some day, and will demand from all an account. The teapot, the old stocking-foot, the linen rag, the willow-pattern tureen, will yield up their barren deposit in many a house: suffer your daughters, at least, to put their money to the exchangers, that they may be enabled at the Master's coming to pay him his own with usury.'

'Rose, did you bring your sampler with you, as I told you?'

'Yes, mother.'

'Sit down, and do a line of marking.'

Rose sat down promptly, and wrought according to orders. After a busy pause of ten minutes, her mother asked –

'Do you think yourself oppressed now? A victim?'

'No, mother.'

'Yet, as far as I understood your tirade, it was a protest against all womanly and domestic employment.'

'You misunderstood it, mother. I should be sorry not to learn to sew: you do right to teach me, and to make me work.'

'Even to the mending of your brother's stockings and the making of sheets?'

'Yes.'

'Where is the use of ranting and spouting about it, then?'

'Am I to do nothing but that? I will do that, and then I will do more. Now, mother, I have said my say. I am twelve years old at present, and not till I am sixteen will I speak again about talents: for four years, I bind myself an industrious apprentice to all you can teach me.'

'You see what my daughters are, Miss Helstone,' observed Mrs Yorke: 'how precociously wise in their own conceits! "I would rather this – I prefer that;" such is Jessie's cuckoo-song: while Rose utters the bolder cry, "I *will*, and I will *not!*"'

'I render a reason, mother: besides, if my cry is bold, it is only heard once in a twelvemonth. About each birthday, the spirit moves me to deliver one oracle respecting my own instruction and management: I utter it and leave it; it is for you, mother, to listen or not.'

'I would advise all young ladies,' pursued Mrs Yorke, 'to study the characters of such children as they chance to meet with before they marry, and have any of their own; to consider well how they would like the responsibility of guiding the careless, the labour of persuading the stubborn, the constant burden and task of training the best.'

'But with love it need not be so very difficult,' interposed Caroline. 'Mothers love their children most dearly – almost better than they love themselves.'

'Fine talk! Very sentimental! There is the rough, practical part of life yet to come to you, young Miss!'

'But, Mrs Yorke, if I take a little baby into my arms – any poor woman's infant for instance, – I feel that I love that helpless thing quite peculiarly, though I am not its mother. I could do almost anything for it willingly, if it were delivered over entirely to my care – if it were quite dependent on me.'

'You *feel!* Yes! yes! I daresay, now: you are led a great deal by your *feelings*, and you think yourself a very sensitive, refined personage, no doubt. Are you aware that, with all these romantic ideas, you have managed to train your features into an habitually lackadaisical expression, better suited to a novel-heroine than to a woman who is to make her way in the real world, by dint of common sense?'

'No; I am not at all aware of that, Mrs Yorke.'

'Look in the glass just behind you. Compare the face you see there with that of any early-rising, hard-working milkmaid.'

'My face is a pale one, but it is not sentimental, and most milkmaids, however red and robust they may be, are more stupid and less practically fitted to make their way in the world than I am. I think more and more correctly than milkmaids in general do; consequently, where they would often, for want of reflection, act weakly, I, by dint of reflection, should act judiciously.'

'Oh, no! you would be influenced by your feelings. You would be guided by impulse.'

'Of course, I should often be influenced by my feelings: they were given me to that end. Whom my feelings teach me to love, I must and *shall* love; and I hope, if ever I have a husband and children, my feelings will induce me to love them. I hope, in that case, all my impulses will be strong in compelling me to love.'

Caroline had a pleasure in saying this with emphasis: she had a pleasure in daring to say it in Mrs Yorke's presence. She did not care what unjust sarcasm might be hurled at her in reply: she flushed, not with anger, but excitement, when the ungenial matron answered, coolly, –

'Don't waste your dramatic effects. That was well said, – it was quite fine; but it is lost on two women – an old wife and an old maid: there should have been a disengaged gentleman present. Is Mr Robert nowhere hid behind the curtains, do you think, Miss Moore?'

Hortense, who during the chief part of the conversation had been in the kitchen superintending the preparations for tea, did not yet quite comprehend the drift of the discourse. She answered, with a puzzled air, that Robert was at Whinbury. Mrs Yorke laughed her own peculiar short laugh.

'Straightforward Miss Moore!' said she, patronizingly. 'It is like you to understand my question so literally, and answer it so simply. *Your* mind comprehends nothing of intrigue. Strange things might go on around you without your being the wiser: you are not of the class the world calls sharp-witted.'

These equivocal compliments did not seem to please Hortense. She drew herself up, puckered her black eyebrows, but still looked puzzled.

'I have ever been noted for sagacity and discernment from childhood,' she returned: for, indeed, on the possession of these qualities, she peculiarly piqued herself.

'You never plotted to win a husband, I'll be bound,' pursued

Mrs Yorke; 'and you have not the benefit of previous experience to aid you in discovering when others plot.'

Caroline felt this kind language where the benevolent speaker intended she should feel it – in her very heart. She could not even parry the shafts: she was defenceless for the present: to answer would have been to avow that the cap fitted. Mrs Yorke, looking at her as she sat with troubled downcast eyes, and cheek burning painfully, and figure expressing in its bent attitude and unconscious tremor all the humiliation and chagrin she experienced, felt the sufferer was fair game. The strange woman had a natural antipathy to a shrinking, sensitive character – a nervous temperament: nor was a pretty, delicate, and youthful face a passport to her affections. It was seldom she met with all these obnoxious qualities combined in one individual: still more seldom she found that individual at her mercy, under circumstances in which she could crush her well. She happened, this afternoon, to be specially bilious and morose: as much disposed to gore as any vicious 'mother of the herd:' lowering her large head, she made a new charge.

'Your cousin Hortense is an excellent sister, Miss Helstone: such ladies as come to try their life's luck here, at Hollow's cottage, may, by a very little clever female artifice, cajole the mistress of the house, and have the game all in their own hands. You are fond of your cousin's society, I dare say, Miss?'

'Of which cousin's?'

'Oh, of the lady's *of course.*'

'Hortense is, and always has been, most kind to me.'

'Every sister, with an eligible single brother, is considered most kind by her spinster friends.'

'Mrs Yorke,' said Caroline, lifting her eyes slowly, their blue orbs at the same time clearing from trouble, and shining steady and full, while the glow of shame left her cheek, and its hue turned pale and settled: 'Mrs Yorke, may I ask what you mean?'

'To give you a lesson on the cultivation of rectitude: to disgust you with craft and false sentiment.'

'Do I need this lesson?'

'Most young ladies of the present day need it. You are quite a modern young lady – morbid, delicate, professing to like retirement; which implies, I suppose, that you find little worthy of your sympathies in the ordinary world. The ordinary world – every-day, honest folks – are better than you think them: much better than any bookish, romancing chit of a girl can be, who hardly ever puts her nose over her uncle, the parson's, garden-wall.'

'Consequently, of whom you know nothing. Excuse me, – indeed, it does not matter whether you excuse me or not – you have attacked me without provocation: I shall defend myself without apology. Of my relations with my two cousins, you are ignorant: in a fit of ill-humour, you have attempted to poison them by gratuitous insinuations, which are far more crafty and false than anything with which you can justly charge me. That I happen to be pale, and sometimes to look diffident, is no business of yours. That I am fond of books, and indisposed for common gossip, is still less your business. That I am a "romancing chit of a girl," is a mere conjecture on your part: I never romanced to you, nor to anybody you know. That I am the parson's niece is not a crime, though you may be narrow-minded enough to think it so. You dislike me: you have no just reason for disliking me; therefore keep the expression of your aversion to yourself. If at any time, in future, you evince it annoyingly, I shall answer even less scrupulously than I have done now.'

She ceased, and sat in white and still excitement. She had spoken in the clearest of tones, neither fast nor loud; but her silver accents thrilled the ear. The speed of the current in her veins was just then as swift as it was viewless.

Mrs Yorke was not irritated at the reproof, worded with a severity so simple, dictated by a pride so quiet. Turning coolly to Miss Moore, she said, nodding her cap approvingly –

'She has spirit in her, after all. Always speak as honestly as you have done just now,' she continued, 'and you'll do.'

'I repel a recommendation so offensive,' was the answer, delivered in the same pure key, with the same clear look. 'I reject counsel poisoned by insinuation. It is my right to speak as I think proper: nothing binds me to converse as you dictate. So far from always speaking as I have done just now, I shall never address any one in a tone so stern, or in language so harsh, unless in answer to unprovoked insult.'

'Mother, you have found your match,' pronounced little Jessie, whom the scene appeared greatly to edify. Rose had heard the whole with an unmoved face. She now said, –

'No: Miss Helstone is not my mother's match – for she allows herself to be vexed: my mother would wear her out in a few weeks. Shirley Keeldar manages better. Mother, you have never hurt Miss Keeldar's feelings yet. She wears armour under her silk dress that you cannot penetrate.'

Mrs Yorke often complained that her children were mutinous. It was strange, that with all her strictness, with all her 'strong-mindedness,' she could gain no command over them: a look from their father had more influence with them than a lecture from her.

Miss Moore – to whom the position of witness to an altercation in which she took no part was highly displeasing, as being an unimportant secondary post – now, rallying her dignity, prepared to utter a discourse which was to prove both parties in the wrong, and to make it clear to each disputant that she had reason to be ashamed of herself, and ought to submit humbly to the superior sense of the individual then addressing her. Fortunately for her audience, she had not harangued above ten minutes, when Sarah's entrance with the tea-tray called her attention, first, to the fact of that damsel having a gilt comb in her hair, and a red necklace round her throat, and secondly, and subsequently to a pointed remonstrance, to the duty of making tea. After the meal, Rose restored her to good humour by bringing her guitar and asking for a song, and afterwards engaging her in an intelligent and sharp cross-examination about guitar-playing and music in general.

Jessie, meantime, directed her assiduities to Caroline. Sitting on a stool at her feet, she talked to her, first about religion and then about politics. Jessie was accustomed at home to drink in a great deal of what her father said on these subjects, and afterwards in company to retail, with more wit and fluency than consistency or discretion, his opinions, antipathies, and preferences. She rated Caroline soundly for being a member of the Established Church, and for having an uncle a clergyman. She informed her that she lived on the country, and ought to work for her living honestly, instead of passing a useless life, and eating the bread of idleness in the shape of tithes. Thence Jessie passed to a review of the Ministry at that time in office, and a consideration of its deserts. She made familiar mention of the names of Lord Castlereagh and Mr Perceval. Each of these personages she adorned with a character that might have separately suited Moloch and Belial. She denounced the war as wholesale murder, and Lord Wellington as a 'hired butcher.'

Her auditress listened with exceeding edification. Jessie had something of the genius of humour in her nature: it was inexpressibly comic to hear her repeating her sire's denunciations in his nervous northern Doric; as hearty a little Jacobin as ever pent a free mutinous spirit in a muslin frock and sash. Not malignant by nature, her language was not so bitter as it was racy, and the expressive little face gave a piquancy to every phrase which held a beholder's interest captive.

Caroline chid her when she abused Lord Wellington; but she listened delighted to a subsequent tirade against the Prince Regent. Jessie quickly read in the sparkle of her hearer's eye, and the laughter hovering round her lips, that at last she had lit on a topic that pleased. Many a time had she heard the fat 'Adonis of fifty' discussed at her father's breakfast-table, and she now gave Mr Yorke's comments on the theme – genuine as uttered by his Yorkshire lips.

But, Jessie, I will write about you no more. This is an autumn evening, wet and wild. There is only one cloud in the sky; but it curtains it from pole to pole. The wind cannot rest: it hurries sobbing over hills of sullen outline, colourless with twilight and mist. Rain has beat all day on that church-tower: it rises dark from the stony enclosure of its graveyard: the nettles, the long grass, and the tombs all drip with wet. This evening reminds me too forcibly of another evening some years ago: a howling, rainy autumn evening too – when certain people who had that day performed a pilgrimage to a grave new-made in a heretic cemetery, sat near a wood-fire on the hearth of a foreign dwelling. They were merry and social, but they each knew that a gap, never to be filled, had been made in their circle. They knew they had lost something whose absence could never be quite atoned for so long as they lived; and they knew that heavy falling rain was soaking into the wet earth which covered their lost darling; and that the sad, sighing gale was mourning above her buried head. The fire warmed them; Life and Friendship yet blessed them; but Jessie lay cold, coffined, solitary – only the sod screening her from the storm.

Mrs Yorke folded up her knitting, cut short the music-lesson and the lecture on politics, and concluded her visit to the cottage, at an hour early enough to ensure her return to Briarmains before the blush of sunset should quite have faded in heaven, or the path up the fields have become thoroughly moist with evening dew.

The lady and her daughters being gone, Caroline felt that she also ought to resume her scarf, kiss her cousin's cheek, and trip away homeward. If she lingered much later, dusk would draw on, and Fanny would be put to the trouble of coming to fetch her: it was both baking and ironing day at the Rectory, she remembered – Fanny would be busy. Still, she could not quit her seat at the little parlour-window. From no point of view could the West look so lovely as from that lattice with the garland of jessamine round it, whose white stars and green leaves seemed now but grey pencil outlines – graceful in form, but colourless in tint – against the gold incarnadined of a summer evening – against the fire-tinged blue of an August sky, at eight o'clock p.m.

Caroline looked at the wicket-gate, beside which holly-oaks spired up tall; she looked at the close hedge of privet and laurel fencing in the garden; her eyes longed to see something more than the shrubs, before they turned from that limited prospect: they longed to see a human figure, of a certain mould and height, pass the hedge and enter the gate. A human figure she at last saw – nay, two: Frederick Murgatroyd went by, carrying a pail of water; Joe Scott followed, dangling on his forefinger the keys of the mill. They were going to lock up mill and stables for the night, and then betake themselves home.

'So must I,' thought Caroline, as she half rose and sighed.

'This is all folly – heart-breaking folly,' she added. 'In the first place, though I should stay till dark, there will be no arrival; because I feel in my heart, Fate has written it down in to-day's page of her eternal book, that I am not to have the pleasure I long for. In the second place, if he stepped in this moment, my presence here would be a chagrin to him, and the consciousness that it must be so would turn half my blood to ice. His hand would, perhaps, be loose and chill, if I put mine into it: his eye would be clouded if I sought its beam. I should look up for that kindling, something I have seen in past days, when my face, or my language, or my disposition had at some happy moment pleased him – I should discover only darkness. I had better go home.'

She took her bonnet from the table where it lay, and was just fastening the ribbon, when Hortense, directing her attention to a splendid bouquet of flowers in a glass on the same table, mentioned that Miss Keeldar had sent them that morning from Fieldhead; and went on to comment on the guests that lady was at present entertaining, on the bustling life she had lately been leading; adding divers conjectures that she did not very well like it, and much wonderment that a person who was so fond of her own way as the heiress, did not find some means of sooner getting rid of this cortège of relatives.

'But they say she actually will not let Mr Sympson and his family go,' she added: 'they wanted much to return to the south last week, to be ready for the reception of the only son, who is expected home from a tour. She insists that her cousin Henry shall come and join his friends here in Yorkshire. I daresay she partly does it to oblige Robert and myself.'

'How to oblige Robert and you?' inquired Caroline.

'Why, my child, you are dull, Don't you know – you must often have heard –'

'Please, ma'am,' said Sarah, opening the door, 'the preserves that you told me to boil in treacle – the congfiters, as you call them – is all burnt to the pan.'

'Les confitures! Elles sont brûlées? Ah, quelle négligence coupable! Coquine de cuisinière – fille insupportable!'

And Mademoiselle, hastily taking from a drawer a large linen apron, and tying it over her black apron, rushed 'éperdue' into the kitchen, whence – to speak truth – exhaled an odour of calcined sweets rather strong than savoury.

The mistress and maid had been in full feud the whole day, on the subject of preserving certain black cherries, hard as marbles, sour as sloes. Sarah held that sugar was the only orthodox condiment to be used in that process; Mademoiselle maintained – and proved it by the practice and experience of her mother, grandmother, and great-grandmother – that treacle, 'mélasse,' was infinitely preferable. She had committed an imprudence in leaving Sarah in charge of the preserving-pan, for her want of sympathy in the nature of its contents had induced a degree of carelessness in watching their confection, whereof the result was – dark and cindery ruin. Hubbub followed: high upbraiding, and sobs rather loud than deep or real.

Caroline, once more turning to the little mirror, was shading her ringlets from her cheek to smooth them under her cottage bonnet, certain that it would not only be useless but unpleasant to stay longer; when, on the sudden opening of the back-door, there fell an abrupt calm in the kitchen: the tongues were checked, pulled up as with bit and bridle. 'Was it – was it – Robert?' He often – almost always – entered by the kitchen way on his return from market. No: it was only Joe Scott, who, having hemmed significantly thrice – every hem being meant as a lofty rebuke to the squabbling womankind – said, –

'Now, I thowt I heerd a crack?'

None answered.

'And,' he continued, pragmatically, 'as t' maister's comed, and as he'll enter through this hoyle, I *con*sidered it desirable to step in and let ye know. A houseful o' women is nivver fit to be comed on wi 'out warning. Here he is: walk forrard, sir. They war playing up queerly, but I think I've quietened 'em.'

Another person – it was now audible – entered. Joe Scott proceeded with his rebukes.

'What d'ye mean by being all i' darkness? Sarah, thou quean, canst t' not light a candle? It war sundown an hour syne. He'll brak' his shins agean some o' yer pots, and tables, and stuff. Tak' tent o' this baking-bowl, sir; they've set it i' yer way, fair as if they did it i' malice.'

To Joe's observations succeeded a confused sort of pause, which Caroline, though she was listening with both her ears, could not understand. It was very brief: a cry broke it – a sound of surprise, followed by the sound of a kiss: ejaculations, but half articulate, succeeded.

'Mon Dieu! mon Dieu! Est-ce que je m'y attendais?' were the words chiefly to be distinguished.

'Et tu te portes toujours bien, bonne sœur?' inquired another voice – Robert's, certainly.

Caroline was puzzled. Obeying an impulse, the wisdom of which she had not time to question, she escaped from the little parlour, by way of leaving the coast clear, and running up-stairs took up a position at the head of the banisters, whence she could make further observations ere presenting herself. It was considerably past sunset now: dusk filled the passage, yet not such deep dusk but that she could presently see Robert and Hortense traverse it.

'Caroline! Caroline!' called Hortense, a moment afterwards, 'venez voir mon frère!'

'Strange!' commented Miss Helstone, 'passing strange! What does this unwonted excitement about such an everyday occurrence as a return from market portend? She has not lost her senses, has she? Surely the burnt treacle has not crazed her?'

She descended in a subdued flutter: yet more was she fluttered when Hortense seized her hand at the parlour-door, and leading her to Robert, who stood in bodily presence, tall and dark against the one window, presented her with a mixture of agitation and formality, as though they had been utter strangers, and this was their first mutual introduction.

Increasing puzzle! He bowed rather awkwardly, and turning from her with a stranger's embarrassment, he met the doubtful light from the window: it fell on his face, and the enigma of the dream (a dream it seemed) was at its height: she saw a visage like and unlike, – Robert, and no Robert.

'What is the matter?' said Caroline. 'Is my sight wrong? Is it my cousin?'

'Certainly, it is your cousin,' asserted Hortense.

Then who was this now coming through the passage, – now entering the room? Caroline, looking round, met a new Robert, – the real Robert, as she felt at once.

'Well,' said he, smiling at her questioning, astonished face, 'which is which?'

'Ah! this is *you*!' was the answer.

He laughed. 'I believe it is *me*: and do you know who *he* is? You never saw him before; but you have heard of him.'

She had gathered her senses now.

'It *can* be only one person: your brother, since it is so like you: my other cousin, Louis.'

'Clever little Œdipus! – you would have baffled the Sphinx!' – but now, see us together. Change places. Change again, to confuse her, Louis. – Which is the old love now, Lina?'

'As if it were possible to make a mistake when you speak! You should have told Hortense to ask. But you are not so much alike: it is only your height, your figure, and complexion that are so similar.'

'And I am Robert, am I not?' asked the new comer, making a first effort to overcome what seemed his natural shyness.

Caroline shook her head gently. A soft, expressive ray from her eye beamed on the real Robert: it said much.

She was not permitted to quit her cousins soon: Robert himself was peremptory in obliging her to remain. Glad, simple, and affable in her demeanour (glad for this night, at least), in light, bright spirits for the time, she was too pleasant an addition to the cottage circle to be willingly parted with by any of them. Louis seemed naturally rather a grave, still, retiring man, but the Caroline of this evening, which was not (as you know, reader) the Caroline of every day, thawed his reserve, and cheered his gravity soon. He sat near her, and talked to her. She already knew his vocation was that of tuition; she learned now he had for some years been the tutor of Mr Sympson's son; that he had been travelling with him, and had accompanied him to the north. She inquired if he liked his post, but got a look in reply which did not invite or license further question. The look woke Caroline's ready sympathy: she thought it a very sad expression to pass over so sensible a face as Louis's: for he *had* a sensible face, – though not handsome, she considered, when seen near Robert's. She turned to make the comparison. Robert was leaning against the wall, a little behind her, turning over the leaves of a book of engravings, and probably listening, at the same time, to the dialogue between her and Louis.

'How could I think them alike?' she asked herself: 'I see now it is Hortense, Louis resembles, not Robert.'

And this was in part true: he had the shorter nose and longer upper-lip of his sister, rather than the fine traits of his brother: he had her mould of mouth and chin – all less decisive, accurate, and dear than those of the young mill-owner. His air, though deliberate and reflective, could scarcely be called prompt and acute. You felt, in sitting near and looking up at him, that a slower and probably a more benignant nature than that of the elder Moore shed calm on your impressions.

Robert – perhaps aware that Caroline's glance had wandered towards and dwelt upon him, though he had neither met nor answered it – put down the book of engravings, and approaching, took a seat at her side. She resumed her conversation with Louis, but, while she talked to him, her thoughts were else-where: her heart beat on the side from which her face was half-averted. She acknowledged a steady, manly, kindly air in Louis; but she bent before the secret power of Robert. To be so near him – though he was silent – though he did not touch so much as her scarf-fringe, or the white hem of her dress – affected her like a spell. Had she been obliged to speak to him *only*, it would have quelled – but, at liberty to address another, it excited her. Her discourse flowed freely: it was gay, playful, eloquent. The indulgent look and placid manner of her auditor encouraged her to ease; the sober pleasure expressed by his smile drew out all that was brilliant in her nature. She felt that this evening she appeared to advantage, and, as Robert was a spectator, the consciousness contented her: had he been called away, collapse would at once have succeeded stimulus.

But her enjoyment was not long to shine full-orbed: a cloud soon crossed it.

Hortense, who for some time had been on the move ordering supper, and was now clearing the little table of some books, &c., to make room for the tray, called Robert's attention to the glass of flowers, the carmine and snow and gold of whose petals looked radiant indeed by candlelight.

'They came from Fieldhead,' she said, 'intended as a gift to you, no doubt: we know who is the favourite there – not I, I'm sure.'

It was a wonder to hear Hortense jest; a sign that her spirits were at high-water mark indeed.

'We are to understand, then, that Robert is the favourite?' observed Louis.

'Mon cher,' replied Hortense, 'Robert – c'est tout ce qu'il y a de plus précieux au monde: à côté de lui, le reste du genre humain n'est que du rebut. N'ai-je pas raison, mon enfant?' she added, appealing to Caroline.

Caroline was obliged to reply, 'Yes' – and her beacon was quenched: her star withdrew, as she spoke.

'Et toi, Robert?' inquired Louis.

'When you shall have an opportunity, ask herself,' was the quiet answer. Whether he reddened or paled Caroline did not examine: she discovered it was late, and she must go home. Home she would go: not even Robert could detain her now.

CHAPTER XXIV

THE VALLEY OF THE SHADOW OF DEATH

THE FUTURE sometimes seems to sob a low warning of the events it is bringing us, like some gathering though yet remote storm, which, in tones of the wind, in flushings of the firmament, in clouds strangely torn, announces a blast strong to strew the sea with wrecks; or commissioned to bring in fog the yellow taint of pestilence, covering white Western isles with the poisoned exhalations of the East, dimming the lattices of English homes with the breath of Indian plague. At other times this Future bursts suddenly, as if a rock had rent, and in it a grave had opened, whence issues the body of one that slept. Ere you are aware, you stand face to face with a shrouded and unthought of Calamity – a new Lazarus.

Caroline Helstone went home from Hollow's cottage in good health, as she imagined. On waking the next morning she felt oppressed with unwonted languor: at breakfast, at each meal of the following day, she missed all sense of appetite: palatable food was as ashes and sawdust to her.

'Am I ill?' she asked, and looked at herself in the glass. Her eyes were bright, their pupils dilated, her cheeks seemed rosier and fuller than usual. 'I look well; why can I not eat?'

She felt a pulse beat fast in her temples: she felt, too, her brain in strange activity: her spirits were raised: hundreds of busy and broken, but brilliant thoughts engaged her mind: a glow rested on them, such as tinged her complexion.

Now followed a hot, parched, thirsty, restless night. Towards morning one terrible dream seized her like a tiger: when she woke, she felt and knew she was ill.

How she had caught the fever (fever it was), she could not tell. Probably in her late walk home, some sweet, poisoned breeze, redolent of honey-dew and miasma, had passed into her lungs and veins, and finding there already a fever of mental excitement, and a languor of long conflict and habitual sadness, had fanned the spark to flame, and left a well-lit fire behind it.

It seemed, however, but a gentle fire: after two hot days and worried nights, there was no violence in the symptoms, and neither her uncle, nor Fanny, nor the doctor, nor Miss Keeldar, when she called, had any fear for her: a few days would restore her, every one believed.

The few days passed, and – though it was still thought it could not long delay – the revival had not begun. Mrs Pryor, who had visited her daily, – being present in her chamber one morning when she had been ill a fortnight – watched her very narrowly for some minutes: she took her hand, and placed her finger on her wrist; then, quietly leaving the chamber, she went to Mr Helstone's study. With him she remained closeted a long time – half the morning. On returning to her sick young friend, she laid aside shawl and bonnet: she stood a while at the bedside, one hand placed in the other, gently rocking herself to and fro, in an attitude and with a movement habitual to her. At last she said, –

'I have sent Fanny to Fieldhead to fetch a few things for me, such as I shall want during a short stay here: it is my wish to remain with you till you are better. Your uncle kindly permits my attendance: will it to yourself be acceptable, Caroline?'

'I am sorry you should take such needless trouble. I do not feel very ill, but I cannot refuse resolutely: it will be such comfort to know you are in the house, to see you sometimes in the room; but don't confine yourself on my account, dear Mrs Pryor. – Fanny nurses me very well.'

Mrs Pryor – bending over the pale little sufferer – was now smoothing the hair under her cap, and gently raising her pillow. As she performed these offices, Caroline, smiling, lifted her face to kiss her.

'Are you free from pain? Are you tolerably at ease?' was inquired in a low, earnest voice, as the self-elected nurse yielded to the caress.

'I think I am almost happy.'

'You wish to drink? Your lips are parched.'

She held a glass filled with some cooling beverage to her mouth.

'Have you eaten anything to-day, Caroline?'

'I cannot eat.'

'But soon your appetite will return: it must return: that is, I pray God it may!'

In laying her again on the couch, she encircled her in her arms; and while so doing, by a movement which seemed scarcely voluntary, she drew her to her heart, and held her close gathered an instant.

'I shall hardly wish to get well, that I may keep you always,' said Caroline.

Mrs Pryor did not smile at this speech: over her features ran a tremor, which for some minutes she was absorbed in repressing.

'You are more used to Fanny than to me,' she remarked, erelong. 'I should think my attendance must seem strange, officious?'

'No: quite natural, and very soothing. You must have been accustomed to wait on sick people, ma'am. You move about the room so softly, and you speak so quietly, and touch me so gently.'

'I am dexterous in nothing, my dear. You will often find me awkward, but never negligent.'

Negligent, indeed, she was not. From that hour, Fanny and Eliza became ciphers in the sick-room: Mrs Pryor made it her domain: she performed all its duties; she lived in it day and night. The patient remonstrated, – faintly, however, from the first, and not at all erelong: loneliness and gloom were now banished from her bedside; protection and solace sat there instead. She and her nurse coalesced in wondrous union. Caroline was usually pained to require or receive much attendance: Mrs Pryor, under ordinary circumstances, had neither the habit nor the art of performing little offices of service; but all now passed with such ease – so naturally, that the patient was as willing to be cherished as the nurse was bent on cherishing: no sign of weariness in the latter ever reminded the former that she ought to be anxious. There was, in fact, no very hard duty to perform; but a hireling might have found it hard.

With all this care, it seemed strange the sick girl did not get well; yet such was the case: she wasted like any snow-wreath in thaw; she faded like any flower in drought. Miss Keeldar, on whose thoughts danger or death seldom intruded, had at first entertained no fears at all for her friend; but seeing her change and sink from time to time when she paid her visits, alarm clutched her heart. She went to Mr Helstone and expressed herself with so much energy, that that gentleman was at last obliged, however unwillingly, to admit the idea that his niece was ill of something more than a migraine; and when Mrs Pryor came and quietly demanded a physician, he said she might send for two, if she liked. One came, but that one was an oracle: he delivered a dark saying of which the future was to solve the mystery, wrote some prescriptions, gave some directions – the whole with an air of crushing authority – pocketed his fee, and went. Probably, he knew well enough he could do no good; but didn't like to say so.

Still, no rumour of serious illness got wind in the neighbourhood. At Hollow's-cottage it was thought that Caroline had only a severe cold, she having written a note to Hortense to that effect; and Mademoiselle contented herself with sending two pots of currant jam, a receipt for a tisane, and a note of advice.

Mrs Yorke being told that a physician had been summoned, sneered at the hypochondriac fancies of the rich and idle, who, she said, having nothing but themselves to think about, must needs send for a doctor if only so much as their little finger ached.

The 'rich and idle,' represented in the person of Caroline, were meantime falling fast into a condition of prostration, whose quickly consummated debility puzzled all who witnessed it, except one; for that one alone reflected how liable is the undermined structure to sink in sudden ruin.

Sick people often have fancies inscrutable to ordinary attendants, and Caroline had one which even her tender nurse could not at first explain. On a certain day in the week, at a certain hour, she would – whether worse or better – entreat to be taken up and dressed, and suffered to sit in her chair near the window. This station she would retain till noon was past: whatever degree of exhaustion or debility her wan aspect betrayed, she still softly put off all persuasion to seek repose until the church-clock had duly tolled mid-day: the twelve strokes sounded, she grew docile, and would meekly lie down. Returned to the couch, she usually buried her face deep in the pillow, and drew the coverlets close round her, as if to shut out the world and sun, of which she was tired: more than once, as she thus lay, a slight convulsion shook the sick-bed, and a faint sob broke the silence round it. These things were not unnoted by Mrs Pryor.

One Tuesday morning, as usual, she had asked leave to rise, and now she sat wrapped in her white dressing-gown, leaning forward in the easy-chair, gazing steadily and patiently from the lattice. Mrs Pryor was seated a little behind, knitting as it seemed, but, in truth, watching her. A change crossed her pale mournful brow, animating its languor; a light shot into her faded eyes, reviving their lustre; she half rose and looked earnestly out. Mrs Pryor, drawing softly near, glanced over her shoulder. From this window was visible the church-yard, beyond it the road, and there, riding sharply by, appeared a horseman. The figure was not yet too remote for recognition: Mrs Pryor had long sight; she knew Mr Moore. Just as an intercepting rising ground concealed him from view, the clock struck twelve.

'May I lie down again?' asked Caroline.

Her nurse assisted her to bed: having laid her down and

drawn the curtain, she stood listening near. The little couch trembled, the suppressed sob stirred the air. A contraction as of anguish altered Mrs Pryor's features; she wrung her hands; half a groan escaped her lips. She now remembered that Tuesday was Whinbury market-day: Mr Moore must always pass the Rectory on his way thither, just ere noon of that day.

Caroline wore continually round her neck a slender braid of silk, attached to which was some trinket. Mrs Pryor had seen the bit of gold glisten; but had not yet obtained a fair view of it. Her patient never parted with it: when dressed it was hidden in her bosom; as she lay in bed she always held it in her hand. That Tuesday afternoon the transient doze – more like lethargy than sleep – which sometimes abridged the long days, had stolen over her: the weather was hot: while turning in febrile restlessness, she had pushed the coverlets a little aside; Mrs Pryor bent to replace them; the small, wasted hand lying nerveless on the sick girl's breast, clasped as usual her jealously-guarded treasure: those fingers whose attenuation it gave pain to see, were now relaxed in sleep: Mrs Pryor gently disengaged the braid, drawing out a tiny locket – a slight thing it was, such as it suited her small purse to purchase: under its crystal face appeared a curl of black hair – too short and crisp to have been severed from a female head.

Some agitated movement occasioned a twitch of the silken chain: the sleeper started and woke. Her thoughts were usually now somewhat scattered on waking; her look generally wandering. Half-rising, as if in terror, she exclaimed:

'Don't take it from me, Robert! Don't! It is my last comfort – let me keep it. I never tell any one whose hair it is – I never show it.'

Mrs Pryor had already disappeared behind the curtain: reclining far back in a deep arm-chair by the bedside, she was withdrawn from view. Caroline looked abroad into the chamber: she thought it empty. As her stray ideas returned slowly, each folding its weak wings on the mind's sad shore, like birds exhausted, – beholding void, and perceiving silence round her, she believed herself alone. Collected, she was not yet: perhaps healthy self-possession and self-control were to be hers no more; perhaps that world the strong and prosperous live in had already rolled from beneath her feet for ever: so, at least, it often seemed to herself. In health, she had never been accustomed to think aloud; but now words escaped her lips unawares.

'Oh! I *should* see him once more before all is over: Heaven *might* favour me thus far!' she cried. 'God grant me a little comfort before I die!' was her humble petition.

'But he will not know I am ill, till I am gone; and he will come when they have laid me out, and I am senseless, cold, and stiff.

'What can my departed soul feel then? Can it see or know what happens to the clay? Can spirits, through any medium, communicate with living flesh? Can the dead at all revisit those they leave? Can they come in the elements? Will wind, water, fire, lend me a path to Moore?

'Is it for nothing the wind sounds almost articulately sometimes – sings as I have lately heard it sing at night – or passes the casement sobbing, as if for sorrow to come? Does nothing, then, haunt it – nothing inspire it?

'Why, it suggested to me words one night: it poured a strain which I could have written down, only I was appalled and dared not rise to seek pencil and paper by the dim watchlight.

'What is that electricity they speak of, whose changes make us well or ill; whose lack or excess blasts; whose even balance revives? What are all those influences that are about us in the atmosphere, that keep playing over our nerves like fingers on stringed instruments, and call forth now a sweet note, and now a wail – now an exultant swell, and, anon, the saddest cadence?

'*Where* is the other world? In *what* will another life consist? Why do I ask? Have I not cause to think that the hour is hasting but too fast when the veil must be rent for me? Do I not know the Grand Mystery is likely to burst prematurely on me? Great Spirit! in whose goodness I confide; whom, as my Father, I have petitioned night and morning from early infancy, help the weak creation of thy hands! Sustain me through the ordeal I dread and must undergo! Give me strength! Give me patience! Give me – oh! *give me* FAITH!'

She fell back on her pillow. Mrs Pryor found means to steal quietly from the room: she re-entered it soon after, apparently as composed as if she had really not overheard this strange soliloquy.

The next day several callers came. It had become known that Miss Helstone was worse. Mr Hall and his sister Margaret arrived; both, after they had been in the sick-room, quitted it in tears: they had found the patient more altered than they expected. Hortense Moore came. Caroline seemed stimulated by her presence: she assured her, smiling, she was not dangerously ill; she talked to her in a low voice, but cheerfully: during her stay, excitement kept up the flush of her complexion: she looked better.

'How is Mr Robert?' asked Mrs Pryor, as Hortense was preparing to take leave.

'He was very well when he left.'

'Left! Is he gone from home?'

It was then explained that some police intelligence about the rioters of whom he was in pursuit, had, that morning, called him away to Birmingham, and probably a fortnight might elapse ere he returned.

'He is not aware that Miss Helstone is very ill?'

'Oh! no. He thought, like me, that she had only a bad cold.'

After this visit, Mrs Pryor took care not to approach Caroline's couch for above an hour: she heard her weep, and dared not look on her tears.

As evening closed in, she brought her some tea. Caroline, opening her eyes from a moment's slumber, viewed her nurse with an unrecognising glance.

'I smelt the honeysuckles in the glen this summer-morning,' she said, 'as I stood at the counting-house window.'

Strange words like these from pallid lips pierce a loving

listener's heart more poignantly than steel. They sound romantic, perhaps, in books: in real life, they are harrowing.

'My darling, do you know me?' said Mrs Pryor.

'I went in to call Robert to breakfast: I have been with him
in the garden: he asked me to go: a heavy dew has refreshed the
flowers: the peaches are ripening.'

'My darling! my darling!' again and again repeated the nurse.

'I thought it was daylight – long after sunrise: it looks dark
– is the moon not set?'

That moon, lately risen, was gazing full and mild upon her:
floating in deep blue space, it watched her unclouded.

'Then it is not morning? I am not at the cottage? Who is
this? – I see a shape at my bedside.'

'It is myself – it is your friend – your nurse – your –. Lean
your head on my shoulder: collect yourself.' (In a lower tone.)
'Oh God, take pity! Give *her* life, and *me* strength! Send me
courage – teach me words!'

Some minutes passed in silence. The patient lay mute and
passive in the trembling arms – on the throbbing bosom of the
nurse.

'I am better now,' whispered Caroline, at last, 'much better –
I feel where I am: this is Mrs Pryor near me: I was dreaming
– I talk when I wake up from dreams: people often do in illness.
How fast your heart beats, ma'am! Do not be afraid.'

'It is not fear, child; only a little anxiety, which will pass.
I have brought you some tea, Cary; your uncle made it himself.
You know he says he can make a better cup of tea than any
housewife can. Taste it. He is concerned to hear that you eat so
little: he would be glad if you had a better appetite.'

'I am thirsty: let me drink.'

She drank eagerly.

'What o'clock is it, ma'am?' she asked.

'Past nine.'

'Not later? Oh! I have yet a long night before me; but the tea
has made me strong: I will sit up.'

Mrs Pryor raised her, and arranged her pillows.

'Thank Heaven! I am not always equally miserable, and ill, and hopeless. The afternoon has been bad since Hortense went: perhaps the evening may be better. It is a fine night, I think? The moon shines clear.'

'Very fine: a perfect summer night. The old church-tower gleams white almost as silver.'

'And does the churchyard look peaceful?'

'Yes, and the garden also: dew glistens on the foliage.'

'Can you see many long weeds and nettles amongst the graves; or do they look turfy and flowery?'

'I see closed daisy-heads, gleaming like pearls on some mounds. Thomas has mown down the dock-leaves and rank grass, and cleared all away.'

'I always like that to be done: it soothes one's mind to see the place in order: and, I dare say, within the church just now that moonlight shines as softly as in my room. It will fall through the east window full on the Helstone monument. When I close my eyes I seem to see poor papa's epitaph in black letters on the white marble. There is plenty of room for other inscriptions underneath.'

'William Farren came to look after your flowers this morning: he was afraid, now you cannot tend them yourself, they would be neglected. He has taken two of your favourite plants home to nurse for you.'

'If I were to make a will, I would leave William all my plants; Shirley my trinkets – except one, which must not be taken off my neck; and you, ma'am, my books.' (After a pause.) 'Mrs Pryor, I feel a longing wish for something.'

'For what, Caroline?'

'You know I always delight to hear you sing: sing me a hymn just now: sing that hymn which begins, –

> "Our God, our help in ages past, –
> Our hope for years to come;

> Our shelter from the stormy blast;
>   Our refuge, haven, home!" '

Mrs Pryor at once complied.

No wonder Caroline liked to hear her sing: her voice, even in speaking, was sweet and silver-clear; in song, it was almost divine: neither flute nor dulcimer has tones so pure. But the tone was secondary compared to the expression which trembled through: a tender vibration from a feeling heart.

The servants in the kitchen, hearing the strain, stole to the stair-foot to listen: even old Helstone, as he walked in the garden, pondering over the unaccountable and feeble nature of women, stood still amongst his borders to catch the mournful melody more distinctly. Why it reminded him of his forgotten dead wife, he could not tell; nor why it made him more concerned than he had hitherto been for Caroline's fading girlhood. He was glad to recollect that he had promised to pay Wynne, the magistrate, a visit that evening. Low spirits and gloomy thoughts were very much his aversion: when they attacked him he usually found means to make them march in double-quick time. The hymn followed him faintly as he crossed the fields: he hastened his customary sharp pace, that he might get beyond its reach.

> 'Thy word commands our flesh to dust, –
>   "Return, ye sons of men:"
> All nations rose from earth at first,
>   And turn to earth again.
>
> 'A thousand ages in thy sight
>   Are like an evening gone;
> Short as the watch that ends the night
>   Before the rising sun.
>
> 'Time, like an ever-rolling stream,
>   Bears all its sons away;
> They fly, forgotten, as a dream
>   Dies at the opening day.

'Like flowery fields, the nations stand,
    Fresh in the morning light;
The flowers beneath the mower's hand
    Lie withering ere 't is night.

'Our God, our help in ages past, –
    Our hope for years to come;
Be thou our guard while troubles last, –
    O Father, be our home!'

'Now sing a song – a Scottish song,' suggested Caroline, when
the hymn was over, – ' "Ye banks and braes o' bonny Doon." '

Again Mrs Pryor obeyed, or essayed to obey. At the close of
the first stanza she stopped; she could get no further: her full
heart flowed over.

'You are weeping at the pathos of the air: come here, and
I will comfort you,' said Caroline, in a pitying accent. Mrs
Pryor came: she sat down on the edge of her patient's bed, and
allowed the wasted arms to encircle her.

'You often soothe me, let me soothe you,' murmured the
young girl, kissing her cheek. 'I hope,' she added, 'it is not for
me you weep?'

No answer followed.

'Do you think I shall not get better? I do not feel *very* ill –
only weak.'

'But your mind, Caroline: your mind is crushed; your heart
is almost broken: you have been so neglected, so repulsed, left
so desolate.'

'I believe grief is, and always has been, my worst ailment.
I sometimes think, if an abundant gush of happiness came on
me, I could revive yet.'

'Do you wish to live?'

'I have no object in life.'

'You love me, Caroline?'

'Very much' – very truly, – inexpressibly sometimes: just now,
I feel as if I could almost grow to your heart.'

'I will return directly, dear,' remarked Mrs Pryor, as she laid Caroline down.

Quitting her, she glided to the door, softly turned the key in the lock, ascertained that it was fast, and came back. She bent over her. She threw back the curtain to admit the moonlight more freely. She gazed intently on her face.

'Then, if you love me,' said she, speaking quickly, with an altered voice: 'if you feel as if – to use your own words – you could "grow to my heart," it will be neither shock nor pain for you to know that *that* heart is the source whence yours was filled; that from *my* veins issued the tide which flows in *yours*; that you are *mine* – my daughter – my own child.'

'Mrs Pryor –!'

'My own child!'

'That is – that means – you have adopted me?'

'It means that, if I have given you nothing else, I at least gave you life; that I bore you – nursed you; that I am your true mother: no other woman can claim the title – it is *mine*.'

'But Mrs James Helstone – but my father's wife, whom I do not remember ever to have seen, she is my mother?'

'She *is* your mother: James Helstone was *my* husband. I say you are *mine*. I have proved it. I thought perhaps you were all his, which would have been a cruel dispensation for me: find it is *not* so. God permitted me to be the parent of my child's mind: it belongs to me: it is my property – my *right*. These features are James's own. He had a fine face when he was young, and not altered by error. Papa, my darling, gave you your blue eyes and soft brown hair: he gave you the oval of your face and the regularity of your lineaments: the outside *he* conferred; but the heart and the brain are *mine*: the germs are from me, and they are improved, they are developed to excellence. I esteem and approve my child as highly as I do most fondly love her.'

'Is what I hear true? Is it no dream?'

'I wish it were as true that the substance and colour of health were restored to your cheek.'

'My own mother! is she one I can be so fond of as I can of you? People generally did not like her, so I have been given to understand.'

'They told you that? Well, your mother now tells you, that, not having the gift to please people generally, for their approbation she does not care: her thoughts are centred in her child: does that child welcome or reject her?'

'But if you *are* my mother, the world is all changed to me. Surely I can live – I should like to recover –'

'You *must* recover. You drew life and strength from my breast when you were a tiny, fair infant, over whose blue eyes I used to weep, fearing I beheld in your very beauty the sign of qualities that had entered my heart like iron, and pierced through my soul like a sword. Daughter! we have been long parted: I return now to cherish you again.'

She held her to her bosom: she cradled her in her arms: she rocked her softly, as if lulling a young child to sleep.

'My mother! My own mother!'

The offspring nestled to the parent: that parent, feeling the endearment and hearing the appeal, gathered her closer still. She covered her with noiseless kisses: she murmured love over her, like a cushat fostering its young.

There was silence in the room for a long while.

'Does my uncle know?'

'Your uncle knows: I told him when I first came to stay with you here.'

'Did you recognise me when we first met at Fieldhead?'

'How could it be otherwise? Mr and Miss Helstone being announced, I was prepared to see my child.'

'It was that then which moved you: I saw you disturbed.'

'You saw nothing, Caroline, I can cover my feelings. You can never tell what an age of strange sensation I lived, during the two minutes that elapsed between the report of your name and your entrance. You can never tell how your look, mien, carriage, shook me.'

'Why? Were you disappointed?'

'What will she be like? I had asked myself; and when I saw what you were like, I could have dropped.'

'Mamma, why?'

'I trembled in your presence. I said I will never own her: she shall never know me.'

'But I said and did nothing remarkable. I felt a little diffident at the thought of an introduction to strangers, that was all.'

'I soon saw you were diffident; that was the first thing which reassured me: had you been rustic, clownish, awkward, I should have been content.'

'You puzzle me.'

'I had reason to dread a fair outside, to mistrust a popular bearing, to shudder before distinction, grace, and courtesy. Beauty and affability had come in my way when I was recluse, desolate, young, and ignorant: a toil-worn governess perishing of uncheered labour, breaking down before her time. These, Caroline, when they smiled on me, I mistook for angels! I followed them home, and when into their hands I had given without reserve my whole chance of future happiness, it was my lot to witness a transfiguration on the domestic hearth: to see the white mask lifted, the bright disguise put away, and opposite me sat down – oh God! I *have* suffered!'

She sank on the pillow.

'I *have* suffered! None saw – none knew: there was no sympathy – no redemption – no redress!'

'Take comfort, mother: it is over now.'

'It is over, and not fruitlessly. I tried to keep the word of His patience: He kept me in the days of my anguish. I was afraid with terror – I was troubled: through great tribulation He brought me through to a salvation revealed in this last time. My fear had torment – He has cast it out: He has given me in its stead perfect love ... But, Caroline –'

Thus she invoked her daughter after a pause.

'Mother!'

'I charge you, when you next look on your father's monu-ment, to respect the name chiselled there. To you he did only good. On you he conferred his whole treasure of beauties; nor added to them one dark defect. All *you* derived from him is excellent. You owe him gratitude. Leave, between him and me, the settlement of our mutual account: meddle not: God is the arbiter. This world's laws never came near us – never! They were powerless as a rotten bulrush to protect me! – impotent as idiot babblings to restrain him! As you said, it is all over now: the grave lies between us. There he sleeps – in that church! To his dust I say this night, what I have never said before, "James, slumber peacefully! See! your terrible debt is cancelled! Look! I wipe out the long, black account with my own hand! James, your child atones: this living likeness of you – this thing with your perfect features – this one good gift you gave me has nestled affectionately to my heart, and tenderly called me 'mother.' Husband! rest forgiven!"'

'Dearest mother, that is right! Can papa's spirit hear us? Is he comforted to know that we still love him?'

'I said nothing of love: I spoke of forgiveness. Mind the truth, child – I said nothing of love! On the threshold of eternity, should he be there to see me enter, will I maintain that.'

'Oh, mother! you must have suffered!'

'Oh, child! the human heart *can* suffer. It can hold more tears than the ocean holds waters. We never know how deep – how wide it is, till misery begins to unbind her clouds, and fill it with rushing blackness.'

'Mother, forget.'

'Forget!' she said, with the strangest spectre of a laugh. 'The north pole will rush to the south, and the headlands of Europe be locked into the bays of Australia ere I forget.'

'Hush, mother! rest! – be at peace!'

And the child lulled the parent, as the parent had erst lulled the child. At last, Mrs Pryor wept: she then grew calmer. She resumed those tender cares agitation had for a moment suspended. Replacing her daughter on the couch, she smoothed the pillow and spread the sheet. The soft hair whose locks were loosened, she rearranged, the damp brow she refreshed with a cool fragrant essence.

'Mamma, let them bring a candle, that I may see you; and tell my uncle to come into this room by-and-by: I want to hear him say that I am your daughter: and, mamma, take your supper here; don't leave me for one minute to-night.'

'Oh, Caroline! it is well you are gentle. You will say to me go, and I shall go; come, and I shall come; do this, and I shall do it. You inherit a certain manner as well as certain features. It will be always "mamma" prefacing a mandate: softly spoken though, from you, thank God!' (she added, under her breath), 'he spoke softly too, once, – like a flute breathing tenderness; and then, when the world was not by to listen, discords that split the nerves and curdled the blood – sounds to inspire insanity.'

'It seems so natural, mamma, to ask you for this and that. I shall want nobody but you to be near me, or to do anything for me; but do not let me be troublesome: check me, if I encroach.'

'You must not depend on me to check you: you must keep guard over yourself. I have little moral courage: the want of it is my bane. It is that which has made me an unnatural parent – which has kept me apart from my child during the ten years which have elapsed since my husband's death left me at liberty to claim her: it was that which first unnerved my arms and permitted the infant I might have retained a while longer, to be snatched prematurely from their embrace.'

'How, mamma?'

'I let you go as a babe, because you were pretty, and I feared your loveliness; deeming it the stamp of perversity. They sent me your portrait, taken at eight years old; that portrait confirmed my fears. Had it shown me a sunburnt little rustic – a heavy, blunt-featured, commonplace child – I should have hastened to claim you; but there, under the silver paper, I saw blooming the delicacy of an aristocratic flower – "little lady" was written on every trait. I had too recently crawled from under the yoke of the fine gentleman – escaped, galled, crushed, paralyzed, dying – to dare to encounter his still finer and most fairy-like representative. My sweet little lady overwhelmed me with dismay: her air of native elegance froze my very marrow. In my experience I had not met with truth, modesty, good principle as the concomitants of beauty. A form so straight and fine, I argued, must conceal a mind warped and cruel. I had little faith in the power of education to rectify such a mind; or rather, I entirely misdoubted my own ability to influence it. Caroline, I dared not undertake to rear you: I resolved to leave you in your uncle's hands. Matthewson Helstone I knew, if an austere, was an upright man. He and all the world thought hardly of me for my strange, unmotherly resolve, and I deserved to be misjudged.'

'Mamma, why did you call yourself Mrs Pryor?'

'It was a name in my mother's family. I adopted it that I might live unmolested. My married name recalled too vividly my married life: I could not bear it. Besides, threats were uttered of forcing me to return to bondage: it could not be; rather a bier for a bed – the grave for a home. My new name sheltered me: I resumed under its screen my old occupation of teaching. At first, it scarcely procured me the means of sustaining life; but how savoury was hunger when I fasted in peace! How safe seemed the darkness and chill of an unkindled hearth, when no lurid reflection from terror crimsoned its desolation! How serene was solitude, when I feared not the irruption of violence and vice!'

'But, mamma, you have been in this neighbourhood before. How did it happen, that when you reappeared here with Miss Keeldar, you were not recognised?'

'I only paid a short visit, as a bride, twenty years ago; and then I was very different to what I am now – slender, almost as slender as my daughter is at this day: my complexion – my very features are changed; my hair, my style of dress – everything is altered. You cannot fancy me a slim young person, attired in scanty drapery of white muslin, with bare arms, bracelets and necklace of beads, and hair disposed in round Grecian curls above my forehead?'

'You must, indeed, have been different. Mamma, I heard the front door open: if it is my uncle coming in, just ask him to step up-stairs, and let me hear his assurance that I am truly awake and collected, and not dreaming or delirious.'

The Rector, of his own accord, was mounting the stairs; and Mrs Pryor summoned him to his niece's apartment.

'She's not worse, I hope?' he inquired, hastily.

'I think her better: she is disposed to converse – she seems stronger.'

'Good!' said he, brushing quickly into the room. 'Ha, Cary! how do? Did you drink my cup of tea? I made it for you just as I like it myself.'

'I drank it every drop, uncle: it did me good – it has made me quite alive. I have a wish for company, so I begged Mrs Pryor to call you in.'

The respected ecclesiastic looked pleased, and yet embarrassed. He was willing enough to bestow his company on his sick niece for ten minutes, since it was her whim to wish it; but what means to employ for her entertainment, he knew not: he hemmed – he fidgeted.

'You'll be up in a trice,' he observed, by way of saying something. 'The little weakness will soon pass off; and then you must drink port-wine – a pipe, if you can – and eat game and oysters: I'll get them for you, if they are to be had anywhere. Bless me! we'll make you as strong as Samson before we've done with you.'

'Who is that lady, uncle, standing beside you at the bedfoot?'

'Good God!' he ejaculated. 'She's not wandering – is she, ma'am?'

Mrs Pryor smiled.

'I am wandering in a pleasant world,' said Caroline, in a soft, happy voice, 'and I want you to tell me whether it is real or visionary. What lady is that? Give her a name, uncle?'

'We must have Dr Rile again, ma'am, or, better still, Mac-Turk: he's less of a humbug. Thomas must saddle the pony, and go for him.'

'No: I don't want a doctor; mamma shall be my only physician. Now, do you understand, uncle?'

Mr Helstone pushed up his spectacles from his nose to his forehead, handled his snuff-box, and administered to himself a portion of the contents. Thus fortified, he answered briefly: –

'I see daylight. You've told her then, ma'am?'

'And is it *true*?' demanded Caroline, rising on her pillow. 'Is she *really* my mother?'

'You won't cry, or make any scene, or turn hysterical, if I answer Yes?'

'Cry? I'd cry if you said *No*. It would be terrible to be disappointed now. But give her a name: how do you call her?'

'I call this stout lady in a quaint black dress, who looks young enough to wear much smarter raiment, if she would – I call her Agnes Helstone: she married my brother James, and is his widow.'

'And my mother?'

'What a little sceptic it is! Look at her small face, Mrs Pryor, scarcely larger than the palm of my hand, alive with acuteness and eagerness.' (To Caroline). – 'She had the trouble of bringing you into the world, at any rate: mind you show your duty to her by quickly getting well, and repairing the waste of these cheeks. Heigho! she used to be plump: what she has done with it all, I can't, for the life of me, divine.'

'If *wishing* to get well will help me, I shall not be long sick. This morning, I had no reason and no strength to wish it.'

Fanny here tapped at the door, and said that supper was ready.

'Uncle, if you please, you may send me a little bit of supper – anything you like, from your own plate. That is wiser than going into hysterics, – is it not?'

'It is spoken like a sage, Cary: see if I don't cater for you judiciously. When women are sensible – and, above all, intelligible – I can get on with them. It is only the vague, superfine sensations, and extremely wire-drawn notions, that put me about. Let a woman ask me to give her an edible or a wearable – be the same a roc's egg or the breastplate of Aaron, a share of St John's locusts and honey or the leathern girdle about his loins – I can, at least, understand the demand: but when they pine for they know not what – sympathy – sentiment – some of these indefinite abstractions – I can't do it: I don't know it; I haven't got it. Madam, accept my arm.'

Mrs Pryor signified that she should stay with her daughter that evening. Helstone, accordingly, left them together. He soon returned, bringing a plate in his own consecrated hand.

'This is chicken,' he said; 'but we'll have partridge to-morrow. Lift her up, and put a shawl over her. On my word, I understand nursing. Now, here is the very same little silver fork you used when you first came to the Rectory: that strikes me as being what you may call a happy thought – a delicate attention. Take it, Cary, and munch away cleverly.'

Caroline did her best. Her uncle frowned to see that her powers were so limited: he prophesied, however, great things for the future; and as she praised the morsel he had brought, and smiled gratefully in his face, he stooped over her pillow, kissed her, and said, with a broken, rugged accent, –

'Good-night, bairnie! God bless thee!'

Caroline enjoyed such peaceful rest that night, circled by her mother's arms, and pillowed on her breast, that she forgot to wish for any other stay; and though more than one feverish dream came to her in slumber, yet, when she woke up panting, so happy and contented a feeling returned with returning consciousness, that her agitation was soothed almost as soon as felt.

As to the mother, she spent the night like Jacob at Peniel. Till break of day, she wrestled with God in earnest prayer.

CHAPTER XXV

THE WEST WIND BLOWS

Not always do those who dare such divine conflict prevail. Night after night the sweat of agony may burst dark on the forehead; the supplicant may cry for mercy with that soundless voice the soul utters when its appeal is to the Invisible. 'Spare my beloved,' it may implore. 'Heal my life's life. Rend not from me what long affection entwines with my whole nature. God of heaven – bend – hear – be clement!' And after this cry and strife, the sun may rise and see him worsted. That opening morn, which used to salute him with the whisper of zephyrs, the carol of skylarks, may breathe, as its first accents, from the dear lips which colour and heat have quitted, –

'Oh! I have had a suffering night. This morning I am worse. I have tried to rise. I cannot. Dreams I am unused to have troubled me.'

Then the watcher approaches the patient's pillow, and sees a new and strange moulding of the familiar features, feels at once that the insufferable moment draws nigh, knows that it is God's will his idol shall be broken, and bends his head, and subdues his soul to the sentence he cannot avert, and scarce can bear.

Happy Mrs Pryor! She was still praying, unconscious that the summer sun hung above the hills, when her child softly woke in her arms. No piteous, unconscious moaning – sound which so wastes our strength that, even if we have sworn to be firm, a rush of unconquerable tears sweeps away the oath – preceded her waking. No space of deaf apathy followed. The first words spoken were not those of one becoming estranged from this world, and already permitted to stray at times into realms foreign to the living. Caroline evidently remembered with clearness what had happened.

'Mamma, I have slept so well. I only dreamed and woke twice.'

Mrs Pryor rose with a start, that her daughter might not see the joyful tears called into her eyes by that affectionate word 'mamma,' and the welcome assurance that followed it.

For many days the mother dared rejoice only with trembling. That first revival seemed like the flicker of a dying lamp: if the flame streamed up bright one moment, the next it sank dim in the socket. Exhaustion followed close on excitement.

There was always a touching endeavour to *appear* better, but too often ability refused to second will; too often the attempt to bear up failed: the effort to eat, to talk, to look cheerful, was unsuccessful. Many an hour passed, during which Mrs Pryor feared that the chords of life could never more be strengthened, though the time of their breaking might be deferred.

During this space the mother and daughter seemed left almost alone in the neighbourhood. It was the close of August: the weather was fine – that is to say, it was very dry and very dusty, for an arid wind had been blowing from the east this month past: very cloudless, too, though a pale haze, stationary in the atmosphere, seemed to rob of all depth of tone the blue of heaven, of all freshness the verdure of earth, and of all glow the light of day. Almost every family in Briarfield was absent on an excursion. Miss Keeldar and her friends were at the sea-side; so were Mrs Yorke's household. Mr Hall and Louis Moore, between whom a spontaneous intimacy seemed to have arisen, the result, probably, of harmony of views and temperament, were gone 'up north' on a pedestrian excursion to the Lakes. Even Hortense, who would fain have staid at home and aided Mrs Pryor in nursing Caroline, had been so earnestly entreated by Miss Mann to accompany her once more to Wormwood Wells, in the hope of alleviating sufferings greatly aggravated by the insalubrious weather, that she felt obliged to comply; indeed, it was not in her nature to refuse a request that at once appealed to her goodness of heart, and – by a confession of dependency – flattered her amour-propre. As for Robert, from Birmingham he had gone on to London, where he still sojourned.

So long as the breath of Asiatic deserts parched Caroline's lips and fevered her veins, her physical convalescence could not keep pace with her returning mental tranquillity: but there came a day when the wind ceased to sob at the eastern gable of the Rectory, and at the oriel window of the church. A little cloud like a man's hand arose in the west: gusts from the same quarter drove it on and spread it wide; wet and tempest prevailed a while. When that was over the sun broke out genially, heaven regained its azure, and earth its green: the livid cholera-tint had vanished from the face of nature: the hills rose clear round the horizon, absolved from that pale malaria-haze.

Caroline's youth could now be of some avail to her, and so could her mother's nurture: both – crowned by God's blessing, sent in the pure west wind blowing soft as fresh through the ever-open chamber lattice – rekindled her long-languishing energies. At last Mrs Pryor saw that it was permitted to hope – a genuine, material convalescence had commenced. It was not merely Caroline's smile which was brighter, or her spirits which were cheered, but a certain look had passed from her face and eye – a look dread and indescribable, but which will easily be recalled by those who have watched the couch of dangerous disease. Long before the emaciated outlines of her aspect began to fill, or its departed colour to return, a more subtle change took place: all grew softer and wanner. Instead of a marble mask and glassy eye, Mrs Pryor saw laid on the pillow a face pale and wasted enough, perhaps more haggard than the other appearance, but less awful; for it was a sick, living girl – not a mere white mould, or rigid piece of statuary.

Now, too, she was not always petitioning to drink. The words 'I am *so* thirsty,' ceased to be her plaint. Sometimes, when she had swallowed a morsel, she would say it had revived her: all descriptions of food were no longer equally distasteful; she could be induced, sometimes, to indicate a preference. With what trembling pleasure and anxious care did not her nurse prepare what was selected! How she watched her as she partook of it!

Nourishment brought strength. She could sit up. Then she longed to breathe the fresh air, to revisit her flowers, to see how the fruit had ripened. Her uncle, always liberal, had bought a garden-chair for her express use: he carried her down in his own arms, and placed her in it himself, and William Farren was there to wheel her round the walks, to show her what he had done amongst her plants, to take her directions for further work.

William and she found plenty to talk about: they had a dozen topics in common; interesting to them, unimportant to the rest of the world. They took a similar interest in animals, birds, insects, and plants: they held similar doctrines about humanity to the lower creation; and had a similar turn for minute observation on points of natural history. The nest and proceedings of some ground-bees, which had burrowed in the turf under an old cherry-tree, was one subject of interest: the haunts of certain hedge-sparrows, and the welfare of certain pearly eggs and callow fledglings, another.

Had 'Chambers' Journal' existed in those days, it would certainly have formed Miss Helstone's and Farren's favourite periodical. She would have subscribed for it; and to him each number would duly have been lent: both would have put implicit faith, and found great savour in its marvellous anecdotes of animal sagacity.

This is a digression; but it suffices to explain why Caroline would have no other hand than William's to guide her chair, and why his society and conversation sufficed to give interest to her garden-airings.

Mrs Pryor, walking near, wondered how her daughter could be so much at ease with a 'man of the people.' *She* found it impossible to speak to him otherwise than stiffly. She felt as if a great gulf lay between her caste and his; and that to cross it, or meet him half-way, would be to degrade herself. She gently asked Caroline, –

'Are you not afraid, my dear, to converse with that person so unreservedly? He may presume, and become troublesomely garrulous.'

'William presume, mamma? You don't know him. He never presumes: he is altogether too proud and sensitive to do so. William has very fine feelings.'

And Mrs Pryor smiled sceptically at the naïve notion of that rough-handed, rough-headed, fustian-clad clown having 'fine feelings.'

Farren, for his part, showed Mrs Pryor only a very sulky brow. He knew when he was misjudged, and was apt to turn unmanageable with such as failed to give him his due.

The evening restored Caroline entirely to her mother, and Mrs Pryor liked the evening; for then, alone with her daughter, no human shadow came between her and what she loved. During the day, she would have her stiff demeanour and cool moments, as was her wont. Between her and Mr Helstone a very respectful but most rigidly ceremonious intercourse was kept up: anything like familiarity would have bred contempt at once in one or both these personages; but by dint of strict civility and well maintained distance, they got on very smoothly.

Towards the servants, Mrs Pryor's bearing was not uncourteous, but shy, freezing, ungenial. Perhaps it was diffidence rather than pride which made her appear so haughty; but, as was to be expected, Fanny and Eliza failed to make the distinction, and she was unpopular with them accordingly. She felt the effect produced: it rendered her at times dissatisfied with herself for faults she could not help; and with all else, dejected, chill, and taciturn.

This mood changed to Caroline's influence, and to that influence alone. The dependent fondness of her nursling, the natural affection of her child, came over her suavely: her frost fell away; her rigidity unbent: she grew smiling and pliant. Not that Caroline made any wordy profession of love – that would ill have suited Mrs Pryor: she would have read therein the proof of insincerity; but she hung on her with easy dependence; she confided in her with fearless reliance: these things contented the mother's heart.

She liked to hear her daughter say 'Mamma, do this.' 'Please, mamma, fetch me that.' 'Mamma, read to me.' 'Sing a little, mamma.'

Nobody else – not one living thing – had ever so claimed her services, so looked for help at her hand. Other people were always more or less reserved and stiff with her, as she was reserved and stiff with them; other people betrayed consciousness of, and annoyance at her weak points: Caroline no more showed such wounding sagacity or reproachful sensitiveness now, than she had done when a suckling of three months old.

Yet Caroline could find fault. Blind to the constitutional defects that were incurable, she had her eyes wide open to the acquired habits that were susceptible of remedy. On certain points she would quite artlessly lecture her parent; and that parent, instead of being hurt, felt a sensation of pleasure in discovering that the girl *dared* lecture her; that she was so much at home with her.

'Mamma, I am determined you shall not wear that old gown any more; its fashion is not becoming: it is too strait in the skirt. You shall put on your black silk every afternoon; in that you look nice: it suits you; and you shall have a black satin dress for Sundays – a real satin – not a satinet or any of the shams. And, mamma, when you get the new one, mind you must wear it.'

'My dear, I thought of the black silk serving me as a best dress for many years yet, and I wished to buy you several things.'

'Nonsense, mamma: my uncle gives me cash to get what I want: you know he is generous enough; and I have set my heart on seeing you in a black satin. Get it soon, and let it be made by a dressmaker of my recommending; let me choose the pattern. You always want to disguise yourself like a grandmother: you would persuade one that you are old and ugly, – not at all! On the contrary, when well dressed and cheerful, you are very comely indeed. Your smile is so pleasant, your teeth are so white, your hair is still such a pretty light colour. And then you speak like a young lady, with such a clear, fine tone, and you sing better than any young lady I ever heard. Why do you wear such dresses and bonnets, mamma, such as nobody else ever wears?'

'Does it annoy you, Caroline?'

'Very much: it vexes me even. People say you are miserly; and yet you are not, for you give liberally to the poor and to religious societies: though your gifts are conveyed so secretly and quietly, that they are known to few except the receivers. But I will be your maid myself: when I get a little stronger I will set to work, and you must be good, mamma, and do as I bid you.'

And Caroline, sitting near her mother, rearranged her muslin handkerchief, and resmoothed her hair.

'My own mamma,' then she went on, as if pleasing herself with the thought of their relationship, 'who belongs to me, and to whom I belong! I am a rich girl now: I have something I can love well, and not be afraid of loving. Mamma, who gave you this little brooch? Let me unpin it and look at it.'

Mrs Pryor, who usually shrank from meddling fingers and near approach, allowed the license complacently.

'Did papa give you this, mamma?'

'My sister gave it me – my only sister, Cary. Would that your aunt Caroline had lived to see her niece!'

'Have you nothing of papa's? – no trinket, no gift of his?'

'I have one thing.'

'That you prize?'

'That I prize.'

'Valuable and pretty?'

'Invaluable and sweet to me.'

'Show it, mamma. Is it here or at Fieldhead?'

'It is talking to me now, leaning on me: its arms are round me.'

'Ah, mamma! you mean your teasing daughter, who will never let you alone; who, when you go into your room, cannot help running to seek for you; who follows you up-stairs and down, like a dog.'

'Whose features still give me such a strange thrill sometimes. I half fear your fair looks yet, child.'

'You don't; you can't. Mamma, I am sorry papa was not good: I do so wish he had been. Wickedness spoils and poisons all pleasant things: it kills love. If you and I thought each other wicked, we could not love each other, could we?'

'And if we could not trust each other, Cary?'

'How miserable we should be! Mother, before I knew you, I had an apprehension that you were not good, that I could not esteem you: that dread damped my wish to see you; and now my heart is elate because I find you perfect, – almost; kind, clever, nice. Your sole fault is that you are old-fashioned, and of that I shall cure you. Mamma, put your work down: read to me. I like your southern accent: it is so pure so soft. It has no rugged burr, no nasal twang, such as almost everyone voice here in the north has. My uncle and Mr Hall say that you are a fine reader, mamma. Mr Hall said he never heard any lady read with such propriety of expression, or purity of accent.'

'I wish I could reciprocate the compliment, Cary; but really, the first time I heard your truly excellent friend read and preach, I could not understand his broad, northern tongue.'

'Could you understand me, mamma? Did I seem to speak roughly?'

'No: I almost wished you had, as I wished you had looked unpolished. Your father, Caroline, naturally spoke well; quite otherwise than your worthy uncle: correctly, gently, smoothly. You inherit the gift.'

'Poor papa! When he was so agreeable, why was he not good?'

'Why, he was *as* he was – and, happily, of that you, child, can form no conception – I cannot tell: it is a deep mystery. The key is in the hands of his Maker: there I leave it.'

'Mamma, you will keep stitching, stitching away: put down the sewing; I am an enemy to it. It cumbers your lap, and I want it for my head: it engages your eyes, and I want them for a book. Here is your favourite – Cowper.'

These importunities were the mother's pleasure. If ever she delayed compliance, it was only to hear them repeated, and to enjoy her child's soft, half-playful, half-petulant urgency. And then, when she yielded, Caroline would say, archly, –

'You will spoil me, mamma. I always thought I should like to be spoiled, and I find it very sweet.'

So did Mrs Pryor.

CHAPTER XXVI

OLD COPY-BOOKS

B Y THE TIME the Fieldhead party returned to Briarfield, Caroline was nearly well. Miss Keeldar, who had received news by post of her friend's convalescence, hardly suffered an hour to elapse between her arrival at home and her first call at the Rectory.

A shower of rain was falling gently, yet fast, on the late flowers and russet autumn shrubs, when the garden-wicket was heard to swing open, and Shirley's well-known form passed the window. On her entrance, her feelings were evinced in her own peculiar fashion. When deeply moved, by serious fears or joys, she was not garrulous. The strong emotion was rarely suffered to influence her tongue; and even her eye refused it more than a furtive and fitful conquest. She took Caroline in her arms, gave her one look, one kiss, then said: –

'You are better.'

And a minute after, – 'I see you are safe now, but take care. God grant your health may be called on to sustain no more shocks!'

She proceeded to talk fluently about the journey. In the midst of vivacious discourse, her eye still wandered to Caroline: there spoke in its light a deep solicitude, some trouble, and some amaze.

'She may be better,' it said; 'but how weak she still is! What peril she has come through!'

Suddenly her glance reverted to Mrs Pryor: it pierced her through.

'When will my governess return to me?' she asked.

'May I tell her all?' demanded Caroline of her mother. Leave being signified by a gesture, Shirley was presently enlightened on what had happened in her absence.

'Very good!' was the cool comment. 'Very good! But it is no news to me.'

'What! Did you know?'

'I guessed long since the whole business. I have heard somewhat of Mrs Pryor's history – not from herself, but from others. With every detail of Mr James Helstone's career and character I was acquainted: an afternoon's sitting and conversation with Miss Mann had rendered me familiar therewith: also he is one of Mrs Yorke's warning-examples – one of the blood-red lights she hangs out to scare young ladies from matrimony. I believe I should have been sceptical about the truth of the portrait traced by such fingers – both these ladies take a dark pleasure in offering to view the dark side of life – but I questioned Mr Yorke on the subject, and he said, – "Shirley, my woman, if you want to know aught about yond' James Helstone, I can only say he was a man-tiger. He was handsome, dissolute, soft, treacherous, courteous, cruel –" Don't cry, Cary; we'll say no more about it.'

'I am not crying, Shirley; or if I am, it is nothing – go on: you are no friend if you withhold from me the truth: I hate that false plan of disguising, mutilating the truth.'

'Fortunately, I have said pretty nearly all that I have to say, except that your uncle himself confirmed Mr Yorke's words: for he too scorns a lie, and deals in none of those conventional subterfuges that are shabbier than lies.'

'But papa is dead: they should let him alone now.'

'They should – and we *will* let him alone. Cry away, Cary, it will do you good: it is wrong to check natural tears; besides, I choose to please myself by sharing an idea that at this moment beams in your mother's eye while she looks at you: every drop blots out a sin. Weep – your tears have the virtue which the rivers of Damascus lacked: like Jordan, they can cleanse a leprous memory.'

'Madam,' she continued, addressing Mrs Pryor, 'did you think I could be daily in the habit of seeing you and your daughter together – marking your marvellous similarity in many points – observing, pardon me – your irrepressible emotions in the presence and still more in the absence of your child, and not form my own conjectures? I formed them, and they are literally correct. I shall begin to think myself shrewd.'

'And you said nothing?' observed Caroline, who soon regained the quiet control of her feelings.

'Nothing. I had no warrant to breathe a word on the subject. *My* business it was not: I abstained from making it such.'

'You guessed so deep a secret, and did not hint that you guessed it?'

'Is that so difficult?'

'It is not like you.'

'How do you know?'

'You are not reserved. You are frankly communicative.'

'I may be communicative, yet know where to stop. In showing my treasure, I may withhold a gem or two – a curious, unbought, graven stone – an amulet, of whose mystic glitter I rarely permit even myself a glimpse. Good-day.'

Caroline thus seemed to get a view of Shirley's character under a novel aspect. Erelong, the prospect was renewed: it opened upon her.

No sooner had she regained sufficient strength to bear a change of scene – the excitement of a little society – than Miss Keeldar sued daily for her presence at Fieldhead. Whether Shirley had become wearied of her honoured relatives is not known: she did not say she was; but she claimed and retained Caroline with an eagerness which proved that an addition to that worshipful company was not unwelcome.

The Sympsons were Church people: of course, the Rector's niece was received by them with courtesy. Mr Sympson proved to be a man of spotless respectability, worrying temper, pious principles, and worldly views; his lady was a very good woman, patient, kind, well-bred. She had been brought up on a narrow system of views – starved on a few prejudices: a mere handful of bitter herbs; a few preferences, soaked till their natural flavour was extracted, and with no seasoning added in the cooking; some excellent principles, made up in a stiff raised-crust of bigotry, difficult to digest: far too submissive was she to complain of this diet, or to ask for a crumb beyond it.

The daughters were an example to their sex. They were tall, with a Roman nose a-piece. They had been educated faultlessly. All they did was well done. History, and the most solid books, had cultivated their minds. Principles and opinions they possessed which could not be mended. More exactly-regulated lives, feelings, manners, habits, it would have been difficult to find anywhere. They knew by heart a certain young-ladies'-school-room code of laws on language, demeanour, &c.; themselves never deviated from its curious little pragmatical provisions; and they regarded with secret, whispered horror, all deviations in others. The Abomination of Desolation was no mystery to them: they had discovered that unutterable Thing in the characteristic others call Originality. Quick were they to recognise the signs of this evil; and wherever they saw its trace – whether in look, word, or deed; whether they read it in the fresh, vigorous style of a book, or listened to it in interesting, unhackneyed, pure, expressive language – they shuddered – they recoiled: danger was above their heads – peril about their steps. What was this strange Thing? Being unintelligible, it must be bad. Let it be denounced and chained up.

Henry Sympson – the only son, and youngest child of the family – was a boy of fifteen. He generally kept with his tutor; when he left him, he sought his cousin Shirley. This boy differed from his sisters: he was little, lame, and pale; his large eyes shone somewhat languidly in a wan orbit: they were, indeed, usually rather dim – but they were capable of illumination: at times, they could not only shine, but blaze: inward emotion could likewise give colour to his cheek and decision to his crippled

movements. Henry's mother loved him; she thought his peculiarities were a mark of election: he was not like other children,
she allowed; she believed him regenerate – a new Samuel –
called of God from his birth: he was to be a clergyman. Mr and
Misses Sympson, not understanding the youth, let him much
alone. Shirley made him her pet; and he made Shirley his
playmate.

In the midst of this family-circle – or rather outside it –
moved the tutor – the satellite.

Yes: Louis Moore was a satellite of the house of Sympson:
connected, yet apart; ever attendant – ever distant. Each member
of that correct family treated him with proper dignity. The father
was austerely civil, sometimes irritable; the mother, being a kind
woman, was attentive, but formal; the daughters saw in him an
abstraction, not a man. It seemed, by their manner, that their
brother's tutor did not live for them. They were learned: so was
he – but not for them. They were accomplished: he had talents
too, imperceptible to their senses. The most spirited sketch from
his fingers was a blank to their eyes; the most original observation from his lips fell unheard on their ears. Nothing could
exceed the propriety of their behaviour.

I should have said, nothing could have equaled it; but I
remembered a fact which strangely astonished Caroline Helstone. It was – to discover that her cousin had absolutely *no*
sympathizing friend at Fieldhead: that to Miss Keeldar he was
as much a mere teacher, as little a gentleman, as little a man, as
to the estimable Misses Sympson.

What had befallen the kind-hearted Shirley that she should
be so indifferent to the dreary position of a fellow-creature thus
isolated under her roof? She was not, perhaps, haughty to him,
but she never noticed him: she let him alone. He came and went,
spoke or was silent, and she rarely recognised his existence.

As to Louis Moore himself, he had the air of a man used to
this life, and who had made up his mind to bear it for a time.
His faculties seemed walled up in him, and were unmurmuring

in their captivity. He never laughed; he seldom smiled; he was uncomplaining. He fulfilled the round of his duties scrupulously. His pupil loved him; he asked nothing more than civility from the rest of the world. It even appeared that he would accept nothing more: in that abode at least; for when his cousin Caroline made gentle overtures of friendship, he did not encourage them; he rather avoided than sought her. One living thing alone, besides his pale, crippled scholar, he fondled in the house, and that was the ruffianly Tartar; who, sullen and impracticable to others, acquired a singular partiality for him: a partiality so marked that sometimes, when Moore, summoned to a meal, entered the room and sat down unwelcomed, Tartar would rise from his lair at Shirley's feet, and betake himself to the taciturn tutor. Once – but once – she noticed the desertion; and holding out her white hand, and speaking softly, tried to coax him back. Tartar looked, slavered, and sighed, as his manner was, but yet disregarded the invitation, and coolly settled himself on his haunches at Louis Moore's side. That gentleman drew the dog's big, black-muzzled head on to his knee, patted him, and smiled one little smile to himself.

An acute observer might have remarked, in the course of the same evening, that after Tartar had resumed his allegiance to Shirley, and was once more couched near her foot-stool, the audacious tutor by one word and gesture fascinated him again. He pricked up his ears at the word; he started erect at the gesture, and came, with head lovingly depressed, to receive the expected caress: as it was given, the significant smile again rippled across Moore's quiet face.

'Shirley,' said Caroline one day, as they two were sitting alone in the summer-house, 'did you know that my cousin Louis was tutor in your uncle's family before the Sympsons came down here?'

Shirley's reply was not so prompt as her responses usually were, but at last she answered, –

'Yes, – of course: I knew it well.'

'I thought you must have been aware of the circumstance.'

'Well! what then?'

'It puzzles me to guess how it chanced that you never mentioned it to me.'

'Why should it puzzle you?'

'It seems odd. I cannot account for it. You talk a great deal, – you talk freely. How was that circumstance never touched on?'

'Because it never was,' and Shirley laughed.

'You are a singular being!' observed her friend: 'I thought I knew you quite well: I begin to find myself mistaken. You were silent as the grave about Mrs Pryor; and now, again, here is another secret. But why you made it a secret is the mystery to me.'

'I never made it a secret: I had no reason for so doing. If you had asked me who Henry's tutor was, I would have told you: besides, I thought you knew.'

'I am puzzled about more things than one in this matter: you don't like poor Louis, – why? Are you impatient at what you perhaps consider his *servile* position? Do you wish that Robert's brother were more highly placed?'

'Robert's brother, indeed!' was the exclamation, uttered in a tone like the accents of scorn; and, with a movement of proud impatience, Shirley snatched a rose from a branch peeping through the open lattice.

'Yes,' repeated Caroline, with mild firmness; 'Robert's brother. He *is* thus closely related to Gérard Moore of the Hollow, though nature has not given him features so handsome, or an air so noble as his kinsman; but his blood is as good, and he is as much a gentleman, were he free.'

'Wise, humble, pious Caroline!' exclaimed Shirley, ironically. 'Men and angels, hear her! We should not despise plain features, nor a laborious yet honest occupation, should we? Look at the subject of your panegyric, – he is there in the garden,' she continued, pointing through an aperture in the clustering creepers; and by that aperture Louis Moore was visible, coming slowly down the walk.

'He is not ugly, Shirley,' pleaded Caroline; 'he is not ignoble; he is sad: silence seals his mind; but I believe him to be intelligent; and be certain, if he had not something very commendable in his disposition, Mr Hall would never seek his society as he does.'

Shirley laughed: she laughed again; each time with a slightly sarcastic sound. 'Well, well,' was her comment. 'On the plea of the man being Cyril Hall's friend and Robert Moore's brother, we'll just tolerate his existence – won't we, Cary? You believe him to be intelligent, do you? Not quite an idiot – eh? Something commendable in his disposition! id est, not an absolute ruffian. Good! Your representations have weight with me; and to prove that they have, should he come this way I will speak to him.'

He approached the summer-house: unconscious that it was tenanted, he sat down on the step. Tartar, now his customary companion, had followed him, and he couched across his feet.

'Old boy!' said Louis, pulling his tawny ear, or rather the mutilated remains of that organ, torn and chewed in a hundred battles, 'the autumn sun shines as pleasantly on us as on the fairest and richest. This garden is none of ours, but we enjoy its greenness and perfume, don't we?'

He sat silent, still caressing Tartar, who slobbered with exceeding affection. A faint twittering commenced among the trees round: something fluttered down as light as leaves: they were little birds, which lighting on the sward at shy distance, hopped as if expectant.

'The small brown elves actually remember that I fed them the other day,' again soliloquized Louis. 'They want some more biscuit: to-day, I forgot to save a fragment. Eager little sprites, I have not a crumb for you.'

He put his hand in his pocket and drew it out empty.

'A want easily supplied,' whispered the listening Miss Keeldar. She took from her reticule a morsel of sweet-cake: for that repository was never destitute of something available to throw to the chickens, young ducks, or sparrows; she crumbled it, and bending over his shoulder, put the crumbs into his hand.

'There,' said she; 'there is a Providence for the improvident.'

'This September afternoon is pleasant,' observed Louis Moore, as – not at all discomposed – he calmly cast the crumbs on to the grass.

'Even for you?'

'As pleasant for me as for any monarch.'

'You take a sort of harsh, solitary triumph in drawing pleasure out of the elements, and the inanimate and lower animate creation.'

'Solitary, but not harsh. With animals I feel I am Adam's son; the heir of him to whom dominion was given over "every living thing that moveth upon the earth." Your dog likes and follows me; when I go into that yard, the pigeons from your dovecot flutter at my feet; your mare in the stable knows me as well as it knows you, and obeys me better.'

'And my roses smell sweet to you, and my trees give you shade.'

'And,' continued Louis, 'no caprice can withdraw these pleasures from me: they are *mine*.'

He walked off: Tartar followed him, as if in duty and affection bound, and Shirley remained standing on the summer-house step. Caroline saw her face as she looked after the rude tutor: it was pale, as if her pride bled inwardly.

'You see,' remarked Caroline, apologetically, 'his feelings are so often hurt, it makes him morose.'

'You see,' retorted Shirley, with ire, 'he is a topic on which you and I shall quarrel if we discuss it often; so drop it henceforward and for ever.'

'I suppose he has more than once behaved in this way,' thought Caroline to herself; 'and that renders Shirley so distant to him: yet I wonder she cannot make allowance for character and circumstances: I wonder the general modesty, manliness, sincerity of his nature, do not plead with her in his behalf. She is not often so inconsiderate – so irritable.'

The verbal testimony of two friends of Caroline's to her cousin's character augmented her favourable opinion of him. William Farren, whose cottage he had visited in company with Mr Hall, pronounced him a 'real gentleman:' there was not such another in Briarfield: he – William – 'could do aught for that man. And then to see how t' bairns liked him, and how t' wife took to him first minute she saw him: he never went into a house but t' childer wor about him directly: them little things wor like as if they'd a keener sense nor grown-up folks i' finding out folk's natures.'

Mr Hall, in answer to a question of Miss Helstone's, as to what he thought of Louis Moore, replied promptly, that he was the best fellow he had met with since he left Cambridge.

'But he is so grave,' objected Caroline.

'Grave! The finest company in the world! Full of odd, quiet, out-of-the-way humour. Never enjoyed an excursion so much in my life as the one I took with him to the Lakes. His understanding and tastes are so superior, it does a man good to be within their influence; and as to his temper and nature, I call them fine.'

'At Fieldhead he looks gloomy, and, I believe, has the character of being misanthropical.'

'Oh! I fancy he is rather out of place there – in a false position. The Sympsons are most estimable people, but not the folks to comprehend him: they think a great deal about form and ceremony, which are quite out of Louis's way.'

'I don't think Miss Keeldar likes him.'

'She doesn't know him – she doesn't know him; otherwise, she has sense enough to do justice to his merits.'

'Well, I suppose she doesn't know him,' mused Caroline to herself, and by this hypothesis she endeavoured to account for what seemed else unaccountable. But such simple solution of the difficulty was not left her long: she was obliged to refuse Miss Keeldar even this negative excuse for her prejudice.

One day she chanced to be in the school-room with Henry Sympson, whose amiable and affectionate disposition had quickly recommended him to her regard. The boy was busied about some mechanical contrivance: his lameness made him fond of sedentary occupation: he began to ransack his tutor's desk for a piece of wax, or twine, necessary to his work. Moore happened to be absent. Mr Hall, indeed, had called for him to take a long walk. Henry could not immediately find the object of his search: he rummaged compartment after compartment; and, at last opening an inner drawer, he came upon – not a ball of cord, or a lump of bees' wax – but a little bundle of small marble-coloured cahiers, tied with tape. Henry looked at them: –

'What rubbish Mr Moore stores up in his desk!' he said: 'I hope he won't keep my old exercises so carefully.'

'What is it?'

'Old copy-books.'

He threw the bundle to Caroline. The packet looked so neat externally, her curiosity was excited to see its contents.

'If they are only copy-books, I suppose I may open them?'

'Oh! yes; quite freely. Mr Moore's desk is half mine – for he lets me keep all sorts of things in it – and I give you leave.'

On scrutiny they proved to be French compositions, written in a hand peculiar but compact, and exquisitely clean and clear. The writing was recognisable: she scarcely needed the further evidence of the name signed at the close of each theme, to tell her whose they were. Yet that name astonished her: Shirley Keeldar, Sympson Grove, —shire' (a southern county), and a date four years back.

She tied up the packet, and held it in her hand, meditating over it. She half felt as if, in opening it, she had violated a confidence.

'They are Shirley's, you see,' said Henry, carelessly.

'Did *you* give them to Mr Moore? She wrote them with Mrs Pryor, I suppose?'

'She wrote them in my school-room at Sympson Grove, when she lived with us there. Mr Moore taught her French: it is his native language.'

'I know . . . Was she a good pupil, Henry?'

'She was a wild, laughing thing, but pleasant to have in the room: she made lesson-time charming. She learned fast – you could hardly tell when or how. French was nothing to her: she spoke it quick – quick; as quick as Mr Moore himself.'

'Was she obedient? Did she give trouble?'

'She gave plenty of trouble in a way: she was giddy, but I liked her. I'm desperately fond of Shirley.'

'*Desperately* fond – you small simpleton! You don't know what you say.'

'I *am desperately* fond of her: she is the light of my eyes: I said so to Mr Moore last night.'

'He would reprove you for speaking with exaggeration.'

'He didn't. He never reproves and reproves, as girls' governesses do. He was reading, and he only smiled into his book, and said that if Miss Keeldar was no more than that, she was less than he took her to be; for I was but a dim-eyed, short-sighted little chap. I'm afraid I am a poor unfortunate, Miss Caroline Helstone. I am a cripple, you know.'

'Never mind, Henry, you are a very nice little fellow; and if God has not given you health and strength, he has given you a good disposition, and an excellent heart and brain.'

'I shall be despised. I sometimes think both Shirley and you despise me.'

'Listen, Henry. Generally, I don't like school-boys: I have a great horror of them. They seem to me little ruffians, who take an unnatural delight in killing and tormenting birds, and insects, and kittens, and whatever is weaker than themselves; but you are so different, I am quite fond of you. You have almost as much sense as a man (far more, God wot,' she muttered to herself, 'than many men); you are fond of reading, and you can talk sensibly about what you read.'

'I *am* fond of reading. I know I have sense, and I know I have feeling.'

Miss Keeldar here entered.

'Henry,' she said, 'I have brought your lunch here: I shall prepare it for you myself.'

She placed on the table a glass of new milk, a plate of something which looked not unlike leather, and a utensil which resembled a toasting-fork.

'What are you two about,' she continued, 'ransacking Mr Moore's desk?'

'Looking at your old copy-books,' returned Caroline.

'My old copy-books?'

'French exercise-books. Look here! They must be held precious: they are kept carefully.'

She showed the bundle. Shirley snatched it up:

'Did not know one was in existence,' she said. 'I thought the whole lot had long since lit the kitchen-fire, or curled the maid's hair at Sympson Grove. What made you keep them, Henry?'

'It is not my doing: I should not have thought of it: it never entered my head to suppose copy-books of value. Mr Moore put them by in the inner drawer of his desk: perhaps he forgot them.'

'C'est cela: he forgot them, no doubt,' echoed Shirley. 'They are extremely well written,' she observed, complacently.

'What a giddy girl you were, Shirley, in those days! I remember you so well: a slim, light creature whom, though you were so tall, I could lift off the floor. I see you with your long, countless curls on your shoulders, and your streaming sash. You used to make Mr Moore lively, that is, at first: I believe you grieved him after a while.'

Shirley turned the closely-written pages and said nothing. Presently she observed, 'That was written one winter afternoon. It was a description of a snow-scene.'

'I remember,' said Henry; 'Mr Moore, when he read it, cried "Voilà le Français gagné!" He said it was well done. Afterwards you made him draw, in sepia, the landscape you described.'

'You have not forgotten then, Hal?'

'Not at all. We were all scolded that day for not coming down to tea when called. I can remember my tutor sitting at his easel, and you standing behind him, holding the candle, and watching him draw the snowy cliff, the pine, the deer couched under it, and the half-moon hung above.'

'Where are his drawings, Harry? Caroline should see them.'

'In his portfolio; but it is padlocked: he has the key.'

'Ask him for it when he comes in.'

'You should ask him, Shirley; you are shy of him now: you are grown a proud lady to him, I noticed that.'

'Shirley, you are a real enigma,' whispered Caroline in her ear. 'What queer discoveries I make day by day now! I, who thought I had your confidence. Inexplicable creature! even this boy reproves you.'

'I have forgotten "Auld Langsyne," you see, Harry,' said Miss Keeldar, answering young Sympson, and not heeding Caroline.

'Which you never should have done. You don't deserve to be a man's morning star, if you have so short a memory.'

'A man's morning star indeed! and by "a man" is meant your worshipful self, I suppose? Come, drink your new milk while it is warm.'

The young cripple rose and limped towards the fire: he had left his crutch near the mantelpiece.

'My poor lame darling!' murmured Shirley, in her softest voice, aiding him.

'Whether do you like me or Mr Sam Wynne best, Shirley?' inquired the boy, as she settled him in an arm-chair.

'Oh, Harry! Sam Wynne is my aversion: you are my pet.'

'Me or Mr Malone?'

'You again, a thousand times.'

'Yet, they are great whiskered fellows, six feet high each.'

'Whereas, as long as you live, Harry, you will never be anything more than a little pale lameter.'

'Yes, I know.'

'You need not be sorrowful. Have I not often told you who was almost as little, as pale, as suffering as you, and yet potent as a giant, and brave as a lion?'

'Admiral Horatio?'

'Admiral Horatio, Viscount Nelson, and Duke of Bronti; great at heart as a Titan; gallant and heroic as all the world and age of chivalry; leader of the might of England; commander of her strength on the deep; hurler of her thunder over the flood.'

'A great man: but I am not warlike, Shirley: and yet my mind is so restless, I burn day and night – for what – I can hardly tell – to be – to do – to suffer, I think.'

'Harry, it is your mind, which is stronger and older than your frame, that troubles you. It is a captive. It lies in physical bondage. But it will work its own redemption yet. Study carefully, not only books but the world. You love nature; love her without fear. Be patient – wait the course of time. You will not be a soldier or a sailor, Henry: but, if you live, you will be – listen to my prophecy – you will be an author – perhaps, a poet.'

'An author! It is a flash – a flash of light to me! I will – I *will*! I'll write a book that I may dedicate it to you.'

'You will write it, that you may give your soul its natural release. Bless me! what am I saying? more than I understand, I believe, or can make good. Here, Hal; here is your toasted oat-cake – eat and live!'

'Willingly!' Here cried a voice outside the open window, 'I know that fragrance of meal bread. Miss Keeldar, may I come in and partake?'

'Mr Hall' (it was Mr Hall, and with him was Louis Moore, returned from their walk), 'there is a proper luncheon laid out in the dining-room, and there are proper people seated round it: you may join that society and share that fare if you please;

but if your ill-regulated tastes lead you to prefer ill-regulated proceedings, step in here, and do as we do.'

'I approve the perfume, and therefore shall suffer myself to be led by the nose,' returned Mr Hall, who presently entered, accompanied by Louis Moore. That gentleman's eye fell on his desk, pillaged.

'Burglars!' said he. 'Henry, you merit the ferule.'

'Give it to Shirley and Caroline – they did it,' was alleged with more attention to effect than truth.

'Traitor and false witness!' cried both the girls. 'We never laid hands on a thing, except in the spirit of laudable inquiry.'

'Exactly so,' said Moore, with his rare smile. 'And what have you ferreted out, in your "spirit of laudable inquiry?"'

He perceived the inner drawer open.

'This is empty,' said he. 'Who has taken –?'

'Here! here!' Caroline hastened to say; and she restored the little packet to its place. He shut it up; he locked it in with a small key attached to his watch-guard; he restored the other papers to order, closed the repository, and sat down without further remark.

'I thought you would have scolded much more, sir,' said Henry. 'The girls deserve reprimand.'

'I leave them to their own consciences.'

'It accuses them of crimes intended as well as perpetrated, sir. If I had not been here, they would have treated your portfolio as they have done your desk; but I told them it was padlocked.'

'And will you have lunch with us?' here interposed Shirley, addressing Moore, and desirous, as it seemed, to turn the conversation.

'Certainly, if I may.'

'You will be restricted to new milk and Yorkshire oat-cake.'

'Va – pour le lait frais!' said Louis. 'But for your oat-cake –!' and he made a grimace.

'He cannot eat it,' said Henry: 'he thinks it is like bran, raised with sour yeast.'

'Come, then, by special dispensation, we will allow him a few cracknels; but nothing less homely.'

The hostess rang the bell and gave her frugal orders, which were presently executed. She herself measured out the milk, and distributed the bread round the cozy circle now enclosing the bright little school-room fire. She then took the post of toaster-general; and kneeling on the rug, fork in hand, fulfilled her office with dexterity. Mr Hall, who relished any homely innovation on ordinary usages, and to whom the husky oat-cake was from custom suave as manna – seemed in his best spirits. He talked and laughed gleefully – now with Caroline, whom he had fixed by his side, now with Shirley, and again with Louis Moore. And Louis met him in congenial spirit: he did not laugh much, but he uttered in the quietest tone the wittiest things. Gravely spoken sentences, marked by unexpected turns and a quite fresh flavour and poignancy, fell easily from his lips. He proved himself to be – what Mr Hall had said he was – excellent company. Caroline marvelled at his humour, but still more at his entire self-possession. Nobody there present seemed to impose on him a sensation of unpleasant restraint: nobody seemed a bore – a check – a chill to him; and yet there was the cool and lofty Miss Keeldar kneeling before the fire, almost at his feet.

But Shirley was cool and lofty no longer – at least not at this moment. She appeared unconscious of the humility of her present position – or if conscious, it was only to taste a charm in its lowliness. It did not revolt her pride that the group to whom she voluntarily officiated as handmaid should include her cousin's tutor: it did not scare her that while she handed the bread and milk to the rest, she had to offer it to him also; and Moore took his portion from her hand as calmly as if he had been her equal.

'You are overheated now,' he said, when she had retained the fork for some time: 'let me relieve you.'

And he took it from her with a sort of quiet authority, to

which she submitted passively – neither resisting him nor thanking him.

'I should like to see your pictures, Louis,' said Caroline, when the sumptuous luncheon was discussed. 'Would not you, Mr Hall?'

'To please you, I should; but, for my own part, I have cut him as an artist. I had enough of him in that capacity in Cumberland and Westmoreland. Many a wetting we got amongst the mountains because he would persist in sitting on a camp-stool, catching effects of rain-clouds, gathering mists, fitful sunbeams, and what not.'

'Here is the portfolio,' said Henry, bringing it in one hand, and leaning on his crutch with the other.

Louis took it, but he still sat as if he wanted another to speak. It seemed as if he would not open it unless the proud Shirley deigned to show herself interested in the exhibition.

'He makes us wait to whet our curiosity,' she said.

'You understand opening it,' observed Louis, giving her the key. 'You spoiled the lock for me once – try now.'

He held it: she opened it; and, monopolizing the contents, had the first view of every sketch herself. She enjoyed the treat – if treat it were – in silence, without a single comment. Moore stood behind her chair and looked over her shoulder, and when she had done, and the others were still gazing, he left his post and paced through the room.

A carriage was heard in the lane – the gate-bell rang: Shirley started.

'There are callers,' she said, 'and I shall be summoned to the room. A pretty figure – as they say – I am to receive company: I and Henry have been in the garden gathering fruit half the morning. Oh, for rest under my own vine and my own fig-tree! Happy is the slavewife of the Indian chief, in that she has no drawing-room duty to perform, but can sit at ease weaving mats, and stringing beads, and peacefully flattening her picaninny's head in an unmolested corner of her wigwam. I'll emigrate to the western woods.'

Louis Moore laughed.

'To marry a White Cloud or a Big Buffalo; and after wedlock to devote yourself to the tender task of digging your lord's maize-field, while he smokes his pipe or drinks fire-water.'

Shirley seemed about to reply, but here the school-room door unclosed, admitting Mr Sympson. That personage stood aghast when he saw the group around the fire.

'I thought you alone, Miss Keeldar,' he said. 'I find quite a party.'

And evidently from his shocked, scandalized air – had he not recognised in one of the party a clergyman – he would have delivered an extempore philippic on the extraordinary habits of his niece: respect for the cloth arrested him.

'I merely wished to announce,' he proceeded, coldly, 'that the family from De Walden Hall, Mr, Mrs, the Misses, and Mr Sam Wynne, are in the drawing-room.' And he bowed, and withdrew.

'The family from De Walden Hall! Couldn't be a worse set,' murmured Shirley.

She sat still, looking a little contumacious, and very much indisposed to stir. She was flushed with the fire; her dark hair had been more than once dishevelled by the morning wind that day; her attire was a light, neatly fitting, but amply flowing dress of muslin; the shawl she had worn in the garden was still draped in a careless fold round her. Indolent, wilful, pictur-esque, and singularly pretty was her aspect – prettier than usual, as if some soft inward emotion – stirred who knows how? – had given new bloom and expression to her features.

'Shirley – Shirley, you ought to go,' whispered Caroline.

'I wonder why?'

She lifted her eyes, and saw in the glass over the fireplace both Mr Hall and Louis Moore gazing at her gravely.

'If,' she said, with a yielding smile – 'if a majority of the present company maintain that the De Walden Hall people have claims on my civility, I will subdue my inclinations to my duty. Let those who think I ought to go, hold up their hands.'

Again consulting the mirror, it reflected an unanimous vote against her.

'You must go,' said Mr Hall, 'and behave courteously, too. You owe many duties to society. It is not permitted you to please only yourself.'

Louis Moore assented with a low 'Hear! hear!'

Caroline, approaching her, smoothed her wavy curls, gave to her attire a less artistic and more domestic grace, and Shirley was put out of the room, protesting still, by a pouting lip, against her dismissal.

'There is a curious charm about her,' observed Mr Hall, when she was gone. 'And now,' he added, 'I must away, for Sweeting is off to see his mother, and there are two funerals.'

'Henry, get your books; it is lesson-time,' said Moore, sitting down to his desk.

'A curious charm!' repeated the pupil, when he and his master were left alone. 'True. Is she not a kind of white witch?' he asked.

'Of whom are you speaking, sir?'

'Of my cousin Shirley.'

'No irrelevant questions. Study in silence.'

Mr Moore looked and spoke sternly – sourly. Henry knew this mood: it was a rare one with his tutor; but when it came he had an awe of it: he obeyed.

CHAPTER XXVII

THE FIRST BLUE-STOCKING

Miss Keeldar and her uncle had characters that would not harmonize, – that never had harmonized. He was irritable, and she was spirited; he was despotic, and she liked freedom; he was worldly, and she, perhaps, romantic.

Not without purpose had he come down to Yorkshire: his mission was clear, and he intended to discharge it conscientiously: he anxiously desired to have his niece married; to make for her a suitable match; give her in charge to a proper husband, and wash his hands of her for ever.

The misfortune was, from infancy upwards, Shirley and he had disagreed on the meaning of the words 'suitable' and 'proper.' She never yet had accepted his definition; and it was doubtful whether, in the most important step of her life, she would consent to accept it.

The trial soon came.

Mr Wynne proposed in form for his son, Samuel Fawthrop Wynne.

'Decidedly suitable! Most proper!' pronounced Mr Sympson. 'A fine unencumbered estate; real substance; good connexions. *It must be done!*'

He sent for his niece to the oak-parlour; he shut himself up there with her alone; he communicated the offer; he gave his opinion; he claimed her consent.

It was withheld.

'No: I shall not marry Samuel Fawthrop Wynne.'

'I ask why? I must have a reason. In all respects he is more than worthy of you.'

She stood on the hearth; she was pale as the white marble slab and cornice behind her; her eyes flashed large, dilated, unsmiling.

'And *I* ask in what sense that young man is worthy of *me*?'

'He has twice your money, – twice your common sense; – equal connexions, – equal respectability.'

'Had he my money counted five score times, I would take no vow to love him.'

'Please to state your objections.'

'He has run a course of despicable, commonplace profligacy. Accept that as the first reason why I spurn him.'

'Miss Keeldar, you shock me!'

'That conduct alone sinks him in a gulf of immeasurable inferiority. His intellect reaches no standard I can esteem: – there is a second stumbling-block. His views are narrow; his feelings are blunt; his tastes are coarse; his manners vulgar.'

'The man is a respectable, wealthy man. To refuse him is presumption on your part.'

'I refuse, point-blank! Cease to annoy me with the subject: I forbid it!'

'Is it your intention ever to marry, or do you prefer celibacy?'

'I deny your right to claim an answer to that question.'

'May I ask if you expect some man of title – some peer of the realm – to demand your hand?'

'I doubt if the peer breathes on whom I would confer it.'

'Were there insanity in the family, I should believe you mad. Your eccentricity and conceit touch the verge of frenzy.'

'Perhaps, ere I have finished, you will see me overleap it.'

'I anticipate no less. Frantic and impracticable girl! Take warning! – I dare you to sully our name by a mésalliance!'

'*Our* name! Am *I* called Sympson?'

'God be thanked that you are not! But be on your guard! – I will not be trifled with!'

'What, in the name of common law and common sense, would you, or could you do, if my pleasure led me to a choice you disapproved?'

'Take care! take care!' (warning her with voice and hand that trembled alike.)

'Why? What shadow of power have you over me? Why should I fear you?'

'Take care, madam!'

'Scrupulous care I will take, Mr Sympson. Before I marry, I am resolved to esteem – to admire – *to love*.'

'Preposterous stuff! – indecorous! – unwomanly!'

'To love with my whole heart. I know I speak in an unknown tongue; but I feel indifferent whether I am comprehended or not.'

'And if this love of yours should fall on a beggar?'

'On a beggar it will never fall. Mendicancy is not estimable.'

'On a low clerk, a play-actor, a play-writer, or – or –'

'Take courage, Mr Sympson! Or what?'

'Any literary scrub, or shabby, whining artist.'

'For the scrubby, shabby, whining, I have no taste: for literature and the arts, I have. And there I wonder how your Fawthrop Wynne would suit me? He cannot write a note without orthographical errors; he reads only a sporting paper: he was the booby of Stilbro' grammar school!'

'Unladylike language! Great God! – to what will she come?' He lifted hands and eyes.

'Never to the altar of Hymen with Sam Wynne.'

'To what will she come? Why are not the laws more stringent, that I might compel her to hear reason?'

'Console yourself, uncle. Were Britain a serfdom, and you the Czar, you could not *compel* me to this step. *I* will write to Mr Wynne. Give yourself no further trouble on the subject.'

Fortune is proverbially called changeful, yet her caprice often takes the form of repeating again and again a similar stroke of luck in the same quarter. It appeared that Miss Keeldar – or her fortune – had by this time made a sensation in the district, and produced an impression in quarters by her unthought of. No less than three offers followed Mr Wynne's – all more or less eligible. All were in succession pressed on her by her uncle, and all in succession she refused. Yet amongst them was more than one gentleman of unexceptionable character, as well as ample wealth. Many besides her uncle asked what she meant, and whom she expected to entrap, that she was so insolently fastidious.

At last, the gossips thought they had found the key to her conduct, and her uncle was sure of it; and, what is more, the discovery showed his niece to him in quite a new light, and he changed his whole deportment to her accordingly.

Fieldhead had, of late, been fast growing too hot to hold them both: the suave aunt could not reconcile them; the daughters froze at the view of their quarrels: Gertrude and Isabella whispered by the hour together in their dressing-room, and became chilled with decorous dread if they chanced to be left alone with their audacious cousin. But, as I have said, a change supervened: Mr Sympson was appeased and his family tranquillized.

The village of Nunnely has been alluded to: its old church, its forest, its monastic ruins. It had also its Hall, called the Priory – an older, a larger, a more lordly abode than any Briarfield or Whinbury owned; and, what is more, it had its man of title – its baronet, which neither Briarfield nor Whinbury could boast. This possession – its proudest and most prized – had for years been nominal only: the present baronet, a young man hitherto resident in a distant province, was unknown on his Yorkshire estate.

During Miss Keeldar's stay at the fashionable watering-place of Cliffbridge, she and her friends had met with and been introduced to Sir Philip Nunnely. They encountered him again and again on the sands, the cliffs, in the various walks, sometimes at the public balls of the place. He seemed solitary; his manner was very unpretending – too simple to be termed affable; rather timid than proud: he did not *condescend* to their society – he seemed *glad* of it.

With any unaffected individual, Shirley could easily and

quickly cement an acquaintance. She walked and talked with Sir Philip; she, her aunt, and cousins, sometimes took a sail in his yacht. She liked him because she found him kind and modest, and was charmed to feel she had the power to amuse him.

One slight drawback there was – where is the friendship without it? – Sir Philip had a literary turn: he wrote poetry, sonnets, stanzas, ballads. Perhaps Miss Keeldar thought him a little too fond of reading and reciting these compositions; perhaps she wished the rhyme had possessed more accuracy – the measure more music – the tropes more freshness – the inspiration more fire; at any rate, she always winced when he recurred to the subject of his poems, and usually did her best to divert the conversation into another channel.

He would beguile her to take moonlight walks with him on the bridge, for the sole purpose, as it seemed, of pouring into her ear the longest of his ballads: he would lead her away to sequestered rustic seats, whence the rush of the surf to the sands was heard soft and soothing; and when he had her all to himself, and the sea lay before them, and the scented shade of gardens spread round, and the tall shelter of cliffs rose behind them, he would pull out his last batch of sonnets, and read them in a voice tremulous with emotion. He did not seem to know, that though they might be rhyme, they were not poetry. It appeared by Shirley's downcast eye and disturbed face that she knew it, and felt heartily mortified by the single foible of this good and amiable gentleman.

Often she tried, as gently as might be, to wean him from this fanatic worship of the Muses: it was his monomania – on all ordinary subjects he was sensible enough; and fain was she to enagage him in ordinary topics. He questioned her sometimes about his place at Nunnely; she was but too happy to answer his interrogatories at length: she never wearied of describing the antique Priory, the wild sylvan park, the hoary church and hamlet; nor did she fail to counsel him to come down and gather his tenantry about him in his ancestral halls.

Somewhat to her surprise Sir Philip followed her advice to the letter; and actually, towards the close of September, arrived at the Priory.

He soon made a call at Fieldhead, and his first visit was not his last: he said – when he had achieved the round of the neighbour-hood – that under no roof had he found such pleasant shelter as beneath the massive oak-beams of the grey manor-house of Briarfield: a cramped, modest dwelling enough, compared with his own – but he liked it.

Presently, it did not suffice to sit with Shirley in her panelled parlour, where others came and went, and where he could rarely find a quiet moment to show her the latest production of his fertile muse; he must have her out amongst the pleasant pastures, and lead her by the still waters. Tête-à-tête ramblings she shunned; so he made parties for her to his own grounds, his glorious forest; to remoter scenes – woods severed by the Wharfe, vales watered by the Aire.

Such assiduity covered Miss Keeldar with distinction. Her uncle's prophetic soul anticipated a splendid future: he already scented the time afar off when, with nonchalant air, and left foot nursed on his right knee, he should be able to make dashingly-familiar allusion to his 'nephew the baronet.' Now, his niece dawned upon him no longer 'a mad girl,' but a 'most sensible woman.' He termed her, in confidential dialogues with Mrs Sympson, 'a truly superior person: peculiar, but very clever.' He treated her with exceeding deference; rose reverently to open and shut doors for her; reddened his face, and gave himself head-aches, with stooping to pick up gloves, handkerchiefs, and other loose property, whereof Shirley usually held but insecure tenure. He would cut mysterious jokes about the superiority of woman's wit over man's wisdom; commence obscure apologies for the blundering mistake he had committed respecting the general-ship, the tactics, of 'a personage not a hundred miles from Fieldhead:' in short, he seemed elate as any 'midden-cock on pattens.'

His niece viewed his manœuvres, and received his innuendoes, with phlegm: apparently, she did not above half comprehend to what aim they tended. When plainly charged with being the preferred of the baronet, she said, she believed he did like her, and for her part she liked him: she had never thought a man of rank – the only son of a proud, fond mother – the only brother of doting sisters – could have so much goodness, and, on the whole, so much sense.

Time proved, indeed, that Sir Philip liked her. Perhaps he had found in her that 'curious charm' noticed by Mr Hall. He sought her presence more and more; and, at last, with a frequency that attested it had become to him an indispensable stimulus. About this time, strange feelings hovered round Fieldhead; restless hopes and haggard anxieties haunted some of its rooms. There was an unquiet wandering of some of the inmates among the still fields round the mansion; there was a sense of expectancy that kept the nerves strained.

One thing seemed clear. Sir Philip was not a man to be despised: he was amiable; if not highly intellectual, he was intelligent. Miss Keeldar could not affirm of him – what she had so bitterly affirmed of Sam Wynne – that his feelings were blunt, his tastes coarse, and his manners vulgar. There was sensibility in his nature; there was a very real, if not a very discriminating, love of the arts; there was the English gentleman in all his deportment: as to his lineage and wealth, both were, of course, far beyond her claims.

His appearance had at first elicited some laughing, though not ill-natured, remarks from the merry Shirley. It was boyish: his features were plain and slight; his hair sandy; his stature insignificant. But she soon checked her sarcasm on this point; she would even fire up if any one else made uncomplimentary allusion thereto. He had 'a pleasing countenance,' she affirmed; 'and there was that in his heart which was better than three Roman noses, than the locks of Absalom, or the proportions of Saul.' A spare and rare shaft she still reserved for his unfortunate poetic propensity: but, even here, she would tolerate no irony save her own.

In short, matters had reached a point which seemed fully to warrant an observation made about this time by Mr Yorke, to the tutor, Louis.

'Yond' brother Robert of yours seems to me to be either a fool or a madman. Two months ago, I could have sworn he had the game all in his own hands; and there he runs the country, and quarters himself up in London for weeks together, and by the time he comes back, he'll find himself checkmated. Louis, "There is a tide in the affairs of men, which, taken at the flood, leads on to fortune; but, once let slip, never returns again." I 'd write to Robert, if I were you, and remind him of that.'

'Robert had views on Miss Keeldar?' inquired Louis, as if the idea were new to him.

'Views I suggested to him myself, and views he might have realized, for she liked him.'

'As a neighbour?'

'As more than that. I have seen her change countenance and colour at the mere mention of his name. Write to the lad, I say, and tell him to come home. He is a finer gentleman than this bit of a baronet, after all.'

'Does it not strike you, Mr Yorke, that for a mere penniless adventurer to aspire to a rich woman's hand is presumptuous – contemptible?'

'Oh! if you are for high notions, and double-refined senti-ment, I've naught to say. I'm a plain, practical man myself; and if Robert is willing to give up that royal prize to a lad-rival – a puling slip of aristocracy – I am quite agreeable. At *his* age, in *his* place, with *his* inducements, I would have acted differently. Neither baronet, nor duke, nor prince, should have snatched my sweetheart from me without a struggle. But you tutors are such solemn chaps: it is almost like speaking to a parson to consult with you.'

*

Flattered and fawned upon as Shirley was just now, it appeared she was not absolutely spoiled – that her better nature did not quite leave her. Universal report had indeed ceased to couple her name with that of Moore, and this silence seemed sanctioned by her own apparent oblivion of the absentee; but that she had not *quite* forgotten him – that she still regarded him, if not with love yet with interest – seemed proved by the increased attention which at this juncture of affairs a sudden attack of illness induced her to show that tutor-brother of Robert's, to whom she habitually bore herself with strange alternations of cool reserve and docile respect: now sweeping past him in all the dignity of the monied heiress and prospective Lady Nunnely, and anon accosting him as abashed schoolgirls are wont to accost their stern professors: bridling her neck of ivory, and curling her lip of carmine, if he encountered her glance, one minute; and the next submitting to the grave rebuke of his eye, with as much contrition as if he had the power to inflict penalties in case of contumacy.

Louis Moore had perhaps caught the fever, which for a few days laid him low, in one of the poor cottages of the district, which he, his lame pupil, and Mr Hall, were in the habit of visiting together. At any rate he sickened, and after opposing to the malady a taciturn resistance for a day or two, was obliged to keep his chamber.

He lay tossing on his thorny bed one evening, Henry, who would not quit him, watching faithfully beside him, when a tap – too light to be that of Mrs Gill or the housemaid – summoned young Sympson to the door.

'How is Mr Moore to-night?' asked a low voice from the dark gallery.

'Come in and see him yourself.'

'Is he asleep?'

'I wish he could sleep. Come and speak to him, Shirley.'

'He would not like it.'

But the speaker stepped in, and Henry, seeing her hesitate on the threshold, took her hand and drew her to the couch.

The shaded light showed Miss Keeldar's form but imperfectly, yet it revealed her in elegant attire. There was a party assembled below, including Sir Philip Nunnely; the ladies were now in the drawing-room, and their hostess had stolen from them to visit Henry's tutor. Her pure white dress, her fair arms and neck, the trembling chainlet of gold circling her throat, and quivering on her breast, glistened strangely amid the obscurity of the sick-room. Her mien was chastened and pensive: she spoke gently.

'Mr Moore, how are you to-night?'

'I have not been very ill, and am now better.'

'I heard that you complained of thirst: I have brought you some grapes: can you taste one?'

'No: but I thank you for remembering me.'

'Just one.'

From the rich cluster that filled a small basket held in her hand, she severed a berry and offered it to his lips. He shook his head, and turned aside his flushed face.

'But what then can I bring you instead? You have no wish for fruit; yet I see that your lips are parched. What beverage do you prefer?'

'Mrs Gill supplies me with toast and water: I like it best.'

Silence fell for some minutes.

'Do you suffer? Have you pain?'

'Very little.'

'What made you ill?'

Silence.

'I wonder what caused this fever? To what do you attribute it?'

'Miasma, perhaps – malaria. This is autumn, a season fertile in fevers.'

'I hear you often visit the sick in Briarfield, and Nunnely too, with Mr Hall: you should be on your guard: temerity is not wise.'

'That reminds me, Miss Keeldar, that perhaps you had better not enter this chamber, or come near this couch. I do not believe my illness is infectious: I scarcely fear (with a sort of smile) *you* will take it; but why should you run even the shadow of a risk? Leave me.'

'Patience: I will go soon; but I should like to do something for you before I depart – any little service –'

'They will miss you below.'

'No, the gentlemen are still at table.'

'They will not linger long: Sir Philip Nunnely is no wine-bibber, and I hear him just now pass from the dining-room to the drawing-room.'

'It is a servant.'

'It is Sir Philip, I know his step.'

'Your hearing is acute.'

'It is never dull, and the sense seems sharpened at present. Sir Philip was here to tea last night. I heard you sing to him some song which he had brought you. I heard him, when he took his departure at eleven o'clock, call you out on the pavement, to look at the evening star.'

'You must be nervously sensitive.'

'I heard him kiss your hand.'

'Impossible!'

'No; my chamber is over the hall, the window just above the front door, the sash was a little raised, for I felt feverish: you stood ten minutes with him on the steps: I heard your discourse, every word, and I heard the salute. Henry, give me some water.'

'Let me give it him.'

But he half rose to take the glass from young Sympson, and declined her attendance.

'And can I do nothing?'

'Nothing: for you cannot guarantee me a night's peaceful rest, and it is all I at present want.'

'You do not sleep well?'

'Sleep has left me.'

'Yet you said you were not very ill?'

'I am often sleepless when in high health.'

'If I had power, I would lap you in the most placid slumber; quite deep and hushed, without a dream.'

'Blank annihilation! I do not ask that.'

'With dreams of all you most desire.'

'Monstrous delusions! The sleep would be delirium, the waking death.'

'Your wishes are not so chimerical: you are no visionary?'

'Miss Keeldar, I suppose you think so; but my character is not, perhaps, quite as legible to you as a page of the last new novel might be.'

'That is possible... But this sleep: I *should* like to woo it to your pillow – to win for you its favour. If I took a book and sat down, and read some pages – ? I can well spare half an hour.'

'Thank you, but I will not detain you.'

'I would read softly.'

'It would not do. I am too feverish and excitable to bear a soft, cooing, vibrating voice close at my ear. You had better leave me.'

'Well, I will go.'

'And no good-night?'

'Yes, sir, yes. Mr Moore, good-night.' (Exit Shirley).

'Henry, my boy, go to bed now: it is time you had some repose.'

'Sir, it would please me to watch at your bed-side all night.'

'Nothing less called for: I am getting better: there, go.'

'Give me your blessing, sir.'

'God bless you, my best pupil!'

'You never call me your dearest pupil!'

'No, nor ever shall.'

Possibly Miss Keeldar resented her former teacher's rejection of her courtesy: it is certain she did not repeat the offer of it. Often as her light step traversed the gallery in the course of a day, it did not again pause at his door; nor did her 'cooing, vibrating voice' disturb a second time the hush of the sick-room. A sick-room, indeed, it soon ceased to be; Mr Moore's good constitution quickly triumphed over his indisposition: in a few days he shook it off, and resumed his duties as tutor.

That 'Auld Langsyne' had still its authority both with preceptor and scholar, was proved by the manner in which he sometimes promptly passed the distance she usually maintained between them, and put down her high reserve with a firm, quiet hand.

One afternoon the Sympson family were gone out to take a carriage airing. Shirley, never sorry to snatch a reprieve from their society, had remained behind, detained by business, as she said. The business – a little letter-writing – was soon despatched after the yard-gates had closed on the carriage: Miss Keeldar betook herself to the garden.

It was a peaceful autumn day. The gilding of the Indian summer mellowed the pastures far and wide. The russet woods stood ripe to be stript, but were yet full of leaf. The purple of heath-bloom, faded but not withered, tinged the hills. The beck wandered down to the Hollow, through a silent district; no wind followed its course, or haunted its woody borders. Fieldhead gardens bore the seal of gentle decay. On the walks, swept that morning, yellow leaves had fluttered down again. Its time of flowers, and even of fruits, was over; but a scantling of apples enriched the trees; only a blossom here and there expanded pale and delicate amidst a knot of faded leaves.

These single flowers – the last of their race – Shirley culled as she wandered thoughtfully amongst the beds. She was fastening into her girdle a hueless and scentless nosegay, when Henry Sympson called to her as he came limping from the house.

'Shirley, Mr Moore would be glad to see you in the schoolroom and to hear you read a little French, if you have no more urgent occupation.'

The messenger delivered his commission very simply, as if it were a mere matter of course.

'Did Mr Moore tell you to say that?'

'Certainly: why not? And now, do come, and let us once more be as we were at Sympson-grove. We used to have pleasant school-hours in those days.'

Miss Keeldar, perhaps, thought that circumstances were changed since then; however she made no remark, but after a little reflection quietly followed Henry.

Entering the school-room, she inclined her head with a decent obeisance, as had been her wont in former times; she removed her bonnet, and hung it up beside Henry's cap. Louis Moore sat at his desk, turning the leaves of a book, open before him, and marking passages with his pencil; he just moved, in acknowledgment of her curtsey, but did not rise.

'You proposed to read to me a few nights ago,' said he. 'I could not hear you then; my attention is now at your service. A little renewed practice in French may not be unprofitable: your accent, I have observed, begins to rust.'

'What book shall I take?'

'Here are the posthumous works of St Pièrre. Read a few pages of the "Fragments de l'Amazone."'

She accepted the chair which he had placed in readiness near his own – the volume lay on his desk – there was but one between them; her sweeping curls drooped so low as to hide the page from him.

'Put back your hair,' he said.

For one moment, Shirley looked not quite certain whether she would obey the request or disregard it: a flicker of her eye beamed furtive on the professor's face; perhaps if he had been looking at her harshly or timidly, or if one undecided line had marked his countenance, she would have rebelled, and the lesson had ended there and then; but he was only awaiting her compliance – as calm as marble, and as cool. She threw the veil of tresses behind her ear. It was well her face owned an agreeable outline, and that her cheek possessed the polish and the roundness of early youth, or, thus robbed of a softening shade, the contours might have lost their grace. But what mattered that in the present society? Neither Calypso nor Eucharis cared to fascinate Mentor.

She began to read. The language had become strange to her tongue; it faltered: the lecture flowed unevenly, impeded by hurried breath, broken by Anglicised tones. She stopped.

'I can't do it. Read me a paragraph, if you please, Mr Moore.'

What *he* read, *she* repeated: she caught his accent in three minutes.

'Très bien,' was the approving comment at the close of the piece.

'C'est presque le Français rattrapé, n'est-ce pas?'

'You could not write French as you once could, I daresay –?'

'Oh! no. I should make strange work of my concords now.'

'You could not compose the devoir of "La Première Femme Savante?"'

'Do you still remember that rubbish?'

'Every line.'

'I doubt you.'

'I will engage to repeat it word for word.'

'You would stop short at the first line.'

'Challenge me to the experiment.'

'I challenge you.'

He proceeded to recite the following: he gave it in French, but we must translate, on pain of being unintelligible to some readers.

'And it came to pass when men began to multiply on the face of the earth, and daughters were born unto them, that the sons of God saw the daughters of men that they were fair; and they took them wives of all which they chose.'

This was in the dawn of time, before the morning stars were set, and while they yet sang together.

The epoch is so remote, the mists and dewy grey of matin twilight veil it with so vague an obscurity, that all distinct feature of custom, all clear line of locality, evade perception and baffle research. It must suffice to know that the world then existed; that men peopled it; that man's nature, with its passions, sympathies, pains, and pleasures, informed the planet and gave it soul.

A certain tribe colonized a certain spot on the globe; of what race this tribe – unknown: in what region that spot – untold. We usually think of the East when we refer to transactions of that date; but who shall declare that there was no life in the West, the South, the North? What is to disprove that this tribe, instead of camping under palm-groves in Asia, wandered beneath island oak-woods rooted in our own seas of Europe?

It is no sandy plain, nor any circumscribed and scant oasis I seem to realize. A forest valley, with rocky sides and brown profundity of shade, formed by tree crowding on tree, descends deep before me. Here, indeed, dwell human beings, but so few, and in alleys so thick branched and over-arched, they are neither heard nor seen. Are they savage? – doubtless. They live by the crook and the bow: half shepherds, half hunters, their flocks wander wild as their prey. Are they happy? – no: not more happy than we are at this day. Are they good? – no: not better than ourselves: their nature is our nature, – human both. There is one in this tribe too often miserable, – a child bereaved of both parents. None cares for this child: she is fed sometimes, but oftener forgotten: a hut rarely receives her: the hollow tree and chill cavern are her home. Forsaken, lost, and wandering, she lives more with the wild beast and bird than with her own kind. Hunger and cold are her comrades: sadness hovers over, and solitude besets her round. Unheeded and unvalued, she should die; but she both lives and grows: the green wilderness nurses her, and becomes to her a mother: feeds her on juicy berry, on saccharine root and nut.

There is something in the air of this clime which fosters life kindly: there must be something, too, in its dews, which heals with sovereign balm. Its gentle seasons exaggerate no passion, no sense; its temperature tends to harmony; its breezes, you would say, bring down from heaven the germ of pure thought, and purer feeling. Not grotesquely fantastic are the forms of cliff and foliage; not violently vivid the colouring of flower and bird: in all the grandeur of these forests there is repose; in all their freshness there is tenderness.

The gentle charm vouchsafed to flower and tree, – bestowed on deer and dove, – has not been denied to the human nursling. All solitary, she has sprung up straight and graceful. Nature cast her features in a fine mould; they have matured in their pure, accurate first lines, unaltered by the shocks of disease. No fierce dry blast has dealt with the surface of her frame; no burning sun has crimped or withered her tresses: her form gleams ivory-white through the trees; her hair flows plenteous, long, and glossy; her eyes not dazzled by vertical fires, beam in the shade large and open, and full and dewy: above those eyes, when the breeze bares her forehead, shines an expanse fair and ample, – a clear, candid page, whereon knowledge, should knowledge ever come, might write a golden record. You see in the desolate young savage nothing vicious or vacant; she haunts the wood harmless and thoughtful: though of what one so untaught can think, it is not easy to divine.

On the evening of one summer day, before the Flood, being utterly alone – for she had lost all trace of her tribe, who had wandered leagues away, she knew not where, – she went up from the vale, to watch Day take leave and Night arrive. A crag, overspread by a tree, was her station: the oak-roots, turfed and mossed, gave a seat: the oak-boughs, thick-leaved, wove a canopy.

Slow and grand the Day withdrew, passing in purple fire, and parting to the farewell of a wild, low chorus from the woodlands. Then Night entered, quiet as death: the wind fell, the birds ceased singing. Now every nest held happy mates, and hart and hind slumbered blissfully safe in their lair.

The girl sat, her body still, her soul astir; occupied, however, rather in feeling than in thinking, – in wishing, than hoping, – in imagining, than projecting. She felt the world, the sky, the night, boundlessly mighty. Of all things, herself seemed to herself the centre, – a small, forgotten atom of life, a spark of soul, emitted inadvertent from the great creative source, and now burning umarked to waste in the heart of a black hollow. She asked, was she thus to burn out and perish, her living light doing no good, never seen, never needed, – a star in an else starless firmament, – which nor shepherd, nor wanderer, nor sage, nor priest, tracked as a guide, or read as a prophecy? Could this be, she demanded, when the flame of her intelligence burned so vivid; when her life beat so true, and real, and potent; when something within her stirred disquieted, and restlessly asserted a God-given strength for which it insisted she should find exercise?

She gazed abroad on Heaven and Evening: Heaven and Evening gazed back on her. She bent down, searching bank, hill, river, spread dim below. All she questioned responded by oracles: she heard, – she was impressed; but she could not understand. Above her head she raised her hands joined together.

'Guidance – help – comfort – come!' was her cry.

There was no voice, nor any that answered.

She waited, kneeling, steadfastly looking up. Yonder sky was sealed: the solemn stars shone alien and remote.

At last, one over-stretched chord of her agony slacked: she thought Something above relented: she felt as if Something far round drew nigher: she heard as if Silence spoke. There was no language, no word, only a tone.

Again – a fine, full, lofty tone, a deep, soft sound, like a storm whispering, made twilight undulate.

Once more, profounder, nearer, clearer, it rolled harmonious.

Yet, again – a distinct voice passed between Heaven and Earth.

'Eva!'

If Eva were not this woman's name, she had none. She rose.

'Here am I.'

'Eva!'

'Oh, Night! (it can be but Night that speaks) I am here!'

The voice, descending, reached Earth.

'Eva!'

'Lord!' she cried, 'behold thine handmaid!'

She had her religion: all tribes held some creed.

'I come: a Comforter!'

'Lord, come quickly!'

The Evening flushed full of hope: the Air panted; the Moon – rising before – ascended large, but her light showed no shape.

'Lean towards me, Eva. Enter my arms; repose thus.'

'Thus I lean, O Invisible, but felt! And what art thou?'

'Eva, I have brought a living draught from heaven. Daughter of Man, drink of my cup!'

'I drink – it is as if sweetest dew visited my lips in a full current. My arid heart revives: my affliction is lightened: my strait and struggle are gone. And the night changes! the wood, the hill, the moon, the wide sky – all change!'

'All change, and for ever. I take from thy vision, darkness: I loosen from thy faculties, fetters! I level in thy path, obstacles: I, with my presence, fill vacancy: I claim as mine the lost atom of life: I take to myself the spark of soul – burning, heretofore, forgotten!'

'Oh, take me! Oh, claim me! This is a god.'

'This is a Son of God: one who feels himself in the portion of life that stirs you: he is suffered to reclaim his own, and so to foster and aid that it shall not perish hopeless.'

'A Son of God! Am I indeed chosen?'

'Thou only in this land. I saw thee that thou wert fair: I knew thee that thou wert mine. To me it is given to rescue, to sustain, to cherish, mine own. Acknowledge in me that Seraph, on earth, named Genius.'

'My glorious Bridegroom! True Dayspring from on high! All I would have, at last I possess. I receive a revelation. The dark hint, the obscure whisper, which have haunted me from child-hood, are interpreted. Thou art He I sought. God-born, take me, thy bride!'

'Unhumbled, I can take what is mine. Did I not give from

the altar the very flame which lit Eva's being? Come again into the heaven whence thou wert sent.'

That Presence, invisible, but mighty, gathered her in like a lamb to the fold; that voice, soft, but all pervading, vibrated through her heart like music. Her eye received no image: and yet a sense visited her vision and her brain as of the serenity of stainless air, the power of sovereign seas, the majesty of marching stars, the energy of colliding elements, the rooted endurance of hills wide based, and, above all, as of the lustre of heroic beauty rushing victorious on the Night, vanquishing its shadows like a diviner Sun.

Such was the bridal-hour of Genius and Humanity. Who shall rehearse the tale of their after-union? Who shall depict its bliss and bale? Who shall tell how He, between whom and the Woman God put enmity, forged deadly plots to break the bond or defile its purity? Who shall record the long strife between Serpent and Seraph? How still the Father of Lies insinuated evil into good – pride into wisdom – grossness into glory – pain into bliss – poison into passion? How the 'dreadless Angel' defied, resisted, and repelled? How, again and again, he refined the polluted cup, exalted the debased emotion, rectified the perverted impulse, detected the lurking venom, baffled the frontless temptation – purified, justified, watched, and withstood? How, by his patience, by his strength, by that unutterable excellence he held from God – his Origin – this faithful Seraph fought for Humanity a good fight through time; and, when Time's course closed, and Death was encountered at the end, barring with fleshless arm the portals of Eternity, how Genius still held close his dying bride, sustained her through the agony of the passage, bore her triumphant into his own home – Heaven; restored her, redeemed, to Jehovah – her Maker; and at last, before Angel and Archangel, crowned her with the crown of Immortality.

Who shall, of these things, write the chronicle?

*

'I never could correct that composition,' observed Shirley, as Moore concluded. 'Your censor-pencil scored it with condemnatory lines, whose signification I strove vainly to fathom.'

She had taken a crayon from the tutor's desk, and was drawing little leaves, fragments of pillars, broken crosses, on the margin of the book.

'French may be half-forgotten, but the habits of the French lesson are retained, I see,' said Louis: 'my books would now, as erst, be unsafe with you. My newly bound St Pièrre would soon be like my Racine: Miss Keeldar, her mark – traced on every page.'

Shirley dropped her crayon as if it burned her fingers.

'Tell me what were the faults of that devoir?' she asked. 'Were they grammatical errors, or did you object to the substance?'

'I never said that the lines I drew were indications of faults at all. You would have it that such was the case, and I refrained from contradiction.'

'What else did they denote?'

'No matter now.'

'Mr Moore,' cried Henry, 'make Shirley repeat some of the pieces she used to say so well by heart.'

'If I ask for any, it will be "Le Cheval Dompté," ' said Moore, trimming with his penknife the pencil Miss Keeldar had worn to a stump.

She turned aside her head; the neck, the clear cheek, forsaken by their natural veil, were seen to flush warm.

'Ah! she has not forgotten, you see, sir,' said Henry, exultant. 'She knows how naughty she was.'

A smile, which Shirley would not permit to expand, made her lip tremble; she bent her face, and hid it half with her arms half in her curls, which, as she stooped, fell loose again.

'Certainly, I was a rebel!' she answered.

'A rebel!' repeated Henry. 'Yes: you and papa had quarrelled terribly, and you set both him and mamma, and Mrs Pryor, and everybody, at defiance: you said he had insulted you –'

'He *had* insulted me,' interposed Shirley.

'And you wanted to leave Sympson Grove directly. You packed your things up, and papa threw them out of your trunk; mamma cried – Mrs Pryor cried; they both stood wringing their hands begging you to be patient, and you knelt on the floor with your things and your upturned box before you, looking, Shirley – looking – why, in one of *your* passions. Your features, in such passions, are not distorted; they are fixed, but quite beautiful: you scarcely look angry, only resolute, and in a certain haste; yet one feels that, at such times, an obstacle cast across your path would be split as with lightning. Papa lost heart, and called Mr Moore.'

'Enough, Henry.'

'No: it is not enough. I hardly know how Mr Moore managed, except that I recollect he suggested to papa that agitation would bring on his gout; and then he spoke quietly to the ladies, and got them away; and afterwards he said to you, Miss Shirley, that it was of no use talking or lecturing now, but that the tea-things were just brought into the school-room, and he was very thirsty, and he would be glad if you would leave your packing for the present and come and make a cup of tea for him and me. You came: you would not talk at first; but soon you softened and grew cheerful. Mr Moore began to tell us about the Continent, the war, and Buonaparte; subjects we were both fond of listening to. After tea he said we should neither of us leave him that evening: he would not let us stray out of his sight, lest we should again get into mischief. We sat one on each side of him: we were so happy. I never passed so pleasant an evening. The next day he gave you, missy, a lecture of an hour, and wound it up by marking you a piece to learn in Bossuet as a punishment-lesson, – "Le Cheval Dompté." You learned it instead of packing up, Shirley. We heard no more of your running away. Mr Moore used to tease you on the subject for a year afterwards.'

'She never said a lesson with greater spirit,' subjoined Moore.

'She then, for the first time, gave me the treat of hearing my native tongue spoken without accent by an English girl.'

'She was as sweet as summer-cherries for a month afterwards,' struck in Henry: 'a good hearty quarrel always left Shirley's temper better than it found it.'

'You talk of me as if I were not present,' observed Miss Keeldar, who had not yet lifted her face.

'Are you sure you *are* present?' asked Moore: 'there have been moments since my arrival here, when I have been tempted to inquire of the lady of Fieldhead if she knew what had become of my former pupil?'

'She is here now.'

'I see her, and humble enough; but I would neither advise Harry, nor others, to believe too implicitly in the humility which one moment can hide its blushing face like a modest little child, and the next lift it pale and lofty as a marble Juno.'

'One man in times of old, it is said, imparted vitality to the statue he had chiselled. Others may have the contrary gift of turning life to stone.'

Moore paused on this observation before he replied to it. His look, at once struck and meditative, said, 'A strange phrase: what may it mean?' He turned it over in his mind, with thought deep and slow, as some German pondering metaphysics.

'You mean,' he said, at last, 'that some men inspire repugnance, and so chill the kind heart.'

'Ingenious!' responded Shirley. 'If the interpretation pleases you, you are welcome to hold it valid. *I* don't care.'

And with that she raised her head, lofty in look, and statue-like in hue, as Louis had described it.

'Behold the metamorphosis!' he said: 'scarce imagined ere it is realized: a lowly nymph develops to an inaccessible goddess. But Henry must not be disappointed of his recitation, and Olympia will deign to oblige him. Let us begin.'

'I have forgotten the very first line.'

'Which I have not. *My* memory, if a slow, is a retentive one.

I acquire deliberately both knowledge and liking: the acquisition grows into my brain, and the sentiment into my breast; and it is not as the rapid springing produce which, having no root in itself, flourishes verdurous enough for a time, but too soon falls withered away. Attention, Henry! Miss Keeldar consents to favour you. "Voyez ce Cheval ardent et impétueux," so it commences.'

Miss Keeldar did consent to make the effort; but she soon stopped.

'Unless I heard the whole repeated, I cannot continue it,' she said.

'Yet it was quickly learned, "soon gained, soon gone," moralized the tutor. He recited the passage deliberately, accurately, with slow, impressive emphasis.

Shirley, by degrees, inclined her ear as he went on. Her face, before turned from him, returned towards him. When he ceased, she took the word up as if from his lips: she took his very tone; she seized his very accent; she delivered the periods as he had delivered them: she reproduced his manner, his pronunciation, his expression.

It was now her turn to petition.

'Recall "Le Songe d'Athalie," ' she entreated, 'and say it.'

He said it for her; she took it from him; she found lively excitement in the pleasure of making his language her own: she asked for further indulgence; all the old school-pieces were revived, and with them Shirley's old school-days.

He had gone through some of the best passages of Racine and Corneille, and then had heard the echo of his own deep tones in the girl's voice, that modulated itself faithfully on his: – 'Le Chène et le Roseau,' that most beautiful of La Fontaine's fables, had been recited, well recited by the tutor, and the pupil had animatedly availed herself of the lesson. Perhaps a simultaneous feeling seized them now that their enthusiasm had kindled to a glow, which the slight fuel of French poetry no longer sufficed to feed; perhaps they longed for a trunk of

English oak to be thrown as a Yule log to the devouring flame.
Moore observed, –

'And these are our best pieces! And we have nothing more
dramatic, nervous, natural!'

And then he smiled and was silent. His whole nature seemed
serenely alight: he stood on the hearth, leaning his elbow on
the mantelpiece, musing not unblissfully.

Twilight was closing on the diminished autumn day: the
school-room windows – darkened with creeping plants, from
which no high October winds had as yet swept the sere foliage
– admitted scarce a gleam of sky; but the fire gave light enough
to talk by.

And now Louis Moore addressed his pupil in French; and
she answered, at first, with laughing hesitation and in broken
phrase: Moore encouraged while he corrected her; Henry joined
in the lesson; the two scholars stood opposite the master, their
arms round each other's waists: Tartar, who long since had
craved and obtained admission, sat sagely in the centre of the
rug, staring at the blaze which burst fitful from morsels of coal
among the red cinders: the group were happy enough, but –

> 'Pleasures are like poppies spread;
> You seize the flower – its bloom is shed.'

The dull, rumbling sound of wheels was heard on the pavement
in the yard.

'It is the carriage returned,' said Shirley; 'and dinner must be
just ready, and I am not dressed.'

A servant came in with Mr Moore's candle and tea: for the
tutor and his pupil usually dined at luncheon time.

'Mr Sympson and the ladies are returned,' she said, 'and Sir
Philip Nunnely is with them.'

'How you did start, and how your hand trembled, Shirley!'
said Henry, when the maid had closed the shutter and was gone.
'But I know why – don't you, Mr Moore? I know what papa
intends. He is a little ugly man, that Sir Philip: I wish he had

not come: I wish sisters and all of them had stayed at De Walden Hall to dine. Shirley should once more have made tea for you and me, Mr Moore, and we would have had a happy evening of it.'

Moore was locking up his desk, and putting away his St Pièrre, – 'That was *your* plan – was it, my boy?'

'Don't you approve it, sir?'

'I approve nothing Utopian. Look Life in its iron face: stare Reality out of its brassy countenance. Make the tea, Henry; I shall be back in a minute.'

He left the room: so did Shirley, by another door,

CHAPTER XXVIII

PHŒBE

S HIRLEY PROBABLY got on pleasantly with Sir Philip that evening, for the next morning she came down in one of her best moods.

'Who will take a walk with me?' she asked, after breakfast. 'Isabella and Gertrude – will you?'

So rare was such an invitation from Miss Keeldar to her female cousins that they hesitated before they accepted it. Their mamma, however; signifying acquiescence in the project, they fetched their bonnets, and the trio set out.

It did not suit these three young persons to be thrown much together: Miss Keeldar liked the society of few ladies: indeed, she had a cordial pleasure in that of none except Mrs Pryor and Caroline Helstone. She was civil, kind, attentive even to her cousins; but still she usually had little to say to them. In the sunny mood of this particular morning, she contrived to enter-tain even the Misses Sympson. Without deviating from her wonted rule of discussing with them only ordinary themes, she imparted to these themes an extraordinary interest: the sparkle of her spirit glanced along her phrases.

What made her so joyous? All the cause must have been in herself. The day was not bright; it was dim – a pale, waning autumn day: the walks through the dun woods were damp; the atmosphere was heavy, the sky overcast; and yet, it seemed that in Shirley's heart lived all the light and azure of Italy, as all its fervour laughed in her grey English eye.

Some directions necessary to be given to her foreman, John, delayed her behind her cousins as they neared Fieldhead on their return; perhaps an interval of twenty minutes elapsed between her separation from them and her re-entrance into the house: in the mean time she had spoken to John, and then she had lingered in the lane at the gate. A summons to luncheon called her in: she excused herself from the meal, and went up-stairs.

'Is not Shirley coming to luncheon?' asked Isabella: 'she said she was not hungry.'

An hour after, as she did not quit her chamber, one of her cousins went to seek her there. She was found sitting at the foot of the bed, her head resting on her hand: she looked quite pale, very thoughtful, almost sad.

'You are not ill?' was the question put.

'A little sick,' replied Miss Keeldar.

Certainly, she was not a little changed from what she had been two hours before.

This change, accounted for only by those three words, explained no otherwise; this change – whencesoever springing, effected in a brief ten minutes – passed like no light summer cloud. She talked when she joined her friends at dinner, talked as usual; she remained with them during the evening; when again questioned respecting her health, she declared herself perfectly recovered: it had been a mere passing faintness; a momentary sensation, not worth a thought: yet it was felt there was a difference in Shirley.

The next day – the day – the week – the fortnight after – this new and peculiar shadow lingered on the countenance, in the manner of Miss Keeldar. A strange quietude settled over her look, her movements, her very voice. The alteration was not so marked as to court or permit questioning, yet it *was* there, and it would not pass away: it hung over her like a cloud which no breeze could stir or disperse. Soon it became evident that to notice this change was to annoy her. First, she shrunk from remark; and, if persisted in, she, with her own peculiar hauteur, repelled it. 'Was she ill?' The reply came with decision.

'I *am not*.'

'Did anything weigh on her mind? Had anything happened to affect her spirits?'

She scornfully ridiculed the idea. 'What did they mean by spirits? She had no spirits, black or white, blue or grey, to affect.'

'Something must be the matter – she was so altered.'

'She supposed she had a right to alter at her ease. She knew she was plainer: if it suited her to grow ugly, why need others fret themselves on the subject?'

'There must be a cause for the change – what was it?'

She peremptorily requested to be let alone.

Then she would make every effort to appear quite gay, and she seemed indignant at herself that she could not perfectly succeed: brief, self-spurning epithets burst from her lips when alone: 'Fool! Coward!' she would term herself. 'Poltroon!' she would say: 'if you must tremble – tremble in secret! Quail where no eye sees you!'

'How dare you' – she would ask herself – 'how dare you show your weakness and betray your imbecile anxieties? Shake them off: rise above them: if you cannot do this, hide them.'

And to hide them, she did her best. She once more became resolutely lively in company. When weary of effort and forced to relax, she sought solitude: not the solitude of her chamber – she refused to mope, shut up between four walls – but that wilder solitude which lies out of doors, and which she could chase, mounted on Zoë, her mare. She took long rides of half a day. Her uncle disapproved, but he dared not remonstrate: it was never pleasant to face Shirley's anger, even when she was healthy and gay; but now that her face showed thin, and her large eye looked hollow, there was something in the darkening of that face and kindling of that eye which touched as well as alarmed.

To all comparative strangers who, unconscious of the alterations in her spirits, commented on the alteration in her looks, she had one reply:

'I am perfectly well: I have not an ailment.'

And health, indeed, she must have had, to be able to bear the exposure to the weather she now encountered. Wet or fair, calm or storm, she took her daily ride over Stilbro' Moor, Tartar keeping up at her side, with his wolf-like gallop, long and untiring.

Twice – three times, the eyes of gossips – those eyes which are everywhere: in the closet and on the hill-top – noticed that instead of turning on Rushedge, the top-ridge of Stilbro' Moor, she rode forwards all the way to the town. Scouts were not wanting to mark her destination there; it was ascertained that she alighted at the door of one Mr Pearson Hall, a solicitor, related to the Vicar of Nunnely: this gentleman and his ancestors had been the agents of the Keeldar family for generations back: some people affirmed that Miss Keeldar was become involved in business speculations connected with Hollow's Mill; that she had lost money, and was constrained to mortgage her land: others conjectured that she was going to be married, and that the settlements were preparing.

Mr Moore and Henry Sympson were together in the school-room: the tutor was waiting for a lesson which the pupil seemed busied in preparing.

'Henry, make haste! the afternoon is getting on.'

'Is it, sir?'

'Certainly. Are you nearly ready with that lesson?'

'No.'

'Not *nearly* ready?'

'I have not construed a line.

Mr Moore looked up: the boy's tone was rather peculiar. 'The task presents no difficulties, Henry; or, if it does, bring them to me: we will work together.'

'Mr Moore, I can do no work.'

'My boy, you are ill.'

'Sir, I am not worse in bodily health than usual, but my heart is full.'

'Shut the book. Come hither, Harry. Come to the fireside.'

Harry limped forward; his tutor placed him a chair: his lips were quivering, his eyes brimming. He laid his crutch on the floor, bent down his head, and wept.

'This distress is not occasioned by physical pain, you say, Harry? You have a grief: – tell it me.'

'Sir, I have such a grief as I never had before. I wish it could be relieved in some way: I can hardly bear it.'

'Who knows but, if we talk it over, we may relieve it? What is the cause? Whom does it concern?'

'The cause, sir, is Shirley: it concerns Shirley.'

'Does it? . . . You think her changed?'

'All who know her think her changed: you too, Mr Moore.'

'Not seriously, – no. I see no alteration but such as a favourable turn might repair in a few weeks: besides, her own word must go for something: she says she is well.'

'There it is, sir: as long as she maintained she was well, I believed her. When I was sad out of her sight, I soon recovered spirits in her presence. Now . . .'

'Well, Harry, now . . . ? Has she said anything to you? You and she were together in the garden two hours this morning: I saw her talking, and you listening. Now, my dear Harry! if Miss Keeldar has said she is ill, and enjoined you to keep her secret, do not obey her. For her life's sake, avow everything. Speak, my boy!'

'*She* say she is ill! I believe, sir, if she were dying, she would smile, and aver "Nothing ails me." '

'What have you learned, then? What new circumstance . . . ?'

'I have learned that she has just made her will.'

'Made her will!'

The tutor and the pupil were silent.

'She told you that?' asked Moore, when some minutes had elapsed.

'She told me quite cheerfully: not as an ominous circumstance, which I felt it to be. She said I was the only person besides her solicitor, Pearson Hall, and Mr Helstone and Mr Yorke, who knew anything about it; and to me, she intimated, she wished specially to explain its provisions.'

'Go on, Harry.'

' "Because," she said, looking down on me with her beautiful eyes, – oh! they *are* beautiful, Mr Moore! I love them, – I love her! She is my star! Heaven must not claim her! She is lovely in this world, and fitted for this world. Shirley is not an angel; she is a woman, and she shall live with men. Seraphs shall not have her! Mr Moore – if one of the "sons of God," with wings wide and bright as the sky, blue and sounding as the sea, having seen that she was fair, descended to claim her, his claim should be withstood – withstood by me – boy and cripple as I am!'

'Henry Sympson, go on, when I tell you.'

' "Because," she said, "if I made no will, and died before you Harry, all my property would go to you; and I do not intend that it should be so, though your father would like it. But you," she said, "will have his whole estate, which is large – larger than Fieldhead; your sisters will have nothing, so I have left them some money: though I do not love them, both together, half so much as I love one lock of your fair hair." She said these words, and she called me her "darling," and let me kiss her. She went on to tell me that she had left Caroline Helstone some money too; that this manor-house, with its furniture and books, she had bequeathed to me, as she did not choose to take the old family place from her own blood; and that all the rest of her property, amounting to about twelve thousand pounds, exclusive of the legacies to my sisters and Miss Helstone, she had willed, not to me, seeing I was already rich, but to a good man, who would make the best use of it that any human being could do: a man, she said, that was both gentle and brave, strong and merciful; a man that might not profess to be pious, but she knew he had the secret of religion pure and undefiled before God. The spirit of love and peace was with him: he visited the fatherless and widows in their affliction, and kept himself unspotted from the world. Then she asked, "Do you approve what I have done, Harry?" I could not answer, – my tears choked me, as they do now.'

Mr Moore allowed his pupil a moment to contend with and master his emotion: he then demanded: –

'What else did she say?'

'When I had signified my full consent to the conditions of her will, she told me I was a generous boy, and she was proud of me: "And now," she added, "in case anything should happen, you will know what to say to Malice when she comes whispering hard things in your ear, insinuating that Shirley has wronged you; that she did not love you. You will know that I *did* love you, Harry; that no sister could have loved you better, my own treasure." Mr Moore, sir, when I remember her voice, and recall her look, my heart beats as if it would break its strings. She *may* go to heaven before me – if God commands it, she *must*; but the rest of my life – and my life will not be long – I am glad of that now – shall be a straight, quick, thoughtful, journey in the path her step has pressed. I thought to enter the vault of the Keeldars before her: should it be otherwise, lay my coffin by Shirley's side.'

Moore answered him with a weighty calm, that offered a strange contrast to the boy's perturbed enthusiasm.

'You are wrong, both of you – you harm each other. If youth once falls under the influence of a shadowy terror, it imagines there will never be full sunlight again – its first calamity it fancies will last a lifetime. What more did she say? Anything more?'

'We settled one or two family points between ourselves.'

'I should rather like to know what –'

'But, Mr Moore, you smile – *I* could not smile to see Shirley in such a mood.'

'My boy, I am neither nervous, nor poetic, nor inexperienced. I see things as they are: you don't as yet. Tell me these family points.'

'Only, sir, she asked me whether I considered myself most of a Keeldar or a Sympson; and I answered I was Keeldar to the core of the heart, and to the marrow of the bones. She said she was glad of it; for, besides her, I was the only Keeldar left in England: and then we agreed on some matters.'

'Well?'

'Well, sir, that if I lived to inherit my father's estate, and her house, I was to take the name of Keeldar, and to make Fieldhead my residence. Henry Shirley Keeldar I said I would be called: and I will. Her name and her manor-house are ages old, and Sympson and Sympson-Grove are of yesterday.'

'Come, you are neither of you going to heaven yet. I have the best hopes of you both, with your proud distinctions – a pair of half-fledged eaglets. Now, what is your inference from all you have told me? put it into words.'

'That Shirley thinks she is going to die.'

'She referred to her health?'

'Not once; but I assure you she is wasting: her hands are growing quite thin, and so is her cheek.'

'Does she ever complain to your mother or sisters?'

'Never. She laughs at them when they question her. Mr Moore, she is a strange being – so fair and girlish: not a man-like woman at all – not an Amazon, and yet lifting her head above both help and sympathy.'

'Do you know where she is now, Henry? Is she in the house, or riding out?'

'Surely not out, sir – it rains fast.'

'True: which, however, is no guarantee that she is not at this moment cantering over Rushedge. Of late she has never permitted weather to be a hinderance to her rides.'

'You remember, Mr Moore, how wet and stormy it was last Wednesday? so wild, indeed, that she would not permit Zoë to be saddled; yet the blast she thought too tempestuous for her mare, she herself faced on foot; that afternoon she walked nearly as far as Nunnely. I asked her, when she came in, if she was not afraid of taking cold. "Not I," she said, "it would be too much good luck for me. I don't know, Harry; but the best thing that could happen to me would be to take a good cold and fever, and so pass off like other Christians." She is reckless, you see, sir.'

'Reckless indeed! Go and find out where she is; and if you can get an opportunity of speaking to her, without attracting attention, request her to come here a minute.'

'Yes, sir.'

He snatched his crutch, and started up to go.

'Harry!'

He returned.

'Do not deliver the message formally. Word it as, in former days, you would have worded an ordinary summons to the school-room.'

'I see, sir; she will be more likely to obey.'

'And Harry –'

'Sir?'

'I will call you when I want you: till then, you are dispensed from lessons.'

He departed. Mr Moore, left alone, rose from his desk.

'I can be very cool and very supercilious with Henry,' he said. 'I can seem to make light of his apprehensions, and look down "du haut de ma grandeur" on his youthful ardour. To *him* I can speak as if, in my eyes, they were both children. Let me see if I can keep up the same rôle with her. I have known the moment when I seemed about to forget it; when Confusion and Submission seemed about to crush me with their soft tyranny; when my tongue faltered, and I have almost let the mantle drop, and stood in her presence, not master – no – but something else. I trust I shall never so play the fool: it is well for a Sir Philip Nunnely to redden when he meets her eye: he may permit himself the indulgence of submission – he may even without disgrace suffer his hand to tremble when it touches hers; but if one of her farmers were to show himself susceptible and senti-mental, he would merely prove his need of a strait waistcoat.

So far I have always done very well. She has sat near me, and I have not shaken – more than my desk. I have encountered her looks and smiles like – why, like a tutor, as I am. Her hand I never yet touched – never underwent that test. Her farmer or her footman I am not – no serf nor servant of hers have I ever been: but I am poor, and it behoves me to look to my self-respect – not to compromise an inch of it. What did she mean by that allusion to the cold people who petrify flesh to marble? It pleased me – I hardly know why – I would not permit myself to inquire – I never do indulge in scrutiny either of her language or coun-tenance; for if I did, I should sometimes forget Common Sense and believe in Romance. A strange, secret ecstasy steals through my veins at moments: I'll not encourage – I'll not remember it. I am resolved, as long as may be, to retain the right to say with Paul – "I am not mad, but speak forth the words of truth and soberness." '

He paused – listening.

'Will she come, or will she not come?' he inquired. 'How will she take the message? naïvely or disdainfully? like a child or like a queen? Both characters are in her nature.

'If she comes, what shall I say to her? How account, firstly, for the freedom of the request? Shall I apologize to her? I could in all humility; but would an apology tend to place us in the positions we ought relatively to occupy in this matter? I *must* keep up the professor, otherwise – I hear a door –.' He waited. Many minutes passed.

'She will refuse me. Henry is entreating her to come: she declines. My petition is presumption in her eyes: let her *only* come, I can teach her to the contrary. I would rather she were a little perverse – it will steel me. I prefer her, cuirassed in pride, armed with a taunt. Her scorn startles me from my dreams – I stand up myself. A sarcasm from her eyes or lips puts strength into every nerve and sinew I have. Some step approaches, and not Henry's . . . .'

The door unclosed; Miss Keeldar came in. The message, it

appeared, had found her at her needle: she brought her work in her hand. That day she had not been riding out: she had evidently passed it quietly. She wore her neat indoor dress and silk apron. This was no Thalestris from the fields, but a quiet domestic character from the fireside. Mr Moore had her at advantage: he should have addressed her at once in solemn accents, and with rigid mien; perhaps he would, had she looked saucy; but her air never showed less of crânerie; a soft kind of youthful shyness depressed her eyelid and mantled on her cheek. The tutor stood silent.

She made a full stop between the door and his desk.

'Did you want me, sir?' she asked.

'I ventured, Miss Keeldar, to send for you – that is, to ask an interview of a few minutes.'

She waited: she plyed her needle.

'Well, sir (not lifting her eyes) – what about?'

'Be seated first. The subject I would broach is one of some moment: perhaps I have hardly a right to approach it: it is possible I ought to frame an apology: it is possible no apology can excuse me. The liberty I have taken arises from a conversation with Henry. The boy is unhappy about your health: all your friends are unhappy on that subject. It is of your health I would speak.'

'I am quite well,' she said briefly.

'Yet changed.'

'That matters to none but myself. We all change.'

'Will you sit down? Formerly, Miss Keeldar, I had some influence with you – have I any now? May I feel that what I am saying is not accounted positive presumption?'

'Let me read some French, Mr Moore, or I will even take a spell at the Latin grammar, and let us proclaim a truce to all sanitary discussions.

'No – no: it is time there were discussions.'

'Discuss away, then, but do not choose me for your text; I am a healthy subject.'

'Do you not think it wrong to affirm, and reaffirm, what is substantially untrue?'

'I say I am well: I have neither cough, pain, nor fever.'

'Is there no equivocation in that assertion? Is it the direct truth?'

'The direct truth.'

Louis Moore looked at her earnestly.

'I can myself,' he said, 'trace no indications of actual disease; but why, then, are you altered?'

'*Am* I altered?'

'We will try: we will seek a proof.'

'How?'

'I ask, in the first place, do you sleep as you used to?'

'I do not: but it is not because I am ill.'

'Have you the appetite you once had?'

'No: but it is not because I am ill.'

'You remember this little ring fastened to my watch-chain? It was my mother's, and is too small to pass the joint of my little finger. You have many a time sportively purloined it: it fitted your forefinger. Try now.'

She permitted the test: the ring dropped from the wasted little hand. Louis picked it up, and re-attached it to the chain. An uneasy flush coloured his brow. Shirley again said: –

'It is not because I am ill.'

'Not only have you lost sleep, appetite, and flesh,' proceeded Moore, 'but your spirits are always at ebb: besides, there is a nervous alarm in your eye – a nervous disquiet in your manner: these peculiarities were not formerly yours.'

'Mr Moore, we will pause here. You have exactly hit it: I am nervous. Now, talk of something else. What wet weather we have! Steady, pouring rain!'

'*You* nervous! Yes: and if Miss Keeldar is nervous, it is not without a cause. Let me reach it. Let me look nearer. The ailment is not physical: I have suspected that. It came in one moment. I know the day. I noticed the change. Your pain is mental.'

'Not at all: it is nothing so dignified – merely nervous. Oh! dismiss the topic.'

'When it is exhausted: not till then. Nervous alarms should always be communicated, that they may be dissipated. I wish I had the gift of persuasion, and could incline you to speak willingly. I believe confession, in your case, would be half-equivalent to cure.'

'No,' said Shirley, abruptly: 'I wish that were at all probable; but I am afraid it is not.'

She suspended her work a moment. She was now seated. Resting her elbow on the table, she leaned her head on her hand. Mr Moore looked as if he felt he had at last gained some footing in this difficult path. She was serious, and in her wish was implied an important admission; after that, she could no longer affirm that *nothing* ailed her.

The tutor allowed her some minutes for repose and reflection, ere he returned to the charge: once, his lips moved to speak; but he thought better of it, and prolonged the pause. Shirley lifted her eye to his: had he betrayed injudicious emotion, perhaps obstinate persistence in silence would have been the result; but he looked calm, strong, trustworthy.

'I had better tell *you* than my aunt,' she said, 'or than my cousins, or my uncle: they would all make such a bustle – and it is that very bustle I dread; the alarm, the flurry, the éclat: in short, I never liked to be the centre of a small domestic whirlpool. You can bear a little shock – eh?'

'A great one, if necessary.'

Not a muscle of the man's frame moved, and yet his large heart beat fast in his deep chest. What was she going to tell him? Was irremediable mischief done?

'Had I thought it right to go to you, I would never have made a secret of the matter one moment,' she continued: 'I would have told at once, and asked advice.'

'Why was it not right to come to me?'

'It might be *right* – I do not mean that; but I could not do

it. I seemed to have no title to trouble you: the mishap concerned me only – I wanted to keep it to myself, and people will
not let me. I tell you, I hate to be an object of worrying attention, or a theme for village gossip. Besides, it may pass away
without result – God knows!'

Moore, though tortured with suspense, did not demand a
quick explanation; he suffered neither gesture, glance, nor word,
to betray impatience. His tranquillity tranquillized Shirley; his
confidence reassured her.

'Great effects may spring from trivial causes,' she remarked,
as she loosened a bracelet from her wrist; then, unfastening her
sleeve, and partially turning it up, –

'Look here, Mr Moore.'

She showed a mark in her white arm; rather a deep though
healed up indentation: something between a burn and a cut.

'I would not show that to any one in Briarfield but you,
because you can take it quietly.'

'Certainly there is nothing in the little mark to shock: its
history will explain.'

'Small as it is, it has taken my sleep away, and made me nervous, thin, and foolish; because, on account of that little mark,
I am obliged to look forward to a possibility that has its terrors.'

The sleeve was readjusted; the bracelet replaced.

'Do you know that you try me!' he said smiling. 'I am a patient
sort of man, but my pulse is quickening.'

'Whatever happens, you will befriend me, Mr Moore. You
will give me the benefit of your self-possession, and not leave
me at the mercy of agitated cowards?'

'I make no promise now. Tell me the tale, and then exact
what pledge you will.'

'It is a very short tale. I took a walk with Isabella and Gertrude
one day, about three weeks ago. They reached home before me:
I stayed behind to speak to John. After leaving him, I pleased
myself with lingering in the lane, where all was very still and
shady: I was tired of chattering to the girls, and in no hurry to

rejoin them. As I stood leaning against the gate-pillar, thinking some very happy thoughts about my future life – for that morning I imagined that events were beginning to turn as I had long wished them to turn –'

'Ah! Nunnely had been with her the evening before!' thought Moore, parenthetically.

'I heard a panting sound; a dog came running up the lane. I know most of the dogs in this neighbourhood; it was Phœbe, one of Mr Sam Wynne's pointers. The poor creature ran with her head down, her tongue hanging out; she looked as if bruised and beaten all over. I called her; I meant to coax her into the house, and give her some water and dinner; I felt sure she had been ill-used: Mr Sam often flogs his pointers cruelly. She was too flurried to know me; and when I attempted to pat her head, she turned and snatched at my arm. She bit it so as to draw blood, then ran panting on. Directly after, Mr Wynne's keeper came up, carrying a gun. He asked if I had seen a dog, I told him I had seen Phœbe.

' "You had better chain up Tartar, ma'am," he said, "and tell your people to keep within the house; I am after Phœbe to shoot her, and the groom is gone another way. She is raging mad." '

Mr Moore leaned back in his chair, and folded his arms across his chest; Miss Keeldar resumed her square of silk canvass, and continued the creation of a wreath of Parmese violets.

'And you told no one, sought no help, no cure: you would not come to me?'

'I got as far as the school-room door; there my courage failed: I preferred to cushion the matter.'

'Why? What can I demand better in this world than to be of use to you?'

'I had no claim.'

'Monstrous! And you did nothing?'

'Yes: I walked straight into the laundry, where they are ironing most of the week, now that I have so many guests in the house. While the maid was busy crimping or starching, I took

an Italian iron from the fire, and applied the light scarlet glowing tip to my arm: I bored it well in: it cauterized the little
wound. Then I went up-stairs.'

'I daresay you never once groaned?'

'I am sure I don't know. I was very miserable. Not firm or
tranquil at all, I think: there was no calm in my mind.'

'There was calm in your person. I remember listening the
whole time we sat at luncheon, to hear if you moved in the
room above: all was quiet.'

'I was sitting at the foot of the bed, wishing Phœbe had not
bitten me.'

'And alone! You like solitude.'

'Pardon me.'

'You disdain sympathy.'

'Do I, Mr Moore?'

'With your powerful mind, you must feel independent of
help, of advice, of society.'

'So be it – since it pleases you.'

She smiled. She pursued her embroidery carefully and quickly;
but her eyelash twinkled, and then it glittered, and then a
drop fell.

Mr Moore leaned forward on his desk, moved his chair,
altered his attitude.

'If it is not so,' he asked, with a peculiar, mellow change in
his voice, 'how is it, then?'

'I don't know.'

'You do know, but you won't speak: all must be locked up in
yourself.'

'Because it is not worth sharing.'

'Because nobody can give the high price you require for your
confidence. Nobody is rich enough to purchase it. Nobody has
the honour, the intellect, the power you demand in your adviser.
There is not a shoulder in England on which you would rest
your hand for support – far less a bosom which you would
permit to pillow your head. Of course you must live alone.'

'I *can* live alone, if need be. But the question is not how to live – but how to die alone. That strikes me in a more grisly light.'

'You apprehend the effects of the virus – ? You anticipate an indefinitely threatening, dreadful doom – ?'

She bowed.

'You are very nervous and womanish.'

'You complimented me two minutes since on my powerful mind.'

'You are very womanish. If the whole affair were coolly examined and discussed, I feel assured it would turn out that there is no danger of your dying at all.'

'Amen! I am very willing to live, if it please God. I have felt life sweet.'

'How can it be otherwise than sweet with your endowments and nature? Do you truly expect that you will be seized with hydrophobia, and die raving mad?'

'I *expect* it, and have *feared* it. Just now, I fear nothing.'

'Nor do I, on your account. I doubt whether the smallest particle of virus mingled with your blood: and if it did, let me assure you that – young, healthy, faultlessly sound as you are – no harm will ensue. For the rest, I shall inquire whether the dog was really mad. I hold she was not mad.'

'Tell nobody that she bit me.'

'Why should I, when I believe the bite innocuous as a cut of this penknife? Make yourself easy: *I* am easy, though I value your life as much as I do my own chance of happiness in eternity. Look up.'

'Why, Mr Moore?'

'I wish to see if you are cheered. Put your work down: raise your head.'

'There –'

'Look at me. Thank you! And is the cloud broken?'

'I fear nothing.'

'Is your mind restored to its own natural sunny clime?'

'I am very content: but I want your promise.'

'Dictate.'

'You know, in case the worst I *have* feared should happen, they will smother me. You need not smile: they will – they always do. My uncle will be full of horror, weakness, precipitation; and that is the only expedient which will suggest itself to him. Nobody in the house will be self-possessed but you: now promise to befriend me – to keep Mr Sympson away from me – not to let Henry come near, lest I should hurt him. Mind – *mind* that you take care of yourself, too: but I shall not injure you, I know I shall not. Lock the chamber-door against the surgeons – turn them out, if they get in. Let neither the young nor the old MacTurk lay a finger on me; nor Mr Graves, their colleague; and, lastly, if I give trouble, with your own hand administer to me a strong narcotic: such a sure dose of laudanum as shall leave no mistake. *Promise to do this.*'

Moore left his desk, and permitted himself the recreation of one or two turns through the room. Stopping behind Shirley's chair, he bent over her, and said, in a low, emphatic voice, –

'I promise all you ask – without comment, without reservation.'

'If female help is needed, call in my housekeeper, Mrs Gill: let her lay me out, if I die. She is attached to me. She wronged me again and again, and again and again I forgave her. She now loves me, and would not defraud me of a pin: confidence has made her honest; forbearance has made her kindhearted. At this day, I can trust both her integrity, her courage, and her affection. Call her; but keep my good aunt and my timid cousins away. Once more, promise.'

'I promise.'

'That is good in you,' she said, looking up at him as he bent above her, and smiling.

'Is it good? Does it comfort?'

'Very much.'

'I will be with you – I and Mrs Gill only – in any, in every extremity where calm and fidelity are needed. No rash or coward hand shall meddle.'

'Yet you think me childish?'

'I do.'

'Ah! you despise me.'

'Do we despise children?'

'In fact, I am neither so strong, nor have I such pride in my strength, as people think, Mr Moore; nor am I so regardless of sympathy; but when I have any grief, I fear to impart it to those I love, lest it should pain them; and to those whom I view with indifference, I cannot condescend to complain. After all, you should not taunt me with being childish; for if you were as unhappy as I have been for the last three weeks, you too would want some friend.'

'We all want a friend, do we not?'

'All of us that have anything good in our natures.'

'Well, you have Caroline Helstone.'

'Yes . . . And you have Mr Hall.'

'Yes . . . Mrs Pryor is a wise, good woman: she can counsel you when you need counsel.'

'For your part, you have your brother Robert.'

'For any right-hand defections, there is the Rev. Matthewson Helstone, M.A., to lean upon; for any left-hand fallings off, there is Hiram Yorke, Esq. Both elders pay you homage.'

'I never saw Mrs Yorke so motherly to any young man as she is to you. I don't know how you have won her heart; but she is more tender to you than she is to her own sons. You have, besides, your sister, Hortense.'

'It appears we are both well provided.'

'It appears so.'

'How thankful we ought to be!'

'Yes.'

'How contented!'

'Yes.'

'For my part, I am almost contented just now, and very

thankful. Gratitude is a divine emotion: it fills the heart, but not to bursting: it warms it, but not to fever. I like to taste leisurely of bliss: devoured in haste, I do not know its flavour.'

Still leaning on the back of Miss Keeldar's chair, Moore watched the rapid motion of her fingers, as the green and purple garland grew beneath them. After a prolonged pause, he again asked, –

'Is the shadow *quite* gone?'

'Wholly. As I *was* two hours since, and as I *am* now, are two different states of existence. I believe, Mr Moore, griefs and fears nursed in silence grow like Titan infants.'

'You will cherish such feelings no more in silence?'

'Not if I dare speak.'

'In using the word "*dare*," to whom do you allude?'

'To you.'

'How is it applicable to me?'

'On account of your austerity and shyness.'

'Why am I austere and shy?'

'Because you are proud.'

'Why am I proud?'

'I should like to know: will you be good enough to tell me?'

'Perhaps, because I am poor, for one reason: poverty and pride often go together.'

'That is such a nice reason: I should be charmed to discover another that would pair with it. Mate that turtle, Mr Moore.'

'Immediately. What do you think of marrying to sober Poverty many-tainted Caprice?'

'Are you capricious?'

'*You* are.'

'A libel. I am steady as a rock: fixed as the Polar Star.'

'I look out at some early hour of the day, and see a fine, perfect rainbow, bright with promise, gloriously spanning the beclouded welkin of life. An hour afterwards I look again – half the arch is gone, and the rest is faded. Still later, the stern sky denies that it ever wore so benign a symbol of hope.'

'Well, Mr Moore, you should contend against these changeful humours: they are your besetting sin. One never knows where to have you.'

'Miss Keeldar, I had once – for two years – a pupil who grew very dear to me. Henry is dear, but she was dearer. Henry never gives me trouble; she – well – she did. I think she vexed me twenty-three hours out of the twenty-four –'

'She was never with you above three hours, or at the most six at a time.'

'She sometimes spilled the draught from my cup, and stole the food from my plate; and when she had kept me unfed for a day (and that did not suit me, for I am a man accustomed to take my meals with reasonable relish, and to ascribe due importance to the rational enjoyment of creature comforts) –'

'I know you do. I can tell what sort of dinners you like best – perfectly well. I know precisely the dishes you prefer –'

'She robbed these dishes of flavour, and made a fool of me besides. I like to sleep well. In my quiet days, when I was my own man, I never quarrelled with the night for being long, nor cursed my bed for its thorns. She changed all this.'

'Mr Moore –'

'And having taken from me peace of mind, and ease of life, she took from me herself; quite coolly, – just as if, when she was gone, the world would be all the same to me. I knew I should see her again at some time. At the end of two years, it fell out that we encountered again under her own roof, where she was mistress. How do you think she bore herself towards me, Miss Keeldar?'

'Like one who had profited well by lessons learned from yourself.'

'She received me haughtily: she meted out a wide space between us, and kept me aloof by the reserved gesture, the rare and alienated glance, the word calmly civil.'

'She was an excellent pupil! Having seen you distant, she at once learned to withdraw. Pray, sir, admire, in her hauteur, a careful improvement on your own coolness.'

'Conscience, and honour, and the most despotic necessity, dragged me apart from her, and kept me sundered with ponderous fetters. She was free: she might have been clement.'

'Never free to compromise her self-respect: to seek where she had been shunned.'

'Then she was inconsistent: she tantalized as before. When I thought I had made up my mind to seeing in her only a lofty stranger, she would suddenly show me such a glimpse of loving simplicity – she would warm me with such a beam of reviving sympathy, she would gladden an hour with converse so gentle, gay, and kindly – that I could no more shut my heart on her image, than I could close that door against her presence. Explain why she distressed me so.'

'She could not bear to be quite outcast; and then she would sometimes get a notion into her head, on a cold, wet day, that the school-room was no cheerful place, and feel it incumbent on her to go and see if you and Henry kept up a good fire; and once there, she liked to stay.'

'But she should not be changeful: if she came at all, she should come oftener.'

'There is such a thing as intrusion.'

'To-morrow, you will not be as you are to-day.'

'I don't know. Will you?'

'I am not mad, most noble Berenice! We may give one day to dreaming, but the next we must awake; and I shall awake to purpose the morning you are married to Sir Philip Nunnely. The fire shines on you and me, and shows us very clearly in the glass, Miss Keeldar; and I have been gazing on the picture all the time I have been talking. Look up! What a difference between your head and mine! – I look old for thirty!'

'You are so grave; you have such a square brow; and your face is sallow. I never regard you as a young man, nor as Robert's junior.'

'Don't you? I thought not. Imagine Robert's clear-cut, handsome face looking over my shoulder. Does not the apparition make vividly manifest the obtuse mould of my heavy traits? There!' (he started) 'I have been expecting that wire to vibrate this last half-hour.'

The dinner-bell rang, and Shirley rose.

'Mr Moore,' she said, as she gathered up her silks, 'have you heard from your brother lately? Do you know what he means by staying in town so long? Does he talk of returning?'

'He talks of returning; but what has caused his long absence I cannot tell. To speak the truth, I thought none in Yorkshire knew better than yourself why he was reluctant to come home.'

A crimson shadow passed across Miss Keeldar's cheek.

'Write to him, and urge him to come,' she said. 'I know there has been no impolicy in protracting his absence thus far: it is good to let the mill stand, while trade is so bad; but he must not abandon the county.'

'I am aware,' said Louis, 'that he had an interview with you the evening before he left, and I saw him quit Fieldhead afterwards. I read his countenance, or *tried* to read it. He turned from me. I divined that he would be long away. Some fine slight fingers have a wondrous knack at pulverizing a man's brittle pride. I suppose Robert put too much trust in his manly beauty and native gentlemanhood. Those are better off who, being destitute of advantage, cannot cherish delusion. But I will write, and say you advise his return.'

'Do not say *I* advise his return, but that his return is advisable.'

The second bell rang, and Miss Keeldar obeyed its call.

CHAPTER XXIX

LOUIS MOORE

Louis Moore was used to a quiet life: being a quiet man, he endured it better than most men would: having a large world of his own in his own head and heart, he tolerated confinement to a small, still corner of the real world very patiently.

How hushed is Fieldhead this evening! All but Moore – Miss Keeldar, the whole family of the Sympsons, even Henry – are gone to Nunnely. Sir Philip would have them come: he wished to make them acquainted with his mother and sisters, who are now at the Priory. Kind gentleman as the Baronet is, he asked the Tutor too; but the Tutor would much sooner have made an appointment with the ghost of the Earl of Huntingdon to meet him, and a shadowy ring of his merry men, under the canopy of the thickest, blackest, oldest oak in Nunnely Forest. Yes, he would rather have appointed tryst with a phantom abbess, or mist-pale nun, among the wet and weedy relics of that ruined sanctuary of theirs, mouldering in the core of the wood. Louis Moore longs to have something near him to-night: but not the boy-baronet, nor his benevolent but stern mother, nor his patrician sisters, nor one soul of the Sympsons.

This night is not calm: the equinox still struggles in its storms. The wild rains of the day are abated: the great single cloud disparts and rolls away from heaven, not passing and leaving a sea all sapphire, but tossed buoyant before a continued, long-sounding, high-rushing moonlight tempest. The Moon reigns glorious, glad of the gale; as glad as if she gave herself to his fierce caress with love. No Endymion will watch for his goddess to-night: there are no flocks out on the mountains; and it is well, for to-night she welcomes Æolus.

Moore – sitting in the school-room – heard the storm roar round the other gable, and along the hall-front: this end was sheltered. He wanted no shelter; he desired no subdued sounds, or screened position.

'All the parlours are empty,' said he: 'I am sick at heart of this cell.'

He left it, and went where the casements, larger and freer than the branch-screened lattice of his own apartment, admitted unimpeded the dark-blue, the silver-fleeced, the stirring and sweeping vision of the autumn night-sky. He carried no candle: unneeded was lamp or fire: the broad and clear, though cloud-crossed and fluctuating beam of the moon shone on every floor and wall.

Moore wanders through all the rooms: he seems following a phantom from parlour to parlour. In the oak-room he stops; this is not chill, and polished, and fireless like the salon: the hearth is hot and ruddy; the cinders tinkle in the intense heat of their clear glow; near the rug is a little worktable, a desk upon it, a chair near it.

Does the vision Moore has tracked occupy that chair? You would think so, could you see him standing before it. There is as much interest now in his eye, and as much significance in his face, as if in this household solitude he had found a living companion, and was going to speak to it.

He makes discoveries. A bag, a small satin bag, hangs on the chair-back. The desk is open, the keys are in the lock; a pretty seal, a silver pen, a crimson berry or two of ripe fruit on a green leaf, a small, clean, delicate glove – these trifles at once decorate and disarrange the stand they strew. Order forbids details in a picture: she puts them tidily away; but details give charm.

Moore spoke.

'Her mark,' he said: 'here she has been – careless, attractive thing! – called away in haste, doubtless, and forgetting to return and put all to rights. Why does she leave fascination in her foot-prints? Whence did she acquire the gift to be heedless, and never offend? There is always something to chide in her, and the reprimand never settles in displeasure on the heart; but, for her lover or her husband, when it had trickled a while in words, would naturally melt from his lips in a kiss. Better pass half an hour in remonstrating with her, than a day in admiring or praising any other woman alive. Am I muttering? – soliloquizing? Stop that.'

He did stop it. He stood thinking; and then he made an arrangement for his evening's comfort.

He dropped the curtains over the broad window and regal moon: he shut out Sovereign and Court and Starry Armies; he added fuel to the hot but fast-wasting fire; he lit a candle, of which there were a pair on the table; he placed another chair opposite that near the work-stand, and then he sat down. His next movement was to take from his pocket a small, thick book of blank paper; to produce a pencil; and to begin to write in a cramp, compact hand. Come near, by all means, reader: do not be shy: stoop over his shoulder fearlessly, and read as he scribbles.

'It is nine o'clock; the carriage will not return before eleven, I am certain. Freedom is mine till then: till then, I may occupy her room; sit opposite her chair; rest my elbow on her table; have her little mementos about me.

'I used rather to like Solitude – to fancy her a somewhat quiet and serious, yet fair nymph; an Oread, descending to me from lone mountain-passes; something of the blue mist of hills in her array, and of their chill breeze in her breath – but much, also, of their solemn beauty in her mien. I once could court her serenely, and imagine my heart easier when I held her to it – all mute, but majestic.

'Since that day I called S. to me in the school-room, and she came and sat so near my side; since she opened the trouble of her mind to me – asked my protection – appealed to my

strength: since that hour I abhor Solitude. Cold abstraction –
fleshless skeleton – daughter – mother – and mate of Death!

'It is pleasant to write about what is near and dear as the core
of my heart: none can deprive me of this little book, and
through this pencil, I can say to it what I will – say what I dare
utter to nothing living – say what I dare not *think* aloud.

'We have scarcely encountered each other since that evening.
Once, when I was alone in the drawing-room, seeing a book of
Henry's she entered, dressed for a concert at Stilbro'. Shyness –
her shyness, not mine – drew a silver veil between us. Much cant
have I heard and read about "maiden modesty;" but, properly
used, and not hackneyed, the words are good and appropriate
words: as she passed to the window, after tacitly but gracefully
recognising me, could call her nothing in my own mind save
"stainless virgin:" to my perception, a delicate splendour robed
her, and the modesty of girlhood was her halo. I may be the
most fatuitous, as I am one of the plainest, of men; but, in truth,
that shyness of hers touched me exquisitely: it flattered my finest
sensations. I looked a stupid block, I dare say: I was alive with a
life of Paradise, as she turned *her* glance from *my* glance, and
softly averted her head to hide the suffusion of her cheek.

'I know this is the talk of a dreamer – of a rapt, romantic
lunatic: I *do* dream: I *will* dream now and then; and if she
has inspired romance into my prosaic composition, how can
I help it?

'What a child she is sometimes! What an unsophisticated,
untaught thing! I see her now, looking up into my face, and
entreating me to prevent them from smothering her, and to be
sure and give her a strong narcotic: I see her confessing that she
was not so self-sufficing, so independent of sympathy, as people
thought: I see the secret tear drop quietly from her eyelash. She
said I thought her childish – and I did. She imagined I despised
her. – Despised her! it was unutterably sweet to feel myself at
once near her and above her: to be conscious of a natural right
and power to sustain her, as a husband should sustain his wife.

'I worship her perfections; but it is her faults, or at least her foibles, that bring her near to me – that nestle her to my heart – that fold her about with my love – and that for a most selfish, but deeply-natural reason: these faults are the steps by which I mount to ascendency over her. If she rose a trimmed, artificial mound, without inequality, what vantage would she offer the foot? It is the natural hill, with its mossy breaks and hollows, whose slope invites ascent – whose summit it is pleasure to gain.

'To leave metaphor. It delights my eye to look on her: she suits me: if I were a king, and she the housemaid that swept my palace-stairs – across all that space between us – my eye would recognise her qualities; a true pulse would beat for her in my heart, though an unspanned gulf made acquaintance impossible. If I were a gentleman, and she waited on me as a servant, I could not help liking that Shirley. Take from her her education – take her ornaments, her sumptuous dress – all extrinsic advantages – take all grace, but such as the symmetry of her form renders inevitable; present her to me at a cottage-door, in a stuff-gown; let her offer me there a draught of water, with that smile – with that warm goodwill with which she now dispenses manorial hospitality – I should like her. I should wish to stay an hour: I should linger to talk with that rustic. I should not feel as I *now* do: I should find in her nothing divine; but whenever I met the young peasant, it would be with pleasure – whenever I left her, it would be with regret.

'How culpably careless in her to leave her desk open, where I know she has money! In the lock hang the keys of all her repositories, of her very jewel-casket. There is a purse in that little satin bag: I see the tassel of silver beads hanging out. That spectacle would provoke my brother Robert: all her little failings would, I know, be a source of irritation to him; if they vex me, it is a most pleasurable vexation: I delight to find her at fault, and were I always resident with her, I am aware she would be no niggard in thus ministering to my enjoyment. She would just give me something to do; to rectify: a theme for my tutor-lectures. I never lecture Henry: never feel disposed to do so: if he does wrong, – and that is very seldom, dear excellent lad! – a word suffices: often I do no more than shake my head; but the moment her "minois mutin" meets my eye, expostulatory words crowd to my lips: from a taciturn man, I believe she would transform me into a talker. Whence comes the delight I take in that talk? It puzzles myself sometimes: the more crâne, malin, taquin is her mood, consequently the clearer occasion she gives me for disapprobation; the more I seek her, the better I like her. She is never wilder than when equipped in her habit and hat; never less manageable than when she and Zoë come in fiery from a race with the wind on the hills; and I confess it – to this mute page I may confess it – I have waited an hour in the court, for the chance of witnessing her return, and for the dearer chance of receiving her in my arms from the saddle. I have noticed (again, it is to this page only I would make the remark) that she will never permit any man but myself to render her that assistance. I have seen her politely decline Sir Philip Nunnely's aid: she is always mighty gentle with her young baronet; mighty tender of his feelings, forsooth, and of his very thin-skinned amour-propre: I have marked her haughtily reject Sam Wynne's. Now I know – my heart knows it, for it has felt it – that she resigns herself to me unreluctantly: is she conscious how my strength rejoices to serve her? I myself am not her slave – I declare it, – but my faculties gather to her beauty, like the genii to the glisten of the lamp. All my knowledge, all my prudence, all my calm, and all my power, stand in her presence humbly waiting a task. How glad they are when a mandate comes! What joy they take in the toil she assigns! Does she know it?

'I have called her careless: it is remarkable that her carelessness never compromises her refinement; indeed, through this very loophole of character, the reality, depth, genuineness of that refinement may be ascertained: a whole garment sometimes covers meagreness and malformation; through a rent sleeve, a fair round arm may be revealed. I have seen and handled many of her possessions, because they are frequently astray. I never saw anything that did not proclaim the lady: nothing sordid, nothing soiled; in one sense she is as scrupulous as, in another, she is unthinking: as a peasant girl, she would go ever trim and cleanly. Look at the pure kid of this little glove, – at the fresh, unsullied satin of the bag.

'What a difference there is between S. and that pearl C. H.! Caroline, I fancy, is the soul of conscientious punctuality and nice exactitude; she would precisely suit the domestic habits of a certain fastidious kinsman of mine: so delicate, dexterous, quaint, quick, quiet; all done to a minute, all arranged to a strawbreadth: she would suit Robert; but what could *I* do with anything so nearly faultless? *She* is my equal; poor as myself; she is certainly pretty: a little Raffaelle head hers; Raffaelle in feature, quite English in expression: all insular grace and purity; but where is there anything to alter, anything to endure, anything to reprimand, to be anxious about? There she is, a lilly of the valley, untinted, needing no tint. What change could improve her? What pencil dare to paint? *My* sweetheart, if I ever have one, must bear nearer affinity to the rose: a sweet, lively delight guarded with prickly peril. *My* wife, if I ever marry, must stir my great frame with a sting now and then: she must furnish use to her husband's vast mass patience. I was not made so enduring to be mated with a lamb: I should find more congenial responsibility in the charge of a young lioness or leopardess. I like few things sweet, but what are likewise pungent; few things bright, but what are likewise hot. I like the summer-day, whose sun makes fruit blush and corn blanch. Beauty is never so beautiful as when, if I tease it, it wreathes back on me with spirit. Fascination is never so imperial as when, roused and half-ireful, she threatens transformation to fierceness. I fear I should tire of the mute, monotonous innocence of the lamb; I should erelong feel as burdensome the nestling dove which never stirred in my bosom; but my patience would exult in stilling the flutterings and training the energies of the restless merlin. In managing the wild instincts of the scarce manageable "bête fauve," my powers would revel.

'Oh, my pupil! Oh, Peri! too mutinous for heaven – too innocent for hell! never shall I do more than see, and worship, and wish for thee. Alas! knowing I could make thee happy, will it be my doom to see thee possessed by those who have not that power?

'However kindly the hand – if it is feeble, it cannot bend Shirley; and she must be bent: it cannot curb her, and she must be curbed.

'Beware! Sir Philip Nunnely! I never see you walking or sitting at her side, and observe her lips compressed, or her brow knit, in resolute endurance of some trait of your character which she neither admires nor likes; in determined toleration of some weakness she believes atoned for by a virtue, but which annoys her, despite that belief: I never mark the grave glow of her face, the unsmiling sparkle of her eye, the slight recoil of her whole frame when you draw a little too near, and gaze a little too expressively, and whisper a little too warmly: I never witness these things, but I think of the fable of Semele reversed.

'It is not the daughter of Cadmus I see: nor do I realize her fatal longing to look on Jove in the majesty of his god-head. It is a priest of Juno that stands before me, watching late and lone at a shrine in an Argive temple. For years of solitary ministry, he has lived on dreams: there is divine madness upon him: he loves the idol he serves, and prays day and night that his frenzy may be fed, and that the Ox-eyed may smile on her votary. She has heard; she will be propitious. All Argos slumbers. The doors of the temple are shut: the priest waits at the altar.

'A shock of heaven and earth is felt – not by the slumbering city; only by that lonely watcher, brave and unshaken in his fanaticism. In the midst of silence, with no preluding sound, he is wrapt in sudden light. Through the roof – through the rent, wide-yawning, vast, white-blazing blue of heaven above, pours a wondrous descent – dread as the down-rushing of stars. He has, what he asked: withdraw – forbear to look – I am blinded. I hear in that fane an unspeakable sound – would that I could not hear it! I see an insufferable glory burning terribly between the pillars. Gods be merciful and quench it!

'A pious Argive enters to make an early offering in the cool dawn of morning. There was thunder in the night: the bolt fell here. The shrine is shivered: the marble pavement round, split and blackened. Saturnia's statue rises chaste, grand, untouched: at her feet, piled ashes lie pale. No priest remains: he who watched will be seen no more.

'There is the carriage! Let me lock up the desk and pocket the keys: she will be seeking them to-morrow: she will have to come to me. I hear her –

' "Mr Moore, have you seen my keys?"

'So she will say in her clear voice, speaking with reluctance, looking ashamed, conscious that this is the twentieth time of asking. I will tantalize her: keep her with me, expecting, doubting; and when I *do* restore them, it shall not be without a lecture. Here is the bag, too, and the purse; the glove – pen – seal. She shall wring them all out of me slowly and separately: only by confession, penitence, entreaty. I never can touch her hand, or a ringlet of her head, or a ribbon of her dress, but I will make privileges for myself: every feature of her face, her bright eyes, her lips, shall go through each change they know, for my pleasure: display each exquisite variety of glance and curve, to delight – thrill – perhaps, more hopelessly to enchain me. If I *must* be her slave, I will not lose my freedom for nothing.'

He locked the desk, pocketed all the property, and went.

CHAPTER XXX

RUSHEDGE, A CONFESSIONAL

EVERYBODY SAID it was high time for Mr Moore to return home: all Briarfield wondered at his strange absence, and Whinbury and Nunnely brought each its separate contribution of amazement.

Was it known why he stayed away? Yes: it was known twenty – forty times over; there being, at least, forty plausible reasons adduced to account for the unaccountable circumstance. Business, it was not – *that* the gossips agreed: he had achieved the business on which he departed long ago: his four ringleaders he had soon scented out and run down; he had attended their trial, heard their conviction and sentence, and seen them safely shipped prior to transportation.

This was known at Briarfield: the newspapers had reported it: the 'Stilbro' Courier' had given every particular, with amplifications. None applauded his perseverance or hailed his success; though the mill-owners were glad of it, trusting that the terrors of Law vindicated would henceforward paralyze the sinister valour of disaffection. Disaffection, however, was still heard muttering to himself. He swore ominous oaths over the drugged beer of alehouses, and drank strange toasts in fiery British gin.

One report affirmed that Moore *dared* not come to Yorkshire: he knew his life was not worth an hour's purchase, if he did.

'I'll tell him that,' said Mr Yorke, when his foreman mentioned the rumour; 'and if *that* does not bring him home full-gallop – nothing will.'

Either that or some other motive prevailed, at last, to recall him. He announced to Joe Scott the day he should arrive at Stilbro', desiring his hackney to be sent to the 'George' for his accommodation; and Joe Scott having informed Mr Yorke, that gentleman made it in his way to meet him.

It was market-day: Moore arrived in time to take his usual place at the market-dinner. As something of a stranger – and as a man of note and action – the assembled manufacturers received him with a certain distinction. Some – who in public would scarcely have dared to acknowledge his acquaintance, lest a little of the hate and vengeance laid up in store for him should perchance have fallen on them – in private hailed him as in some sort their champion. When the wine had circulated, their respect would have kindled to enthusiasm, had not Moore's unshaken nonchalance held it in a damp, low, smouldering state.

Mr Yorke – the permanent president of these dinners – witnessed his young friend's bearing with exceeding compla-cency. If one thing could stir his temper or excite his contempt more than another, it was to see a man befooled by flattery, or elate with popularity. If one thing smoothed, soothed, and charmed him especially, it was the spectacle of a public character incapable of relishing his publicity: *incapable*, I say; disdain would but have incensed – it was indifference that appeased his rough spirit.

Robert, leaning back in his chair, quiet and almost surly, while the clothiers and blanket-makers vaunted his prowess and rehearsed his deeds – many of them interspersing their flatteries with coarse invectives against the operative class – was a delectable sight for Mr Yorke. His heart tingled with the pleasing conviction that these gross eulogiums shamed Moore deeply, and made him half scorn himself and his work. On abuse, on reproach, on calumny, it is easy to smile; but painful indeed is the panegyric of those we condemn. Often had Moore gazed with a brilliant countenance over howling crowds from a hostile hustings: he had breasted the storm of unpopularity with gallant bearing and soul elate; but he drooped his head under the half-bred tradesmen's praise, and shrank chagrined before their congratulations.

Yorke could not help asking him how he liked his supporters, and whether he did not think they did honour to his cause. 'But it is a pity, lad,' he added, 'that you did not hang these four samples of the Unwashed. If you had managed *that* feat, the gentry here would have riven the horses out of the coach, yoked to a score of asses, and drawn you into Stilbro' like a conquering general.'

Moore soon forsook the wine, broke from the party, and took the road. In less than five minutes Mr Yorke followed him: they rode out of Stilbro' together.

It was early to go home, but yet it was late in the day: the last ray of the sun had already faded from the cloud-edges, and the October night was casting over the moorlands the shadow of her approach.

Mr Yorke – moderately exhilarated with his moderate libations, and not displeased to see young Moore again in Yorkshire, and to have him for his comrade during the long ride home – took the discourse much to himself. He touched briefly, but scoffingly, on the trials and the conviction; he passed thence to the gossip of the neighbourhood, and, erelong, he attacked Moore on his own personal concerns.

'Bob, I believe you are worsted; and you deserve it. All was smooth. Fortune had fallen in love with you: she had decreed you the first prize in her wheel – twenty thousand pounds: she only required that you should hold your hand out and take it. And what did you do? You called for a horse and rode a-hunting to Warwickshire. Your sweet-heart – Fortune, I mean – was perfectly indulgent. She said, "I'll excuse him: he's young." She waited like "Patience on a monument," till the chase was over, and the vermin-prey run down. She expected you would come back then, and be a good lad: you might still have had her first prize.

'It capped her beyond expression, and me too, to find that,

instead of thundering home in a breakneck gallop, and laying your assize-laurels at her feet, you coolly took coach up to London. What you have done there, Satan knows: nothing in this world, I believe, but sat and sulked: your face was never lily-fair, but it is olive-green now. You're not as bonnie as you were, man.'

'And who is to have this prize you talk so much about?'

'Only a baronet: that is all. I have not a doubt in my own mind you've lost her: she will be Lady Nunnely before Christmas.'

'Hem! Quite probable.'

'But she need not to have been. Fool of a lad! I swear you might have had her!'

'By what token, Mr Yorke?'

'By every token. By the light of her eyes, the red of her cheeks: red they grew when your name was mentioned, though of custom they are pale.'

'My chance is quite over, I suppose?'

'It ought to be; but try: it is worth trying. I call this Sir Philip milk and water. And then he writes verses, they say – tags rhymes. *You* are above that, Bob, at all events.'

'Would you advise me to propose, late as it is, Mr Yorke? at the eleventh hour?'

'You can but make the experiment, Robert. If she has a fancy for you – and, on my conscience, I believe she has, or had – she will forgive much. But, my lad, you are laughing: is it at me? You had better girn at your own perverseness. I see, however, you laugh at the wrong side of your mouth: you have as sour a look at this moment as one need wish to see.'

'I have so quarrelled with myself, Yorke. I have so kicked against the pricks, and struggled in a strait waistcoat, and dislocated my wrists with wrenching them in handcuffs, and battered my hard head, by driving it against a harder wall.'

'Ha! I'm glad to hear that. Sharp exercise yon'! I hope it has done you good; ta'en some of the self-conceit out of you?'

'Self-conceit! What is it? Self-respect, self-tolerance, even, what are they? Do you sell the articles? Do you know anybody who does? Give an indication: they would find in me a liberal chapman. I would part with my last guinea this minute to buy.'

'Is it so with you, Robert? I find that spicy. I like a man to speak his mind. What has gone wrong?'

'The machinery of all my nature; the whole enginery of this human mill: the boiler, which I take to be the heart, is fit to burst.'

'That suld be putten i' print: it's striking. It's almost blank verse. Ye'll be jingling into poetry just e' now. If the afflatus comes, give way, Robert; never heed me: I'll bear it this whet (time).'

'Hideous, abhorrent, base blunder! You may commit in a moment what you will rue for years – what life cannot cancel.'

'Lad, go on. I call it pie, nuts, sugar-candy. I like the taste uncommonly. Go on: it will do you good to talk: the moor is before us now, and there is no life for many a mile round.'

'I *will* talk. I am not ashamed to tell. There is a sort of wild cat in my breast, and I choose that you shall hear how it can yell.'

'To me it is music. What grand voices you and Louis have! When Louis sings – tones off like a soft, deep bell, I've felt myself tremble again. The night is still: it listens: it is just leaning down to you, like a black priest to a blacker penitent. Confess, lad: smooth naught down: be candid as a convicted, justified, sanctified methody at an experience-meeting. Make yourself as wicked as Beelzebub: it will ease your mind.'

'As mean as Mammon, you would say. Yorke, if I got off horseback and laid myself down across the road, would you have the goodness to gallop over me – backwards and forwards – about twenty times?'

'Wi' all the pleasure in life, if there were no such thing as a coroner inquest.'

'Hiram Yorke, I certainly believed she loved me. I have seen her eyes sparkle radiantly when she has found me out in a crowd: she has flushed up crimson when she has offered me her hand, and said, "How do you do, Mr Moore?"

'My name had a magical influence over her: when others uttered it, she changed countenance, – I know she did. She pronounced it herself in the most musical of her many musical tones. She was cordial to me; she took an interest in me; she was anxious about me; she wished me well; she sought, she seized every opportunity to benefit me. I considered, paused, watched, weighed, wondered: I could come to but one conclusion – this is love.

'I looked at her, Yorke: I saw, in her, youth and a species of beauty. I saw power in her. Her wealth offered me the redemption of my honour and my standing. I owed her gratitude. She had aided me substantially and effectually by a loan of five thousand pounds. Could I remember these things? Could I believe she loved me? Could I hear wisdom urge me to marry her, and disregard every dear advantage, disbelieve every flattering suggestion, disdain every well-weighed counsel, turn and leave her? Young, graceful, gracious, – my benefactress, attached to me, enamoured of me, – I used to say so to myself; dwell on the word; mouth it over and over again; swell over it with a pleasant, pompous complacency, – with an admiration dedicated entirely to myself, and unimpaired even by esteem for her; indeed, I smiled in deep secrecy at her naïveté and simplicity, in being the first to love, and to show it. That whip of yours seems to have a good heavy handle, Yorke: you can swing it about your head and knock me out of the saddle, if you choose. I should rather relish a loundering whack.'

'Tak' patience, Robert, till the moon rises, and I can see you. Speak plain out, – did you love her, or not? I could like to know: I feel curious.'

'Sir . . . Sir – I say – she is very pretty, in her own style, and very attractive. She has a look, at times, of a thing made out of fire and air, at which I stand and marvel, without a thought of clasping and kissing it. I felt in her a powerful magnet to my interest and vanity: I never felt as if nature meant her to be my other and better self. When a question on that head rushed upon me, I flung it off, saying brutally, I should be rich with her, and ruined without her: vowing I would be practical, and not romantic.'

'A very sensible resolve. What mischief came of it, Bob?'

'With this sensible resolve, I walked up to Fieldhead one night last August: it was the very eve of my departure for Birmingham – for – you see – I wanted to secure fortune's splendid prize: I had previously despatched a note, requesting a private inter-view. I found her at home, and alone.

'She received me without embarrassment, for she thought I came on business: *I* was embarrassed enough, but determined. I hardly know how I got the operation over; but I went to work in a hard, firm fashion, – frightful enough, I daresay. I sternly offered myself – my fine person – with my debts, of course, as a settlement.

'It vexed me; it kindled my ire, to find that she neither blushed, trembled, nor looked down. She responded: –

' "I doubt whether I have understood you, Mr Moore."

'And I had to go over the whole proposal twice, and word it as plainly as A B C, before she would fully take it in. And then, what did she do? Instead of faltering a sweet Yes, or maintaining a soft, confused silence (which would have been as good) she started up, walked twice fast through the room, in the way that *she* only does, and no other woman, and ejaculated, –

' "God bless me!" '

'Yorke, I stood on the hearth, backed by the mantelpiece; against it I leaned, and prepared for anything – everything. I knew my doom, and I knew myself. There was no misunder-standing her aspect and voice. She stopped and looked at me.

' "God bless me!" she pitilessly repeated, in that shocked, indignant, yet saddened accent. "You have made a strange pro-posal – strange from *you*: and if you knew how strangely you worded it, and looked it, you would be startled at yourself. You spoke like a brigand who demanded my purse, rather than like a lover who asked my heart."

'A queer sentence, was it not, Yorke? and I knew, as she uttered it, it was true as queer. Her words were a mirror in which I saw myself.

'I looked at her, dumb and wolfish: she at once enraged and shamed me.

' "Gérard Moore, you know you don't love Shirley Keeldar." I might have broken out into false swearing: vowed that I did love her; but I could not lie in her pure face: I could not perjure myself in her truthful presence. Besides, such hollow oaths would have been vain as void: she would no more have believed me than she would have believed the ghost of Judas, had he broken from the night and stood before her. Her female heart had finer perceptions than to be cheated into mistaking my half-coarse, half-cold admiration, for true-throbbing, manly love.

'What next happened? you will say, Mr Yorke.

'Why, she sat down in the window-seat and cried. She cried passionately: her eyes not only rained, but lightened. They flashed, open, large, dark, haughty, upon me: they said – "You have pained me: you have outraged me: you have deceived me."

'She added words soon to looks.

' "I *did* respect – I *did* admire – I *did* like you," she said: "yes – as much as if you were my brother: and *you* – *you* want to make a speculation of me. You would immolate me to that mill – your Moloch!"

'I had the common sense to abstain from any word of excuse – any attempt at palliation: I stood to be scorned.

'Sold to the devil for the time being, I was certainly infatuated: when I did speak, what do you think I said?

' "Whatever my own feelings were, I was persuaded *you* loved *me*, Miss Keeldar."

'Beautiful! – was it not? She sat quite confounded. "Is it Robert Moore that speaks?" I heard her mutter. "Is it a man – or something lower?"

' "Do you mean," she asked aloud – "do you mean you thought I loved you as we love those we wish to marry?"

'It *was* my meaning; and I said so.

' "You conceived an idea obnoxious to a woman's feelings," was her answer: "you have announced it in a fashion revolting to a woman's soul. You insinuate that all the frank kindness I have shown you has been a complicated, a bold, and an immodest manœuvre to ensnare a husband: you imply that at last you come here out of pity to offer me your hand, because I have courted you. Let me say this: – Your sight is jaundiced: you have seen wrong. Your mind is warped: you have judged wrong. Your tongue betrays you: you now speak wrong. I never loved you. Be at rest there. My heart is as pure of passion for you as yours is barren of affection for me."

'I hope I was answered, Yorke?

' "I seem to be a blind, besotted sort of person," was my remark.

' "*Loved* you!" she cried. "Why, I have been as frank with you as a sister – never shunned you – never feared you. You cannot, she affirmed, triumphantly – "you cannot make me tremble with your coming, nor accelerate my pulse by your influence."

'I alleged that often, when she spoke to me, she blushed, and that the sound of my name moved her.

' "Not for *your* sake!" she declared, briefly: I urged explanation, but could get none.

' "When I sat beside you at the school-feast, did you think I loved you then? When I stopped you in Maythorn-lane, did you think I loved you then? When I called on you in the counting-house – when I walked with you on the pavement – did you think I loved you then?"

'So she questioned me; and I said I did.

'By the Lord! Yorke – she rose – she grew tall – she expanded and refined almost to flame: there was a trembling all through her, as in live coal, when its vivid vermilion is hottest.

' "That is to say, that you have the worst opinion of me: that you deny me the possession of all I value most. That is to say, that I am a traitor to all my sisters: that I have acted as no woman can act, without degrading herself and her sex: that I have sought where the incorrupt of my kind naturally scorn and abhor to seek." She and I were silent, for many a minute. "Lucifer – Star of the Morning!" she went on, "thou art fallen. You – once high in my esteem – are hurled down: you – once intimate in my friendship – are cast out. Go!"

'I went not: I had heard her voice tremble – seen her lip quiver: I knew another storm of tears would fall; and then, I believed, some calm and some sunshine must come, and I would wait for it.

'As fast, but more quietly than before, the warm rain streamed down: there was another sound in her weeping – a softer, more regretful sound. While I watched, her eyes lifted to me a gaze more reproachful than haughty – more mournful than incensed.

' "Oh, Moore!" said she: "it was worse than Et tu, Brute!"

'I relieved myself by what should have been a sigh, but it became a groan. A sense of Cain-like desolation made my breast ache.

' "There has been error in what I have done," I said, "and it has won me bitter wages; which I will go and spend far from her who gave them."

'I took my hat. All the time, I could not have borne to depart so; and I believed she would not let me. Nor would she, but for the mortal pang I had given her pride, that cowed her compassion and kept her silent.

'I was obliged to turn back of my own accord when I reached the door, to approach her and to say, "Forgive me."

' "I could, if there was not myself to forgive, too," was her reply; "but to mislead a sagacious man so far, I must have done wrong."

'I broke out suddenly with some declamation I do not remember: I know that it was sincere, and that my wish and aim were to absolve her to herself: in fact, in her case, self-accusation was a chimera.

'At last, she extended her hand. For the first time I wished to take her in my arms and kiss her. I *did* kiss her hand many times.

' "Some day we shall be friends again," she said, "when you have had time to read my actions and motives in a true light, and not so horribly to misinterpret them. Time may give you the right key to all: then, perhaps, you will comprehend me; and then we shall be reconciled."

'Farewell drops rolled slow down her cheeks: she wiped them away.

' "I am sorry for what has happened – deeply sorry," she sobbed. So was I, God knows! Thus were we severed.'

'A queer tale!' commented Mr Yorke.

'I'll do it no more,' vowed his companion: 'never more will I mention marriage to a woman, unless I feel love. Henceforth, Credit and Commerce may take care of themselves. Bankruptcy may come when it lists. I have done with slavish fear of disaster. I mean to work diligently, wait patiently, bear steadily. Let the worst come – I will take an axe and an emigrant's berth, and go out with Louis to the West – he and I have settled it. No woman shall ever again look at me as Miss Keeldar looked – ever again feel towards me as Miss Keeldar felt: in no woman's presence will I ever again stand at once such a fool and such a knave – such a brute and such a puppy.'

'Tut!' said the imperturbable Yorke, 'you make too much of it; but still, I say, I am capped: firstly, that she did not love you; and, secondly, that you did not love her. You are both young; you are both handsome; you are both well enough for wit, and even for temper – take you on the right side: what ailed you, that you could not agree?'

'We never *have* been – never *could* be *at home* with each other, Yorke. Admire each other as we might at a distance, still we jarred when we came very near. I have sat at one side of a room

and observed her at the other; perhaps in an excited, genial
moment, when she had some of her favourites round her – her
old beaux, for instance, yourself and Helstone, with whom she
is so playful, pleasant, and eloquent. I have watched her when
she was most natural, most lively, and most lovely; my judgment
has pronounced her beautiful: beautiful she is, at times, when
her mood and her array partake of the splendid. I have drawn a
little nearer, feeling that our terms of acquaintance gave me the
right of approach; I have joined the circle round her seat, caught
her eye, and mastered her attention; then we have conversed;
and others – thinking me, perhaps, peculiarly privileged – have
withdrawn by degrees, and left us alone. Were we happy thus
left? For myself, I must say, No. Always a feeling of constraint
came over me; always I was disposed to be stern and strange.
We talked politics and business: no soft sense of domestic intimacy ever opened our hearts, or thawed our language, and made
it flow easy and limpid. If we had confidences, they were confidences of the counting-house, not of the hearth. Nothing in her
cherished affection in me – made me better, gentler: she only
stirred my brain and whetted my acuteness: she never crept into
my heart or influenced its pulse; and for this good reason, no
doubt, because I had not the secret of making her love me.'

'Well, lad, it is a queer thing. I might laugh at thee, and reckon
to despise thy refinements; but as it is dark night and we are by
ourselves, I don't mind telling thee that thy talk brings back a
glimpse of my own past life. Twenty-five years ago, I tried to
persuade a beautiful woman to love me, and she would not. I had
not the key to her nature: she was a stone wall to me, doorless
and windowless.'

'But you loved *her*, Yorke: you worshipped Mary Cave: your
conduct, after all, was that of a man – never of a fortune-hunter.'

'Ay! I *did* love her; but then she was beautiful as the moon
we do *not* see to-night: there is naught like her in these days:
Miss Helstone, maybe, has a look of her, but nobody else.'

'Who has a look of her?'

'That black-coated tyrant's niece; that quiet, delicate Miss Helstone. Many a time I have put on my spectacles to look at the lassie in church, because she has gentle blue een, wi' long lashes; and, when she sits in shadow, and is very still and very pale, and is, happen, about to fall asleep wi' the length of the sermon and the heat of the biggin' – she is as like one of Canova's marbles as aught else.'

'Was Mary Cave in that style?'

'Far grander! Less lass-like and flesh-like. You wondered why she hadn't wings and a crown. She was a stately, peaceful angel – was my Mary.'

'And you could not persuade her to love you?'

'Not with all I could do; though I prayed Heaven many a time, on my bended knees, to help me.'

'Mary Cave was not what you think her, Yorke – I have seen her picture at the Rectory. She is no angel, but a fair, regular-featured, taciturn-looking woman – rather too white and lifeless for my taste. But – supposing she had been something better than she was –'

'Robert,' interrupted Yorke, 'I could fell you off your horse at this moment. However, I'll hold my hand. Reason tells me you are right, and I am wrong. I know well enough that the passion I still have is only the remnant of an illusion. If Miss Cave had possessed either feeling or sense, she could not have been so perfectly impassible to my regard as she showed herself – she must have preferred me to that copper-faced despot.'

'Supposing, Yorke, she had been educated (no women were educated in those days); supposing she had possessed a thoughtful, original mind, a love of knowledge, a wish for information, which she took an artless delight in receiving from your lips, and having measured out to her by your hand; supposing her conversation – when she sat at your side – was fertile, varied, imbued with a picturesque grace and genial interest, quiet-flowing but clear and bounteous; supposing that when you stood near her by chance, or when you sat near her by design, comfort at once became your atmosphere, and content your element; supposing that whenever her face was under your gaze, or her idea filled your thoughts, you gradually ceased to be hard and anxious, and pure affection, love of home, thirst for sweet discourse, unselfish longing to protect and cherish, replaced the sordid, cankering calculations of your trade; supposing – with all this – that many a time, when you had been so happy as to possess your Mary's little hand, you had felt it tremble as you held it – just as a warm little bird trembles when you take it from its nest; supposing you had noticed her shrink into the background on your entrance into a room, yet if you sought her in her retreat she welcomed you with the sweetest smile that ever lit a fair virgin face, and only turned her eyes from the encounter of your own, lest their clearness should reveal too much; supposing, in short, your Mary had been – not cold, but modest; not vacant, but reflective; not obtuse, but sensitive; not inane, but innocent; not prudish, but pure – would you have left her to court another woman for her wealth?'

Mr Yorke raised his hat, wiped his forehead with his handkerchief.

'The moon is up,' was his first not quite relevant remark, pointing with his whip across the moor. 'There she is, rising into the haze, staring at us wi' a strange red glower. She is no more silver than old Helstone's brow is ivory. What does she mean by leaning her cheek on Rushedge i' that way, and looking at us wi' a scowl and a menace?'

'Yorke, if Mary had loved you silently, yet faithfully – chastely, yet fervently – as you would wish your wife to love, would you have left her?'

'Robert!' he lifted his arm: he held it suspended, and paused. 'Robert! this is a queer world, and men are made of the queerest dregs that Chaos churned up in her ferment. I might swear sounding oaths – oaths that would make the poachers think there was a bittern booming in Bilberry Moss – that, in the case you put, Death only should have parted me from Mary. But

I have lived in the world fifty-five years; I have been forced to study human nature; and – to speak a dark truth – the odds are, if Mary had loved and not scorned me; if I had been secure of her affection, certain of her constancy, been irritated by no doubts, stung by no humiliations – the odds are' (he let his hand fall heavy on the saddle) – 'the odds are, I should have left her!'

They rode side by side in silence. Ere either spoke again, they were on the other side of Rushedge: Briarfield lights starred the purple skirt of the moor. Robert, being the youngest, and having less of the past to absorb him than his comrade, recommenced first.

'I believe – I daily find it proved – that we can get nothing in this world worth keeping, not so much as a principle or a conviction, except out of purifying flame, or through strengthening peril. We err; we fall; we are humbled – then we walk more carefully. We greedily eat and drink poison out of the gilded cup of vice, or from the beggar's wallet of avarice; we are sickened, degraded; everything good in us rebels against us; our souls rise bitterly indignant against our bodies; there is a period of civil war; if the soul has strength, it conquers and rules thereafter.'

'What art thou going to do now, Robert? What are thy plans?'

'For my private plans, I'll keep them to myself; which is very easy, as at present I have none: no private life is permitted a man in my position, a man in debt. For my public plans, my views are a little altered. While I was in Birmingham, I looked a little into reality, considered closely, and at their source, the causes of the present troubles of this country; I did the same in London. Unknown, I could go where I pleased, mix with whom I would. I went where there was want of food, of fuel, of clothing; where there was no occupation and no hope. I saw some, with naturally elevated tendencies and good feelings, kept down amongst sordid privations and harassing griefs. I saw many originally low, and to whom lack of education left scarcely anything but animal wants, disappointed in those wants, ahungered, athirst, and desperate as famished animals: I saw what taught my brain a new lesson, and filled my breast with fresh feelings. I have no intention to profess more softness or sentiment than I have hitherto professed; mutiny and ambition I regard as I have always regarded them: I should resist a riotous mob just as heretofore: I should open on the scent of a runaway ringleader as eagerly as ever, and run him down as relentlessly, and follow him up to condign punishment as rigorously; but I should do it now chiefly for the sake and the security of those he misled. Something there is to look to, Yorke, beyond a man's personal interest: beyond the advancement of well-laid schemes; beyond even the discharge of dishonouring debts. To respect himself, a man must believe he renders justice to his fellow-men. Unless I am more considerate to ignorance, more forbearing to suffering, than I have hitherto been, I shall scorn myself as grossly unjust. What now?' he said, addressing his horse, which, hearing the ripple of water, and feeling thirsty, turned to a way-side trough, where the moonbeam was playing in a crystal eddy.

'Yorke,' pursued Moore, 'ride on: I must let him drink.'

Yorke accordingly rode slowly forwards, occupying himself. as he advanced, in discriminating, amongst the many lights now spangling the distance, those of Briarmains. Stilbro' Moor was left behind; plantations rose dusk on either hand; they were descending the hill; below them lay the valley with its populous parish: they felt already at home.

Surrounded no longer by heath, it was not startling to Mr Yorke to see a hat rise, and to hear a voice speak behind the wall. The words, however, were peculiar.

'When the wicked perisheth, there is shouting,' it said; and added, 'As the whirlwind passeth, so is the wicked no more (with a deeper growl); terrors take hold of him as waters; hell is naked before him. He shall die without knowledge.'

A fierce flash and sharp crack violated the calm of night. Yorke, ere he turned, knew the four convicts of Birmingham were avenged.

CHAPTER XXXI

UNCLE AND NIECE

THE DIE WAS CAST. Sir Philip Nunnely knew it: Shirley knew it: Mr Sympson knew it. That evening, when all the Fieldhead family dined at Nunnely Priory, decided the business.

Two or three things conduced to bring the baronet to a point. He had observed that Miss Keeldar looked pensive and delicate. This new phase in her demeanour smote him on his weak or poetic side: a spontaneous sonnet brewed in his brain; and while it was still working there, one of his sisters persuaded his ladye-love to sit down to the piano and sing a ballad – one of Sir Philip's own ballads. It was the least elaborate, the least affected – out of all comparison the best of his numerous efforts.

It chanced that Shirley, the moment before, had been gazing from a window down on the park; she had seen that stormy moonlight which 'le Professeur Louis' was, perhaps, at the same instant contemplating from her own oak-parlour lattice; she had seen the isolated trees of the domain – broad, strong, spreading oaks, and high-towering heroic beeches – wrestling with the gale. Her ear had caught the full roar of the forest lower down; the swift rushing of clouds, the moon, to the eye, hasting swifter still, had crossed her vision: she turned from sight and sound – touched, if not rapt – wakened, if not inspired.

She sang, as requested. There was much about love in the ballad: faithful love that refused to abandon its object; love that disaster could not shake; love that, in calamity, waxed fonder, in poverty clung closer. The words were set to a fine old air – in themselves they were simple and sweet: perhaps, when read, they wanted force; when *well* sung, they wanted nothing. Shirley sang them well: she breathed into the feeling, softness; she poured round the passion, force: her voice was fine that evening; its expressions dramatic: she impressed all, and charmed one.

On leaving the instrument, she went to the fire, and sat down on a seat – semi-stool, semi-cushion: the ladies were round her – none of them spoke. The Misses Sympson and the Misses Nunnely looked upon her, as quiet poultry might look on an egret, an ibis, or any other strange fowl. What made her sing so? *They* never sang so. Was it *proper* to sing with such expression, with such originality – so unlike a school-girl? Decidedly not: it was strange; it was unusual. What was *strange* must be *wrong*; what was *unusual* must be *improper*. Shirley was judged.

Moreover, old Lady Nunnely eyed her stonily from her great chair by the fireside: her gaze said, –

'This woman is not of mine or my daughters' kind: I object to her as my son's wife.'

Her son catching the look, read its meaning: he grew alarmed: what he so wished to win, there was danger he might lose. He must make haste.

The room they were in had once been a picture-gallery. Sir Philip's father – Sir Monckton – had converted it into a saloon; but still it had a shadowy, long-withdrawing look. A deep recess with a window – a recess that held one couch, one table, and a fairy cabinet, formed a room within a room. Two persons standing there might interchange a dialogue, and, so it were neither long nor loud, none be the wiser.

Sir Philip induced two of his sisters to perpetrate a duet; he gave occupation to the Misses Sympson: the elder ladies were conversing together. He was pleased to remark that, meantime, Shirley rose to look at the pictures. He had a tale to tell about one ancestress, whose dark beauty seemed as that of a flower of the south: he joined her, and began to tell it.

There were mementos of the same lady in the cabinet adorning the recess; and while Shirley was stooping to examine the missal and the rosary on the inlaid shelf, and while the Misses

Nunnely indulged in a prolonged screech, guiltless of expression, pure of originality, perfectly conventional and absolutely unmeaning, Sir Philip stooped too, and whispered a few hurried sentences. At first, Miss Keeldar was struck so still, you might have fancied that whisper a charm which had changed her to a statue; but she presently looked up and answered. They parted. Miss Keeldar returned to the fire, and resumed her seat: the baronet gazed after her, then went and stood behind his sisters. Mr Sympson – Mr Sympson only – had marked the pantomime.

That gentleman drew his own conclusions. Had he been as acute as he was meddling, as profound as he was prying, he might have found that in Sir Philip's face whereby to correct his inference. Ever shallow, hasty, and positive he went home quite cock-a-hoop.

He was not a man that kept secrets well: when elate on a subject, he could not avoid talking about it. The next morning, having occasion to employ his son's tutor as his secretary, he must needs announce to him, in mouthing accents, and with much flimsy pomp of manner, that he had better hold himself prepared for a return to the south, at an early day, as the important business which had detained him (Mr Sympson) so long in Yorkshire, was now on the eve of fortunate completion: his anxious and laborious efforts were likely, at last, to be crowned with the happiest success: a truly eligible addition was about to be made to the family connexions.

'In Sir Philip Nunnely?' Louis Moore conjectured.

Whereupon Mr Sympson treated himself simultaneously to a pinch of snuff and a chuckling laugh, checked only by a sudden choke of dignity, and an order to the tutor to proceed with business.

For a day or two, Mr Sympson continued as bland as oil; but also he seemed to sit on pins, and his gait, when he walked, emulated that of a hen treading a hot girdle. He was for ever looking out of the window, and listening for chariot-wheels: Bluebeard's wife – Sisera's mother – were nothing to him. He waited when the matter should be opened in form; when himself should be consulted; when lawyers should be summoned; when settlement discussions, and all the delicious worldly fuss, should pompously begin.

At last there came a letter; he himself handed it to Miss Keeldar out of the bag: he knew the handwriting; he knew the crest on the seal. He did not see it opened and read, for Shirley took it to her own room; nor did he see it answered, for she wrote her reply shut up, and was very long about it, – the best part of a day. He questioned her whether it was answered; she responded, 'Yes.'

Again he waited – waited in silence – absolutely not daring to speak: kept mute by something in Shirley's face, – a very awful something – inscrutable to him as the writing on the wall to Belshazzar. He was moved more than once to call Daniel, in the person of Louis Moore, and to ask an interpretation; but his dignity forbade the familiarity. Daniel himself, perhaps, had his own private difficulties connected with that baffling bit of translation: he looked like a student for whom grammars are blank, and dictionaries dumb.

Mr Sympson had been out, to while away an anxious hour in the society of his friends at De Walden Hall. He returned a little sooner than was expected; his family and Miss Keeldar were assembled in the oak-parlour; addressing the latter, he requested her to step with him into another room: he wished to have with her a '*strictly* private interview.'

She rose, asking no questions, and professing no surprise.

'Very well, sir,' she said in the tone of a determined person, who is informed that the dentist is come to extract that large double tooth of his, from which he has suffered such a purgatory this month past. She left her sewing and her thimble in the window-seat, and followed her uncle where he led.

Shut into the drawing-room, the pair took seats, each in an arm-chair, placed opposite, a few yards between them.

'I have been to De Walden Hall,' said Mr Sympson. He paused. Miss Keeldar's eyes were on the pretty white and green carpet. *That* information required no response: she gave none.

'I have learned,' he went on, slowly, – 'I have learned a circumstance which surprises me.'

Resting her cheek on her forefinger, she waited to be told what circumstance.

'It seems that Nunnely Priory is shut up; that the family are gone back to their place in —shire. It seems that the baronet – that the baronet – that Sir Philip himself has accompanied his mother and sisters.'

'Indeed!' said Shirley.

'May I ask if you share the amazement with which I received this news?'

'No, sir.'

'*Is* it news to you?'

'Yes, sir.'

'I mean – I mean –' pursued Mr Sympson, now fidgeting in his chair, quitting his hitherto brief and tolerably clear phraseology, and returning to his customary wordy, confused, irritable style; 'I mean to have a *thorough* explanation. I will *not* be put off. I – I – shall *insist* on being heard; and on – on having my own way. My questions *must* be answered. I will have clear, satisfactory replies. I am not to be trifled with. Silence!

'It is a strange and an extraordinary thing – a very singular – a most odd thing! I thought all was right: knew no other: and there – the family are gone!'

'I suppose, sir, they had a right to go.'

'*Sir Philip is gone!*' (with emphasis).

Shirley raised her brows: 'Bon voyage!' said she.

'This will not do: this must be altered, ma'am.'

He drew his chair forward; he pushed it back; he looked perfectly incensed, and perfectly helpless.

'Come, come, now, uncle,' expostulated Shirley, 'do not begin to fret and fume, or we shall make no sense of the business.

Ask me what you want to know: I am as willing to come to an explanation as you: I promise you truthful replies.'

'I want – I demand to know, Miss Keeldar, whether Sir Philip has made you an offer?'

'He has.'

'You avow it?'

'I avow it. But now, go on: consider that point settled.'

'He made you an offer that night we dined at the Priory?'

'It is enough to say that he made it. Go on.'

'He proposed in the recess – in the room that used to be a picture-gallery – that Sir Monckton converted into a saloon?'

No answer.

'You were both examining a cabinet: I saw it all: my sagacity was not at fault – it never is. Subsequently, you received a letter from him. On what subject – of what nature were the contents?'

'No matter.'

'Ma'am, is that the way in which you speak to me?'

Shirley's foot tapped quick on the carpet.

'There you sit, silent and sullen – *you* who promised truthful replies!'

'Sir, I have answered you thus far: proceed.'

'I should like to see that letter.'

'You *cannot* see it.'

'I *must* and *shall*, ma'am. I am your guardian.'

'Having ceased to be a ward, I have no guardian.'

'Ungrateful being! Reared by me as my own daughter –'

'Once more, uncle, have the kindness to keep to the point. Let us both remain cool. For my part, I do not wish to get into a passion; but, you know, once drive me beyond certain bounds, I care little what I say: I am not then soon checked. Listen! You have asked me whether Sir Philip made me an offer: that question is answered. What do you wish to know next?'

'I desire to know whether you accepted or refused him? and know it I will.'

'Certainly: you ought to know it. I refused him.'

'Refused him! You – *you*. Shirley Keeldar, *refused* Sir Philip Nunnely?'

'I did.'

The poor gentleman bounced from his chair, and first rushed, and then trotted, through the room.

'There it is! There it is! There it is!'

'Sincerely speaking, I am sorry, uncle, you are so disappointed.'

Concession – contrition – never do any good with some people. Instead of softening and conciliating, they but embolden and harden them: of that number was Mr Sympson.

'*I* disappointed! What is it to me? Have *I* an interest in it? You would insinuate, perhaps, that I have motives?'

'Most people have motives, of some sort, for their actions.'

'She accuses me to my face! I – that have been a parent to her – she charges with bad motives!'

'*Bad* motives, I did not say.'

'And now you prevaricate. You have no principles!'

'Uncle, you tire me: I want to go away.'

'Go you shall not! I will be answered. What are your intentions, Miss Keeldar?'

'In what respect?'

'In respect of matrimony.'

'To be quiet – and to do just as I please.'

'Just as you please! The words are to the last degree indecorous.'

'My Sympson, I advise you not to become insulting: you know I will not bear that.'

'You read French. Your mind is poisoned with French novels. You have imbibed French principles.'

'The ground you are treading now returns a mighty hollow sound under your feet. Beware!'

'It will end in infamy, sooner or later: I have foreseen it all along.'

'Do you assert, sir, that something in which *I* am concerned will end in infamy?'

'That it will – that it will. You said just now you would act as you please. You acknowledge no rules – no limitations.'

'Silly stuff! and vulgar as silly!'

'Regardless of decorum, you are prepared to fly in the face of propriety.'

'You tire me, uncle.'

'What, madam – *what* could be your reasons for refusing Sir Philip?'

'At last, there is another sensible question: I shall be glad to reply to it. Sir Philip is too young for me: I regard him as a boy: all his relations – his mother especially – would be annoyed if he married me: such a step would embroil him with them: I am not his equal in the world's estimation.'

'Is that all?'

'Our dispositions are not compatible.'

'Why, a more amiable gentleman never breathed.'

'He is very amiable – very excellent – truly estimable, but *not my master*: not in one point. I could not trust myself with his happiness: I would not undertake the keeping of it for thousands: I will accept no hand which cannot hold me in check.'

'I thought you liked to do as you please: you are vastly inconsistent.'

'When I promise to obey, it shall be under the conviction that I can keep that promise: I could not obey a youth like Sir Philip. Besides, he would never command me: he would expect me always to rule – to guide, and I have no taste whatever for the office.'

'*You* no taste for swaggering, and subduing, and ordering, and ruling?'

'Not my husband: only my uncle,'

'Where is the difference?'

'There *is* a slight difference: that is certain. And I know full well, any man who wishes to live in decent comfort with me as a husband must be able to control me.'

'I wish you had a real tyrant.'

'A tyrant would not hold me for a day – not for an hour. I would rebel – break from him – defy him.'

'Are you not enough to bewilder one's brain with your self-contradiction?'

'It is evident I bewilder your brain.'

'You talk of Sir Philip being young: he is two-and-twenty.'

'My husband must be thirty, with the sense of forty.'

'You had better pick out some old man – some white-headed or bald-headed swain.'

'No, thank you.'

'You could lead some doting fool: you might pin him to your apron.'

'I might do that with a boy: but it is not my vocation. Did I not say I prefer a *master*? One in whose presence I shall feel obliged and disposed to be good. One whose control my impatient temper must acknowledge. A man whose approbation can reward – whose displeasure punish me. A man I shall feel it impossible not to love, and very possible to fear.'

'What is there to hinder you from doing all this with Sir Philip? He is a baronet; a man of rank, property, connexions, far above yours. If you talk of intellect, he is a poet: he writes verses: which you, I take it, cannot do, with all your cleverness.'

'Neither his title, wealth, pedigree, nor poetry, avail to invest him with the power I describe. These are feather-weights: they want ballast: a measure of sound, solid practical sense would have stood him in better stead with me.'

'You and Henry rave about poetry: you used to catch fire like tinder on the subject when you were a girl.'

'Oh! uncle, there is nothing really valuable in this world, there is nothing glorious in the world to come, that is not poetry!'

'Marry a poet then, in God's name!'

'Show him me, and I will.'

'Sir Philip.'

'Not at all. You are almost as good a poet as he.'

'Madam, you are wandering from the point.'

'Indeed, uncle, I wanted to do so; and I shall be glad to lead you away with me. Do not let us get out of temper with each other: it is not worth while.'

'Out of temper, Miss Keeldar! I should be glad to know who is out of temper?'

'*I* am not, yet.'

'If you mean to insinuate that *I* am, I consider that you are guilty of impertinence.'

'You will be soon, if you go on at that rate.'

'There it is! With your pert tongue, you would try the patience of a Job.'

'I know I should.'

'No levity, Miss! This is not a laughing matter. It is an affair I am resolved to probe thoroughly, convinced that there is mischief at the bottom. You described just now, with far too much freedom for your years and sex, the sort of individual you would prefer as a husband. – Pray, did you paint from the life?'

Shirley opened her lips; but instead of speaking she only glowed rose-red.

'I shall have an answer to that question,' affirmed Mr Sympson, assuming vast courage and consequence on the strength of this symptom of confusion.

'It was an historical picture, uncle, from several originals.'

'Several originals! Bless my heart!'

'I have been in love several times.'

'This is cynical.'

'With heroes of many nations.'

'What next –?'

'And philosophers.'

'She is mad –'

'Don't ring the bell, uncle; you will alarm my aunt.'

'Your poor dear aunt, what a niece has she!'

'Once I loved Socrates.'

'Pooh! No trifling, ma'am.'

'I admired Themistocles, Leonidas, Epaminondas.'

'Miss Keeldar –'

'To pass over a few centuries, Washington was a plain man, but I liked him: but, to speak of the actual present –'

'Ah! the actual present.'

'To quit crude school-girl fancies, and come to realities.'

'Realities! That is the test to which you shall be brought, ma'am.'

'To avow before what altar I now kneel – to reveal the present idol of my soul –'

'You will make haste about it, if you please; it is near luncheon time, and confess *you shall.*'

'Confess, I must: my heart is full of the secret; it must be spoken: I only wish you were Mr Helstone instead of Mr Sympson, you would sympathize with me better.'

'Madam – it is a question of common sense and common prudence, not of sympathy and sentiment, and so on. Did you say it was Mr Helstone?'

'Not precisely, but as near as may be: they are rather alike.'

'I will know the name – I will have particulars.'

'They positively *are* rather alike; their very faces are not dissimilar – a pair of human falcons – and dry, direct, decided both. But my hero is the mightier of the two: his mind has the clearness of the deep sea, the patience of its rocks, the force of its billows.'

'Rant and fustian!'

'I daresay he can be harsh as a saw-edge, and gruff as a hungry raven.'

'Miss Keeldar, does the person reside in Briarfield? answer me that.'

'Uncle – I am going to tell you – his name is trembling on my tongue.'

'Speak, girl!'

'That was well said, uncle. "Speak, girl!" it is quite tragic. England has howled savagely against this man, uncle; and she will one day roar exultingly over him. He has been unscared by the howl, and he will be unelated by the shout.'

'I said she was mad – she is.'

'This country will change and change again in her demeanour to him: he will never change in his duty to her. Come, cease to chafe, uncle, I 'll tell you his name.'

'You shall tell me, or –'

'Listen! Arthur Wellesley, Lord Wellington.'

Mr Sympson rose up furious: he bounced out of the room, but immediately bounced back again, shut the door, and resumed his seat.

'Ma'am you *shall* tell me *this*: will your principles permit you to marry a man without money – a man below you?'

'Never a man below me.'

(In a high voice.) 'Will you, Miss Keeldar, marry a poor man?'

'What right have you, Mr Sympson, to ask me?'

'I insist upon knowing.'

'You don't go the way to know.'

'My family respectability shall not be compromised.'

'A good resolution: keep it.'

'Madam, it is you who shall keep it.'

'Impossible, sir, since I form no part of your family.'

'Do you disown us?'

'I disdain your dictatorship.'

'Whom *will* you marry, Miss Keeldar?'

'Not Mr Sam Wynne, because I scorn him: not Sir Philip Nunnely, because I *only* esteem him.'

'Whom have you in your eye?'

'Four rejected candidates.'

'Such obstinacy could not be, unless you were under improper influence.'

'What do you mean? There are certain phrases potent to

make my blood boil, – improper influence! What old woman's cackle is that?'

'Are you a young lady?'

'I am a thousand times better: I am an honest woman, and as such I will be treated.'

'Do you know (leaning mysteriously forward, and speaking with ghastly solemnity), do you know the whole neighbourhood teems with rumours respecting you and a bankrupt tenant of yours – the foreigner Moore?'

'Does it?'

'It does. Your name is in every mouth.'

'It honours the lips it crosses, and I wish to the gods it may purify them.'

'Is it *that* person who has power to influence you?'

'Beyond any whose cause you have advocated.'

'It is he you will marry?'

'He is handsome, and manly, and commanding.'

'You declare it to my face! The Flemish knave! The low trader!'

'He is talented, and venturous, and resolute. Prince is on his brow, and ruler in his bearing.'

'She glories in it! She conceals nothing! No shame, no fear!'

'When we speak the name of Moore, shame should be forgotten and fear discarded: the Moores know only honour and courage.'

'I say she is mad.'

'You have taunted me till my blood is up. You have worried me till I turn again.'

'That Moore is the brother of my son's tutor. Would you let the Usher call you Sister?'

Bright and broad shone Shirley's eye, as she fixed it on her questioner now.

'No: no. Not for a province of possession, – not for a century of life.'

'You cannot separate the husband from his family.'

'What then?'

'Mr Louis Moore's sister you will be.'

'Mr Sympson ... I am sick at heart with all this weak trash: I will bear no more. Your thoughts are not my thoughts, your aims are not my aims, your gods are not my gods. We do not view things in the same light; we do not measure them by the same standard; we hardly speak in the same tongue. Let us part.

'It is not,' she resumed, much excited, – 'It is not that I hate you; you are a good sort of man: perhaps you mean well in your way; but we cannot suit: we are ever at variance. You annoy me with small meddling, with petty tyranny; you exasperate my temper, and make and keep me passionate. As to your small maxims, your narrow rules, your little prejudices, aversions, dogmas, bundle them off: Mr Sympson – go, offer them a sacrifice to the deity you worship; I'll none of them: I wash my hands of the lot. I walk by another creed, light, faith, and hope, than you.'

'Another creed! I believe she is an infidel.'

'An infidel to *your* religion; an atheist to *your* god.'

'An – atheist!!!'

'Your god, sir, is the World. In my eyes, you too, if not an infidel, are an idolater. I conceive that you ignorantly worship: in all things you appear to me too superstitious. Sir, your god, your great Bel, your fish-tailed Dagon, rises before me as a demon. You, and such as you, have raised him to a throne, put on him a crown, given him a sceptre. Behold how hideously he governs! See him busied at the work he likes best – making marriages. He binds the young to the old, the strong to the imbecile. He stretches out the arm of Mezentius, and fetters the dead to the living. In his realm there is hatred – secret hatred: there is disgust – unspoken disgust: there is treachery – family treachery: there is vice – deep, deadly, domestic vice. In his dominions, children grow unloving between parents who have never loved: infants are nursed on deception from their very birth; they are reared in an atmosphere corrupt with lies. Your god rules at the bridal of kings – look at your royal dynasties! your deity is the deity of foreign aristocracies – analyze the blue blood of Spain! Your god is the Hymen of France – what is French domestic life? All that surrounds him hastens to decay: all declines and degenerates under his sceptre. *Your* god is a masked Death.'

'This language is terrible! My daughters and you must associate no longer, Miss Keeldar: there is danger in such companionship. Had I known you a little earlier – but, extraordinary as I thought you, I could not have believed –'

'Now, sir, do you begin to be aware that it is useless to scheme for me? That, in doing so, you but sow the wind to reap the whirlwind? I sweep your cobweb-projects from my path, that I may pass on unsullied. I am anchored on a resolve you cannot shake. My heart, my conscience shall dispose of my hand – *they only*. Know this at last.'

Mr Sympson was becoming a little bewildered.

'Never heard such language!' he muttered again and again. 'Never was so addressed in my life – never was so used.'

'You are quite confused, sir. You had better withdraw, or I will.'

He rose hastily.

'We must leave this place: they must pack up at once.'

'Do not hurry my aunt and cousins: give them time.'

'No more intercourse: she's not proper.'

He made his way to the door; he came back for his handkerchief; he dropped his snuff-box: leaving the contents scattered on the carpet, he stumbled out: Tartar lay outside across the mat – Mr Sympson almost fell over him: in the climax of his exasperation he hurled an oath at the dog, and a coarse epithet at his mistress.

'Poor Mr Sympson! He is both feeble and vulgar,' said Shirley to herself. 'My head aches, and I am tired,' she added; and leaning her head upon a cushion, she softly subsided from excitement to repose. One, entering the room a quarter of an hour afterwards, found her asleep. When Shirley had been agitated, she generally took this natural refreshment: it would come at her call.

The intruder paused in her unconscious presence, and said – 'Miss Keeldar.'

Perhaps his voice harmonized with some dream into which she was passing – it did not startle, it hardly roused her: without opening her eyes, she but turned her head a little, so that her cheek and profile, before hidden by her arm, became visible: she looked rosy, happy, half-smiling, but her eyelashes were wet; she had wept in slumber; or perhaps, before dropping asleep, a few natural tears had fallen after she had heard that epithet: no man – no woman is always strong, always able to bear up against the unjust opinion – the vilifying word: calumny, even from the mouth of a fool, will sometimes cut into unguarded feelings. Shirley looked like a child that had been naughty and punished, but was now forgiven and at rest.

'Miss Keeldar,' again said the voice: this time it woke her; she looked up and saw at her side Louis Moore – not close at her side, but standing, with arrested step, two or three yards from her.

'Oh, Mr Moore!' she said; 'I was afraid it was my uncle again: he and I have quarrelled.'

'Mr Sympson should let you alone,' was the reply: 'can he not see that you are as yet far from strong?'

'I assure you he did not find me weak: I did not cry when he was here.'

'He is about to evacuate Fieldhead – so he says. He is now giving orders to his family: he has been in the school-room issuing commands in a manner which, I suppose, was a continuation of that with which he has harassed you.'

'Are you and Henry to go?'

'I believe, as far as Henry is concerned, that was the tenor of his scarcely-intelligible directions; but he may change all to-morrow: he is just in that mood when you cannot depend on his consistency for two consecutive hours: I doubt whether he will leave you for weeks yet. To myself he addressed some words which will require a little attention and comment by-and-by, when I have time to bestow on them. At the moment he came in, I was busied with a note I had got from Mr Yorke – so fully busied that I cut short the interview with him somewhat abruptly: I left him raving: here is the note – I wish you to see it – it refers to my brother Robert.' And he looked at Shirley.

'I shall be glad to hear news of him: is he coming home?'

'He is come: he is in Yorkshire: Mr Yorke went yesterday to Stilbro' to meet him.'

'Mr Moore – something is wrong –?'

'Did my voice tremble? He is now at Briarmains – and I am going to see him.'

'What has occurred?'

'If you turn so pale I shall be sorry I have spoken. It might have been worse: Robert is not dead, but much hurt.'

'Oh! sir; it is you who are pale. Sit down near me.'

'Read the note – let me open it.'

Miss Keeldar read the note: it briefly signified that last night Robert Moore had been shot at from behind the wall of Milldean plantation, at the foot of the Brow; that he was wounded severely, but it was hoped not fatally: of the assassin, or assassins, nothing was known – they had escaped. 'No doubt,' Mr Yorke observed, 'it was done in revenge: it was a pity ill-will had ever been raised; but that could not be helped now.'

'He is my only brother,' said Louis, as Shirley returned the note. 'I cannot hear unmoved that ruffians have laid in wait for him, and shot him down like some wild beast from behind a wall.'

'Be comforted: be hopeful. He will get better – I know he will.'

Shirley, solicitous to soothe, held her hand over Mr Moore's, as it lay on the arm of the chair: she just touched it lightly, scarce palpably.

'Well, give me your hand,' he said; 'it will be for the first time: it is in a moment of calamity – give it me.'

Awaiting neither consent nor refusal, he took what he asked.

'I am going to Briarmains now,' he went on. 'I want you to step over to the Rectory, and tell Caroline Helstone what has happened: will you do this? she will hear it best from you.'

'Immediately,' said Shirley, with docile promptitude. 'Ought I to say that there is no danger?'

'Say so.'

'You will come back soon, and let me know more?'

'I will either come or write.'

'Trust me for watching over Caroline. I will communicate with your sister, too; but, doubtless, she is already with Robert?'

'Doubtless; or will be soon. Good-morning, now.'

'You will bear up, come what may?'

'We shall see that.'

Shirley's fingers were obliged to withdraw from the Tutor: Louis was obliged to relinquish that hand folded, clasped, hidden in his own.

'I thought I should have had to support her,' he said, as he walked towards Briarmains, 'and it is she who has made me strong. That look of pity – that gentle touch! No down was ever softer – no elixir more potent! It lay like a snow-flake: it thrilled like lightning. A thousand times I have longed to possess that hand – to have it in mine. I *have* possessed it – for five minutes I held it. Her fingers and mine can never be strangers more – having met once, they must meet again.'

CHAPTER XXXII

THE SCHOOLBOY AND THE WOOD-NYMPH

B RIARMAINS BEING nearer than the Hollow, Mr Yorke had conveyed his young comrade there. He had seen him laid in the best bed of the house, as carefully as if he had been one of his own sons. The sight of his blood, welling from the treacherously-inflicted wound, made him indeed the son of the Yorkshire gentleman's heart. The spectacle of the sudden event; of the tall, straight shape prostrated in its pride across the road; of the fine southern head laid low in the dust; of that youth in prime flung at once before him pallid, lifeless, helpless – this was the very combination of circumstances to win for the victim Mr Yorke's liveliest interest.

No other hand was there to raise – to aid; no other voice to question kindly; no other brain to concert measures: he had to do it all himself. This utter dependence of the speechless, bleeding youth (as a youth he regarded him) on his benevolence, secured that benevolence most effectually. Well did Mr Yorke like to have power, and to use it: he had now between his hands power over a fellow-creature's life: it suited him.

No less perfectly did it suit his saturnine better-half: the incident was quite in her way, and to her taste. Some women would have been terror-struck to see a gory man brought in over their threshold, and laid down in their hall in the 'howe of the night.' There, you would suppose, was subject-matter for hysterics. No: Mrs Yorke went into hysterics when Jessie would not leave the garden to come to her knitting, or when Martin proposed starting for Australia, with a view to realize freedom, and escape the tyranny of Matthew; but an attempted murder near her door – a half-murdered man in her best bed – set her straight, cheered her spirits, gave her cap the dash of a turban.

Mrs Yorke was just the woman who, while rendering miserable the drudging life of a simple maid-servant, would nurse like a heroine an hospital full of plague patients. She almost loved Moore: her tough heart almost yearned towards him, when she found him committed to her charge, – left in her arms, as dependent on her as her youngest-born in the cradle. Had she seen a domestic, or one of her daughters, give him a draught of water, or smooth his pillow, she would have boxed the intruder's ears. She chased Jessie and Rose from the upper realm of the house: she forbade the housemaids to set their foot in it.

Now, if the accident had happened at the Rectory gates, and old Helstone had taken in the martyr, neither Yorke nor his wife would have pitied him: they would have adjudged him right served for his tyranny and meddling: as it was, he became, for the present, the apple of their eye.

Strange! Louis Moore was permitted to come, – to sit down on the edge of the bed, and lean over the pillow, – to hold his brother's hand, and press his pale forehead with his fraternal lips: and Mrs Yorke bore it well. She suffered him to stay half the day there; she once suffered him to sit up all night in the chamber; she rose herself at five o'clock of a wet November morning, and with her own hands lit the kitchen fire, and made the brothers a breakfast, and served it to them herself. Majestically arrayed in a boundless flannel wrapper, a shawl, and her nightcap, she sat and watched them eat, as complacently as a hen beholds her chickens feed. Yet she gave the cook warning that day for venturing to make and carry up to Mr Moore a basin of sago-gruel; and the housemaid lost her favour because, when Mr Louis was departing, she brought him his surtout aired from the kitchen, and like a 'forward piece,' as she was, helped him on with it, and accepted, in return, a smile, a 'thank you, my girl,' and a shilling. Two ladies called one day, pale and anxious, and begged earnestly, humbly, to be allowed to see Mr Moore one instant: Mrs Yorke hardened her heart, and sent them packing, – not without opprobrium.

But how was it when Hortense Moore came? – Not so bad as might have been expected: the whole family of the Moores really seemed to suit Mrs Yorke so as no other family had ever suited her. Hortense and she possessed an exhaustless mutual theme of conversation in the corrupt propensities of servants. Their views of this class were similar: they watched them with the same suspicion, and judged them with the same severity. Hortense, too, from the very first, showed no manner of jealousy of Mrs Yorke's attentions to Robert: she let her keep the post of nurse with little interference; and, for herself, found ceaseless occupation in fidgeting about the house, holding the kitchen under surveillance, reporting what passed there, and, in short, making herself generally useful. Visiters, they both of them agreed in excluding sedulously from the sick-room. They held the young millowner captive, and hardly let the air breathe or the sun shine on him.

Mr MacTurk, the surgeon to whom Moore's case had been committed, pronounced his wound of a dangerous, but, he trusted, not of a hopeless character. At first, he wished to place with him a nurse of his own selection; but this neither Mrs Yorke nor Hortense would hear of: they promised faithful observance of directions. He was left, therefore, for the present, in their hands.

Doubtless, they executed the trust to the best of their ability; but something got wrong: the bandages were displaced, or tampered with; great loss of blood followed. MacTurk, being summoned, came with steed afoam. He was one of those surgeons whom it is dangerous to vex: abrupt in his best moods; in his worst, savage. On seeing Moore's state, he relieved his feelings by a little flowery language, with which it is not necessary to strew the present page. A bouquet or two of the choicest blossoms fell on the unperturbed head of one Mr Graves, a stony young assistant, he usually carried about with him; with a second nosegay he gifted another young gentleman in his train – an interesting facsimile of himself, being, indeed, his own son; but the full corbeille of blushing bloom fell to the lot of meddling womankind, en masse.

For the best part of one winter night, himself and satellites were busied about Moore. There, at his bedside, shut up alone with him in his chamber, they wrought and wrangled over his exhausted frame. They three were on one side of the bed, and Death on the other. The conflict was sharp: it lasted till day broke, when the balance between the belligerents seemed so equal that both parties might have claimed the victory.

At dawn, Graves and young MacTurk were left in charge of the patient, while the senior went himself in search of additional strength, and secured it in the person of Mrs Horsfall, the best nurse on his staff. To this woman he gave Moore in charge, with the sternest injunctions respecting the responsibility laid on her shoulders. She took this responsibility stolidly, as she did also the easy chair at the bed-head. That moment she began her reign.

Mrs Horsfall had one virtue, – orders received from MacTurk she obeyed to the letter: the Ten Commandments were less binding in her eyes than her surgeon's dictum. In other respects, she was no woman, but a dragon. Hortense Moore fell effaced before her; Mrs Yorke withdrew – crushed: yet both these women were personages of some dignity in their own estimation, and of some bulk in the estimation of others. Perfectly cowed by the breadth, the height, the bone, and the brawn of Mrs Horsfall, they retreated to the back-parlour. She, for her part, sat up-stairs when she liked, and downstairs when she preferred it: she took her dram three times a-day, and her pipe of tobacco four times.

As to Moore, no one now ventured to inquire about him: Mrs Horsfall had him at dry-nurse: it was she who was to do for him; and the general conjecture now ran that she did for him accordingly.

Morning and evening MacTurk came to see him: his case, thus complicated by a new mischance, was become one of interest in the surgeon's eyes: he regarded him as a damaged piece of clock-work, which it would be creditable to his skill to set a-going again. Graves and young MacTurk – Moore's sole other visiters – contemplated him in the light in which they were wont to contemplate the occupant for the time being of the dissecting-room at Stilbro' Infirmary.

Robert Moore had a pleasant time of it: in pain; in danger; too weak to move; almost too weak to speak; a sort of giantess his keeper; the three surgeons his sole society. Thus he lay though the diminishing days and lengthening nights of the whole drear month of November.

In the commencement of his captivity, Moore used feebly to resist Mrs Horsfall: he hated the sight of her rough bulk, and dreaded the contact of her hard hands; but she taught him docility in a trice. She made no account whatever of his six feet – his manly thews and sinews: she turned him in his bed as another woman would have turned a babe in its cradle. When he was good, she addressed him as 'my dear,' and 'honey'; and when he was bad, she sometimes shook him. Did he attempt to speak when MacTurk was there, she lifted her hand and bade him 'hush!' like a nurse checking a forward child. If she had not smoked – if she had not taken gin, it would have been better, he thought; but she did both. Once – in her absence – he intimated to MacTurk, that 'that woman was a dram-drinker.'

'Pooh! my dear sir; they are all so,' was the reply he got for his pains. 'But Horsfall has this virtue,' added the surgeon, – 'drunk or sober, she always remembers to obey *me*.'

At length the latter autumn passed: its fogs, its rains withdrew from England their mourning and their tears; its winds swept on to sigh over lands far away. Behind November came deep winter; clearness, stillness, frost accompanying.

A calm day had settled into a crystalline evening; the world wore a North Pole colouring: all its lights and tints looked like the 'reflets'* of white, or violet, or pale green gems. The hills wore a lilac-blue; the setting sun had purple in its red; the sky was ice, all silvered azure; when the stars rose, they were of white crystal – not gold; grey, or cerulean, or faint emerald hues – cool, pure, and transparent – tinged the mass of the landscape.

What is this by itself in a wood no longer green, no longer even russet; a wood, neutral tint – this dark blue moving object? Why, it is a schoolboy – a Briarfield grammar-schoolboy – who has left his companions, now trudging home by the high road, and is seeking a certain tree, with a certain mossy mound at its root – convenient as a seat. Why is he lingering here? – the air is cold, and the time wears late. He sits down: what is he thinking about? Does he feel the chaste charm nature wears to-night? A pearl-white moon smiles through the grey trees: Does he care for her smile?

Impossible to say; for he is silent, and his countenance does not speak: as yet, it is no mirror to reflect sensation, but rather a mask to conceal it. This boy is a stripling of fifteen – slight, and tall of his years; in his face there is as little of amenity as of servility: his eye seems prepared to note any incipient attempt to control or overreach him, and the rest of his features indicate faculties alert for resistance. Wise ushers avoid unnecessary interference with that lad. To break him in by severity would be a useless attempt; to win him by flattery would be an effort worse than useless. He is best let alone. Time will educate, and experience train him.

Professedly, Martin Yorke (it is a young Yorke, of course) tramples on the name of poetry: talk sentiment to him, and you would be answered by sarcasm. Here he is, wandering alone, waiting duteously on Nature, while she unfolds a page of stern, of silent, and of solemn poetry, beneath his attentive gaze.

---

*Find me an English word as good, reader, and I will gladly dispense with the French word. Reflections won't do.

Being seated, he takes from his satchel a book – not the Latin grammar, but a contraband volume of Fairy tales; there will be light enough yet for an hour to serve his keen young vision: besides, the moon waits on him – her beam, dim and vague as yet, fills the glade where he sits.

He reads: he is led into a solitary mountain region; all round him rude and desolate, shapeless, and almost colourless. He hears bells tinkle on the wind; forth-riding from the formless folds of the mist, dawns on him the brightest vision – a green-robed lady, on a snow-white palfrey; he sees her dress, her gems, and her steed; she arrests him with some mysterious question: he is spell-bound, and must follow her into Fairy-land.

A second legend bears him to the seashore: there tumbles in a strong tide, boiling at the base of dizzy cliffs: it rains and blows. A reef of rocks, black and rough, stretches far into the sea; all along, and among, and above these crags, dash and flash, sweep and leap, swells, wreaths, drifts of snowy spray. Some lone wanderer is out on these rocks, treading, with cautious step, the wet, wild sea-weed; glancing down into hollows where the brine lies fathoms deep and emerald-clear, and seeing there wilder, and stranger, and huger vegetation, than is found on land, with treasure of shells – some green, some purple, some pearly – clustered in the curls of the snaky plants. He hears a cry. Looking up, and forward, he sees, at the bleak point of the reef, a tall, pale thing – shaped like man, but made of spray – transparent, tremulous, awful: it stands not alone: they are all human figures that wanton in the rocks – a crowd of foam-women – a band of white, evanescent Nereides.

Hush! – shut the book: hide it in the satchel. – Martin hears a tread. He listens: No – Yes: Once more, the dead leaves, lightly crushed, rustle on the wood-path. Martin watches: the trees part, and a woman issues forth.

She is a lady dressed in dark silk, a veil covering her face. Martin never met a lady in this wood before – nor any female, save, now and then, a village-girl come to gather nuts. To-night, the apparition does not displease him. He observes, as she approaches, that she is neither old nor plain, but, on the contrary, very youthful; and, but that he now recognises her for one whom he has often wilfully pronounced ugly, he would deem that he discovered traits of beauty behind the thin gauze of that veil.

She passes him, and says nothing. He knew she would: all women are proud monkeys – and he knows no more conceited doll than that Caroline Helstone. The thought is hardly hatched in his mind, when the lady retraces those two steps she had got beyond him, and, raising her veil, reposes her glance on his face, while she softly asks: –

'Are you one of Mr Yorke's sons?'

No human evidence would ever have been able to persuade Martin Yorke that he blushed when thus addressed; yet blush he did, to the ears.

'I am,' he said, bluntly; and encouraged himself to wonder, superciliously, what would come next.

'You are Martin, I think?' was the observation that followed.

It could not have been more felicitous: it was a simple sentence – very artlessly, a little timidly, pronounced; but it chimed in harmony to the youth's nature: it stilled him like a note of music.

Martin had a keen sense of his personality: he felt it right and sensible that the girl should discriminate him from his brothers. Like his father, he hated ceremony: it was acceptable to hear a lady address him as 'Martin,' and not Mr Martin, or Master Martin, which form would have lost her his good graces for ever. Worse, if possible, than ceremony, was the other extreme of slipshod familiarity: the slight tone of bashfulness – the scarcely-perceptible hesitation – was considered perfectly in place.

'I am Martin,' he said.

'Are your father and mother well?' – (it was lucky she did not say *papa* and *mamma*: that would have undone all,) – 'and Rose and Jessie?'

'I suppose so.'

'My cousin Hortense is still at Briarmains?'

'Oh, yes!'

Martin gave a comic half-smile and demi-groan: the half-smile was responded to by the lady, who could guess in what sort of odour Hortense was likely to be held by the young Yorkes.

'Does your mother like her?'

'They suit so well about the servants, they can't help liking each other.'

'It is cold to-night.'

'Why are you out so late?'

'I lost my way in this wood.'

Now, indeed, Martin allowed himself a refreshing laugh of scorn.

'Lost your way in the mighty forest of Briarmains! You deserve never more to find it.'

'I never was here before, and I believe I am trespassing now: you might inform against me if you chose, Martin, and have me fined: it is your father's wood.'

'I should think I knew that; but since you are so simple as to lose your way, I will guide you out.'

'You need not: I have got into the track now: I shall be right. Martin,' (a little quickly), 'how is Mr Moore?'

Martin had heard certain rumours: it struck him that it might be amusing to make an experiment.

'Going to die. Nothing can save him. All hope flung over-board!'

She put her veil aside. She looked into his eyes, and said, –

'To die!'

'To die. All along of the women, my mother and the rest: they did something about his bandages that finished everything: he would have got better but for them. I am sure they should be arrested, cribbed, tried, and brought in for Botany Bay, at the very least.'

The questioner, perhaps, did not hear this judgment: she stood motionless. In two minutes, without another word, she moved forwards: no good-night, no further inquiry. This was not amusing, nor what Martin had calculated on: he expected something dramatic and demonstrative: it was hardly worth while to frighten the girl, if she would not entertain him in return. He called, –

'Miss Helstone!'

She did not hear or turn. He hastened after and overtook her.

'Come. Are you uneasy about what I said?'

'You know nothing about death, Martin: you are too young for me to talk to concerning such a thing.'

'Did you believe me? It's all flummery! Moore eats like three men: they are always making sago or tapioca, or something good for him: I never go into the kitchen but there is a saucepan on the fire, cooking him some dainty. I think I will play the old soldier, and be fed on the fat of the land like him.'

'Martin! Martin!' here her voice trembled, and she stopped.

'It is exceedingly wrong of you, Martin: you have almost killed me.'

Again she stopped: she leaned against a tree, trembling, shuddering, and as pale as death.

Martin contemplated her with inexpressible curiosity. In one sense it was, as he would have expressed it, 'nuts' to him to see this: it told him so much, and he was beginning to have a great relish for discovering secrets; in another sense, it reminded him of what he had once felt when he had heard a blackbird lamenting for her nestlings, which Matthew had crushed with a stone, and that was not a pleasant feeling. Unable to find anything very appropriate to *say*, in order to comfort her, he began to cast about in his mind what he could *do*: he smiled: the lad's smile gave wondrous transparency to his physiognomy.

'Eureka!' he cried. 'I'll set all straight by-and-by. You are better now, Miss Caroline: walk forward,' he urged.

Not reflecting that it would be more difficult for Miss

Helstone than for himself to climb a wall or penetrate a hedge, he piloted her by a short cut which led to no gate. The consequence was he had to help her over some formidable obstacles, and, while he railed at her for helplessness, he perfectly liked to feel himself of use.

'Martin, before we separate, assure me seriously, and on your word of honour, that Mr Moore is better.'

'How very much you think of that Moore!'

'No – but – many of his friends may ask me, and I wish to be able to give an authentic answer.'

'You may tell them he is well enough, only idle: you may tell them that he takes mutton-chops for dinner, and the best of arrowroot for supper. I intercepted a basin myself one night on its way up-stairs, and ate half of it.'

'And who waits on him, Martin? Who nurses him?'

'Nurses him? – the great baby! Why, a woman as round and big as our largest water-butt – a rough, hard-favoured old girl. I make no doubt she leads him a rich life: nobody else is let near him: he is chiefly in the dark. It is my belief she knocks him about terribly in that chamber. I listen at the wall sometimes when I am in bed, and I think I hear her thumping him. You should see her fist: she could hold half a dozen hands like yours in her one palm. After all, notwithstanding the chops and jellies he gets, I would not be in his shoes. In fact, it is my private opinion that she eats most of what goes up on the tray to Mr Moore. I wish she may not be starving him.'

Profound silence and meditation on Caroline's part, and a sly watchfulness on Martin's.

'You never see him, I suppose, Martin?'

'I? No: I don't care to see him, for my own part.'

Silence again.

'Did not you come to our house once with Mrs Pryor, about five weeks since, to ask after him?' again inquired Martin.

'Yes.'

'I dare say you wished to be shown up-stairs?'

'We *did* wish it: we entreated it; but your mother declined.'

'Ay! she declined. I heard it all: she treated you as it is her pleasure to treat visiters now and then: she behaved to you rudely and harshly.'

'She was not kind; for, you know Martin, we are relations, and it is natural we should take an interest in Mr Moore. But here we must part: we are at your father's gate.'

'Very well – what of that? I shall walk home with you.'

'They will miss you, and wonder where you are.'

'Let them . . . I can take care of myself, I suppose.'

Martin knew that he had already incurred the penalty of a lecture, and dry bread for tea. No matter, the evening had furnished him with an adventure: it was better than muffins and toast.

He walked home with Caroline. On the way he promised to see Mr Moore, in spite of the dragon who guarded his chamber, and appointed an hour on the next day, when Caroline was to come to Briarmains Wood and get tidings of him: he would meet her at a certain tree. The scheme led to nothing: still he liked it.

Having reached home, the dry bread and the lecture were duly administered to him, and he was dismissed to bed at an early hour. He accepted his punishment with the toughest stoicism.

Ere ascending to his chamber he paid a secret visit to the dining-room, a still, cold, stately apartment, seldom used; for the family customarily dined in the back parlour. He stood before the mantelpiece, and lifted his candle to two pictures hung above – female heads: one, a type of serene beauty – happy and innocent; the other, more lovely – but forlorn and desperate.

'She looked like *that*,' he said, gazing on the latter sketch, 'when she sobbed, turned white, and leaned against the tree.'

'I suppose,' he pursued, when he was in his room, and seated on the edge of his pallet-bed, – 'I suppose she is, what they call, "*in love*;" yes, *in love* with that long thing in the next chamber. Whisht! is that Horsfall clattering him? I wonder he does not yell out. It really sounds as if she had fallen on him tooth and nail; but I suppose she is making the bed. I saw her at it once – she hit into the mattresses as if she was boxing. It is queer, Zillah (they call her Zillah) – Zillah Horsfall is a woman, and Caroline Helstone is a woman: they are two individuals of the same species – not much alike though. Is she a pretty girl, that Caroline? I suspect she is – very nice to look at – something so clear in her face – so soft in her eyes. I approve of her looking at me; it does me good. She has long eyelashes: their shadow seems to rest where she gazes, and to instil peace and thought. If she behaves well, and continues to suit me, as she has suited me to-day, I may do her a good turn. I rather relish the notion of circumventing my mother and that ogress, old Horsfall. Not that I like humouring Moore; but whatever I do I'll be paid for, and in coin of my own choosing: I know what reward I will claim – one displeasing to Moore, and agreeable to myself.'

He turned into bed.

CHAPTER XXXIII

MARTIN'S TACTICS

IT WAS NECESSARY to the arrangement of Martin's plan, that
he should stay at home that day. Accordingly, he found no
appetite for breakfast; and, just about school-time, took a severe
pain about his heart, which rendered it advisable that, instead
of setting out to the grammar-school with Mark, he should
succeed to his father's arm-chair by the fireside, and also to his
morning-paper. This point being satisfactorily settled, and
Mark being gone to Mr Sumner's class, and Matthew and Mr
Yorke withdrawn to the counting-house, three other exploits,
nay four, remained to be achieved.

The first of these was to realize the breakfast he had not yet
tasted, and with which his appetite of fifteen could ill afford to
dispense; the second, third, fourth, to get his mother, Miss
Moore, and Mrs Horsfall successively, out of the way before
four o'clock that afternoon.

The first was, for the present, the most pressing, since the
work before him demanded an amount of energy which the
present empty condition of his youthful stomach did not seem
likely to supply.

Martin knew the way to the larder; and knowing this way, he
took it. The servants were in the kitchen, breakfasting solemnly
with closed doors; his mother and Miss Moore were airing themselves on the lawn, and discussing the closed doors aforesaid:
Martin, safe in the larder, made fastidious selection from its
stores. His breakfast had been delayed – he was determined it
should be recherché: it appeared to him that a variety on his
usual somewhat insipid fare of bread and milk was both desirable

and advisable: the savoury and the salutary he thought might be combined. There was a store of rosy apples laid in straw upon a shelf; he picked out three. There was pastry upon a dish; he selected an apricot-puff and a damson tart. On the plain household bread his eye did not dwell; but he surveyed with favour some currant tea-cakes, and condescended to make choice of one. Thanks to his clasp-knife, he was able to appropriate a wing of fowl and a slice of ham; a cantlet of cold custard-pudding he thought would harmonize with these articles; and having made this final addition to his booty, he at length sallied forth into the hall.

He was already half-way across – three steps more would have anchored him in the harbour of the back-parlour – when the front door opened, and there stood Matthew. Better far had it been the Old Gentleman, in full equipage of horns, hoofs, and tail.

Matthew, sceptic and scoffer, had already failed to subscribe a prompt belief in that pain about the heart: he had muttered some words, amongst which the phrase 'shamming Abraham' had been very distinctly audible; and the succession to the arm-chair and newspaper had appeared to affect him with mental spasms: the spectacle now before him, the apples, the tarts, the tea-cake, the fowl, ham and pudding, offered evidence but too well calculated to inflate his opinion of his own sagacity.

Martin paused 'interdit' one minute, one instant; the next he knew his ground, and pronounced all well. With the true perspicacity 'des âmes élites,' he at once saw how this – at first sight untoward event – might be turned to excellent account: he saw how it might be so handled as to secure the accomplishment of his second task, viz. the disposal of his mother. He knew that a collision between him and Matthew always suggested to Mrs Yorke the propriety of a fit of hysterics; he further knew that, on the principle of calm succeeding to storm, after a morning of hysterics, his mother was sure to indulge in an afternoon of bed. This would accommodate him perfectly.

The collision duly took place in the hall. A dry laugh, an insulting sneer, a contemptuous taunt, met by a nonchalant but most cutting reply, were the signals. They rushed at it. Martin, who usually made little noise on these occasions, made a great deal now. In flew the servants, Mrs Yorke, Miss Moore: no female hand could separate them: Mr Yorke was summoned.

'Sons,' said he, 'one of you must leave my roof if this occurs again: I will have no Cain and Abel strife here.'

Martin now allowed himself to be taken off: he had been hurt; he was the youngest and slightest: he was quite cool, in no passion: he even smiled, content that the most difficult part of the labour he had set himself was over.

Once he seemed to flag in the course of the morning.

'It is not worth while to bother myself for that Caroline,' he remarked. But, a quarter of an hour afterwards, he was again in the dining-room, looking at the head with dishevelled tresses and eyes turbid with despair.

'Yes,' he said, 'I made her sob, shudder, almost faint: I'll see her smile before I've done with her: besides, I want to outwit all these womenites.'

Directly after dinner, Mrs Yorke fulfilled her son's calculation, by withdrawing to her chamber. Now for Hortense.

That lady was just comfortably settled to stocking-mending in the back-parlour, when Martin – laying down a book which, stretched on the sofa (he was still indisposed, according to his own account), he had been perusing in all the voluptuous ease of a yet callow pacha – lazily introduced some discourse about Sarah, the maid at the Hollow. In the course of much verbal meandering, he insinuated information that this damsel was said to have three suitors, Frederic Murgatroyd, Jeremiah Pighills, and John-of-Mally's-of-Hannah's-of-Deb's; and that Miss Mann had affirmed she knew for a fact, that, now the girl was left in sole charge of the cottage, she often had her swains to meals, and entertained them with the best the house afforded.

It needed no more. Hortense could not have lived another

hour without betaking herself to the scene of these nefarious transactions, and inspecting the state of matters in person. Mrs Horsfall remained.

Martin, master of the field now, extracted from his mother's work-basket a bunch of keys; with these he opened the sideboard cupboard, produced thence a black bottle and a small glass, placed them on the table, nimbly mounted the stairs, made for Mr Moore's door, tapped, the nurse opened.

'If you please, ma'am, you are invited to step into the back-parlour and take some refreshmment: you will not be disturbed: the family are out.'

He watched her down; he watched her in; himself shut the door: he knew she was safe.

The hard work was done; now for the pleasure. He snatched his cap, and away for the wood.

It was yet but half-past three; it had been a fine morning, but the sky looked dark now: it was beginning to snow; the wind blew cold; the wood looked dismal, the old tree grim. Yet Martin approved the shadow on his path: he found a charm in the spectral aspect of the doddered oak.

He had to wait: to and fro he walked, while the flakes fell faster; and the wind, which at first had but moaned, pitifully howled.

'She is long in coming,' he muttered, as he glanced along the narrow track. 'I wonder,' he subjoined, 'what I wish to see her so much for? She is not coming for me. But I have power over her, and I want her to come that I may use that power.'

He continued his walk.

'Now,' he resumed, when a further period had elapsed, 'if she fails to come, I shall hate and scorn her.'

It struck four: he heard the church-clock far away. A step so quick, so light, that, but for the rustling of leaves, it would scarcely have sounded on the wood-walk, checked his impatience. The wind blew fiercely now, and the thickened white storm waxed bewildering; but on she came, and not dismayed.

'Well, Martin,' she said eagerly, 'how is he?'

'It is queer how she thinks of *him*,' reflected Martin: 'the blinding snow and bitter cold are nothing to her, I believe: yet she is but a "chitty-faced creature," as my mother would say. I could find in my heart to wish I had a cloak to wrap her in.'

Thus meditating to himself, he neglected to answer Miss Helstone.

'You have seen him?'

'No.'

'Oh! You promised you would.'

'I mean to do better by you than that. Didn't I say, *I* don't care to see him?'

'But now it will be so long before I get to know anything certain about him, and I am sick of waiting. Martin, *do* see him, and give him Caroline Helstone's regards, and say she wished to know how he was, and if anything could be done for his comfort.'

'I wont.'

'You are changed: you were so friendly last night.'

'Come: we must not stand in this wood; it is too cold.'

'But, before I go, promise me to come again to-morrow with news.'

'No such thing; I am much too delicate to make and keep such appointments in the winter season: if you know what a pain I had in my chest this morning, and how I went without breakfast, and was knocked down besides, you 'd feel the impropriety of bringing me here in the snow. Come, I say.'

'Are you really delicate, Martin?'

'Don't I look so?'

'You have rosy cheeks.'

'That's hectic. Will you come – or you won't?'

'Where?'

'With me. I was a fool not to bring a cloak: I would have made you cozy.'

'You are going home: my nearest road lies in the opposite direction.'

'Put your arm through mine. I'll take care of you.'

'But, the wall – the hedge – it is such hard work climbing, and you are too slender and young to help me without hurting yourself.'

'You shall go through the gate.'

'But –'

'But! – but! Will you trust me or not?'

She looked into his face.

'I think I will. Anything rather than return as anxious as I came.'

'I can't answer for that. This, however, I promise you; be ruled by me, and you shall see Moore yourself.'

'See him myself?'

'Yourself.'

'But, dear Martin, does he know?'

'Ah! I'm dear now. No: he doesn't know.'

'And your mother and the others?'

'All is right.'

Caroline fell into a long silent fit of musing, but still she walked on with her guide: they came in sight of Briarmains.

'Have you made up your mind?' he asked.

She was silent.

'Decide. We are just on the spot. *I won't* see him – that I tell you – except to announce your arrival.'

'Martin, you are a strange boy, and this is a strange step; but all I feel *is* and *has* been, for a long time, strange. I will see him.'

'Having said that, you will neither hesitate nor retract?'

'No.'

'Here we are, then. Do not be afraid of passing the parlour-window: no one will see you. My father and Matthew are at the mill; Mark is at school; the servants are in the back-kitchen; Miss Moore is at the cottage; my mother in her bed; and Mrs Horsfall in Paradise. Observe – I need not ring: I open the door; the hall is empty; the staircase quiet; so is the gallery: the whole house and all its inhabitants are under a spell, which I will not break till you are gone.'

'Martin, I trust you.'

'You never said a better word. Let me take your shawl: I will shake off the snow and dry it for you. You are cold and wet: never mind; there is a fire up-stairs. Are you ready?'

'Yes.'

'Follow me.'

He left his shoes on the mat; mounted the stair unshod; Caroline stole after, with noiseless step: there was a gallery, and there was a passage; at the end of that passage Martin paused before a door and tapped: he had to tap twice – thrice: a voice, known to one listener, at last said, –'

'Come in.'

The boy entered briskly.

'Mr Moore, a lady called to inquire after you: none of the women were about: it is washing-day, and the maids are over the crown of the head in soap-suds in the back-kitchen; so I asked her to step up.'

'Up here, sir?'

'Up here, sir; but if you object, she shall go down again.'

'Is this a place, or am I a person to bring a lady to, you absurd lad?'

'No: so I'll take her off.'

'Martin, you will stay here. Who is she?'

'Your grandmother from that château on the Scheldt Miss Moore talks about.'

'Martin,' said the softest whisper at the door, 'don't be foolish.'

'Is she there?' inquired Moore, hastily. He had caught an imperfect sound.

'She is there, fit to faint: she is standing on the mat, shocked at your want of filial affection.'

'Martin, you are an evil cross between an imp and a page. What is she like?'

'More like me than you; for she is young and beautiful.'

'You are to show her forward. Do you hear?'

'Come, Miss Caroline.'

'Miss Caroline!' repeated Moore.

And when Miss Caroline entered, she was encountered in the middle of the chamber by a tall, thin, wasted figure, who took both her hands.

'I give you a quarter of an hour,' said Martin, as he withdrew: 'no more. Say what you have to say in that time: till it is past, I will wait in the gallery: nothing shall approach: I'll see you safe away. Should you persist in staying longer, I leave you to your fate.'

He shut the door. In the gallery he was as elate as a king: he had never been engaged in an adventure he liked so well; for no adventure had ever invested him with so much importance, or inspired him with so much interest.

'You are come at last,' said the meagre man, gazing on his visitress with hollow eyes.

'Did you expect me before?'

'For a month – near two months, we have been very near; and I have been in sad pain, and danger, and misery, Cary.'

'I could not come.'

'Couldn't you? But the Rectory and Briarmains are very near: not two miles apart.'

There was pain – there was pleasure in the girl's face as she listened to these implied reproaches: it was sweet – it was bitter to defend herself.

'When I say I could not come, I mean I could not see you; for I came with mamma the very day we heard what had happened. Mr MacTurk then told us it was impossible to admit any stranger.'

'But afterwards – every fine afternoon these many weeks past I have waited and listened. Something here, Cary, (laying his hand on his breast), told me it was impossible but that you should think of me. Not that I merit thought; but we are old acquaintance; we are cousins.'

'I came again, Robert: mamma and I came again.'

'Did you? Come, that is worth hearing: since you came again, we will sit down and talk about it.'

They sat down. Caroline drew her chair up to his. The air was now dark with snow: an Iceland blast was driving it wildly. This pair neither heard the long 'wuthering' rush, nor saw the white burden it drifted: each seemed conscious but of one thing – the presence of the other.

'So mamma and you came again?'

'And Mrs Yorke did treat us strangely. We asked to see you. "No," said she; "not in my house. I am at present responsible for his life: it shall not be forfeited for half an hour's idle gossip." But I must not tell you all she said: it was very disagreeable. However, we came yet again – mamma, Miss Keeldar, and I. This time we thought we should conquer, as we were three against one, and Shirley was on our side. But Mrs Yorke opened such a battery.'

Moore smiled. 'What did she say?'

'Things that astonished us. Shirley laughed at last; I cried; mamma was seriously annoyed: we were all three driven from the field. Since that time I have only walked once a-day past the house, just for the satisfaction of looking up at your window, which I could distinguish by the drawn curtains. I really dared not come in.'

'I *have* wished for you, Caroline.'

'I did not know that. I never dreamt one instant that you thought of me. If I had but most distantly imagined such a possibility –'

'Mrs Yorke would still have beaten you.'

'She would not. Stratagem should have been tried, if persuasion failed. I would have come to the kitchen door; the servant should have let me in; and I would have walked straight upstairs. In fact, it was far more the fear of intrusion – the fear of yourself, that baffled me, than the fear of Mrs Yorke.'

'Only last night, I despaired of ever seeing you again.

Weakness has wrought terrible depression in me – terrible depressions.'

'And you sit alone?'

'Worse than alone.'

'But you must be getting better, since you can leave your bed?'

'I doubt whether I shall live: I see nothing for it, after such exhaustion, but decline.'

'You – you shall go home to the Hollow.'

'Dreariness would accompany – nothing cheerful come near me.'

'I *will* alter this: this *shall* be altered, were there ten Mrs Yorkes to do battle with.'

'Cary, you make me smile.'

'Do smile: smile again. Shall I tell you what I should like?'

'Tell me anything – only keep talking. I am Saul: but for music I should perish.'

'I should like you to be brought to the Rectory, and given to me and mamma.'

'A precious gift! I have not laughed since they shot me till now.'

'Do you suffer pain, Robert?'

'Not so much pain now; but I am hopelessly weak, and the state of my mind is inexpressible – dark, barren, impotent. Do you not read it all in my face? I look a mere ghost.'

'Altered, yet I should have known you anywhere: but I understand your feelings: I experienced something like it. Since we met, I too have been very ill.'

'*Very* ill?'

'I thought I should die. The tale of my life seemed told. Every night, just at midnight, I used to wake from awful dreams – and the book lay open before me at the last page, where was written "Finis." I had strange feelings.'

'You speak my experience.'

'I believed I should never see you again; and I grew so thin – as thin as you are now: I could do nothing for myself –

neither rise nor lie down; and I could not eat – yet, you see I am better.'

'Comforter! sad as sweet: I am too feeble to say what I feel; but, while you speak, I *do* feel.'

'Here I am at your side, where I thought never more to be: here I speak to you – I see you listen to me willingly – look at me kindly. Did I count on that? I despaired.'

Moore sighed – a sigh so deep, it was nearly a groan: he covered his eyes with his hand.

'May I be spared to make some atonement!'

Such was his prayer.

'And for what?'

'We will not touch on it now, Cary: unmanned as I am, I have not the power to cope with such a topic. Was Mrs Pryor with you during your illness?'

'Yes,' (Caroline smiled brightly) – 'you know she is mamma?'

'I have heard: Hortense told me; but that tale too I will receive from yourself. Does she add to your happiness?'

'What! mamma? She is *dear* to me; *how* dear I cannot say. I was altogether weary, and she held me up.'

'I deserve to hear that in a moment when I can scarce lift my hand to my head. I deserve it.'

'It is no reproach against you.'

'It is a coal of fire heaped on my head; and so is every word you address to me, and every look that lights your sweet face. Come still nearer, Lina, and give me your hand – if my thin fingers do not scare you.'

She took those thin fingers between her two little hands – she bent her head 'et les effleura de ses lèvres' (I put that in French, because the word 'effleurer' is an exquisite word). Moore was much moved: a large tear or two coursed down his hollow cheek.

'I'll keep these things in my heart, Cary: that kiss I will put by, and you shall hear of it again one day.'

'Come out!' cried Martin, opening the door. 'Come away – you have had twenty minutes instead of a quarter of an hour.'

'She will not stir yet – you hempseed.'

'I dare not stay longer, Robert.'

'Can you promise to return?'

'No, she can't,' responded Martin. 'The thing musn't become customary: I can't be troubled. It's very well for once: I'll not have it repeated.'

'*You*'ll not have it repeated!'

'Hush! don't vex him – we could not have met to-day but for him: but I will come again, if it is your wish that I should come.'

'It *is* my wish – my *one* wish – almost the only wish I can feel.'

'Come this minute: my mother has coughed, got up, set her feet on the floor. Let her only catch you on the stairs, Miss Caroline: you're not to bid him good-bye' (stepping between her and Moore), – 'you are to march.'

'My shawl, Martin.'

'I have it. I'll put it on for you when you are in the hall.'

He made them part: he would suffer no farewell but what could be expressed in looks: he half carried Caroline down the stairs. In the hall he wrapped her shawl round her, and – but that his mother's tread then creaked in the gallery, and but that a sentiment of diffidence – the proper, natural, therefore the noble impulse of his boy's heart, held him back, he would have claimed his reward – he would have said, 'Now, Miss Caroline, for all this give me one kiss.' But ere the words had passed his lips, she was across the snowy road, rather skimming than wading the drifts.

'She is my debtor, and I *will* be paid.'

He flattered himself that it was opportunity, not audacity, which had failed him: he misjudged the quality of his own nature, and held it for something lower than it was.

CHAPTER XXXIV

CASE OF DOMESTIC PERSECUTION –
REMARKABLE INSTANCE OF PIOUS
PERSEVERANCE IN THE DISCHARGE OF
RELIGIOUS DUTIES

MARTIN, HAVING known the taste of excitement, wanted a second draught; having felt the dignity of power, he loathed to relinquish it. Miss Helstone – that girl he had always called ugly, and whose face was now perpetually before his eyes, by day and by night, in dark and in sunshine – had once come within his sphere: it fretted him to think the visit might never be repeated.

Though a schoolboy, he was no ordinary schoolboy: he was destined to grow up an original. At a few years later date, he took great pains to pare and polish himself down to the pattern of the rest of the world, but he never succeeded: an unique stamp marked him always. He now sat idle at his desk in the grammar-school, casting about in his mind for the means of adding another chapter to his commenced romance: he did not yet know how many commenced life-romances are doomed never to get beyond the first – or, at most, the second chapter. His Saturday half-holiday he spent in the wood with his book of fairy legends, and that other unwritten book of his imagination.

Martin harboured an irreligious reluctance to see the approach of Sunday. His father and mother – while disclaiming community with the Establishment – failed not duly, once on the sacred day, to fill their large pew in Briarfield church with the whole of their blooming family. Theoretically, Mr Yorke placed all sects and churches on a level: Mrs Yorke awarded the palm to Moravians and Quakers, on account of that crown of humility by these worthies worn: neither of them were ever known, however, to set foot in a conventicle.

Martin, I say, disliked Sunday, because the morning service was long, and the sermon usually little to his taste: this Saturday afternoon, however, his woodland musings disclosed to him a new-found charm in the coming day.

It proved a day of deep snow: so deep, that Mrs Yorke, during breakfast, announced her conviction that the children, both boys and girls, would be better at home: and her decision that, instead of going to church, they should sit silent for two hours in the back-parlour, while Rose and Martin alternately read a succession of sermons – John Wesley's Sermons: John Wesley, being a Reformer and an Agitator, had a place both in her own and her husband's favour.

'Rose will do as she pleases,' said Martin, not looking up from the book which, according to his custom then and in after-life, he was studying over his bread and milk.

'Rose will do as she is told, and Martin too,' observed the mother.

'I am going to church.'

So her son replied, with the ineffable quietude of a true Yorke, who knows his will and means to have it, and who, if pushed to the wall, will let himself be crushed to death, provided no way of escape can be found – but will never capitulate.

'It is not fit weather,' said the father.

No answer: the youth read studiously; he slowly broke his bread and sipped his milk.

'Martin hates to go to church, but he hates still more to obey,' said Mrs Yorke.

'I suppose I am influenced by pure perverseness?'

'Yes – you are.'

'Mother – I *am not*.'

'By what, then, are you influenced?'

'By a complication of motives; the intricacies of which I

should as soon think of explaining to you as I should of turning myself inside out to exhibit the internal machinery of my frame.'

'Hear Martin! Hear him!' cried Mr Yorke. 'I must see and have this lad of mine brought up to the Bar: Nature meant him to live by his tongue. Hesther, your third son must certainly be a lawyer: he has the stock in trade – brass, self-conceit, and words – words – words.'

'Some bread, Rose, if you please,' requested Martin, with intense gravity, serenity, phlegm: the boy had naturally a low, plaintive voice, which, in his 'dour' moods, rose scarcely above a lady's whisper: the more inflexibly stubborn the humour, the softer, the sadder the tone. He rang the bell, and gently asked for his walking-shoes.

'But, Martin,' urged his sire, 'there is drift all the way – a man could hardly wade through it. However, lad,' he continued, seeing that the boy rose as the church-bell began to toll, 'this is a case wherein I would by no means balk the obdurate chap of his will. Go to church by all means. There is a pitiless wind, and a sharp, frozen sleet, besides the depth underfoot. Go out into it, since thou prefers it to a warm fireside.'

Martin quietly assumed his cloak, comforter, and cap, and deliberately went out.

'My father has more sense than my mother,' he pronounced. 'How women miss it! They drive the nail into the flesh, thinking they are hammering away at insensate stone.'

He reached church early.

'Now, if the weather frightens her (and it is a real December tempest), or if that Mrs Pryor objects to her going out, and I should miss her after all, it will vex me: but, tempest or tornado, hail or ice, she *ought* to come; and, if she has a mind worthy of her eyes and features, she *will* come: she will be here for the chance of seeing me, as I am here for the chance of seeing her: she will want to get a word respecting her confounded sweetheart, as I want to get another flavour of what I think the essence of life: a taste of existence, with the spirit preserved in it, and not evaporated. Adventure is to stagnation what champagne is to flat porter.'

He looked round. The church was cold, silent, empty, but for one old woman. As the chimes subsided, and the single bell tolled slowly, another and another elderly parishioner came dropping in, and took a humble station in the free sittings. It is always the frailest, the oldest, and the poorest that brave the worst weather, to prove and maintain their constancy to dear old mother Church: this wild morning, not one affluent family attended, not one carriage party appeared – all the lined and cushioned pews were empty; only on the bare oaken seats sat ranged the grey-haired elders and feeble paupers.

'I'll scorn her, if she doesn't come,' muttered Martin shortly and savagely to himself. The Rector's shovel-hat had passed the porch: Mr Helstone and his clerk were in the vestry.

The bells ceased – the reading-desk was filled – the doors were closed – the service commenced: void stood the Rectory-pew – she was not there: Martin scorned her.

'Worthless thing! Vapid thing! Commonplace humbug! Like all other girls – weakly, selfish, shallow!'

Such was Martin's liturgy.

'She is not like our picture: her eyes are not large and expressive: her nose is not straight, delicate, Hellenic: her mouth has not that charm I thought it had – which, I imagined, could beguile me of sullenness in my worst moods. What is she? A thread-paper, a doll, a toy – a *girl*, in short.'

So absorbed was the young cynic, he forgot to rise from his knees at the proper place, and was still in an exemplary attitude of devotion when – the litany over – the first hymn was given out. To be so caught did not contribute to soothe him: he started up red (for he was so sensitive to ridicule as any girl). To make the matter worse, the church-door had re-opened, and the aisles were filling: patter, patter, patter, a hundred little feet trotted in. It was the Sunday-scholars. According to Briarfield winter custom, these children had till now been kept where there was a warm stove, and only led into church just before the Communion and Sermon.

The little ones were settled first, and at last, when the boys and the younger girls were all arranged – when the organ was swelling high, and the choir and congregation were rising to uplift a spiritual song – a tall class of young women came quietly in, closing the procession. Their teacher, having seen them seated, passed into the Rectory-pew. The French-grey cloak and small beaver bonnet were known to Martin: it was the very costume his eyes had ached to catch. Miss Helstone had not suffered the storm to prove an impediment: after all, she was come to church. Martin probably whispered his satisfaction to his hymn-book; at any rate, he therewith hid his face two minutes.

Satisfied or not, he had time to get very angry with her again before the sermon was over; she had never once looked his way: at least, he had not been so lucky as to encounter a glance.

'If,' he said – 'if she takes no notice of me; if she shows I am not in her thoughts, I shall have a worse, a meaner opinion of her than ever. Most despicable would it be to come for the sake of those sheep-faced Sunday-scholars, and not for my sake, or that long skeleton Moore's.'

The sermon found an end; the benediction was pronounced; the congregation dispersed: she had not been near him.

Now, indeed, as Martin set his face homeward, he felt that the sleet was sharp, and the east wind cold.

His nearest way lay through some fields: it was a dangerous, because an untrodden way: he did not care; he would take it. Near the second stile rose a clump of trees: was that an umbrella waiting there? Yes: an umbrella held with evident difficulty against the blast: behind it fluttered a French-grey cloak. Martin grinned as he toiled up the steep encumbered field, difficult to the foot as a slope in the upper realms of Etna. There was an inimitable look in his face when, having gained the stile, he seated himself coolly thereupon, and thus opened a conference which, for his own part, he was willing to prolong indefinitely.

'I think you had better strike a bargain: exchange me for Mrs Pryor.'

'I was not sure whether you would come this way, Martin; but I thought I would run the chance: there is no such thing as getting a quiet word spoken in the church or churchyard.'

'Will you agree? Make over Mrs Pryor to my mother, and put me in her skirts?'

'As if I could understand you! What puts Mrs Pryor into your head?'

'You call her "mamma," don't you?'

'She *is* my mamma.'

'Not possible – or so inefficient, so careless a mamma – I should make a five times better one. You *may* laugh: I have no objection to see you laugh: your teeth – I hate ugly teeth; but yours are as pretty as a pearl necklace, and a necklace, of which the pearls are very fair, even, and well matched too.'

'Martin, what now? I thought the Yorkes never paid compliments?'

'They have not done till this generation; but I feel as if it were my vocation to turn out a new variety of the Yorke species. I am rather tired of my own ancestors: we have traditions going back for four ages – tales of Hiram, which was the son of Hiram, which was the son of Samuel, which was the son of John, which was the son of Zerubbabel Yorke. All, from Zerubbabel down to the last Hiram, were such as you see my father. Before that, there was a Godfrey: we have his picture; it hangs in Moore's bedroom: it is like me. Of his character we know nothing; but I am sure it was different to his descendants: he has long curling dark hair; he is carefully and cavalierly dressed. Having said that he is like me, I need not add that he is handsome.'

'You are not handsome, Martin.'

'No; but wait a while: just let me take my time: I mean to begin from this day to cultivate, to polish – and we shall see.'

'You are a very strange – a very unaccountable boy, Martin; but don't imagine you ever will be handsome: you cannot.'

'I mean to try. But we were talking about Mrs Pryor: she must be the most unnatural mamma in existence, coolly to let her daughter come out in this weather. Mine was in such a rage, because I would go to church: she was fit to fling the kitchen-brush after me.'

'Mamma was very much concerned about me; but I am afraid I was obstinate: I *would* go.'

'To see me?'

'Exactly: I thought of nothing else. I greatly feared the snow would hinder you from coming: you don't know how pleased I was to see you all by yourself in the pew.'

'*I* came to fulfil my duty, and set the parish a good example. And so you were obstinate, were you? I should like to see you obstinate, I should. Wouldn't I have you in good discipline if I owned you? Let me take the umbrella.'

'I can't stay two minutes: our dinner will be ready.'

'And so will ours; and we have always a hot dinner on Sundays. Roast goose to-day, with apple-pie and rice-pudding. I always contrive to know the bill of fare: well, I like these things uncommonly; but I 'll make the sacrifice, if you will.'

'We have a cold dinner: my uncle will allow no unnecessary cooking on the Sabbath. But I must return: the house would be in commotion, if I failed to appear.'

'So will Briarmains, bless you! I think I hear my father sending out the overlooker and five of the dyers, to look in six directions for the body of his prodigal son in the snow; and my mother repenting her of her many misdeeds towards me, now I am gone.'

'Martin, how is Mr Moore?'

'*That* is what you came for – just to say that word.'

'Come, tell me quickly.'

'Hang him! he is no worse; but as ill-used as ever – mewed up, kept in solitary confinement. They mean to make either an idiot or a maniac of him, and take out a commission of lunacy. Horsfall starves him: you saw how thin he was.'

'You were very good the other day, Martin.'

'What day? I am always good – a model.'

'When will you be so good again?'

'I see what you are after; but you'll not wheedle me: I am no cat's paw.'

'But it must be done: it is quite a right thing, and a necessary thing.'

'How you encroach! Remember, I managed the matter of my own free will before.'

'And you will again.'

'I won't: the business gave me far too much trouble: I like my ease.'

'Mr Moore wishes to see me, Martin; and I wish to see him.'

'I daresay' (coolly).

'It is too bad of your mother to exclude his friends.'

'Tell her so.'

'His own relations.'

'Come and blow her up.'

'You know that would advance nothing. Well, I shall stick to my point. See him I will. If you won't help me, I'll manage without help.'

'Do: there is nothing like self-reliance – self-dependence.'

'I have no time to reason with you now; but I consider you provoking. Good-morning.'

Away she went – the umbrella shut; for she could not carry it against the wind.

'She is not vapid; she is not shallow,' said Martin. 'I shall like to watch, and mark how she will work her way without help. If the storm were not of snow, but of fire – such as came refreshingly down on the cities of the plain – she would go through it to procure five minutes' speech of that Moore. Now, I consider I have had a pleasant morning: the disappointments got time on: the fears and fits of anger only made that short discourse pleasanter, when it came at last. She expected to coax me at once: she'll not manage that in one effort: she shall come again, again, and yet again. It would please me to put her in a passion – to make her cry: I want to discover how far she will go – what she will do and dare – to get her will. It seems strange and new to find one human being thinking so much about another as she thinks about Moore. – But it is time to go home: my appetite tells me the hour: won't I walk into that goose? – and we'll try whether Matthew or I shall get the largest cut of the apple-pie to-day.'

CHAPTER XXXV

WHEREIN MATTERS MAKE SOME PROGRESS, BUT NOT MUCH

MARTIN HAD planned well: he had laid out a dexterously concerted scheme for his private amusement; but older and wiser schemers than he are often doomed to see their finest-spun projects swept to annihilation by the sudden broom of Fate – that fell housewife, whose red arm none can control. In the present instance, this broom was manufactured out of the tough fibres of Moore's own stubborn purpose, bound tight with his will. He was now resuming his strength, and making strange head against Mrs Horsfall. Each morning he amazed that matron with a fresh astonishment. First, he discharged her from her valet-duties: he would dress himself. Then, he refused the coffee she brought him: he would breakfast with the family. Lastly, he forbade her his chamber. On the same day, amidst the outcries of all the women in the place, he put his head out of doors. The morning after, he followed Mr Yorke to his counting-house, and requested an envoy to fetch a chaise from the Red-House Inn. He was resolved, he said, to return home to the Hollow that very afternoon. Mr Yorke, instead of opposing, aided and abetted him: the chaise was sent for, though Mrs Yorke declared the step would be his death. It came. Moore, little disposed to speak, made his purse do duty for his tongue: he expressed his gratitude to the servants and to Mrs Horsfall, by the chink of his coin. The latter personage approved and understood this language perfectly; it made amends for all previous contumacy: she and her patient parted the best friends in the world.

The kitchen visited and soothed, Moore betook himself to the parlour: he had Mrs Yorke to appease: not quite so easy a task as the pacification of her housemaids. There she sat plunged in sullen dudgeon; the gloomiest speculations on the depths of man's ingratitude absorbing her thoughts. He drew near and bent over her; she was obliged to look up, if it were only to bid him 'avaunt.' There was beauty still in his pale, wasted features; there was earnestness, and a sort of sweetness – for he was smiling – in his hollow eyes.

'Good-bye!' he said; and as he spoke the smile glittered and melted. He had no iron mastery of his sensations now: a trifling emotion made itself apparent in his present weak state.

'And what are you going to leave us for?' she asked: 'we will keep you, and do anything in the world for you, if you will only stay till you are stronger.'

'Good-bye!' he again said: and added, 'you have been a mother to me: give your wilful son one embrace.'

Like a foreigner, as he was, he offered her first one cheek, then the other: she kissed him.

'What a trouble – what a burden I have been to you!' he muttered.

'You are the worst trouble now, headstrong youth!' was the answer. 'I wonder who is to nurse you at Hollow's cottage: your sister Hortense knows no more about such matters than a child.'

'Thank God! for I have had nursing enough to last me my life.'

Here the little girls came in; Jessie crying, Rose quiet, but grave. Moore took them out into the hall to soothe, pet, and kiss them. He knew it was not in their mother's nature to bear to see any living thing caressed but herself: she would have felt annoyed had he fondled a kitten in her presence.

The boys were standing about the chaise as Moore entered it; but for them he had no farewell. To Mr Yorke he only said, –

'You have a good riddance of me: that was an unlucky shot

for you, Yorke; it turned Briarmains into an hospital. Come and see me at the cottage soon.'

He drew up the glass; the chaise rolled away. In half an hour he alighted at his own garden-wicket. Having paid the driver and dismissed the vehicle, he leaned on that wicket an instant, at once to rest and to muse.

'Six months ago I passed out at this gate,' said he, 'a proud, angry, disappointed man; I come back sadder and wiser: weakly enough, but not worried. A cold, grey, yet quiet world lies round – a world where, if I hope little, I fear nothing. All slavish terrors of embarrassment have left me: let the worst come, I can work, as Joe Scott does, for an honourable living: in such doom, I yet see some hardship, but no degradation. Formerly, pecuniary ruin was equivalent in my eyes to personal dishonour. It is not so now: I know the difference. Ruin *is* an evil; but one for which I am prepared: the day of whose coming I know, for I have calculated. I can yet put it off six months – not an hour longer: if things by that time alter – which is not probable; if fetters, which now seem indissoluble, should be loosened from our trade (of all things the most unlikely to happen) I might conquer in this long struggle yet – I might – Good God! what might I not do? But the thought is a brief madness: let me see things with sane eyes. Ruin will come, lay her axe to my fortune's roots, and hew them down. I shall snatch a sapling, I shall cross the sea, and plant it in American woods. Louis will go with me. Will none but Louis go? I cannot tell – I have no right to ask.'

He entered the house.

It was afternoon, twilight yet out of doors: starless and moonless twilight; for, though keenly freezing with a dry black frost, heaven wore a mask of clouds congealed and fast-locked. The mill-dam too was frozen: the Hollow was very still: indoors it was already dark. Sarah had lit a good fire in the parlour; she was preparing tea in the kitchen.

'Hortense,' said Moore, as his sister bustled up to help him off with his cloak, 'I am pleased to come home.'

Hortense did not feel the peculiar novelty of this expression coming from her brother, who had never before called the cottage his home; and to whom its narrow limits had always heretofore seemed rather restrictive than protective: still, whatever contributed to his happiness pleased her; and she expressed herself to that effect.

He sat down, but soon rose again: he went to the window; he came back to the fire.

'Hortense!'

'Mon frère?'

'This little parlour looks very clean and pleasant: unusually bright, somehow.'

'It is true, brother: I have had the whole house thoroughly and scrupulously cleaned in your absence.'

'Sister, I think on this first day of your return home, you ought to have a friend or so to tea; if it were only to see how fresh and spruce you have made the little place.'

'True, brother: if it were not late, I might send for Miss Mann.'

'So you might; but it really is too late to disturb that good lady; and the evening is much too cold for her to come out.'

'How thoughtful in you, dear Gérard! We must put it off till another day.'

'I want some one to-day, dear sister: some quiet guest, who would tire neither of us.'

'Miss Ainley?'

'An excellent person, they say; but she lives too far off. Tell Harry Scott to step up to the Rectory with a request from you, that Caroline Helstone should come and spend the evening with you.'

'Would it not be better to-morrow, dear brother?'

'I should like her to see the place as it is just now: its brilliant cleanliness and perfect neatness are so much to your credit.'

'It might benefit her in the way of example.'

'It might and must: she ought to come.'

He went into the kitchen.

'Sarah, delay tea half an hour.' He then commissioned her to despatch Harry Scott to the Rectory, giving her a twisted note hastily scribbled in pencil by himself, and addressed 'Miss Helstone.'

Scarcely had Sarah time to get impatient under the fear of damage to her toast already prepared, when the messenger returned; and with him the invited guest.

She entered through the kitchen, quietly tripped up Sarah's stairs to take off her bonnet and furs, and came down as quietly, with her beautiful curls nicely smoothed; her graceful merino dress and delicate collar all trim and spotless; her gay little work-bag in her hand. She lingered to exchange a few kindly words with Sarah; and to look at the new tortoise-shell kitten basking on the kitchen hearth; and to speak to the canary-bird, which a sudden blaze from the fire had startled on its perch; and then she betook herself to the parlour.

The gentle salutation, the friendly welcome, were interchanged in such tranquil sort as befitted cousins meeting; a sense of pleasure, subtle and quiet as a perfume, diffused itself through the room; the newly kindled lamp burned up bright; the tray and the singing urn were brought in.

'I am pleased to come home,' repeated Mr Moore.

They assembled round the table. Hortense chiefly talked. She congratulated Caroline on the evident improvement in her health: her colour and her plump cheeks were returning, she remarked. It was true: there was an obvious change in Miss Helstone: all about her seemed elastic; depression, fear, forlornness, were withdrawn: no longer crushed, and saddened, and slow, and drooping, she looked like one who had tasted the cordial of heart's-ease, and been lifted on the wing of hope.

After tea, Hortense went up-stairs: she had not rummaged her drawers for a month past, and the impulse to perform that operation was now become resistless. During her absence, the talk passed into Caroline's hands: she took it up with ease; she fell into her best tone of conversation. A pleasing facility and elegance of language gave fresh charm to familiar topics: a new music in the always soft voice gently surprised and pleasingly captivated the listener; unwonted shades and lights of expression elevated the young countenance with character, and kindled it with animation.

'Caroline, you look as if you had heard good tidings,' said Moore, after earnestly gazing at her for some minutes.

'Do I?'

'I sent for you this evening that I might be cheered; but you cheer me more than I had calculated.'

'I am glad of that. And I *really* cheer you?'

'You look brightly; move buoyantly; speak musically.'

'It is pleasant to be here again.'

'Truly it is pleasant: I feel it so. And to see health on your cheek, and hope in your eye, is pleasant, Cary: but what is this hope, and what is the source of this sunshine I perceive about you?'

'For one thing, I am happy in mamma: I love her so much, and she loves me. Long and tenderly she nursed me; now, when her care has made me well, I can occupy myself for and with her all the day. I say it is my turn to attend to her; and I *do* attend to her: I am her waiting-woman, as well as her child: I like – you would laugh if you knew what pleasure I have in making dresses and sewing for her. She looks so nice now, Robert: I will not let her be old-fashioned. And then, she is charming to talk to: full of wisdom; ripe in judgment; rich in information; exhaustless in stores her observant faculties have quietly amassed. Every day that I live with her, I like her better; I esteem her more highly; I love her more tenderly.'

' *That* for one thing, then, Cary: you talk in such a way about "mamma", it is enough to make one jealous of the old lady.'

'She is not old, Robert.'

'Of the young lady, then.'

'She does not pretend to be young.'

'Well – of the matron. But you said, "mamma's" affection was *one* thing that made you happy: now for the other thing.'

'I am glad you are better.'

'What besides?'

'I am glad we are friends.'

'You and I?'

'Yes: I once thought we never should be.'

'Cary, some day I mean to tell you a thing about myself that is not to my credit, and, consequently, will not please you.'

'Ah! – don't! I cannot bear to think ill of you.'

'And I cannot bear that you should think better of me than I deserve.'

'Well, but I half know your "thing": indeed, I believe I know all about it.'

'You do not.'

'I believe I do.'

'Whom does it concern besides me?'

She coloured; she hesitated; she was silent.

'Speak, Cary! – whom does it concern?'

She tried to utter a name, and could not.

'Tell me: there is none present but ourselves: be frank.'

'But if I guess wrong?'

'I will forgive. Whisper, Cary.'

He bent his ear to her lips: still she would not, or could not, speak clearly to the point. Seeing that Moore waited, and was resolved to hear something, she at last said, –

'Miss Keeldar spent a day at the Rectory about a week since. The evening came on very wintry, and we persuaded her to stay all night.'

'And you and she curled your hair together?'

'How do you know that?'

'And then you chatted; and she told you –'

'It was not at curling-hair time; so you are not as wise as you think: and besides, she didn't tell me.'

'You slept together afterwards?'

'We occupied the same room and bed. We did not sleep much: we talked the whole night through.'

'I'll be sworn you did! and then it all came out – tant pis. I would rather you had heard it from myself.'

'You are quite wrong: she did not tell me what you suspect: she is not the person to proclaim such things; but yet I inferred something from parts of her discourse: I gathered more from rumour, and I made out the rest by instinct.'

'But if she did not tell you that I wanted to marry her for the sake of her money, and that she refused me indignantly and scornfully (you need neither start nor blush; nor yet need you prick your trembling fingers with your needle: that is the plain truth, whether you like it or not) – if such was not the subject of her august confidences, on what point did they turn? You say you talked the whole night through: what about?'

'About things we never thoroughly discussed before, intimate friends as we have been: but you hardly expect I should tell you?'

'Yes, yes, Cary – you will tell me: you said we were friends; and friends should always confide in each other.'

'But you are sure you won't repeat it?'

'Quite sure.'

'Not to Louis?'

'Not even to Louis? What does Louis care for young ladies' secrets?'

'Robert – Shirley is a curious, magnanimous being.'

'I daresay: I can imagine there are both odd points and grand points about her.'

'I have found her chary in showing her feelings; but when they rush out, river-like, and pass full and powerful before you, – almost without leave from her – you gaze, wonder, you admire, and – I think – love her.'

'You saw this spectacle?'

'Yes: at dead of night; when all the house was silent, and starlight, and the cold reflection from the snow glimmered in our chamber, – then I saw Shirley's heart.'

'Her heart's core? Do you think she showed you that?'

'Her heart's core.'

'And how was it?'

'Like a shrine, -- for it was holy; like snow, – for it was pure; like flame, – for it was warm; like death, – for it was strong.'

'Can she love? Tell me that.'

'What think you?'

'She has loved none that have loved her yet.'

'Who are those that have loved her?'

He named a list of gentlemen, closing with Sir Philip Nunnely.

'She has loved none of these.'

'Yet some of them were worthy of a woman's affection.'

'Of some women's; but not of Shirley's.'

'Is she better than others of her sex?'

'She is peculiar, and more dangerous to take as a wife – rashly.'

'I can imagine that.'

'She spoke of you –'

'Oh! she did! I thought you denied it.'

'She did not speak in the way you fancy; but I asked her, and I would make her tell me what she thought of you, or rather, how she felt towards you. I wanted to know: I had long wanted to know.'

'So had I; but let us hear: she thinks meanly – she feels contemptuously, doubtless?'

'She thinks of you almost as highly as a woman can think of a man. You know she can be eloquent: I yet feel in fancy the glow of the language in which her opinion was conveyed.'

'But how does she feel?'

'Till you shocked her (she said you had shocked her, but she would not tell me how), she felt as a sister feels towards a brother of whom she is at once fond and proud.'

'I'll shock her no more, Cary, for the shock rebounded on myself till I staggered again: but that comparison about sister and brother is all nonsense: she is too rich and proud to entertain fraternal sentiments for me.'

'You don't know her, Robert; and somehow, I fancy *now* (I had other ideas formerly), that you cannot know her: you and she are not so constructed as to be able thoroughly to understand each other.'

'It may be so. I esteem her; I admire her; and yet my impressions concerning her are harsh – perhaps uncharitable. I believe, for instance, that she is incapable of love –'

'Shirley incapable of love!'

'That she will never marry: I imagine her jealous of compromising her pride, of relinquishing her power, of sharing her property.'

'Shirley has hurt your amour-propre.'

'She did hurt it – though I had not an emotion of tenderness, not a spark of passion for her.'

'Then, Robert, it was very wicked in you to want to marry her.'

'And very mean, my little pastor, my pretty priestess. I never wanted to kiss Miss Keeldar in my life, though she has fine lips, scarlet and round, as ripe cherries; or, if I did wish it, it was the mere desire of the eye.'

'I doubt, now, whether you are speaking the truth: the grapes or the cherries are sour – "hung too high." '

'She has a pretty figure, a pretty face, beautiful hair: I acknowledge all her charms and feel none of them; or only feel them in a way she would disdain. I suppose I was truly tempted, by the mere gilding of the bait. Caroline, what a noble fellow your Robert is – great, good, disinterested, and then so pure!'

'But not perfect: he made a great blunder once, and we will hear no more about it.'

'And shall we think no more about it, Cary? Shall we not despise him in our heart, gentle but just, compassionate but upright?'

'Never! We will remember that with what measure we mete it shall be measured unto us, and so we will give no scorn – only affection.'

'Which won't satisfy, I warn you of that. Something besides affection – something far stronger, sweeter, warmer – will be demanded one day: is it there to give?'

Caroline was moved – much moved.

'Be calm, Lina,' said Moore, soothingly; 'I have no intention, because I have no right, to perturb your mind now, nor for months to come: don't look as if you would leave me: we will make no more agitating allusions: we will resume our gossip. Do not tremble, look me in the face: see what a poor, pale, grim phantom I am – more pitiable than formidable.'

She looked shyly. 'There is something formidable still, pale as you are,' she said, as her eye fell under his.

'To return to Shirley,' pursued Moore; 'is it your opinion that she is ever likely to marry?'

'She loves.'

'Platonically – theoretically – all humbug!'

'She loves, what I call, sincerely.'

'Did she say so?'

'I cannot affirm that she said so: no such confession as, I love this man or that, passed her lips.'

'I thought not.'

'But the feeling made its way in spite of her, and I saw it. She spoke of one man in a strain not to be misunderstood: her voice alone was sufficient testimony. Having wrung from her an opinion on your character, I demanded a second opinion of – another person about whom I had my conjectures; though they were the most tangled and puzzled conjectures in the world. I would *make* her speak: I shook her, I chid her, I pinched her fingers when she tried to put me off with gibes and jests in her queer, provoking way, and at last, out it came: the voice, I say, was enough; hardly raised above a whisper, and yet such a soft vehemence in its tones. There was no confession – no confidence in the matter: to these things she cannot condescend; but I am sure that man's happiness is dear to her as her own life.'

'Who is it?'

'I charged her with the fact; she did not deny; she did not avow, but looked at me: I saw her eyes by the snow-gleam. It was quite enough: I triumphed over her mercilessly.'

'What right had *you* to triumph? Do you mean to say you are fancy-free?'

'Whatever *I* am, Shirley is a bondswoman. Lioness! She has found her captor. Mistress she may be of all round her – but her own mistress she is not.'

'So you exulted at recognising a fellow-slave in one so fair and imperial?'

'I did; Robert, you say right, in one so fair and imperial.'

'You confess it – a *fellow*-slave?'

'I confess nothing; but I say that haughty Shirley is no more free than was Hagar.'

'And who, pray, is the Abraham; the hero of a patriarch who has achieved such a conquest?'

'You still speak scornfully, and cynically, and sorely; but I will make you change your note before I have done with you.'

'We will see that: can she marry this Cupidon?'

'Cupidon! he is just about as much a Cupidon as you are a Cyclops.'

'Can she marry him?'

'You will see.'

'I want to know his name, Cary.'

'Guess it.'

'Is it any one in this neighbourhood?'

'Yes, in Briarfield parish.'

'Then it is some person unworthy of her. I don't know a soul in Briarfield parish her equal.'

'Guess.'

'Impossible. I suppose she is under a delusion, and will plunge into some absurdity after all.'

Caroline smiled.

'Do *you* approve the choice?' asked Moore.

'Quite, *quite.*'

'Then I *am* puzzled; for the head which owns this bounteous fall of hazel curls is an excellent little thinking machine, most accurate in its working: it boasts a correct, steady judgment, inherited from "mamma," I suppose.'

'And I *quite* approve, and mamma was charmed.'

' "Mamma" charmed! Mrs Pryor. It can't be romantic then?'

'It is romantic, but it is also right.'

'Tell me, Cary. Tell me out of pity: I am too weak to be tantalized.'

'You shall be tantalized: it will do you no harm: you are not so weak as you pretend.'

'I have twice this evening had some thoughts of falling on the floor at your feet.'

'You had better not: I shall decline to help you up.'

'And worshipping you downright. My mother was a Roman Catholic; you look like the loveliest of her pictures of the Virgin: I think I will embrace her faith, and kneel and adore.'

'Robert, Robert, sit still; don't be absurd: I will go to Hortense, if you commit extravagances.'

'You have stolen my senses: just now nothing will come into my mind but "les litanies de la sainte Vièrge. Rose céleste, reine des Anges!" '

' "Tour d'ivoire, maison d'or": is not that the jargon? Well, sit down quietly, and guess your riddle.'

'But, "mamma" charmed! There's the puzzle.'

'I'll tell you what mamma said when I told her: "Depend upon it, my dear, such a choice will make the happiness of Miss Keeldar's life." '

'I'll guess once, and no more. It is old Helstone. She is going to be your aunt.'

'I'll tell my uncle; I'll tell Shirley!' cried Caroline, laughing gleefully. 'Guess again, Robert; your blunders are charming.'

'It is the parson, Hall.'

'Indeed, no: he is mine, if you please.'

'Yours! Ay! the whole generation of women in Briarfield seem to have made an idol of that priest: I wonder why: he is bald, sand-blind, grey-haired.'

'Fanny will be here to fetch me, before you have solved the riddle, if you don't make haste.'

'I'll guess no more, I am tired: and then I don't care. Miss Keeldar may marry "le grand Turc" for me.'

'Must I whisper?'

'That you must, and quickly: here comes Hortense; come near, a little nearer, my own Lina: I care for the whisper more than the words.'

She whispered: Robert gave a start, a flash of the eye, a brief laugh: Miss Moore entered, and Sarah followed behind, with information that Fanny was come. The hour of converse was over.

Robert found a moment to exchange a few more whispered sentences: he was waiting at the foot of the staircase, as Caroline descended after putting on her shawl.

'Must I call Shirley a noble creature now?' he asked.

'If you wish to speak the truth, certainly.'

'Must I forgive her?'

'Forgive her? Naughty Robert! Was she in the wrong, or were you?'

'Must I at length love her downright, Cary?'

Caroline looked keenly up, and made a movement towards him, something between the loving and the petulant.

'Only give the word, and I'll try to obey you.'

'Indeed, you must not love her: the bare idea is perverse.'

'But then she is handsome, peculiarly handsome: hers is a beauty that grows on you: you think her but graceful, when you first see her; you discover her to be beautiful, when you have known her for a year.'

'It is not you who are to say these things. Now, Robert, be good.'

'Oh! Cary, I have no love to give. Were the goddess of beauty to woo me, I could not meet her advances: there is no heart which I can call mine in this breast.'

'So much the better: you are a great deal safer without: good-night.'

'Why must you always go, Lina, at the very instant when I most want you to stay?'

'Because you most wish to retain when you are most certain to lose.'

'Listen; one other word. Take care of your own heart: do you hear me?'

'There is no danger.'

'I am not convinced of that: the Platonic parson, for instance.'

'Who? Malone?'

'Cyril Hall: I owe more than one twinge of jealousy to that quarter.'

'As to you, you have been flirting with Miss Mann: she showed me the other day a plant you had given her. — Fanny, I am ready.'

CHAPTER XXXVI

WRITTEN IN THE SCHOOLROOM

Louis Moore's doubts, respecting the immediate evacuation of Fieldhead by Mr Sympson, turned out to be perfectly well founded. The very next day after the grand quarrel about Sir Philip Nunnely, a sort of reconciliation was patched up between uncle and niece: Shirley, who could never find in her heart to be or to seem inhospitable (except in the single instance of Mr Donne), begged the whole party to stay a little longer: she begged in such earnest, it was evident she wished it, for some reason. They took her at her word: indeed, the uncle could not bring himself to leave her quite unwatched – at full liberty to marry Robert Moore, as soon as that gentleman should be able (Mr Sympson piously prayed this might never be the case) to reassert his supposed pretensions to her hand. They all stayed.

In his first rage against all the house of Moore, Mr Sympson had so conducted himself towards Mr Louis, that that gentleman – patient of labour or suffering, but intolerant of coarse insolence – had promptly resigned his post, and could now be induced to resume and retain it only till such time as the family should quit Yorkshire: Mrs Sympson's entreaties prevailed with him thus far; his own attachment to his pupil constituted an additional motive for concession; and probably he had a third motive, stronger than either of the other two: probably he would have found it very hard indeed to leave Fieldhead just now.

Things went on, for some time, pretty smoothly; Miss Keeldar's health was re-established; her spirits resumed their flow: Moore had found means to relieve her from every nervous apprehension; and, indeed, from the moment of giving him her confidence, every fear seemed to have taken wing: her heart became as lightsome, her manner as careless, as those of a little child, that, thoughtless of its own life or death, trusts all respon-sibility to its parents. He and William Farren – through whose medium he made inquiries concerning the state of Phœbe – agreed in asserting that the dog was not mad: that it was only ill-usage which had driven her from home: for it was proved that her master was in the frequent habit of chastising her viol-ently. Their assertion might, or might not, be true: the groom and gamekeeper affirmed to the contrary; both asserting that, if hers was not a clear case of hydrophobia, there was no such disease. But to this evidence Louis Moore turned an incredulous ear: he reported to Shirley only what was encouraging: she believed him; and, right or wrong, it is certain that in her case the bite proved innocuous.

November passed; December came: the Sympsons were now really departing; it was incumbent on them to be at home by Christmas; their packages were preparing; they were to leave in a few days. One winter evening, during the last week of their stay, Louis Moore again took out his little blank book, and discoursed with it as follows: –

'She is lovelier than ever. Since that little cloud was dispelled, all the temporary waste and wanness have vanished. It was mar-vellous to see how soon the magical energy of youth raised her elastic, and revived her blooming.

'After breakfast this morning, when I had seen her, and listened to her, and – so to speak – felt her, in every sentient atom of my frame, I passed from her sunny presence into the chill drawing-room. Taking up a little gilt volume, I found it to contain a selection of lyrics. I read a poem or two: whether the spell was in me or in the verse, I know not, but my heart filled genially – my pulse rose: I glowed, notwithstanding the frost-air. I, too, am young as yet; though she said she never considered me young, I am barely thirty: there are moments when life – for no other reason than my own youth – beams with sweet hues upon me.

'It was time to go to the school-room: I went. That same school-room is rather pleasant in a morning; the sun then shines through the low lattice; the books are in order; there are no papers strewn about; the fire is clear and clean; no cinders have fallen, no ashes accumulated. I found Henry there, and he had brought with him Miss Keeldar: they were together.

'I said she was lovelier than ever: she is. A fine rose, not deep but delicate, opens on her cheek; her eye, always dark, clear, and speaking, utters now a language I cannot render – it is the utterance, seen not heard, through which angels must have communed when there was "silence in heaven." Her hair was always dusk as night, and fine as silk; her neck was always fair, flexible, polished – but both have now a new charm: the tresses are soft as shadow, the shoulders they fall on wear a goddess-grace. Once I only *saw* her beauty, now I *feel* it.

'Henry was repeating his lesson to her before bringing it to me – one of her hands was occupied with the book, he held the other: that boy gets more than his share of privileges; he dares caress and is caressed. What indulgence and compassion she shows him! Too much: if this went on, Henry, in a few years, when his soul was formed, would offer it on her altar as I have offered mine.

'I saw her eyelid flitter when I came in, but she did not look up: *now* she hardly ever gives me a glance. She seems to grow silent too – to *me* she rarely speaks, and, when I am present, she says little to others. In my gloomy moments, I attribute this change to indifference, – aversion, – what not? In my sunny intervals I give it another meaning: I say, were I her equal, I could find in this shyness – coyness, and in that coyness – love. As it is, dare I look for it? What could I do with it, if found?

'This morning I dared, at least, contrive an hour's com-munion for her and me; I dared not only *wish* – but *will* an interview with her: I dared summon solitude to guard us. Very decidedly I called Henry to the door: without hesitation, I said, "Go where you will, my boy; but, till I call you, return not here."

'Henry, I could see, did not like his dismissal: that boy is young, but a thinker: his meditative eye shines on me strangely sometimes: he half feels what links me to Shirley; he half guesses that there is a dearer delight in the reserve with which I am treated, than in all the endearments he is allowed. The young, lame, half-grown lion would growl at me now and then, because I have tamed his lioness and am her keeper, did not the habit of discipline and the instinct of affection hold him subdued. Go, Henry; you must learn to take your share of the bitter of life with all of Adam's race that have gone before, or will come after you: your destiny can be no exception to the common lot: be grateful that your love is overlooked thus early, before it can claim any affinity to passion: an hour's fret, a pang of envy, suffice to express what you feel: Jealousy hot as the sun above the line, Rage destructive as the tropic storm, the clime of your sensations ignores – as yet.

'I took my usual seat at the desk, quite in my usual way: I am blessed in that power to cover all inward ebullition with outward calm. No one who looks at my slow face can guess the vortex sometimes whirling in my heart, and engulfing thought, and wrecking prudence. Pleasant is it to have the gift to proceed peacefully and powerfully in your course without alarming by one eccentric movement. It was not my present intention to utter one word of love to her, or to reveal one glimpse of the fire in which I wasted. Presumptuous, I never have been; presumptuous, I never will be: rather than even *seem* selfish and interested, I would resolutely rise, gird my loins, part and leave her, and seek, on the other side of the globe, a new life, cold and barren as the rock the salt tide daily washes. My design this morning was to take of her a near scrutiny – to read a line in the page of her heart: before I left, I determined to know *what* I was leaving.

'I had some quills to make into pens: most men's hands would have trembled when their hearts were so stirred; mine went to work steadily, and my voice, when I called it into exercise, was firm.

' "This day-week you will be alone at Fieldhead, Miss Keeldar."

' "Yes: I rather think my uncle's intention to go is a settled one now."

' "He leaves you dissatisfied."

' "He is not pleased with me."

' "He departs as he came – no better for his journey: this is mortifying."

' "I trust the failure of his plans will take from him all inclination to lay new ones."

' "In his way, Mr Sympson honestly wished you well. All he has done, or intended to do, he believed to be for the best."

' "You are kind to undertake the defence of a man who has permitted himself to treat you with so much insolence."

' "I never feel shocked at, or bear malice for, what is spoken in character; and most perfectly in character was that vulgar and violent onset against me, when he had quitted you worsted."

' "You cease now to be Henry's tutor?"

' "I shall be parted from Henry for a while – (if he and I live we shall meet again somehow, for we love each other) – and be ousted from the bosom of the Sympson family for ever. Happily this change does not leave me stranded: it but hurries into premature execution designs long formed."

' "No change finds you off your guard: I was sure, in your calm way, you would be prepared for sudden mutation. I always think you stand in the world like a solitary but watchful, thoughtful archer in a wood; and the quiver on your shoulder holds more arrows than one; your bow is provided with a second string. Such too is your brother's wont. You two might go forth homeless hunters to the loneliest western wilds; all would be well with you. The hewn tree would make you a hut, the cleared forest yield you fields from its stripped bosom, the buffalo would feel your rifle-shot, and with lowered horns and hump pay homage at your feet."

' "And any Indian tribe of Black-feet, or Flat-heads, would afford us a bride, perhaps?" '

' "No (hesitating): I think not. The savage is sordid: I think, – that is, I *hope*, – you would neither of you share your hearth with that to which you could not give your heart."

' "What suggested the wild West to your mind, Miss Keeldar? Have you been with me in spirit when I did not see you? Have you entered into my day-dreams, and beheld my brain labouring at its scheme of a future?"

'She had separated a slip of paper for lighting tapers – a spill, as it is called – into fragments: she threw morsel by morsel into the fire, and stood pensively watching them consume. She did not speak.

' "How did you learn what you seem to know about my intentions?"

' "I know nothing: I am only discovering them now: I spoke at hazard."

"Your hazard sounds like divination. A tutor I will never be again: never take a pupil after Henry and yourself: not again will I sit habitually at another man's table – no more be the appendage of a family. I am now a man of thirty: I have never been free since I was a boy of ten. I have such a thirst for freedom – such a deep passion to know her and call her mine – such a day-desire and night-longing to win her and possess her, I will not refuse to cross the Atlantic for her sake: her I will follow deep into virgin woods. Mine it shall not be to accept a savage girl as a slave – she could not be a wife. I know no white woman whom I love that would accompany me; but I am certain Liberty will await me, sitting under a pine: when I call her she will come to my log-house, and she shall fill my arms."

'She could not hear me speak so unmoved, and she *was* moved. It was right – I meant to move her. She could not answer me, nor could she look at me: I should have been sorry if she could have done either. Her cheek glowed as if a crimson flower, through whose petals the sun shone, had cast its light upon it. On the white lid and dark lashes of her downcast eye, trembled all that is graceful in the sense of half-painful, half-pleasing shame.

'Soon she controlled her emotion, and took all her feelings under command. I saw she had felt insurrection, and was waking to empire – she sat down. There was that in her face which I could read: it said, I see the line which is my limit – nothing shall make me pass it. I feel – I know how far I may reveal my feelings, and when I must clasp the volume. I have advanced to a certain distance, as far as the true and sovereign and undegraded nature of my kind permits – now here I stand rooted. My heart may break if it is baffled: let it break – it shall never dishonour me – it shall never dishonour my sisterhood in me. Suffering before degradation! death before treachery!

'I, for my part, said, "If she were poor, I would be at her feet. If she were lowly, I would take her in my arms. Her Gold and her Station are two griffins, that guard her on each side. Love looks and longs, and dares not: Passion hovers round, and is kept at bay: Truth and Devotion are scared. There is nothing to lose in winning her – no sacrifice to make – it is all clear gain, and therefore unimaginably difficult."

'Difficult or not, something must be done; something must be said. I could not, and would not, sit silent with all that beauty modestly mute in my presence. I spoke thus; and still I spoke with calm: quiet as my words were, I could hear they fell in a tone distinct, round, and deep.

' "Still, I know I shall be strangely placed with that mountain nymph, Liberty. She is, I suspect, akin to that Solitude which I once wooed, and from which I now seek a divorce. These Oreads are peculiar: they come upon you with an unearthly charm, like some starlight evening; they inspire a wild but not warm delight; their beauty is the beauty of spirits: their grace is not the grace of life, but of seasons or scenes in Nature: theirs is the dewy bloom of morning – the languid flush of evening – the peace of the moon – the changefulness of clouds. I want and will have something different. This elfish splendour looks chill to my vision, and feels frozen to my touch. I am not a poet: I cannot live with abstractions. You, Miss Keeldar, have sometimes, in your laughing satire, called me a material philosopher, and implied that I live sufficiently for the substantial. Certainly I feel material from head to foot; and glorious as Nature is, and deeply as I worship her with the solid powers of a solid heart, I would rather behold her through the soft human eyes of a loved and lovely wife, than through the wild orbs of the highest goddess of Olympus."

' "Juno could not cook a buffalo steak as you like it," said she.

' "She could not: but I will tell you who could – some young, penniless, friendless orphan girl. I wish I could find such a one: pretty enough for me to love, with something of the mind and heart suited to my taste: not uneducated – honest and modest. I care nothing for attainments; but I would fain have the germ of those sweet natural powers which nothing acquired can rival: any temper Fate wills, – I can manage the hottest. To such a creature as this, I should like to be first tutor and then husband. I would teach her my language, my habits, and my principles, and then I would reward her with my love."

' "*Reward* her! lord of the creation! *Reward* her!" ejaculated she, with a curled lip.

' "And be repaid a thousandfold."

' "If she willed it, Monseigneur."

' "And she *should* will it."

' "You have stipulated for any temper Fate wills. Compulsion is flint and a blow to the metal of some souls."

' "And love the spark it elicits."

' "Who cares for the love that is but a spark – seen, flown upward, and gone?"

' "I must find my orphan girl. Tell me how, Miss Keeldar."

' "Advertise; and be sure you add, when you describe the qualifications, she must be a good plain cook."

' "I must find her; and when I do find her, I shall marry her."

' "Not you!" and her voice took a sudden accent of peculiar scorn.

'I liked this: I had roused her from the pensive mood in which I had first found her: I would stir her further.

' "Why doubt it?"

' "*You* marry!"

' "Yes, – of course; nothing more evident than that I can, and shall."

' "The contrary is evident, Mr Moore."

'She charmed me in this mood: waxing disdainful, half insulting, pride, temper, derision, blent in her large fine eye, that had, just now, the look of a merlin's.

' "Favour me with your reasons for such an opinion, Miss Keeldar."

' "How will *you* manage to marry, I wonder?"

' "I shall manage it with ease and speed when I find the proper person."

' "Accept celibacy!" (and she made a gesture with her hand as if she gave me something) "take it as your doom!"

' "No: you cannot give what I already have. Celibacy has been mine for thirty years. If you wish to offer me a gift, a parting present, a keepsake, you must change the boon."

' "Take worse, then!"

' "How? What?"

'I now felt, and looked, and spoke eagerly. I was unwise to quit my sheet-anchor of calm even for an instant: it deprived me of an advantage and transferred it to her. The little spark of temper dissolved in sarcasm, and eddied over her countenance in the ripples of a mocking smile.

' "Take a wife that has paid you court to save your modesty, and thrust herself upon you to spare your scruples."

' "Only show me where."

' "Any stout widow that has had a few husbands already, and can manage these things."

' "She must not be rich then. Oh these riches!"

' "Never would you have gathered the produce of the gold-bearing garden. You have not courage to confront the sleepless dragon: you have not craft to borrow the aid of Atlas!"

' "You look hot and haughty."

' "And you far haughtier. Yours is the monstrous pride which counterfeits humility."

' "I am a dependant: I know my place."

' "I am a woman: I know mine."

' "I am poor: I must be proud."

' "I have received ordinances, and own obligations stringent as yours."

'We had reached a critical point now, and we halted and looked at each other. *She* would not give in, I felt. Beyond this, I neither felt nor saw. A few moments yet were mine: the end was coming – I heard its rush – but not come; I would dally, wait, talk, and when impulse urged, I would act. I am never in a hurry: I never was in a hurry in my whole life. Hasty people drink the nectar of existence scalding hot: taste it cool as dew. I proceeded: –

' "Apparently, Miss Keeldar, you are as little likely to marry as myself: I know you have refused three, nay, four advantageous offers, and, I believe, a fifth. Have you rejected Sir Philip Nunnely?"

'I put this question suddenly and promptly.

' "Did you think I should take him?"

' "I thought you might."

' "On what grounds, may I ask?"

' "Conformity of rank; age; pleasing contrast of temper, for *he* is mild and amiable; harmony of intellectual tastes."

' "A beautiful sentence! Let us take it to pieces. 'Conformity of rank.' – He is quite above me: compare my grange with his palace, if you please: I am disdained by his kith and kin. 'Suitability of age.' – We were born in the same year; consequently, he is still a boy, while I am a woman: ten years his senior to all intents and purposes. 'Contrast of temper.' – Mild and amiable, is he: I – what? Tell me."

' "Sister of the spotted, bright, quick, fiery leopard."

' "And you would mate me with a kid – the Millennium being yet millions of centuries from mankind; being yet, indeed, an archangel high in the seventh heaven, uncommissioned to descend – ? Unjust barbarian! 'Harmony of intellectual tastes.' – He is fond of poetry, and I hate it –"

' "Do you? That is news."

' "I absolutely shudder at the sight of metre or at the sound of rhyme, whenever I am at the Priory or Sir Philip at Fieldhead. Harmony, indeed! When did I whip up syllabub sonnets, or string stanzas fragile as fragments of glass? and when did I betray a belief that those penny-beads were genuine brilliants?"

' "You might have the satisfaction of leading him to a higher standard – of improving his tastes."

' "Leading and improving! teaching and tutoring! bearing and forbearing! Pah! My husband is not to be my baby. I am not to set him his daily lesson and see that he learns it, and give him a sugar-plum if he is good, and a patient, pensive, pathetic lecture if he is bad. But it is like a tutor to talk of the 'satisfaction of teaching' – I suppose *you* think it the finest employment in the world. I don't – I reject it. Improving a husband! No. I shall insist upon my husband improving me, or else we part."

' "God knows it is needed!"

' "What do you mean by that, Mr Moore?"

' "What I say. Improvement is imperatively needed."

' "If you were a woman you would school Monsieur, votre mari, charmingly: it would just suit you; schooling is your vocation."

' "May I ask whether, in your present just and gentle mood, you mean to taunt me with being a tutor?"

' "Yes – bitterly; and with anything else you please: any defect of which you are painfully conscious."

' "With being poor, for instance?"

' "Of course; that will sting you; you are sore about your poverty: you brood over that."

' "With having nothing but a very plain person to offer the woman who may master my heart?"

' "Exactly. You have a habit of calling yourself plain. You are sensitive about the cut of your features, because they are not quite on an Apollo-pattern. You abuse them more than is need-ful, in the faint hope that others may say a word in their behalf – which won't happen. Your face is nothing to boast of, certainly: not a pretty line, nor a pretty tint, to be found therein."

' "Compare it with your own."

' "It looks like a god of Egypt: a great sand-buried stone head; or rather I will compare it to nothing so lofty: it looks like Tartar: you are my mastiff's cousin: I think you as much like him as a man can be like a dog."

' "Tartar is your dear companion. In summer, when you rise early, and run out into the fields to wet your feet with the dew, and freshen your cheek and uncurl your hair with the breeze, you always call him to follow you: you call him sometimes with a whistle that you learned from me. In the solitude of your wood, when you think nobody but Tartar is listening, you whistle the very tunes you imitated from my lips, or sing the very songs you have caught up by ear from my voice: I do not ask whence flows the feeling which you pour into these songs, for I know it flows out of your heart, Miss Keeldar. In the winter evenings, Tartar lies at your feet: you suffer him to rest his head on your perfumed lap; you let him couch on the borders of your satin raiment: his rough hide is familiar with the contact of your hand: I once saw you kiss him on that snow-white beauty-spot which stars his broad forehead. It is dangerous to say I am like Tartar: it suggests to me a claim to be treated like Tartar."

' "Perhaps, sir, you can extort as much from your penniless and friendless young orphan-girl, when you find her."

' "Oh! could I find her such as I imagine her. Something to tame first, and teach afterwards: to break in, and then to fondle. To lift the destitute proud thing out of poverty; to establish power over, and then to be indulgent to the capricious moods that never were influenced and never indulged before; to see her alternately irritated and subdued about twelve times in the twenty-four hours; and perhaps, eventually, when her training was accomplished, to behold her the exemplary and patient mother of about a dozen children, only now and then lending little Louis a cordial cuff by way of paying the interest of the vast debt she owes his father. Oh!" (I went on) "my orphan-girl would give me many a kiss; she would watch on the threshold for my coming home of an evening; she would run into my arms; should keep my hearth as bright as she would make it warm. God bless the sweet idea! Find her I must."

'Her eyes emitted an eager flash, her lips opened; but she reclosed them, and impetuously turned away.

' "Tell me, tell me where she is, Miss Keeldar!"

'Another movement: all haughtiness, and fire, and impulse.

' "I must know. You *can* tell me. You *shall* tell me."

' "I *never will.*"

'She turned to leave me. Could I now let her part as she had always parted from me? No: I had gone too far not to finish. I had come too near the end not to drive home to it. All the encumbrance of doubt, all the rubbish of indecision must be removed at once, and the plain truth must be ascertained. She must take her part, and tell me what it was. I must take mine, and adhere to it.

' "A minute, madam," I said, keeping my hand on the door-handle before I opened it. "We have had a long conversation this morning, but the last word has not been spoken yet: it is yours to speak it."

' "May I pass?"

' "No. I guard the door. I would almost rather die than let you leave me just now, without speaking the word I demand."

' "What dare you expect me to say?"

' "What I am dying and perishing to hear; what I *must* and *will* hear; what you dare not now suppress."

' "Mr Moore, I hardly know what you mean: you are not like yourself."

'I suppose I hardly was like my usual self, for I scared her; that I could see: it was right; she must be scared to be won.

' "You *do* know what I mean, and for the first time I stand before you *myself*. I have flung off the tutor, and beg to introduce you to the man: and, remember, he is a gentleman."

'She trembled. She put her hand to mine as if to remove it from the lock; she might as well have tried to loosen, by her soft touch, metal welded to metal. She felt she was powerless, and receded; and again she trembled.

'What change I underwent, I cannot explain; but out of her emotion passed into me a new spirit. I neither was crushed nor elated by her lands and gold; I thought not of them, cared not for them: they were nothing: dross that could not dismay me. I saw only herself; her young beautiful form; the grace, the majesty, the modesty of her girlhood.

' "My pupil," I said.

' "My master," was the low answer.

' "I have a thing to tell you."

'She waited with declined brow, and ringlets drooped.

' "I have to tell you, that for four years you have been growing into your tutor's heart, and that you are rooted there now. I have to declare that you have bewitched me, in spite of sense and experience, and difference of station and estate: you have so looked, and spoken, and moved; so shown me your faults and your virtues – beauties rather; they are hardly so stern as virtues, – that I love you – love you with my life and strength. It is out now."

'She sought what to say, but could not find a word: she tried to rally; but vainly. I passionately repeated that I loved her.

' "Well, Mr Moore, what then?" was the answer I got; uttered in a tone that would have been petulant, if it had not faltered.

' "Have you nothing to say to me? Have you no love for me?"

' "A little bit."

' "I am not to be tortured: I will not even play at present."

' "I don't want to play; I want to go."

' "I wonder you dare speak of going at this moment. *You* go! What! with my heart in your hand, to lay it on your toilet and pierce it with your pins? From my presence you do not stir; out of my reach you do not stray, till I receive a hostage – pledge for pledge – your heart for mine."

' "The thing you want is mislaid – lost some time since: let me go and seek it."

' "Declare that it is where your keys often are – in my possession."

' "You ought to know. And where are my keys, Mr Moore? indeed and truly, I have lost them again; and Mrs Gill wants some money, and I have none, except this sixpence."

'She took the coin out of her apron-pocket, and showed it in her palm. I could have trifled with her; but it would not do: life and death were at stake. Mastering at once the sixpence and the hand that held it, I demanded, –

' "Am I to die without you, or am I to live for you?"

' "Do as you please: far be it from me to dictate your choice."

' "You shall tell me with your own lips, whether you doom me to exile, or call me to hope."

' "Go. I can bear to be left."

' "Perhaps, I too *can* bear to leave you: but reply, Shirley, my pupil, my sovereign – reply."

' "Die without me, if you will. Live for me if you dare."

' "I am not afraid of you, my leopardess: I *dare* live for and with you, from this hour till my death. Now, then, I have you: you are mine: I will never let you go. Wherever my home be, I have chosen my wife. If I stay in England, in England you will stay; if I cross the Atlantic, you will cross it also: our lives are riveted; our lots intertwined."

' "And are we equal then, sir? Are we equal at last?"

' "You are younger, frailer, feebler, more ignorant than I."

' "Will you be good to me, and never tyrannize?"

' "Will you let me breathe, and not bewilder me? You must not smile at present. The world swims and changes round me. The sun is a dizzying scarlet blaze; the sky a violet vortex whirling over me."

'I am a strong man, but I staggered as I spoke. All creation was exaggerated: colour grew more vivid; motion more rapid; life itself more vital. I hardly saw her for a moment; but I heard her voice – pitilessly sweet. She would not subdue one of her charms in compassion: perhaps she did not know what I felt.

' "You name me leopardess: remember, the leopardess is tameless," said she.

' "Tame or fierce, wild or subdued, you are *mine*."

' "I am glad I know my keeper, and am used to him. Only his voice will I follow; only his hand shall manage me; only at his feet will I repose."

'I took her back to her seat, and sat down by her side: I wanted to hear her speak again: I could never have enough of her voice and her words.

' "How much do you love me?" I asked.

' "Ah! you know: I will not gratify you: will not flatter."

' "I don't know half enough: my heart craves to be fed. If you knew how hungry and ferocious it is, you would hasten to stay it with a kind word or two."

' "Poor Tartar!" said she, touching and patting my hand: "poor fellow; stalwart friend; Shirley's pet and favourite, lie down!"

' "But I will not lie down till I am fed with one sweet word."

'And at last she gave it.

' "Dear Louis, be faithful to me: never leave me. I don't care for life, unless I may pass it at your side."

' "Something more."

'She gave me a change: it was not her way to offer the same dish twice.

' "Sir!" she said, starting up, "at your peril, you ever again name such sordid things as money, or poverty, or inequality. It will be absolutely dangerous to torment me with these maddening scruples. I defy you to do it."

'My face grew hot. I did once more wish I were not so poor, or she were not so rich. She saw the transient misery; and then, indeed, she caressed me. Blent with torment, I experienced rapture.

' "Mr Moore," said she, looking up with a sweet, open, earnest countenance, "teach me and help me to be good. I do not ask you to take off my shoulders all the cares and duties of property; but I ask you to share the burden, and to show me how to sustain my part well. Your judgment is well-balanced; your heart is kind; your principles are sound. I know you are wise; I feel you are benevolent; I believe you are conscientious. Be my companion through life; be my guide where I am ignorant: be my master where I am faulty; be my friend always!"

' "So help me God, I will!" '

Yet again, a passage from the blank book, if you like, reader; if you don't like it, pass it over: –

'The Sympsons are gone; but not before discovery and explanation. My manner must have betrayed something, or my looks: I was quiet, but I forgot to be guarded sometimes. I stayed longer in the room than usual; I could not bear to be out of her presence; I returned to it, and basked in it, like Tartar in the sun. If she left the oak-parlour, instinctively I rose, and left it too. She chid me for this procedure more than once: I did it with a vague, blundering idea of getting a word with her in the hall, or elsewhere. Yesterday, towards dusk, I had her to myself for five minutes, by the hall-fire: we stood side by side; she was railing at me, and I was enjoying the sound of her voice: the young ladies passed, and looked at us; we did not separate: erelong, they repassed, and again looked. Mrs Sympson came; we did not move: Mr Sympson opened the dining-room door; Shirley flashed him back full payment for his spying gaze: she curled her lip, and tossed her tresses. The glance she gave was at once explanatory and defiant; it said – "I like Mr Moore's society, and I dare you to find fault with my taste."

'I asked, "Do you mean him to understand how matters are?"

' "I do," said she; "but I leave the development to chance. There will be a scene. I neither invite it nor fear it – only, you must be present; for I am inexpressibly tired of facing him solus. I don't like to see him in a rage; he then puts off all his fine proprieties and conventional disguises, and the real human being below is what you would call 'commun, plat, bas – vilain et un peu méchant.' His ideas are not clean, Mr Moore; they want scouring with soft soap and fuller's earth. I think, if he could add his imagination to the contents of Mrs Gill's bucking-basket, and let her boil it in her copper, with rain-water and bleaching-powder (I hope you think me a tolerable laundress), it would do him incalculable good."

'This morning, fancying I heard her descend somewhat early, I was down instantly. I had not been deceived: there she was, busy at work, in the breakfast-parlour, of which the housemaid was completing the arrangement and dusting. She had risen betimes to finish some little keepsake she intended for Henry. I got only a cool reception; which I accepted till the girl was gone, taking my book to the window-seat very quietly. Even when we were alone, I was slow to disturb her: to sit with her in sight was happiness, and the proper happiness, for early morning – serene, incomplete, but progressive. Had I been obtrusive, I knew I should have encountered rebuff. "Not at home to suitors," was written on her brow; therefore, I read on – stole, now and then, a look; watched her countenance soften and open, as she felt I respected her mood, and enjoyed the gentle content of the moment.

'The distance between us shrank, and the light hoar-frost thawed insensibly: ere an hour elapsed, I was at her side, watching her sew, gathering her sweet smiles and her merry words, which fell for me abundantly. We sat, as we had a right to sit, side by side: my arm rested on her chair; I was near enough to count the stitches of her work, and to discern the eye of her needle. The door suddenly opened.

'I believe, if I had just then started from her, she would have despised me: thanks to the phlegm of my nature, I rarely start. When I am well-off, bien, comfortable, I am not soon stirred: bien I was – très bien – consequently, immutable: no muscle moved. I hardly looked to the door.

' "Good-morning, uncle," said she, addressing that personage; who paused on the threshold in a state of petrifaction.

' "Have you been long down-stairs, Miss Keeldar, and alone with Mr Moore?"

' "Yes, a very long time: we both came down early; it was scarcely light."

' "The proceeding is improper –"

' "It was at first: I was rather cross, and not civil; but you will perceive that we are now friends."

' "I perceive more than you would wish me to perceive."

' "Hardly, sir," said I: "we have no disguises. Will you permit me to intimate, that any further observations you have to make may as well be addressed to mine. Henceforward, I stand between Miss Keeldar and all annoyance."

' "*You!* What have *you* to do with Miss Keeldar?"

' "To protect, watch over, serve her."

' "You, sir? – you, the tutor?"

' "Not one word of insult, sir," interposed she: "not one syllable of disrespect to Mr Moore, in this house."

' "Do you take his part?"

' "*His* part! Oh, yes!"

'She turned to me with a sudden, fond movement, which I met by circling her with my arm. She and I both rose.

' "Good Ged!" was the cry from the morning-gown ❙
quivering at the door. *Ged*, I think, must be the cogn❙
of Mr Sympson's Lares: when hard-pressed, he always inv❙
this idol.

' "Come forward, uncle: you shall hear all. Tell him al❙
Louis."

' "I dare him to speak! The beggar! the knave! the specious
hypocrite! the vile, insinuating, infamous menial! Stand apart
from my niece, sir: let her go!"

'She clung to me with energy. "I am near my future husband,"
she said: "who dares touch him or me?"

' "Her husband!" he raised and spread his hands: he dropped
into a seat.

' "A while ago, you wanted much to know whom I meant
to marry: my intention was then formed, but not mature for
communication; now it is ripe, sun-mellowed, perfect: take the
crimson-peach – take Louis Moore!"

' "But" (savagely) "you *shall not* have him – he *shall not*
have you."

' "I would die before I would have another. I would die if
I might not have him."

'He uttered words with which this page shall never be
polluted.

'She turned white as death: she shook all over: she lost her
strength. I laid her down on the sofa: just looked to ascertain
that she had not fainted – of which, with a divine smile, she
assured me; I kissed her, and then, if I were to perish, I cannot
give a clear account of what happened in the course of the
next five minutes: she has since – through tears, laughter, and
trembling – told me that I turned terrible, and gave myself to
the demon; she says I left her, made one bound across the room
– that Mr Sympson vanished through the door as if shot from
a cannon – I also vanished, and she heard Mrs Gill scream.

'Mrs Gill was still screaming when I came to my senses: I was
then in another apartment – the oak-parlour, I think: I held

anding
omen
okes
633

hed into a chair, and my hand was on

n his head – I was strangling him, I

d wringing her hands, entreating

.at moment, and felt at once as cool as

.rs Gill to fetch the Red-House Inn chaise

informed Mr Sympson he must depart from

. the instant it came: though half-frightened out of his

., he declared he would not. Repeating the former order,

I added a commission to fetch a constable. I said: –

' "You *shall* go – by fair means or foul."

'He threatened prosecution – I cared for nothing: I had stood over him once before, not quite so fiercely as now, but full as austerely. It was one night when burglars attempted the house at Sympson-Grove; and in his wretched cowardice he would have given a vain alarm, without daring to offer defence: I had then been obliged to protect his family and his abode by mastering himself – and I had succeeded. I now remained with him till the chaise came: I marshalled him to it, he scolding all the way. He was terribly bewildered, as well as enraged; he would have resisted me, but knew not how: he called for his wife and daughters to come. I said they should follow him as soon as they could prepare: the smoke, the fume, the fret of his demeanour was inexpressible, but it was a fury incapable of producing a deed: that man, properly handled, must ever remain impotent. I know he will never touch me with the law: I know his wife, over whom he tyrannizes in trifles, guides him in matters of importance. I have long since earned her undying mother's gratitude by my devotion to her boy: in some of Henry's ailments I have nursed him – better, she said, than any woman could nurse: she will never forget that. She and her daughters quitted me to-day, in mute wrath and consternation – but she respects me. When Henry clung to my neck, as I lifted him into the carriage and placed him by her side – when I arranged her own wrapping to make her warm, though she turned her head from me, I saw the tears start to her eyes. She will but the more zealously advocate my cause, because she has left me in anger. I am glad of this: not for my own sake, but for that of my life and idol – my Shirley.'

Once again he writes – a week after: –

'I am now at Stilbro': I have taken up my temporary abode with a friend – a professional man – in whose business I can be useful. Every day I ride over to Fieldhead. How long will it be before I can call that place my home, and its mistress mine? I am not easy – not tranquil: I am tantalized – sometimes tortured. To see her now, one would think she had never pressed her cheek to my shoulder, or clung to me with tenderness or trust. I feel unsafe: she renders me miserable: I am shunned when I visit her: she withdraws from my reach. Once, this day, I lifted her face, resolved to get a full look down her deep, dark eyes: difficult to describe what I read there! Pantheress! – beautiful forest-born! – wily, tameless, peerless nature! She gnaws her chain: I see the white teeth working at the steel! She has dreams of her wild woods, and pinings after virgin freedom. I wish Sympson would come again, and oblige her again to entwine her arms about me. I wish there was danger she should lose me, as there is risk I shall lose her. No: final loss, I do not fear; but long delay –

'It is now night – midnight. I have spent the afternoon and evening at Fieldhead. Some hours ago she passed me, coming down the oak-staircase to the hall: she did not know I was standing in the twilight, near the staircase-window, looking at the frost-bright constellations. How closely she glided against the banisters! How shyly shone her large eyes upon me! How evanescent, fugitive, fitful, she looked, – slim and swift as a Northern Streamer!

'I followed her into the drawing-room: Mrs Pryor and Caroline Helstone were both there: she has summoned them to bear her company awhile. In her white evening dress; with her long hair flowing full and wavy; with her noiseless step, her pale cheek, her eye full of night and lightning, she looked, I thought, spirit-like, – a thing made of an element, – the child of a breeze and a flame, – the daughter of ray and rain-drop, – a thing never to be overtaken, arrested, fixed. I wished I could avoid following her with my gaze, as she moved here and there, but it was impossible. I talked with the other ladies as well as I could, but still I looked at her. She was very silent: I think she never spoke to me, – not even when she offered me tea. It happened that she was called out a minute by Mrs Gill. I passed into the moon-lit hall, with the design of getting a word as she returned; nor in this did I fail.

' "Miss Keeldar, stay one instant!" said I, meeting her.

' "Why? – the hall is too cold.'

' "It is not cold for me: at my side, it should not be cold for you."

' "But I shiver."

' "With fear, I believe. What makes you fear me? You are quiet and distant: why?"

' "I may well fear what looks like a great dark goblin meeting me in the moonlight."

' "*Do not – do not* pass! – stay with me awhile: let us exchange a few quiet words. It is three days since I spoke to you alone: such changes are cruel."

' "I have no wish to be cruel," she responded, softly enough: indeed, there was softness in her whole deportment, – in her face, in her voice; but there was also reserve, and an air fleeting, evanishing, intangible.

' "You certainly give me pain," said I. "It is hardly a week since you called me your future husband, and treated me as such; now I am once more the tutor for you: I am addressed as Mr Moore, and Sir; your lips have forgotten Louis."

' "No, Louis, no: it is an easy, liquid name; not soon forgotten."

' "Be cordial to Louis, then: approach him, – let him approach."

' "I *am* cordial," said she, hovering aloof like a white shadow.

' "Your voice is very sweet, and very low," I answered, quietly advancing: "you seem subdued, but still startled."

' "No, – quite calm, and afraid of nothing," she assured me.

' "Of nothing but your votary."

'I bent a knee to the flags at her feet.

' "You see I am in a new world, Mr Moore. I don't know myself, – I don't know you: but rise; when you do so, I feel troubled and disturbed."

'I obeyed: it would not have suited me to retain that attitude long. I courted serenity and confidence for her, and not vainly: she trusted, and clung to me again.

' "Now, Shirley," I said, "you can conceive I am far from happy in my present uncertain unsettled state."

' "Oh, yes; you *are* happy!" she cried, hastily: "you don't know how happy you are! – any change will be for the worse!"

' "Happy or not, I cannot bear to go on so much longer: you are too generous to require it."

' "Be reasonable, Louis, – be patient! I like you because you are patient."

' "Like me no longer, then, – love me instead: fix our marriage-day. Think of it to-night, and decide."

'She breathed a murmur, inarticulate yet expressive; darted, or melted, from my arms – and I lost her.'

CHAPTER XXXVII

THE WINDING-UP

YES, READER, we must settle accounts now. I have only briefly to narrate the final fates of some of the personages whose acquaintance we have made in this narrative, and then you and I must shake hands, and for the present separate.

Let us turn to the Curates, – to the much-loved, though long-neglected. Come forward, modest merit! Malone, I see, promptly answers the invocation: he knows his own description when he hears it.

No, Peter Augustus, we can have nothing to say to you: it won't do. Impossible to trust ourselves with the touching tale of your deeds and destinies. Are you not aware, Peter, that a discriminating public has its crotchets: that the unvarnished truth does not answer; that plain facts will not digest? Do you not know that the squeak of the real pig is no more relished now than it was in days of yore? Were I to give the catastrophe of your life and conversation, the public would sweep off in shrieking hysterics, and there would be a wild cry for sal-volatile and burnt feathers. 'Impossible!' would be pronounced here: 'untrue!' would be responded there. 'Inartistic!' would be solemnly decided. Note well! Whenever you present the actual, simple truth, it is, somehow, always denounced as a lie: they disown it, cast it off, throw it on the parish; whereas the product of your own imagination, the mere figment, the sheer fiction, is adopted, petted, termed pretty, proper, sweetly natural: the little, spurious wretch gets all the comfits, – the honest, lawful bantling, all the cuffs. Such is the way of the world, Peter; and, as you are the legitimate urchin, rude, unwashed, and naughty, you must stand down.

Make way for Mr Sweeting.

Here he comes, with his lady on his arm; the most splendid and the weightiest woman in Yorkshire: Mrs Sweeting, formerly Miss Dora Sykes. They were married under the happiest auspices. Mr Sweeting having been just inducted to a comfortable living, and Mr Sykes being in circumstances to give Dora a handsome portion. They lived long and happily together, beloved by their parishioners, and by a numerous circle of friends.

There! I think the varnish has been put on very nicely.

Advance, Mr Donne.

This gentleman turned out admirably: far better than either you or I could possibly have expected, reader. He, too, married a most sensible, quiet, lady-like little woman: the match was the making of him: he became an exemplary domestic character, and a truly active parish-priest (as a pastor, he, to his dying day, conscientiously refused to act). The outside of the cup and platter he burnished up with the best polishing-powder; the furniture of the altar and temple he looked after with the zeal of an upholsterer, – the care of a cabinet-maker. His little school, his little church, his little parsonage, all owed their erection to him; and they did him credit: each was a model in its way: if uniformity and taste in architecture had been the same thing as consistency and earnestness in religion, what a shepherd of a Christian flock Mr Donne would have made! There was one art in the mastery of which nothing mortal ever surpassed Mr Donne – it was that of begging. By his own unassisted efforts, he begged all the money for all his erections. In this matter he had a grasp of plan, a scope of action quite unique: he begged of high and low, – of the shoeless cottage brat and the coronetted duke: he sent out begging-letters far and wide – to old Queen Charlotte, to the princesses her daughters, to her sons the royal dukes, to the Prince Regent, to Lord Castlereagh, to every member of the ministry then in office; and, what is more remarkable, he screwed something out of every one of these personages. It is on record that he got five pounds from the close-fisted old lady, Queen Charlotte, and two guineas from the royal profligate, her eldest son. When Mr Donne set out on begging expeditions, he armed himself in a complete suit of brazen mail: that you had given a hundred pounds yesterday, was, with him, no reason why you should not give two hundred to-day: he would tell you so to your face, and, ten to one, get the money out of you: people gave to get rid of him. After all, he did some good with the cash; he was useful in his day and generation.

Perhaps I ought to remark, that on the premature and sudden vanishing of Mr Malone from the stage of Briarfield parish (you cannot know how it happened, reader; your curiosity must be robbed to pay your elegant love of the pretty and pleasing), there came as his successor another Irish curate, Mr Macarthey. I am happy to be able to inform you, *with truth*, that this gentleman did as much credit to his country as Malone had done it discredit: he proved himself as decent, decorous, and conscientious, as Peter was rampant, boisterous, and – (this last epithet I choose to suppress, because it would let the cat out of the bag). He laboured faithfully in the parish: the schools, both Sunday and day schools, flourished under his sway like green bay-trees. Being human, of course he had his faults; these, however, were proper, steady-going, clerical faults; what many would call virtues: the circumstance of finding himself invited to tea with a Dissenter would unhinge him for a week; the spectacle of a Quaker wearing his hat in the church, the thought of an unbaptized fellow-creature being interred with Christian rites – these things could make strange havoc in Mr Macarthey's physical and mental economy; otherwise, he was sane and rational, diligent and charitable.

I doubt not a justice-loving public will have remarked, ere this, that I have thus far shown a criminal remissness in pursuing, catching, and bringing to condign punishment the would-be

assassin of Mr Robert Moore: here was a fine opening to lead
my willing readers a dance, at once decorous and exciting: a
dance of law and gospel, of the dungeon, the dock, and the
'dead-thraw.' You might have liked it, reader, but *I* should not:
I and my subject would presently have quarrelled, and then I
should have broken down: I was happy to find that facts perfectly exonerated me from the attempt. The murderer was never
punished; for the good reason, that he was never caught; the
result of the further circumstance, that he was never pursued.
The magistrates made a shuffling, as if they were going to rise
and do valiant things; but, since Moore himself, instead of
urging and leading them as heretofore, lay still on his little
cottage-couch, laughing in his sleeve and sneering with every
feature of his pale, foreign face, they considered better of it; and,
after fulfilling certain indispensable forms, prudently resolved to
let the matter quietly drop: which they did.

Mr Moore knew who had shot him, and all Briarfield knew:
it was no other than Michael Hartley, the half-crazed weaver
once before alluded to, a frantic Antinomian in religion, and a
mad leveller in politics; the poor soul died of delirium tremens
a year after the attempt on Moore, and Robert gave his wretched
widow a guinea to bury him.

The winter is over and gone: spring has followed with beamy
and shadowy, with flowery and showery flight: we are now in
the heart of summer – in mid-June, – the June of 1812.

It is burning weather: the air is deep azure and red gold: it
fits the time; it fits the age; it fits the present spirit of the nations.
The nineteenth century wantons in its giant adolescence: the
Titan-boy uproots mountains in his game, and hurls rocks in
his wild sport. This summer, Bonaparte is in the saddle: he and
his host scour Russian deserts: he has with him Frenchmen and
Poles, Italians and children of the Rhine, six hundred thousand
strong. He marches on old Moscow: under old Moscow's walls
the rude Cossack waits him. Barbarian stoic! he waits without

fear of the boundless ruin rolling on. He puts his trust in a snow-cloud: the Wilderness, the Wind, and the Hail-Storm are his refuge: his allies are the elements – Air, Fire, Water. And what are these? Three terrible archangels ever stationed before the throne of Jehovah. They stand clothed in white, girdled with golden girdles; they uplift vials, brimming with the wrath of God. Their time is the day of vengeance; their signal, the word of the Lord of Hosts, 'thundering with the voice of His excellency.'

'Hast thou entered into the treasures of the snow? or hast thou seen the treasures of the hail, which I have reserved against the time of trouble, against the day of battle and war?

'Go your ways: pour out the vials of the wrath of God upon the earth.'

It is done: the earth is scorched with fire: the sea becomes 'as the blood of a dead man:' the islands flee away; the mountains are not found.

In this year, Lord Wellington assumed the reins in Spain: they made him Generalissimo, for their own salvation's sake. In this year, he took Badajos, he fought the field of Vittoria, he captured Pampeluna, he stormed St Sebastian; in this year, he won Salamanca.

Men of Manchester! I beg your pardon for this slight résumé of warlike facts: but it is of no consequence. Lord Wellington is, for you, only a decayed old gentleman now: I rather think some of you have called him a 'dotard' – you have taunted him with his age, and the loss of his physical vigour. What fine heroes you are yourselves! Men like you have a right to trample on what is mortal in a demigod. Scoff at your ease – your scorn can never break his grand, old heart.

But come, friends, whether Quakers or Cotton-printers, let us hold a Peace-Congress, and let out our venom quietly. We have been talking with unseemly zeal about bloody battles and butchering generals; we arrive now at a triumph in your line. On the 18th of June 1812, the Orders in Council were repealed,

and the blockaded ports thrown open. You know very well –
such of you as are old enough to remember – you made Yorkshire and Lancashire shake with your shout on that occasion:
the ringers cracked a bell in Briarfield belfry; it is dissonant to
this day. The Association of Merchants and Manufacturers
dined together at Stilbro', and one and all went home in such
a plight as their wives would never wish to witness more.
Liverpool started and snorted like a river-horse roused amongst
his reeds by thunder. Some of the American merchants felt
threatenings of apoplexy, and had themselves bled: all, like wise
men, at this first moment of prosperity, prepared to rush into
the bowels of speculation, and to delve new difficulties, in whose
depths they might lose themselves at some future day. Stocks,
which had been accumulating for years, now went off in a
moment, in the twinkling of an eye; warehouses were lightened,
ships were laden; work abounded, wages rose: the good time
seemed come. These prospects might be delusive, but they were
brilliant – to some they were even true. At that epoch, in that
single month of June, many a solid fortune was realized.

When a whole province rejoices, the humblest of its inhabitants
tastes a festal feeling: the sound of public bells rouses the most
secluded abode, as if with a call to be gay. And so Caroline
Helstone thought, when she dressed herself more carefully than
usual on the day of this trading triumph, and went, attired in
her neatest muslin, to spend the afternoon at Fieldhead, there
to superintend certain millinery preparations for a great event:
the last appeal in these matters being reserved for her un-
impeachable taste. She decided on the wreath, the veil, the dress
to be worn at the altar: she chose various robes and fashions for
more ordinary occasions, without much reference to the bride's
opinion; that lady, indeed, being in a somewhat impracticable
mood.

Louis had presaged difficulties, and he had found them:
in fact, his mistress had shown herself exquisitely provoking;

putting off her marriage day by day, week by week, month by month. At first coaxing him with soft pretences of procrastination, and in the end rousing his whole deliberate but determined nature to revolt against her tyranny, at once so sweet and so intolerable.

It had needed a sort of tempest-shock to bring her to the point; but there she was at last, fettered to a fixed day: there she lay, conquered by love, and bound with a vow.

Thus vanquished and restricted, she pined, like any other chained denizen of deserts. Her captor alone could cheer her; his society only could make amends for the lost privilege of liberty: in his absence, she sat or wandered alone; spoke little, and ate less.

She furthered no preparations for her nuptials; Louis was himself obliged to direct all arrangements: he was virtually master of Fieldhead, weeks before he became so nominally: the least presumptuous, the kindest master that ever was; but with his lady absolute. She abdicated without a word or a struggle. 'Go to Mr Moore; ask Mr Moore,' was her answer when applied to for orders. Never was wooer of wealthy bride so thoroughly absolved from the subaltern part; so inevitably compelled to assume a paramount character.

In all this, Miss Keeldar partly yielded to her disposition; but a remark she made a year afterwards proved that she partly also acted on system. 'Louis,' she said, 'would never have learned to rule, if she had not ceased to govern: the incapacity of the sovereign had developed the powers of the premier.'

It had been intended that Miss Helstone should act as bridesmaid at the approaching nuptials; but Fortune had destined her another part.

She came home in time to water her plants. She had performed this little task. The last flower attended to was a rose-tree, which bloomed in a quiet green nook at the back of the house. This plant had received the refreshing shower: she was now resting a minute. Near the wall stood a fragment of sculptured stone –

a monkish relic; once, perhaps, the base of a cross: she mounted it, that she might better command the view. She had still the watering-pot in one hand; with the other, her pretty dress was held lightly aside, to avoid trickling drops: she gazed over the wall, along some lonely fields; beyond three dusk trees, rising side by side against the sky; beyond a solitary thorn, at the head of a solitary lane far off: she surveyed the dusk moors, where bonfires were kindling: the summer evening was warm; the bell-music was joyous; the blue smoke of the fires looked soft; their red flame bright: above them, in the sky whence the sun had vanished, twinkled a silver point – the Star of Love.

Caroline was not unhappy that evening; far otherwise: but as she gazed she sighed, and as she sighed a hand circled her, and rested quietly on her waist; Caroline thought she knew who had drawn near: she received the touch unstartled.

'I am looking at Venus, mamma: see, she is beautiful. How white her lustre is, compared with the deep red of the bonfires!'

The answer was a closer caress; and Caroline turned, and looked, not into Mrs Pryor's matron face, but up at a dark manly visage. She dropped her watering-pot, and stepped down from the pedestal.

'I have been sitting with "mamma" an hour,' said the intruder. 'I have had a long conversation with her. Where, meantime, have you been?'

'To Fieldhead. Shirley is as naughty as ever, Robert: she will neither say Yes nor No to any question put. She sits alone: I cannot tell whether she is melancholy or nonchalant: if you rouse her, or scold her, she gives you a look half wistful, half reckless, which sends you away as queer and crazed as herself. What Louis will make of her, I cannot tell: for my part, if I were a gentleman, I think I would not dare undertake her.'

'Never mind them: they were cut out for each other. Louis, strange to say, likes her all the better for these freaks: he will manage her, if any one can. She tires him, however: he has had a stormy courtship for such a calm character; but you see it all ends in victory for him. Caroline, I have sought you to ask an audience. Why are those bells ringing?'

'For the repeal of your terrible law; the Orders you hate so much. You are pleased, are you not?'

'Yesterday evening at this time, I was packing some books for a sea-voyage: they were the only possessions, except some clothes, seeds, roots, and tools, which I felt free to take with me to Canada. I was going to leave you.'

'To leave me? To leave *me?*'

Her little fingers fastened on his arm: she spoke and looked affrighted.

'Not now – not now. Examine my face; yes, look at me well: is the despair of parting legible thereon?'

She looked into an illuminated countenance, whose characters were all beaming, though the page itself was dusk: this face, potent in the majesty of its traits, shed down on her hope, fondness, delight.

'Will the repeal do you good; much good – *immediate* good?' she inquired.

'The repeal of the Orders in Council saves me. Now I shall not turn bankrupt; now I shall not give up business; now I shall not leave England; now I shall be no longer poor; now I can pay my debts; now all the cloth I have in my warehouses will be taken off my hands, and commissions given me for much more: this day lays for my fortunes abroad, firm foundation; on which, for the first time in my life, I can securely build.'

Caroline devoured his words: she held his hand in hers; she drew a long breath.

'You are saved? Your heavy difficulties are lifted?'

'They are lifted: I breathe: I can act.'

'At last! Oh! Providence is kind. Thank Him, Robert.'

'I do thank Providence.'

'And I also, for your sake!' She looked up devoutly.

'Now, I can take more workmen; give better wages; lay wiser and more liberal plans; do some good; be less selfish: *now,*

Caroline, I can have a house – a home which I can truly call mine – and *now* –'

He paused; for his deep voice was checked.

'And *now*,' he resumed – 'now I can think of marriage; *now* I can seek a wife.'

This was no moment for her to speak: she did not speak.

'Will Caroline, who meekly hopes to be forgiven as she forgives – will she pardon all I have made her suffer – all that long pain I have wickedly caused her – all that sickness of body and mind she owed to me? Will she forget what she knows of my poor ambition – my sordid schemes? Will she let me expiate these things? Will she suffer me to prove that, as I once deserted cruelly, trifled wantonly, injured basely, I can now love faithfully, cherish fondly, treasure tenderly?'

His hand was in Caroline's still: a gentle pressure answered him.

'Is Caroline mine?'

'Caroline is yours.'

'I will prize her: the sense of her value is here, in my heart; the necessity for her society is blended with my life: not more jealous shall I be of the blood whose flow moves my pulses, than of her happiness and well-being.'

'I love you, too, Robert, and will take faithful care of you.'

'Will you take faithful care of me? – faithful care! as if that rose should promise to shelter from tempest this hard, grey stone? But she *will* care for me, in her way: these hands will be the gentle ministrants of every comfort I can taste. I know the being I seek to entwine with my own will bring me a solace – a charity – a purity – to which, of myself, I am a stranger.'

Suddenly, Caroline was troubled; her lip quivered.

'What flutters my dove?' asked Moore, as she nestled to, and then uneasily shrank from him.

'Poor mamma! I am all mamma has: must I leave her?'

'Do you know, I thought of that difficulty: I and "mamma" have discussed it.'

'Tell me what you wish – what you would like – and I will consider if it is possible to consent; but I cannot desert her, even for you: I cannot break her heart, even for your sake.'

'She was faithful when I was false – was she not? I never came near your sick-bed, and she watched it ceaselessly.'

'What must I do? Anything but leave her.'

'At my wish, you never shall leave her.'

'She may live very near us?'

'With us – only she will have her own rooms and servant: for this she stipulates herself.'

'You know she has an income, that, with her habits, makes her quite independent?'

'She told me that, with a gentle pride that reminded me of somebody else.'

'She is not at all interfering, and incapable of gossip.'

'I know her, Cary: but if – instead of being the personification of reserve and discretion – she were something quite opposite, I should not fear her.'

'Yet she will be your mother-in-law?' The speaker gave an arch little nod: Moore smiled.

'Louis and I are not of the order of men who fear their mothers-in-law, Cary: our foes never have been, nor will be, those of our own household. I doubt not, my mother-in-law will make much of me.'

'That she will – in her quiet way, you know. She is not demonstrative; and when you see her silent, or even cool, you must not fancy her displeased – it is only a manner she has. Be sure to let me interpret for her, whenever she puzzles you: always believe my account of the matter, Robert.'

'Oh, implicitly! Jesting apart, I feel that she and I will suit – on ne peut mieux. Hortense, you know, is exquisitely susceptible – in our French sense of the word – and not, perhaps, always reasonable in her requirements; yet – dear, honest girl – I never painfully wounded her feelings, or had a serious quarrel with her, in my life.'

'No: you are most generously considerate – indeed, most tenderly indulgent to her; and you will be considerate with mamma. You are a gentleman all through, Robert, to the bone, and nowhere so perfect a gentleman as at your own fireside.'

'An eulogium I like: it is very sweet. I am well pleased my Caroline should view me in this light.'

'Mamma just thinks of you as I do.'

'Not quite, I hope?'

'She does not want to marry you – don't be vain; but she said to me the other day, "My dear, Mr Moore has pleasing manners; he is one of the few gentlemen I have seen who combine politeness with an air of sincerity." '

' "Mamma" is rather a misanthropist, is she not? Not the best opinion of the sterner sex?'

'She forbears to judge them as a whole, but she has her exceptions whom she admires. Louis and Mr Hall, and, of late – yourself. She did not like you once: I knew that, because she would never speak of you. But, Robert –'

'Well, what now? What is the new thought?'

'You have not seen my uncle yet?'

'I have: "mamma" called him into the room. He consents conditionally: if I prove that I can keep a wife, I may have her; and I *can* keep her better than he thinks – better than I choose to boast.'

'If you get rich, you will do good with your money, Robert?'

'I *will* do good; you shall tell me how: indeed, I have some schemes of my own, which you and I will talk about on our own hearth one day. I have seen the necessity of doing good: I have learned the downright folly of being selfish. Caroline, I foresee what I will now foretell. This war *must* erelong draw to a close: Trade is likely to prosper for some years to come: there may be a brief misunderstanding between England and America, but that will not last. What would you think if, one day – perhaps ere another ten years elapse – Louis and I divide Briarfield parish betwixt us? Louis, at any rate, is certain of power and property:

he will not bury his talents: he is a benevolent fellow, and has besides an intellect of his own of no trifling calibre. His mind is slow but strong: it must work: it may work deliberately, but it will work well. He will be made magistrate of the district – Shirley says he shall: she would proceed impetuously and prematurely to obtain for him this dignity, if he would let her, but he will not; as usual, he will be in no haste: ere he has been master of Fieldhead a year, all the district will feel his quiet influence, and acknowledge his unassuming superiority: a magistrate is wanted – they will, in time, invest him with the office voluntarily and unreluctantly. Everybody admires his future wife: and everybody will, in time, like him: he is of the "pâte" generally approved, "bon comme le pain" – daily bread for the most fastidious; good for the infant and the aged, nourishing for the poor, wholesome for the rich. Shirley, in spite of her whims and oddities, her dodges and delays, has an infatuated fondness for him: she will one day see him as universally beloved as even *she* could wish: he will also be universally esteemed, considered, consulted, depended on – too much so: his advice will be always judicious, his help always good-natured – erelong, both will be in inconvenient request: he will have to impose restrictions. As for me, if I succeed as I intend to do, my success will add to his and Shirley's income: I can double the value of their mill-property: I can line yonder barren Hollow with lines of cottages, and rows of cottage-gardens –'

'Robert! And root up the copse?'

'The copse shall be firewood ere five years elapse: the beautiful wild ravine shall be a smooth descent; the green natural terrace shall be a paved street: there shall be cottages in the dark ravine, and cottages on the lonely slopes: the rough pebbled track shall be an even, firm, broad, black, sooty road, bedded with the cinders from my mill: and my mill, Caroline – my mill shall fill its present yard.'

'Horrible! You will change our blue hill-country air into the Stilbro' smoke atmosphere.'

'I will pour the waters of Pactolus through the valley of Briarfield.'

'I like the beck a thousand times better.'

'I will get an act for enclosing Nunnely Common, and parcelling it out into farms.'

'Stilbro' Moor, however, defies you, thank Heaven! What can you grow in Bilberry Moss! What will flourish on Rushedge?'

'Caroline, the houseless, the starving, the unemployed, shall come to Hollow's mill from far and near; and Joe Scott shall give them work, and Louis Moore, Esq., shall let them a tenement, and Mrs Gill shall mete them a portion till the first pay-day.'

She smiled up in his face.

'Such a Sunday-school as you will have, Cary! such collections as you will get! such a day-school as you and Shirley, and Miss Ainley, will have to manage between you! The mill shall find salaries for a master and mistress, and the Squire or the Clothier shall give a treat once a-quarter.'

She mutely offered a kiss, an offer taken unfair advantage of, to the extortion of about a hundred kisses.

'Extravagant day-dreams!' said Moore, with a sigh and smile, 'yet perhaps we may realize some of them. Meantime, the dew is falling: Mrs Moore, I shall take you in.'

It is August: the bells clash out again, not only through Yorkshire but through England: from Spain, the voice of a trumpet has sounded long: it now waxes louder and louder; it proclaims Salamanca won. This night is Briarfield to be illuminated. On this day the Fieldhead tenantry dine together; the Hollow's mill work-people will be assembled for a like festal purpose; the schools have a grand treat. This morning there were two marriages solemnized in Briarfield church, – Louis Gérard Moore, Esq., late of Antwerp, to Shirley, daughter of the late Charles Cave Keeldar, Esq. of Fieldhead: Robert Gérard Moore, Esq., of Hollow's mill, to Caroline, niece of the Rev. Matthew-son Helstone, M.A., Rector of Briarfield.

The ceremony, in the first instance, was performed by Mr Helstone; Hiram Yorke, Esq. of Briarmains, giving the bride away. In the second instance, Mr Hall, Vicar of Nunnely, officiated. Amongst the bridal train, the two most noticeable personages were the youthful bridesmen, Henry Sympson and Martin Yorke.

I suppose Robert Moore's prophecies were, partially, at least, fulfilled. The other day I passed up the Hollow, which tradition says was once green, and lone, and wild; and there I saw the manufacturer's day-dreams embodied in substantial stone and brick and ashes – the cinder-black highway, the cottages, and the cottage-gardens; there I saw a mighty mill, and a chimney, ambitious as the tower of Babel. I told my old housekeeper when I came home where I had been.

'Ay!' said she; 'this world has queer changes. I can remember the old mill being built – the very first it was in all the district; and then, I can remember it being pulled down, and going with my lake-lasses (companions) to see the foundation-stone of the new one laid: the two Mr Moores made a great stir about it; they were there, and a deal of fine folk beside, and both their ladies; very bonnie and grand they looked; but Mrs Louis was the grandest, she always wore such handsome dresses: Mrs Robert was quieter-like. Mrs Louis smiled when she talked: she had a real happy, glad, good-natured look; but she had een that pierced a body through: there is no such ladies now-a-days.'

'What was the Hollow like then, Martha?'

'Different to what it is now; but I can tell of it clean different again: when there was neither mill, nor cot, nor hall, except Fieldhead, within two miles of it. I can tell, one summer-evening, fifty years syne, my mother coming running in just at the edge of dark, almost fleyed out of her wits, saying, she had seen a fairish (fairy) in Fieldhead Hollow; and that was the last fairish that ever was seen on this country side (though they've been heard within these forty years). A lonesome spot it was – and a bonnie spot – full of oak trees and nut trees. It is altered now.'

The story is told. I think I now see the judicious reader putting on his spectacles to look for the moral. It would be an insult to his sagacity to offer directions. I only say, God speed him in the quest!

THE PROFESSOR

PREFACE

THIS LITTLE BOOK was written before either *Jane Eyre* or *Shirley*, and yet no indulgence can be solicited for it on the plea of a first attempt. A first attempt it certainly was not, as the pen which wrote it had been previously worn a good deal in a practice of some years. I had not indeed published anything before I commenced *The Professor*, but in many a crude effort, destroyed almost as soon as composed, I had got over any such taste as I might once have had for ornamented and redundant composition, and come to prefer what was plain and homely. At the same time I had adopted a set of principles on the subject of incident, etc., such as would be generally approved in theory, but the result of which, when carried out into practice, often procures for an author more surprise than pleasure.

I said to myself that my hero should work his way through life as I had seen real living men work theirs – that he should never get a shilling he had not earned – that no sudden turns should lift him in a moment to wealth and high station; that whatever small competency he might gain, should be won by the sweat of his brow; that, before he could find so much as an arbour to sit down in, he should master at least half the ascent of 'the Hill of Difficulty'; that he should not even marry a beautiful girl or a lady of rank. As Adam's son he should share Adam's doom, and drain throughout life a mixed and moderate cup of enjoyment.

In the sequel, however, I find that publishers in general scarcely approved of this system, but would have liked something more imaginative and poetical – something more consonant with a highly wrought fancy, with a taste for pathos, with sentiments more tender, elevated, unworldly. Indeed, until an author has tried to dispose of a manuscript of this kind, he can never know what stores of romance and sensibility lie hidden in breasts he would not have suspected of casketing such treasures. Men in business are usually thought to prefer the real; on trial the idea will be often found fallacious: a passionate preference for the wild, wonderful, and thrilling – the strange, startling, and harrowing – agitates divers souls that show a calm and sober surface.

Such being the case, the reader will comprehend that to have reached him in the form of a printed book, this brief narrative must have gone through some struggles – which indeed it has. And after all, its worst struggle and strongest ordeal is yet to come; but it takes comfort – subdues fear – leans on the staff of a moderate expectation – and mutters under its breath, while lifting its eye to that of the public.

> He that is low need fear no fall.'

CURRER BELL

The foregoing preface was written by my wife with a view to the publication of *The Professor*, shortly after the appearance of *Shirley*. Being dissuaded from her intention, the authoress made some use of the materials in a subsequent work – *Villette*. As, however, these two stories are in most respects unlike, it has been represented to me that I ought not to withhold *The Professor* from the public. I have therefore consented to its publication.

A. B. NICHOLLS

Haworth Parsonage,
September 22nd, 1856.

CHAPTER I

INTRODUCTORY

T HE OTHER DAY, in looking over my papers, I found in my desk the following copy of a letter, sent by me a year since to an old school acquaintance: –

'DEAR CHARLES, – I think when you and I were at Eton together, we were neither of us what could be called popular characters: you were a sarcastic, observant, shrewd, cold-blooded creature; my own portrait I will not attempt to draw, but I cannot recollect that it was a strikingly attractive one – can you? What animal magnetism drew thee and me together I know not; certainly I never experienced anything of the Pylades and Orestes sentiment for you, and I have reason to believe that you, on your part, were equally free from all romantic regard to me. Still, out of school hours we walked and talked continually together; when the theme of conversation was our companions or our masters we understood each other, and when I recurred to some sentiment of affection, some vague love of an excellent or beautiful object, whether in animate or in inanimate nature, your sardonic coldness did not move me. I felt myself superior to that check *then* as I do *now*.

'It is a long time since I wrote to you, and a still longer time since I saw you. Chancing to take up a newspaper of your county the other day, my eye fell on your name. I began to think of old times; to run over the events which have transpired since we separated; and I sat down and commenced this letter. What you have been doing I know not; but you shall hear, if you choose to listen, how the world has wagged with me.

659

'First, after leaving Eton, I had an interview with my maternal uncles, Lord Tynedale and the Hon. John Seacombe. They asked me if I would enter the Church, and my uncle the nobleman offered me the living of Seacombe, which is in his gift, if I would; then my other uncle, Mr Seacombe, hinted that when I became rector of Seacombe-cum-Scaife, I might perhaps be allowed to take, as mistress of my house and head of my parish, one of my six cousins, his daughters, all of whom I greatly dislike.

'I declined both the Church and matrimony. A good clergyman is a good thing, but I should have made a very bad one. As to the wife – oh, how like a nightmare is the thought of being bound for life to one of my cousins! No doubt they are accomplished and pretty; but not an accomplishment, not a charm of theirs, touches a chord in my bosom. To think of passing the winter evenings by the parlour fireside of Seacombe Rectory alone with one of them – for instance, the large and well-modelled statue, Sarah – no; I should be a bad husband, under such circumstances, as well as a bad clergyman.

'When I had declined my uncles' offers they asked me "what I intended to do?" I said I should reflect. They reminded me that I had no fortune, and no expectation of any, and, after a considerable pause, Lord Tynedale demanded sternly, "Whether I had thoughts of following my father's steps and engaging in trade?" Now, I had had no thoughts of the sort. I do not think that my turn of mind qualifies me to make a good tradesman; my taste, my ambition does not lie in that way; but such was the scorn expressed in Lord Tynedale's countenance as he pronounced the word *trade* – such the contemptuous sarcasm of his tone – that I was instantly decided. My father was but a name to me, yet that name I did not like to hear mentioned with a sneer to my very face. I answered then, with haste and warmth, "I cannot do better than follow in my father's steps; yes, I will be a tradesman." My uncles did not remonstrate; they and I parted with mutual disgust. In reviewing this transaction,

I find that I was quite right to shake off the burden of Tynedale's patronage, but a fool to offer my shoulders instantly for the reception of another burden – one which might be more intolerable, and which certainly was yet untried.

'I wrote instantly to Edward – you know Edward – my only brother, ten years my senior, married to a rich millowner's daughter, and now possessor of the mill and business which was my father's before he failed. You are aware that my father – once reckoned a Crœsus of wealth – became bankrupt a short time previous to his death, and that my mother lived in destitution for some six months after him, unhelped by her aristocratical brothers, whom she had mortally offended by her union with Crimsworth, the —shire manufacturer. At the end of the six months she brought me into the world, and then herself left it without, I should think, much regret, as it contained little hope or comfort for her.

'My father's relations took charge of Edward, as they did of me, till I was nine years old. At that period it chanced that the representation of an important borough in our county fell vacant; Mr Seacombe stood for it. My uncle Crimsworth, an astute mercantile man, took the opportunity of writing a fierce letter to the candidate, stating that if he and Lord Tynedale did not consent to do something towards the support of their sister's orphan children, he would expose their relentless and malignant conduct towards that sister, and do his best to turn the circumstances against Mr Seacombe's election. That gentleman and Lord T. knew well enough that the Crimsworths were an unscrupulous and determined race; they knew also that they had influence in the borough of X—; and, making a virtue of necessity, they consented to defray the expenses of my education. I was sent to Eton, where I remained ten years, during which space of time Edward and I never met. He, when he grew up, entered into trade, and pursued his calling with such diligence, ability and success, that now, in his thirtieth year, he was fast making a fortune. Of this I was apprised by the occasional short letters

I received from him, some three or four times a year; which said letters never concluded without some expression of determined enmity against the house of Seacombe, and some reproach to me for living, as he said, on the bounty of that house. At first, while still in boyhood, I could not understand why, as I had no parents, I should not be indebted to my uncles Tynedale and Seacombe for my education; but as I grew up, and heard by degrees of the persevering hostility, the hatred till death evinced by them against my father – of the sufferings of my mother – of all the wrongs, in short, of our house – then did I conceive shame of the dependence in which I lived, and form a resolution no more to take bread from hands which had refused to minister to the necessities of my dying mother. It was by these feelings I was influenced when I refused the Rectory of Seacombe, and the union with one of my patrician cousins.

'An irreparable breach thus being effected between my uncles and myself, I wrote to Edward; told him what had occurred, and informed him of my intention to follow his steps and be a tradesman. I asked, moreover, if he could give me employment. His answer expressed no approbation of my conduct, but he said I might come down to —shire, if I liked, and he would "see what could be done in the way of furnishing me with work". I repressed all – even *mental* comment on his note – packed my trunk and carpet-bag, and started for the North directly.

'After two days' travelling (railroads were not then in existence) I arrived, one wet October afternoon, in the town of X—. I had always understood that Edward lived in this town, but on inquiry I found that it was only Mr Crimsworth's mill and warehouse which were situated in the smoky atmosphere of Bigben Close; his *residence* lay four miles out, in the country.

'It was late in the evening when I alighted at the gates of the habitation designated to me as my brother's. As I advanced up the avenue, I could see through the shades of twilight, and the dank gloomy mists which deepened those shades, that the house was large, and the grounds surrounding it sufficiently spacious.

I paused a moment on the lawn in front, and leaning my back against a tall tree which rose in the centre, I gazed with interest on the exterior of Crimsworth Hall.

' "Edward is rich," thought I to myself. "I believed him to be doing well – but I did not know he was master of a mansion like this." Cutting short all marvelling, speculation, conjecture, etc., I advanced to the front door and rang. A man-servant opened it – I announced myself – he relieved me of my wet cloak and carpet-bag, and ushered me into a room furnished as a library, where there was a bright fire, and candles burning on the table; he informed me that his master was not yet returned from X— market, but that he would certainly be at home in the course of half an hour.

'Being left to myself, I took the stuffed easy chair, covered with red morocco, which stood by the fireside, and while my eyes watched the flames dart from the glowing coals, and the cinders fall at intervals on the hearth, my mind busied itself in conjectures concerning the meeting about to take place. Amidst much that was doubtful in the subject of these conjectures, there was one thing tolerably certain – I was in no danger of encountering severe disappointment; from this, the moderation of my expectations guaranteed me. I anticipated no over-flowings of fraternal tenderness; Edward's letters had always been such as to prevent the engendering or harbouring of delusions of this sort. Still, as I sat awaiting his arrival, I felt eager – very eager – I cannot tell you why; my hand, so utterly a stranger to the grasp of a kindred hand, clenched itself to repress the tremor with which impatience would fain have shaken it.

'I thought of my uncles; and as I was engaged in wondering whether Edward's indifference would equal the cold disdain I had always experienced from them, I heard the avenue gates open: wheels approached the house; Mr Crimsworth had arrived; and after the lapse of some minutes, and a brief dialogue between himself and the servant in the hall, his tread drew near the library door – that tread alone announced the master of the house.

'I still retained some confused recollection of Edward as he was ten years ago – a tall, wiry, raw youth; *now*, as I rose from my seat and turned towards the library door, I saw a fine-looking and powerful man, light-complexioned, well-made, and of athletic proportions; the first glance made me aware of an air of promptitude and sharpness, shown as well in his movements as in his port, his eye, and the general expression of his face. He greeted me with brevity, and, in the moment of shaking hands, scanned me from head to foot; he took his seat in the morocco-covered arm-chair, and motioned me to another seat.

' "I expected you would have called at the counting-house in the Close," said he; and his voice, I noticed, had an abrupt accent, probably habitual to him; he spoke also with a guttural northern tone, which sounded harsh in my ears, accustomed to the silvery utterance of the South.

' "The landlord of the inn, where the coach stopped, directed me here," said I. "I doubted at first the accuracy of his information, not being aware that you had such a residence as this."

' "Oh, it is all right!" he replied, "only I was kept half an hour behind time, waiting for you – that is all. I thought you must be coming by the eight o'clock coach."

'I expressed regret that he had had to wait; he made no answer, but stirred the fire, as if to cover a moment of impatience; then he scanned me again.

'I felt an inward satisfaction that I had not, in the first moment of meeting, betrayed any warmth, any enthusiasm; that I had saluted this man with a quiet and steady phlegm.

' "Have you quite broken with Tynedale and Seacombe?" he asked hastily.

' "I do not think I shall have any further communication with them; my refusal of their proposals will, I fancy, operate as a barrier against all future intercourse."

' "Why," said he, "I may as well remind you at the very

outset of our connection, that 'no man can serve two masters'. Acquaintance with Lord Tynedale will be incompatible with assistance from me." There was a kind of gratuitous menace in his eye as he looked at me in finishing this observation.

'Feeling no disposition to reply to him, I contented myself with an inward speculation on the differences which exist in the constitution of men's minds. I do not know what inference Mr Crimsworth drew from my silence – whether he considered it a symptom of contumacity or an evidence of my being cowed by his peremptory manner. After a long and hard stare at me, he rose sharply from his seat.

' "To-morrow," said he, "I shall call your attention to some other points; but now it is supper-time, and Mrs Crimsworth is probably waiting; will you come?"

'He strode from the room, and I followed. In crossing the hall, I wondered what Mrs Crimsworth might be. "Is she," thought I, "as alien to what I like as Tynedale, Seacombe, the Misses Seacombe – as the affectionate relative now striding before me? or is she better than these? Shall I, in conversing with her, feel free to show something of my real nature; or –" Further conjectures were arrested by my entrance into the dining-room.

'A lamp, burning under a shade of ground-glass, showed a handsome apartment, wainscoted with oak; supper was laid on the table; by the fireplace, standing as if waiting our entrance, appeared a lady; she was young, tall, and well shaped; her dress was handsome and fashionable: so much my first glance sufficed to ascertain. A gay salutation passed between her and Mr Crimsworth; she chid him, half playfully, half poutingly, for being late; her voice (I always take voices into the account in judging of character) was lively – it indicated, I thought, good animal spirits. Mr Crimsworth soon checked her animated scolding with a kiss – a kiss that still told of the bridegroom (they had not yet been married a year); she took her seat at the supper-table in first-rate spirits. Perceiving me, she begged my pardon for not noticing me before, and then shook hands with me, as ladies do when a flow of good-humour disposes them to be cheerful to all, even the most indifferent of their acquaintance. It was now further obvious to me that she had a good complexion, and features sufficiently marked but agreeable; her hair was red – quite red. She and Edward talked much, always in a vein of playful contention; she was vexed, or pretended to be vexed, that he had that day driven a vicious horse in the gig, and he made light of her fears. Sometimes she appealed to me.

' "Now, Mr William, isn't it absurd in Edward to talk so? He says he will drive Jack, and no other horse, and the brute has thrown him twice already."

'She spoke with a kind of lisp, not disagreeable, but childish. I soon saw also that there was more than girlish – a somewhat infantine expression in her by no means small features; this lisp and expression were, I have no doubt, a charm in Edward's eyes, and would be so to those of most men, but they were not to mine. I sought her eye, desirous to read there the intelligence which I could not discern in her face or hear in her conversation; it was merry, rather small; by turns I saw vivacity, vanity, coquetry, look out through its irid, but I watched in vain for a glimpse of soul. I am no Oriental; white necks, carmine lips and cheeks, clusters of bright curls do not suffice for me without that Promethean spark which will live after the roses and lilies are faded, the burnished hair grown grey. In sunshine, in prosperity, the flowers are very well; but how many wet days are there in life – November seasons of disaster, when a man's hearth and home would be cold indeed, without the clear, cheering gleam of intellect.

'Having perused the fair page of Mrs Crimsworth's face, a deep, involuntary sigh announced my disappointment; she took it as a homage to her beauty, and Edward, who was evidently proud of his rich and handsome young wife, threw on me a glance – half ridicule, half ire.

'I turned from them both, and gazing wearily round the

room, I saw two pictures set in the oak panelling – one on each side the mantelpiece. Ceasing to take part in the bantering conversation that flowed on between Mr and Mrs Crimsworth, I bent my thoughts to the examination of these pictures. They were portraits – a lady and a gentleman, both costumed in the fashion of twenty years ago. The gentleman was in the shade. I could not see him well. The lady had the benefit of a full beam from the softly shaded lamp. I presently recognized her; I had seen this picture before in childhood; it was my mother; that and the companion picture being the only heirlooms saved out of the sale of my father's property.

'The face, I remembered, had pleased me as a boy, but *then* I did not understand it; *now* I knew how rare that class of face is in the world, and I appreciated keenly its thoughtful, yet gentle expression. The serious grey eye possessed for me a strong charm, as did certain lines in the features indicative of most true and tender feeling. I was sorry it was only a picture.

'I soon left Mr and Mrs Crimsworth to themselves; a servant conducted me to my bedroom; in closing my chamber-door, I shut out all intruders – you, Charles, as well as the rest. – Good-bye for the present,

WILLIAM CRIMSWORTH.'

To this letter I never got an answer; before my old friend received it, he had accepted a Government appointment in one of the colonies, and was already on his way to the scene of his official labours. What has become of him since, I know not.

The leisure time I have at command, and which I intended to employ for his private benefit, I shall now dedicate to that of the public at large. My narrative is not exciting, and above all, not marvellous; but it may interest some individuals, who, having toiled in the same vocation as myself, will find in my experience frequent reflections of their own. The above letter will serve as an introduction. I now proceed.

CHAPTER II

A FINE October morning succeeded to the foggy evening
that had witnessed my first introduction to Crimsworth
Hall. I was early up and walking in the large, park-like meadow
surrounding the house. The autumn sun, rising over the
—shire hills, disclosed a pleasant country: woods brown and
mellow varied the fields from which the harvest had been lately
carried; a river, gliding between the woods, caught on its surface
the somewhat cold gleam of the October sun and sky; at frequent intervals along the banks of the river, tall, cylindrical
chimneys, almost like slender round towers, indicated the factories which the trees half concealed; here and there mansions,
similar to Crimsworth Hall, occupied agreeable sites on the
hillside; the country wore, on the whole, a cheerful, active,
fertile look. Steam, trade, machinery had long banished from
it all romance and seclusion. At a distance of five miles, a valley,
opening between the low hills, held in its cup the great town
of X—. A dense, permanent vapour brooded over this locality
– there lay Edward's 'Concern'.

I forced my eye to scrutinize this prospect, I forced my mind
to dwell on it for a time, and when I found that it communicated no pleasurable emotion to my heart – that it stirred in
me none of the hopes a man ought to feel when he sees laid
before him the scene of his life's career – I said to myself,
'William, you are a rebel against circumstances; you are a fool,
and know not what you want; you have chosen trade and you
shall be a tradesman. Look!' I continued mentally – 'Look at
the sooty smoke in that hollow, and know that there is your post!
There you cannot dream, you cannot speculate and theorize –
there you shall out and work!'

Thus self-schooled, I returned to the house. My brother was

in the breakfast-room. I met him collectedly – I could not meet him cheerfully; he was standing on the rug, his back to the fire – how much did I read in the expression of his eye as my glance encountered his, when I advanced to bid him good-morning; how much that was contradictory to my nature! He said 'Good-morning' abruptly and nodded, and then he snatched, rather than took, a newspaper from the table, and began to read it with the air of a master who seizes a pretext to escape the bore of conversing with an underling. It was well I had taken a resolution to endure for a time, or his manner would have gone far to render insupportable the disgust I had just been endeavouring to subdue. I looked at him: I measured his robust frame and powerful proportions; I saw my own reflection in the mirror over the mantelpiece; I amused myself with comparing the two pictures. In fact I resembled him, though I was not so handsome; my features were less regular; I had a darker eye, and a broader brow – in form I was greatly inferior – thinner, slighter, not so tall. As an animal, Edward excelled me far; should he prove as paramount in mind as in person I must be a slave – for I must expect from him no lion-like generosity to one weaker than himself, his cold, avaricious eye, his stern, forbidding manner told me he would not spare. Had I then force of mind to cope with him? I did not know; I had never been tried.

Mrs Crimsworth's entrance divided my thoughts for a moment. She looked well, dressed in white, her face and her attire shining in morning and bridal freshness. I addressed her with the degree of ease her last night's careless gaiety seemed to warrant, but she replied with coolness and restraint: her husband had tutored her; she was not to be too familiar with his clerk.

As soon as breakfast was over Mr Crimsworth intimated to me that they were bringing the gig round to the door, and that in five minutes he should expect me to be ready to go down with him to X—. I did not keep him waiting; we were soon dashing at a rapid rate along the road. The horse he drove was the same vicious animal about which Mrs Crimsworth had expressed her fears the night before. Once or twice Jack seemed disposed to turn restive, but a vigorous and determined application of the whip from the ruthless hand of his master soon compelled him to submission, and Edward's dilated nostril expressed his triumph in the result of the contest; he scarcely spoke to me during the whole of the brief drive, only opening his lips at intervals to damn his horse.

X— was all stir and bustle when we entered it; we left the clean streets where there were dwelling-houses and shops, churches and public buildings; we left all these, and turned down to a region of mills and warehouses; thence we passed through two massive gates into a great paved yard, and we were in Bigben Close, and the mill was before us, vomiting soot from its long chimney, and quivering through its thick brick walls with the commotion of its iron bowels. Workpeople were passing to and fro; a waggon was being laden with pieces. Mr Crimsworth looked from side to side, and seemed at one glance to comprehend all that was going on; he alighted, and leaving his horse and gig to the care of a man who hastened to take the reins from his hand, he bid me follow him to the counting-house. We entered it; a very different place from the parlours of Crimsworth Hall – a place for business, with a bare, planked floor, a safe, two high desks and stools and some chairs. A person was seated at one of the desks, who took off his square cap when Mr Crimsworth entered, and in an instant was again absorbed in his occupation of writing or calculating – I know not which.

Mr Crimsworth, having removed his mackintosh, sat down by the fire. I remained standing near the hearth; he said presently –

'Steighton, you may leave the room; I have some business to transact with this gentleman. Come back when you hear the bell.'

The individual at the desk rose and departed, closing the door as he went out. Mr Crimsworth stirred the fire, then folded his arms, and sat a moment thinking, his lips compressed, his brow knit. I had nothing to do but to watch him – how well his features were cut! what a handsome man he was! Whence, then, came that air of contraction – that narrow and hard aspect on his forehead, in all his lineaments?

Turning to me he began abruptly: –

'You are come down to —shire to learn to be a tradesman?'

'Yes, I am.'

'Have you made up your mind on the point? Let me know that at once.'

'Yes.'

'Well, I am not bound to help you, but I have a place here vacant, if you are qualifed for it. I will take you on trial. What can you do? Do you know anything besides that useless trash of college learning – Greek, Latin, and so forth?'

'I have studied mathematics.'

'Stuff! I dare say you have.'

'I can read and write French and German.'

'Hum!' He reflected a moment, then opening a drawer in a desk near him took out a letter, and gave it to me.

'Can you read that?' he asked.

It was a German commercial letter; I translated it; I could not tell whether he was gratified or not – his countenance remained fixed.

'It is well,' he said, after a pause, 'that you are acquainted with something useful, something that may enable you to earn your board and lodging; since you know French and German, I will take you as second clerk to manage the foreign corres-pondence of the house. I shall give you a good salary – £90 a year – and now,' he continued, raising his voice, 'hear once for all what I have to say about our relationship, and all that sort of humbug! I must have no nonsense on that point; it would never suit me. I shall excuse you nothing on the plea of being my brother; if I find you stupid, negligent, dissipated, idle, or possessed of any faults detrimental to the interests of the house, I shall dismiss you as I would any other clerk. Ninety pounds a year are good wages, and I expect to have the full value of my money out of you; remember, too, that things are on a practical footing in my establishment – business-like habits, feelings, and ideas, suit me best. Do you understand?'

'Partly,' I replied. 'I suppose you mean that I am to do my work for my wages; not to expect favour from you, and not to depend on you for any help but what I earn; that suits me exactly, and on these terms I will consent to be your clerk.'

I turned on my heel, and walked to the window; this time I did not consult his face to learn his opinion: what it was I do not know, nor did I then care. After a silence of some minutes he recommenced: –

'You perhaps expect to be accommodated with apartments at Crimsworth Hall, and to go and come with me in the gig. I wish you, however, to be aware that such an arrangement would be quite inconvenient to me. I like to have the seat in my gig at liberty for any gentleman whom for business reasons I may wish to take down to the hall for a night or so. You will seek out lodgings in X—.'

Quitting the window, I walked back to the hearth.

'Of course I shall seek out lodgings in X—,' I answered. 'It would not suit me either to lodge at Crimsworth Hall.'

My tone was quiet. I always speak quietly. Yet Mr Crimsworth's blue eye became incensed; he took his revenge rather oddly. Turning to me he said bluntly –

'You are poor enough, I suppose; how do you expect to live till your quarter's salary becomes due?'

'I shall get on,' said I.

'How do you expect to live?' he repeated in a louder voice.

'As I can, Mr Crimsworth.'

'Get into debt at your peril! that's all,' he answered. 'For aught I know you may have extravagant aristocratic habits: if you have, drop them; I tolerate nothing of the sort here, and I will never give you a shilling extra, whatever liabilities you may incur – mind that.'

'Yes, Mr Crimsworth, you will find I have a good memory.'

I said no more. I did not think the time was come for much parley. I had an instinctive feeling that it would be folly to let one's temper effervesce often with such a man as Edward. I said to myself, 'I will place my cup under this continual dropping; it shall stand there still and steady; when full, it will run over of itself – meantime patience. Two things are certain. I am capable of performing the work Mr Crimsworth has set me; I can earn my wages conscientiously, and those wages are sufficient to enable me to live. As to the fact of my brother assuming towards me the bearing of a proud, harsh master, the fault is his, not mine, and shall his injustice, his bad feeling, turn me at once aside from the path I have chosen? No; at least, ere I deviate, I will advance far enough to see whither my career tends. As yet I am only pressing in at the entrance – a strait gate enough; it ought to have a good terminus.' While I thus reasoned, Mr Crimsworth rang a bell; his first clerk, the individual dismissed previously to our conference, re-entered.

'Mr Steighton,' said he, 'show Mr William the letters from Voss Brothers, and give him English copies of the answers; he will translate them.'

Mr Steighton, a man of about thiry-five, with a face at once sly and heavy, hastened to execute this order; he laid the letters on the desk, and I was soon seated at it, and engaged in rendering the English answers into German. A sentiment of keen pleasure accompanied this first effort to earn my own living – a sentiment neither poisoned nor weakened by the presence of the taskmaster, who stood and watched me for some time as I wrote. I thought he was trying to read my character, but I felt as secure against his scrutiny as if I had had on a casque with the visor down – or rather I showed him my countenance with the confidence that one would show an unlearned man a letter written in Greek; he might see lines, and trace characters, but he could make nothing of them; my nature was not his nature, and its signs were to him like the words of an unknown tongue. Ere long he turned away abruptly, as if baffled, and left the counting-house; he returned to it but twice in the course of that day; each time he mixed and swallowed a glass of brandy-and-water, the materials for making which he extracted from a cupboard on one side of the fireplace; having glanced at my translations – he could read both French and German – he went out again in silence.

CHAPTER III

I SERVED Edward as his second clerk faithfully, punctually, diligently. What was given me to do I had the power and the determination to do well. Mr Crimsworth watched sharply for defects, but found none; he set Timothy Steighton, his favourite and head man, to watch also. Tim was baffled; I was as exact as himself, and quicker. Mr Crimsworth made inquiries as to how I lived, whether I got into debt – no, my accounts with my landlady were always straight. I had hired small lodgings, which I contrived to pay for out of a slender fund – the accumulated savings of my Eton pocket-money; for, as it had ever been abhorrent to my nature to ask pecuniary assistance, I had early acquired habits of self-denying economy; husbanding my monthly allowance with anxious care, in order to obviate the danger of being forced, in some moment of future exigency, to beg additional aid. I remember many called me miser at the time, and I used to couple the reproach with this consolation – better to be misunderstood now than repulsed hereafter. At this day I had my reward; I had had it before, when on parting with my irritated uncles one of them threw down on the table before me a £5 note, which I was able to leave there, saying that my travelling expenses were already provided for. Mr Crimsworth employed Tim to find out whether my landlady had any complaint to make on the score of my morals; she answered that she believed I was a very religious man, and asked Tim, in her turn, if he thought I had any intention of going into the Church some day; for, she said, she had had young curates to lodge in her house who were nothing equal to me for steadiness and quietness. Tim was 'a religious man' himself, indeed, he was 'a joined Methodist', which did not (be it understood) prevent him from being at

675

the same time an ingrained rascal, and he came away much
posed at hearing this account of my piety. Having imparted it
to Mr Crimsworth, that gentleman, who himself frequented
no place of worship, and owned no God but Mammon, turned
the information into a weapon of attack against the equability
of my temper. He commenced a series of covert sneers, of which
I did not at first perceive the drift, till my landlady happened
to relate the conversation she had had with Mr Steighton;
this enlightened me; afterwards I came to the counting-house
prepared, and managed to receive the millowner's blasphemous
sarcasms, when next levelled at me, on a buckler of impenetrable
indifference. Ere long he tired of wasting his ammunition on
a statue, but he did not throw away the shafts – he only kept
them quiet in his quiver.

Once during my clerkship I had an invitation to Crimsworth
Hall; it was on the occasion of a large party given in honour of
the master's birthday; he had always been accustomed to invite
his clerks on similar anniversaries, and could not well pass me
over; I was, however, kept strictly in the background. Mrs
Crimsworth, elegantly dressed in satin and lace, blooming in
youth and health, vouchsafed me no more notice than was
expressed by a distant move; Crimsworth, of course, never spoke
to me; I was introduced to none of the band of young ladies,
who, enveloped in silvery clouds of white gauze and muslin, sat
in array against me on the opposite side of a long and large
room; in fact, I was fairly isolated, and could but contemplate
the shining ones from afar, and when weary of such a dazzling
scene, turn for a change to the consideration of the carpet
pattern. Mr Crimsworth, standing on the rug, his elbow supported by the marble mantelpiece, and about him a group of
very pretty girls, with whom he conversed gaily – Mr Crimsworth, thus placed, glanced at me; I looked weary, solitary, kept
down like some desolate tutor or governess; he was satisfied.

Dancing began; I should have liked well enough to be introduced to some pleasing and intelligent girl, and to have freedom

and opportunity to show that I could both feel and communicate the pleasure of social intercourse – that I was not, in short, a block, or a piece of furniture, but an acting, thinking, sentient man. Many smiling faces and graceful figures glided past me, but the smiles were lavished on other eyes, the figures sustained by other hands than mine. I turned away tantalized, left the dancers, and wandered into the oak-panelled dining-room. No fibre of sympathy united me to any living thing in this house; I looked for and found my mother's picture. I took a wax taper from a stand, and held it up. I gazed long, earnestly; my heart grew to the image. My mother, I perceived, had bequeathed to me much of her features and countenance – her forehead, her eyes, her complexion. No regular beauty pleases egotistical human beings so much as a softened and refined likeness of themselves; for this reason, fathers regard with complacency the lineaments of their daughters' faces, where frequently their own similitude is found flatteringly associated with softness of hue and delicacy of outline. I was just wondering how that picture, to me so interesting, would strike an impartial spectator, when a voice close behind me pronounced the words –

'Humph! there's some sense in that face.'

I turned; at my elbow stood a tall man, young, though probably five or six years older than I – in other respects of an appearance the opposite to commonplace; though just now, as I am not disposed to paint his portrait in detail, the reader must be content with the silhouette I have just thrown off; it was all I myself saw of him for the moment: I did not investigate the colour of his eyebrows, nor of his eyes either; I saw his stature, and the outline of his shape; I saw, too, his fastidious-looking *retroussé* nose; these observations, few in number, and general in character (the last excepted), sufficed, for they enabled me to recognize him.

'Good evening, Mr Hunsden,' muttered I with a bow, and then, like a shy noodle as I was, I began moving away – and why? Simply because Mr Hunsden was a manufacturer and a millowner, and I was only a clerk, and my instinct propelled me from my superior. I had frequently seen Hunsden in Bigben Close, where he came almost weekly to transact business with Mr Crimsworth, but I had never spoken to him, nor he to me, and I owed him a sort of involuntary grudge, because he had more than once been the tacit witness of insults offered by Edward to me. I had the conviction that he could only regard me as a poor-spirited slave, wherefore I now went about to shun his presence and eschew his conversation.

'Where are you going?' asked he, as I edged off sideways. I had already noticed that Mr Hunsden indulged in abrupt forms of speech, and I perversely said to myself –

'He thinks he may speak as he likes to a poor clerk; but my mood is not, perhaps, so supple as he deems it, and his rough freedom pleases me not at all.'

I made some slight reply, rather indifferent than courteous, and continued to move away. He coolly planted himself in my path.

'Stay here awhile,' said he: 'it is so hot in the dancing-room; besides, you don't dance; you have not had a partner to-night.'

He was right, and as he spoke neither his look, tone, nor manner displeased me; my *amour-propre* was propitiated; he had not addressed me out of condescension, but because, having repaired to the cool dining-room for refreshment, he now wanted someone to talk to, by way of temporary amusement. I hate to be condescended to, but I like well enough to oblige; I stayed.

'That is a good picture,' he continued, recurring to the portrait.

'Do you consider the face pretty?' I asked.

'Pretty! no – how can it be pretty, with sunk eyes and hollow cheeks? but it is peculiar; it seems to think. You could have a talk with that woman, if she were alive, on other subjects than dress, visiting, and compliments.'

I agreed with him, but did not say so. He went on.

'Not that I admire a head of that sort; it wants character and force; there's too much of the sen-si-tive (so he articulated it, curling his lip at the same time) in that mouth; besides, there is Aristocrat written on the brow and defined in the figure; I hate your aristocrats.'

'You think, then, Mr Hunsden, that patrician descent may be read in a distinctive cast of form and features?'

'Patrician descent be hanged! Who doubts that your lordlings may have their "distinctive cast of form and features" as much as we — shire tradesmen have ours? But which is the best? Not theirs, assuredly. As to their women, it is a little different: they cultivate beauty from childhood upwards, and may by care and training attain to a certain degree of excellence in that point, just like the Oriental odalisques. Yet even this superiority is doubtful. Compare the figure in that frame with Mrs Edward Crimsworth – which is the finer animal?'

I replied quietly: 'Compare yourself and Mr Edward Crimsworth, Mr Hunsden.'

'Oh, Crimsworth is better filled up than I am, I know; besides, he has a straight nose, arched eyebrows, and all that; but these advantages – if they are advantages – he did not inherit from his mother, the patrician, but from his father, old Crimsworth, who, *my* father says, was as veritable a — shire blue-dyer as ever put indigo in a vat; yet withal the handsomest man in the three Ridings. It is you, William, who are the aristocrat of your family, and you are not as fine a fellow as your plebeian brother by a long chalk.'

There was something in Mr Hunsden's point-blank mode of speech which rather pleased me than otherwise, because it set me at my ease. I continued the conversation with a degree of interest.

'How do you happen to know that I am Mr Crimsworth's brother? I thought you and everybody else looked upon me only in the light of a poor clerk.'

'Well, and so we do; and what are you but a poor clerk? You

do Crimsworth's work, and he gives you wages – shabby wages they are, too.'

I was silent. Hunsden's language now bordered on the impertinent, still his manner did not offend me in the least – it only piqued my curiosity; I wanted him to go on, which he did in a little while.

'This world is an absurd one,' said he.

'Why so, Mr Hunsden?'

'I wonder you should ask: you are yourself a strong proof of the absurdity I allude to.'

I was determined he should explain himself of his own accord, without my pressing him so to do – so I resumed my silence.

'Is it your intention to become a tradesman?' he inquired presently.

'It was my serious intention three months ago.'

'Humph! the more fool you – you look like a tradesman! What a practical business-like face you have!'

'My face is as the Lord made it, Mr Hunsden.'

'The Lord never made either your face or head for X—. What good can your bumps of ideality, comparison, self-esteem, conscientiousness, do you here? But if you like Bigben Close, stay there; it's your own affair, not mine.'

'Perhaps I have no choice.'

'Well, I care naught about it – it will make little difference to me what you do or where you go; but I'm cool now – I want to dance again; and I see such a fine girl sitting in the corner of the sofa there by her mamma; see if I don't get her for a partner in a jiffy! There's Waddy – Sam Waddy making up to her; won't I cut him out?'

And Mr Hunsden strode away. I watched him through the open folding-doors; he outstripped Waddy, applied for the hand of the fine girl, and led her off triumphant. She was a tall, well-made, full-formed, dashingly dressed young woman much in the style of Mrs E. Crimsworth; Hunsden whirled her through the waltz with spirit; he kept at her side during the remainder of the evening, and I read in her animated and gratified countenance that he succeeded in making himself perfectly agreeable. The mamma too (a stout person in a turban – Mrs Lupton by name) looked well pleased; prophetic visions probably flattered her inward eye. The Hunsdens were of an old stem; and scornful as Yorke (such was my late interlocutor's name) professed to be of the advantages of birth, in his secret heart he knew well and fully appreciated the distinction his ancient, if not high lineage conferred on him in a mushroom-place like X—, concerning whose inhabitants it was proverbially said, that not one in a thousand knew his own grandfather. Moreover, the Hunsdens, once rich, were still independent; and report affirmed that Yorke bade fair, by his success in business, to restore to pristine prosperity the partially decayed fortunes of his house. These circumstances considered, Mrs Lupton's broad face might well wear a smile of complacency as she contemplated the heir of Hunsden Wood occupied in paying assiduous court to her darling Sarah Martha. I, however, whose observations, being less anxious, were likely to be more accurate, soon saw that the grounds for maternal self-congratulation were slight indeed; the gentleman appeared to me much more desirous of making, than susceptible of receiving an impression. I know not what it was in Mr Hunsden that, as I watched him (I had nothing better to do), suggested to me, every now and then, the idea of a foreigner. In form and features he might be pronounced English, though even there one caught a dash of something Gallic; but he had no English shyness: he had learnt somewhere, somehow, the art of setting himself quite at his ease, and of allowing no insular timidity to intervene as a barrier between him and his convenience or pleasure. Refinement he did not affect, yet vulgar he could not be called; he was not odd – no quiz – yet he resembled no one else I had ever seen before; his general bearing intimated complete, sovereign satisfaction with himself; yet, at times, an indescribable shade passed like an eclipse over his countenance, and seemed to me like the sign of a sudden and strong inward doubt of himself, his words and actions – an energetic discontent at his life or his social position, his future prospects or his mental attainments – I know not which; perhaps, after all, it might only be a bilious caprice.

CHAPTER IV

No man likes to acknowledge that he has made a mistake in the choice of his profession, and every man, worthy of the name, will row long against wind and tide before he allows himself to cry out, 'I am baffled!' and submits to be floated passively back to land. From the first week of my residence in X— I felt my occupation irksome. The thing itself – the work of copying and translating business letters – was a dry and tedious task enough, but had that been all, I should long have borne with the nuisance; I am not of an impatient nature, and influenced by the double desire of getting my living and justifying to myself and others the resolution I had taken to become a tradesman, I should have endured in silence the rust and cramp of my best faculties; I should not have whispered, even inwardly, that I longed for liberty; I should have pent in every sigh by which my heart might have ventured to intimate its distress under the closeness, smoke, monotony, and joyless tumult of Bigben Close, and its panting desire for freer and fresher scenes; I should have set up the image of Duty, the fetish of Perseverance, in my small bedroom at Mrs King's lodgings, and they two should have been my household gods, from which my darling, my cherished-in-secret, Imagination, the tender and the mighty, should never, either by softness or strength, have severed me. But this was not all; the antipathy which had sprung up between myself and my employer, striking deeper root and spreading denser shade daily, excluded me from every glimpse of the sunshine of life; and I began to feel like a plant growing in humid darkness out of the slimy walls of a well.

Antipathy is the only word which can express the feeling Edward Crimsworth had for me – a feeling, in a great measure, involuntary, and which was liable to be excited by every, the most trifling movement, look, or word of mine. My southern accent annoyed him; the degree of education evinced in my language irritated him; my punctuality, industry, and accuracy fixed his dislike, and gave it the high flavour and poignant relish of envy; he feared that I too should one day make a successful tradesman. Had I been in anything inferior to him, he would not have hated me so thoroughly, but I knew all that he knew, and, what was worse, he suspected that I kept the padlock of silence on mental wealth in which he was no sharer. If he could have once placed me in a ridiculous or mortifying position, he would have forgiven me much, but I was guarded by three faculties – Caution, Tact, Observation; and prowling and prying as was Edward's malignity, it could never baffle the lynx-eyes of these, my natural sentinels. Day by day did his malice watch my tact, hoping it would sleep, and prepared to steal snake-like on its slumber; but tact, if it be genuine, never sleeps.

I had received my first quarter's wages, and was returning to my lodgings, possessed heart and soul with the pleasant feeling that the master who had paid me grudged every penny of that hard-earned pittance – (I had long ceased to regard Mr Crimsworth as my brother – he was a hard, grinding master; he wished to be an inexorable tyrant: that was all). Thoughts, not varied but strong, occupied my mind; two voices spoke within me; again and again they uttered the same monotonous phrases. One said 'William, your life is intolerable.' The other: 'What can you do to alter it?' I walked fast, for it was a cold, frosty night in January; as I approached my lodgings, I turned from a general view of my affairs to the particular speculation as to whether my fire would be out; looking towards the window of my sitting-room, I saw no cheering red gleam.

'That slut of a servant has neglected it as usual,' said I, 'and I shall see nothing but pale ashes if I go in; it is a fine starlight night – I will walk a little farther.'

It *was* a fine night, and the streets were dry and even clean for X—; there was a crescent curve of moonlight to be seen by the parish church tower, and hundreds of stars shone keenly bright in all quarters of the sky.

Unconsciously I steered my course towards the country; I had got into Grove Street, and began to feel the pleasure of seeing dim trees at the extremity, round a suburban house, when a person leaning over the iron gate of one of the small gardens which front the neat dwelling-houses in this street, addressed me as I was hurrying with quick stride past.

'What the deuce is the hurry? Just so must Lot have left Sodom, when he expected fire to pour down upon it, out of burning brass clouds.'

I stopped short, and looked towards the speaker. I smelt the fragrance and saw the red spark of a cigar; the dusk outline of a man, too, bent towards me over the wicket.

'You see I am meditating in the field at eventide,' continued this shade. 'God knows it's cool work! especially as instead of Rebecca on a camel's hump, with bracelets on her arms and a ring in her nose, Fate sends me only a counting-house clerk, in a grey tweed wrapper.'

The voice was familiar to me – its second utterance enabled me to seize the speaker's identity.

'Mr Hunsden! good evening.'

'Good evening, indeed! yes, but you would have passed me without recognition if I had not been so civil as to speak first.'

'I did not know you.'

'A famous excuse! You ought to have known me; I knew you, though you were going ahead like a steam-engine. Are the police after you?'

'It wouldn't be worth their while; I'm not of consequence enough to attract them.'

'Alas, poor shepherd! Alack and welladay! What a theme for regret, and how down in the mouth you must be, judging from the sound of your voice! But since you're not running from the police, from whom are you running? – the devil?'

'On the contrary, I am going post to him.'

'That is well – you're just in luck: this is Tuesday evening; there are scores of market gigs and carts returning to Dinneford to-night; and he, or some of his, have a seat in all regularly; so if you'll step in and sit half an hour in my bachelor's parlour, you may catch him as he passes without much trouble. I think though you'd better let him alone to-night, he'll have so many customers to serve; Tuesday is his busy day in X— and Dinneford; come in, at all events.'

He swung the wicket open as he spoke.

'Do you really wish me to go in?' I asked.

'As you please – I'm alone; your company for an hour or two would be agreeable to me; but, if you don't choose to favour me so far, I'll not press the point. I hate to bore any one.'

It suited me to accept the invitation as it suited Hunsden to give it. I passed through the gate, and followed him to the front door, which he opened; thence we traversed a passage, and entered his parlour; the door being shut, he pointed me to an arm-chair by the hearth; I sat down, and glanced round me.

It was a comfortable room, at once snug and handsome; the bright grate was filled with a genuine —shire fire, red, clear, and generous, no penurious South-of-England ember happed in the corner of a grate. On the table a shaded lamp diffused around a soft, pleasant, and equal light; the furniture was almost luxurious for a young bachelor, comprising a couch and two very easy chairs; bookshelves filled the recesses on each side of the mantelpiece; they were well-furnished, and arranged with perfect order. The neatness of the room suited my taste; I hate irregular and slovenly habits. From what I saw I concluded that Hunsden's ideas on that point corresponded with my own. While he removed from the centre-table to the sideboard a few pamphlets and periodicals, I ran my eye along the shelves of the bookcase nearest me. French and German works predominated, the old French dramatists, sundry modern authors, Thiers, Villemain, Paul de Kock, George Sand, Eugène Sue; in

German – Goethe, Schiller, Zschokke, Jean Paul Richter; in English there were works on Political Economy. I examined no further, for Mr Hunsden himself recalled my attention.

'You shall have something,' said he, 'for you ought to feel disposed for refreshment after walking nobody knows how far on such a Canadian night as this; but it shall not be brandy-and-water, and it shall not be a bottle of port, nor ditto of sherry. I keep no such poison. I have Rhein-wein for my own drinking, and you may choose between that and coffee.'

Here again Hunsden suited me: if there was one generally received practice I abhorred more than another, it was the habitual imbibing of spirits and strong wines. I had, however, no fancy for his acid German nectar, but I liked coffee, so I responded –

'Give me some coffee, Mr Hunsden.'

I perceived my answer pleased him; he had doubtless expected to see a chilling effect produced by his steady announcement that he would give me neither wine nor spirits; he just shot one searching glance at my face to ascertain whether my cordiality was genuine or a mere feint of politeness. I smiled, because I quite understood him; and, while I honoured his conscientious firmness, I was amused at his mistrust; he seemed satisfied, rang the bell, and ordered coffee, which was presently brought; for himself, a bunch of grapes and half a pint of something sour sufficed. My coffee was excellent; I told him so, and expressed the shuddering pity with which his anchorite fare inspired me. He did not answer, and I scarcely think heard my remark. At that moment one of those momentary eclipses I before alluded to had come over his face, extinguishing his smile, and replacing, by an abstracted and alienated look, the customarily shrewd, bantering glance of his eye. I employed the interval of silence in a rapid scrutiny of his physiognomy. I had never observed him closely before; and, as my sight is very short, I had gathered only a vague, general idea of his appearance; I was surprised now, on examination, to perceive how small, and even feminine, were his lineaments; his tall figure, long and dark locks, his voice and general bearing, had impressed me with the notion of something powerful and massive; not at all: – my own features were cast in a harsher and squarer mould than his. I discerned that there would be contrasts between his inward and outward man; contentions too; for I suspected his soul had more of will and ambition than his body had of fibre and muscle. Perhaps, in these incompatibilities of the 'physique' with the 'morale', lay the secret of that fitful gloom; he *would* but *could* not, and the athletic mind scowled scorn on its more fragile companion. As to his good looks, I should have liked to have a woman's opinion on that subject; it seemed to me that his face might produce the same effect on a lady that a very piquant and interesting, though scarcely pretty, female face would on a man. I have mentioned his dark locks – they were brushed sideways above a white and sufficiently expansive forehead; his cheek had a rather hectic freshness; his features might have done well on canvas, but indifferently in marble: they were plastic: character had set a stamp upon each; expression re-cast them at her pleasure, and strange metamorphoses she wrought, giving him now the mien of a morose bull, and anon that of an arch and mischievous girl; more frequently, the two semblances were blent, and a queer, composite countenance they made.

Starting from his silent fit, he began –

'William! what a fool you are to live in those dismal lodgings of Mrs King's, when you might take rooms here in Grove Street, and have a garden like me!'

'I should be too far from the mill.'

'What of that? It would do you good to walk there and back two or three times a day; besides, are you such a fossil that you never wish to see a flower or a green leaf?'

'I am no fossil.'

'What are you then? You sit at that desk in Crimsworth's counting-house day by day and week by week, scraping with a pen on paper, just like an automaton; you never get up; you never say you are tired; you never ask for a holiday; you never take change or relaxation; you give way to no excess of an evening; you neither keep wild company, nor indulge in strong drink.'

'Do you, Mr Hunsden?'

'Don't think to pose me with short questions; your case and mine are diametrically different, and it is nonsense attempting to draw a parallel. I say, that when a man endures patiently what ought to be unendurable, he is a fossil.'

'Whence do you acquire the knowledge of my patience?'

'Why, man, do you suppose you are a mystery? The other night you seemed surprised at my knowing to what family you belonged; now you find subject for wonderment in my calling you patient. What do you think I do with my eyes and ears? I've been in your counting-house more than once when Crimsworth has treated you like a dog; called for a book, for instance, and when you gave him the wrong one, or what he chose to consider the wrong one, flung it back almost in your face; desired you to shut or open the door as if you had been his flunkey; to say nothing of your position at the party about a month ago, where you had neither place nor partner, but hovered about like a poor shabby, hanger-on; and how patient you were under each and all of these circumstances!'

'Well, Mr Hunsden, what then?'

'I can hardly tell you what then; the conclusion to be drawn as to your character depends upon the nature of the motives which guide your conduct; if you are patient because you expect to make something eventually out of Crimsworth, notwithstanding his tyranny, or perhaps by means of it, you are what the world calls an interested and mercenary, but may be a very wise fellow; if you are patient because you think it a duty to meet insult with submission, you are an essential sap, and in no shape the man for my money; if you are patient because your nature is phlegmatic, flat, inexcitable, and that you cannot get up to the pitch of resistance, why, God made you to be crushed; and lie down by all means, and lie flat, and let Juggernaut ride well over you.'

Mr Hunsden's eloquence was not, it will be perceived, of the smooth and oily order. As he spoke, he pleased me ill. I seemed to recognize in him one of those characters who, sensitive enough themselves, are selfishly relentless towards the sensitiveness of others. Moreover, though he was neither like Crimsworth nor Lord Tynedale, yet he was acrid, and, I suspected, overbearing in his way: there was a tone of despotism in the urgency of the very reproaches by which he aimed at goading the oppressed into rebellion against the oppressor. Looking at him still more fixedly than I had yet done, I saw written in his eye and mien a resolution to arrogate to himself a freedom so unlimited, that it might often trench on the just liberty of his neighbours. I rapidly ran over these thoughts, and then I laughed a low and involuntary laugh, moved thereto by a slight inward revelation of the inconsistency of man. It was as I thought: Hunsden had expected me to take with calm his incorrect and offensive surmises, his bitter and haughty taunts; and himself was chafed by a laugh scarce louder than a whisper.

His brow darkened, his thin nostril dilated a little.

'Yes,' he began, 'I told you that you were an aristocrat, and who but an aristocrat would laugh such a laugh as that, and look such a look? A laugh frigidly jeering; a look lazily mutinous; gentlemanlike irony, patrician resentment. What a nobleman you would have made, William Crimsworth! You are cut out for one; pity Fortune has baulked Nature! Look at the features, figure, even to the hands – distinction all over – ugly distinction! Now, if you'd only an estate and a mansion, and a park, and a title, how you could play the exclusive, maintain the rights of your class, train your tenantry in habits of respect to the peerage, oppose at every step the advancing power of the people, support your rotten order, and be ready for its sake to wade knee-deep in churls' blood; as it is, you've no power; you can do nothing;

you're wrecked and stranded on the shores of commerce; forced into collision with practical men, with whom you cannot cope, for *you'll never be a tradesman.*'

The first part of Hunsden's speech moved me not at all, or, if it did, it was only to wonder at the perversion into which prejudice had twisted his judgment of my character; the concluding sentence, however, not only moved, but shook me; the blow it gave was a severe one, because Truth wielded the weapon. If I smiled now, it was only in disdain of myself.

Hunsden saw his advantage; he followed it up.

'You'll make nothing by trade,' continued he; 'nothing more than the crust of dry bread and the draught of fair water on which you now live; your only chance of getting a competency lies in marrying a rich widow, or running away with an heiress.'

'I leave such shifts to be put in practice by those who devise them,' said I, rising.

'And even that is hopeless,' he went on coolly. 'What widow would have you? Much less, what heiress? You're not bold and venturesome enough for the one, nor handsome and fascinating enough for the other. You think perhaps you look intelligent and polished; carry your intellect and refinement to market, and tell me in a private note what price is bid for them.'

Mr Hunsden had taken his tone for the night; the string he struck was out of tune, he would finger no other. Averse to discord, of which I had enough every day and all day long, I concluded, at last, that silence and solitude were preferable to jarring converse. I bade him a good-night.

'What! Are you going, lad? Well, good-night: you'll find the door.' And he sat still in front of the fire, while I left the room and the house. I had got a good way on my return to my lodgings before I found out that I was walking very fast, and breathing very hard, and that my nails were almost stuck into the palms of my clenched hands, and that my teeth were set fast; on making this discovery, I relaxed both my pace, fists, and jaws, but I could not so soon cause the regrets rushing rapidly through my mind to slacken their tide. Why did I make myself a tradesman? Why did I enter Hunsden's house this evening? Why, at dawn to-morrow, must I repair to Crimsworth's mill? All that night did I ask myself these questions, and all that night fiercely demanded of my soul an answer. I got no sleep; my head burned, my feet froze; at last the factory bells rang, and I sprang from my bed with other slaves.

CHAPTER V

THERE is a climax to everything, to every state of feeling as well as to every position in life. I turned this truism over in my mind as, in the frosty dawn of a January morning, I hurried down the steep and now icy street which descended from Mrs King's to the Close. The factory workpeople had preceded me by nearly an hour, and the mill was all lighted up and in full operation when I reached it. I repaired to my post in the counting-house as usual; the fire there, but just lit, as yet only smoked; Steighton was not yet arrived. I shut the door and sat down at the desk; my hands, recently washed in half-frozen water, were still numb; I could not write till they had regained vitality, so I went on thinking, and still the theme of my thoughts was the 'climax'. Self-dissatisfaction troubled exceedingly the current of my meditations.

'Come, William Crimsworth,' said my conscience, or whatever it is that within ourselves takes ourselves to task – 'Come, get a clear notion of what you would have, or what you would not have. You talk of a climax; pray has your endurance reached its climax? It is not four months old. What a fine resolute fellow you imagined yourself to be when you told Tynedale you would tread in your father's steps, and a pretty treading you are likely to make of it! How well you like X—! Just at this moment how redolent of pleasant associations are its streets, its shops, its warehouses, its factories! How the prospect of this day cheers you! Letter-copying till noon, solitary dinner at your lodgings, letter-copying till evening, solitude; for you neither find pleasure in Brown's, nor Smith's, nor Nicholl's, nor Eccles' company; and as to Hunsden, you fancied there was pleasure to be derived from his society – he! he! how did you like the taste you had of him last night? – was it sweet? Yet he is a talented, an original-minded man, and even he does not like you; your self-respect defies you to like him; he has always seen you to disadvantage; he always will see you to disadvantage; your positions are unequal, and were they on the same level your minds could not assimilate; never hope, then, to gather the honey of friendship out of that thorn-guarded plant. Hollo, Crimsworth! where are your thoughts tending? You leave the recollection of Hunsden as a bee would a rock, as a bird a desert; and your aspirations spread eager wings towards a land of visions where, now in advancing daylight – in X— daylight – you dare to dream of congeniality, repose, union. Those three you will never meet in this world; they are angels. The souls of just men made perfect may encounter them in heaven, but your soul will never be made perfect. Eight o'clock strikes! your hands are thawed, get to work!'

'Work? why should I work?' said I sullenly: 'I cannot please though I toil like a slave.' 'Work, work!' reiterated the inward voice. 'I may work, it will do no good,' I growled; but nevertheless I drew out a packet of letters and commenced my task – task thankless and bitter as that of the Israelite crawling over the sun-baked fields of Egypt in search of straw and stubble wherewith to accomplish his tale of bricks.

About ten o'clock I heard Mr Crimsworth's gig turn into the yard, and in a minute or two he entered the counting-house. It was his custom to glance his eye at Steighton and myself, to hang up his mackintosh, stand a minute with his back to the fire, and then walk out. To-day he did not deviate from his usual habits; the only difference was that when he looked at me, his brow, instead of being merely hard, was surly; his eye, instead of being cold, was fierce. He studied me a minute or two longer than usual, but went out in silence.

Twelve o'clock arrived; the bell rang for a suspension of labour; the workpeople went off to their dinners; Steighton, too, departed, desiring me to lock the counting-house door and take the key with me. I was tying up a bundle of papers, and putting them in their place, preparatory to closing my desk, when Crimsworth reappeared at the door, and, entering, closed it behind him.

'You'll stay here a minute,' said he, in a deep, brutal voice, while his nostrils distended and his eye shot a spark of sinister fire.

Alone with Edward I remembered our relationship, and remembering that forgot the difference of position; I put away deference and careful forms of speech; I answered with simple brevity.

'It is time to go home,' I said, turning the key in my desk.

'You'll stay here!' he reiterated. 'And take your hand off that key! leave it in the lock!'

'Why?' asked I. 'What cause is there for changing my usual plans?'

'Do as I order,' was the answer, 'and no questions! You are my servant; obey me! What have you been about–?' He was going on in the same breath when an abrupt pause announced that rage had for the moment got the better of articulation.

'You may look, if you wish to know,' I replied. 'There is the open desk, there are the papers.'

'Confound your insolence! What have you been about?'

'Your work, and have done it well.'

'Hypocrite and twaddler! Smooth-faced, snivelling grease-horn!' (this last term is, I believe, purely —shire, and alludes to the horn of black, rancid whale-oil, usually to be seen suspended to cart-wheels, and employed for greasing the same).

'Come, Edward Crimsworth, enough of this. It is time you and I wound up accounts. I have now given your service three months' trial, and I find it the most nauseous slavery under the sun. Seek another clerk. I stay no longer.'

'What! do you dare to give me notice? Stop at least for your wages.' He took down the heavy gig whip hanging beside his mackintosh.

I permitted myself to laugh with a degree of scorn I took no pains to temper or hide. His fury boiled up, and when he had sworn half a dozen vulgar, impious oaths, without, however, venturing to lift the whip, he continued –

'I've found you out and know you thoroughly, you mean, whining lickspittle! What have you been saying all over X— about me? Answer me that!'

'You? I have neither inclination nor temptation to talk about you.'

'You lie! It is your practice to talk about me; it is your constant habit to make public complaint of the treatment you receive at my hands. You have gone and told it far and near that I give you low wages and knock you about like a dog. I wish you were a dog! I'd set to this minute, and never stir from the spot till I'd cut every strip of flesh from your bones with this whip.'

He flourished this tool. The end of the lash just touched my forehead. A warm excited thrill ran through my veins, my blood seemed to give a bound, and then raced fast and hot along its channels. I got up nimbly, came round to where he stood, and faced him.

'Down with your whip!' said I, 'and explain this instant what you mean.'

'Sirrah! to whom are you speaking?'

'To you. There is no one else present, I think. You say I have been calumniating you – complaining of your low wages and bad treatment. Give your grounds for these assertions.'

Crimsworth had no dignity, and when I sternly demanded an explanation, he gave one in a loud, scolding voice.

'Grounds! you shall have them; and turn to the light that I may see your brazen face blush black, when you hear yourself proved to be a liar and a hypocrite. At a public meeting in the Town-hall yesterday, I had the pleasure of hearing myself insulted by the speaker opposed to me in the question under discussion, by allusions to my private affairs; by cant about monsters without natural affection, family despots, and such trash; and when I rose to answer, I was met by a shout from the filthy mob, where the mention of your name enabled me at once to detect the quarter in which this base attack had originated. When I looked round, I saw that treacherous villain, Hunsden, acting as fugleman. I detected you in close conversation with Hunsden at my house a month ago, and I know that you were at Hunsden's rooms last night. Deny it if you dare.'

'Oh, I shall not deny it! And if Hunsden hounded on the people to hiss you, he did quite right. You deserve popular execration; for a worse man, a harder master, a more brutal brother than you are has seldom existed.'

'Sirrah! sirrah!' reiterated Crimsworth; and to complete his apostrophe, he cracked the whip straight over my head.

A minute sufficed to wrest it from him, break it in two pieces, and throw it under the grate. He made a headlong rush at me, which I evaded, and said –

'Touch me, and I'll have you up before the nearest magistrate.'

Men like Crimsworth, if firmly and calmly resisted, always abate something of their exorbitant insolence; he had no mind to be brought before a magistrate, and I suppose he saw I meant what I said. After an odd and long stare at me, at once bull-like and amazed, he seemed to bethink himself that, after all, his money gave him sufficient superiority over a beggar like me, and that he had in his hands a surer and more dignified mode of revenge than the somewhat hazardous one of personal chastisement.

'Take your hat,' said he. 'Take what belongs to you, and go out at that door; get away to your parish, you pauper: beg, steal, starve, get transported, do what you like; but at your peril venture again into my sight! If ever I hear of your setting foot on an inch of ground belonging to me, I'll hire a man to cane you.'

'It is not likely you'll have the chance; once off your premises, what temptation can I have to return to them? I leave a prison,

I leave a tyrant; I leave what is worse than the worst that can lie before me, so no fear of my coming back.'

'Go, or I'll make you!' exclaimed Crimsworth.

I walked deliberately to my desk, took out such of its contents as were my own property, put them in my pocket, locked the desk, and placed the key on the top.

'What are you abstracting from that desk?' demanded the millowner. 'Leave all behind in its place, or I'll send for a policeman to search you.'

'Look sharp about it, then,' said I, and I took down my hat, drew on my gloves, and walked leisurely out of the counting-house – walked out of it to enter it no more.

I recollect that when the mill-bell rang the dinner-hour, before Mr Crimsworth entered, and the scene above related took place, I had had rather a sharp appetite, and had been waiting somewhat impatiently to hear the signal of feeding-time. I forgot it now, however; the images of potatoes and roast mutton were effaced from my mind by the stir and tumult which the transaction of the last half-hour had there excited. I only thought of walking, that the action of my muscles might harmonize with the action of my nerves; and walk I did, fast and far. How could I do otherwise? A load was lifted off my heart; I felt light and liberated. I had got away from Bigben Close without a breach of resolution; without injury to my self-respect. I had not forced circumstances; circumstances had freed me. Life was again open to me; no longer was its horizon limited by the high black wall surrounding Crimsworth's mill. Two hours had elapsed before my sensations had so far subsided as to leave me calm enough to remark for what wider and clearer boundaries I had exchanged that sooty girdle. When I did look up, lo! straight before me lay Grovetown, a village of villas about five miles out of X——. The short winter day, as I perceived from the far-declined sun, was already approaching its close; a chill frost-mist was rising from the river on which X—— stands, and along whose banks the road I had taken lay;

it dimmed the earth, but did not obscure the clear icy blue of the January sky. There was a great stillness near and far; the time of the day favoured tranquillity, as the people were all employed within-doors, the hour of evening release from the factories not being yet arrived; a sound of full-flowing water alone pervaded the air, for the river was deep and abundant, swelled by the melting of a late snow. I stood awhile, leaning over a wall; and looking down at the current: I watched the rapid rush of its waves. I desired memory to take a clear and permanent impression of the scene, and treasure it for future years. Grovetown church clock struck four; looking up, I beheld the last of that day's sun, glinting red through the leafless boughs of some very old oak-trees surrounding the church – its light coloured and characterized the picture as I wished. I paused yet a moment, till the sweet, slow sound of the bell had quite died out of the air; then ear, eye, and feeling satisfied, I quitted the wall and once more turned my face towards X—.

CHAPTER VI

I RE-ENTERED the town a hungry man; the dinner I had forgotten recurred seductively to my recollection; and it was with a quick step and sharp appetite I ascended the narrow street leading to my lodgings. It was dark when I opened the front door and walked into the house. I wondered how my fire would be; the night was cold, and I shuddered at the prospect of a grate full of sparkless cinders. To my joyful surprise, I found, on entering my sitting-room, a good fire and a clean hearth. I had hardly noticed this phenomenon, when I became aware of another subject for wonderment; the chair I usually occupied near the hearth was already filled; a person sat there with his arms folded on his chest, and his legs stretched out on the rug. Short-sighted as I am, doubtful as was the gleam of the firelight, a moment's examination enabled me to recognize in this person my acquaintance, Mr Hunsden. I could not of course be much pleased to see him, considering the manner in which I had parted from him the night before, and as I walked to the hearth, stirred the fire, and said coolly, 'Good evening,' my demeanour evinced as little cordiality as I felt; yet I wondered in my own mind what had brought him there; and I wondered, also, what motives had induced him to interfere so actively between me and Edward; it was to him, it appeared, that I owed my welcome dismissal; still I could not bring myself to ask him questions, to show any eagerness of curiosity; if he chose to explain, he might, but the explanation should be a perfectly voluntary one on his part; I thought he was entering upon it.

'You owe me a debt of gratitude,' were the first words.

'Do I?' said I; 'I hope it is not a large one, for I am much too poor to charge myself with heavy liabilities of any kind.'

'Then declare yourself bankrupt at once, for this liability is a ton weight at least. When I came in I found your fire out, and I had it lit again, and made that sulky drab of a servant stay and blow at it with the bellows till it had burnt up properly; now, say "Thank you!" '

'Not till I have had something to eat; I can thank nobody while I am so famished.'

I rang the bell and ordered tea and some cold meat.

'Cold meat!' exclaimed Hunsden, as the servant closed the door, 'what a glutton you are, man! Meat with tea! you'll die of eating too much.'

'No, Mr Hunsden, I shall not.' I felt a necessity for contradicting him; I was irritated with hunger, and irritated at seeing him there, and irritated at the continued roughness of his manner.

'It is over-eating that makes you so ill-tempered,' said he.

'How do you know?' I demanded. 'It is like you to give a pragmatical opinion without being acquainted with any of the circumstances of the case; I have had no dinner.'

What I said was petulant and snappish enough, and Hunsden only replied by looking in my face and laughing.

'Poor thing!' he whined after a pause. 'It has had no dinner, has it? What! I suppose its master would not let it come home. Did Crimsworth order you to fast by way of punishment, William?'

'No, Mr Hunsden.' Fortunately at this sulky juncture, tea was brought in, and I fell to upon some bread and butter and cold beef directly. Having cleared a plateful, I became so far humanized as to intimate to Mr Hunsden 'that he need not sit there staring, but might come to the table and do as I did, if he liked.'

'But I don't like in the least,' said he, and therewith he summoned the servant by a fresh pull of the bell-rope, and intimated a desire to have a glass of toast-and-water. 'And some more coal,' he added; 'Mr Crimsworth shall keep a good fire while I stay.'

His orders being executed, he wheeled his chair round to the table, so as to be opposite me.

'Well,' he proceeded. 'You are out of work, I suppose.'

'Yes,' said I; and not disposed to show the satisfaction I felt on this point, I, yielding to the whim of the moment, took up the subject as though I considered myself aggrieved rather than benefited by what had been done. 'Yes – thanks to you, I am. Crimsworth turned me off at a minute's notice, owing to some interference of yours at a public meeting, I understand.'

'Ah! what! he mentioned that! He observed me signalling the lads, did he? What had he to say about his friend Hunsden – anything sweet?'

'He called you a treacherous villain.'

'Oh, he hardly knows me yet! I'm one of those shy people who don't come out all at once, and he is only just beginning to make my acquaintance, but he'll find I've some good qualities – excellent ones! The Hunsdens were always unrivalled at tracking a rascal; a downright, dishonourable villain is their natural prey – they could not keep off him wherever they met him; you used the word pragmatical just now – that word is the property of our family; it has been applied to us from generation to generation; we have fine noses for abuses; we scent a scoundrel a mile off; we are reformers born, radical reformers; and it was impossible for me to live in the same town as Crimsworth, to come into weekly contact with him, to witness some of his conduct to you (for whom personally I care nothing; I only consider the brutal injustice with which he violated your natural claim to equality) – I say it was impossible for me to be thus situated and not feel the angel or the demon of my race at work within me. I followed my instinct, opposed a tyrant, and broke a chain.'

Now this speech interested me much, both because it brought out Hunsden's character, and because it explained his motives; it interested me so much that I forgot to reply to it, and sat silent, pondering over a throng of ideas it had suggested.

'Are you grateful to me?' he asked, presently.

In fact I was grateful, or almost so, and I believe I half liked him at the moment, notwithstanding his proviso that what he had done was not out of regard for me. But human nature is perverse. Impossible to answer his blunt question in the affirmative, so I disclaimed all tendency to gratitude, and advised him, if he expected any reward for his championship, to look for it in a better world, as he was not likely to meet with it here. In reply he termed me 'a dry-hearted, aristocratic scamp', whereupon I again charged him with having taken the bread out of my mouth.

'Your bread was dirty, man!' cried Hunsden – 'dirty and unwholesome! It came through the hands of a tyrant, for I tell you Crimsworth is a tyrant, – a tyrant to his workpeople, a tyrant to his clerks, and will some day be a tyrant to his wife.'

'Nonsense! bread is bread, and a salary is a salary. I've lost mine, and through your means.'

'There's sense in what you say, after all,' rejoined Hunsden. 'I must say I am rather agreeably surprised to hear you make so practical an observation as that last. I had imagined now, from my previous observation of your character, that the sentimental delight you would have taken in your newly regained liberty would, for a while at least, have effaced all ideas of forethought and prudence. I think better of you for looking steadily to the needful.'

'Looking steadily to the needful! How can I do otherwise? I must live, and to live I must have what you call "the needful", which I can only get by working. I repeat it, you have taken my work from me.'

'What do you mean to do?' pursued Hunsden coolly. 'You have influential relations; I suppose they'll soon provide you with another place.'

'Influential relations? Who? I should like to know their names.'

'The Seacombes.'

'Stuff! I have cut them.'

Hunsden looked at me incredulously.

'I have,' said I, 'and that definitively.'

'You must mean they have cut you, William.'

'As you please. They offered me their patronage on condition of my entering the Church; I declined both the terms and the recompense; I withdrew from my cold uncles, and preferred throwing myself into my elder brother's arms, from whose affectionate embrace I am now torn by the cruel intermeddling of a stranger – of yourself, in short.'

I could not repress a half-smile as I said this; a similar demi-manifestation of feeling appeared at the same moment on Hunsden's lips.

'Oh, I see!' said he, looking into my eyes, and it was evident he *did* see right down into my heart. Having sat a minute or two with his chin resting on his hand, diligently occupied in the continued perusal of my countenance, he went on –

'Seriously, have you then nothing to expect from the Seacombes?'

'Yes, rejection and repulsion. Why do you ask me twice? How can hands stained with the ink of a counting-house, soiled with the grease of a wool-warehouse, ever again be permitted to come into contact with aristocratic palms?'

'There would be a difficulty, no doubt; still you are such a complete Seacombe in appearance, feature, language, almost manner, I wonder they should disown you.'

'They have disowned me; so talk no more about it.'

'Do you regret it, William?'

'No.'

'Why not, lad?'

'Because they are not people with whom I could ever have had any sympathy.'

'I say you are one of them.'

'That merely proves that you know nothing at all about it; I am my mother's son, but not my uncles' nephew.'

'Still – one of your uncles is a lord, though rather an obscure and not a very wealthy one, and the other a right honourable: you should consider worldly interest.'

'Nonsense, Mr Hunsden. You know or may know that even had I desired to be submissive to my uncles, I could not have stooped with a good enough grace ever to have won their favour. I should have sacrificed my own comfort and not have gained their patronage in return.'

'Very likely – so you calculated your wisest plan was to follow your own devices at once?'

'Exactly. I must follow my own devices – I must till the day of my death; because I can neither comprehend, adopt, nor work out those of other people.'

Hunsden yawned. 'Well,' said he, 'in all this, I see but one thing clearly – that is, that the whole affair is no business of mine.' He stretched himself and again yawned. 'I wonder what time it is?' he went on: 'I have an appointment for seven o'clock.'

'Three-quarters past six by my watch.'

'Well, then, I'll go.' He got up. 'You'll not meddle with trade again?' said he, leaning his elbow on the mantelpiece.

'No; I think not.'

'You would be a fool if you did. Probably, after all, you'll think better of your uncles' proposal and go into the Church.'

'A singular regeneration must take place in my whole inner and outer man before I do that. A good clergyman is one of the best of men.'

'Indeed! Do you think so?' interrupted Hunsden, scoffingly.

'I do, and no mistake. But I have not the peculiar points which go to make a good clergyman; and rather than adopt a profession for which I have no vocation, I would endure extremities of hardship from poverty.'

'You're a mighty difficult customer to suit. You won't be a tradesman or a parson; you can't be a lawyer, or a doctor, or a gentleman, because you've no money. I'd recommend you to travel.'

'What! without money?'

'You must travel in search of money, man. You can speak French – with a vile English accent, no doubt – still, you can speak it. Go on to the Continent, and see what will turn up for you there.'

'God knows I should like to go!' exclaimed I with involuntary ardour.

'Go: what the deuce hinders you? You may get to Brussels, for instance, for five or six pounds, if you know how to manage with economy.'

'Necessity would teach me if I didn't.'

'Go, then, and let your wits make a way for you when you get there. I know Brussels almost as well as I know X—, and I am sure it would suit such a one as you better than London.'

'But occupation, Mr Hunsden! I must go where occupation is to be had; and how could I get recommendation, or introduction, or employment at Brussels?'

'There speaks the organ of caution. You hate to advance a step before you know every inch of the way. You haven't a sheet of paper and a pen-and-ink?'

'I hope so,' and I produced writing materials with alacrity; for I guessed what he was going to do. He sat down, wrote a few lines, folded, sealed, and addressed a letter, and held it out to me.

'There, Prudence, there's a pioneer to hew down the first rough difficulties of your path. I know well enough, lad, you are not one of those who will run their neck into a noose without seeing how they are to get it out again, and you're right there. A reckless man is my aversion, and nothing should ever persuade me to meddle with the concerns of such a one. Those who are reckless for themselves are generally ten times more so for their friends.'

'This is a letter of introduction, I suppose?' said I, taking the epistle.

'Yes. With that in your pocket you will run no risk of finding yourself in a state of absolute destitution, which, I know, you would regard as a degradation – so should I, for that matter. The person to whom you will present it generally has two or three respectable places depending upon his recommendation.'

'That will just suit me,' said I.

'Well, and where's your gratitude?' demanded Mr Hunsden; 'don't you know how to say "Thank you"?'

'I've fifteen pounds and a watch, which my godmother, whom I never saw, gave me eighteen years ago,' was my rather irrelevant answer; and I further avowed myself a happy man, and professed that I did not envy any being in Christendom.

'And your gratitude?'

'I shall be off presently, Mr Hunsden – to-morrow, if all be well: I'll not stay a day longer in X— than I'm obliged.'

'Very good – but it will be decent to make due acknowledgment for the assistance you have received; be quick! It is just going to strike seven: I'm waiting to be thanked.'

'Just stand out of the way, will you, Mr Hunsden? I want a key that is on the corner of the mantelpiece. I'll pack my portmanteau before I go to bed.'

The house clock struck seven.

'The lad is a heathen,' said Hunsden, and taking his hat from a sideboard, he left the room, laughing to himself. I had half an inclination to follow him: I really intended to leave X— the next morning, and should certainly not have another opportunity of bidding him good-bye. The front door banged to.

'Let him go,' said I; 'we shall meet again some day.'

CHAPTER VII

READER, perhaps you were never in Belgium? Haply you don't know the physiognomy of the country? You have not its lineaments defined upon your memory, as I have them on mine?

Three – nay four – pictures line the four-walled cell where are stored for me the records of the past. First, Eton. All in that picture is in far perspective, receding, diminutive; but freshly coloured, green, dewy, with a spring sky, piled with glittering yet showery clouds; for my childhood was not all sunshine – it had its overcast, its cold, its stormy hours. Second, X—, huge, dingy; the canvas cracked and smoked; a yellow sky, sooty clouds; no sun, no azure; the verdure of the suburbs blighted and sullied – a very dreary scene.

Third, Belgium; and I will pause before this landscape. As to the fourth, a curtain covers it, which I may hereafter withdraw, or may not, as suits my convenience and capacity. At any rate, for the present it must hang undisturbed. Belgium! name unromantic and unpoetic, yet name that whenever uttered has in my ear a sound, in my heart an echo, such as no other assemblage of syllables, however sweet or classic, can produce. Belgium! I repeat the word, now as I sit alone near midnight. It stirs my world of the past like a summons to resurrection; the graves unclose, the dead are raised; thoughts, feelings, memories that slept, are seen by me ascending from the clods – haloed most of them – but while I gaze on their vapoury forms, and strive to ascertain definitely their outline, the sound which wakened them dies, and they sink, each and all, like a light wreath of mist, absorbed in the mould, recalled to urns, resealed in monuments. Farewell, luminous phantoms!

This is Belgium, reader. Look! don't call the picture a flat or a dull one – it was neither flat nor dull to me when I first beheld it. When I left Ostend on a mild February morning, and found myself on the road to Brussels, nothing could look vapid to me. My sense of enjoyment possessed an edge whetted to the finest, untouched, keen, exquisite. I was young; I had good health; pleasure and I had never met; no indulgence of hers had enervated or sated one faculty of my nature. Liberty I clasped in my arms for the first time, and the influence of her smile and embrace revived my life like the sun and the west wind. Yes, at that epoch I felt like a morning traveller who doubts not that from the hill he is ascending he shall behold a glorious sunrise; what if the track be strait, steep, and stony? he sees it not; his eyes are fixed on that summit, flushed already, flushed and gilded, and having gained it he is certain of the scene beyond. He knows that the sun will face him, that his chariot is even now coming over the eastern horizon, and that the herald breeze he feels on his cheek is opening for the god's career a clear, vast path of azure, amidst clouds soft as pearl and warm as flame. Difficulty and toil were to be my lot, but sustained by energy, drawn on by hopes as bright as vague, I deemed such a lot no hardship. I mounted now the hill in shade; there were pebbles, inequalities, briars in my path, but my eyes were fixed on the crimson peak above; my imagination was with the refulgent firmament beyond, and I thought nothing of the stones turning under my feet, or of the thorns scratching my face and hands.

I gazed often, and always with delight, from the window of the diligence (these, be it remembered, were not the days of trains and railroads). Well! and what did I see? I will tell you faithfully. Green, reedy swamps; fields fertile but flat, cultivated in patches that made them look like magnified kitchen-gardens; belts of cut trees, formal as pollard willows, skirting the horizon; narrow canals, gliding slow by the roadside; painted Flemish farm-houses; some very dirty hovels; a grey, dead sky; wet road, wet fields, wet house-tops: not a beautiful, scarcely a picturesque object met my eye along the whole route; yet to me all was beautiful, all was more than picturesque. It continued fair so long as daylight lasted, though the moisture of many preceding damp days had sodden the whole country; as it grew dark, however, the rain recommenced, and it was through streaming and starless darkness my eye caught the first gleam of the lights of Brussels. I saw little of the city but its lights that night. Having alighted from the diligence, a fiacre conveyed me to the Hôtel de —, where I had been advised by a fellow-traveller to put up; having eaten a traveller's supper, I retired to bed, and slept a traveller's sleep.

Next morning I awoke from prolonged and sound repose with the impression that I was yet in X—, and perceiving it to be broad daylight I started up, imagining that I had overslept myself and should be behind time at the counting-house. The momentary and painful sense of restraint vanished before the revived and reviving consciousness of freedom, as, throwing back the white curtains of my bed, I looked forth into a wide, lofty foreign chamber; how different from the small and dingy, though not uncomfortable, apartment I had occupied for a night or two at a respectable inn in London while waiting for the sailing of the packet! Yet far be it from me to profane the memory of that dingy little room! It, too, is dear to my soul; for there, as I lay in quiet and darkness, I first heard the great bell of St Paul's telling London it was midnight, and well do I recall the deep, deliberate tones, so full charged with colossal phlegm and force. From the small, narrow window of that room, I first saw *the* dome, looming through a London mist. I suppose the sensations, stirred by those first sounds, first sights, are felt but once; treasure them, Memory; seal them in urns, and keep them in safe niches! Well – I rose. Travellers talk of the apartments in foreign dwellings being bare and uncomfortable; I thought my chamber looked stately and cheerful. It had such large windows – *croisées* that opened like doors, with such broad, clear panes of glass; such a great looking-glass

stood on my dressing-table – such a fine mirror glittered over
the mantelpiece – the painted floor looked so clean and glossy;
when I had dressed and was descending the stairs, the broad
marble steps almost awed me, and so did the lofty hall into
which they conducted. On the first landing I met a Flemish
housemaid: she had wooden shoes, a short red petticoat, a
printed cotton bedgown, her face was broad, her physiognomy
eminently stupid; when I spoke to her in French, she answered
me in Flemish, with an air the reverse of civil; yet I thought
her charming; if she was not pretty or polite, she was, I
conceived, very picturesque; she reminded me of the female
figures in certain Dutch paintings I had seen in other years at
Seacombe Hall.

I repaired to the public room; that, too, was very large and
very lofty, and warmed by a stove; the floor was black, and the
stove was black, and most of the furniture was black: yet I never
experienced a freer sense of exhilaration than when I sat down
at a very long, black table (covered, however, in part by a white
cloth), and, having ordered breakfast, began to pour out my
coffee from a little black coffee-pot. The stove might be dismal-
looking to some eyes, not to mine, but it was indisputably very
warm, and there were two gentlemen seated by it talking in
French; impossible to follow their rapid utterance, or comprehend much of the purport of what they said – yet French, in
the mouths of Frenchmen, or Belgians (I was not then sensible
of the horrors of the Belgian accent), was as music to my
ears. One of these gentlemen presently discerned me to be an
Englishman – no doubt from the fashion in which I addressed
the waiter; for I would persist in speaking French in my execrable South-of-England style, though the man understood
English. The gentleman, after looking towards me once or
twice, politely accosted me in very good English; I remember
I wished to God that I could speak French as well; his fluency
and correct pronunciation impressed me for the first time with
a due notion of the cosmopolitan character of the capital I was

in; it was my first experience of that skill in living languages I afterwards found to be so general in Brussels.

I lingered over my breakfast as long as I could; while it was there on the table, and while that stranger continued talking to me, I was a free, independent traveller; but at last the things were removed, the two gentlemen left the room; suddenly the illusion ceased, reality and business came back. I, a bondsman just released from the yoke, freed for one week from twenty-one years of constraint, must, of necessity, resume the fetters of dependency. Hardly had I tasted the delight of being without a master when duty issued her stern mandate: 'Go forth and seek another service.' I never linger over a painful and necessary task; I never take pleasure before business, it is not in my nature to do so; impossible to enjoy a leisurely walk over the city, though I perceived the morning was very fine, until I had presented Mr Hunsden's letter of introduction, and got fairly on to the track of a new situation. Wrenching my mind from liberty and delight, I seized my hat, and forced my reluctant body out of the Hôtel de — into the foreign street.

It was a fine day, but I would not look at the blue sky nor at the stately houses round me; my mind was bent on one thing, finding out 'Mr Brown, Numero —, Rue Royale', for so my letter was addressed. By dint of inquiry I succeeded; I stood at last at the desired door, knocked, asked for Mr Brown, and was admitted.

Being shown into a small breakfast-room, I found myself in the presence of an elderly gentleman – very grave, business-like, and respectable-looking. I presented Mr Hunsden's letter; he received me very civilly. After a little desultory conversation he asked me if there was anything in which his advice or experience could be of use. I said, 'Yes,' and then proceeded to tell him that I was not a gentleman of fortune, travelling for pleasure, but an ex-counting-house clerk, who wanted employment of some kind, and that immediately too. He replied that as a friend of Mr Hunsden's he would be willing to assist me as well as he could. After some meditation he named a place in a mercantile house at Liège, and another in a bookseller's shop at Louvain.

'Clerk and shopman!' murmured I to myself. 'No.' I shook my head. I had tried the high stool; I hated it; I believed there were other occupations that would suit me better; besides I did not wish to leave Brussels.

'I know of no place in Brussels,' answered Mr Brown, 'unless indeed you were disposed to turn your attention to teaching. I am acquainted with the director of a large establishment who is in want of a professor of English and Latin.'

I thought two minutes, then I seized the idea eagerly.

'The very thing, sir!' said I.

'But,' asked he, 'do you understand French well enough to teach Belgian boys English?'

Fortunately I could answer this question in the affirmative; having studied French under a Frenchman, I could speak the language intelligibly though not fluently. I could also read it well and write it decently.

'Then,' pursued Mr Brown, 'I think I can promise you the place, for Monsieur Pelet will not refuse a professor recommended by me; but come here again at five o'clock this afternoon, and I will introduce you to him.'

The word 'professor' struck me. 'I am not a professor,' said I.

'Oh,' returned Mr Brown, 'professor, here in Belgium, means a teacher, that is all.'

My conscience thus quieted, I thanked Mr Brown, and, for the present, withdrew. This time I stepped out into the street with a relieved heart; the task I had imposed on myself for that day was executed. I might now take some hours of holiday. I felt free to look up. For the first time I remarked the sparkling clearness of the air, the deep blue of the sky, the gay, clean aspect of the whitewashed or painted houses; I saw what a fine street was the Rue Royale, and, walking leisurely along its broad pavement, I continued to survey its stately hotels, till the palisades, the gates, and trees of the park appearing in sight, offered to my eye a new attraction. I remember, before entering the park, I stood awhile to contemplate the statue of General Belliard, and then I advanced to the top of the great staircase just beyond, and I looked down into a narrow back street, which I afterwards learnt was called the Rue d'Isabelle. I well recollect that my eye rested on the green door of a rather large house opposite, where, on a brass plate, was inscribed, 'Pensionnat de Demoiselles'. Pensionnat! The word excited an uneasy sensation in my mind; it seemed to speak of restraint. Some of the demoiselles, externats no doubt, were at that moment issuing from the door – I looked for a pretty face amongst them, but their close, little French bonnets hid their features; in a moment they were gone.

I had traversed a good deal of Brussels before five o'clock arrived, but punctually as that hour struck I was again in the Rue Royale. Re-admitted to Mr Brown's breakfast-room, I found him as before, seated at the table, and he was not alone – a gentleman stood by the hearth. Two words of introduction designated him as my future master. 'M. Pelet, Mr Crimsworth; Mr Crimsworth, M. Pelet.' A bow on each side finished the ceremony. I don't know what sort of a bow I made; an ordinary one, I suppose, for I was in a tranquil, commonplace frame of mind; I felt none of the agitation which had troubled my first interview with Edward Crimsworth. M. Pelet's bow was extremely polite, yet not theatrical, scarcely French; he and I were presently seated opposite to each other. In a pleasing voice, low and, out of consideration to my foreign ears, very distinct and deliberate, M. Pelet intimated that he had just been receiving from 'le respectable M. Brown', an account of my attainments and character, which relieved him from all scruple as to the propriety of engaging me as professor of English and Latin in his establishment; neverthless, for form's sake, he would put a few questions to test my powers. He did, and expressed in flattering terms his satisfaction at my answers.

The subject of salary next came on; it was fixed at one thousand francs per annum, besides board and lodging. 'And in addition,' suggested M. Pelet, 'as there will be some hours in each day during which your services will not be required in my establishment, you may, in time, obtain employment in other seminaries, and thus turn your vacant moments to profitable account.'

I thought this very kind, and indeed I found afterwards that the terms on which M. Pelet had engaged me were really liberal for Brussels; instruction being extremely cheap there on account of the number of teachers. It was further arranged that I should be installed in my new post the very next day, after which M. Pelet and I parted.

Well, and what was he like? and what were my impressions concerning him? He was a man of about forty years of age, of middle size, and rather emaciated figure; his face was pale, his cheeks were sunk, and his eyes hollow; his features were pleasing and regular, they had a French turn (for M. Pelet was no Fleming, but a Frenchman both by birth and parentage), yet the degree of harshness inseparable from Gallic lineaments was, in his case, softened by a mild blue eye, and a melancholy, almost suffering, expression of countenance; his physiognomy was 'fine et spirituelle'. I use two French words because they define better than any English terms the species of intelligence with which his features were imbued. He was altogether an interesting and prepossessing personage. I wondered only at the utter absence of all the ordinary characteristics of his profession, and almost feared he could not be stern and resolute enough for a schoolmaster. Externally at least M. Pelet presented an absolute contrast to my late master, Edward Crimsworth.

Influenced by the impression I had received of his gentleness, I was a good deal surprised when, on arriving the next day at my new employer's house, and being admitted to a first view of what was to be the sphere of my future labours, namely, the large, lofty, and well-lighted schoolrooms, I beheld a numerous assemblage of pupils, boys of course, whose collective appearance showed all the signs of a full, flourishing, and well-disciplined seminary. As I traversed the classes in company with M. Pelet, a profound silence reigned on all sides, and if by chance a murmur or a whisper arose, one glance from the pensive eye of this most gentle pedagogue stilled it instantly. It was astonishing, I thought, how so mild a check could prove so effectual. When I had perambulated the length and breadth of the classes, M. Pelet turned and said to me –

'Would you object to taking the boys as they are, and testing their proficiency in English?'

The proposal was unexpected. I had thought I should have been allowed at least a day to prepare; but it is a bad omen to commence any career by hesitation, so I just stepped to the professor's desk near which we stood, and faced the circle of my pupils. I took a moment to collect my thoughts, and likewise to frame in French the sentence by which I proposed to open business. I made it as short as possible:–

'Messieurs, prenez vos livres de lecture.'

'Anglais ou Français, monsieur?' demanded a thick-set moon-faced young Flamand in a blouse. The answer was fortunately easy:–

'Anglais.'

I determined to give myself as little trouble as possible in this lesson; it would not do yet to trust my unpractised tongue with the delivery of explanations; my accent and idiom would be too open to the criticisms of the young gentlemen before me, relative to whom I felt it would be necessary at once to take up an advantageous position, and I proceeded to employ means accordingly.

'Commencez!' cried I, when they had all produced their books. The moon-faced youth (by name Jules Vanderkelkov, as I afterwards learnt) took the first sentence. The 'livre de lecture' was the 'Vicar of Wakefield', much used in foreign schools because it is supposed to contain prime samples of conversational English; it might, however, have been a Runic scroll for any resemblance the words, as enunciated by Jules, bore to the language in ordinary use amongst the natives of Great Britain. My God! how he did snuffle, snort, and wheeze! All he said was said in his throat and nose, for it is thus the Flamands speak, but I heard him to the end of his paragraph without proffering a word of correction, whereat he looked vastly self-complacent, convinced, no doubt, that he had acquitted himself like a real born and bred 'Anglais'. In the same unmoved silence I listened to a dozen in rotation, and when the twelfth had concluded with splutter, hiss, and mumble, I solemnly laid down the book.

'Arrêtez!' said I. There was a pause, during which I regarded them all with a steady and somewhat stern gaze; a dog, if stared at hard enough and long enough, will show symptoms of embarrassment, and so at length did my bench of Belgians. Perceiving that some of the faces before me were beginning to look sullen, and others ashamed, I slowly joined my hands, and ejaculated in a deep 'voix de poitrine' –

'Comme c'est affreux!'

They looked at each other, pouted, coloured, swung their heels; they were not pleased, I saw, but they were impressed, and in the way I wished them to be. Having thus taken them down a peg in their self-conceit, the next step was to raise myself in their estimation; not a very easy thing, considering that I hardly dared to speak for fear of betraying my own deficiencies.

'Ecoutez, messieurs!' said I, and I endeavoured to throw into my accents the compassionate tone of a superior being, who, touched by the extremity of the helplessness, which at first only excited his scorn, deigns at length to bestow aid. I then began at the very beginning of the 'Vicar of Wakefield', and read, in a slow, distinct voice, some twenty pages, they all the while sitting mute and listening with fixed attention; by the time I had done nearly an hour had elapsed. I then rose and said –

'C'est assez pour aujourd'hui, messieurs; demain nous recommencerons, et j'espère que tout ira bien.'

With this oracular sentence I bowed, and in company with M. Pelet quitted the schoolroom.

'C'est bien! c'est très bien!' said my principal as we entered his parlour. 'Je vois que monsieur a de l'adresse; cela me plaît, car, dans l'instruction, l'adresse fait tout autant que le savoir.'

From the parlour M. Pelet conducted me to my apartment, my 'chambre', as Monsieur said with a certain air of complacency. It was a very small room, with an excessively small bed, but M. Pelet gave me to understand that I was to occupy it quite alone, which was of course a great comfort. Yet, though so limited in dimensions, it had two windows. Light not being taxed in Belgium, the people never grudge its admission into their houses; just here, however, this observation is not very *à propos*, for one of these windows was boarded up; the open window looked into the boys' playground. I glanced at the other, as wondering what aspect it would present if disencumbered of the boards. M. Pelet read, I suppose, the expression of my eye; he explained –

'La fenêtre fermée donne sur un jardin appartenant à un pensionnat de demoiselles,' said he, 'et les convenances exigent – enfin, vous comprenez – n'est-ce pas, monsieur?'

'Oui, oui,' was my reply, and I looked of course quite satisfied; but when M. Pelet had retired and closed the door after him, the first thing I did was to scrutinize closely the nailed boards, hoping to find some chink or crevice which I might enlarge, and so get a peep at the consecrated ground. My researches were vain, for the boards were well joined and strongly nailed. It is astonishing how disappointed I felt. I thought it would have been so pleasant to have looked out upon a garden planted with flowers and trees, so amusing to have watched the demoiselles at their play; to have studied female character in a variety of phases, myself the while sheltered from view by a modest muslin curtain, whereas, owing doubtless to the absurd scruples of some old duenna of a directress, I had now only the option of looking at a bare gravelled court, with an enormous 'pas de géant' in the middle, and the monotonous walls and windows of a boys' schoolhouse round. Not only then, but many a time after, especially in moments of weariness and low spirits, did I look with dissatisfied eyes on that most tantalizing board, longing to tear it away and get a glimpse of the green region which I imagined to lie beyond. I knew a tree grew close up to the window, for though there were as yet no leaves to rustle, I often heard at night the tapping of branches against the panes. In the daytime, when I listened attentively, I could hear, even through the boards, the voices of the demoiselles in their hours of recreation, and, to speak the honest truth, my sentimental reflections were occasionally a trifle disarranged by the not quite silvery, in fact the too often brazen sounds, which, rising from the unseen paradise below, penetrated clamorously into my solitude. Not to mince matters, it really seemed to me a doubtful case whether the lungs of Mdlle Reuter's girls or those of M. Pelet's boys were the strongest, and when it came to shrieking the girls indisputably beat the boys hollow. I forgot to say, by the by, that Reuter was the name of the old lady who had had my window boarded up. I say old, for such I, of course, concluded her to be, judging from her cautious chaperon-like proceedings; besides, nobody ever spoke of her as young. I remember I was very much amused when I first heard her Christian name; it was Zoraïde – Mademoiselle Zoraïde Reuter. But the Continental nations do allow themselves vagaries in the choice of names, such as we sober English never run into. I think, indeed, we have too limited a list to choose from.

Meantime my path was gradually growing smooth before me. I, in a few weeks, conquered the teasing difficulties inseparable from the commencement of almost every career. Ere long I had acquired as much facility in speaking French as set me at my ease with my pupils: and as I had encountered them on a right footing at the very beginning, and continued tenaciously to retain the advantage I had early gained, they never attempted mutiny, which circumstance, all who are in any degree acquainted with the ongoings of Belgian schools, and who know the relation in which professors and pupils too frequently stand towards each other in those establishments, will consider an important and uncommon one. Before concluding this chapter I will say a word on the system I pursued with regard to my classes: my experience may possibly be of use to others.

It did not require very keen observation to detect the character of the youth of Brabant, but it needed a certain degree of tact to adapt one's measures to their capacity. Their intellectual faculties were generally weak, their animal propensities strong; thus there was at once an impotence and a kind of inert force in their natures; they were dull, but they were also singularly stubborn, heavy as lead and, like lead, most difficult to move. Such being the case, it would have been truly absurd to exact from them much in the way of mental exertion; having short memories, dense intelligence, feeble reflective powers, they recoiled with repugnance from any occupation that demanded close study or deep thought. Had the abhorred effort been extorted from them by injudicious and arbitrary measures on the part of the Professor, they would have resisted as obstinately, as clamorously, as desperate swine; and though not brave singly, they were relentless acting *en masse*.

I understood that before my arrival in M. Pelet's establishment, the combined insubordination of the pupils had effected the dismissal of more than one English master. It was necessary, then, to exact only the most moderate application from natures so little qualified to apply – to assist, in every practicable way, understandings so opaque and contracted – to be ever gentle, considerate, yielding even, to a certain point, with dispositions so irrationally perverse; but, having reached that culminating point of indulgence, you must fix your foot, plant it, root it in rock – become immutable as the towers of Ste Gudule; for a step – but half a step farther, and you would plunge headlong into the gulf of imbecility; there lodged, you would speedily receive proofs of Flemish gratitude and magnanimity in showers of Brabant saliva and handfuls of Low-Country mud. You might smooth to the utmost the path of learning, remove every pebble from the track; but then you must finally insist with decision on the pupil taking your arm and allowing himself to be led quietly along the prepared road. When I had brought down my lesson to the lowest level of my dullest pupil's capacity – when I had shown myself the mildest, the most tolerant of masters – a word of impertinence, a movement of disobedience, changed me at once into a despot. I offered them but one alternative – submission and acknowledgement of error, or ignominious expulsion. This system answered, and my influence, by degrees, became established on a firm basis. 'The boy is father to the man,' it is said; and so I often thought when I looked at my boys and remembered the political history of their ancestors. Pelet's school was merely an epitome of the Belgian nation.

CHAPTER VIII

A<small>ND</small> P<small>ELET</small> himself? How did I continue to like him? Oh, extremely well! Nothing could be more smooth, gentlemanlike, and even friendly, than his demeanour to me. I had to endure from him neither cold neglect, irritating interference, nor pretentious assumption of superiority. I fear, however, two poor, hard-worked Belgian ushers in the establishment could not have said as much; to them the director's manner was invariably dry, stern and cool. I believe he perceived once or twice that I was a little shocked at the difference he made between them and me, and accounted for it by saying, with a quiet, sarcastic smile –

'Ce ne sont que des Flamands – allez!'

And then he took his cigar gently from his lips and spat on the painted floor of the room in which we were sitting. Flamands certainly they were, and both had the true Flamand physiognomy, where intellectual inferiority is marked in lines none can mistake; still they were men, and, in the main, honest men; and I could not see why their being aboriginals of the flat, dull soil should serve as a pretext for treating them with perpetual severity and contempt. This idea of injustice somewhat poisoned the pleasure I might otherwise have derived from Pelet's soft, affable manner to myself. Certainly it was agreeable, when the day's work was over, to find one's employer an intelligent and cheerful companion; and if he was sometimes a little sarcastic and sometimes a little too insinuating, and if I did discover that his mildness was more a matter of appearance than of reality – if I did occasionally suspect the existence of flint or steel under an external covering of velvet – still we are none of us perfect; and weary as I was of the atmosphere of brutality and insolence in which I had constantly lived at X—, I had no inclination now, on casting anchor in calmer regions, to institute at once a prying search after defects that were scrupulously withdrawn and carefully veiled from my view. I was willing to take Pelet for what he seemed – to believe him benevolent and friendly until some untoward event should prove him otherwise. He was not married, and I soon perceived he had all a Frenchman's, all a Parisian's notions about matrimony and women. I suspected a degree of laxity in his code of morals, there was something so cold and *blasé* in his tone whenever he alluded to what he called 'le beau sexe'; but he was too gentlemanlike to intrude topics I did not invite, and as he was really intelligent and really fond of intellectual subjects of discourse, he and I always found enough to talk about, without seeking themes in the mire. I hated his fashion of mentioning love; I abhorred, from my soul, mere licentiousness. He felt the difference of our notions, and, by mutual consent, we kept off ground debatable.

Pelet's house was kept and his kitchen managed by his mother, a real old Frenchwoman; she had been handsome – at least she told me so, and I strove to believe her; she was now ugly, as only Continental old women can be; perhaps, though, her style of dress made her look uglier than she really was. Indoors she would go about without cap, her grey hair strangely dishevelled; then, when at home, she seldom wore a gown – only a shabby cotton camisole, shoes, too, were strangers to her feet, and in lieu of them she sported roomy slippers, trodden down at the heels. On the other hand, whenever it was her pleasure to appear abroad, as on Sundays, and fête-days, she would put on some very brilliant-coloured dress, usually of thin texture, a silk bonnet with a wreath of flowers, and a very fine shawl. She was not, in the main, an ill-natured old woman, but an incessant and most indiscreet talker; she kept chiefly in and about the kitchen, and seemed rather to avoid her son's august presence; of him, indeed, she evidently stood in awe. When he reproved her, his reproofs were bitter and unsparing; but he seldom gave himself that trouble.

Madame Pelet had her own society, her own circle of chosen visitors, whom, however, I seldom saw, as she generally entertained them in what she called her 'cabinet', a small den of a place adjoining the kitchen, and descending into it by one or two steps. On these steps, by the by, I have not unfrequently seen Madame Pelet seated with a trencher on her knee, engaged in the threefold employment of eating her dinner, gossiping with her favourite servant, the housemaid, and scolding her antagonist, the cook; she never dined, and seldom indeed took any meal with her son; and as to showing her face at the boys' table, that was quite out of the question. These details will sound very odd in English ears, but Belgium is not England, and its ways are not our ways.

Madame Pelet's habits of life, then, being taken into consideration, I was a good deal surprised when, one Thursday evening (Thursday was always a half-holiday), as I was sitting all alone in my apartment, correcting a huge pile of English and Latin exercises, a servant tapped at the door, and, on its being opened, presented Madame Pelet's compliments, and she would be happy to see me to take my 'goûter' (a meal which answers to our English 'tea') with her in the dining-room.

'Plaît-il?' said I, for I thought I must have misunderstood, the message and invitation were so unusual; the same words were repeated. I accepted, of course, and as I descended the stairs, I wondered what whim had entered the old lady's brain; her son was out – gone to pass the evening at the Salle of the Grande Harmonie or some other club of which he was a member. Just as I laid my hand on the handle of the dining-room door, a queer idea glanced across my mind.

'Surely she's not going to make love to me,' said I. 'I've heard of old Frenchwomen doing odd things in that line; and the goûter? They generally begin such affairs with eating and drinking, I believe.'

There was a fearful dismay in this suggestion of my excited imagination, and if I had allowed myself time to dwell upon it, I should no doubt have cut there and then, rushed back to my chamber, and bolted myself in; but whenever a danger or a horror is veiled with uncertainty, the primary wish of the mind is to ascertain first the naked truth, reserving the expedient of flight for the moment when its dread anticipation shall be realized. I turned the door-handle, and in an instant had crossed the fatal threshold, closed the door behind me, and stood in the presence of Madame Pelet.

Gracious heavens! The first view of her seemed to confirm my worst apprehensions. There she sat, dressed out in a light green muslin gown, on her head a lace cap with flourishing red roses in the frill; her table was carefully spread; there were fruit, cakes, and coffee, with a bottle of something – I did not know what. Already the cold sweat started on my brow, already I glanced back over my shoulder at the closed door, when, to my unspeakable relief, my eye, wandering wildly in the direction of the stove, rested upon a second figure, seated in a large fauteuil beside it. This was a woman, too, and, moreover, an old woman, and as fat and as rubicund as Madame Pelet was meagre and yellow; her attire was likewise very fine, and spring flowers of different hues circled in a bright wreath the crown of her violet-coloured velvet bonnet.

I had only time to make these general observations when Madame Pelet, coming forward with what she intended should be a graceful and elastic step, thus accosted me –

'Monsieur is indeed most obliging to quit his books, his studies, at the request of an insignificant person like me – will monsieur complete his kindness by allowing me to present him to my dear friend Madame Reuter, who resides in the neighbouring house – the young ladies' school?'

'Ah!' thought I, 'I knew she was old,' and I bowed and took my seat. Madame Reuter placed herself at the table opposite to me.

'How do you like Belgium, monsieur?' asked she, in an accent of the broadest Bruxellois. I could now well distinguish the difference between the fine and pure Parisian utterance of M. Pelet, for instance, and the guttural enunciation of the Flamands. I answered politely, and then wondered how so coarse and clumsy an old woman as the one before me should be at the head of a ladies' seminary which I had always heard spoken of in terms of high commendation. In truth there was something to wonder at. Madame Reuter looked more like a joyous, free-living Flemish fermière, or even a maîtresse d'auberge, than a staid, grave, rigid directrice de pensionnat. In general the Continental, or at least the Belgian old women permit themselves a licence of manners, speech, and aspect, such as our venerable granddames would recoil from as absolutely disreputable, and Madame Reuter's jolly face bore evidence that she was no exception to the rule of her country; there was a twinkle and leer in her left eye; her right she kept habitually half shut, which I thought very odd indeed. After several vain attempts to comprehend the motives of these two droll old creatures for inviting me to join them at their goûter, I at last fairly gave it up, and resigning myself to inevitable mystification, I sat and looked first at one, then at the other, taking care meantime to do justice to the confitures, cakes, and coffee, with which they amply supplied me. They, too, ate, and that with no delicate appetite, and having demolished a large portion of the solids, they proposed a 'petit verre'. I declined. Not so Mesdames Pelet and Reuter; each mixed herself what I thought rather a stiff tumbler of punch, and, placing it on a stand near the stove, they drew up their chairs to that convenience, and invited me to do the same. I obeyed; and being seated fairly between them, I was thus addressed first by Madame Pelet, then by Madame Reuter.

'We will now speak of business,' said Madame Pelet, and she went on to make an elaborate speech, which, being interpreted, was to the effect that she had asked for the pleasure of my company that evening in order to give her friend Madame Reuter an opportunity of broaching an important proposal, which might turn out greatly to my advantage.

'Pourvu que vous soyez sage,' said Madame Reuter, 'et à vrai dire, vous en avez bien l'air. Take one drop of the punch' (or *ponche*, as she pronounced it); 'it is an agreeable and wholesome beverage after a full meal.'

I bowed, but again declined it. She went on –

'I feel,' said she, after a solemn sip – 'I feel profoundly the importance of the commission with which my dear daughter has entrusted me, for you are aware, monsieur, that it is my daughter who directs the establishment in the next house?'

'Ah! I thought it was yourself, madame?' Though, indeed, at that moment I recollected that it was called Mademoiselle, not Madame Reuter's pensionnat.

'I! oh, no! I manage the house and look after the servants, as my friend Madame Pelet does for Monsieur her son – nothing more. Ah! you thought I gave lessons in class – did you?'

And she laughed loud and long, as though the idea tickled her fancy amazingly.

'Madame is in the wrong to laugh,' I observed; 'if she does not give lessons, I am sure it is not because she cannot'; and I whipped out a white pocket-handkerchief and wafted it, with a French grace, past my nose, bowing at the same time.

'Quel charmant jeune homme!' murmured Madame Pelet in a low voice. Madame Reuter, being less sentimental, as she was Flamand and not French, only laughed again.

'You are a dangerous person, I fear,' said she; 'if you can forge compliments at that rate, Zoraïde will positively be afraid of you; but if you are good, I will keep your secret, and not tell her how well you can flatter. Now, listen what sort of a proposal she makes to you. She has heard that you are an excellent professor, and as she wishes to get the very best masters for her school (car Zoraïde fait tout comme une reine, c'est une véritable maîtresse-femme), she has commissioned me to step over this afternoon, and sound Madame Pelet as to the possibility of engaging you. Zoraïde is a wary general; she never advances without first examining well her ground. I don't think she would be pleased if she knew I had already disclosed her intentions to you; she did not order me to go so far, but I thought there would be no harm in letting you into the secret, and Madame Pelet was of the same opinion. Take care, however, you don't betray either of us to Zoraïde – to my daughter, I mean, she is so discreet and circumspect herself she cannot understand that one should find pleasure in gossiping a little –'

'C'est absolument comme mon fils!' cried Madame Pelet.

'All the world is so changed since our girlhood!' rejoined the other: 'young people have such old heads now. But to return, monsieur. Madame Pelet will mention the subject of your giving lessons in my daughter's establishment to her son, and he will speak to you; and then to-morrow you will step over to our house and ask to see my daughter, and you will introduce the subject as if the first intimation of it had reached you from M. Pelet himself, and be sure you never mention my name, for I would not displease Zoraïde on any account.'

'Bien! bien!' interrupted I – for all this chatter and circumlocution began to bore me very much; 'I will consult M. Pelet, and the thing shall be settled as you desire. Good evening, mesdames – I am infinitely obliged to you.'

'Comment! vous vous en allez déjà?' exclaimed Madame Pelet.

'Prenez encore quelquechose, monsieur; une pomme cuite, des biscuits, encore une tasse de café?'

'Merci, merci, madame – au revoir.' And I backed at last out of the apartment.

Having regained my own room, I set myself to turn over in my mind the incident of the evening. It seemed a queer affair altogether, and queerly managed; the two old women had made quite a little intricate mess of it; still I found that the uppermost feeling in my mind on the subject was one of satisfaction. In the first place it would be a change to give lessons in another seminary, and then to teach young ladies would be an occupation so interesting – to be admitted at all into a ladies' boarding-school would be an incident so new in my life. 'Besides,' thought I, as I glanced at the boarded window, 'I shall now at last see the mysterious garden: I shall gaze both on the angels and their Eden.'

CHAPTER IX

MONSIEUR PELET could not of course object to the proposal made by Mdlle Reuter; permission to accept such additional employment, should it offer, having formed an article of the terms on which he had engaged me. It was, therefore, arranged in the course of the next day that I should be at liberty to give lessons in Mdlle Reuter's establishment four afternoons in every week.

When evening came I prepared to step over in order to seek a conference with Mademoiselle herself on the subject; I had not had time to pay the visit before, having been all day closely occupied in class. I remember very well that before quitting my chamber, I held a brief debate with myself as to whether I should change my ordinary attire for something smarter. At last I concluded it would be a waste of labour. 'Doubtless,' thought I, 'she is some stiff old maid; for though the daughter of Madame Reuter, she may well number upwards of forty winters; besides, if it were otherwise, if she be both young and pretty, I am not handsome, and no dressing can make me so, therefore I'll go as I am.' And off I started, cursorily glancing sideways as I passed the toilet-table, surmounted by a looking-glass: a thin irregular face I saw, with sunk, dark eyes under a large, square forehead, complexion destitute of bloom or attraction; something young, but not youthful, no object to win a lady's love, no butt for the shafts of Cupid.

I was soon at the entrance of the pensionnat, in a moment I had pulled the bell; in another moment the door was opened, and within appeared a passage paved alternately with black and white marble; the walls were painted in imitation of marble also; and at the far end opened a glass door, through which I saw shrubs and grass-plat, looking pleasant in the sunshine of the mild spring evening – for it was now the middle of April.

This, then, was my first glimpse of *the* garden; but I had not time to look long, the portress, after having answered in the affirmative my question as to whether her mistress was at home, opened the folding-doors of a room to the left, and having ushered me in, closed them behind me. I found myself in a salon with a very well-painted, highly varnished floor; chairs and sofas covered with white draperies, a green porcelain stove, walls hung with pictures in gilt frames, a gilt pendule and other ornaments on the mantelpiece, a large lustre pendent from the centre of the ceiling, mirrors, consoles, muslin curtains, and a handsome centre-table completed the inventory of furniture. All looked extremely clean and glittering, but the general effect would have been somewhat chilling had not a second large pair of folding-doors, standing wide open, and disclosing another and smaller salon, more snugly furnished, offered some relief to the eye. This room was carpeted, and therein was a piano, a couch, a chiffonnière – above all, it contained a lofty window with a crimson curtain, which, being undrawn, afforded another glimpse of the garden, through the large, clear panes, round which some leaves of ivy, some tendrils of vine were trained.

'Monsieur Creemsvort, n'est-ce pas?' said a voice behind me; and, starting involuntarily, I turned. I had been so taken up with the contemplation of the pretty little salon that I had not noticed the entrance of a person into the larger room. It was, however, Mdlle Reuter who now addressed me, and stood close beside me; and when I had bowed with instantaneously recovered sang-froid – for I am not easily embarrassed – I commenced the conversation by remarking on the pleasant aspect of her little cabinet, and the advantage she had over M. Pelet in possessing a garden.

'Yes,' she said, 'she often thought so'; and added, 'it is my garden, monsieur, which makes me retain this house, otherwise

I should probably have removed to larger and more commodious premises long since; but you see I could not take my garden with me, and I should scarcely find one so large and pleasant anywhere else in town.'

I approved her judgment.

'But you have not seen it yet,' said she, rising; 'come to the window and take a better view.' I followed her; she opened the sash, and leaning out I saw in full the enclosed demesne which had hitherto been to me an unknown region. It was a long, not very broad strip of cultured ground, with an alley bordered by enormous old fruit trees down the middle; there was a sort of lawn, a parterre of rose-trees, some flower-borders, and, on the far side, a thickly planted copse of lilacs, laburnums, and acacias. It looked pleasant, to me – very pleasant, so long a time had elapsed since I had seen a garden of any sort. But it was not only on Mdlle Reuter's garden that my eyes dwelt; when I had taken a view of her well-trimmed beds and budding shrubberies, I allowed my glance to come back to herself, nor did I hastily withdraw it.

I had thought to see a tall, meagre, yellow, conventual image in black, with a close white cap, bandaged under the chin like a nun's head-gear; whereas, there stood by me a little and roundly formed woman, who might indeed be older than I, but was still young; she could not, I thought, be more than six or seven and twenty; she was as fair as a fair Englishwoman; she had no cap; her hair was nut-brown, and she wore it in curls; pretty her features were not, nor very soft, nor very regular, but neither were they in any degree plain, and I already saw cause to deem them expressive. What was their predominant cast? Was it sagacity? – sense? Yes, I thought so; but I could scarcely as yet be sure. I discovered, however, that there was a certain serenity of eye, and freshness of complexion, most pleasing to behold. The colour on her cheek was like the bloom on a good apple, which is as sound at the core as it is red on the rind.

Mdlle Reuter and I entered upon business. She said she was

not absolutely certain of the wisdom of the step she was about
to take, because I was so young, and parents might possibly
object to a professor like me for their daughters: 'But it is often
well to act on one's own judgment,' said she, 'and to lead
parents, rather than be led by them. The fitness of a professor
is not a matter of age; and, from what I have heard, and from
what I observe myself, I would much rather trust you than
M. Ledru, the music-master, who is a married man of near fifty.'

I remarked that I hoped she would find me worthy of her
good opinion; that if I knew myself, I was incapable of betraying
any confidence reposed in me. 'Du reste,' said she, 'the surveillance will be strictly attended to.' And then she proceeded to
discuss the subject of terms. She was very cautious, quite on
her guard; she did not absolutely bargain, but she warily
sounded me to find out what my expectations might be; and
when she could not get me to name a sum, she reasoned and
reasoned with a fluent yet quiet circumlocution of speech, and
at last nailed me down to five hundred francs per annum – not
too much, but I agreed. Before the negotiation was completed,
it began to grow a little dusk. I did not hasten it, for I liked
well enough to sit and hear her talk; I was amused with the
sort of business talent she displayed. Edward could not have
shown himself more practical, though he might have evinced
more coarseness and urgency; and then she had so many
reasons, so many explanations; and, after all, she succeeded in
proving herself quite disinterested and even liberal. At last she
concluded, she could say no more, because, as I acquiesced in
all things, there was no further ground for the exercise of her
parts of speech. I was obliged to rise. I would rather have sat a
little longer; what had I to return to but my small empty
room? And my eyes had a pleasure in looking at Mdlle Reuter,
especially now, when the twilight softened her features a little,
and, in the doubtful dusk, I could fancy her forehead as open
as it was really elevated, her mouth touched with turns of
sweetness as well as defined in lines of sense. When I rose to

go, I held out my hand, on purpose, though I knew it was contrary to the etiquette of foreign habits; she smiled, and said –

'Ah! c'est comme tous les Anglais,' but gave me her hand very kindly.

'It is the privilege of my country, mademoiselle,' said I; 'and, remember, I shall always claim it.'

She laughed a little, quite good-naturedly, and with the sort of tranquillity obvious in all she did – a tranquillity which soothed and suited me singularly, at least I thought so that evening. Brussels seemed a very pleasant place to me when I got out again into the street, and it appeared as if some cheerful, eventful, upward-tending career were even then opening to me, on that selfsame mild, still April night. So impressionable a being is man, or at least such a man as I was in those days.

CHAPTER X

NEXT DAY the morning hours seemed to pass very slowly at M. Pelet's; I wanted the afternoon to come that I might go again to the neighbouring pensionnat and give my first lesson within its pleasant precincts; for pleasant they appeared to me. At noon the hour of recreation arrived; at one o'clock we had lunch; this got on the time, and at last Ste Gudule's deep bell, tolling slowly two, marked the moment for which I had been waiting.

At the foot of the narrow back-stairs that descended from my room, I met M. Pelet.

'Comme vous avez l'air rayonnant!' said he. 'Je ne vous ai jamais vu aussi gai. Que s'est-il donc passé?'

'Apparemment que j'aime les changements,' replied I.

'Ah! je comprends – c'est cela – soyez sage seulement. Vous êtes bien jeune – trop jeune pour le rôle que vous allez jouer; il faut prendre garde – savez-vous?'

'Mais quel danger y a-t-il?'

'Je n'en sais rien – ne vous laissez pas aller à de vives impressions – voilà tout.'

I laughed: a sentiment of exquisite pleasure played over my nerves at the thought that 'vives impressions' were likely to be created; it was the deadness, the sameness of life's daily ongoings that had hitherto been my bane; my blouse-clad élèves in the boys' seminary never stirred in me any 'vives impressions', except it might be occasionally some of anger. I broke from M. Pelet, and as I strode down the passage he followed me with one of his laughs – a very French, rakish, mocking sound.

Again I stood at the neighbouring door, and soon was re-admitted into the cheerful passage with its clear dove-colour, imitation-marble walls. I followed the portress, and descending a step, and making a turn, I found myself in a sort of corridor; a side-door opened, Mdlle Reuter's little figure, as graceful as it was plump, appeared. I could now see her dress in full daylight; a neat, simple mousseline-laine gown fitted her compact round shape to perfection – delicate little collar and manchettes of lace, trim Parisian brodequins showed her neck, wrists, and feet, to complete advantage; but how grave was her face as she came suddenly upon me! Solicitude and business were in her eye – on her forehead; she looked almost stern. Her 'Bon jour, monsieur,' was quite polite, but so orderly, so commonplace, it spread directly a cool, damp towel over my 'vives impressions'. The servant turned back when her mistress appeared, and I walked slowly along the corridor, side by side with Mdlle Reuter.

'Monsieur will give a lesson in the first class to-day,' said she; 'dictation or reading will perhaps be the best thing to begin with, for those are the easiest forms of communicating instruction in a foreign language; and, at the first, a master naturally feels a little unsettled.'

She was quite right, as I had found from experience; it only remained for me to acquiesce. We proceeded now in silence. The corridor terminated in a hall, large, lofty, and square; a glass door on one side showed within a long, narrow refectory, with tables, an armoire, and two lamps; it was empty; large glass doors, in front, opened on the playground and garden; a broad staircase ascended spirally on the opposite side; the remaining wall showed a pair of great folding-doors, now closed, and admitting, doubtless, to the classes.

Mdlle Reuter turned her eye laterally on me, to ascertain, probably, whether I was collected enough to be ushered into her sanctum sanctorum. I suppose she judged me to be in a tolerable state of self-government, for she opened the door, and I followed her through. A rustling sound of uprising greeted our entrance; without looking to the right or left, I walked straight up the lane between two sets of benches and desks, and took possession of the empty chair and isolated desk raised on an estrade, of one step high, so as to command one division; the other division being under the surveillance of a maîtresse similarly elevated. At the back of the estrade, and attached to a movable partition dividing this schoolroom from another beyond, was a large tableau of wood painted black and varnished; a thick crayon of white chalk lay on my desk for the convenience of elucidating any grammatical or verbal obscurity which might occur in my lessons by writing it upon the tableau; a wet sponge appeared beside the chalk, to enable me to efface the marks when they had served the purpose intended.

I carefully and deliberately made these observations before allowing myself to take one glance at the benches before me; having handled the crayon, looked back at the tableau, fingered the sponge in order to ascertain that it was in a right state of moisture, I found myself cool enough to admit of looking calmly up and gazing deliberately round me.

At first I observed that Mdlle Reuter had already glided away, she was nowhere visible; a maîtresse or teacher, the one who occupied the corresponding estrade to my own, alone remained to keep guard over me; she was a little in the shade, and, with my short-sight, I could only see that she was of a thin, bony figure and rather tallowy complexion, and that her attitude, as she sat, partook equally of listlessness and affectation. More obvious, more prominent, shone on by the full light of the large window, were the occupants of the benches just before me, of whom some were girls of fourteen, fifteen, sixteen, some young women from eighteen (as it appeared to me) up to twenty; the most modest attire, the simplest fashion of wearing the hair, were apparent in all; and good features, ruddy, blooming complexions, large and brilliant eyes, forms full, even to solidity, seemed to abound. I did not bear the first view like a stoic; I was dazzled, my eyes fell, and in a voice somewhat low I murmured –

'Prenez vos cahiers de dictée, mesdemoiselles.'

Not so had I bid the boys at Pelet's take their reading-books. A rustle followed, and an opening of desks; behind the lifted lids which momentarily screened the heads bent down to search for exercise-books, I heard tittering and whispers.

'Eulalie, je suis prête à pâmer de rire,' observed one.

'Comme il a rougi en parlant!'

'Oui, c'est un véritable blanc-bec.'

'Tais-toi, Hortense – il nous écoute.'

And now the lids sank and the heads reappeared; I had marked three, the whisperers, and I did not scruple to take a very steady look at them as they emerged from their temporary eclipse. It is astonishing what ease and courage their little phrases of flippancy had given me; the idea by which I had been awed was that the youthful beings before me, with their dark nun-like robes and softly braided hair, were a kind of half-angels. The light titter, the giddy whisper, had already in some measure relieved my mind of that fond and oppressive fancy.

The three I allude to were just in front, within half a yard of my estrade, and were among the most womanly-looking present. Their names I knew afterwards, and may as well mention now; they were Eulalie, Hortense, Caroline. Eulalie was tall, and very finely shaped: she was fair, and her features were those of a Low-Country Madonna; many a 'figure de Vierge' have I seen in Dutch pictures exactly resembling hers; there were no angles in her shape or in her face, all was curve and roundness – neither thought, sentiment, nor passion disturbed by line or flush the equality of her pale, clear skin; her noble bust heaved with her regular breathing, her eyes moved a little – by these evidences of life alone could I have distinguished her from some large handsome figure moulded in wax. Hortense was of middle size and stout, her form was ungraceful, her face striking, more alive and brilliant than Eulalie's, her hair was dark brown, her complexion richly coloured; there were frolic and mischief in her eye: consistency and good sense she might possess, but none of her features betokened those qualities.

Caroline was little, though evidently full grown; raven-black hair, very dark eyes, absolutely regular features, with a colourless olive complexion, clear as to the face and sallow about the neck, formed in her that assemblage of points whose union many persons regard as the perfection of beauty. How, with the tintless pallor of her skin and the classic straightness of her lineaments, she managed to look sensual, I don't know. I think her lips and eyes contrived the affair between them, and the result left no uncertainty on the beholder's mind. She was sensual now, and in ten years' time she would be coarse – promise plain was written in her face of much future folly.

If I looked at these girls with little scruple, they looked at me with still less. Eulalie raised her unmoved eye to mine, and seemed to expect, passively but securely, an impromptu tribute to her majestic charms. Hortense regarded me boldly, and giggled at the same time, while she said, with an air of impudent freedom –

'Dictez-nous quelquechose de facile pour commencer, monsieur.'

Caroline shook her loose ringlets of abundant but somewhat coarse hair over her rolling black eyes; parting her lips, as full as those of a hot-blooded Maroon, she showed her well-set teeth sparkling between them, and treated me at the same time to a smile 'de sa façon'. Beautiful as Pauline Borghese, she looked at the moment scarcely purer than Lucrèce de Borgia. Caroline was of noble family. I heard her lady-mother's character afterwards, and then I ceased to wonder at the precocious accomplishments of the daughter. These three, I at once saw, deemed themselves the queens of the school, and conceived that by their splendour they threw all the rest into the shade. In less than five minutes they had thus revealed to me their characters, and in less than five minutes I had buckled on a breastplate of steely indifference, and let down a visor of impassable austerity.

'Take your pens and commence writing,' said I, in as dry

and trite a voice as if I had been addressing only Jules Vanderkelkov and Co.

The dictée now commenced. My three belles interrupted me
perpetually with little silly questions and uncalled-for remarks,
to some of which I made no answer, and to others replied very
quietly and briefly.

'Comment dit-on point et virgule en Anglais, monsieur?'

'Semi-colon, mademoiselle.'

'Simi-collong? Ah, comme c'est drôle!' (giggle).

'J'ai une si mauvaise plume – impossible d'écrire!'

'Mais, monsieur – je ne sais pas suivre – vous allez si vite.'

'Je n'ai rien compris, moi!'

Here a general murmur arose, and the teacher, opening her
lips for the first time, ejaculated –

'Silence, mesdemoiselles!'

No silence followed – on the contrary, the three ladies in
front began to talk more loudly.

'C'est si difficile, l'Anglais!'

'Je déteste la dictée.'

'Quel ennui d'écrire quelquechose que l'on ne comprend
pas!'

Some of those behind laughed: a degree of confusion began
to pervade the class; it was necessary to take prompt measures.

'Donnez-moi votre cahier,' said I to Eulalie in an abrupt
tone; and bending over, I took it before she had time to
give it.

'Et vous, mademoiselle – donnez-moi le vôtre,' continued I,
more mildly, addressing a little pale, plain-looking girl who sat
in the first row of the other division, and whom I had remarked
as being at once the ugliest and the most attentive in the room;
she rose up, walked over to me, and delivered her book with a
grave, modest curtsy. I glanced over the two dictations; Eulalie's
was slurred, blotted, and full of silly mistakes – Sylvie's (such
was the name of the ugly little girl) was clearly written, it contained no error against sense, and but few faults of orthography.

I coolly read aloud both exercises, marking the faults – then I looked at Eulalie.

'C'est honteux!' said I, and I deliberately tore her dictation in four parts, and presented her with the fragments. I returned Sylvie her book with a smile, saying –

'C'est bien – je suis content de vous.'

Sylvie looked calmly pleased, Eulalie swelled like an incensed turkey, but the mutiny was quelled: the conceited coquetry and futile flirtation of the first bench were exchanged for a taciturn sullenness, much more convenient to me, and the rest of my lesson passed without interruption.

A bell clanging out in the yard announced the moment for the cessation of school labours. I heard our own bell at the same time, and that of a certain public college immediately after. Order dissolved instantly; up started every pupil, I hastened to seize my hat, bow to the maîtresse, and quit the room before the tide of externats should pour from the inner class, where I knew near a hundred were prisoned, and whose rising tumult I already heard.

I had scarcely crossed the hall and gained the corridor, when Mdlle Reuter came again upon me.

'Step in here a moment,' said she, and she held open the door of the side-room from whence she had issued on my arrival; it was a *salle-à-manger*, as appeared from the beaufet and the armoire vitrée, filled with glass and china, which formed part of its furniture. Ere she had closed the doors on me and herself, the corridor was already filled with day-pupils, tearing down their cloaks, bonnets, and cabas from the wooden pegs on which they were suspended; the shrill voice of a maîtresse was heard at intervals vainly endeavouring to enforce some sort of order; vainly, I say: discipline there was none in these rough ranks, and yet this was considered one of the best-conducted schools in Brussels.

'Well, you have given your first lesson,' began Mdlle Reuter in the most calm, equable voice, as though quite unconscious of the chaos from which we were separated only by a single wall.

'Were you satisfied with your pupils, or did any circumstance in their conduct give you cause for complaint? Conceal nothing from me, repose in me entire confidence.'

Happily, I felt in myself complete power to manage my pupils without aid; the enchantment, the golden haze which had dazzled my perspicacity at first, had been a good deal dissipated. I cannot say I was chagrined or downcast by the contrast which the reality of a pensionnat de demoiselles presented to my vague ideal of the same community; I was only enlightened and amused; consequently, I felt in no disposition to complain to Mdlle Reuter, and I received her considerate invitation to confidence with a smile.

'A thousand thanks, mademoiselle, all has gone very smoothly.'

She looked more than doubtful.

'Et les trois demoiselles du premier banc?' said she.

'Ah! tout va au mieux!' was my answer, and Mdlle Reuter ceased to question me; but her eye – not large, not brilliant, not melting or kindling, but astute, penetrating, practical – showed she was even with me; it let out a momentary gleam, which said plainly, 'Be as close as you like, I am not dependent on your candour; what you would conceal I already know.'

By a transition so quiet as to be scarcely perceptible, the directress's manner changed; the anxious business air passed from her face, and she began chatting about the weather and the town, and asking in neighbourly wise after M. and Madame Pelet. I answered all her little questions; she prolonged her talk, I went on following its many little windings; she sat so long, said so much, varied so often the topics of discourse, that it was not difficult to perceive she had a particular aim in thus detaining me. Her mere words could have afforded no clue to this aim, but her countenance aided; while her lips uttered only affable commonplaces, her eyes reverted continually to my face.

Her glances were not given in full, but out of the corners, so quietly, so stealthily, yet I think I lost not one. I watched her as keenly as she watched me; I perceived soon that she was feeling after my real character; she was searching for salient points, and weak points, and eccentric points; she was applying now this test, now that, hoping in the end to find some chink, some niche, where she could put in her little firm foot and stand upon my neck – mistress of my nature. Do not mistake me, reader, it was no amorous influence she wished to gain – at that time it was only the power of the politician to which she aspired; I was now installed as a professor in her establishment, and she wanted to know where her mind was superior to mine – by what feeling or opinion she could lead me.

I enjoyed the game much, and did not hasten its conclusion; sometimes I gave her hopes, beginning a sentence rather weakly, when her shrewd eye would light up – she thought she had me; having led her a little way, I delighted to turn round and finish with sound, hard sense, whereat her countenance would fall. At last a servant entered to announce dinner; the conflict being thus necessarily terminated, we parted without having gained any advantage on either side: Mdlle Reuter had not even given me an opportunity of attacking her with feeling, and I had managed to baffle her little schemes of craft. It was a regular drawn battle. I again held out my hand when I left the room, she gave me hers: it was a small and white hand, but how cool! I met her eye too in full – obliging her to give me a straightforward look; this last test went against me: it left her as it found her – moderate, temperate, tranquil; me it disappointed.

'I am growing wiser,' thought I, as I walked back to M. Pelet's. 'Look at this little real woman; is she like the women of novelists and romancers? To read of female character as depicted in Poetry and Fiction, one would think it was made up of sentiment, either for good or bad – here is a specimen, and a most sensible and respectable specimen, too, whose staple ingredient is abstract reason. No Talleyrand was ever more passionless than Zoraïde Reuter!' So I thought then; I found afterwards that blunt susceptibilities are very consistent with strong propensities.

CHAPTER XI

I HAD indeed had a very long talk with the crafty little politician, and on regaining my quarters I found that dinner was half over. To be late at meals was against a standing rule of the establishment, and had it been one of the Flemish ushers who thus entered after the removal of the soup and the commencement of the first course, M. Pelet would probably have greeted him with a public rebuke, and would certainly have mulcted him both of soup and fish; as it was, that polite though partial gentleman only shook his head, and as I took my place, unrolled my napkin, and said my heretical grace to myself, he civilly despatched a servant to the kitchen, to bring me a plate of 'purée aux carottes' (for this was a maigre-day), and before sending away the first course, reserved for me a portion of the stock-fish of which it consisted. Dinner being over, the boys rushed out for their evening play; Kint and Vandam (the two ushers) of course followed them. Poor fellows! if they had not looked so very heavy, so very soulless, so very indifferent to all things in heaven above or in the earth beneath, I could have pitied them greatly for the obligation they were under to trail after those rough lads everywhere and at all times; even as it was, I felt disposed to scout myself as a privileged prig when I turned to ascend to my chamber, sure to find there, if not enjoyment, at least liberty; but this evening (as had often happened before) I was to be still further distinguished.

'Eh bien, mauvais sujet!' said the voice of M. Pelet behind me, as I set my foot on the first step of the stair, 'où allez-vous? Venez à la salle-à-manger, que je vous gronde un peu.'

'I beg pardon, monsieur,' said I, as I followed him to his private sitting-room, 'for having returned so late – it was not my fault.'

'That is just what I want to know,' rejoined M. Pelet, as he ushered me into the comfortable parlour with a good wood-fire – for the stove had now been removed for the season. Having rung the bell he ordered 'Coffee for two', and presently he and I were seated, almost in English comfort, one on each side of the hearth, a little round table between us, with a coffee-pot, a sugar-basin, and two large white china cups. While M. Pelet employed himself in choosing a cigar from a box, my thoughts reverted to the two outcast ushers, whose voices I could hear even now crying hoarsely for order in the playground.

'C'est une grande responsabilité, que la surveillance,' observed I.

'Plaît-il?' dit M. Pelet.

I remarked that I thought Messieurs Vandam and Kint must sometimes be a little fatigued with their labours.

'Des bêtes de somme, – des bêtes de somme,' murmured scornfully the director. Meantime I offered him his cup of coffee.

'Servez-vous, mon garçon,' said he blandly, when I had put a couple of huge lumps of Contintental sugar into his cup. 'And now tell me why you stayed so long at Mdlle Reuter's. I know that lessons conclude, in her establishment as in mine, at four o'clock, and when you returned it was past five.'

'Mademoiselle wished to speak with me, monsieur.'

'Indeed! on what subject? if one may ask.'

'Mademoiselle talked about nothing, monsieur.'

'A fertile topic! And did she discourse thereon in the school-room, before the pupils?'

'No; like you, monsieur, she asked me to walk into her parlour.'

'And Madame Reuter – the old duenna – my mother's gossip, was there, of course?'

'No, monsieur; I had the honour of being quite alone with mademoiselle.'

'C'est joli – cela,' observed M. Pelet, and he smiled and looked into the fire.

'Honi soit qui mal y pense,' murmured I, significantly.

'Je connais un peu ma petite voisine – voyez-vous?'

'In that case, monsieur will be able to aid me in finding out what was mademoiselle's reason for making me sit before her sofa one mortal hour, listening to the most copious and fluent dissertation on the merest frivolities.'

'She was sounding your character.'

'I thought so, monsieur.'

'Did she find out your weak point?'

'What is my weak point?'

'Why, the sentimental. Any woman sinking her shaft deep enough will at last reach a fathomless spring of sensibility in thy breast, Crimsworth.'

I felt the blood stir about my heart and rise warm to my cheek.

'Some women might, monsieur.'

'Is Mdlle Reuter of the number? Come, speak frankly, mon fils; elle est encore jeune, plus âgée que toi peut-être, mais juste assez pour unir la tendresse d'une petite maman à l'amour d'une épouse dévouée; n'est-ce pas que cela t'irait supérieurement?'

'No, monsieur; I should like my wife to be my wife, and not my half mother.'

'She is then a little too old for you?'

'No, monsieur, not a day too old if she suited me in other things.'

'In what does she not suit you, William? She is personally agreeable, is she not?'

'Very; her hair and complexion are just what I admire; and her turn of form, though quite Belgian, is full of grace.'

'Bravo! and her face? her features? How do you like them?'

'A little harsh, especially her mouth.'

'Ah, yes! her mouth,' said M. Pelet, and he chuckled inwardly. 'There is character about her mouth – firmness – but she has a very pleasant smile; don't you think so?'

'Rather crafty.'

'True, but that expression of craft is owing to her eyebrows; have you remarked her eyebrows?'

I answered that I had not.

'You have not seen her looking down then?' said he.

'No.'

'It is a treat, notwithstanding. Observe her when she has some knitting, or some other woman's work in hand, and sits the image of peace, calmly intent on her needles and her silk, some discussion meantime going on around her, in the course of which peculiarities of character are being developed, or important interests canvassed; she takes no part in it; her humble, feminine mind is wholly with her knitting; none of her features move; she neither presumes to smile approval, nor frown disapprobation; her little hands assiduously ply their unpretending task; if she can only get this purse finished, or this bonnet-grec completed, it is enough for her. If gentlemen approach her chair, a deeper quiescence, a meeker modesty settles on her features, and clothes her general mien; observe then her eyebrows, et dîtes-moi s'il n'y a pas du chat dans l'un et du renard dans l'autre.'

'I will take careful notice the first opportunity,' said I.

'And then,' continued M. Pelet, 'the eyelid will flicker, the light-coloured lashes be lifted a second, and a blue eye, glancing out from under the screen, will take its brief, sly, searching survey, and retreat again.'

I smiled, and so did Pelet, and after a few minutes' silence, I asked –

'Will she ever marry, do you think?'

'Marry! Will birds pair? Of course it is both her intention and resolution to marry when she finds a suitable match, and no one is better aware than herself of the sort of impression she is capable of producing; no one likes better to captivate in a quiet way. I am mistaken if she will not yet leave the print of her stealing steps on thy heart, Crimsworth.'

'Of her steps? Confound it, no! My heart is not a plank to be walked on.'

'But the soft touch of a patte de velours will do it no harm.'

'She offers me no patte de velours; she is all form and reserve with me.'

'That to begin with; let respect be the foundation, affection the first floor, love the superstructure; Mdlle Reuter is a skilful architect.'

'And interest, M. Pelet – interest? Will not mademoiselle consider that point?'

'Yes, yes, no doubt; it will be the cement between every stone. And now we have discussed the directress, what of the pupils? N'y a-t-il pas de belles études parmi ces jeunes têtes?'

'Studies of character? Yes; curious ones, at least, I imagine; but one cannot divine much from a first interview.'

'Ah, you affect discretion; but tell me, now, were you not a little abashed before those blooming young creatures?'

'At first, yes; but I rallied and got through with all due sang-froid.'

'I don't believe you.'

'It is true, notwithstanding. At first I thought them angels, but they did not leave me long under that delusion; three of the eldest and handsomest undertook the task of setting me right, and they managed so cleverly that in five minutes I knew *them*, at least, for what they were – three arrant coquettes.'

'Je les connais!' exclaimed M. Pelet. 'Elles sont toujours au premier rang à l'église et à la promenade; une blonde superbe, une jolie espiègle, une belle brune.'

'Exactly.'

'Lovely creatures, all of them – heads for artists; what a group they would make, taken together! Eulalie (I know their names), with her smooth braided hair and calm ivory brow. Hortense, with her rich chestnut locks so luxuriantly knotted, plaited, twisted, as if she did not know how to dispose of all their abundance, with her vermilion lips, damask cheek, and roguish, laughing eye. And Caroline de Blémont! Ah, there is beauty! beauty in perfection. What a cloud of sable curls about the face of a houri! What fascinating lips! What glorious black eyes! Your Byron would have worshipped her, and you – you cold, frigid islander! – you played the austere, the insensible in the presence of an Aphrodite so exquisite?'

I might have laughed at the director's enthusiasm had I believed it real, but there was something in his tone which indicated got-up raptures. I felt he was only affecting fervour in order to put me off my guard, to induce me to come out in return, so I scarcely even smiled. He went on –

'Confess, William, do not the mere good looks of Zoraïde Reuter appear dowdyish and commonplace compared with the splendid charms of some of her pupils?'

The question discomposed me, but I now felt plainly that my principal was endeavouring (for reasons best known to himself – at that time I could not fathom them) to excite ideas and wishes in my mind alien to what was right and honourable. The iniquity of the instigation proved its antidote, and when he further added –

'Each of those three beautiful girls will have a handsome fortune; and with a little address, a gentlemanlike, intelligent young fellow like you might make himself master of the hand, heart, and purse of any one of the trio.'

I replied by a look and an interrogative 'Monsieur?' which startled him.

He laughed a forced laugh, affirmed that he had only been joking, and demanded whether I could possibly have thought him in earnest. Just then the bell rang; the play-hour was over; it was an evening on which M. Pelet was accustomed to read passages from the drama and the belles lettres to his pupils. He did not wait for my answer, but rising, left the room, humming as he went some gay strain of Béranger's.

CHAPTER XII

D AILY, as I continued my attendance at the seminary of
Mdlle Reuter, did I find fresh occasions to compare the
ideal with the real. What had I known of female character
previously to my arrival at Brussels? Precious little. And what
was my notion of it? Something vague, slight, gauzy, glittering;
now when I came in contact with it I found it to be a palpable
substance enough; very hard, too, sometimes, and often heavy;
there was metal in it, both lead and iron.

Let the idealists, the dreamers about earthly angels and
human flowers, just look here while I open my portfolio and
show them a sketch or two, pencilled after nature. I took
these sketches in the second-class schoolroom of Mdlle Reuter's
establishment, where about a hundred specimens of the genus
'jeune fille' collected together offered a fertile variety of subject.
A miscellaneous assortment they were, differing both in caste
and country: as I sat on my estrade and glanced over the long
range of desks, I had under my eye French, English, Belgians,
Austrians, and Prussians. The majority belonged to the class
bourgeois; but there were many countesses, there were the
daughters of two generals and of several colonels, captains, and
government employés; these ladies sat side by side with young
females destined to be demoiselles de magasins, and with some
Flamandes, genuine aborigines of the country. In dress all were
nearly similar, and in manners there was small difference; exceptions there were to the general rule, but the majority gave the
tone to the establishment, and that tone was rough, boisterous,
marked by a point-blank disregard of all forbearance towards
each other or their teachers; an eager pursuit by each individual
of her own interest and convenience; and a coarse indifference
to the interest and convenience of every one else. Most of them

could lie with audacity when it appeared advantageous to do so. All understood the art of speaking fair when a point was to be gained, and could with consummate skill and at a moment's notice turn the cold shoulder the instant civility ceased to be profitable. Very little open quarrelling ever took place amongst them; but backbiting and talebearing were universal. Close friendships were forbidden by the rules of the school, and no one girl seemed to cultivate more regard for another than was just necessary to secure a companion when solitude would have been irksome. They were each and all supposed to have been reared in utter unconsciousness of vice. The precautions used to keep them ignorant, if not innocent, were innumerable. How was it, then, that scarcely one of those girls having attained the age of fourteen could look a man in the face with modesty and propriety? An air of bold, impudent flirtation, or a loose, silly leer, was sure to answer the most ordinary glance from a masculine eye. I know nothing of the arcana of the Roman Catholic religion, and I am not a bigot in matters of theology, but I suspect the root of this precocious impurity, so obvious, so general in Popish countries, is to be found in the discipline, if not the doctrines, of the Church of Rome. I record what I have seen: these girls belonged to what are called the respectable ranks of society; they had all been carefully brought up, yet was the mass of them mentally depraved. So much for the general view: now for one or two selected specimens.

The first picture is a full length of Aurelia Koslow, a German fräulein, or rather a half-breed between German and Russian. She is eighteen years of age, and has been sent to Brussels to finish her education; she is of middle size, stiffly made, body long, legs short, bust much developed but not compactly moulded, waist disproportionately compressed by an inhumanly braced corset, dress carefully arranged, large feet tortured into small bottines, head small, hair smoothed, braided, oiled, and gummed to perfection; very low forehead, very diminutive and vindictive grey eyes, somewhat Tartar features, rather flat nose, rather high cheek-bones, yet the ensemble not positively ugly; tolerably good complexion. So much for person. As to mind, deplorably ignorant and ill-informed; incapable of writing or speaking correctly even German, her native tongue, a dunce in French, and her attempts at learning English a mere farce, yet she has been at school twelve years; but as she invariably gets her exercises, of every description, done by a fellow-pupil, and reads her lessons off a book concealed in her lap, it is not wonderful that her progress has been so snail-like. I do not know what Aurelia's daily habits of life are, because I have not the opportunity of observing her at all times; but from what I see of the state of her desk, books, and papers, I should say she is slovenly and even dirty; her outward dress, as I have said, is well attended to, but in passing behind her bench I have remarked that her neck is grey for want of washing, and her hair, so glossy with gum and grease, is not such as one feels tempted to pass the hand over, much less to run the fingers through. Aurelia's conduct in class, at least when I am present, is something extraordinary, considered as an index of girlish innocence. The moment I enter the room, she nudges her next neighbour and indulges in a half-suppressed laugh. As I take my seat on the estrade, she fixes her eye on me; she seems resolved to attract, and, if possible, monopolize my notice: to this end she launches at me all sorts of looks, languishing, provoking, leering, laughing. As I am found quite proof against this sort of artillery – for we scorn what, unasked, is lavishly offered – she has recourse to the expedient of making noises; sometimes she sighs, sometimes groans, sometimes utters in-articulate sounds, for which language has no name. If, in walk-ing up the schoolroom, I pass near her, she puts out her foot that it may touch mine; if I do not happen to observe the manœuvre, and my boot comes in contact with her brodequin, she affects to fall into convulsions of suppressed laughter; if I notice the snare and avoid it, she expresses her mortification in sullen muttering, where I hear myself abused in bad French pronounced with an intolerable Low-German accent.

Not far from Mdlle Koslow sits another young lady by name Adèle Dronsart: this is a Belgian, rather low of stature, in form heavy, with broad waist, short neck and limbs, good red and white complexion, features well chiselled and regular, well-cut eyes of a clear brown colour, light brown hair, good teeth, age not much above fifteen, but as full-grown as a stout young Englishwoman of twenty. This portrait gives the idea of a somewhat dumpy but good-looking damsel, does it not? Well, when I looked along the row of young heads, my eye generally stopped at this of Adèle's; her gaze was ever waiting for mine, and it frequently succeeded in arresting it. She was an unnatural-looking being – so young, fresh, blooming, yet so Gorgon-like. Suspicion, sullen ill-temper were on her forehead, vicious propensities in her eye, envy and panther-like deceit about her mouth. In general she sat very still; her massive shape looked as if it could not bend much, nor did her large head – so broad at the base, so narrow towards the top – seem made to turn readily on her short neck. She had but two varieties of expression; the prevalent one a forbidding, dissatisfied scowl, varied sometimes by a most pernicious and perfidious smile. She was shunned by her fellow-pupils, for, bad as many of them were, few were as bad as she.

Aurelia and Adèle were in the first division of the second class; the second division was headed by a pensionnaire named Juanna Trista. This girl was of mixed Belgian and Spanish origin; her Flemish mother was dead, her Catalonian father was a merchant residing in the — Isles, where Juanna had been born and whence she was sent to Europe to be educated. I wonder that any one, looking at the girl's head and coun-tenance, would have received her under their roof. She had precisely the same shape of skull as Pope Alexander the Sixth; her organs of benevolence, veneration, conscientiousness, adhe-siveness, were singularly small, those of self-esteem, firmness, destructiveness, combativeness, preposterously large; her head sloped up in the penthouse shape, was contracted about the forehead, and prominent behind; she had rather good, though large and marked features; her temperament was fibrous and bilious, her complexion pale and dark, hair and eyes black, form angular and rigid but proportionate, age fifteen.

Juanna was not very thin, but she had a gaunt visage, and her 'regard' was fierce and hungry; narrow as was her brow, it presented space enough for the legible graving of two words, Mutiny and Hate; in some one of her other lineaments – I think the eye – cowardice had also its distinct cipher. Mdlle Trista thought fit to trouble my first lessons with a coarse work-day sort of turbulence; she made noises with her mouth like a horse, she ejected her saliva, she uttered brutal expressions; behind and below her were seated a band of very vulgar, inferior-looking Flamandes, including two or three examples of that deformity of person and imbecility of intellect whose frequency in the Low Countries would seem to furnish proof that the climate is such as to induce degeneracy of the human mind and body; these, I soon found, were completely under her influence, and with their aid she got up and sustained a swinish tumult, which I was constrained at last to quell by ordering her and two of her tools to rise from their seats, and, having kept them standing five minutes, turning them bodily out of the schoolroom: the accomplices into a large place adjoining called the grande salle; the principal into a cabinet, of which I closed the door and pocketed the key. This judgment I executed in the presence of Mdlle Reuter, who looked much aghast at beholding so decided a proceeding – the most severe that had ever been ventured on in her establishment. Her look of affright I answered with one of composure, and finally with a smile, which perhaps flattered and certainly soothed her. Juanna Trista remained in Europe long enough to repay, by malevolence and ingratitude, all who had ever done her a good turn; and she then went to join her father in the — Isles, exulting in the thought that she should there have slaves, whom, as she said, she could kick and strike at will.

These three pictures are from the life. I possess others, as marked and as little agreeable, but I will spare my reader the exhibition of them.

Doubtless it will be thought that I ought now, by way of contrast, to show something charming; some gentle virgin head, circled with a halo, some sweet personification of innocence, clasping the dove of peace to her bosom. No: I saw nothing of the sort, and therefore cannot portray it. The pupil in the school possessing the happiest disposition was a young girl from the country, Louise Path; she was sufficiently benevolent and obliging, but not well taught nor well mannered; moreover, the plague-spot of dissimulation was in her also; honour and principle were unknown to her, she had scarcely heard their names. The least exceptionable pupil was the poor little Sylvie I have mentioned once before. Sylvie was gentle in manners, intelligent in mind; she was even sincere, as far as her religion would permit her to be so, but her physical organization was defective; weak health stunted her growth and chilled her spirits, and then, destined as she was for the cloister, her whole soul was warped to a conventual bias, and in the tame, trained subjection of her manner, one read that she had already pre-pared herself for her future course of life, by giving up her independence of thought and action into the hands of some despotic confessor. She permitted herself no original opinion, no preference of companion or employment; in everything she was guided by another. With a pale, passive, automaton air, she went about all day long doing what she was bid; never what she liked, or what, from innate conviction, she thought it right to do. The poor little future religieuse had been early taught to make the dictates of her own reason and conscience quite subordinate to the will of her spiritual director. She was the model pupil of Mdlle Reuter's establishment; pale, blighted image, where life lingered feebly, but whence the soul had been conjured by Romish wizard-craft!

A few English pupils there were in this school, and these might be divided into two classes. 1st: The Continental English – the daughters chiefly of broken adventurers, whom debt or dishonour had driven from their own country. These poor girls had never known the advantages of settled homes, decorous example, or honest Protestant education; resident a few months now in one Catholic school, now in another, as their parents wandered from land to land – from France to Germany, from Germany to Belgium – they had picked up some scanty instruction, many bad habits, losing every notion even of the first elements of religion and morals, and acquiring an imbecile indifference to every sentiment that can elevate humanity; they were distinguishable by a habitual look of sullen dejection, the result of crushed self-respect and constant browbeating from their Popish fellow-pupils, who hated them as English, and scorned them as heretics.

The second class were British English. Of these I did not encounter half a dozen during the whole time of my attendance at the seminary; their characteristics were clean but careless dress, ill-arranged hair (compared with the tight and trim foreigners), erect carriage, flexible figures, white and taper hands, features more irregular, but also more intellectual than those of the Belgians, grave and modest countenances, a general air of native propriety and decency; by this last circumstance alone I could at a glance distinguish the daughter of Albion and nursling of Protestantism from the foster-child of Rome, the *protégée* of Jesuitry: proud, too, was the aspect of these British girls; at once envied and ridiculed by their Continental associates, they warded off insult with austere civility, and met hate with mute disdain; they eschewed company-keeping, and in the midst of numbers seemed to dwell isolated.

The teachers presiding over this mixed multitude were three in number, all French – their names, Mdlles Zéphyrine, Pélagie, and Suzette; the two last were commonplace personages enough; their look was ordinary, their manner was ordinary, their temper was ordinary, their thoughts, feelings and views were all ordinary – were I to write a chapter on the subject I could not elucidate it further. Zéphyrine was somewhat more distinguished in appearance and deportment than Pélagie and Suzette, but in character a genuine Parisian coquette, perfidious, mercenary, and dry-hearted. A fourth maîtresse I sometimes saw who seemed to come daily to teach needlework, or netting, or lace-mending, or some such flimsy art; but of her I never had more than a passing glimpse, as she sat in the carré, with her frames and some dozen of the elder pupils about her, consequently I had no opportunity of studying her character, or even of observing her person much; the latter, I remarked, had a very girlish air for a maîtresse, otherwise it was not striking; of character I should think she possessed but little, as her pupils seemed constantly 'en révolte' against her authority. She did not reside in the house; her name, I think, was Mdlle Henri.

Amidst this assemblage of all that was insignificant and defective, much that was vicious and repulsive (by that last epithet many would have described the two or three stiff, silent, decently behaved, ill-dressed British girls), the sensible, sagacious, affable directress shone like a steady star over a marsh full of Jack-o'-lanthorns; profoundly aware of her superiority, she derived an inward bliss from that consciousness which sustained her under all the care and responsibility inseparable from her position; it kept her temper calm, her brow smooth, her manner tranquil. She liked – as who would not? – on entering the schoolroom, to feel that her sole presence sufficed to diffuse that order and quiet which all the remonstrances, and even commands, of her underlings frequently failed to enforce; she liked to stand in comparison, or rather contrast, with those who surrounded her, and to know that in personal as well as mental advantages, she bore away the undisputed palm of preference – (the three teachers were all plain). Her pupils she managed with such indulgence and address, taking always on herself the office of recompenser and eulogist, and abandoning to her subalterns every invidious task of blame and punishment, that they all regarded her with deference, if not with affection; her teachers did not love her, but they submitted because they were her inferiors in everything; the various masters who attended her school were each and all in some way or other under her influence: over one she had acquired power by her skilful management of his bad temper; over another by little attentions to his petty caprices; a third she had subdued by flattery; a fourth – a timid man – she kept in awe by a sort of austere decision of mien; me, she still watched, still tried by the most ingenious tests – she roved round me, baffled, yet persevering; I believe she thought I was like a smooth and bare precipice, which offered neither jutting stone nor tree-root, nor tuft of grass to aid the climber. Now she flattered with exquisite tact, now she moralized, now she tried how far I was accessible to mercenary motives, then she disported on the brink of affection – knowing that some men are won by weakness – anon, she talked excellent sense, aware that others have the folly to admire judgment. I found it at once pleasant and easy to evade all these efforts; it was sweet, when she thought me nearly won, to turn round and to smile in her very eyes, half scornfully, and then to witness her scarcely veiled, though mute mortification. Still she persevered, and at last, I am bound to confess it, her finger, essaying, proving every atom of the casket, touched its secret spring, and for a moment the lid sprung open; she laid her hand on the jewel within; whether she stole and broke it, or whether the lid shut again with a snap on her fingers, read on, and you shall know.

It happened that I came one day to give a lesson when I was indisposed; I had a bad cold and a cough; two hours' incessant talking left me very hoarse and tired; as I quitted the school-room, and was passing along the corridor, I met Mdlle Reuter; she remarked, with an anxious air, that I looked very pale and tired. 'Yes,' I said, 'I was fatigued': and then, with increased interest, she rejoined, 'You shall not go away till you have had some refreshment.' She persuaded me to step into the parlour, and was very kind and gentle while I stayed. The next day she was kinder still; she came herself into the class to see that the windows were closed, and that there was no draught; she exhorted me with friendly earnestness not to over-exert myself; when I went away, she gave me her hand unasked, and I could not but mark, by a respectful and gentle pressure, that I was sensible of the favour, and grateful for it. My modest demonstration kindled a little merry smile on her countenance; I thought her almost charming. During the remainder of the evening, my mind was full of impatience for the afternoon of the next day to arrive, that I might see her again.

I was not disappointed, for she sat in the class during the whole of my subsequent lesson, and often looked at me almost with affection. At four o'clock she accompanied me out of the schoolroom, asking with solicitude after my health, then scolding me sweetly because I spoke too loud and gave myself too much trouble; I stopped at the glass door which led into the garden, to hear her lecture to the end; the door was open, it was a very fine day, and while I listened to the soothing reprimand, I looked at the sunshine and flowers and felt very happy. The day-scholars began to pour from the schoolrooms into the passage.

'Will you go into the garden a minute or two,' asked she, 'till they are gone?'

I descended the steps without answering, but I looked back as much as to say –

'You will come with me?'

In another minute I and the directress were walking side by side down the alley bordered with fruit-trees, whose white blossoms were then in full blow as well as their tender green leaves. The sky was blue, the air still, the May afternoon was full of brightness and fragrance. Released from the stifling class, surrounded with flowers and foliage, with a pleasing, smiling, affable woman at my side – how did I feel? Why, very enviably.

It seemed as if the romantic visions my imagination had suggested of this garden, while it was yet hidden from me by the jealous boards, were more than realized; and, when a turn in the alley shut out the view of the house, and some tall shrubs excluded M. Pelet's mansion, and screened us momentarily from the other houses, rising amphitheatre-like round this green spot, I gave my arm to Mdlle Reuter, and led her to a garden-chair, nestled under some lilacs near. She sat down; I took my place at her side. She went on talking to me with that ease which communicates ease, and, as I listened, a revelation dawned in my mind that I was on the brink of falling in love. The dinner-bell rang, both at her house and M. Pelet's; we were obliged to part; I detained her a moment as she was moving away.

'I want something,' said I.

'What?' asked Zoraïde naïvely.

'Only a flower.'

'Gather it then – or two, or twenty, if you like.'

'No – one will do – but you must gather it, and give it to me.'

'What a caprice!' she exclaimed, but she raised herself on her tip-toes, and, plucking a beautiful branch of lilac, offered it to me with grace. I took it, and went away, satisfied for the present, and hopeful for the future.

Certainly that May day was a lovely one, and it closed in moonlight night of summer warmth and serenity. I remember this well; for, having sat up late that evening correcting devoirs, and feeling weary and a little oppressed with the closeness of my small room, I opened the often-mentioned boarded window, whose boards, however, I had persuaded old Madame Pelet to have removed since I had filled the post of professor in the pensionnat de demoiselles, as, from that time, it was no longer 'inconvenant' for me to overlook my own pupils at their sports. I sat down in the window-seat, rested my arm on the sill and leaned out: above me was the clear-obscure of a cloudless night sky – splendid moonlight subdued the tremulous sparkle of the stars – below lay the garden, varied with silvery lustre and deep shade, and all fresh with dew – a grateful perfume exhaled from the closed blossoms of the fruit-trees – not a leaf stirred, the night was breezeless. My window looked directly down upon a certain walk of Mdlle Reuter's garden called 'l'allée défendue', so named because the pupils were forbidden to enter it on account of its proximity to the boys' school. It was here that the lilacs and laburnums grew especially thick; this was the most sheltered nook in the enclosure, its shrubs screened the garden-chair where that afternoon I had sat with the young directress. I need not say that my thoughts were chiefly with her as I leaned from the lattice, and let my eye roam, now over the walks and borders of the garden, now along the many-windowed front of the house which rose white beyond the masses of foliage. I wondered in what part of the building was situated her apartment; and a single light, shining through the persiennes of one croisée, seemed to direct me to it.

'She watches late,' thought I, 'for it must be now near mid-night. She is a fascinating little woman,' I continued in voiceless soliloquy; 'her image forms a pleasant picture in memory; I know she is not what the world calls pretty – no matter, there is harmony in her aspect, and I like it; her brown hair, her blue eye, the freshness of her cheek, the whiteness of her neck, all suit my taste. Then I respect her talent; the idea of marrying a doll or a fool was always abhorrent to me: I know that a pretty doll, a fair fool, might do well enough for the honeymoon; but when passion cooled, how dreadful to find a lump of wax and wood laid in my bosom, a half idiot clasped in my arms, and to remember that I had made of this my equal – nay, my idol – to know that I must pass the rest of my dreary life with a creature incapable of understanding what I said, of appreciating what I thought or of sympathizing with what I felt! Now, Zoraïde Reuter,' thought I, 'has tact, "caractère", judgment, discretion; has she heart? What a good, simple little smile played about her lips when she gave me the branch of lilacs!

I have thought her crafty, dissembling, interested sometimes, it is true; but may not much that looks like cunning and dissimulation in her conduct be only the efforts made by a bland temper to traverse quietly perplexing difficulties? And as to interest, she wishes to make her way in the world, no doubt, and who can blame her? Even if she be truly deficient in sound principle, is it not rather her misfortune than her fault? She has been brought up a Catholic: had she been born an Englishwoman, and reared a Protestant, might she not have added straight integrity to all her other excellences? Supposing she were to marry an English and Protestant husband, would she not, rational, sensible as she is, quickly acknowledge the superiority of right over expediency, honesty over policy? It would be worth a man's while to try the experiment; to-morrow I will renew my observations. She knows that I watch her: how calm she is under scrutiny! it seems rather to gratify than annoy her.' Here a strain of music stole in upon my monologue, and suspended it; it was a bugle, very skilfully played, in the neighbourhood of the park, I thought, or on the Place Royale. So sweet were the tones, so subduing their effect at that hour, in the midst of silence and under the quiet reign of moonlight, I ceased to think, that I might listen more intently. The strain retreated, its sound waxed fainter and was soon gone; my ear prepared to repose on the absolute hush of midnight once more. No. What murmur was that which, low, and yet near and approaching nearer, frustrated the expectation of total silence? It was someone conversing – yes, evidently, an audible though subdued voice spoke in the garden immediately below me. Another answered: the first voice was that of a man, the second that of a woman; and a man and a woman I saw coming slowly down the alley. Their forms were at first in shade, I could but discern a dusk outline of each, but a ray of moonlight met them at the termination of the walk, when they were under my very nose, and revealed very plainly, very unequivocally, Mdlle Zoraïde Reuter, arm-in-arm, or hand-in-hand (I forget which), with my principal, confidant, and counsellor, M. François Pelet. And M. Pelet was saying –

'A quand donc le jour des noces, ma bien-aimée?'

And Mdlle Reuter answered –

'Mais, François, tu sais bien qu'il me serait impossible de me marier avant les vacances.'

'June, July, August, a whole quarter!' exclaimed the director. 'How can I wait so long? – I who am ready, even now, to expire at your feet with impatience!'

'Ah! if you die, the whole affair will be settled without any trouble about notaries and contracts; I shall only have to order a slight mourning dress, which will be much sooner prepared that the nuptial trousseau.'

'Cruel Zoraïde! you laugh at the distress of one who loves you so devotedly as I do: my torment is your sport; you scruple not to stretch my soul on the rack of jealousy; for, deny it as you will, I am certain you have cast encouraging glances on that schoolboy, Crimsworth; he has presumed to fall in love, which he dared not have done unless you had given him room to hope.'

'What do you say, François? Do you say Crimsworth is in love with me?'

'Over head and ears.'

'Has he told you so?'

'No – but I see it in his face: he blushes whenever your name is mentioned.'

A little laugh of exulting coquetry announced Mdlle Reuter's gratification of this piece of intelligence (which was a lie, by the by – I had never been so far gone as that, after all). M. Pelet proceeded to ask what she intended to do with me, intimating pretty plainly, and not very gallantly, that it was nonsense for her to think of taking such a 'blanc-bec' as a husband, since she must be at least ten years older than I (was she then thirty-two? I should not have thought it). I heard her disclaim any intentions on the subject – the director, however, still pressed her to give a definite answer.

'François,' said she, 'you are jealous,' and still she laughed; then, as if suddenly recollecting that this coquetry was not consistent with the character for modest dignity she wished to establish, she proceeded in a demure voice: 'Truly, my dear François, I will not deny that this young Englishman may have made some attempts to ingratiate himself with me; but, so far from giving him any encouragement, I have always treated him with as much reserve as it was possible to combine with civility; affianced as I am to you, I would give no man false hopes; believe me, dear friend.'

Still Pelet uttered murmurs of distrust – so I judged, at least, from her reply.

'What folly! How could I prefer an unknown foreigner to you? And then – not to flatter your vanity – Crimsworth could not bear comparison with you either physically or mentally; he is not a handsome man at all; some may call him gentlemanlike and intelligent looking, but for my part –'

The rest of the sentence was lost in the distance, as the pair, rising from the chair in which they had been seated, moved away. I waited their return, but soon the opening and shutting of a door informed me that they had re-entered the house; I listened a little longer, all was perfectly still; I listened more than an hour – at last I heard M. Pelet come in and ascend to his chamber. Glancing once more towards the long front of the garden-house, I perceived that its solitary light was at length extinguished; so, for a time, was my faith in love and friendship. I went to bed, but something feverish and fiery had got into my veins which prevented me from sleeping much that night.

CHAPTER XIII

Next morning I rose with the dawn, and having dressed myself and stood half an hour, my elbow leaning on the chest of drawers, considering what means I should adopt to restore my spirits, fagged with sleeplessness, to their ordinary tone – for I had no intention of getting up a scene with M. Pelet, reproaching him with perfidy, sending him a challenge, or performing other gambadoes of the sort – I hit at last on the expedient of walking out in the cool of the morning to a neighbouring establishment of baths, and treating myself to a bracing plunge. The remedy produced the desired effect. I came back at seven o'clock steadied and invigorated, and was able to greet M. Pelet, when he entered to breakfast, with an unchanged and tranquil countenance; even a cordial offering of the hand and the flattering appellation of 'mon fils', pronounced in that caressing tone with which Monsieur had, of late days especially, been accustomed to address me, did not elicit any external sign of the feeling which, though subdued, still glowed at my heart. Not that I nursed vengeance – no; but the sense of insult and treachery lived in me like a kindling, though as yet smothered coal. God knows I am not by nature vindictive; I would not hurt a man because I can no longer trust or like him; but neither my reason nor feelings are of the vacillating order – they are not of that sandlike sort where impressions, if soon made, are as soon effaced. Once convinced that my friend's disposition is incompatible with my own, once assured that he is indelibly stained with certain defects obnoxious to my principles, and I dissolve the connection. I did so with Edward. As to Pelet, the discovery was yet new; should I act thus with him? It was the question I placed before my mind as I stirred my cup of coffee with a half-pistolet (we never had spoons), Pelet meantime being seated opposite, his pallid face looking as knowing and more haggard than usual, his blue eye turned, now sternly on his boys and ushers, and now graciously on me.

'Circumstances must guide me,' said I; and meeting Pelet's false glance and insinuating smile, I thanked heaven that I had last night opened my window and read by the light of a full moon the true meaning of that guileful countenance. I felt half his master, because the reality of his nature was now known to me; smile and flatter as he would, I saw his soul lurk behind his smile, and heard in every one of his smooth phrases a voice interpreting their treacherous import.

But Zoraïde Reuter? Of course her defection had cut me to the quick? That sting must have gone too deep for any consolations of philosophy to be available in curing its smart? Not at all. The night fever over, I looked about for balm to that wound also, and found some nearer home than at Gilead. Reason was my physician; she began by proving that the prize I had missed was of little value: she admitted that, physically, Zoraïde might have suited me, but affirmed that our souls were not in harmony, and that discord must have resulted from the union of her mind with mine. She then insisted on the suppression of all repining, and commanded me rather to rejoice that I had escaped a snare. Her medicament did me good. I felt its strengthening effect when I met the directress the next day; its stringent operation on the nerves suffered no trembling, no faltering; it enabled me to face her with firmness, to pass her with ease. She had held out her hand to me – that I did not choose to see. She had greeted me with a charming smile – it fell on my heart like light on stone. I passed on to the estrade, she followed me; her eye, fastened on my face, demanded of every feature the meaning of my changed and careless manner. 'I will give her an answer,' thought I; and, meeting her gaze full, arresting, fixing her glance, I shot into her eyes, from my own, a look, where there was no respect, no love, no tenderness, no gallantry; where the strictest analysis could detect nothing but scorn, hardihood, irony. I made her bear it, and feel it; her steady countenance did not change, but her colour rose, and she approached me as if fascinated. She stepped on to the estrade, and stood close by my side; she had nothing to say. I would not relieve her embarrassment, and negligently turned over the leaves of a book.

'I hope you feel quite recovered to-day,' at last she said, in a low tone.

'And I, mademoiselle, hope that you took no cold last night in consequence of your late walk in the garden.'

Quick enough of comprehension, she understood me directly; her face became a little blanched – a very little – but no muscle in her rather marked features moved; and, calm and self-possessed, she retired from the estrade, taking her seat quietly at a little distance, and occupying herself with netting a purse. I proceeded to give my lesson; it was a 'Composition', *i.e.* I dictated certain general questions, of which the pupils were to compose the answers from memory, access to books being forbidden. While Mdlle Eulalie, Hortense, Caroline, etc., were pondering over the string of rather abstruse grammatical interrogatories I had propounded, I was at liberty to employ the vacant half-hour in further observing the directress herself. The green silk purse was progressing fast in her hands; her eyes were bent upon it; her attitude, as she sat netting within two yards of me, was still yet guarded; in her whole person were expressed at once, and with equal clearness, vigilance and repose – a rare union! Looking at her, I was forced, as I had often been before, to offer her good sense, her wondrous self-control, the tribute of involuntary admiration. She had felt that I had withdrawn from her my esteem; she had seen contempt and coldness in my eye, and to her, who coveted the approbation of all around her, who thirsted after universal good opinion, such discovery must have been an acute wound. I had witnessed its effect in the momentary pallor of her cheek – cheek unused to vary; yet how quickly, by dint of self-control, had she recovered her composure! With what quiet dignity she now sat, almost at my side, sustained by her sound and vigorous sense; no trembling in her somewhat lengthened, though shrewd upper lip, no coward shame on her austere forehead!

'There is metal there,' I said, as I gazed. 'Would that there were fire also, living ardour to make the steel glow – then I could love her.'

Presently I discovered that she knew I was watching her, for she stirred not, she lifted not her crafty eyelid; she but glanced down from her netting to her small foot, peeping from the soft folds of her purple merino gown; thence her eye reverted to her hand, ivory white, with a bright garnet ring on the fore-finger, and a light frill of lace round the wrist; with a scarcely perceptible movement she turned her head, causing her nut-brown curls to wave gracefully. In these slight signs I read that the wish of her heart, the design of her brain, was to lure back the game she had scared. A little incident gave her the opportunity of addressing me again.

While all was silence in the class – silence but for the rustling of copy-books and the travelling of pens over their pages – a leaf of the large folding-door, opening from the hall, unclosed, admitting a pupil who, after making a hasty obeisance, en-sconced herself with some appearance of trepidation, probably occasioned by her entering so late, in a vacant seat at the desk nearest the door. Being seated, she proceeded, still with an air of hurry and embarrassment, to open her cabas, to take out her books; and, while I was waiting for her to look up, in order to make out her identity – for, short-sighted as I was, I had not recognized her at her entrance – Mdlle Reuter, leaving her chair, approached the estrade.

'Monsieur Creemsvort,' she said, in a whisper: for when the schoolrooms were silent, the directress always moved with velvet tread, and spoke in the most subdued key, enforcing order and stillness fully as much by example as by precept: 'Monsieur Creemsvort, that young person, who has just entered, wishes to have the advantage of taking lessons with you in English; she is not a pupil of the house; she is, indeed, in one sense, a teacher, for she gives instruction in lace-mending, and in little varieties of ornamental needlework. She very properly proposes to qualify herself for a higher department of education, and has asked permission to attend your lessons, in order to perfect her knowledge of English, in which language she has, I believe, already made some progress; of course it is my wish to aid her in an effort so praiseworthy; you will permit her, then, to benefit by your instruction – n'est-ce pas, monsieur?' And Mdlle Reuter's eyes were raised to mine with a look at once naïve, benign, and beseeching.

I replied, 'Of course,' very laconically, almost abruptly.

'Another word,' she said, with softness: 'Mdlle Henri has not received a regular education; perhaps her natural talents are not of the highest order: but I can assure you of the excellence of her intentions, and even of the amiability of her disposition. Monsieur will then, I am sure, have the goodness to be considerate with her at first, and not expose her backwardness, her inevitable deficiencies, before the young ladies, who, in a sense, are her pupils. Will Monsieur Creemsvort favour me by attending to this hint?' I nodded. She continued with subdued earnestness –

'Pardon me, monsieur, if I venture to add that what I have just said is of importance to the poor girl; she already experiences great difficulty in impressing these giddy young things with a due degree of deference for her authority, and should that difficulty be increased by new discoveries of her incapacity, she might find her position in my establishment too painful to be retained; a circumstance I should much regret for her sake, as she can ill afford to lose the profits of her occupation here.'

Mdlle Reuter possessed marvellous tact; but tact the most exquisite, unsupported by sincerity, will sometimes fail of its effect; thus, on this occasion, the longer she preached about the necessity of being indulgent to the governess-pupil, the more impatient I felt as I listened. I discerned so clearly that while her professed motive was a wish to aid the dull, though well-meaning Mdlle Henri, her real one was no other than a design to impress me with an idea of her own exalted goodness and tender considerateness; so having again hastily nodded assent to her remarks, I obviated their renewal by suddenly demanding the compositions, in a sharp accent, and stepping from the estrade, I proceeded to collect them. As I passed the governess-pupil, I said to her –

'You have come in too late to receive a lesson to-day; try to be more punctual next time.'

I was behind her, and could not read in her face the effect of my not very civil speech. Probably I should not have troubled myself to do so, had I been full in front; but I observed that she immediately began to slip her books into her cabas again; and, presently, after I had returned to the estrade, while I was arranging the mass of compositions, I heard the folding-door again open and close; and, on looking up, I perceived her place vacant. I thought to myself, 'She will consider her first attempt at taking a lesson in English something of a failure'; and I wondered whether she had departed in the sulks, or whether stupidity had induced her to take my words too literally, or, finally, whether my irritable tone had wounded her feelings. The last notion I dismissed almost as soon as I had conceived it, for not having seen any appearance of sensitiveness in any human face since my arrival in Belgium, I had begun to regard it almost as a fabulous quality. Whether her physiognomy announced it I could not tell, for her speedy exit had allowed me no time to ascertain the circumstance. I had, indeed, on two or three previous occasions, caught a passing view of her (as I believe has been mentioned before); but I never stopped to scrutinize either her face or person, and had but the most vague idea of her general appearance. Just as I had finished rolling up the compositions, the four o'clock bell rang; with my accustomed alertness in obeying that signal, I grasped my hat and evacuated the premises.

CHAPTER XIV

I F I WAS punctual in quitting Mdlle Reuter's domicile, I was at least equally punctual in arriving there; I came the next day at five minutes before two, and on reaching the schoolroom door, before I opened it, I heard a rapid, gabbling sound, which warned me that the 'prière du midi' was not yet concluded. I waited the termination thereof; it would have been impious to intrude my heretical presence during its progress. How the repeater of the prayer did cackle and splutter! I never before or since heard language enounced with such steam-engine haste. 'Notre Père qui êtes au ciel' went off like a shot; then followed an address to Marie 'vierge céleste, reine des anges, maison d'or, tour d'ivoire!' and then an invocation to the saint of the day; and then down they all sat, and the solemn (?) rite was over; and I entered, flinging the door wide and striding in fast, as it was my wont to do now; for I had found that in entering with aplomb, and mounting the estrade with emphasis, consisted the grand secret of ensuring immediate silence. The folding-doors between the two classes, opened for the prayer, were instantly closed; a maîtresse, work-box in hand, took her seat at her appropriate desk; the pupils sat still with their pens and books before them; my three beauties in the van, now well humbled by a demeanour of consistent coolness, sat erect with their hands folded quietly on their knees; they had given up giggling and whispering to each other, and no longer ventured to utter pert speeches in my presence; they now only talked to me occasionally with their eyes, by means of which organs they could still, however, say very audacious and coquettish things. Had affection, goodness, modesty, real talent, ever employed those bright orbs as interpreters, I do not think I could have refrained from giving a kind and encouraging, perhaps an ardent reply now and then; but as it was, I found pleasure in answering the glance of vanity with the gaze of stoicism. Youthful, fair, brilliant as were many of my pupils, I can truly say that in me they never saw any other bearing than such as an austere, though just, guardian might have observed towards them. If any doubt the accuracy of this assertion, as inferring more conscientious self-denial or Scipio-like self-control than they feel disposed to give me credit for, let them take into consideration the following circumstances, which, while detracting from my merit, justify my veracity.

Know, O incredulous reader! that a master stands in a somewhat different relation towards a pretty, light-headed, probably ignorant girl, to that occupied by a partner at a ball, or a gallant on the promenade. A professor does not meet his pupil to see her dressed in satin and muslin, with hair perfumed and curled, neck scarcely shaded by aerial lace, round white arms circled with bracelets, feet dressed for the gliding dance. It is not his business to whirl her through the waltz, to feed her with compliments, to heighten her beauty by the flush of gratified vanity. Neither does he encounter her on the smooth-rolled, tree-shaded Boulevard, in the green and sunny park, whither she repairs clad in her becoming walking-dress, her scarf thrown with grace over her shoulders, her little bonnet scarcely screening her curls, the red rose under its brim adding a new tint to the softer rose on her cheek; her face and eyes, too, illumined with smiles, perhaps as transient as the sunshine of the gala-day, but also quite as brilliant; it is not his office to walk by her side, to listen to her lively chat, to carry her parasol, scarcely larger than a broad green leaf, to lead in a ribbon her Blenheim spaniel or Italian greyhound. No: he finds her in the schoolroom, plainly dressed, with books before her. Owing to her education or her nature, books are to her a nuisance, and she opens them with aversion, yet her teacher must instil into her mind the contents of these books; that mind resists the admission of grave information, it recoils, it grows restive, sullen tempers are shown, disfiguring frowns spoil the symmetry of the face, sometimes coarse gestures banish grace from the deportment, while mut- tered expressions, redolent of native and ineradicable vulgarity, desecrate the sweetness of the voice. Where the temperament is serene though the intellect be sluggish, an unconquerable dull- ness opposes every effort to instruct. Where there is cunning but not energy, dissimulation, falsehood, a thousand schemes and tricks are put in play to evade the necessity of application; in short, to the tutor, female youth, female charms are like tapestry hangings of which the wrong side is continually turned towards him; and even when he sees the smooth, neat external surface he so well knows what knots, long stitches, and jagged ends are behind that he has scarce a temptation to admire too fondly the seemly forms and bright colours exposed to general view.

Our likings are regulated by our circumstances. The artist prefers a hilly country because it is picturesque; the engineer a flat one because it is convenient; the man of pleasure likes what he calls 'a fine woman' – she suits him; the fashionable young gentleman admires the fashionable young lady – she is of his kind; the toilworn, fagged, probably irritable tutor, blind almost to beauty, insensible to airs and graces, glories chiefly in certain mental qualities: application, love of knowledge, natural capa- city, docility, truthfulness, gratefulness, are the charms that attract his notice and win his regard. These he seeks, but seldom meets; these, if by chance he finds, he would fain retain for ever, and when separation deprives him of them he feels as if some ruthless hand had snatched from him his only ewe-lamb. Such being the case, and the case it is, my readers will agree with me that there was nothing either very meritorious or very marvellous in the integrity and moderation of my conduct at Mdlle Reuter's pensionnat de demoiselles.

My first business this afternoon consisted in reading the list of places for the month, determined by the relative correctness of the compositions given the preceding day. The list was headed, as usual, by the name of Sylvie, that plain, quiet little girl I have described before as being at once the best and ugliest pupil in the establishment; the second place had fallen to the lot of a certain Léonie Ledru, a diminutive, sharp-featured, and parchment-skinned creature of quick wits, frail conscience, and indurated feelings; a lawyer-like thing, of whom I used to say that, had she been a boy, she would have made a model of an unprincipled, clever attorney. Then came Eulalie, the proud beauty, the Juno of the school, whom six long years of drilling in the simple grammar of the English language had compelled, despite the stiff phlegm of her intellect, to acquire a mechanical acquaintance with most of its rules. No smile, no trace of pleasure or satisfaction appeared in Sylvie's nun-like passive face as she heard her name read first. I always felt saddened by the sight of that poor girl's absolute quiescence on all occasions, and it was my custom to look at her, to address her, as seldom as possible; her extreme docility, her assiduous perseverance, would have recommended her warmly to my good opinion; her modesty, her intelligence, would have induced me to feel most kindly – most affectionately towards her, notwithstanding the almost ghastly plainness of her features, the disproportion of her form, the corpse-like lack of animation in her countenance, had I not been aware that every friendly word, every kindly action, would be reported by her to her confessor, and by him misinter-preted and poisoned. Once I laid my hand on her head, in token of approbation; I thought Sylvie was going to smile, her dim eye almost kindled; but, presently, she shrank from me; I was a man and a heretic; she, poor child! a destined nun and devoted Cath-olic; thus a fourfold wall of separation divided her mind from mine. A pert smirk, and a hard glance of triumph, was Léonie's method of testifying her gratification; Eulalie looked sullen and envious – she had hoped to be first. Hortense and Caroline exchanged a reckless grimace on hearing their names read out somewhere near the bottom of the list; the brand of mental inferiority was considered by them as no disgrace, their hopes for the future being based solely on their personal attractions.

This affair arranged, the regular lesson followed. During a brief interval, employed by the pupils in ruling their books, my eye, ranging carelessly over the benches, observed, for the first time, that the farthest seat in the farthest row – a seat usually vacant – was again filled by the new scholar, the Mdlle Henri so ostentatiously recommended to me by the directress. To-day I had on my spectacles; her appearance, therefore, was clear to me at the first glance; I had not to puzzle over it. She looked young; yet, had I been required to name her exact age, I should have been somewhat nonplussed; the slightness of her figure might have suited seventeen; a certain anxious and preoccupied expression of face seemed the indication of riper years. She was dressed, like all the rest, in a dark stuff gown and a white collar; her features were dissimilar to any there, not so rounded, more defined, yet scarcely regular. The shape of her head too was different, the superior part more developed, the base considerably less. I felt assured, at first sight, that she was not a Belgian; her complexion, her countenance, her lineaments, her figure, were all distinct from theirs, and, evidently, the type of another race – of a race less gifted with fullness of flesh and plenitude of blood; less jocund, material, unthinking. When I first cast my eyes on her, she sat looking fixedly down, her chin resting on her hand, and she did not change her attitude till I commenced the lesson. None of the Belgian girls would have retained one position, and that a reflective one, for the same length of time. Yet, having intimated that her appearance was peculiar, as being unlike that of her Flemish companions, I have little more to say respecting it; I can pronounce no encomiums on her beauty, for she was not beautiful; nor offer condolence on her plainness, for neither was she plain; a careworn character of forehead, and a corresponding moulding of the mouth, struck me with a sentiment resembling surprise, but these traits would probably have passed unnoticed by any less crotchety observer.

Now, reader, though I have spent more than a page in describing Mdlle Henri, I know well enough that I have left on your mind's eye no distinct picture of her; I have not painted her complexion, nor her eyes, nor her hair, nor even drawn the outline of her shape. You cannot tell whether her nose was aquiline or *retroussé*, whether her chin was long or short, her face square or oval; nor could I the first day, and it is not my intention to communicate to you at once a knowledge I myself gained by little and little.

I gave a short exercise which they all wrote down. I saw the new pupil was puzzled at first with the novelty of the form and language; once or twice she looked at me with a sort of painful solicitude, as not comprehending at all what I meant; then she was not ready when the others were, she could not write her phrases so fast as they did; I would not help her, I went on relentless. She looked at me; her eye said most plainly, 'I cannot follow you.' I disregarded the appeal, and, carelessly leaning back in my chair, glancing from time to time with a *nonchalant* air out of the window, I dictated a little faster. On looking towards her again, I perceived her face clouded with embarrassment, but she was still writing on most diligently; I paused a few seconds; she employed the interval in hurriedly re-perusing what she had written, and shame and discomfiture were apparent in her countenance; she evidently found she had made great nonsense of it. In ten minutes more the dictation was complete, and having allowed a brief space in which to correct it, I took their books; it was with a reluctant hand Mdlle Henri gave up hers, but, having once yielded it to my possession, she composed her anxious face, as if, for the present, she had resolved to dismiss regret, and had made up her mind to be thought unprecedentedly stupid. Glancing over her exercises, I found that several lines had been omitted, but what was written contained very few faults; I instantly inscribed 'Bon' at the bottom of the page, and returned it to her; she smiled, at first incredulously, then as if reassured, but did not lift her eyes; she could look at me, it seemed, when perplexed and bewildered, but not when gratified; I thought that scarcely fair.

CHAPTER XV

Some time elapsed before I again gave a lesson in the first class; the holiday of Whitsuntide occupied three days, and on the fourth it was the turn of the second division to receive my instructions. As I made the transit of the carré I observed, as usual, the band of sewers surrounding Mdlle Henri; there were only about a dozen of them, but they made as much noise as might have sufficed for fifty; they seemed very little under her control; three or four at once assailed her with importunate requirements; she looked harassed, she demanded silence, but in vain. She saw me, and I read in her eye pain that a stranger should witness the insubordination of her pupils; she seemed to entreat order – her prayers were useless; then I remarked that she compressed her lips and contracted her brow; and her countenance, if I read it correctly, said – 'I have done my best; I seem to merit blame notwithstanding; blame me then who will.' I passed on; as I closed the schoolroom door, I heard her say, suddenly and sharply, addressing one of the eldest and most turbulent of the lot –

'Amélia Müllenberg, ask me no question, and request of me no assistance, for a week to come; during that space of time I will neither speak to you nor help you.'

The words were uttered with emphasis – nay, with vehemence – and a comparative silence followed; whether the calm was permanent, I know not; two doors now closed between me and the carré.

Next day was appropriated to the first class; on my arrival I found the directress seated, as usual, in a chair between the two estrades, and before her was standing Mdlle Henri, in an attitude (as it seemed to me) of somewhat reluctant attention. The directress was knitting and talking at the same time. Amidst the hum of a large schoolroom, it was easy so to speak in the ear of one person, as to be heard by that person alone, and it was thus Mdlle Reuter parleyed with her teacher. The face of the latter was a little flushed, not a little troubled; there was vexation in it, whence resulting I know not, for the directress looked very placid indeed; she could not be scolding in such gentle whispers, and with so equable a mien: no, it was presently proved that her discourse had been of the most friendly tendency, for I heard the closing words –

'C'est assez, ma bonne amie; à present je ne veux pas vous retenir davantage.'

Without reply, Mdlle Henri turned away; dissatisfaction was plainly evinced in her face, and a smile, slight and brief, but bitter, distrustful, and, I thought, scornful, curled her lip as she took her place in the class; it was a secret, involuntary smile, which lasted but a second; an air of depression succeeded, chased away presently by one of attention and interest, when I gave the word for all the pupils to take their reading-books. In general I hated the reading-lesson; it was such a torture to the ear to listen to their uncouth mouthing of my native tongue, and no effort of example or precept on my part ever seemed to effect the slightest improvement in their accent. To-day, each in her appropriate key, lisped, stuttered, mumbled, and jabbered as usual; about fifteen had racked me in turn, and my auricular nerve was expecting with resignation the discords of the sixteenth, when a full, though low, voice read out, in clear, correct English –

'On his way to Perth, the king was met by a Highland woman, calling herself a prophetess; she stood at the side of the ferry by which he was about to travel to the north, and cried with a loud voice, "My lord the king, if you pass this water you will never return again alive!" ' – (*vide* the *History of Scotland*).

I looked up in amazement; the voice was a voice of Albion; the accent was pure and silvery; it only wanted firmness, and assurance, to be the counterpart of what any well-educated lady in Essex or Middlesex might have enounced, yet the speaker or reader was no other than Mdlle Henri, in whose grave, joyless face I saw no mark of consciousness that she had performed any extraordinary feat. No one else evinced surprise either. Mdlle Reuter knitted away assiduously; I was aware, however, that at the conclusion of the paragraph, she had lifted her eyelid and honoured me with a glance sideways; she did not know the full excellency of the teacher's style of reading, but she perceived that her accent was not that of the others, and wanted to discover what I thought; I masked my visage with indifference, and ordered the next girl to proceed.

When the lesson was over, I took advantage of the confusion caused by breaking up to approach Mdlle Henri; she was standing near the window and retired as I advanced; she thought I wanted to look out, and did not imagine that I could have anything to say to her. I took her exercise-book out of her hand; as I turned over the leaves I addressed her –

'You have had lessons in English before?' I asked.

'No, sir.'

'No! you read it well; you have been in England?'

'Oh, no!' with some animation.

'You have been in English families?'

Still the answer was 'No'. Here my eye, resting on the flyleaf of the book, saw written, 'Frances Evans Henri'.

'Your name?' I asked.

'Yes, sir.'

My interrogations were cut short; I heard a little rustling behind me, and close at my back was the directress, professing to be examining the interior of a desk.

'Mademoiselle,' said she, looking up and addressing the teacher, 'you will have the goodness to go and stand in the corridor, while the young ladies are putting on their things, and try to keep some order.'

Mdlle Henri obeyed.

'What splendid weather!' observed the directress cheerfully, glancing at the same time from the window. I assented and was withdrawing. 'What of your new pupil, monsieur?' continued she, following my retreating steps. 'Is she likely to make progress in English?'

'Indeed, I can hardly judge. She possesses a pretty good accent; of her real knowledge of the language I have as yet had no opportunity of forming an opinion.'

'And her natural capacity, monsieur? I have had my fears about that: can you relieve me by an assurance at least of its average power?'

'I see no reason to doubt its average power, mademoiselle, but really I scarcely know her, and have not had time to study the calibre of her capacity. I wish you a very good afternoon.'

She still pursued me. 'You will observe, monsieur, and tell me what you think; I could so much better rely on your opinion than on my own; women cannot judge of these things as men can, and, excuse my pertinacity, monsieur, but it is natural I should feel interested about this poor little girl (pauvre petite); she has scarcely any relations, her own efforts are all she has to look to, her acquirements must be her sole fortune; her present position has once been mine, or nearly so; it is then but natural I should sympathize with her; and sometimes, when I see the difficulty she has in managing pupils, I feel quite chagrined. I doubt not she does her best, her intentions are excellent; but, monsieur, she wants tact and firmness. I have talked to her on the subject, but I am not fluent, and probably did not express myself with clearness; she never appears to comprehend me. Now, would you occasionally, when you see an opportunity, slip in a word of advice to her on the subject; men have so much more influence than women have – they argue so much more logically than we do; and you, monsieur, in particular, have so paramount a power of making yourself obeyed; a word of advice from you could not but do her good; even if she were sullen and headstrong (which I hope she is not), she would scarcely refuse to listen to you; for my own part, I can truly say that I never attend one of your lessons without deriving benefit from witnessing your management of the pupils. The other masters are a constant source of anxiety to me; they cannot impress the young ladies with sentiments of respect, nor restrain the levity natural to youth: in you, monsieur, I feel the most absolute confidence; try then to put this poor child into the way of controlling our giddy, high-spirited Brabantoises. But, monsieur, I would add one word more; don't alarm her *amour-propre*; beware of inflicting a wound there. I reluctantly admit that in that particular she is blamably – some would say ridiculously – susceptible. I fear I have touched this sore point inadvertently, and she cannot get over it.'

During the greater part of this harangue my hand was on the lock of the outer door; I now turned it.

'Au revoir, mademoiselle,' said I, and I escaped. I saw the directress's stock of words was yet far from exhausted. She looked after me, she would fain have detained me longer. Her manner towards me had been altered ever since I had begun to treat her with hardness and indifference: she almost cringed to me on every occasion; she consulted my countenance incessantly, and beset me with innumerable little officious attentions. Servility creates despotism. This slavish homage, instead of softening my heart, only pampered whatever was stern and exacting in its mood. The very circumstance of her hovering round me like a fascinated bird, seemed to transform me into a rigid pillar of stone; her flatteries irritated my scorn, her blandishments confirmed my reserve. At times I wondered what she meant by giving herself such trouble to win me, when the more profitable Pelet was already in her nets, and when, too, she was aware that I possessed her secret, for I had not scrupled to tell her as much: but the fact is that as it was her nature to doubt the reality and undervalue the worth of modesty, affection, disinterestedness – to regard these qualities as foibles of character – so it was equally her tendency to consider pride, hardness, selfishness, as proofs of strength. She would trample on the neck of humility, she would kneel at the feet of disdain; she would meet tenderness with secret contempt, indifference she would woo with ceaseless assiduities. Benevolence, devotedness, enthusiasm, were her antipathies; for dissimulation and self-interest she had a preference – they were real wisdom in her eyes; moral and physical degradation, mental and bodily inferiority, she regarded with indulgence; they were foils capable of being turned to good account as set-offs for her own endowments. To violence, injustice, tyranny, she succumbed – they were her natural masters; she had no propensity to hate, no impulse to resist them; the indignation their behests awake in some hearts was unknown in hers. From all this it resulted that the false and selfish called her wise, the vulgar and debased termed her charitable, the insolent and unjust dubbed her amiable, the conscientious and benevolent generally at first accepted as valid her claim to be considered one of themselves; but ere long the plating of pretension wore off, the real material appeared below, and they laid her aside as a deception.

CHAPTER XVI

IN THE course of another fortnight I had seen sufficient of Frances Evans Henri to enable me to form a more definite opinion of her character. I found her possessed in a somewhat remarkable degree of at least two good points, viz. perseverance and a sense of duty; I found she was really capable of applying to study, of contending with difficulties. At first I offered her the same help which I had always found it necessary to confer on the others; I began with unloosing for her each knotty point, but I soon discovered that such help was regarded by my new pupil as degrading; she recoiled from it with a certain proud impatience. Hereupon I appointed her long lessons, and left her to solve alone any perplexities they might present. She set to the task with serious ardour, and having quickly accomplished one labour, eagerly demanded more. So much for her perseverance; as to her sense of duty, it evinced itself thus: she liked to learn, but hated to teach; her progress as a pupil depended upon herself, and I saw that on herself she could calculate with certainty; her success as a teacher rested partly, perhaps chiefly, upon the will of others; it cost her a most painful effort to enter into conflict with this foreign will, to endeavour to bend it into subjection to her own; for in what regarded people in general the action of her will was impeded by many scruples; it was as unembarrassed as strong where her own affairs were concerned, and to it she could at any time subject her inclination, if that inclination went counter to her convictions of right; yet when called upon to wrestle with the propensities, the habits, the faults of others, of children especially, who are deaf to reason, and, for the most part, insensate to persuasion, her will sometimes almost refused to act; then came in the sense of duty, and forced the reluctant will into operation. A wasteful expense of energy and labour was frequently the consequence; Frances toiled for and with her pupils like a drudge, but it was long ere her conscientious exertions were rewarded by anything like docility on their part, because they saw that they had power over her, inasmuch as by resisting her painful attempts to convince, persuade, control – by forcing her to the employment of coercive measures – they could inflict upon her exquisite suffering. Human beings – human children especially – seldom deny themselves the pleasure of exercising a power which they are conscious of possessing, even though that power consist only in a capacity to make others wretched; a pupil whose sensations are duller than those of his instructor, while his nerves are tougher and his bodily strength perhaps greater, has an immense advantage over that instructor, and he will generally use it relentlessly, because the very young, very healthy, very thoughtless, know neither how to sympathize nor how to spare. Frances, I fear, suffered much; a continual weight seemed to oppress her spirits; I have said she did not live in the house, and whether in her own abode, wherever that might be, she wore the same preoccupied, unsmiling, sorrowfully resolved air that always shaded her features under the roof of Mdlle Reuter, I could not tell.

One day I gave, as a devoir, the trite little anecdote of Alfred tending cakes in the herdsman's hut, to be related with amplifications. A singular affair most of the pupils made of it; brevity was what they had chiefly studied; the majority of the narratives were perfectly unintelligible; those of Sylvie and Léonie Ledru alone pretended to anything like sense and connection. Eulalie, indeed, had hit upon a clever expedient for at once ensuring accuracy and saving trouble; she had obtained access somehow to an abridged history of England, and had copied the anecdote out fair. I wrote on the margin of her production, 'Stupid and deceitful', and then tore it down the middle.

Last in the pile of single-leaved devoirs, I found one of several sheets, neatly written out and stitched together; I knew the hand, and scarcely needed the evidence of the signature 'Frances Evans Henri' to confirm my conjecture as to the writer's identity.

Night was my usual time for correcting devoirs, and my own room the usual scene of such task – task most onerous hitherto; and it seemed strange to me to feel rising within me an incipient sense of interest, as I snuffed the candle and addressed myself to the perusal of the poor teacher's manuscript.

'Now,' thought I, 'I shall see a glimpse of what she really is; I shall get an idea of the nature and extent of her powers; not that she can be expected to express herself well in a foreign tongue, but still, if she has any mind, here will be a reflection of it.'

The narrative commenced by a description of a Saxon peasant's hut, situated within the confines of a great, leafless, winter forest; it represented an evening in December; flakes of snow were falling, and the herdsman foretold a heavy storm; he summoned his wife to aid him in collecting their flock, roaming far away on the pastoral banks of the Thone; he warns her that it will be late ere they return. The good woman is reluctant to quit her occupation of baking cakes for the evening meal; but acknowledging the primary importance of securing the herds and flocks, she puts on her sheepskin mantle; and, addressing a stranger who rests half-reclined on a bed of rushes near the hearth, bids him mind the bread till her return.

'Take care, young man,' she continues, 'that you fasten the door well after us; and, above all, open to none in our absence; whatever sound you hear, stir not, and look not out. The night will soon fall; this forest is most wild and lonely; strange noises are often heard therein after sunset; wolves haunt these glades, and Danish warriors infest the country; worse things are talked of; you might chance to hear, as it were, a child cry, and on opening the door to afford it succour, a great black bull, or a shadowy goblin dog, might rush over the threshold; or, more awful still, if something flapped, as with wings, against the lattice, and then a raven or a white dove flew in and settled on the hearth, such a visitor would be a sure sign of misfortune to the house; therefore, heed my advice, and lift the latchet for nothing.'

Her husband calls her away, both depart. The stranger, left alone, listens awhile to the muffled snow-wind, the remote, swollen sound of the river, and then he speaks.

'It is Christmas Eve,' says he, 'I mark the date; here I sit alone on a rude couch of rushes, sheltered by the thatch of a herdsman's hut; I, whose inheritance was a kingdom, owe my night's harbourage to a poor serf; my throne is usurped, my crown presses the brow of an invader; I have no friends; my troops wander broken in the hills of Wales; reckless robbers spoil my country; my subjects lie prostrate, their breasts crushed by the heel of the brutal Dane. Fate! thou hast done thy worst, and now thou standest before me resting thy hand on thy blunted blade. Aye; I see thine eye confront mine and demand why I still live, why I still hope. Pagan demon, I credit not thine omnipotence, and so cannot succumb to thy power. My God, whose Son, as on this night, took on Him the form of man, and for man vouchsafed to suffer and bleed, controls thy hand, and without His behest thou canst not strike a stroke. My God is sinless, eternal, allwise – in Him is my trust; and though stripped and crushed by thee – though naked, desolate, void of resource – I do not despair, I cannot despair: were the lance of Guthrum now wet with my blood, I should not despair. I watch, I toil, I hope, I pray; Jehovah, in His own time, will aid.'

I need not continue the quotation: the whole devoir was in the same strain. There were errors of orthography, there were foreign idioms, there were some faults of construction, there were verbs irregular transformed into verbs regular; it was mostly made up, as the above example shows, of short and somewhat rude sentences, and the style stood in great need of polish and sustained dignity; yet such as it was, I had hitherto seen nothing like it in the course of my professorial experience. The girl's mind had conceived a picture of the hut, of the two peasants, of the crownless king; she had imagined the wintry forest, she had recalled the old Saxon ghost-legends, she had appreciated Alfred's courage under calamity, she had remembered his Christian education, and had shown him, with the rooted confidence of those primitive days, relying on the scriptural Jehovah for aid against the mythological Destiny. This she had done without a hint from me: I had given the subject, but not said a word about the manner of treating it.

'I will find, or make, an opportunity of speaking to her,' I said to myself as I rolled the devoir up; 'I will learn what she has of English in her besides the name of Frances Evans; she is no novice in the language, that is evident, yet she told me she had neither been in England, nor taken lessons in English, nor lived in English families.'

In the course of my next lesson, I made a report of the other devoirs, dealing out praise and blame in very small retail parcels, according to my custom, for there was no use in blaming severely, and high encomiums were rarely merited. I said nothing of Mdlle Henri's exercise, and, spectacles on nose, I endeavoured to decipher in her countenance her sentiments at the omission. I wanted to find out whether in her existed a consciousness of her own talents. 'If she thinks she did a clever thing in composing that devoir, she will now look mortified,' thought I. Grave as usual, almost sombre, was her face; as usual, her eyes were fastened on the cahier open before her; there was something, I thought, of expectation in her attitude, as I concluded a brief review of the last devoir, and when, casting it from me and rubbing my hands, I bade them take their grammars, some slight change did pass over her air and mien, as though she now relinquished a faint prospect of pleasant excitement: she had been waiting for something to be discussed in which she had a degree of interest; the discussion was not to come on, so expectation sank back, shrunk and sad, but attention, promptly filling up the void, repaired in a moment the transient collapse of feature; still, I felt, rather than saw, during the whole course of the lesson, that a hope had been wrenched from her, and that if she did not show distress, it was because she would not.

At four o'clock, when the bell rang and the room was in immediate tumult, instead of taking my hat and starting from the estrade, I sat still a moment. I looked at Frances, she was putting her books into her cabas; having fastened the button, she raised her head; encountering my eye, she made a quiet, respectful obeisance, as bidding good afternoon, and was turning to depart.

'Come here,' said I, lifting my finger at the same time. She hesitated; she could not hear the words amidst the uproar now pervading both schoolrooms; I repeated the sign; she approached; again she paused within half a yard of the estrade, and looked shy, and still doubtful whether she had mistaken my meaning.

'Step up,' I said, speaking with decision. It is the only way of dealing with diffident, easily embarrassed characters, and with some slight manual aid I presently got her placed just where I wanted her to be, that is, between my desk and the window, where she was screened from the rush of the second division, and where no one could sneak behind her to listen.

'Take a seat,' I said, placing a tabouret; and I made her sit down. I knew what I was doing would be considered a very strange thing, and, what was more, I did not care. Frances knew it also, and, I fear, by an appearance of agitation and trembling, that she cared much. I drew from my pocket the rolled-up devoir.

'This is yours, I suppose?' said I, addressing her in English, for I now felt sure she could speak English.

'Yes,' she answered distinctly; and as I unrolled it and laid it out flat on the desk before her with my hand upon it, and a pencil in that hand, I saw her moved, and, as it were, kindled; her depression beamed as a cloud might behind which the sun is burning.

'This devoir has numerous faults,' said I. 'It will take you some years of careful study before you are in a condition to write English with absolute correctness. Attend: I will point out some principal defects.' And I went through it carefully, noting every error, and demonstrating why they were errors, and how the words or phrases ought to have been written. In the course of this sobering process she became calm. I now went on –

'As to the substance of your devoir, Mdlle Henri, it has surprised me; I perused it with pleasure, because I saw in it some proofs of taste and fancy. Taste and fancy are not the highest gifts of the human mind, but such as they are you possess them – not probably in a paramount degree, but in a degree beyond what the majority can boast. You may then take courage; cultivate the faculties that God and nature have bestowed on you, and do not fear in any crisis of suffering, under any pressure of injustice, to derive free and full consolation from the consciousness of their strength and rarity.'

'Strength and rarity!' I repeated to myself; 'aye, the words are probably true,' for on looking up, I saw the sun had dissevered its screening cloud, her countenance was transfigured, a smile shone in her eyes – a smile almost triumphant; it seemed to say –

'I am glad you have been forced to discover so much of my nature; you need not so carefully moderate your language. Do you think I am myself a stranger to myself? What you tell me in terms so qualified, I have known fully from a child.'

She did say this as plainly as a frank and flashing glance could, but in a moment the glow of her complexion, the radiance of her aspect, had subsided; if strongly conscious of her talents, she was equally conscious of her harassing defects, and the remembrance of these obliterated for a single second, now reviving with sudden force, at once subdued the too vivid characters in which her sense of her powers had been expressed. So quick was the revulsion of feeling, I had not time to check her triumph by reproof; ere I could contract my brows to a frown she had become serious and almost mournful-looking.

'Thank you, sir,' said she, rising. There was gratitude both in her voice and in the look with which she accompanied it. It was time, indeed, for our conference to terminate; for, when I glanced around, behold all the boarders (the day-scholars had departed) were congregated within a yard or two of my desk, and stood staring with eyes and mouths wide open; the three maîtresses formed a whispering knot in one corner, and close at my elbow was the directress, sitting on a low chair, calmly clipping the tassels of her finished purse.

CHAPTER XVII

AFTER ALL I had profited but imperfectly by the opportunity I had so boldly achieved of speaking to Mdlle
Henri; it was my intention to ask her how she came to be
possessed of two English baptismal names, Frances and Evans,
in addition to her French surname; also whence she derived
her good accent. I had forgotten both points, or, rather, our
colloquy had been so brief that I had not had time to bring
them forward; moreover, I had not half tested her powers of
speaking English; all I had drawn from her in that language
were the words 'Yes', and 'Thank you, sir'. 'No matter,'
I reflected. 'What has been left incomplete now, shall be finished
another day.' Nor did I fail to keep the promise thus made to
myself. It was difficult to get even a few words of particular
conversation with one pupil among so many; but, according
to the old proverb, 'Where there is a will, there is a way'; and
again and again I managed to find an opportunity for exchanging a few words with Mdlle Henri, regardless that envy stared
and detraction whispered whenever I approached her.

'Your book an instant.' Such was the mode in which I often
began these brief dialogues; the time was always just at the
conclusion of the lesson; and motioning to her to rise, I installed
myself in her place, allowing her to stand deferentially at my
side; for I esteemed it wise and right in her case to enforce
strictly all forms ordinarily in use between master and pupil;
the rather because I perceived that in proportion as my manner
grew austere and magisterial, hers became easy and self-
possessed – an odd contradiction, doubtless, to the ordinary
effect in such cases; but so it was.

'A pencil,' said I, holding out my hand without looking at
her. (I am now about to sketch a brief report of the first of these

conferences.) She gave me one, and while I underlined some errors in a grammatical exercise she had written, I observed –

'You are not a native of Belgium?'

'No.'

'Nor of France?'

'No.'

'Where, then, is your birthplace?'

'I was born at Geneva.'

'You don't call Frances and Evans Swiss names, I presume?'

'No, sir; they are English names.'

'Just so; and is it the custom of the Genevese to give their children English appellatives?'

'Non, monsieur; mais –'

'Speak English, if you please.'

'Mais –'

'English –'

'But' (slowly and with embarrassment) 'my parents were not all the two Genevese.'

'Say *both*, instead of "all the two", mademoiselle.'

'Not *both* Swiss; my mother was English.'

'Ah! and of English extraction?'

'Yes – her ancestors were all English.'

'And your father?'

'He was Swiss.'

'What besides? What was his profession?'

'Ecclesiastic – pastor – he had a church.'

'Since your mother is an Englishwoman, why do you not speak English with more facility?'

'Maman est morte, il y a dix ans.'

'And you do homage to her memory by forgetting her language? Have the goodness to put French out of your mind so long as I converse with you – keep to English.'

'C'est si difficile, monsieur, quand on n'en a plus l'habitude.'

'You had the habitude formerly, I suppose? Now answer me in your mother-tongue.'

'Yes, sir, I spoke the English more than the French when I was a child.'

'Why do you not speak it now?'

'Because I have no English friends.'

'You live with your father, I suppose?'

'My father is dead.'

'You have brothers and sisters?'

'Not one.'

'Do you live alone?'

'No – I have an aunt – ma tante Julienne.'

'Your father's sister?'

'Justement, monsieur.'

'Is that English?'

'No – but I forget –'

'For which, mademoiselle, if you were a child I should certainly devise some slight punishment; at your age – you must be two or three and twenty, I should think?'

'Pas encore, monsieur – en un mois j'aurai dix-neuf ans.'

'Well, nineteen is a mature age, and, having attained it, you ought to be so solicitous for your own improvement, that it should not be needful for a master to remind you twice of the expediency of your speaking English whenever practicable.'

To this wise speech I received no answer; and, when I looked up, my pupil was smiling to herself a much-meaning, though not very gay smile; it seemed to say, 'He talks of he knows not what': it said this so plainly, that I determined to request information on the point concerning which my ignorance seemed to be thus tacitly affirmed.

'Are you solicitous for your own improvement?'

'Rather.'

'How do you prove it, mademoiselle?'

An odd question, and bluntly put; it excited a second smile.

'Why, monsieur, I am not inattentive – am I? I learn my lessons well –'

'Oh, a child can do that! and what more do you do?'

'What more can I do?'

'Oh, certainly, not much; but you are a teacher, are you not, as well as a pupil?'

'Yes.'

'You teach lace-mending?'

'Yes.'

'A dull, stupid occupation; do you like it?'

'No – it is tedious.'

'Why do you pursue it? Why do you not rather teach history, geography, grammar, even arithmetic?'

'Is monsieur certain that I am myself thoroughly acquainted with these studies?'

'I don't know; you ought to be at your age.'

'But I never was at school, monsieur.'

'Indeed! What then were your friends – what was your aunt about? She is very much to blame.'

'No, monsieur, no – my aunt is good – she is not to blame – she does what she can; she lodges and nourishes me' (I report Mdlle Henri's phrases literally, and it was thus she translated from the French). 'She is not rich; she has only an annuity of twelve hundred francs, and it would be impossible for her to send me to school.'

'Rather,' thought I to myself on hearing this; but I continued, in the dogmatical tone I had adopted –

'It is sad, however, that you should be brought up in ignorance of the most ordinary branches of education; had you known something of history and grammar you might, by degrees, have relinquished your lace-mending drudgery, and risen in the world.'

'It is what I mean to do.'

'How? By a knowledge of English alone? That will not suffice; no respectable family will receive a governess whose whole stock of knowledge consists in a familiarity with one foreign language.'

'Monsieur, I know other things.'

'Yes, yes; you can work with Berlin wools, and embroider handkerchiefs and collars – that will do little for you.'

Mdlle Henri's lips were unclosed to answer, but she checked herself, as thinking the discussion had been sufficiently pursued, and remained silent.

'Speak,' I continued impatiently; 'I never like the appearance of acquiescence when the reality is not there; and you had a contradiction at your tongue's end.'

'Monsieur, I have had many lessons both in grammar, history, geography, and arithmetic. I have gone through a course of each study.'

'Bravo! but how did you manage it, since your aunt could not afford to send you to school?'

'By lace-mending; by the thing monsieur despises so much.'

'Truly! And now, mademoiselle, it will be a good exercise for you to explain to me in English how such a result was produced by such means.'

'Monsieur, I begged my aunt to have me taught lace-mending soon after we came to Brussels, because I knew it was a métier, a trade which was easily learnt, and by which I could earn some money very soon. I learnt it in a few days and I quickly got work, for all the Brussels ladies have old lace – very precious – which must be mended all the times it is washed. I earned money a little, and this money I gave for lessons in the studies I have mentioned; some of it I spent in buying books, English books especially; soon I shall try to find a place of governess, or schoolteacher, when I can write and speak English well; but it will be difficult, because those who know I have been a lace-mender will despise me, as the pupils here despise me. Pourtant j'ai mon projet,' she added in a lower tone.

'What is it?'

'I will go and live in England; I will teach French there.'

The words were pronounced emphatically. She said 'England'

as you might suppose an Israelite of Moses' days would have said Canaan.

'Have you a wish to see England?'

'Yes, and an intention.'

And here a voice, the voice of the directress, interposed –

'Mademoiselle Henri, je crois qu'il va pleuvoir; vous feriez bien, ma bonne amie, de retourner chez vous tout de suite.'

In silence, without a word of thanks for this officious warning, Mdlle Henri collected her books; she moved to me respectfully, endeavoured to move to her superior, though the endeavour was almost a failure, for her head seemed as if it would not bend, and thus departed.

Where there is one grain of perseverance or wilfulness in the composition, trifling obstacles are ever known rather to stimulate than discourage. Mdlle Reuter might as well have spared herself the trouble of giving that intimation about the weather (by the by her prediction was falsified by the event – it did not rain that evening). At the close of the next lesson I was again at Mdlle Henri's desk. Thus did I accost her –

'What is your idea of England, mademoiselle? Why do you wish to go there?'

Accustomed by this time to the calculated abruptness of my manner, it no longer discomposed or surprised her, and she answered with only so much of hesitation as was rendered inevitable by the difficulty she experienced in improvising the translation of her thoughts from French to English.

'England is something unique, as I have heard and read; my idea of it is vague, and I want to go there to render my idea clear, definite.'

'Hum! How much of England do you suppose you could see if you went there in the capacity of a teacher? A strange notion you must have of getting a clear and definite idea of a country! All you could see of Great Britain would be the interior of a school, or at most of one or two private dwellings.'

'It would be an English school; they would be English dwellings.'

'Indisputably; but what then? What would be the value of observations made on a scale so narrow?'

'Monsieur, might one not learn something by analogy? An – échantillon – a – a sample often serves to give an idea of the whole; besides, narrow and wide are words comparative, are they not? All my life would perhaps seem narrow in your eyes – all the life of a – that little animal subterranean – une taupe – comment dit-on?'

'Mole.'

'Yes – a mole, which lives underground, would seem narrow even to me.'

'Well, mademoiselle – what then? Proceed.'

'Mais, monsieur, vous me comprenez.'

'Not in the least; have the goodness to explain.'

'Why, monsieur, it is just so. In Switzerland I have done but little, learnt but little, and seen but little; my life there was in a circle; I walked the same round every day; I could not get out of it; had I rested – remained there even till my death, I should never have enlarged it, because I am poor and not skilful, I have not great acquirements; when I was quite tired of this round, I begged my aunt to go to Brussels; my existence is no larger here, because I am no richer or higher; I walk in as narrow a limit, but the scene is changed; it would change again if I went to England. I knew something of the bourgeois of Geneva, now I know something of the bourgeois of Brussels; if I went to London, I should know something of the bourgeois of London. Can you make any sense out of what I say, monsieur, or is it all obscure?'

'I see, I see – now let us advert to another subject; you propose to devote your life to teaching, and you are a most unsuccessful teacher; you cannot keep your pupils in order.'

A flush of painful confusion was the result of this harsh

remark; she bent her head to the desk, but soon raising it replied –

'Monsieur, I am not a skilful teacher, it is true, but practice improves; besides, I work under difficulties; here I only teach sewing, I can show no power in sewing, no superiority – it is a subordinate art; then I have no associates in this house, I am isolated; I am, too, a heretic, which deprives me of influence.'

'And in England you would be a foreigner; that too would deprive you of influence, and would effectually separate you from all around you; in England you would have as few connections, as little importance as you have here.'

'But I should be learning something; for the rest, there are probably difficulties for such as I everywhere, and if I must contend, and perhaps be conquered, I would rather submit to English pride than to Flemish coarseness; besides, monsieur –'

She stopped – not evidently from any difficulty in finding words to express herself, but because discretion seemed to say, 'You have said enough.'

'Finish your phrase,' I urged.

'Besides, monsieur, I long to live once more among Protestants; they are more honest than Catholics; a Romish school is a building with porous walls, a hollow floor, a false ceiling; every room in this house, monsieur, has eye-holes and ear-holes, and what the house is, the inhabitants are – very treacherous; they all think it lawful to tell lies; they all call it politeness to profess friendship where they feel hatred.'

'All?' said I; 'you mean the pupils – the mere children – inexperienced, giddy things, who have not learnt to distinguish the difference between right and wrong?'

'On the contrary, monsieur – the children are the most sincere; they have not yet had time to become accomplished in duplicity; they will tell lies, but they do it unartificially, and you know they are lying; but the grown-up people are very false; they deceive strangers, they deceive each other –'

A servant here entered –

'Mdlle Henri – Mdlle Reuter vous prie de vouloir bien conduire la petite de Dorlodot chez elle, elle vous attend dans le cabinet de Rosalie la portière – c'est que sa bonne n'est pas venue la chercher – voyez-vous.'

'Eh bien! est-ce que je suis sa bonne – moi?' demanded Mdlle Henri; then smiling, with that same bitter, derisive smile I had seen on her lips before, she hastily rose and made her exit.

CHAPTER XVIII

T HE YOUNG Anglo-Swiss evidently derived both pleasure
and profit from the study of her mother-tongue. In teaching her I did not, of course, confine myself to the ordinary
school routine; I made instruction in English a channel for
instruction in literature. I prescribed to her a course of reading;
she had a little selection of English classics, a few of which had
been left her by her mother, and the others she had purchased
with her own penny fee. I lent her some more modern works;
all these she read with avidity, giving me, in writing, a clear
summary of each work when she had perused it. Composition,
too, she delighted in. Such occupation seemed the very breath
of her nostrils, and soon her improved productions wrung from
me the avowal that those qualities in her I had termed taste
and fancy ought rather to have been denominated judgment
and imagination. When I intimated so much, which I did as
usual in dry and stinted phrase, I looked for the radiant and
exulting smile my one word of eulogy had elicited before; but
Frances coloured. If she did smile, it was very softly and shyly;
and instead of looking up to me with a conquering glance, her
eyes rested on my hand, which, stretched over her shoulder,
was writing some directions with a pencil on the margin of her
book.

'Well, are you pleased that I am satisfied with your progress?'
I asked.

'Yes,' said she slowly, gently, the blush that had half subsided
returning.

'But I do not say enough, I suppose?' I continued. 'My
praises are too cool?'

She made no answer, and, I thought, looked a little sad.
I divined her thoughts, and should much have liked to have

responded to them, had it been expedient to do so. She was
not now very ambitious of my admiration – not eagerly desirous
of dazzling me; a little affection – ever so little – pleased her
better than all the panegyrics in the world. Feeling this, I stood
a good while behind her, writing on the margin of her book.
I could hardly quit my station or relinquish my occupation;
something retained me bending there, my head very near hers,
and my hand near hers too; but the margin of a copy-book is
not an illimitable space – so, doubtless, the directress thought;
and she took occasion to walk past in order to ascertain by
what art I prolonged so disproportionately the period necessary
for filling it. I was obliged to go. Distasteful effort – to leave
what we most prefer!

Frances did not become pale or feeble in consequence of her
sedentary employment; perhaps the stimulus it communicated
to her mind counterbalanced the inaction it imposed on her
body. She changed, indeed, changed obviously and rapidly; but
it was for the better. When I first saw her, her countenance was
sunless, her complexion colourless; she looked like one who
had no source of enjoyment, no store of bliss anywhere in the
world; now the cloud had passed from her mien, leaving space
for the dawn of hope and interest, and those feelings rose like
a clear morning, animating what had been depressed, tinting
what had been pale. Her eyes, whose colour I had not at first
known, so dim were they with repressed tears, so shadowed
with ceaseless dejection, now, lit by a ray of the sunshine that
cheered her heart, revealed irids of bright hazel – irids large
and full, screened with long lashes; and pupils instinct with
fire. That look of wan emaciation which anxiety or low spirits
often communicates to a thoughtful, thin face, rather long than
round, having vanished from hers; a clearness of skin almost
bloom, and a plumpness almost embonpoint, softened the
decided lines of her features. Her figure shared in this beneficial
change; it became rounder, and as the harmony of her form
was complete and her stature of the graceful middle height,

one did not regret (or at least *I* did not regret) the absence of confirmed fullness, in contours, still slight, though compact, elegant, flexible – the exquisite turning of waist, wrist, hand, foot, and ankle satisfied completely my notions of symmetry, and allowed a lightness and freedom of movement which corresponded with my ideas of grace.

Thus improved, thus wakened to life, Mdlle Henri began to take a new footing in the school; her mental power, manifested gradually but steadily, ere long extorted recognition even from the envious; and when the young and healthy saw that she could smile brightly, converse gaily, move with vivacity and alertness, they acknowledged in her a sisterhood of youth and health, and tolerated her as of their kind accordingly.

To speak truth, I watched this change much as a gardener watches the growth of a precious plant, and I contributed to it too, even as the said gardener contributes to the development of his favourite. To me it was not difficult to discover how I could best foster my pupil, cherish her starved feelings, and induce the outward manifestation of that inward vigour which sunless drought and blighting blast had hitherto forbidden to expand. Constancy of attention – a kindness as mute as watchful, always standing by her, cloaked in the rough garb of austerity, and making its real nature known only by a rare glance of interest, or a cordial and gentle word; real respect masked with seeming imperiousness, directing, urging her actions, yet helping her too, and that with devoted care: these were the means I used, for these means best suited Frances' feelings, as susceptible as deep vibrating – her nature at once proud and shy.

The benefits of my system became apparent also in her altered demeanour as a teacher; she now took her place amongst her pupils with an air of spirit and firmness which assured them at once that she meant to be obeyed – and obeyed she was. They felt they had lost their power over her. If any girl had rebelled, she would no longer have taken her rebellion to heart; she possessed a source of comfort they could not drain, a pillar of support they could not overthrow: formerly, when insulted, she wept; now, she smiled.

The public reading of one of her devoirs achieved the revelation of her talents to all and sundry; I remember the subject – it was an emigrant's letter to his friends at home. It opened with simplicity; some natural and graphic touches disclosed to the reader the scene of virgin forest and great, New-World river – barren of sail and flag – amidst which the epistle was supposed to be indited. The difficulties and dangers that attend a settler's life were hinted at; and in the few words said on that subject, Mdlle Henri failed not to render audible the voice of resolve, patience, endeavour. The disasters which had driven him from his native country were alluded to; stainless honour, inflexible independence, indestructible self-respect there took the word. Past days were spoken of; the grief of parting, the regrets of absence, were touched upon; feeling, forcible and fine, breathed eloquent in every period. At the close, consolation was suggested; religious faith became there the speaker, and she spoke well.

The devoir was powerfully written in language at once chaste and choice, in a style nerved with vigour and graced with harmony.

Mdlle Reuter was quite sufficiently acquainted with English to understand it when read or spoken in her presence, though she could neither speak nor write it herself. During the perusal of this devoir, she sat placidly busy, her eyes and fingers occupied with the formation of a 'rivière', or open-work hem round a cambric handkerchief; she said nothing, and her face and forehead, clothed with a mask of purely negative expression, were as blank of comment as her lips. As neither surprise, pleasure, approbation, nor interest were evinced in her countenance, so no more were disdain, envy, annoyance, weariness; if that inscrutable mien said anything, it was simply this –

'The matter is too trite to excite an emotion, or call forth an opinion.'

As soon as I had done, a hum rose; several of the pupils, pressing round Mdlle Henri, began to beset her with compliments; the composed voice of the directress was now heard –

'Young ladies, such of you as have cloaks and umbrellas will hasten to return home before the shower becomes heavier' (it was raining a little); 'the remainder will wait till their respective servants arrive to fetch them.' And the school dispersed, for it was four o'clock.

'Monsieur, a word,' said Mdlle Reuter, stepping on to the estrade, and signifying, by a movement of the hand, that she wished me to relinquish, for an instant, the castor I had clutched.

'Mademoiselle, I am at your service.'

'Monsieur, it is of course an excellent plan to encourage effort in young people by making conspicuous the progress of any particularly industrious pupil; but do you not think that in the present instance, Mdlle Henri can hardly be considered as a concurrent with the other pupils? She is older than most of them, and has had advantages of an exclusive nature for acquiring a knowledge of English; on the other hand, her sphere of life is somewhat beneath theirs; under these circumstances, a public distinction, conferred upon Mdlle Henri, may be the means of suggesting comparisons, and exciting feelings such as would be far from advantageous to the individual forming their object. The interest I take in Mdlle Henri's real welfare makes me desirous of screening her from annoyances of this sort; besides, monsieur, as I have before hinted to you, the sentiment of *amour-propre* has a somewhat marked preponderance in her character; celebrity has a tendency to foster this sentiment, and in her it should be rather repressed – she rather needs keeping down than bringing forward; and then I think, monsieur – it appears to me that ambition, *literary* ambition especially, is not a feeling to be cherished in the mind of a woman; would not Mdlle Henri be much safer and happier if taught to believe that in the quiet discharge of social duties consists her real vocation, than if stimulated to aspire after applause and publicity? She may never marry; scanty as are her resources, obscure as are her connections, uncertain as is her health (for I think her consumptive, her mother died of that complaint), it is more than probable she never will; I do not see how she can rise to a position whence such a step would be possible; but even in celibacy it would be better for her to retain the character and habits of a respectable, decorous female.'

'Indisputably, mademoiselle,' was my answer. 'Your opinion admits of no doubt'; and, fearful of the harangue being renewed, I retreated under cover of that cordial sentence of assent.

At the date of a fortnight after the little incident noted above, I find it recorded in my diary that a hiatus occurred in Mdlle Henri's usually regular attendance in class. The first day or two I wondered at her absence, but did not like to ask an explanation of it; I thought indeed some chance word might be dropped which would afford me the information I wished to obtain, without my running the risk of exciting silly smiles and gossiping whispers by demanding it. But when a week passed and the seat at the desk near the door still remained vacant, and when no allusion was made to the circumstance by any individual of the class – when, on the contrary, I found that all observed a marked silence on the point – I determined, *coûte que coûte*, to break the ice of this silly reserve. I selected Sylvie as my informant, because from her I knew that I should at least get a sensible answer, unaccompanied by wriggle, titter, or other flourish of folly.

'Où donc est Mdlle Henri?' I said one day as I returned an exercise-book I had been examining.

'Elle est partie, monsieur.'

'Partie! et pour combien de temps? Quand reviendra-t-elle?'

'Elle est partie pour toujours, monsieur; elle ne reviendra plus.'

'Ah!' was my involuntary exclamation; then, after a pause –

'En êtes-vous bien sûre, Sylvie?'

'Oui, oui, monsieur, mademoiselle la directrice nous l'a dit elle-même il y a deux ou trois jours.'

And I could pursue my inquiries no further; time, place, and circumstances forbade my adding another word. I could neither comment on what had been said, nor demand further particulars. A question as to the reason of the teacher's departure, as to whether it had been voluntary or otherwise, was indeed on my lips, but I suppressed it – there were listeners all round. An hour after, in passing Sylvie in the corridor as she was putting on her bonnet, I stopped short and asked –

'Sylvie, do you know Mdlle Henri's address? I have some books of hers,' I added carelessly, 'and I should wish to send them to her.'

'No, monsieur,' replied Sylvie; 'but perhaps Rosalie, the portress, will be able to give it you.'

Rosalie's cabinet was just at hand; I stepped in and repeated the inquiry. Rosalie – a smart French grisette – looked up from her work with a knowing smile, precisely the sort of smile I had been so desirous to avoid exciting. Her answer was prepared; she knew nothing whatever of Mdlle Henri's address – had never known it. Turning from her with impatience – for I believed she lied and was hired to lie – I almost knocked down someone who had been standing at my back; it was the directress. My abrupt movement made her recoil two or three steps. I was obliged to apologize, which I did more concisely than politely. No man likes to be dogged, and in the very irritable mood in which I then was the sight of Mdlle Reuter thoroughly incensed me. At the moment I turned her countenance looked hard, dark, and inquisitive; her eyes were bent upon me with an expression of almost hungry curiosity. I had scarce caught this phase of physiognomy ere it had vanished; a bland smile played on her features; my harsh apology was received with good-humoured facility.

'Oh, don't mention it, monsieur; you only touched my hair with your elbow; it is no worse, only a little dishevelled.' She shook it back, and passing her fingers through her curls, loosened them into more numerous and flowing ringlets. Then she went on with vivacity –

'Rosalie, I was coming to tell you to go instantly and close the windows of the salon; the wind is rising, and the muslin curtains will be covered with dust.'

Rosalie departed. 'Now,' thought I, 'this will not do; Mdlle Reuter thinks her meanness in eavesdropping is screened by her art in devising a pretext, whereas the muslin curtains she speaks of are not more transparent than this same pretext.' An impulse came over me to thrust the flimsy screen aside, and confront her craft boldly with a word or two of plain truth. 'The rough-shod foot treads most firmly on slippery ground,' thought I; so I began –

'Mademoiselle Henri has left your establishment – been dismissed, I presume?'

'Ah, I wished to have a little conversation with you, monsieur,' replied the directress with the most natural and affable air in the world; 'but we cannot talk quietly here; will monsieur step into the garden a minute?' And she preceded me, stepping out through the glass door I have before mentioned.

'There,' said she, when we had reached the centre of the middle alley, and when the foliage of shrubs and trees, now in their summer pride, closing behind and around us, shut out the view of the house, and thus imparted a sense of seclusion even to this little plot of ground in the very core of a capital.

'There! one feels quiet and free when there are only pear-trees and rose-bushes about one; I dare say you, like me, monsieur, are sometimes tired of being eternally in the midst of life; of having human faces always round you, human eyes always upon you, human voices always in your ear. I am sure I often wish intensely for liberty to spend a whole month in the country at some little farm-house, bien gentille, bien propre, tout entourée de champs et de bois; quelle vie charmante que la vie champêtre! N'est-ce pas, monsieur?'

'Cela dépend, mademoiselle.'

'Que le vent est bon et frais!' continued the directress; and she was right there, for it was a south wind, soft and sweet. I carried my hat in my hand, and this gentle breeze, passing through my hair, soothed my temples like balm. Its refreshing effect, however, penetrated no deeper than the mere surface of the frame; for as I walked by the side of Mdlle Reuter, my heart was still hot within me, and while I was musing the fire burned; then spake I with my tongue –

'I understand Mdlle Henri is gone from hence, and will not return?'

'Ah, true! I meant to have named the subject to you some days ago, but my time is completely taken up, I cannot do half the things I wish: have you never experienced what it is, monsieur, to find the day too short by twelve hours for your numerous duties?'

'Not often. Mdlle Henri's departure was not voluntary, I presume? If it had been, she would certainly have given me some intimation of it, being my pupil.'

'Oh, did she not tell you? that was strange; for my part, I never thought of adverting to the subject; when one has so many things to attend to, one is apt to forget little incidents that are not of primary importance.'

'You consider Mdlle Henri's dismission, then, as a very insignificant event?'

'Dismission? Ah! she was not dismissed; I can say with truth, monsieur, that since I became the head of this establishment no master or teacher has ever been *dismissed* from it.'

'Yet some have left it, mademoiselle?'

'Many; I have found it necessary to change frequently – a change of instructors is often beneficial to the interests of a school; it gives life and variety to the proceedings; it amuses the pupils, and suggests to the parents the idea of exertion and progress.'

'Yet when you are tired of a professor or maîtresse, you scruple to dismiss them?'

'No need to have recourse to such extreme measures, I assure you. Allons, monsieur le professeur – asseyons-nous; je vais vous donner une petite leçon dans votre état d'instituteur.' (I wish I might write all she said to me in French – it loses sadly by being translated into English.) We had now reached *the* garden-chair; the directress sat down, and signed to me to sit by her, but I only rested my knee on the seat, and stood leaning my head and arm against the embowering branch of a huge laburnum, whose golden flowers, blent with the dusky green leaves of a lilac-bush, formed a mixed arch of shade and sunshine over the retreat. Mdlle Reuter sat silent for a moment; some novel movements were evidently working in her mind, and they showed their nature on her astute brow; she was meditating some *chef d'œuvre* of policy. Convinced by several months' experience that the affectation of virtues she did not possess was unavailing to ensnare me – aware that I had read her real nature, and would believe nothing of the character she gave out as being hers – she had determined, at last, to try a new key, and see if the lock of my heart would yield to that; a little audacity, a word of truth, a glimpse of the real. 'Yes, I will try,' was her inward resolve; and then her blue eye glittered upon me – it did not flash – nothing of flame ever kindled in its temperate gleam.

'Monsieur fears to sit by me?' she inquired playfully.

'I have no wish to usurp Pelet's place,' I answered, for I had got the habit of speaking to her bluntly – a habit begun in anger, but continued because I saw that, instead of offending, it fascinated her. She cast down her eyes, and drooped her eyelids; she sighed uneasily; she turned with an anxious gesture, as if she would give me the idea of a bird that flutters in its cage, and would fain fly from its jail and jailer, and seek its natural mate and pleasant nest.

'Well – and your lesson?' I demanded briefly.

'Ah!' she exclaimed, recovering herself, 'you are so young, so frank and fearless, so talented, so impatient of imbecility, so disdainful of vulgarity, you need a lesson; here it is then: far more is to be done in this world by dexterity than by strength; but, perhaps, you knew that before, for there is delicacy as well as power in your character – policy, as well as pride?'

'Go on,' said I; and I could hardly help smiling, the flattery was so piquant, so finely seasoned. She caught the prohibited smile, though I passed my hand over my mouth to conceal it; and again she made room for me to sit beside her. I shook my head, though temptation penetrated to my senses at the moment, and once more I told her to go on.

'Well, then, if ever you are at the head of a large establishment, dismiss nobody. To speak truth, monsieur (and to you I will speak truth), I despise people who are always making rows, blustering, sending off one to the right, and another to the left, urging and hurrying circumstances. I'll tell you what I like best to do, monsieur, shall I?' She looked up again; she had compounded her glance well this time – much archness, more deference, a spicy dash of coquetry, an unveiled consciousness of capacity. I nodded; she treated me like the great Mogul; so I became the great Mogul as far as she was concerned.

'I like, monsieur, to take my knitting in my hands, and to sit quietly down in my chair; circumstances defile past me; I watch their march; so long as they follow the course I wish, I say nothing, and do nothing; I don't clap my hands, and cry out, 'Bravo! How lucky I am!' to attract the attention and envy of my neighbours – I am merely passive; but when events fall out ill – when circumstances become adverse – I watch very vigilantly; I knit on still, and still I hold my tongue; but every now and then, monsieur, I just put my toe out – so – and give the rebellious circumstance a little secret push, without noise, which sends it the way I wish, and I am successful after all, and nobody has seen my expedient. So, when teachers or masters become troublesome and inefficient – when, in short, the interests of the school would suffer from their retaining their places – I mind my knitting, events progress, circumstances glide past; I see one which, if pushed ever so little awry, will render untenable the post I wish to have vacated – the deed is done – the stumbling-block removed – and no one saw me: I have not made an enemy, I am rid of an incumbrance.'

A moment since, and I thought her alluring; this speech concluded, I looked on her with distaste. 'Just like you,' was my cold answer. 'And in this way you have ousted Mdlle Henri? You wanted her office, therefore you rendered it intolerable to her?'

'Not at all, monsieur, I was merely anxious about Mdlle Henri's health; no, your moral sight is clear and piercing, but there you have failed to discover the truth. I took – I have always taken a real interest in Mdlle Henri's welfare; I did not like her going out in all weathers; I thought it would be more advantageous for her to obtain a permanent situation; besides, I considered her now qualified to do something more than teach sewing. I reasoned with her; left the decision to herself; she saw the correctness of my views, and adopted them.'

'Excellent! and now, mademoiselle, you will have the goodness to give me her address.'

'Her address!' and a sombre and stony change came over the mien of the directress. 'Her address? Ah! – well – I wish I could oblige you, monsieur, but I cannot, and I will tell you why; whenever I myself asked her for her address, she always evaded the inquiry. I thought – I may be wrong – but I *thought* her motive for doing so was a natural, though mistaken reluctance to introduce me to some, probably, very poor abode; her means were narrow, her origin obscure; she lives somewhere, doubtless, in the "basse ville".'

'I'll not lose sight of my best pupil yet,' said I, 'though she were born of beggars and lodged in a cellar; for the rest, it is absurd to make a bugbear of her origin to me – I happen to know that she was a Swiss pastor's daughter, neither more nor less; and, as to her narrow means, I care nothing for the poverty of her purse as long as her heart overflows with affluence.'

'Your sentiments are perfectly noble, monsieur,' said the directress, affecting to suppress a yawn; her sprightliness was now extinct, her temporary candour shut up; the little, red-coloured, piratical-looking pennon of audacity she had allowed to float a minute in the air, was furled, and the broad sober-hued flag of dissimulation again hung low over the citadel. I did not like her thus, so I cut short the *tête-à-tête* and departed.

CHAPTER XIX

NOVELISTS SHOULD never allow themselves to weary of the study of real life. If they observed this duty conscientiously, they would give us fewer pictures chequered with vivid contrasts of light and shade; they would seldom elevate their heroes and heroines to the heights of rapture – still seldomer sink them to the depths of despair; for if we rarely taste the fullness of joy in this life, we yet more rarely savour the acrid bitterness of hopeless anguish; unless, indeed, we have plunged like beasts into sensual indulgence, abused, strained, stimulated, again over-strained, and, at last, destroyed our faculties for enjoyment; then, truly, we may find ourselves without support, robbed of hope. Our agony is great, and how can it end? We have broken the spring of our powers; life must be all suffering – too feeble to conceive faith – death must be darkness – God, spirits, religion can have no place in our collapsed minds, where linger only hideous and polluting recollections of vice; and time brings us on to the brink of the grave, and dissolution flings us in – a rag eaten through and through with disease, wrung together with pain, stamped into the churchyard sod by the inexorable heel of despair.

But the man of regular life and rational mind never despairs. He loses his property – it is a blow – he staggers a moment; then, his energies, roused by the smart, are at work to seek a remedy; activity soon mitigates regret. Sickness affects him; he takes patience – endures what he cannot cure. Acute pain racks him; his writhing limbs know not where to find rest; he leans on Hope's anchors. Death takes from him what he loves; roots up, and tears violently away, the stem round which his affections were twined – a dark, dismal time, a frightful wrench – but some morning Religion looks into his desolate house with sunrise, and says, that in another world, another life, he shall meet his kindred again. She speaks of that world as a place unsullied by sin – of that life as an era unembittered by suffering; she mightily strengthens her consolation by connecting with it two ideas – which mortals cannot comprehend, but on which they love to repose – Eternity, Immortality; and the mind of the mourner, being filled with an image, faint yet glorious, of heavenly hills all light and peace – of a spirit resting there in bliss – of a day when his spirit shall also alight there, free and disembodied – of a reunion perfected by love, purified from fear – he takes courage – goes out to encounter the necessities and discharge the duties of life; and, though sadness may never lift her burden from his mind, Hope will enable him to support it.

Well – and what suggested all this? and what is the inference to be drawn therefrom? What suggested it, is the circumstance of my best pupil – my treasure – being snatched from my hands, and put away out of my reach; the inference to be drawn from it is – that, being a steady, reasonable man, I did not allow the resentment, disappointment, and grief, engendered in my mind by this evil chance, to grow there to any monstrous size; nor did I allow them to monopolize the whole space of my heart; I pent them, on the contrary, in one strait and secret nook. In the daytime, too, when I was about my duties, I put them on the silent system; and it was only after I had closed the door of my chamber at night that I somewhat relaxed my severity towards these morose nurslings, and allowed vent to their language of murmurs; then, in revenge, they sat on my pillow, haunted my bed, and kept me awake with their long, midnight cry.

A week passed. I had said nothing more to Mdlle Reuter. I had been calm in my demeanour to her, though stony cold and hard. When I looked at her, it was with the glance fitting to be bestowed on one who I knew had consulted jealousy as an adviser, and employed treachery as an instrument – the glance of quiet disdain and rooted distrust. On Saturday evening, ere I left the house, I stept into the *salle-à-manger*, where she was sitting alone, and, placing myself before her, I asked, with the same tranquil tone and manner that I should have used had I put the question for the first time –

'Mademoiselle, will you have the goodness to give me the address of Frances Evans Henri?'

A little surprised, but not disconcerted, she smilingly disclaimed any knowledge of that address, adding, 'Monsieur has perhaps forgotten that I explained all about that circumstance before – a week ago?'

'Mademoiselle,' I continued, 'you would greatly oblige me by directing me to that young person's abode.'

She seemed somewhat puzzled; and, at last, looking up with an admirably counterfeited air of naïveté, she demanded, 'Does Monsieur think I am telling an untruth?'

Still avoiding to give her a direct answer, I said, 'It is not then your intention, mademoiselle, to oblige me in this particular?'

'But, monsieur, how can I tell you what I do not know?'

'Very well; I understand you perfectly, mademoiselle, and now I have only two or three words more to say. This is the last week in July; in another month the vacation will commence; have the goodness to avail yourself of the leisure it will afford you to look out for another English master – at the close of August, I shall be under the necessity of resigning my post in your establishment.'

I did not wait for her comments on this announcement, but bowed and immediately withdrew.

That same evening, soon after dinner, a servant brought me a small packet; it was directed in a hand I knew, but had not hoped so soon to see again; being in my own apartment and alone, there was nothing to prevent my immediately opening it; it contained four five-franc pieces, and a note in English.

'MONSIEUR, – I came to Mdlle Reuter's house yesterday, at the time when I knew you would be just about finishing your lesson, and asked if I might go into the schoolroom and speak to you. Mdlle Reuter came out and said you were already gone; it had not yet struck four, so I thought she must be mistaken, but concluded it would be vain to call another day on the same errand. In one sense a note will do as well – it will wrap up the 20 francs, the price of the lessons I have received from you; and if it will not fully express the thanks I owe you in addition – if it will not bid you good-bye as I could wish to have done – if it will not tell you, as I long to do, how sorry I am that I shall probably never see you more – why, spoken words would hardly be more adequate to the task. Had I seen you, I should probably have stammered out something feeble and unsatisfactory – something belying my feelings rather than explaining them; so it is perhaps as well that I was denied admission to your presence. You often remarked, monsieur, that my devoirs dwelt a great deal on fortitude in bearing grief – you said I introduced that theme too often; I find indeed that it is much easier to write about a severe duty than to perform it, for I am oppressed when I see and feel to what a reverse fate has condemned me; you were kind to me, monsieur – very kind; I am afflicted – I am heartbroken to be quite separated from you; soon I shall have no friend on earth. But it is useless troubling you with my distresses. What claim have I on your sympathy? None; I will then say no more. – Farewell, monsieur,

F. E. HENRI.'

I put up the note in my pocket-book. I slipped the five-franc pieces into my purse – then I took a turn through my narrow chamber.

'Mdlle Reuter talked about her poverty,' said I, 'and she is poor; yet she pays her debts and more. I have not yet given her a quarter's lessons, and she has sent me a quarter's due. I wonder of what she deprived herself to scrape together the twenty francs – I wonder what sort of a place she has to live in, and what sort of a woman her aunt is, and whether she is likely to get employment to supply the place she has lost. No doubt she will have to trudge about long enough from school to school, to inquire here, and apply there – be rejected in this place, disappointed in that. Many an evening she'll go to her bed tired and unsuccessful. And the directress would not let her in to bid me good-bye? I might not have the chance of standing with her for a few minutes at a window in the schoolroom and exchanging some half-dozen of sentences – getting to know where she lived – putting matters in train for having all things arranged to my mind? No address on the note' – I continued, drawing it again from the pocket-book and examining it on each side of the two leaves: 'women are women, that is certain, and always do business like women; men mechanically put a date and address to their communications. And these five-franc pieces?' – (I hauled them forth from my purse) – 'if she had offered me them herself instead of tying them up with a thread of green silk in a kind of Lilliputian packet, I could have thrust them back into her little hand, and shut up the small, taper fingers over them – so – and compelled her shame, her pride, her shyness, all to yield to a little bit of determined Will – now where is she? How can I get at her?'

Opening my chamber door I walked down into the kitchen.

'Who brought the packet?' I asked of the servant who had delivered it to me.

'Un petit commissionnaire, monsieur.'

'Did he say anything?'

'Rien.'

And I wended my way up the back-stairs, wondrously the wiser for my inquiries.

'No matter,' said I to myself, as I again closed the door. 'No matter – I'll seek her through Brussels.'

And I did. I sought her day by day whenever I had a moment's leisure, for four weeks; I sought her on Sundays all day long; I sought her on the Boulevards, in the Allée Verte, in the Park; I sought her in Ste Gudule and St Jacques; I sought her in the two Protestant chapels; I attended these latter at the German,

French and English services, not doubting that I should meet
her at one of them. All my researches were absolutely fruitless;
my security on the last point was proved by the event to be
equally groundless with my other calculations. I stood at the
door of each chapel after the service, and waited till every
individual had come out, scrutinizing every gown draping a
slender form, peering under every bonnet covering a young
head. In vain; I saw girlish figures pass me, drawing their black
scarfs over their sloping shoulders, but none of them had the
exact turn and air of Mdlle Henri's; I saw pale and thoughtful
faces 'encadrées' in bands of brown hair, but I never found her
forehead, her eyes, her eyebrows. All the features of all the faces
I met seemed frittered away, because my eye failed to recognize
the peculiarities it was bent upon – an ample space of brow
and a large, dark, and serious eye, with a fine but decided line
of eyebrow traced above.

'She has probably left Brussels – perhaps is gone to England,
as she said she would,' muttered I, inwardly, as on the afternoon
of the fourth Sunday, I turned from the door of the chapel-
royal which the doorkeeper had just closed and locked, and
followed in the wake of the last of the congregation, now
dispersed and dispersing over the square. I had soon outwalked
the couples of English gentlemen and ladies. (Gracious goodness! why don't they dress better? My eye is yet filled with
visions of the high-flounced, slovenly, and tumbled dresses in
costly silk and satin; of the large, unbecoming collars in expensive lace; of the ill-cut coats and strangely fashioned pantaloons
which every Sunday, at the English service, filled the chairs of
the chapel-royal, and after it, issuing forth into the square,
came into disadvantageous contrast with freshly and trimly
attired foreign figures, hastening to attend salut at the church
of Coburg.) I had passed these pairs of Britons, and the groups
of pretty British children, and the British footmen and waiting-
maids; I had crossed the Place Royale, and got into the Rue
Royale, thence I had diverged into the Rue de Louvain – an

old and quiet street. I remember that, feeling a little hungry, and not desiring to go back and take my share of the 'goûter', now on the refectory-table at Pelet's – to wit, pistolets and water – I stepped into a baker's and refreshed myself on a *couc* (?) – it is a Flemish word, I don't know how to spell it – *à Corinthe* – *anglice*, a currant bun – and a cup of coffee; and then I strolled on towards the Porte de Louvain. Very soon I was out of the city, and slowly mounting the hill, which ascends from the gate, I took my time; for the afternoon, though cloudy, was very sultry, and not a breeze stirred to refresh the atmosphere. No inhabitant of Brussels need wander far to search for solitude; let him but move half a league from his own city and he will find her brooding still and blank over the wide fields, so drear though so fertile, spread out treeless and trackless round the capital of Brabant. Having gained the summit of the hill, and having stood and looked long over the cultured but lifeless campaign, I felt a wish to quit the high road, which I had hitherto followed, and get in among those tilled grounds – fertile as the beds of a Brobdingnagian kitchen-garden – spreading far and wide even to the boundaries of the horizon, where, from a dusk green, distance changed them to a sullen blue, and confused their tints with those of the livid and thunderous-looking sky. Accordingly I turned up a by-path to the right; I had not followed it far ere it brought me, as I expected, into the fields, amidst which, just before me, stretched a long and lofty white wall enclosing, as it seemed from the foliage showing above, some thickly planted nursery of yew and cypress, for of that species were the branches resting on the pale parapets, and crowding gloomily about a massive cross, planted doubtless on a central eminence and extending its arms, which seemed of black marble, over the summits of those sinister trees I approached, wondering to what house this well-protected garden appertained; I turned the angle of the wall, thinking to see some stately residence; I was close upon great iron gates; there was a hut serving for a lodge near, but I had no occasion to apply for the key – the gates were open; I pushed one leaf back – rain had rusted its hinges, for it groaned dolefully as they revolved. Thick planting embowered the entrance. Passing up the avenue, I saw objects on each hand which, in their own mute language of inscription and sign, explained clearly to what abode I had made my way. This was the house appointed for all living; crosses, monuments, and garlands of everlastings announced 'The Protestant Cemetery, outside the gate of Louvain.'

The place was large enough to afford half an hour's strolling without the monotony of treading continually the same path; and, for those who love to peruse the annals of graveyards, here was variety of inscription enough to occupy the attention for double or treble that space of time. Hither people of many kindreds, tongues, and nations had brought their dead for interment; and here, on pages of stone, of marble, and of brass, were written names, dates, last tributes of pomp or love, in English, in French, in German, and Latin. Here the Englishman had erected a marble monument over the remains of his Mary Smith or Jane Brown, and inscribed it only with her name. There the French widower had shaded the grave of his Elmire or Celestine with a brilliant thicket of roses, amidst which a little tablet rising bore an equally bright testimony to her count-less virtues. Every nation, tribe, and kindred mourned after its own fashion; and how soundless was the mourning of all! My own tread, though slow and upon smooth-rolled paths, seemed to startle, because it formed the sole break to a silence otherwise total. Not only the winds, but the very fitful, wandering airs were that afternoon, as by common consent, all fallen asleep in their various quarters; the north was hushed, the south silent, the east sobbed not, nor did the west whisper. The clouds in heaven were condensed and dull, but apparently quite motion-less. Under the trees of this cemetery nestled a warm, breathless gloom, out of which the cypresses stood up straight and mute, above which the willows hung low and still; where the flowers,

as languid as fair, waited listless for night dew or thunder-
shower; where the tombs, and those they hid, lay impassible to
sun or shadow, to rain or drought.

Importuned by the sound of my own footsteps, I turned off
upon the turf, and slowly advanced to a grove of yews; I saw
something stir among the stems; I thought it might be a broken
branch swinging, my short-sighted vision had caught no form,
only a sense of motion; but the dusky shade passed on, appearing and disappearing at the openings in the avenue. I soon
discerned it was a living thing, and a human being; and, drawing
nearer, I perceived it was a woman, pacing slowly to and fro,
and evidently deeming herself alone as I had deemed myself
alone, and meditating as I had been meditating. Ere long she
returned to a seat which I fancy she had but just quitted, or
I should have caught sight of her before. It was in a nook,
screened by a clump of trees; there was the white wall before
her, and a little stone set up against the wall, and at the foot of
the stone was an allotment of turf freshly turned up, a new-
made grave. I put on my spectacles, and passed softly close
behind her; glancing at the inscription on the stone, I read,
'Julienne Henri, died at Brussels, aged sixty. August 10th,
18—.' Having perused the inscription, I looked down at the
form sitting bent and thoughtful just under my eyes, unconscious of the vicinity of any living thing; it was a slim,
youthful figure in mourning apparel of the plainest black stuff,
with a little, simple, black crape bonnet; I felt, as well as saw,
who it was; and, moving neither hand nor foot, I stood for
some moments enjoying the security of conviction. I had sought
her for a month, and had never discovered one of her traces –
never met a hope, or seized a chance of encountering her anywhere. I had been forced to loosen my grasp on expectation;
and, but an hour ago, had sunk slackly under the discouraging
thought that the current of life, and the impulse of destiny, had
swept her for ever from my reach; and, behold, while bending
suddenly earthward beneath the pressure of despondency –

while following with my eyes the track of sorrow on the turf of a graveyard – here was my lost jewel dropped on the tear-fed herbage, nestling in the mossy and mouldy roots of yew-trees.

Frances sat very quiet, her elbow on her knee, and her head on her hand. I knew she could retain a thinking attitude a long time without change; at last, a tear fell; she had been looking at the name on the stone before her, and her heart had no doubt endured one of those constrictions with which the desolate living, regretting the dead, are, at times, so sorely oppressed. Many tears rolled down, which she wiped away, again and again, with her handkerchief; some distressed sobs escaped her, and then, the paroxysm over, she sat quiet as before. I put my hand gently on her shoulder; no need further to prepare her, for she was neither hysterical nor liable to fainting-fits; a sudden push, indeed, might have startled her, but the contact of my quiet touch merely woke attention as I wished; and though she turned quickly, yet so lightning-swift is thought – in some minds especially – I believe the wonder of what – the consciousness of who it was that thus stole unawares on her solitude, had passed through her brain, and flashed into her heart, even before she had effected that hasty movement; at least, Amazement had hardly opened her eyes and raised them to mine, ere Recognition informed their irids with most speaking brightness. Nervous surprise had hardly discomposed her features ere a sentiment of most vivid joy shone clear and warm on her whole countenance. I had hardly time to observe that she was wasted and pale, ere called to feel a responsive inward pleasure by the sense of most full and exquisite pleasure glowing in the animated flush, and shining in the expansive light, now diffused over my pupil's face. It was the summer sun flashing out after the heavy summer shower; and what fertilizes more rapidly than that beam, burning almost like fire in its ardour?

I hate boldness – that boldness which is of the brassy brow and insensate nerves; but I love the courage of the strong heart, the fervour of the generous blood; I loved with passion the light of Frances Evans' clear hazel eye when it did not fear to look straight into mine; I loved the tones with which she uttered the words –

'Mon maître! mon maître!'

I loved the movement with which she confided her hand to my hand; I loved her as she stood there, penniless and parentless; for a sensualist charmless, for me a treasure – my best object of sympathy on earth, thinking such thoughts as I thought, feeling such feelings as I felt, my ideal of the shrine in which to seal my stores of love; personification of discretion and forethought, of diligence and perseverance, of self-denial and self-control – those guardians, those trusty keepers of the gift I longed to confer on her – the gift of all my affections; model of truth and honour, of independence and conscientiousness – those refiners and sustainers of an honest life; silent possessor of a well of tenderness, of a flame, as genial as still, as pure as quenchless, of natural feeling, natural passion – those sources of refreshment and comfort to the sanctuary of home. I knew how quietly and how deeply the well bubbled in her heart; I knew how the more dangerous flame burned safely under the eye of reason; I had seen when the fire shot up a moment high and vivid, when the accelerated heat troubled life's current in its channels; I had seen reason reduce the rebel, and humble its blaze to embers. I had confidence in Frances Evans; I had respect for her, and as I drew her arm through mine, and led her out of the cemetery, I felt I had another sentiment, as strong as confidence, as firm as respect, more fervid than either – that of love.

'Well, my pupil,' said I, as the ominous-sounding gate swung to behind us – 'Well, I have found you again: a month's search has seemed long, and I little thought to have discovered my lost sheep straying amongst graves.'

Never had I addressed her but as 'Mademoiselle' before, and to speak thus was to take up a tone new to both her and me. Her answer apprised me that this language ruffled none of her feelings, woke no discord in her heart –

'Mon maître,' she said, 'have you troubled yourself to seek me? I little imagined you would think much of my absence, but I grieved bitterly to be taken away from you. I was sorry for that circumstance when heavier troubles ought to have made me forget it.'

'Your aunt is dead?'

'Yes, a fortnight since, and she died full of regret, which I could not chase from her mind; she kept repeating, even during the last night of her existence, 'Frances, you will be so lonely when I am gone, so friendless': she wished, too, that she could have been buried in Switzerland, and it was I who persuaded her in her old age to leave the banks of Lake Leman, and to come, only as it seems to die, in this flat region of Flanders. Willingly would I have observed her last wish, and taken her remains back to our own country, but that was impossible; I was forced to lay her here.'

'She was ill but a short time, I presume?'

'But three weeks. When she began to sink I asked Mdlle Reuter's leave to stay with her and wait on her; I readily got leave.'

'Do you return to the pensionnat?' I demanded hastily.

'Monsieur, when I had been at home a week Mdlle Reuter called one evening, just after I had got my aunt to bed; she went into her room to speak to her, and was extremely civil and affable, as she always is; afterwards she came and sat with me a long time, and just as she rose to go away, she said: "Mademoiselle, I shall not soon cease to regret your departure from my establishment, though indeed it is true that you have taught your class of pupils so well that they are all quite accomplished in the little works you manage so skilfully, and have not the slightest need of further instruction; my second teacher must in future supply your place, with regard to the younger pupils, as well as she can, though she is indeed an inferior artiste to you, and doubtless it will be your part now to assume a higher position in your calling; I am sure you will everywhere

find schools and families willing to profit by your talents."
And then she paid me my last quarter's salary. I asked, as
mademoiselle would no doubt think, very bluntly, if she
designed to discharge me from her establishment. She smiled
at my inelegance of speech, and answered that "our connection
as employer and employed was certainly dissolved, but that she
hoped still to retain the pleasure of my acquaintance; she should
always be happy to see me as a friend"; and then she said something about the excellent condition of the streets, and the long
continuance of fine weather, and went away quite cheerful.'

I laughed inwardly; all this was so like the directress – so like
what I had expected and guessed of her conduct; and then the
exposure and proof of her lie, unconsciously afforded by
Frances: – 'She had frequently applied for Mdlle Henri's
address,' forsooth; 'Mdlle Henri had always evaded giving it,'
etc., etc., and here I found her a visitor at the very house of
whose locality she had professed absolute ignorance!

Any comments I might have intended to make on my pupil's
communication were checked by the plashing of large raindrops
on our faces and on the path, and by the muttering of a distant
but coming storm. The warning obvious in stagnant air and
leaden sky had already induced me to take the road leading
back to Brussels, and now I hastened my own steps and those
of my companion, and, as our way lay downhill, we got on
rapidly. There was an interval after the fall of the first broad
drops before heavy rain came on; in the meantime we had
passed through the Porte de Louvain, and were again in the city.

'Where do you live?' I asked; 'I will see you safe home.'

'Rue Notre Dame aux Neiges,' answered Frances.

It was not far from the Rue de Louvain, and we stood on
the doorsteps of the house we sought ere the clouds, severing
with loud peal and shattered cataract of lightning, emptied
their livid folds in a torrent, heavy, prone, and broad.

'Come in! come in!' said Frances, as, after putting her into
the house, I paused ere I followed: the word decided me;

I stepped across the threshold, shut the door on the rushing, flashing, whitening storm, and followed her upstairs to her apartments. Neither she nor I were wet; a projection over the door had warded off the straight-descending flood; none but the first large drops had touched our garments; one minute more and we should not have had a dry thread on us.

Stepping over a little mat of green wool, I found myself in a small room with a painted floor and a square of green carpet in the middle; the articles of furniture were few, but all bright and exquisitely clean; order reigned through its narrow limits – such order as it soothed my punctilious soul to behold. And I had hesitated to enter the abode, because I apprehended after all that Mdlle Reuter's hint about its extreme poverty might be too well founded, and I feared to embarrass the lace-mender by entering her lodgings unawares! Poor the place might be; poor, truly, it was; but its neatness was better than elegance, and had but a bright little fire shone on that clean hearth, I should have deemed it more attractive than a palace. No fire was there, however, and no fuel laid ready to light; the lace-mender was unable to allow herself that indulgence, especially now when, deprived by death of her sole relative, she had only her own unaided exertions to rely on. Frances went into an inner room to take off her bonnet, and she came out a model of frugal neatness, with her well-fitting black stuff dress, so accurately defining her elegant bust and taper waist, with her spotless white collar turned back from a fair and shapely neck, with her plenteous brown hair arranged in smooth bands on her temples, and in a large Grecian plait behind: ornaments she had none – neither brooch, ring, nor ribbon; she did well enough without them – perfection of fit, proportion of form, grace of carriage, agreeably supplied their place. Her eye, as she re-entered the small sitting-room, instantly sought mine, which was just then lingering on the hearth; I knew she read at once the sort of inward ruth and pitying pain which the chill vacancy of that hearth stirred in my soul: quick to penetrate, quick to determine, and quicker to put in practice, she had in a moment tied a holland apron round her waist; then she disappeared, and reappeared with a basket; it had a cover; she opened it, and produced wood and coal; deftly and compactly she arranged them in the grate.

'It is her whole stock, and she will exhaust it out of hospitality,' thought I.

'What are you going to do?' I asked; 'not surely to light a fire this hot evening? I shall be smothered.'

'Indeed, monsieur, I feel it very chilly since the rain began; besides, I must boil the water for my tea, for I take tea on Sundays; you will be obliged to try and bear the heat.'

She had struck a light; the wood was already in a blaze; and truly, when contrasted with the darkness, the wild tumult of the tempest without, that peaceful glow which began to beam on the now animated hearth, seemed very cheering. A low, purring sound, from some quarter, announced that another being, besides myself, was pleased with the change; a black cat, roused by the light from its sleep on a little cushioned footstool, came and rubbed its head against Frances' gown as she knelt; she caressed it, saying it had been a favourite with her 'pauvre tante Julienne'.

The fire being lit, the hearth swept, and a small kettle of a very antique pattern, such as I thought I remembered to have seen in old farm-houses in England, placed over the now ruddy flame, Frances' hands were washed, and her apron removed in an instant; then she opened a cupboard, and took out a tea-tray, on which she had soon arranged a china tea-equipage, whose pattern, shape, and size denoted a remote antiquity; a little, old-fashioned silver spoon was deposited in each saucer; and a pair of silver tongs, equally old-fashioned, were laid on the sugar-basin; from the cupboard, too, was produced a tiny silver cream-ewer, not larger than an egg-shell. While making these preparations, she chanced to look up, and, reading curiosity in my eyes, she smiled and asked –

'Is this like England, monsieur?'

'Like the England of a hundred years ago,' I replied.

'Is it truly? Well, everything on this tray is at least a hundred years old: these cups, these spoons, this ewer are all heirlooms; my great-grandmother left them to my grandmother, she to my mother, and my mother brought them with her from England to Switzerland, and left them to me; and, ever since I was a little girl, I have thought I should like to carry them back to England, whence they came.'

She put some pistolets on the table; she made the tea, as foreigners do make tea – *i.e.* at the rate of a teaspoonful to half a dozen cups; she placed me in a chair, and, as I took it, she asked, with a sort of exultation –

'Will it make you think yourself at home for a moment?'

'If I had a home in England, I believe it would recall it,' I answered; and, in truth, there was a sort of illusion in seeing the fair-complexioned, English-looking girl presiding at the English meal, and speaking in the English language.

'You have then no home?' was her remark.

'None, nor ever have had. If ever I possess a home, it must be of my own making, and the task is yet to begin.' And, as I spoke, a pang, new to me, shot across my heart: it was a pang of mortification at the humility of my position, and the inadequacy of my means; while with that pang was born a strong desire to do more, earn more, be more, possess more; and in the increased possessions, my roused and eager spirit panted to include the home I had never had, the wife I inwardly vowed to win.

Frances' tea was little better than hot water, sugar, and milk; and her pistolets, with which she could not offer me butter, were sweet to my palate as manna.

The repast over, and the treasured plate and porcelain being washed and put by, the bright table rubbed still brighter, 'le chat de ma tante Julienne' also being fed with provisions brought forth on a plate for its special use, a few stray cinders, and a scattering of ashes too, being swept from the hearth, Frances at last sat down; and then, as she took a chair opposite to me, she betrayed, for the first time, a little embarrassment, and no wonder, for indeed I had unconsciously watched her rather too closely, followed all her steps and all her movements a little too perseveringly with my eyes, for she mesmerized me by the grace and alertness of her action – by the deft, cleanly, and even decorative effect resulting from each touch of her slight and fine fingers; and when, at last, she subsided to stillness, the intelligence of her face seemed beauty to me, and I dwelt on it accordingly. Her colour, however, rising, rather than settling with repose, and her eyes remaining downcast, though I kept waiting for the lids to be raised that I might drink a ray of the light I loved – a light where fire dissolved in softness, where affection tempered penetration, where, just now at least, pleasure played with thought – this expectation not being gratified, I began at last to suspect that I had probably myself to blame for the disappointment; I must cease gazing, and begin talking, if I wished to break the spell under which she now sat motionless; so recollecting the composing effect which an authoritative tone and manner had ever been wont to produce on her, I said –

'Get one of your English books, mademoiselle, for the rain yet falls heavily, and will probably detain me half an hour longer.'

Released, and set at ease, up she rose, got her book, and accepted at once the chair I placed for her at my side. She had selected 'Paradise Lost' from her shelf of classics, thinking, I suppose, the religious character of the book best adapted it to Sunday; I told her to begin at the beginning, and while she read Milton's invocation to that heavenly muse, who on the 'secret top of Oreb or Sinai' had taught the Hebrew shepherd how in the womb of chaos the conception of a world had originated and ripened, I enjoyed, undisturbed, the treble pleasure of having her near me, hearing the sound of her voice – a sound sweet and satisfying in my ear – and looking, by intervals, at her face: of this last privilege, I chiefly availed myself when I found fault with an intonation, a pause, or an emphasis; as long as I dogmatized, I might also gaze, without exciting too warm a flush.

'Enough,' said I, when she had gone through some half-dozen pages (a work of time with her, for she read slowly and paused often to ask and receive information), 'enough; and now the rain is ceasing, and I must soon go.' For indeed, at that moment, looking towards the window, I saw it all blue; the thunder-clouds were broken and scattered, and the setting August sun sent a gleam like the reflection of rubies through the lattice. I got up; I drew on my gloves.

'You have not yet found another situation to supply the place of that from which you were dismissed by Mdlle Reuter?'

'No, monsieur; I have made inquiries everywhere, but they all ask me for references; and to speak truth, I do not like to apply to the directress, because I consider she acted neither justly nor honourably towards me; she used underhand means to set my pupils against me, and thereby render me unhappy while I held my place in her establishment, and she eventually deprived me of it by a masked and hypocritical manœuvre, pretending that she was acting for my good, but really snatching from me my chief means of subsistence, at a crisis when not only my own life, but that of another, depended on my exertions: of her I will never more ask a favour.'

'How, then, do you propose to get on? How do you live now?'

'I have still my lace-mending trade; with care it will keep me from starvation, and I doubt not by dint of exertion to get better employment yet; it is only a fortnight since I began to try; my courage or hopes are by no means worn out yet.'

'And if you get what you wish, what then? what are your ultimate views?'

'To save enough to cross the Channel: I always look to England as my Canaan.'

'Well, well – ere long I shall pay you another visit; good evening now,' and I left her rather abruptly; I had much ado to resist a strong inward impulse, urging me to take a warmer, more expressive leave: what so natural as to fold her for a moment in a close embrace, to imprint one kiss on her cheek or forehead? I was not unreasonable – that was all I wanted; satisfied in that point, I could go away content; and Reason denied me even this; she ordered me to turn my eyes from her face, and my steps from her apartment – to quit her as dryly and coldly as I would have quitted old Madame Pelet. I obeyed, but I swore rancorously to be avenged one day. 'I'll earn a right to do as I please in this matter, or I'll die in the contest. I have one object before me now – to get that Genevese girl for my wife; and my wife she shall be – that is, provided she has as much, or half as much regard for her master as he has for her. And would she be so docile, so smiling, so happy under my instructions if she had not? Would she sit at my side when I dictate or correct, with such a still, contented, halcyon mien?' For I had ever remarked, that however sad or harassed her countenance might be when I entered a room, yet after I had been near her, spoken to her a few words, given her some directions, uttered perhaps some reproofs, she would, all at once, nestle into a nook of happiness, and look up serene and revived. The reproofs suited her best of all: while I scolded she would chip away with her pen-knife at a pencil or a pen, fidgeting a little, pouting a little, defending herself by mono-syllables; and when I deprived her of the pen or pencil, fearing it would be all cut away, and when I interdicted even the monosyllabic defence, for the purpose of working up the sub-dued excitement a little higher, she would at last raise her eyes and give me a certain glance, sweetened with gaiety, and pointed with defiance, which, to speak truth, thrilled me as nothing had ever done, and made me, in a fashion (though happily she did not know it), her subject, if not her slave. After such little scenes her spirits would maintain their flow, often for some hours, and, as I remarked before, her health therefrom took a sustenance and vigour which, previously to the event of her aunt's death and her dismissal, had almost recreated her whole frame.

It has taken me several minutes to write these last sentences; but I had thought all their purport during the brief interval of descending the stairs from Frances' room. Just as I was opening the outer door, I remembered the twenty francs which I had not restored; I paused: impossible to carry them away with me; difficult to force them back on their original owner; I had now seen her in her own humble abode, witnessed the dignity of her poverty, the pride of order, the fastidious care of conservatism, obvious in the arrangement and economy of her little home; I was sure she would not suffer herself to be excused paying her debts; I was certain the favour of indemnity would be accepted from no hand, perhaps least of all from mine: yet these four five-franc pieces were a burden to my self-respect, and I must get rid of them. An expedient – a clumsy one no doubt, but the best I could devise – suggested itself to me. I darted up the stairs, knocked, re-entered the room as if in haste –

'Mademoiselle, I have forgotten one of my gloves; I must have left it here.'

She instantly rose to seek it; as she turned her back, I – being now at the hearth – noiselessly lifted a little vase – one of a set of china ornaments, as old-fashioned as the tea-cups – slipped the money under it, then saying – 'Oh, here is my glove! I had dropped it within the fender; good evening, mademoiselle,' I made my second exit.

Brief as my impromptu return had been, it had afforded me time to pick up a heartache; I remarked that Frances had already removed the red embers of her cheerful little fire from the grate: forced to calculate every item, to save in every detail, she had instantly on my departure retrenched a luxury too expensive to be enjoyed alone.

'I am glad it is not yet winter,' thought I; 'but in two months more come the winds and rains of November; would to God that before then I could earn the right, and the power, to shovel coals into that grate *ad libitum*!'

Already the pavement was drying; a balmy and fresh breeze stirred the air, purified by lightning; I left the West behind me, where spread a sky like opal; azure inmingled with crimson: the enlarged sun, glorious in Tyrian tints, dipped his brim already; stepping, as I was, eastward, I faced a vast bank of clouds, but also I had before me the arch of an evening rainbow; a perfect rainbow – high, wide, vivid. I looked long; my eye drank in the scene, and I suppose my brain must have absorbed it; for that night, after lying awake in pleasant fever a long time, watching the silent sheet-lightning, which still played among the retreating clouds, and flashed silvery over the stars, I at last fell asleep; and then in a dream were reproduced the setting sun, the bank of clouds, the mighty rainbow. I stood, methought, on a terrace; I leaned over a parapeted wall; there was space below me, depth I could not fathom, but hearing an endless dash of waves, I believed it to be the sea – sea spread to the horizon; sea of changeful green and intense blue: all was soft in the distance; all vapour-veiled. A spark of gold glistened on the line between water and air, floated up, approached, enlarged, changed; the object hung midway between heaven and earth, under the arch of the rainbow; the soft but dusk clouds diffused behind. It hovered as on wings; pearly, fleecy, gleaming air streamed like raiment round it: light, tinted with carnation, coloured what seemed face and limbs; a large star shone with still lustre on an angel's forehead; an uplifted arm and hand, glancing like a ray, pointed to the bow overhead, and a voice in my heart whispered –

'Hope smiles on Effort!'

CHAPTER XX

A COMPETENCY was what I wanted; a competency it was now my aim and resolve to secure; but never had I been farther from the mark. With August the school-year (l'année scolaire) closed, the examinations concluded, the prizes were adjudged, the schools dispersed, the gates of all colleges, the doors of all pensionnats shut, not to be reopened till the beginning or middle of October. The last day of August was at hand, and what was my position? Had I advanced a step since the commencement of the past quarter? On the contrary, I had receded one. By renouncing my engagement as English master in Mdlle Reuter's establishment, I had voluntarily cut off £20 from my yearly income; I had diminished my £60 per annum to £40, and even that sum I now held by a very precarious tenure.

It is some time since I made any reference to M. Pelet. The moonlight walk is, I think, the last incident recorded in this narrative where that gentleman cuts any conspicuous figure: the fact is, since that event, a change had come over the spirit of our intercourse. He, indeed, ignorant that the still hour, a cloudless moon, and an open lattice had revealed to me the secret of his selfish love and false friendship, would have continued smooth and complaisant as ever; but I grew spiny as a porcupine, and inflexible as a blackthorn cudgel; I never had a smile for his raillery, never a moment for his society; his invitations to take coffee with him in his parlour were invariably rejected, and very stiffly and sternly rejected too; his jesting allusions to the directress (which he still continued) were heard with a grim calm very different from the petulant pleasure they were formerly wont to excite. For a long time Pelet bore with my frigid demeanour very patiently; he even increased his attentions; but finding that even a cringing politeness failed to thaw or move me, he at last altered too; in his turn he cooled; his invitations ceased; his countenance became suspicious and overcast, and I read in the perplexed yet brooding aspect of his brow a constant examination and comparison of premises, and an anxious endeavour to draw thence some explanatory inference. Ere long, I fancy, he succeeded, for he was not without penetration; perhaps, too, Mdlle Zoraïde might have aided him in the solution of the enigma; at any rate I soon found that the uncertainty of doubt had vanished from his manner; renouncing all pretence of friendship and cordiality, he adopted a reserved, formal, but still scrupulously polite deportment. This was the point to which I had wished to bring him, and I was now again comparatively at my ease. I did not, it is true, like my position in his house; but being freed from the annoyance of false professions and double-dealing I could endure it, especially as no heroic sentiment of hatred or jealousy of the director distracted my philosophical soul; he had not, I found, wounded me in a very tender point, the wound was so soon and so radically healed, leaving only a sense of contempt for the treacherous fashion in which it had been inflicted, and a lasting mistrust of the hand which I had detected attempting to stab in the dark.

This state of things continued till about the middle of July, and then there was a little change; Pelet came home one night, an hour after his usual time, in a state of unequivocal intoxication, a thing anomalous with him; for if he had some of the worst faults of his countrymen, he had also one at least of their virtues, *i.e.* sobriety. So drunk, however, was he on this occasion, that after having roused the whole establishment (except the pupils, whose dormitory, being over the classes in a building apart from the dwelling-house, was consequently out of the reach of disturbance) by violently ringing the hall-bell and ordering lunch to be brought in immediately, for he imagined it was noon, whereas the city bells had just tolled midnight; after having furiously rated the servants for their want of punctuality, and gone near to chastise his poor old mother, who advised him to go to bed, he began raving dreadfully about 'le maudit Anglais, Creemsvort'. I had not yet retired; some German books I had got hold of had kept me up late; I heard the uproar below, and could distinguish the director's voice exalted in a manner as appalling as it was unusual. Opening my door a little, I became aware of a demand on his part for 'Creemsvort' to be brought down to him that he might cut his throat on the hall-table and wash his honour, which he affirmed to be in a dirty condition, in infernal British blood. 'He is either mad or drunk,' thought I, 'and in either case the old woman and the servants will be the better of a man's assistance,' so I descended straight to the hall. I found him staggering about, his eyes in a fine frenzy rolling – a pretty sight he was, a just medium between the fool and the lunatic.

'Come, M. Pelet,' said I, 'you had better go to bed,' and I took hold of his arm. His excitement, of course, increased greatly at sight and touch of the individual for whose blood he had been making application: he struggled and struck with fury – but a drunken man is no match for a sober one; and, even in his normal state, Pelet's worn-out frame could not have stood against my sound one. I got him upstairs, and, in process of time, to bed. During the operation he did not fail to utter comminations which, though broken, had a sense in them; while stigmatizing me as the treacherous spawn of a perfidious country, he, in the same breath, anathematized Zoraïde Reuter; he termed her 'femme sotte et vicieuse', who, in a fit of lewd caprice, had thrown herself away on an unprincipled adven-turer; directing the point of the last appellation by a furious blow, obliquely aimed at me. I left him in the act of bounding elastically out of the bed into which I had tucked him; but, as I took the precaution of turning the key in the door behind me, I retired to my own room, assured of his safe custody till morning, and free to draw undisturbed conclusions from the scene I had just witnessed.

Now, it was precisely about this time that the directress, stung by my coldness, bewitched by my scorn, and excited by the preference she suspected me of cherishing for another, had fallen into a snare of her own laying – was herself caught in the meshes of the very passion with which she wished to entangle me. Conscious of the state of things in that quarter, I gathered, from the condition in which I saw my employer, that his ladye-love had betrayed the alienation of her affections – inclinations, rather, I would say; affection is a word at once too warm and too pure for the subject – had let him see that the cavity of her hollow heart, emptied of his image, was now occupied by that of his usher. It was not without some surprise that I found myself obliged to entertain this view of the case; Pelet, with his old-established school, was so convenient, so profitable a match – Zoraïde was so calculating, so interested a woman – I wondered mere personal preference could, in her mind, have prevailed for a moment over worldly advantage: yet, it was evident, from what Pelet said, that, not only had she repulsed him, but had even let slip expressions of partiality for me. One of his drunken exclamations was, 'And the jade doats on your youth, you raw blockhead! and talks of your noble deportment, as she calls your accursed English formality – and your pure morals, forsooth! des mœurs de Caton a-t-elle dit – sotte!' Hers, I thought, must be a curious soul, where, in spite of a strong, natural tendency to estimate unduly advantages of wealth and station, the sardonic disdain of a fortuneless subordinate had wrought a deeper impression than could be imprinted by the most flattering assiduities of a prosperous *chef d'institution.* I smiled inwardly; and strange to say, though my *amour-propre* was excited not disagreeably by the conquest, my better feelings remained untouched. Next day, when I saw the directress, and when she made an excuse to meet me in the corridor, and besought my notice by a demeanour and look subdued to Helot humility, I could not love, I could scarcely pity her. To answer briefly and dryly some insinuating inquiry about my health – to pass her by with a stern bow – was all I could; her presence and manner had then, and for some time previously and subsequently, a singular effect upon me; they sealed up all that was good, elicited all that was noxious in my nature; sometimes they enervated my senses, but they always hardened my heart. I was aware of the detriment done, and quarrelled with myself for the change. I had ever hated a tyrant; and, behold, the possession of a slave, self-given, went near to transform me into what I abhorred! There was at once a sort of low gratification in receiving this luscious incense from an attractive and still young worshipper; and an irritating sense of degradation in the very experience of the pleasure. When she stole about me with the soft step of a slave, I felt at once barbarous and sensual as a pasha. I endured her homage sometimes; sometimes I rebuked it. My indifference or harshness served equally to increase the evil I desired to check.

'Que le dédain lui sied bien!' I once overheard her say to her mother: 'il est beau comme Apollon quand il sourit de son air hautain.'

And the jolly old dame laughed, and said she thought her daughter was bewitched, for I had no point of a handsome man about me, except being straight and without deformity. 'Pour moi,' she continued, 'il me fait tout l'effet d'un chat-huant, avec ses bésicles.'

Worthy old girl! I could have gone and kissed her had she not been a little too old, too fat, and too red-faced; her sensible, truthful words seemed so wholesome, contrasted with the morbid illusions of her daughter.

When Pelet awoke on the morning after his frenzy fit, he retained no recollection of what had happened the previous night, and his mother fortunately had the discretion to refrain from informing him that I had been a witness of his degradation. He did not again have recourse to wine for curing his griefs, but even in his sober mood he soon showed that the iron of jealousy had entered into his soul. A thorough Frenchman, the national characteristic of ferocity had not been omitted by nature in compounding the ingredients of his character; it had appeared first in his access of drunken wrath, when some of his demonstrations of hatred to my person were of a truly fiendish character, and now it was more covertly betrayed by momentary contractions of the features, and flashes of fierceness in his light blue eyes, when their glance chanced to encounter mine. He absolutely avoided speaking to me; I was now spared even the falsehood of his politeness. In this state of our mutual relations my soul rebelled, sometimes almost ungovernably, against living in the house and discharging the service of such a man; but who is free from the constraint of circumstances? At that time, I was not: I used to rise each morning eager to shake off his yoke, and go out with my portmanteau under my arm, if a beggar, at least a freeman; and in the evening, when I came back from the pensionnat de demoiselles, a certain pleasant voice in my ear; a certain face, so intelligent, yet so docile, so reflective, yet so soft, in my eyes; a certain cast of character, at once proud and pliant, sensitive and sagacious, serious and ardent, in my head; a certain tone of feeling, fervid and modest, refined and practical, pure and powerful, delighting and troubling my memory – visions of new ties I longed to contract, of new duties I longed to undertake, had taken the rover and the rebel out of me, and had shown endurance of my hated lot in the light of a Spartan virtue.

But Pelet's fury subsided; a fortnight sufficed for its rise, progress and extinction: in that space of time the dismissal of the obnoxious teacher had been effected in the neighbouring house, and in the same interval I had declared my resolution to follow and find out my pupil, and upon my application for her address being refused, I had summarily resigned my own post. This last act seemed at once to restore Mdlle Reuter to her senses; her sagacity, her judgment, so long misled by a fascinating delusion, struck again into the right track the moment that delusion vanished. By the right track, I do not mean the steep and difficult path of principle – in that path she never trod; but the plain highway of common sense, from which she had of late widely diverged. When there she carefully sought, and, having found, industriously pursued the trail of her old suitor, M. Pelet. She soon overtook him. What arts she employed to soothe and blind him I know not, but she succeeded both in allaying his wrath and hoodwinking his discernment, as was soon proved by the alteration in his mien and manner; she must have managed to convince him that I neither was, nor ever had been, a rival of his, for the fortnight of fury against me terminated in a fit of exceeding graciousness and amenity, not unmixed with a dash of exulting self-complacency, more ludi-crous than irritating. Pelet's bachelor's life had been passed in proper French style with due disregard to moral restraint, and I thought his married life promised to be very French also. He often boasted to me what a terror he had been to certain husbands of his acquaintance; I perceived it would not now be difficult to pay him back in his own coin.

The crisis drew on. No sooner had the holidays commenced than note of preparation for some momentous event sounded all through the premises of Pelet; painters, polishers, and uphol-sterers were immediately set to work, and there was talk of 'la chambre de Madame', 'le salon de Madame'. Not deeming it probable that the old duenna at present graced with that title in our house, had inspired her son with such enthusiasm of filial piety as to induce him to fit up apartments expressly for her use, I concluded, in common with the cook, the two housemaids, and the kitchen-scullion, that a new and more juvenile Madame was destined to be the tenant of these gay chambers.

Presently official announcement of the coming event was put forth. In another week's time M. François Pelet, directeur, and Mdlle Zoraïde Reuter, directrice, were to be joined together in the bands of matrimony. Monsieur, in person, heralded the fact to me; terminating his communication by an obliging expression of his desire that I should continue, as heretofore, his ablest assistant and most trusted friend; and a proposition to raise my salary by an additional two hundred francs per annum. I thanked him, gave no conclusive answer at the time, and, when he had left me, threw off my blouse, put on my coat, and set out on a long walk outside the Porte de Flandre, in order, as I thought, to cool my blood, calm my nerves, and shake my disarranged ideas into some order. In fact, I had just received what was virtually my dismissal. I could not conceal, I did not desire to conceal from myself the conviction that, being now certain that Mdlle Reuter was destined to become Madame Pelet, it would not do for me to remain a dependent dweller in the house, which was soon to be hers. Her present demeanour towards me was deficient neither in dignity nor propriety; but I knew her former feeling was unchanged. Decorum now repressed, and Policy masked it, but Opportunity would be too strong for either of these – Temptation would shiver their restraints.

I was no pope – I could not boast infallibility: in short, if I stayed, the probability was that, in three months' time, a practical modern French novel would be in full process of concoction under the roof of the unsuspecting Pelet. Now, modern French novels are not to my taste, either practically or theoretically. Limited as had yet been my experience of life, I had once had the opportunity of contemplating, near at hand, an example of the results produced by a course of interesting and romantic domestic treachery. No golden halo of fiction was about this example, I saw it bare and real, and it was very loathsome. I saw a mind degraded by the practice of mean subterfuge, by the habit of perfidious deception, and a body depraved by the infectious influence of the vice-polluted soul. I had suffered much from the forced and prolonged view of this spectacle; those sufferings I did not now regret, for their simple recollection acted as a most wholesome antidote to temptation. They had inscribed on my reason the conviction that unlawful pleasure, trenching on another's rights, is delusive and envenomed pleasure – its hollowness disappoints at the time, its poison cruelly tortures afterwards, its effects deprave for ever.

From all this resulted the conclusion that I must leave Pelet's and that instantly; 'but,' said Prudence, 'you know not where to go, nor how to live'; and then the dream of true love came over me: Frances Henri seemed to stand at my side; her slender waist to invite my arm; her hand to court my hand; I felt it was made to nestle in mine, I could not relinquish my right to it, nor could I withdraw my eyes for ever from hers, where I saw so much happiness, such a correspondence of heart with heart; over whose expression I had such influence; where I could kindle bliss, infuse awe, stir deep delight, rouse sparkling spirit, and sometimes waken pleasurable dread. My hopes to win and possess, my resolutions to work and rise, rose in array against me; and here I was about to plunge into the gulf of absolute destitution; 'and all this,' suggested an inward voice, 'because you fear an evil which may never happen!' 'It will happen; you *know* it will,' answered that stubborn monitor, Conscience. 'Do what you feel is right; obey me, and even in the sloughs of want I will plant for you firm footing.' And then, as I walked fast along the road, there rose upon me a strange, inly-felt idea of some Great Being, unseen, but all present, who in His beneficence desired only my welfare, and now watched the struggle of good and evil in my heart, and waited to see whether I should obey His voice, heard in the whispers of my conscience, or lend an ear to the sophisms by which His enemy and mine – the Spirit of Evil – sought to lead me astray. Rough and steep was the path indicated by divine suggestion; mossy and declining the green way along which Temptation strewed flowers; but whereas, methought, the Deity of Love, the Friend of all that exists, would smile well-pleased were I to gird up my loins and address myself to the rude ascent; so, on the other hand, each inclination to the velvet declivity seemed to kindle a gleam of triumph on the brow of the man-hating, God-defying demon. Sharp and short I turned round; fast I retraced my steps; in half an hour I was again at M. Pelet's: I sought him in his study; brief parley, concise explanation sufficed; my manner proved that I was resolved; he, perhaps, at heart approved my decision. After twenty minutes' conversation, I re-entered my own room, self-deprived of the means of living, self-sentenced to leave my present home, with the short notice of a week in which to provide another.

CHAPTER XXI

Directly as I closed the door, I saw laid on the table two letters; my thought was, that they were notes of invitation from the friends of some of my pupils; I had received such marks of attention occasionally, and with me, who had no friends, correspondence of more interest was out of the question; the postman's arrival had never yet been an event of interest to me since I came to Brussels. I laid my hand carelessly on the documents, and coldly and slowly glancing at them, I prepared to break the seals; my eye was arrested and my hand too; I saw what excited me, as if I had found a vivid picture where I expected only to discover a blank page: on one cover was an English postmark; on the other, a lady's clear, fine autograph; the last I opened first: –

'Monsieur, – I found out what you had done the very morning after your visit to me; you might be sure I should dust the china every day; and, as no one but you had been in my room for a week, and as fairy-money is not current in Brussels, I could not doubt who left the twenty francs on the chimney-piece. I thought I heard you stir the vase when I was stooping to look for your glove under the table, and I wondered you should imagine it had got into such a little cup. Now, monsieur, the money is not mine, and I shall not keep it; I will not send it in this note because it might be lost – besides, it is heavy; but I will restore it to you the first time I see you, and you must make no difficulties about taking it; because, in the first place, I am sure, monsieur, you can understand that one likes to pay one's debts; that it is satisfactory to owe no man anything; and, in the second place, I can now very well afford to be honest, as I am provided with a situation. The last circumstance is, indeed, the reason of my writing to you, for it is pleasant to communicate good news; and, in these days, I have only my master to whom I can tell anything.

'A week ago, monsieur, I was sent for by Mrs Wharton, an English lady; her eldest daughter was going to be married, and some rich relation having made her a present of a veil and dress in costly old lace, as precious, they said, almost as jewels, but a little damaged by time, I was commissioned to put them in repair. I had to do it at the house; they gave me, besides, some embroidery to complete, and nearly a week elapsed before I had finished everything. While I worked, Miss Wharton often came into the room and sat with me, and so did Mrs Wharton; they made me talk English; asked how I had learned to speak it so well; then they inquired what I knew besides – what books I had read; soon they seemed to make a sort of wonder of me, considering me no doubt as a learned grisette. One afternoon, Mrs Wharton brought in a Parisian lady to test the accuracy of my knowledge of French; the result of it was that, owing probably in a great degree to the mother's and daughter's good-humour about the marriage, which inclined them to do beneficent deeds, and partly, I think, because they are naturally benevolent people, they decided that the wish I had expressed to do something more than mend lace was a very legitimate one; and the same day they took me in their carriage to Mrs D.'s, who is the directress of the first English school at Brussels. It seems she happened to be in want of a French lady to give lessons in geography, history, grammar, and composition, in the French language. Mrs Wharton recommended me very warmly; and, as two of her younger daughters are pupils in the house, her patronage availed to get me the place. It was settled that I am to attend six hours daily (for, happily, it was not required that I should live in the house; I should have been sorry to leave my lodgings), and, for this, Mrs D. will give me twelve hundred francs per annum.

'You see, therefore, monsieur, that I am now rich; richer

almost than I ever hoped to be: I feel thankful for it, especially as my sight was beginning to be injured by constant working at fine lace; and I was getting, too, very weary of sitting up late at nights, and yet not being able to find time for reading or study. I began to fear that I should fall ill, and be unable to pay my way; this fear is now, in a great measure, removed; and, in truth, monsieur, I am very grateful to God for the relief; and I feel it necessary, almost, to speak of my happiness to someone who is kind-hearted enough to derive joy from seeing others joyful. I could not, therefore, resist the temptation of writing to you; I argued with myself it is very pleasant to me to write, and it will not be exactly painful, though it may be tiresome, to monsieur to read. Do not be too angry with my circum-locution and inelegancies of expression, and, believe me, your attached pupil,

F. E. HENRI.'

Having read this letter, I mused on its contents for a few moments – whether with sentiments pleasurable or otherwise I will hereafter note – and then took up the other. It was directed in a hand to me unknown – small and rather neat; neither masculine nor exactly feminine; the seal bore a coat of arms, concerning which I could only decipher that it was not that of the Seacombe family, consequently the epistle could be from none of my almost forgotten, and certainly quite forget-ting patrician relations. From whom, then, was it? I removed the envelope; the note folded within ran as follows: –

'I have no doubt in the world that you are doing well in that greasy Flanders; living probably on the fat of the unctuous land; sitting like a black-haired, tawny-skinned, long-nosed Israelite by the flesh-pots of Egypt; or like a rascally son of Levi near the brass cauldrons of the sanctuary, and every now and then plunging in a consecrated hook, and drawing out of the sea of broth the fattest of heave-shoulders and the fleshiest of wave-breasts. I know this, because you never write to any one in England. Thankless dog that you are! I, by the sovereign efficacy of my recommendation, got you the place where you are now living in clover, and yet not a word of gratitude, or even acknowledgment, have you ever offered in return; but I am coming to see you, and small conception can you, with your addled aristocratic brains, form of the sort of moral kicking I have, ready packed in my carpet-bag, destined to be presented to you immediately on my arrival.

'Meantime I know all about your affairs, and have just got information, by Brown's last letter, that you are said to be on the point of forming an advantageous match with a pursy little Belgian schoolmistress – a Mdlle Zénobie, or some such name. Won't I have a look at her when I come over? And this you may rely on: if she pleases my taste, or if I think it worth while in a pecuniary point of view, I'll pounce on your prize and bear her away triumphant in spite of your teeth. Yet I don't like dumpies either, and Brown says she is little and stout – the better fitted for a wiry, starved-looking chap like you.

'Be on the look-out, for you know neither the day nor hour when your — (I don't wish to blaspheme, so I'll leave a blank) – cometh. – Yours truly,

HUNSDEN YORKE HUNSDEN.'

'Humph!' said I; and ere I laid the letter down, I again glanced at the small, neat handwriting, not a bit like that of a mercantile man, nor, indeed, of any man except Hunsden himself. They talk of affinities between the autograph and the character: what affinity was there here? I recalled the writer's peculiar face and certain traits I suspected, rather than knew, to appertain to his nature, and I answered, 'A great deal.'

Hunsden, then, was coming to Brussels, and coming I knew not when; coming charged with the expectation of finding me on the summit of prosperity, about to be married, to step into a warm nest, to lie comfortably down by the side of a snug, well-fed little mate.

'I wish him joy of the fidelity of the picture he has painted,' thought I. 'What will he say when, instead of a pair of plump turtle-doves, billing and cooing in a bower of roses, he finds a single lean cormorant, standing mateless and shelterless on poverty's bleak cliff? Oh, confound him! Let him come, and let him laugh at the contrast between rumour and fact. Were he the devil himself, instead of being merely very like him, I'd not condescend to get out of his way, or to forge a smile or a cheerful word wherewith to avert his sarcasm.'

Then I recurred to the other letter: that struck a chord whose sound I could not deaden by thrusting my fingers into my ears, for it vibrated within; and though its swell might be exquisite music, its cadence was a groan.

That Frances was relieved from the pressure of want, that the curse of excessive labour was taken off her, filled me with happiness; that her first thought in prosperity should be to augment her joy by sharing it with me, met and satisfied the wish of my heart. Two results of her letter were then pleasant, sweet as two draughts of nectar; but applying my lips for the third time to the cup, they were excoriated as with vinegar and gall.

Two persons whose desires are moderate may live well enough in Brussels on an income which would scarcely afford a respectable maintenance for one in London: and that, not because the necessaries of life are so much dearer in the latter capital, or taxes so much higher than in the former, but because the English surpass in folly all the nations on God's earth, and are more abject slaves to custom, to opinion, to the desire to keep up a certain appearance, than the Italians are to priestcraft, the French to vainglory, the Russians to their Czar, or the Germans to black beer. I have seen a degree of sense in the modest arrangement of one homely Belgian household, that might put to shame the elegance, the superfluities, the luxuries, the strained refinements of a hundred genteel English mansions. In Belgium, provided you can make money, you may save it; this is scarcely possible in England; ostentation there lavishes in a month what industry has earned in a year. More shame to all classes in that most bountiful and beggarly country for their servile following of Fashion; I could write a chapter or two on this subject, but must forbear, at least for the present. Had I retained my £60 per annum I could, now that Frances was in possession of £50, have gone straight to her this very evening, and spoken out the words which, repressed, kept fretting my heart with fever; our united income would, as we should have managed it, have sufficed well for our mutual support; since we lived in a country where economy was not confounded with meanness, where frugality in dress, food, and furniture was not synonymous with vulgarity in these various points. But the placeless usher, bare of resource, and unsupported by connections, must not think of this; such a sentiment as love, such a word as marriage, were misplaced in his heart, and on his lips. Now for the first time did I truly feel what it was to be poor; now did the sacrifice I had made in casting from me the means of living put on a new aspect; instead of a correct, just, honourable act, it seemed a deed at once light and fanatical; I took several turns in my room, under the goading influence of most poignant remorse; I walked a quarter of an hour from the wall to the window; and at the window, self-reproach seemed to face me; at the wall, self-disdain: all at once out spoke Conscience –

'Down, stupid tormentors!' cried she; 'the man has done his duty; you shall not bait him thus by thoughts of what might have been; he relinquished a temporary and contingent good to avoid a permanent and certain evil; he did well. Let him reflect now, and when your blinding dust and deafening hum subside, he will discover a path.'

I sat down; I propped my forehead on both my hands; I thought and thought an hour – two hours; vainly. I seemed like one sealed in a subterranean vault, who gazes at utter blackness; at blackness ensured by yard-thick stone walls around, and by piles of building above, expecting light to penetrate through granite, and through cement firm as granite. But there are chinks, or there may be chinks, in the best adjusted masonry; there was a chink in my cavernous cell; for, eventually, I saw, or seemed to see, a ray – pallid, indeed, and cold, and doubtful, but still a ray, for it showed that narrow path which conscience had promised. After two, three hours' torturing research in brain and memory, I disinterred certain remains of circumstances, and conceived a hope that by putting them together an expedient might be framed, and a resource discovered. The circumstances were briefly these: –

Some three months ago M. Pelet had, on the occasion of his fête, given the boys a treat, which treat consisted in a party of pleasure to a certain place of public resort in the outskirts of Brussels, of which I do not at this moment remember the name, but near it were several of those lakelets called étangs; and there was one étang, larger than the rest, where on holidays people were accustomed to amuse themselves by rowing round it in little boats. The boys having eaten an unlimited quantity of 'gaufres', and drank several bottles of Louvain beer, amid the shades of a garden made and provided for such crams, petitioned the director for leave to take a row on the étang. Half a dozen of the eldest succeeded in obtaining leave, and I was commissioned to accompany them as surveillant. Among the half-dozen happened to be a certain Jean Baptiste Vandenhuten, a most ponderous young Flamand, not tall, but even now, at the early age of sixteen, possessing a breadth and depth of personal development truly national. It chanced that Jean was the first lad to step into the boat; he stumbled, rolled to one side, the boat revolted at his weight and capsized. Vandenhuten sank like lead, rose, sank again. My coat and waistcoat were off in an instant; I had not been brought up at Eton and boated and bathed and swam there ten long years for nothing; it was a natural and easy act for me to leap to the rescue. The lads and the boatmen yelled; they thought there would be two deaths by drowning instead of one; but as Jean rose the third time, I clutched him by one leg and the collar, and in three minutes more both he and I were safe landed. To speak heaven's truth, my merit in the action was small indeed, for I had run no risk, and subsequently did not even catch cold from the wetting; but when M. and Madame Vandenhuten, of whom Jean Baptiste was the sole hope, came to hear of the exploit, they seemed to think I had evinced a bravery and devotion which no thanks could sufficiently repay. Madame, in particular was 'certain I must have dearly loved their sweet son, or I would not thus have hazarded my own life to save his'. Monsieur, an honest-looking, though phlegmatic man, said very little, but he would not suffer me to leave the room till I had promised that in case I ever stood in need of help I would, by applying to him, give him a chance of discharging the obligation under which he affirmed I had laid him. These words, then, were my glimmer of light; it was here I found my sole outlet; and in truth, though the cold light roused, it did not cheer me; nor did the outlet seem such as I should like to pass through. Right I had none to M. Vandenhuten's good offices; it was not on the ground of merit I could apply to him; no, I must stand on that of necessity: I had no work; I wanted work; my best chance of obtaining it lay in securing his recommendation. This I knew could be had by asking for it; not to ask because the request revolted my pride and contradicted my habits, would, I felt, be an indulgence of false and indolent fastidiousness. I might repent the omission all my life; I would not then be guilty of it.

That evening I went to M. Vandenhuten's; but I had bent the bow and adjusted the shaft in vain; the string broke. I rang the bell at the great door (it was a large, handsome house in an expensive part of the town); a man-servant opened; I asked for M. Vandenhuten; M. Vandenhuten and family were all out of town – gone to Ostend – did not know when they would be back. I left my card, and retraced my steps.

CHAPTER XXII

A WEEK is soon gone; *le jour des noces* arrived; the marriage was solemnized at St Jacques; Mdlle Zoraïde became Madame Pelet, *née* Reuter; and, in about an hour after this transformation, 'the happy pair', as newspapers phrase it, were on their way to Paris; where, according to previous arrangement, the honeymoon was to be spent. The next day I quitted the pensionnat. Myself and my chattels (some books and clothes) were soon transferred to a modest lodging I had hired in a street not far off. In half an hour my clothes were arranged in a commode, my books on a shelf, and the 'flitting' was effected. I should not have been unhappy that day had not one pang tortured me – a longing to go to the Rue Notre Dame aux Neiges, resisted, yet irritated by an inward resolve to avoid that street till such time as the mist of doubt should clear from my prospects.

It was a sweet September evening – very mild, very still; I had nothing to do; at that hour I knew Frances would be equally released from occupation; I thought she might possibly be wishing for her master, I knew I wished for my pupil. Imagination began with her low whispers, infusing into my soul the soft tale of pleasures that might be.

'You will find her reading or writing,' said she; 'you can take your seat at her side; you need not startle her peace by undue excitement; you need not embarrass her manner by unusual action or language. Be as you always are; look over what she has written; listen while she reads; chide her, or quietly approve; you know the effect of either system; you know her smile when pleased, you know the play of her looks when roused; you have the secret of awakening what expression you will, and you can choose amongst that pleasant variety. With you she will sit silent as long as it suits you to talk alone; you can hold her under a potent spell; intelligent as she is, eloquent as she can be, you can seal her lips, and veil her bright countenance with diffidence; yet, you know, she is not all monotonous mildness; you have seen, with a sort of strange pleasure, revolt, scorn, austerity, bitterness, lay energetic claim to a place in her feelings and physiognomy; you know that few could rule her as you do; you know she might break, but never bend under the hand of Tyranny and Injustice, but Reason and Affection can guide her by a sign. Try their influence now. Go – they are not passions; you may handle them safely.'

'I will *not* go,' was my answer to the sweet temptress. 'A man is master of himself to a certain point, but not beyond it. Could I seek Frances to-night, could I sit with her alone in a quiet room, and address her only in the language of Reason and Affection?'

'No,' was the brief, fervent reply of that Love which had conquered and now controlled me.

Time seemed to stagnate; the sun would not go down; my watch ticked, but I thought the hands were paralysed.

'What a hot evening!' I cried, throwing open the lattice; for, indeed, I had seldom felt so feverish. Hearing a step ascending the common stair, I wondered whether the *locataire*, now mounting to his apartments, were as unsettled in mind and condition as I was, or whether he lived in the calm of certain resources, and in the freedom of unfettered feelings. What! was he coming in person to solve the problem hardly proposed in inaudible thought? He had actually knocked at the door – at *my* door; a smart, prompt rap; and, almost before I could invite him in, he was over the threshold, and had closed the door behind him.

'And how are you?' asked an indifferent, quiet voice, in the English language; while my visitor, without any sort of bustle or introduction, put his hat on the table, and his gloves into his hat, and drawing the only arm-chair the room afforded a little forward, seated himself tranquilly therein.

'Can't you speak?' he inquired in a few moments, in a tone whose nonchalance seemed to intimate that it was much the same thing whether I answered or not. The fact is, I found it desirable to have recourse to my good friends 'les bésicles'; not exactly to ascertain the identity of my visitor – for I already knew him, confound his impudence! – but to see how he looked – to get a clear notion of his mien and countenance. I wiped the glasses very deliberately, and put them on quite as deliberately; adjusting them so as not to hurt the bridge of my nose, or get entangled in my short tufts of dun hair. I was sitting in the window-seat, with my back to the light, and I had him *vis-à-vis*; a position he would much rather have had reversed; for, at any time, he preferred scrutinizing to being scrutinized. Yes, it was *he*, and no mistake, with his six feet of length arranged in a sitting attitude; with his dark travelling surtout with its velvet collar, his grey pantaloons, his black stock, and *his* face, the most original one Nature ever modelled, yet the least obtrusively so; not one feature that could be termed marked or odd, yet the effect of the whole unique. There is no use in attempting to describe what is indescribable. Being in no hurry to address him, I sat and stared at my ease.

'Oh, that's your game – is it?' said he at last. 'Well, we'll see about which is the soonest tired.' And he slowly drew out a fine cigar-case, picked one to his taste, lit it, took a book from the shelf convenient to his hand, then, leaning back, proceeded to smoke and read as tranquilly as if he had been in his own room, in Grove Street, —shire, England. I knew he was capable of continuing in that attitude till midnight, if he conceived the whim, so I rose, and taking the book from his hand, I said –

'You did not ask for it, and you shall not have it.'

'It is silly and dull,' he observed 'so I have not lost much'; then the spell being broken, he went on, 'I thought you lived at Pelet's; I went there this afternoon, expecting to be starved to death by sitting in a boarding-school drawing-room, and they told me you were gone, had departed this morning; you had left your address behind you though, which I wondered at; it was a more practical and sensible precaution than I should have imagined you capable of. Why did you leave?'

'Because M. Pelet has just married the lady whom you and Mr Brown assigned to me as my wife.'

'Oh indeed!' replied Hunsden with a short laugh; 'so you've lost both your wife and your place?'

'Precisely so.'

I saw him give a quick covert glance all round my room; he marked its narrow limits, its scanty furniture: in an instant he had comprehended the state of matters – had absolved me from the crime of prosperity. A curious effect this discovery wrought in his strange mind; I am morally certain that if he had found me installed in a handsome parlour, lounging on a soft couch, with a pretty, wealthy wife at my side, he would have hated me; a brief, cold, haughty visit would in such a case have been the extreme limit of his civilities, and never would he have come near me more, so long as the tide of fortune bore me smoothly on its surface; but the painted furniture, the bare walls, the cheerless solitude of my room relaxed his rigid pride, and I know not what softening change had taken place both in his voice and look ere he spoke again.

'You have got another place?'

'No.'

'You are in the way of getting one?'

'No.'

'That is bad; have you applied to Brown?'

'No, indeed.'

'You had better; he often has it in his power to give useful information in such matters.'

'He served me once very well; I have no claim on him, and sin not in the humour to bother him again.'

'Oh, if you're bashful, and dread being intrusive, you need only commission me. I shall see him to-night; I can put in a word.'

'I beg you will not, Mr Hunsden; I am in your debt already; you did me an important service when I was at X—; got me out of a den where I was dying: that service I have never repaid, and at present I decline positively adding another item to the account.'

'If the wind sits that way, I'm satisfied. I thought my un-exampled generosity in turning you out of that accursed counting-house would be duly appreciated some day: "Cast your bread on the waters, and it shall be found after many days," say the Scriptures. Yes, that's right, lad – make much of me – I'm a nonpareil: there's nothing like me in the common herd. In the meantime, to put all humbug aside and talk sense for a few moments, you would be greatly the better of a situa-tion, and what is more, you are a fool if you refuse to take one from any hand that offers it.'

'Very well, Mr Hunsden; now you have settled that point, talk of something else. What news from X—?'

'I have not settled that point, or at least there is another to settle before we get to X—. Is this Miss Zénobie' (Zoraïde, interposed I) – 'well, Zoraïde – is she really married to Pelet?'

'I tell you yes – and if you don't believe me, go and ask the curé of St Jacques.'

'And your heart is broken?'

'I am not aware that it is; it feels all right – beats as usual.'

'Then your feelings are less superfine than I took them to be; you must be a coarse, callous character, to bear such a thwack without staggering under it.'

'Staggering under it? What the deuce is there to stagger under in the circumstance of a Belgian schoolmistress marrying a French schoolmaster? The progeny will doubtless be a strange hybrid race; but that's their look-out – not mine.'

'He indulges in scurrilous jests and the bride was his affianced one!'

'Who said so?'

'Brown.'

'I'll tell you what, Hunsden – Brown is an old gossip.'

'He is; but in the meantime, if his gossip be founded on less than fact – if you took no particular interest in Miss Zoraïde – why, O youthful pedagogue! did you leave your place in consequence of her becoming Madame Pelet?'

'Because –' I felt my face grow a little hot; 'because – in short, Mr Hunsden, I decline answering any more questions,' and I plunged my hands deep in my breeches pockets.

Hunsden triumphed: his eyes – his laugh announced victory.

'What the deuce are you laughing at, Mr Hunsden?'

'At your exemplary composure. Well, lad, I'll not bore you; I see how it is: Zoraïde has jilted you – married some one richer, as any sensible woman would have done if she had had the chance.'

I made no reply – I let him think so, not feeling inclined to enter into an explanation of the real state of things, and as little to forge a false account; but it was not easy to blind Hunsden; my very silence, instead of convincing him that he had hit the truth, seemed to render him doubtful about it; he went on –

'I suppose the affair has been conducted as such affairs always are amongst rational people: you offered her your youth and your talents – such as they are – in exchange for her position and money: I don't suppose you took appearance, or what is called *love*, into the account – for I understand she is older than you, and, Brown says, rather sensible-looking than beautiful. She, having then no chance of making a better bargain, was at first inclined to come to terms with you, but Pelet – the head of a flourishing school – stepped in with a higher bid; she accepted, and he has got her: a correct transaction – perfectly so – business-like and legitimate. And now we'll talk of something else.'

'Do,' said I, very glad to dismiss the topic, and especially glad to have baffled the sagacity of my cross-questioner – if, indeed, I had baffled it; for though his words now led away from the dangerous point, his eyes, keen and watchful, seemed still preoccupied with the former idea.

'You want to hear news from X—? And what interest can you have in X—? You left no friends there, for you made none. Nobody ever asks after you – neither man nor woman; and if I mention your name in company, the men look as if I had spoken of Prester John, and the women sneer covertly. Our X— belles must have disliked you. How did you excite their displeasure?'

'I don't know. I seldom spoke to them – they were nothing to me. I considered them only as something to be glanced at from a distance; their dresses and faces were often pleasing enough to the eye: but I could not understand their conversation, nor even read their countenances. When I caught snatches of what they said, I could never make much of it; and the play of their lips and eyes did not help me at all.'

'That was your fault, not theirs. There are sensible as well as handsome women in X—; women it is worth any man's while to talk to, and with whom I can talk with pleasure: but you had and have no pleasant address; there is nothing in you to induce a woman to be affable. I have remarked you sitting near the door in a room full of company, bent on hearing, not on speaking; on observing, not on entertaining; looking frigidly shy at the commencement of a party, confusingly vigilant about the middle, and insultingly weary towards the end. Is that the way, do you think, ever to communicate pleasure or excite interest? No; and if you are generally unpopular, it is because you deserve to be so.'

'Content!' I ejaculated.

'No, you are not content; you see beauty always turning its back on you; you are mortified and then you sneer. I verily believe all that is desirable on earth – wealth, reputation, love – will for ever to you be the ripe grapes on the high trellis: you'll look up at them; they will tantalize in you the lust of the eye; but they are out of reach: you have not the address to fetch a ladder, and you'll go away calling them sour.'

Cutting as these words might have been under some circumstances, they drew no blood now. My life was changed; my experience had been varied since I left X—, but Hunsden could not know this; he had seen me only in the character of Mr Crimsworth's clerk – a dependant amongst wealthy strangers, meeting disdain with a hard front, conscious of an unsocial and unattractive exterior, refusing to sue for notice which I was sure would be withheld, declining to evince an admiration which I knew would be scorned as worthless. He could not be aware that since then youth and loveliness had been to me everyday objects; that I had studied them at leisure and closely, and had seen the plain texture of truth under the embroidery of appearance; nor could he, keen-sighted as he was, penetrate into my heart, search my brain, and read my peculiar sympathies and antipathies; he had not known me long enough, or well enough, to perceive how low my feelings would ebb under some influences, powerful over most minds; how high, how fast they would flow under other influences, that perhaps acted with the more intense force on me because they acted on me alone. Neither could he suspect for an instant the history of my communications with Mdlle Reuter; secret to him and to all others was the tale of her strange infatuation; her blandishments, her wiles had been seen but by me, and to me only were they known; but they had changed me, for they had proved that I *could* impress. A sweeter secret nestled deeper in my heart; one full of tenderness and as full of strength; it took the sting out of Hunsden's sarcasm; it kept me unbent by shame, and unstirred by wrath. But of all this I could say nothing – nothing decisive at least; uncertainty sealed my lips, and during the interval of silence by which alone I replied to Mr Hunsden, I made up my mind to be for the present wholly misjudged by him, and misjudged I was; he thought he had been rather too hard upon me, and that I was crushed by the weight of his upbraidings; so to reassure me he said, doubtless I should mend some day; I was only at the beginning of life yet; and since happily I was not quite without sense, every false step I made would be a good lesson.

Just then I turned my face a little to the light; the approach of twilight, and my position in the window-seat, had, for the last ten minutes, prevented him from studying my countenance; as I moved, however, he caught an expression which he thus interpreted –

'Confound it! How doggedly self-approving the lad looks! I thought he was fit to die with shame, and there he sits grinning smiles, as good as to say, "Let the world wag as it will, I've the philosopher's stone in my waistcoat pocket, and the elixir of life in my cupboard; I'm independent of both Fate and Fortune!"'

'Hunsden – you spoke of grapes; I was thinking of a fruit I like better than your X— hot-house grapes – an unique fruit, growing wild, which I have marked as my own, and hope one day to gather and taste. It is of no use your offering me the draught of bitterness, or threatening me with death by thirst: I have the anticipation of sweetness on my palate; the hope of freshness on my lips; I can reject the unsavoury, and endure the exhausting.'

'For how long?'

'Till the next opportunity for effort; and as the prize of success will be a treasure after my own heart, I'll bring a bull's strength to the struggle.'

'Bad luck crushes bulls as easily as bullaces; and, I believe, the fury dogs you: you were born with a wooden spoon in your mouth, depend on it.'

'I believe you; and I mean to make my wooden spoon do the work of some people's silver ladles: grasped firmly, and handled nimbly, even a wooden spoon will shovel up broth.'

Hunsden rose. 'I see,' said he; 'I suppose you're one of those who develop best unwatched, and act best unaided – work your own way. Now, I'll go.' And, without another word, he was going; at the door he turned.

'Crimsworth Hall is sold,' said he.

'Sold!' was my echo.

'Yes; you know, of course, that your brother failed three months ago?'

'What! Edward Crimsworth?'

'Precisely; and his wife went home to her father's; when affairs went awry, his temper sympathized with them; he used her ill; I told you he would be a tyrant to her some day; as to him –'

'Aye, as to him – what has become of him?'

'Nothing extraordinary – don't be alarmed; he put himself under the protection of the court, compounded with his creditors – tenpence in the pound; in six weeks set up again, coaxed back his wife, and is flourishing like a green bay-tree.'

'And Crimsworth Hall – was the furniture sold too?'

'Everything – from the grand piano down to the rolling-pin.'

'And the contents of the oak dining-room – were they sold?'

'Of course; why should the sofas and chairs of that room be held more sacred than those of any other?'

'And the pictures?'

'What pictures? Crimsworth had no special collection that I know of – he did not profess to be an amateur.'

'There were two portraits, one on each side the mantelpiece; you cannot have forgotten them, Mr Hunsden; you once noticed that of the lady –'

'Oh, I know! the thin-faced gentlewoman with a shawl put on like drapery. – Why, as a matter of course, it would be sold among the other things. If you had been rich, you might have bought it, for I remember you said it represented your mother: you see what it is to be without a sou.'

I did. 'But surely,' I thought to myself, 'I shall not always be so poverty-stricken; I may one day buy it back yet. – Who purchased it? do you know?' I asked.

'How is it likely? I never inquired who purchased anything; there spoke the unpractical man – to imagine all the world is interested in what interests himself. Now, good-night – I'm off for Germany to-morrow morning; I shall be back here in six weeks, and possibly I may call and see you again; I wonder whether you'll be still out of place!' he laughed, as mockingly, as heartlessly as Mephistopheles, and so laughing, vanished.

Some people, however indifferent they may become after a considerable space of absence, always contrive to leave a pleasant impression just at parting; not so Hunsden; a conference with him affected one like a draught of Peruvian bark; it seemed a concentration of the specially harsh, stringent, bitter; whether, like bark, it invigorated, I scarcely knew.

A ruffled mind makes a restless pillow; I slept little on the night after this interview; towards morning I began to doze, but hardly had my slumber become sleep, when I was roused from it by hearing a noise in my sitting-room, to which my bedroom adjoined – a step, and a shoving of furniture; the movement lasted barely two minutes; with the closing of the door it ceased. I listened; not a mouse stirred; perhaps I had dreamt it; perhaps a *locataire* had made a mistake, and entered my apartment instead of his own. It was yet but five o'clock; neither I nor the day were wide awake; I turned, and was soon unconscious. When I did rise, about two hours later, I had forgotten the circumstance; the first thing I saw, however, on quitting my chamber, recalled it; just pushed in at the door of my sitting-room, and still standing on end, was a wooden packing-case – a rough deal affair, wide but shallow; a porter had doubtless shoved it forward, but seeing no occupant of the room, had left it at the entrance.

'That is none of mine,' thought I, approaching; 'it must be meant for somebody else.' I stooped to examine the address:

'Wm Crimsworth, Esq., No. –, — St, Brussels.'

I was puzzled, but concluding that the best way to obtain information was to ask within, I cut the cords and opened the case. Green baize enveloped its contents, sewn carefully at the sides; I ripped the packthread with my pen-knife, and still, as the seam gave way, glimpses of gilding appeared through the widening interstices. Boards and baize being at length removed, I lifted from the case a large picture, in a magnificent frame; leaning it against a chair, in a position where the light from the window fell favourably upon it, I stepped back – already I had mounted my spectacles. A portrait-painter's sky (the most sombre and threatening of welkins), and distant trees of a conventional depth of hue, raised in full relief a pale, pensive-looking female face, shadowed with soft dark hair, almost blending with the equally dark clouds; large solemn eyes looked reflectively into mine; a thin cheek rested on a delicate little hand; a shawl, artistically draped, half hid, half showed a slight figure. A listener (had there been one) might have heard me, after ten minutes' silent gazing, utter the word, 'Mother!' I might have said more – but with me, the first word uttered aloud in soliloquy rouses consciousness; it reminds me that only crazy people talk to themselves, and then I think out my monologue, instead of speaking it. I had thought a long while, and a long while had contemplated the intelligence, the sweetness, and – alas! the sadness also of those fine grey eyes, the mental power of that forehead, and the rare sensibility of that serious mouth, when my glance, travelling downwards, fell on a narrow billet, stuck in the corner of the picture, between the frame and the canvas. Then I first asked, 'Who sent this picture? Who thought of me, saved it out of the wreck of Crimsworth Hall, and now commits it to the care of its natural keeper?' I took the note from its niche; thus it spoke: –

'There is a sort of stupid pleasure in giving a child sweets, a fool his bells, a dog a bone. You are repaid by seeing the child besmear his face with sugar; by witnessing how the fool's ecstasy makes a greater fool of him than ever; by watching the dog's nature come out over his bone. In giving William Crimsworth his mother's picture, I give him sweets, bells, and bone all in one; what grieves me is, that I cannot behold the result; I would have added five shillings more to my bid if the auctioneer could only have promised me that pleasure.

H.Y.H.

'P.S. – You said last night you positively declined adding another item to your account with me: don't you think I've saved you that trouble?'

I muffled the picture in its green baize covering, restored it to the case, and having transported the whole concern to my bedroom, put it out of sight under my bed. My pleasure was now poisoned by pungent pain; I determined to look no more till I could look at my ease. If Hunsden had come in at that moment, I should have said to him, 'I owe you nothing, Hunsden – not a fraction of a farthing: you have paid yourself in taunts.'

Too anxious to remain any longer quiescent, I had no sooner breakfasted than I repaired once more to M. Vandenhuten's, scarcely hoping to find him at home; for a week had barely elapsed since my first call; but fancying I might be able to glean information as to the time his return was expected. A better result awaited me than I had anticipated, for though the family were yet at Ostend, M. Vandenhuten had come over to Brussels on business for the day. He received me with the quiet kindness of a sincere though not excitable man. I had not sat five minutes alone with him in his bureau, before I became aware of a sense of ease in his presence, such as I rarely experienced with strangers. I was surprised at my own composure, for, after all, I had come on business to me exceedingly painful – that of soliciting a favour. I asked on what basis the calm rested – I feared it might be deceptive. Ere long I caught a glimpse of the ground, and at once I felt assured of its solidity; I knew where I was.

M. Vandenhuten was rich, respected, and influential; I, poor, despised, and powerless; so we stood to the world at large as members of the world's society; but to each other, as a pair of human beings, our positions were reversed. The Dutchman (he was not Flamand, but pure Hollandais) was slow, cool, of rather dense intelligence, though sound and accurate judgment; the Englishman far more nervous, active, quicker both to plan and to practise, to conceive and to realize. The Dutchman was benevolent, the Englishman susceptible; in short our characters dovetailed, but my mind having more fire and action than his, instinctively assumed and kept the predominance.

This point settled, and my position well ascertained, I addressed him on the subject of my affairs with that genuine frankness which full confidence can alone inspire. It was a pleasure to him to be so appealed to; he thanked me for giving him this opportunity of using a little exertion in my behalf. I went on to explain to him that my wish was not so much to be helped, as to be put into the way of helping myself; of him I did not want exertion – that was to be my part – but only information and recommendation. Soon after I rose to go. He held out his hand at parting – an action of greater significance with foreigners than with Englishmen. As I exchanged a smile with him, I thought the benevolence of his truthful face was better than the intelligence of my own. Characters of my order experience a balm-like solace in the contact of such souls as animated the honest breast of Victor Vandenhuten.

The next fortnight was a period of many alternations; my existence during its lapse resembled a sky of one of those autumnal nights which are specially haunted by meteors and falling stars. Hopes and fears, expectations and disappointments, descended in glancing showers from zenith to horizon; but all were transient, and darkness followed swift each vanishing apparition. M. Vandenhuten aided me faithfully; he set me on the track of several places, and himself made efforts to secure them for me; but for a long time solicitation and recommendation were vain – the door either shut in my face when I was about to walk in, or another candidate, entering before me, rendered my further advance useless. Feverish and roused, no disappointment arrested me; defeat following fast on defeat served as stimulants to will. I forgot fastidiousness, conquered reserve, thrust pride from me: I asked, I persevered, I remonstrated, I dunned. It is so that openings are forced into the guarded circle where Fortune sits dealing favours round. My perseverance made me known; my importunity made me remarked. I was inquired about; my former pupils' parents, gathering the reports of their children, heard me spoken of as talented, and they echoed the word: the sound, bandied about at random, came at last to ears which, but for its universality, it might never have reached; and at the very crisis when I had tried my last effort and knew not what to do, Fortune looked in at me one morning, as I sat in drear and almost desperate deliberation on my bedstead, nodded with the familiarity of an old acquaintance – though God knows I had never met her before – and threw a prize into my lap.

In the second week of October, 18—, I got the appointment of English professor to all classes of — College, Brussels, with a salary of three thousand francs per annum; and the certainty of being able, by dint of the reputation and publicity accompanying the position, to make as much more by private lessons. The official notice, which communicated this information, mentioned also that it was the strong recommendation of M. Vandenhuten, négociant, which had turned the scale of choice in my favour.

No sooner had I read the announcement than I hurried to M. Vandenhuten's bureau, pushed the document under his nose, and when he had perused it, took both his hands, and thanked him with unrestrained vivacity. My vivid words and emphatic gesture moved his Dutch calm to unwonted sensation. He said he was happy – glad to have served me; but he had done nothing meriting such thanks. He had not laid out a centime – only scratched a few words on a sheet of paper.

Again I repeated to him –

'You have made me quite happy, and in a way that suits me; I do not feel an obligation irksome, conferred by your kind hand; I do not feel disposed to shun you because you have done me a favour; from this day you must consent to admit me to your intimate acquaintance, for I shall hereafter recur again and again to the pleasure of your society.'

'Ainsi soit-il,' was the reply, accompanied by a smile of benignant content. I went away with its sunshine in my heart.

CHAPTER XXIII

IT WAS two o'clock when I returned to my lodgings; my dinner, just brought in from a neighbouring hotel, smoked on the table; I sat down, thinking to eat – had the plate been heaped with potsherds and broken glass, instead of boiled beef and haricots, I could not have made a more signal failure: appetite had forsaken me. Impatient of seeing food which I could not taste, I put it all aside into a cupboard, and then demanded, 'What shall I do till evening?' for before six pm it would be vain to seek the Rue Notre Dame aux Neiges; its inhabitant (for me it had but one) was detained by her vocation elsewhere. I walked in the streets of Brussels, and I walked in my own room from two o'clock till six; never once in that space of time did I sit down. I was in my chamber when the last-named hour struck; I had just bathed my face and feverish hands, and was standing near the glass; my cheek was crimson, my eye was flame, still all my features looked quite settled and calm. Descending swiftly the stair and stepping out, I was glad to see Twilight drawing on in clouds; such shade was to me like a grateful screen, and the chill of latter Autumn, breathing in a fitful wind from the north-west, met me as a refreshing coolness. Still I saw it was cold to others, for the women I passed were wrapped in shawls, and the men had their coats buttoned close.

When are we quite happy? Was I so then? No; an urgent and growing dread worried my nerves, and had worried them since the first moment good tidings had reached me. How was Frances? It was ten weeks since I had seen her, six since I had heard from her, or of her. I had answered her letter by a brief note, friendly but calm, in which no mention of continued correspondence or further visits was made. At that hour my bark hung on the topmost curl of a wave of fate, and I knew not on what shoal the onward rush of the billow might hurl it; I would not then attach her destiny to mine by the slightest thread; if doomed to split on the rock, or run aground on the sand-bank, I was resolved no other vessel should share my disaster: but six weeks was a long time; and could it be that she was still well and doing well? Were not all sages agreed in declaring that happiness finds no climax on earth? Dared I think that but half a street now divided me from the full cup of contentment – the draught drawn from waters said to flow only in heaven?

I was at the door; I entered the quiet house; I mounted the stairs; the lobby was void and still, all the doors closed; I looked for the neat green mat; it lay duly in its place.

'Signal of hope!' I said, and advanced. 'But I will be a little calmer; I am not going to rush in, and get up a scene directly.' Forcibly staying my eager step, I paused on the mat.

'What an absolute hush! Is she in? Is anybody in?' I demanded to myself. A little tinkle, as of cinders falling from a grate, replied; a movement – a fire was gently stirred; and the slight rustle of life continuing, a step paced equably backwards and forwards, backwards and forwards, in the apartment. Fascinated, I stood, more fixedly fascinated when a voice rewarded the attention of my strained ear – so low, so self-addressed, I never fancied the speaker otherwise than alone; solitude might speak thus in a desert, or in the hall of a forsaken house.

> ' "And ne'er but once, my son," he said,
>   "Was yon dark cavern trod;
> In persecution's iron days,
>   When the land was left by God.
> From Bewley's bog, with slaughter red,
>   A wanderer hither drew;
> And oft he stopp'd and turn'd his head,
>   As by fits the night-winds blew.

> For trampling round by Cheviot-edge
> Were heard the troopers keen;
> And frequent from the Whitelaw ridge
> The death-shot flash'd between," ' etc. etc.

The old Scotch ballad was partly recited, then dropt; a pause ensued; then another strain followed, in French, of which the purport, translated, ran as follows:

> 'I gave, at first, attention close;
> Then interest warm ensued;
> From interest, as improvement rose
> Succeeded gratitude.
>
> Obedience was no effort soon,
> And labour was no pain;
> If tired, a word, a glance alone
> Would give me strength again.
>
> From others of the studious band,
> Ere long he singled me;
> But only by more close demand,
> And sterner urgency.
>
> The task he from another took,
> From me he did reject,
> He would no slight omission brook,
> And suffer no defect.
>
> If my companions went astray,
> He scarce their wanderings blam'd;
> If I but falter'd in the way,
> His anger fiercely flam'd.'

Something stirred in an adjoining chamber; it would not do to be surprised eavesdropping; I tapped hastily, and as hastily entered. Frances was just before me; she had been walking slowly in her room, and her step was checked by my advent: Twilight only was with her, and tranquil, ruddy Firelight; to these sisters, the Bright and the Dark, she had been speaking, ere I entered, in poetry. Sir Walter Scott's voice, to her a foreign, far-off sound, a mountain echo, had uttered itself in the first stanzas; the second, I thought, from the style and the substance, was the language of her own heart. Her face was grave, its expression concentrated; she bent on me an unsmiling eye – an eye just returning from abstraction, just awaking from dreams: well-arranged was her simple attire, smooth her dark hair, orderly her tranquil room; but what – with her thoughtful look, her serious self-reliance, her bent to meditation and haply inspiration – what had she to do with love? 'Nothing,' was the answer of her own sad, though gentle countenance; it seemed to say, 'I must cultivate fortitude and cling to poetry; one is to be my support and the other my solace through life. Human affections do not bloom, nor do human passions glow for me.' Other women have such thoughts. Frances, had she been as desolate as she deemed, would not have been worse off than thousands of her sex. Look at the rigid and formal race of old maids – the race whom all despise; they have fed themselves, from youth upwards, on maxims of resignation and endurance. Many of them get ossified with the dry diet; self-control is so continually their thought, so perpetually their object, that at last it absorbs the softer and more agreeable qualities of their nature; and they die mere models of austerity, fashioned out of a little parchment and much bone. Anatomists will tell you that there is a heart in the withered old maid's carcase – the same as in that of any cherished wife or proud mother in the land. Can this be so? I really don't know; but feel inclined to doubt it.

I came forward, bade Frances 'Good evening', and took my seat. The chair I had chosen was one she had probably just left; it stood by a little table where were her open desk and papers.

I know not whether she had fully recognized me at first, but she did so now; and in a voice, soft but quiet, she returned my greeting. I had shown no eagerness; she took her cue from me, and evinced no surprise. We met as we had always met, as master and pupil – nothing more. I proceeded to handle the papers; Frances, observant and serviceable, stepped into an inner room, brought a candle, lit it, placed it by me; then drew the curtain over the lattice, and having added a little fresh fuel to the already bright fire, she drew a second chair to the table and sat down at my right hand, a little removed. The paper on the top was a translation of some grave French author into English, but underneath lay a sheet with stanzas; on this I laid my hands. Frances half rose, made a movement to recover the captured spoil, saying, that was nothing – a mere copy of verses. I put my resistance with the decision I knew she never long opposed; but on this occasion her fingers had fastened on the paper. I had quietly to unloose them; their hold dissolved to my touch; her hand shrunk away; my own would fain have followed it, but for the present I forbade such impulse. The first page of the sheet was occupied with the lines I had over-heard; the sequel was not exactly the writer's own experience, but a composition by portions of that experience suggested. Thus while egotism was avoided, the fancy was exercised, and the heart satisfied. I translate as before, and my translation is nearly literal; it continued thus:

> 'When sickness stay'd awhile my course,
>   He seem'd impatient still,
> Because his pupil's flagging force
>   Could not obey his will.
>
> One day when summoned to the bed
>   Where pain and I did strive,
> I heard him, as he bent his head,
>   Say, "God, she *must* revive!"

I felt his hand, with gentle stress,
    A moment laid on mine,
And wished to mark my consciousness
    By some responsive sign.

But pow'rless then to speak or move,
    I only felt, within,
The sense of Hope, the strength of Love,
    Their healing work begin.

And as he from the room withdrew,
    My heart his steps pursued;
I long'd to prove, by efforts new,
    My speechless gratitude.

When once again I took my place,
    Long vacant, in the class,
Th' unfrequent smile across his face
    Did for one moment pass.

The lessons done; the signal made
    Of glad release and play,
He, as he passed, an instant stay'd,
    One kindly word to say:

"Jane, till to-morrow you are free
    From tedious task and rule;
This afternoon I must not see
    That yet pale face in school.

"Seek in the garden-shades a seat,
    Far from the play-ground din;
The sun is warm, the air is sweet:
    Stay till I call you in."

A long and pleasant afternoon
   I passed in those green bowers;
All silent, tranquil, and alone
    With birds, and bees, and flowers.

Yet, when my master's voice I heard
    Call, from the window, "Jane!"
I entered, joyful, at the word,
    The busy house again.

He, in the hall, paced up and down;
    He paused as I passed by;
His forehead stern relaxed its frown:
    He raised his deep-set eye.

"Not quite so pale," he murmured low.
    "Now, Jane, go rest awhile,"
And as I smiled, his smoothened brow
    Returned as glad a smile.

My perfect health restored, he took
    His mien austere again;
And, as before, he would not brook
    The slightest fault from Jane.

The longest task, the hardest theme
    Fell to my share as erst,
And still I toiled to place my name
    In every study first.

He yet begrudged and stinted praise,
    But I had learnt to read
The secret meaning of his face,
    And that was my best meed.

Even when his hasty temper spoke
   In tones that sorrow stirred,
My grief was lulled as soon as woke
   By some relenting word.

And when he lent some precious book,
   Or gave some fragrant flower,
I did not quail to Envy's look,
   Upheld by Pleasure's power.

At last our school ranks took their ground;
   The hard-fought field I won;
The prize, a laurel wreath, was bound
   My throbbing forehead on.

Low at my master's knee I bent,
   The offered crown to meet;
Its green leaves through my temples sent
   A thrill as wild as sweet.

The strong pulse of Ambition struck
   In every vein I owned;
At the same instant, bleeding broke
   A secret, inward wound.

The hour of triumph was to me
   The hour of sorrow sore;
A day hence I must cross the sea,
   Ne'er to recross it more.

An hour hence, in my master's room,
   I with him sat alone,
And told him what a dreary gloom
   O'er joy had parting thrown.

He little said; the time was brief,
  The ship was soon to sail,
And while I sobbed in bitter grief,
  My master but looked pale.

They called in haste; he bade me go,
  Then snatched me back again;
He held me fast and murmured low,
  "Why will they part us, Jane?

"Were you not happy in my care?
  Did I not faithful prove?
Will others to my darling bear
  As true, as deep a love?

"O God, watch o'er my foster-child!
  O guard her gentle head
When winds are high and tempests wild
  Protection round her spread!

"They call again; leave then my breast;
  Quit thy true shelter, Jane;
But when deceived, repulsed, opprest,
  Come home to me again!"'

I read – then dreamily made marks on the margin with my
pencil; thinking all the while of other things; thinking that
'Jane' was now at my side; no child, but a girl of nineteen; and
she might be mine, so my heart affirmed; Poverty's curse was
taken off me; Envy and Jealousy were far away, and unapprized
of this our quiet meeting; the frost of the Master's manner
might melt; I felt the thaw coming fast whether I would or
not; no further need for the eye to practise a hard look, for the
brow to compress its expanse into a stern fold: it was now
permitted to suffer the outward revelation of the inward glow

– to seek, demand, elicit an answering ardour. While musing thus, I thought that the grass on Hermon never drank the fresh dews of sunset more gratefully than my feelings drank the bliss of this hour.

Frances rose, as if restless; she passed before me to stir the fire, which did not want stirring; she lifted and put down the little ornaments on the mantelpiece; her dress waved within a yard of me; slight, straight, and elegant, she stood erect on the hearth.

There are impulses we can control; but there are others which control us, because they attain us with a tiger-leap, and are our masters ere we have seen them. Perhaps, though, such impulses are seldom altogether bad; perhaps Reason, by a process as brief as quiet, a process that is finished ere felt, has ascertained the sanity of the deed Instinct meditates, and feels justified in remaining passive while it is performed. I know I did not reason, I did not plan or intend, yet, whereas one moment I was sitting solus on the chair near the table, the next, I held Frances on my knee, placed there with sharpness and decision, and retained with exceeding tenacity.

'Monsieur!' cried Frances, and was still: not another word escaped her lips; sorely confounded she seemed during the lapse of the first few moments; but the amazement soon subsided; terror did not succeed, nor fury: after all, she was only a little nearer than she had ever been before, to one she habitually respected and trusted; embarrassment might have impelled her to contend, but self-respect checked resistance where resistance was useless.

'Frances, how much regard have you for me?' was my demand. No answer; the situation was yet too new and surprising to permit speech. On this consideration, I compelled myself for some seconds to tolerate her silence, though impatient of it: presently, I repeated the same question – probably not in the calmest of tones; she looked at me; my face, doubtless, was no model of composure, my eyes no still wells of tranquillity.

'Do speak,' I urged; and a very low, hurried, yet still arch voice said –

'Monsieur, vous me faites mal; de grâce lâchez un peu ma main droite.'

In truth I became aware that I was holding the said 'main droite' in a somewhat ruthless grasp: I did as desired; and, for the third time, asked more gently –

'Frances, how much regard have you for me?'

'Mon maître, j'en ai beaucoup,' was the truthful rejoinder.

'Frances, have you enough to give yourself to me as my wife? – to accept me as your husband?'

I felt the agitation of the heart, I saw 'the purple light of love' cast its glowing reflection on cheeks, temples, neck; I desired to consult the eye, but sheltering lash and lid forbade.

'Monsieur,' said the soft voice at last, – 'Monsieur désire savoir si je consens – si – enfin, si je veux me marier avec lui?'

'Justement.'

'Monsieur sera-t-il aussi bon mari qu'il a été bon maître?'

'I will try, Frances.'

A pause; then with a new, yet still subdued inflexion of the voice – an inflexion which provoked while it pleased me – accompanied, too, by a 'sourire à la fois fin et timide' in perfect harmony with the tone –

'C'est-à-dire, monsieur sera toujours un peu entêté, exigeant, volontaire—?'

'Have I been so, Frances?'

'Mais oui; vous le savez bien.'

'Have I been nothing else?'

'Mais oui; vous avez été mon meilleur ami.'

'And what, Frances, are you to me?'

'Votre dévouée élève, qui vous aime de tout son cœur.'

'Will my pupil consent to pass her life with me? Speak English now, Frances.'

Some moments were taken for reflection; the answer, pronounced slowly, ran thus –

'You have always made me happy; I like to hear you speak; I like to see you; I like to be near you; I believe you are very good, and very superior; I know you are stern to those who are careless and idle, but you are kind, very kind to the attentive and industrious, even if they are not clever. Master, I should be *glad* to live with you always'; and she made a sort of movement, as if she would have clung to me, but restraining herself she only added with earnest emphasis – 'Master, I consent to pass my life with you.'

'Very well, Frances.'

I drew her a little nearer to my heart; I took a first kiss from her lips, thereby sealing the compact, now framed between us; afterwards she and I were silent, nor was our silence brief. Frances' thoughts, during this interval, I know not, nor did I attempt to guess them; I was not occupied in searching her countenance, nor in otherwise troubling her composure. The peace I felt, I wished her to feel; my arm, it is true, still detained her; but with a restraint that was gentle enough, so long as no opposition tightened it. My gaze was on the red fire; my heart was measuring its own content; it sounded and sounded, and found the depth fathomless.

'Monsieur,' at last said my quiet companion, as stirless in her happiness as a mouse in its terror. Even now in speaking she scarcely lifted her head.

'Well, Frances?' I like unexaggerated intercourse; it is not my way to overpower with amorous epithets, any more than to worry with selfishly importunate caresses.

'Monsieur est raisonnable, n'est-ce pas?'

'Yes; especially when I am requested to be so in English; but why do you ask me? You see nothing vehement or obstrusive in my manner; am I not tranquil enough?'

'Ce n'est pas cela –' began Frances.

'English!' I reminded her.

'Well, monsieur, I wished merely to say, that I should like, of course, to retain my employment of teaching. You will teach still, I suppose, monsieur?'

'Oh, yes! It is all I have to depend on.'

'Bon! – I mean good. Thus we shall have both the same profession. I like that; and my efforts to get on will be as unrestrained as yours – will they not, monsieur?'

'You are laying plans to be independent of me,' said I.

'Yes, monsieur; I must be no incumbrance to you – no burden in any way.'

'But, Frances, I have not yet told you what my prospects are. I have left M. Pelet's; and after nearly a month's seeking, I have got another place, with a salary of three thousand francs a year, which I can easily double by a little additional exertion. Thus you see it would be useless for you to fag yourself by going out to give lessons; on six thousand francs you and I can live, and live well.'

Frances seemed to consider. There is something flattering to man's strength, something consonant to his honourable pride, in the idea of becoming the providence of what he loves – feeding and clothing it, as God does the lilies of the field. So, to decide her resolution, I went on –

'Life has been painful and laborious enough to you so far, Frances; you require complete rest; your twelve hundred francs would not form a very important addition to our income, and what sacrifice of comfort to earn it! Relinquish your labours: you must be weary, and let me have the happiness of giving you rest.'

I am not sure whether Frances had accorded due attention to my harangue; instead of answering me with her usual respectful promptitude, she only sighed and said –

'How rich you are, monsieur!' and then she stirred uneasily in my arms. 'Three thousand francs!' she murmured, 'while I get only twelve hundred!' She went on faster. 'However, it must be so for the present; and, monsieur, were you not saying something about my giving up my place? Oh, no! I shall hold it fast'; and her little fingers emphatically tightened on mine.

'Think of my marrying you to be kept by you, monsieur! I could not do it; and how dull my days would be! You would be away teaching in close, noisy schoolrooms, from morning till evening, and I should be lingering at home, unemployed and solitary; I should get depressed and sullen, and you would soon tire of me.'

'Frances, you could read and study – two things you like so well.'

'Monsieur, I could not; I like a contemplative life, but I like an active life better; I must act in some way, and act with you. I have taken notice, monsieur, that people who are only in each other's company for amusement, never really like each other so well, or esteem each other so highly, as those who work together, and perhaps suffer together.'

'You speak God's truth,' said I at last, 'and you shall have your own way, for it is the best way. Now, as a reward for such ready consent, give me a voluntary kiss.'

After some hesitation, natural to a novice in the art of kissing, she brought her lips into very shy and gentle contact with my forehead; I took the small gift as a loan, and repaid it promptly, and with generous interest.

I know not whether Frances was really much altered since the time I first saw her; but, as I looked at her now, I felt that she was singularly changed for me; the sad eye, the pale cheek, the dejected and joyless countenance I remembered as her early attributes, were quite gone, and now I saw a face dressed in graces; smile, dimple, and rosy tint rounded its contours and brightened its hues. I had been accustomed to nurse a flattering idea that my strong attachment to her proved some particular perspicacity in my nature; she was not handsome, she was not rich, she was not even accomplished, yet was she my life's treasure; I must then be a man of peculiar discernment. To-night my eyes opened on the mistake I had made; I began to suspect that it was only my tastes which were unique, not my power of discovering and appreciating the superiority of moral worth over physical charms. For me, Frances had physical charms: in her there was no deformity to get over; none of those prominent defects of eyes, teeth, complexion, shape, which hold at bay the admiration of the boldest male champions of intellect (for women can love a downright ugly man if he be but talented); had she been either 'édentée, myope, rugueuse, ou bossue', my feelings towards her might still have been kindly, but they could never have been impassioned; I had affection for the poor little misshapen Sylvie, but for her I could never have had love. It is true Frances' mental points had been the first to interest me, and they still retained the strongest hold on my preference; but I liked the graces of her person too. I derived a pleasure, purely material, from contemplating the clearness of her brown eyes, the fairness of her fine skin, the purity of her well-set teeth, the proportion of her delicate form; and that pleasure I could ill have dispensed with. It appeared, then, that I too was a sensualist, in my temperate and fastidious way.

Now, reader, during the last two pages I have been giving you honey fresh from flowers, but you must not live entirely on food so luscious; taste then a little gall – just a drop, by way of change.

At a somewhat late hour I returned to my lodgings: having temporarily forgotten that man had any such coarse cares as those of eating and drinking, I went to bed fasting. I had been excited and in action all day, and had tasted no food since eight that morning; besides, for a fortnight past, I had known no rest either of body or mind; the last few hours had been a sweet delirium, it would not subside now and, till long after midnight, broke with troubled ecstasy the rest I so much needed. At last I dozed, but not for long; it was yet quite dark when I awoke, and my waking was like that of Job when a spirit passed before his face, and like him, 'the hair of my flesh stood up'. I might continue the parallel, for in truth, though I saw nothing, yet, 'a thing was secretly brought unto me, and mine ear received a little thereof; there was silence, and I heard a voice', saying – 'In the midst of life we are in death.'

That sound, and the sensation of chill anguish accompanying it, many would have regarded as supernatural; but I recognized it at once as the effect of reaction. Man is ever clogged with his mortality, and it was my mortal nature which now faltered and plained; my nerves which jarred and gave a false sound, because the soul, of late rushing headlong to an aim, had overstrained the body's comparative weakness. A horror of great darkness fell upon me; I felt my chamber invaded by one I had known formerly, but had thought for ever departed. I was temporarily a prey to hypochondria.

She had been my acquaintance, nay, my guest, once before in boyhood; I had entertained her at bed and board for a year; for that space of time I had her to myself in secret; she lay with me, she ate with me, she walked out with me, showing me nooks in woods, hollows in hills, where we could sit together, and where she could drop her drear veil over me, and so hide sky and sun, grass and green tree; taking me entirely to her death-cold bosom, and holding me with arms of bone. What tales she would tell me at such hours! What songs she would recite in my ears! How she would discourse to me of her own country – the grave – and again and again promise to conduct me there ere long; and, drawing me to the very brink of a black, sullen river, show me, on the other side, shores unequal with mound, monument, and tablet, standing up in a glimmer more hoary than moonlight. 'Necropolis!' she would whisper, pointing to the pale piles, and add, 'It contains a mansion prepared for you.'

But my boyhood was lonely, parentless; uncheered by brother or sister; and there was no marvel that, just as I rose to youth, a sorceress, finding me lost in vague mental wanderings, with many affections and few objects, glowing aspirations and gloomy prospects, strong desires and slender hopes, should lift up her illusive lamp to me in the distance, and lure me to her vaulted home of horrors. No wonder her spells *then* had power; but *now*, when my course was widening, my prospect brightening; when my affections had found a rest; when my desires, folding wings, weary with long flight, had just alighted on the very lap of fruition, and nestled there warm, content, under the caress of a soft hand – why did hypochondria accost me now?

I repulsed her as one would a dreaded and ghastly concubine coming to embitter a husband's heart towards his young bride; in vain; she kept her sway over me for that night and the next day, and eight succeeding days. Afterwards, my spirits began slowly to recover their tone; my appetite returned, and in a fortnight I was well. I had gone about as usual all the time, and had said nothing to anybody of what I felt; but I was glad when the evil spirit departed from me, and I could again seek Frances, and sit at her side, freed from the dreadful tyranny of my demon.

CHAPTER XXIV

ONE FINE, frosty Sunday in November, Frances and I took a long walk; we made the tour of the city by the Boulevards; and, afterwards, Frances being a little tired, we sat down on one of those wayside seats placed under the trees, at intervals, for the accommodation of the weary. Frances was telling me about Switzerland; the subject animated her; and I was just thinking that her eyes spoke full as eloquently as her tongue, when she stopped and remarked –

'Monsieur, there is a gentleman who knows you.'

I looked up; three fashionably dressed men were just then passing – Englishmen, I knew by their air and gait as well as by their features; in the tallest of the trio I at once recognized Mr Hunsden; he was in the act of lifting his hat to Frances; afterwards, he made a grimace at me, and passed on.

'Who is he?'

'A person I knew in England.'

'Why did he bow to me? He does not know me.'

'Yes, he does know you, in his way.'

'How, monsieur?' (She still called me 'monsieur'; I could not persuade her to adopt any more familiar term.)

'Did you not read the expression of his eyes?'

'Of his eyes? No. What did they say?'

'To you they said, "How do you do, Wilhelmina Crimsworth?" To me, "So you have found your counterpart at last; there she sits, the female of your kind!" '

'Monsieur, you could not read all that in his eyes; he was so soon gone.'

'I read that and more, Frances; I read that he will probably call on me this evening, or on some future occasion shortly;

and I have no doubt he will insist on being introduced to you; shall I bring him to your rooms?'

'If you please, monsieur – I have no objection; I think, indeed, I should rather like to see him nearer; he looks so original.'

As I had anticipated, Mr Hunsden came that evening. The first thing he said was –

'You need not begin boasting, Monsieur le Professeur; I know about your appointment to — College, and all that; Brown has told me.' Then he intimated that he had returned from Germany but a day or two since; afterwards, he abruptly demanded whether that was Madame Pelet-Reuter with whom he had seen me on the Boulevards. I was going to utter a rather emphatic negative, but on second thoughts I checked myself, and, seeming to assent, asked what he thought of her?

'As to her, I'll come to that directly; but first I've a word for you. I see you are a scoundrel; you've no business to be promenading about with another man's wife. I thought you had sounder sense than to get mixed up in foreign hodge-podge of this sort.'

'But the lady?'

'She's too good for you evidently; she is like you, but something better than you – no beauty, though; yet when she rose (for I looked back to see you both walk away) I thought her figure and carriage good. These foreigners understand grace. What the devil has she done with Pelet? She has not been married to him three months – he must be a spoon!'

I would not let the mistake go too far; I did not like it much.

'Pelet? How your head runs on Mons. and Madame Pelet! You are always talking about them. I wish to the gods you had wed Mdlle Zoraïde yourself!'

'Was that young gentlewoman not Mdlle Zoraïde?'

'No; nor Madame Zoraïde either.'

'Why did you tell a lie, then?'

'I told no lie; but you are in such a hurry. She is a pupil of mine – a Swiss girl.'

'And of course you are going to be married to her? Don't deny that.'

'Married! I think I shall – if Fate spares us both ten weeks longer. That is my little wild strawberry, Hunsden, whose sweetness made me careless of your hot-house grapes.'

'Stop! No boasting – no heroics; I won't bear them. What is she? To what *caste* does she belong?'

I smiled. Hunsden unconsciously laid stress on the word *caste*, and in fact, republican, lordhater as he was, Hunsden was as proud of his old —shire blood, of his descent and family standing, respectable and respected through long generations back, as any peer in the realm of his Norman race and Conquest-dated title. Hunsden would as little have thought of taking a wife from a *caste* inferior to his own, as a Stanley would think of mating with a Cobden. I enjoyed the surprise I should give; I enjoyed the triumph of my practice over his theory; and leaning over the table, and uttering the words slowly but with repressed glee, I said concisely –

'She is a lace-mender.'

Hunsden examined me. He did not *say* he was surprised, but surprised he was; he had his own notions of good breeding. I saw he suspected I was going to take some very rash step; but repressing declamation or remonstrance, he only answered –

'Well, you are the best judge of your own affairs. A lace-mender may make a good wife as well as a lady; but of course you have taken care to ascertain thoroughly that since she has not education, fortune, or station, she is well furnished with such natural qualities as you think most likely to conduce to your happiness. Has she many relations?'

'None in Brussels.'

'That is better. Relations are often the real evil in such cases. I cannot but think that a train of inferior connections would have been a bore to you to your life's end.'

After sitting in silence a little while longer, Hunsden rose and was quietly bidding me good evening; the polite, considerate manner in which he offered me his hand (a thing he had never done before) convinced me that he thought I had made a terrible fool of myself; and that, ruined and thrown away as I was, it was no time for sarcasm or cynicism, or indeed for anything but indulgence and forbearance.

'Good-night, William,' he said, in a really soft voice, while his face looked benevolently compassionate. 'Good-night, lad. I wish you and your future wife much prosperity; and I hope she will satisfy your fastidious soul.'

I had much ado to refrain from laughing as I beheld the magnanimous pity of his mien; maintaining, however, a grave air, I said –

'I thought you would have liked to have seen Mdlle Henri?'

'Oh, that is the name! Yes – if it would be convenient, I should like to see her – but –.' He hesitated.

'Well?'

'I should on no account wish to intrude.'

'Come, then,' said I. We set out. Hunsden no doubt regarded me as a rash, imprudent man, thus to show my poor little grisette sweetheart, in her poor little unfurnished grenier; but he prepared to act the real gentleman, having, in fact, the kernel of that character, under the harsh husk it pleased him to wear by way of mental mackintosh. He talked affably, and even gently, as we went along the street; he had never been so civil to me in his life. We reached the house, entered, ascended the stair; on gaining the lobby, Hunsden turned to mount a narrower stair which led to a higher story; I saw his mind was bent on the attics.

'Here, Mr Hunsden,' said I quietly, tapping at Frances' door. He turned; in his genuine politeness he was a little disconcerted at having made the mistake; his eye reverted to the green mat, but he said nothing.

We walked in, and Frances rose from her seat near the table

to receive us; her mourning attire gave her a recluse, rather conventual, but withal very distinguished look; its grave simplicity added nothing to beauty, but much to dignity; the finish of the white collar and manchettes sufficed for a relief to the merino gown of solemn black; ornament was forsworn. Frances curtsied with sedate grace, looking, as she always did, when one first accosted her, more a woman to respect than to love; I introduced Mr Hunsden, and she expressed her happiness at making his acquaintance in French. The pure and polished accent, the low yet sweet and rather full voice, produced their effect immediately; Hunsden spoke French in reply; I had not heard him speak that language before; he managed it very well. I retired to the window-seat; Mr Hunsden, at his hostess's invitation, occupied a chair near the hearth; from my position I could see them both, and the room too, at a glance. The room was so clean and bright, it looked like a little polished cabinet; a glass filled with flowers in the centre of the table, a fresh rose in each china cup on the mantelpiece gave it an air of *fête*. Frances was serious, and Mr Hunsden subdued, but both mutually polite; they got on at the French swimmingly: ordinary topics were discussed with great state and decorum; I thought I had never seen two such models of propriety, for Hunsden (thanks to the constraint of the foreign tongue) was obliged to shape his phrases, and measure his sentences, with a care that forbade any eccentricity. At last England was mentioned, and Frances proceeded to ask questions. Animated by degrees, she began to change, just as a grave night-sky changes at the approach of sunrise: first it seemed as if her forehead cleared, then her eyes glittered, her features relaxed and became quite mobile; her subdued complexion grew warm and transparent; to me, she now looked pretty; before, she had only looked ladylike.

She had many things to say to the Englishman just fresh from his island-country, and she urged him with an enthusiasm of curiosity, which ere long thawed Hunsden's reserve as fire thaws a congealed viper. I use this not very flattering comparison because he vividly reminded me of a snake waking from torpor, as he erected his tall form, reared his head, before a little declined, and putting back his hair from his broad Saxon forehead, showed unshaded the gleam of almost savage satire which his interlocutor's tone of eagerness and look of ardour had sufficed at once to kindle in his soul and elicit from his eyes: he was himself, as Frances was herself, and in none but his own language would he now address her.

'You understand English?' was the prefatory question.

'A little.'

'Well, then, you shall have plenty of it; and first, I see you've not much more sense than some others of my acquaintance' (indicating me with his thumb), 'or else you'd never turn rabid about that dirty little country called England; for rabid, I see you are; I read Anglophobia in your looks, and hear it in your words. Why, mademoiselle, is it possible that anybody with a grain of rationality should feel enthusiasm about a mere name, and that name England? I thought you were a lady-abbess five minutes ago, and respected you accordingly; and now I see you are a sort of Swiss sibyl, with high Tory and high Church principles!'

'England is your country?' asked Frances.

'Yes.'

'And you don't like it?'

'I'd be sorry to like it! A little corrupt, venal, lord-and-king-cursed nation, full of mucky pride (as they say in —shire), and helpless pauperism; rotten with abuses, worm-eaten with prejudices!'

'You might say so of almost every state; there are abuses and prejudices everywhere, and I thought fewer in England than in other countries.'

'Come to England and see. Come to Birmingham and Manchester; come to St Giles' in London, and get a practical notion of how our system works. Examine the footprints of our august aristocracy; see how they walk in blood, crushing hearts as they go. Just put your head in at English cottage doors; get a glimpse of Famine crouched torpid on black hearth-stones; of Disease lying bare on beds without coverlets, of Infamy wantoning viciously with Ignorance, though indeed Luxury is her favourite paramour, and princely halls are dearer to her than thatched hovels –'

'I was not thinking of the wretchedness and vice in England; I was thinking of the good side – of what is elevated in your character as a nation.'

'There is no good side – none at least of which you can have any knowledge; for you cannot appreciate the efforts of industry, the achievements of enterprise, or the discoveries of science; narrowness of education and obscurity of position quite incapacitate you from understanding those points; and as to historical and poetical associations, I will not insult you, mademoiselle, by supposing that you alluded to such humbug.'

'But I did partly.'

Hunsden laughed – his laugh of unmitigated scorn.

'I did, Mr Hunsden. Are you of the number of those to whom such associations give no pleasure?'

'Mademoiselle, what is an association? I never saw one. What is its length, breadth, weight, value – aye, *value*? What price will it bring in the market?'

'Your portrait, to any one who loved you, would, for the sake of association, be without price.'

That inscrutable Hunsden heard this remark and felt it rather acutely, too, somewhere; for he coloured – a thing not unusual with him, when hit unawares on a tender point. A sort of trouble momentarily darkened his eye, and I believe he filled up the transient pause succeeding his antagonist's home-thrust, by a wish that someone did love him as he would like to be loved – someone whose love he could unreservedly return.

The lady pursued her temporary advantage.

'If your world is a world without associations, Mr Hunsden,

I no longer wonder that you hate England so. I don't clearly know what Paradise is, and what angels are; yet taking it to be the most glorious region I can conceive, and angels the most elevated existences – if one of them – if Abdiel the Faithful himself' (she was thinking of Milton) 'were suddenly stripped of the faculty of association, I think he would soon rush forth from "the everduring gates", leave heaven, and seek what he had lost in hell. Yes, in the very hell from which he turned "with retorted scorn".'

Frances' tone in saying this was as marked as her language, and it was when the word 'hell' twanged off from her lips with a somewhat startling emphasis, that Hunsden deigned to bestow one slight glance of admiration. He liked something strong, whether in man or woman; he liked whatever dared to clear conventional limits. He had never before heard a lady say 'hell' with that uncompromising sort of accent, and the sound pleased him from a lady's lips; he would fain have had Frances to strike the string again, but it was not in her way. The display of eccentric vigour never gave her pleasure, and it only sounded in her voice or flashed in her countenance when extraordinary circumstances – and those generally painful – forced it out of the depths where it burned latent. To me, once or twice, she had, in intimate conversation, uttered venturous thoughts in nervous language; but when the hour of such manifestation was past, I could not recall it; it came of itself and of itself departed. Hunsden's excitations she put by soon with a smile, and, recurring to the theme of disputation, said –

'Since England is nothing, why do the Continental nations respect her so?'

'I should have thought no child would have asked that question,' replied Hunsden, who never at any time gave information without reproving for stupidity those who asked it of him. 'If you had been my pupil, as I suppose you once had the misfortune to be that of a deplorable character not a hundred miles off, I would have put you in the corner for such a confession of ignorance. Why, mademoiselle, can't you see that it is our *gold* which buys us French politeness, German good-will, and Swiss servility?' and he sneered diabolically.

'Swiss!' said Frances, catching the word 'servility'. 'Do you call my countrymen servile?' And she started up. I could not suppress a low laugh; there was ire in her glance and defiance in her attitude. 'Do you abuse Switzerland to me, Mr Hunsden? Do you think I have no associations? Do you calculate that I am prepared to dwell only on what vice and degradation may be found in Alpine villages, and to leave quite out of my heart the social greatness of my countrymen, and our blood-earned freedom, and the natural glories of our mountains? You're mistaken – you're mistaken!'

'Social greatness? Call it what you will, your countrymen are sensible fellows; they make a marketable article of what to you is an abstract idea; they have, ere this, sold their social greatness and also their blood-earned freedom to be the servants of foreign kings.'

'You never were in Switzerland?'

'Yes – I have been there twice.'

'You know nothing of it.'

'I do.'

'And you say the Swiss are mercenary, as a parrot says "Poor Poll", or as the Belgians here say the English are not brave, or as the French accuse them of being perfidious: there is no justice in your dictums.'

'There is truth.'

'I tell you, Mr Hunsden, you are a more unpractical man than I am an unpractical woman, for you don't acknowledge what really exists; you want to annihilate individual patriotism and national greatness as an atheist would annihilate God and his own soul, by denying their existence.'

'Where are you flying to? You are off at a tangent – I thought we were talking about the mercenary nature of the Swiss.'

'We were – and if you proved to me that the Swiss are

mercenary to-morrow (which you cannot do) I should love Switzerland still.'

'You would be mad, then – mad as a March hare – to indulge in a passion for millions of shiploads of soil, timber, snow, and ice.'

'Not so mad as you who love nothing.'

'There's a method in my madness; there's none in yours.'

'Your method is to squeeze the sap out of creation and make manure of the refuse, by way of turning it to what you call use.'

'You cannot reason at all,' said Hunsden; 'there is no logic in you.'

'Better to be without logic than without feeling,' retorted Frances, who was now passing backwards and forwards from her cupboard to the table, intent, if not on hospitable thoughts, at least on hospitable deeds, for she was laying the cloth, and putting plates, knives and forks thereon.

'Is that a hit at me, mademoiselle? Do you suppose I am without feeling?'

'I suppose you are always interfering with your own feelings, and those of other people, and dogmatizing about the irrationality of this, that, and the other sentiment, and then ordering it to be suppressed because you imagine it to be inconsistent with logic.'

'I do right.'

Frances had stepped out of sight into a sort of little pantry; she soon reappeared.

'You do right? Indeed, no! You are much mistaken if you think so. Just be so good as to let me get to the fire, Mr Hunsden; I have something to cook.' (An interval occupied in settling a casserole on the fire; then, while she stirred its contents:) 'Right! as if it were right to crush any pleasurable sentiment that God has given to man, especially any sentiment that, like patriotism, spreads man's selfishness in wider circles' (fire stirred, dish put down before it).

'Were you born in Switzerland?'

'I should think so, or else why should I call it my country?'

'And where did you get your English features and figure?'

'I am English, too; half the blood in my veins is English; thus I have a right to a double power of patriotism, possessing an interest in two noble, free, and fortunate countries.'

'You had an English mother?'

'Yes, yes; and you, I suppose, had a mother from the moon or from Utopia, since not a nation in Europe has a claim on your interest?'

'On the contrary, I'm a universal patriot, if you could understand me rightly: my country is the world.'

'Sympathies so widely diffused must be very shallow: will you have the goodness to come to table. Monsieur' (to me who appeared to be now absorbed in reading by moonlight) – 'Monsieur, supper is served.'

This was said in quite a different voice to that in which she had been bandying phrases with Mr Hunsden – not so short, graver and softer.

'Frances, what do you mean by preparing supper? we had no intention of staying.'

'Ah, monsieur, but you have stayed, and supper is prepared; you have only the alternative of eating it.'

The meal was a foreign one, of course; it consisted in two small but tasty dishes of meat prepared with skill and served with nicety; a salad and 'fromage français', completed it. The business of eating interposed a brief truce between the belligerents, but no sooner was supper disposed of than they were at it again. The fresh subject of dispute ran on the spirit of religious intolerance which Mr Hunsden affirmed to exist strongly in Switzerland, notwithstanding the professed attachment of the Swiss to freedom. Here Frances had greatly the worst of it, not only because she was unskilled to argue, but because her own real opinions on the point in question happened to coincide pretty nearly with Mr Hunsden's, and she only contradicted him out of opposition. At last she gave in, confessing that she thought as he thought, but bidding him take notice that she did not consider herself beaten.

'No more did the French at Waterloo,' said Hunsden.

'There is no comparison between the cases,' rejoined Frances; 'mine was a sham fight.'

'Sham or real, it's up with you.'

'No; though I have neither logic nor wealth of words, yet in a case where my opinion really differed from yours, I would adhere to it when I had not another word to say in its defence; you should be baffled by dumb determination. You speak of Waterloo; your Wellington ought to have been conquered there, according to Napoleon; but he persevered in spite of the laws of war, and was victorious in defiance of military tactics. I would do as he did.'

'I'll be bound for it you would; probably you have some of the same sort of stubborn stuff in you.'

'I should be sorry if I had not; he and Tell were brothers, and I'd scorn the Swiss, man or woman, who had none of the much-enduring nature of our heroic William in his soul.'

'If Tell was like Wellington, he was an ass.'

'Does not *ass* mean *baudet*?' asked Frances, turning to me.

'No, no,' replied I, 'it means an *esprit-fort*; and now,' I continued, as I saw that fresh occasion of strife was brewing between these two, 'it is high time to go.'

Hunsden rose. 'Good-bye,' said he to Frances; 'I shall be off for this glorious England to-morrow, and it may be twelve months or more before I come to Brussels again; whenever I do come I'll seek you out, and you shall see if I don't find means to make you fiercer than a dragon. You've done pretty well this evening, but next interview you shall challenge me outright. Meantime you're doomed to become Mrs William Crimsworth, I suppose; poor young lady! but you have a spark of spirit; cherish it, and give the Professor the full benefit thereof.'

'Are you married, Mr Hunsden?' asked Frances, suddenly.

'No. I should have thought you might have guessed I was a Benedict by my look.'

'Well, whenever you marry don't take a wife out of Switzerland; for if you begin blaspheming Helvetia, and cursing the cantons – above all, if you mention the word *ass* in the same breath with the name Tell (for ass *is* baudet, I know; though Monsieur is pleased to translate it *esprit-fort*) your mountain maid will some night smother her Breton-bretonnant, even as your own Shakespeare's Othello smothered Desdemona.'

'I am warned,' said Hunsden; 'and so are you, lad' (nodding to me). 'I hope yet to hear of a travesty of the Moor and his gentle lady, in which the parts shall be reversed according to the plan just sketched – you, however, being in my nightcap. Farewell, mademoiselle!' He bowed on her hand, absolutely like Sir Charles Grandison on that of Harriet Byron; adding – 'Death from such fingers would not be without charms.'

'Mon Dieu!' murmured Frances, opening her large eyes and lifting her distinctly arched brows; 'c'est qu'il fait des compliments! je ne m'y suis pas attendu.' She smiled, half in ire, half in mirth, curtsied with foreign grace, and so they parted.

No sooner had we got into the street than Hunsden collared me.

'And that is your lace-mender?' said he; 'and you reckon you have done a fine, magnanimous thing in offering to marry her? You, a scion of Seacombe, have proved your disdain of social distinctions by taking up with an *ouvrière*! And I pitied the fellow, thinking his feelings had misled him, and that he had hurt himself by contracting a low match!'

'Just let go my collar, Hunsden.'

On the contrary, he swayed me to and fro; so I grappled him round the waist. It was dark; the street lonely and lampless. We had then a tug for it; and after we had both rolled on the pavement, and with difficulty picked ourselves up, we agreed to walk on more soberly.

'Yes, that's my lace-mender,' said I; 'and she is to be mine for life – God willing.'

'God is not willing – you can't suppose it; what business have you to be suited so well with a partner? And she treats you with a sort of respect, too, and says, "Monsieur", and modulates her tone in addressing you, actually, as if you were something superior! She could not evince more deference to such a one as I, were she favoured by fortune to the supreme extent of being my choice instead of yours.'

'Hunsden, you're a puppy. But you've only seen the title-page of my happiness; you don't know the tale that follows; you cannot conceive the interest and sweet variety and thrilling excitement of the narrative.'

Hunsden – speaking low and deep, for we had now entered a busier street – desired me to hold my peace, threatening to do something dreadful if I stimulated his wrath further by boasting. I laughed till my sides ached. We soon reached his hotel; before he entered it, he said –

'Don't be vainglorious. Your lace-mender is too good for you, but not good enough for me; neither physically nor morally does she come up to my ideal of a woman. No; I dream of something far beyond that pale-faced, excitable little Helvetian (by the by she has infinitely more of the nervous mobile Paris-ienne in her than of the robust "jungfrau"). Your Mdlle Henri is in person chétive, in mind sans caractère, compared with the queen of my visions. You, indeed, may put up with that minois chiffoné; but when I marry I must have straighter and more harmonious features, to say nothing of a nobler and better developed shape than that perverse, ill-thriven child can boast.'

'Bribe a seraph to fetch you a coal of fire from heaven, if you will,' said I, 'and with it kindle life in the tallest, fattest, most boneless, fullest-blooded of Rubens' painted women – leave me only my Alpine peri, and I'll not envy you.'

With a simultaneous movement, each turned his back on the other. Neither said 'God bless you'; yet on the morrow the sea was to roll between us.

CHAPTER XXV

In two months more Frances had fulfilled the time of mourning for her aunt. One January morning – the first of the New Year holidays – I went in a fiacre, accompanied only by M. Vandenhuten, to the Rue Notre Dame aux Neiges, and having alighted alone and walked upstairs, I found Frances apparently waiting for me, dressed in a style scarcely appropriate to that cold, bright frosty day. Never till now had I seen her attired in any other than black or sad-coloured stuff; and there she stood by the window, clad all in white, and white of a most diaphanous texture; her array was very simple, to be sure, but it looked imposing and festal because it was so clear, full, and floating; a veil shadowed her head, and hung below her knee, a little wreath of pink flowers fastened it to her thickly tressed Grecian plait, and thence it fell softly on each side of her face. Singular to state, she was, or had been crying; when I asked her if she were ready, she said 'Yes, monsieur', with something very like a checked sob; and when I took a shawl, which lay on the table, and folded it round her, not only did tear after tear course unbidden down her cheek, but she shook to my ministration like a reed. I said I was sorry to see her in such low spirits, and requested to be allowed an insight into the origin thereof. She only said, 'It was impossible to help it', and then voluntarily, though hurriedly, putting her hand into mine, accompanied me out of the room, and ran downstairs with a quick, uncertain step, like one who was eager to get some formidable piece of business over. I put her into the fiacre. M. Vandenhuten received her, and seated her beside himself, we drove all together to the Protestant chapel, went through a certain service in the Common Prayer Book, and she and I came out married. M. Vandenhuten had given the bride away.

We took no bridal trip; our modesty, screened by the peaceful obscurity of our station, and the pleasant isolation of our circumstances, did not exact that additional precaution. We repaired at once to a small house I had taken in the faubourg nearest to that part of the city where the scene of our avocations lay.

Three or four hours after the wedding ceremony, Frances, divested of her bridal snow, and attired in a pretty lilac gown of warmer materials, a piquant black silk apron, and a lace collar with some finishing decoration of lilac ribbon, was kneeling on the carpet of a neatly furnished though not spacious parlour, arranging on the shelves of a chiffonnière some books, which I handed to her from the table. It was snowing fast out of doors; the afternoon had turned out wild and cold; the leaden sky seemed full of drifts, and the street was already ankle-deep in the white downfall. Our fire burned bright, our new habitation looked brilliantly clean and fresh, the furniture was all arranged, and there were but some articles of glass, china, books, etc., to put in order. Frances found in this business occupation till tea-time, and then, after I had distinctly instructed her how to make a cup of tea in rational English style, and after she had got over the dismay occasioned by seeing such an extravagant amount of material put into the pot, she administered to me a proper British repast, at which there wanted neither candles nor urn, firelight nor comfort.

Our week's holiday glided by, and we readdressed ourselves to labour. Both my wife and I began in good earnest with the notion that we were working people, destined to earn our bread by exertion, and that of the most assiduous kind. Our days were thoroughly occupied; we used to part every morning at eight o'clock, and not meet again till five p.m.; but into what sweet rest did the turmoil of each busy day decline! Looking down the vista of memory, I see the evenings passed in that little parlour like a long string of rubies circling the dusk brow of the past. Unvaried were they as each cut gem, and like each gem brilliant and burning.

A year and a half passed. One morning (it was a *fête*, and we had the day to ourselves) Frances said to me, with a suddenness peculiar to her when she had been thinking long on a subject, and at last, having came to a conclusion, wished to test its soundness by the touchstone of my judgment –

'I don't work enough.'

'What now?' demanded I, looking up from my coffee, which I had been deliberately stirring while enjoying, in anticipation, a walk I purposed to take with Frances, that fine summer day (it was June), to a certain farm-house in the country, where we were to dine. 'What now?' and I saw at once, in the serious ardour of her face, a project of vital importance.

'I am not satisfied,' returned she: 'you are now earning eight thousand francs a year' (it was true; my efforts, punctuality, the fame of my pupils' progress, the publicity of my station, had so far helped me on), 'while I am still at my miserable twelve hundred francs. I *can* do better, and I *will*.'

'You work as long and as diligently as I do, Frances.'

'Yes, monsieur, but I am not working in the right way, and I am convinced of it.'

'You wish to change – you have a plan for progress in your mind; go and put on your bonnet; and, while we take our walk, you shall tell me of it.'

'Yes, monsieur.'

She went – as docile as a well-trained child; she was a curious mixture of tractability and firmness: I sat thinking about her, and wondering what her plan could be, when she re-entered.

'Monsieur, I have given Minnie' (our bonne) 'leave to go out too, as it is so very fine; so will you be kind enough to lock the door, and take the key with you?'

'Kiss me, Mrs Crimsworth,' was my not very apposite reply; but she looked so engaging in her light summer dress and little cottage bonnet, and her manner in speaking to me was then, as always, so unaffectedly and suavely respectful, that my heart expanded at the sight of her, and a kiss seemed necessary to content its importunity.

'There, monsieur.'

'Why do you always call me "Monsieur"? Say "William".'

'I cannot pronounce your W; besides, "Monsieur" belongs to you; I like it best.'

Minnie having departed in clean cap and smart shawl, we, too, set out, leaving the house solitary and silent – silent, at least, but for the ticking of the clock. We were soon clear of Brussels; the fields received us, and then the lanes, remote from carriage-resounding *chaussées*. Ere long we came upon a nook, so rural, green, and secluded, it might have been a spot in some pastoral English province; a bank of short and mossy grass, under a hawthorn, offered a seat too tempting to be declined; we took it, and when we had admired and examined some English-looking wild-flowers growing at our feet, I recalled Frances' attention and my own to the topic touched on at breakfast.

'What was her plan?' A natural one – the next step to be mounted by us, or, at least, by her, if she wanted to rise in her profession. She proposed to begin a school. We already had the means for commencing on a careful scale, having lived greatly within our income. We possessed, too, by this time, an extensive and eligible connection, in the sense advantageous to our business; for, though our circle of visiting acquaintance continued as limited as ever, we were now widely known in schools and families as teachers. When Frances had developed her plan, she intimated, in some closing sentences, her hopes for the future. If we only had good health and tolerable success, we might, she was sure, in time realize an independency; and that, perhaps, before we were too old to enjoy it; then both she and I would rest; and what was to hinder us from going to live in England? England was still her Promised Land.

I put no obstacle in her way; raised no objection; I knew she was not one who could live quiescent and inactive, or even comparatively inactive. Duties she must have to fulfil, and important duties; work to do – and exciting, absorbing, profitable work; strong faculties stirred in her frame, and they demanded full nourishment, free exercise: mine was not the hand ever to starve or cramp them; no, I delighted in offering them sustenance, and in clearing them wider space for action.

'You have conceived a plan, Frances,' said I, 'and a good plan; execute it; you have my free consent, and wherever and whenever my assistance is wanted, ask and you shall have.'

Frances' eyes thanked me almost with tears; just a sparkle or two, soon brushed away; she possessed herself of my hand too, and held it for some time very close clasped in both her own, but she said no more than, 'Thank you, monsieur.'

We passed a divine day, and came home late, lighted by a full summer moon.

Ten years rushed now upon me with dusty, vibrating, unresting wings; years of bustle, action, unslacked endeavour; years in which I and my wife, having launched ourselves in the full career of progress, as progress whirls on in European capitals, scarcely knew repose, were strangers to amusement, never thought of indulgence, and yet, as our course ran side by side, as we marched hand in hand, we neither murmured, repented, nor faltered. Hope indeed cheered us; health kept us up; harmony of thought and deed smoothed many difficulties, and, finally, success bestowed every now and then encouraging reward on diligence. Our school became one of the most popular in Brussels, and as by degrees we raised our terms and elevated our system of education, our choice of pupils grew more select, and at length included the children of the best families in Belgium. We had, too, an excellent connection in England, first opened by the unsolicited recommendation of Mr Hunsden, who having been over, and having abused me for my prosperity in set terms, went back, and soon after sent a leash of young —shire heiresses – his cousins; as he said, 'to be polished off by Mrs Crimsworth'.

As to this same Mrs Crimsworth, in one sense she was become another woman, though in another she remained unchanged. So different was she under different circumstances, I seemed to possess two wives. The faculties of her nature, already disclosed when I married her, remained fresh and fair; but other faculties shot up strong, branched out broad, and quite altered the external character of the plant. Firmness, activity, and enterprise, covered with grave foliage, poetic feeling, and fervour; but these flowers were still there, preserved pure and dewy under the umbrage of later growth and hardier nature: perhaps I only in the world knew the secret of their existence, but to me they were ever ready to yield an exquisite fragrance and present a beauty as chaste as radiant.

In the daytime my house and establishment were conducted by Madame the directress, a stately and elegant woman, bearing much anxious thought on her large brow; much calculated dignity in her serious mien: immediately after breakfast I used to part with this lady; I went to my college, she to her schoolroom; returning for an hour in the course of the day, I found her always in class, intently occupied: silence, industry, observance, attending on her presence. When not actually teaching, she was overlooking and guiding by eye and gesture; she then appeared vigilant and solicitous. When communicating instruction, her aspect was more animated; she seemed to feel a certain enjoyment in the occupation. The language in which she addressed her pupils, though simple and unpretending, was never trite or dry; she did not speak from routine formulas – she made her own phrases as she went on, and very nervous and impressive phrases they frequently were; often, when elucidating favourite points of history, or geography, she would wax genuinely eloquent in her earnestness. Her pupils, or at least the elder and more intelligent amongst them, recognized well the language of a superior mind; they felt too, and some of them received the impression of elevated sentiments; there was little fondling between mistress and girls, but some of Frances' pupils in time learnt to love her sincerely, all of them beheld her with respect; her general demeanour towards them was serious; sometimes benignant when they pleased her with their progress and attention, always scrupulously refined and considerate. In cases where reproof or punishment was called for she was usually forbearing enough; but if any took advantage of that forbearance, which sometimes happened, a sharp, sudden, and lightning-like severity taught the culprit the extent of the mistake committed. Sometimes a gleam of tenderness softened her eyes and manner, but this was rare; only when a pupil was sick, or when it pined after home, or in the case of some little motherless child, or of one much poorer than its companion, whose scanty wardrobe and mean appointments brought on it the contempt of the jewelled young countesses and silk-clad misses. Over such feeble fledgelings the directress spread a wing of kindliest protection: it was to their bedside she came at night to tuck them warmly in; it was after them she looked in winter to see that they always had a comfortable seat by the stove; it was they who by turns were summoned to the salon to receive some little dole of cake or fruit – to sit on a footstool at the fireside – to enjoy home comforts, and almost home liberty, for an evening together – to be spoken to gently and softly, comforted, encouraged, cherished – and when bedtime came, dismissed with a kiss of true tenderness. As to Julia and Georgiana G——, daughters of an English baronet, as to Mdlle Mathilde de ——, heiress of a Belgian count, and sundry other children of patrician race, the directress was careful of them as of the others, anxious for their progress, as for that of the rest – but it never seemed to enter her head to distinguish them by a mark of preference; one girl of noble blood she loved dearly – a young Irish baroness – Lady Catherine ——; but it was for her enthusiastic heart and clever head, for her generosity and her genius – the title and rank went for nothing.

My afternoons were spent also in college, with the exception of an hour that my wife daily exacted of me for her establishment, and with which she would not dispense. She said I must spend that time amongst her pupils to learn their characters, to be *au courant* with everything that was passing in the house, to become interested in what interested her, to be able to give her my opinion on knotty points when she required it, and this she did constantly, never allowing my interest in the pupils to fall asleep, and never making any change of importance without my cognizance and consent. She delighted to sit by me when I gave my lessons (lessons in literature), her hands folded on her knee, the most fixedly attentive of any present. She rarely addressed me in class; when she did it was with an air of marked deference; it was her pleasure, her joy to make me still the master in all things.

At six o'clock p.m. my daily labours ceased. I then came home, for my home was my heaven; ever at that hour, as I entered our private sitting-room, the lady-directress vanished from before my eyes, and Frances Henri, my own little lace-mender, was magically restored to my arms; much disappointed she would have been if her master had not been as constant to the tryste as herself, and if his truthful kiss had not been prompt to answer her soft 'Bon soir, monsieur'.

Talk French to me she would, and many a punishment she has had for her wilfulness. I fear the choice of chastisement must have been injudicious, for instead of correcting the fault, it seemed to encourage its renewal. Our evenings were our own; that recreation was necessary to refresh our strength for all the due discharge of our duties; sometimes we spent them all in conversation, and my young Genevese, now that she was thoroughly accustomed to her English professor, now that she loved him too absolutely to fear him much, reposed in him a confidence so unlimited that topics of conversation could no more be wanting with him than subjects for communion with her own heart. In those moments, happy as a bird with its mate, she would show me what she had of vivacity, of mirth, of originality in her well-dowered nature. She would show, too, some stores of raillery, of 'malice', and would vex, tease, pique me sometimes about what she called my 'bizarreries anglaises', my 'caprices insulaires', with a wild and witty wickedness that made a perfect white demon of her while it lasted. This was rare, however, and the elfish freak was always short: sometimes when driven a little hard in the war of words – for her tongue did ample justice to the pith, the point, the delicacy of her native French, in which language she always attacked me – I used to turn upon her with my old decision, and arrest bodily the sprite that teased me. Vain idea! no sooner had I grasped hand or arm than the elf was gone; the provocative smile quenched in the expressive brown eyes, and a ray of gentle homage shone under the lids in its place. I had seized a mere vexing fairy, and found a submissive and supplicating little mortal woman in my arms. Then I made her get a book, and read English to me for an hour by way of penance. I frequently dosed her with Wordsworth in this way, and Wordsworth steadied her soon; she had a difficulty in comprehending his deep, serene, and sober mind; his language, too, was not facile to her; she had to ask questions, to sue for explanations, to be like a child and a novice, and to acknowledge me as her senior and director. Her instinct instantly penetrated and possessed the meaning of more ardent and imaginative writers. Byron excited her; Scott she loved; Wordsworth only she puzzled at, wondered over, and hesitated to pronounce an opinion upon.

But whether she read to me, or talked with me; whether she teased me in French, or entreated me in English; whether she jested with wit, or inquired with deference; narrated with interest, or listened with attention; whether she smiled *at* me or *on* me, always at nine o'clock I was left – abandoned. She would extricate herself from my arms, quit my side, take her lamp, and be gone. Her mission was upstairs; I have followed her sometimes and watched her. First she opened the door of the dortoir (the pupils' chamber), noiselessly she glided up the long room between the two rows of white beds, surveyed all the sleepers; if any were wakeful, especially if any were sad, spoke to them and soothed them; stood some minutes to ascertain that all was safe and tranquil; trimmed the watchlight which burned in the apartment all night, then withdrew, closing the door behind her without sound. Thence she glided to our own chamber; it had a little cabinet within; this she sought; there, too, appeared a bed, but one, and that a very small one; her face (the night I followed and observed her) changed as she approached this tiny couch; from grave it warmed to earnest; she shaded with one hand the lamp she held in the other; she bent above the pillow and hung over a child asleep; its slumber (that evening at least, and usually, I believe) was sound and calm; no tear wet its dark eyelashes; no fever heated its round cheek; no ill dream discomposed its budding features. Frances gazed, she did not smile, and yet the deepest delight filled, flushed her face; feeling, pleasurable, powerful, worked in her whole frame, which still was motionless. I saw, indeed, her heart heave, her lips were a little apart, her breathing grew somewhat hurried; the child smiled; then at last the mother smiled too, and said in low soliloquy, 'God bless my little son!' She stooped closer over him, breathed the softest of kisses on his brow, covered his minute hand with hers, and at last started up and came away. I regained the parlour before her. Entering it two minutes later she said quietly as she put down her extinguished lamp –

'Victor rests well: he smiled in his sleep; he has your smile, monsieur.'

The said Victor was of course her own boy, born in the third year of our marriage: his Christian name had been given him in honour of M. Vandenhuten, who continued always our trusty and well-beloved friend.

Frances was then a good and dear wife to me, because I was to her a good, just, and faithful husband. What she would have been had she married a harsh, envious, careless man – a profligate, a prodigal, a drunkard, or a tyrant – is another question, and one which I once propounded to her. Her answer, given after some reflection was –

'I should have tried to endure the evil or cure it for awhile; and when I found it intolerable and incurable, I should have left my torturer suddenly and silently.'

'And if law or might had forced you back again?'

'What, to a drunkard, a profligate, a selfish spendthrift, an unjust fool?'

'Yes.'

'I would have gone back; again assured myself whether or not his vice and my misery were capable of remedy; and if not, have left him again.'

'And if again forced to return, and compelled to abide?'

'I don't know,' she said hastily. 'Why do you ask me, monsieur?'

I would have an answer, because I saw a strange kind of spirit in her eye, whose voice I determined to waken.

'Monsieur, if a wife's nature loathes that of the man she is wedded to, marriage must be slavery. Against slavery all right thinkers revolt, and though torture be the price of resistance, torture must be dared: though the only road to freedom lie through the gates of death, those gates must be passed; for freedom is indispensable. Then, monsieur, I would resist as far as my strength permitted; when that strength failed I should be sure of a refuge. Death would certainly screen me both from bad laws and their consequences.'

'Voluntary death, Frances?'

'No, monsieur. I'd have courage to live out every throe of anguish fate assigned me, and principle to contend for justice and liberty to the last.'

'I see you would have made no patient Grizzle. And now, supposing fate had merely assigned you the lot of an old maid, what then? How would you have liked celibacy?'

'Not much, certainly. An old maid's life must doubtless be void and vapid – her heart strained and empty. Had I been an old maid I should have spent existence in efforts to fill the void and ease the aching. I should have probably failed, and died weary and disappointed, despised and of no account, like other single women. But I'm not an old maid,' she added quickly. 'I should have been, though, but for my master. I should never have suited any man but Professor Crimsworth – no other gentleman, French, English, or Belgian, would have thought me amiable or handsome; and I doubt whether I should have cared for the approbation of many others, if I could have obtained it. Now, I have been Professor Crimsworth's wife eight years, and what is he in my eyes? Is he honourable, beloved – ?' She stopped, her voice was cut off, her eyes suddenly suffused. She and I were standing side by side; she threw her arms round me, and strained me to her heart with passionate earnestness: the energy of her whole being glowed in her dark and then dilated eye, and crimsoned her animated cheek; her look and movement were like inspiration; in one there was such a flash, in the other such a power. Half an hour afterwards, when she had become calm, I asked where all that wild vigour was gone which had transformed her erewhile and made her glance so thrilling and ardent – her action so rapid and strong. She looked down, smiling softly and passively –

'I cannot tell where it is gone, monsieur,' said she, 'but I know that, whenever it is wanted, it will come back again.'

Behold us now at the close of the ten years, and we have realized an independency. The rapidity with which we attained this end had its origin in three reasons: – Firstly, we worked so hard for it; secondly, we had no incumbrances to delay success; thirdly, as soon as we had capital to invest, two well-skilled counsellors, one in Belgium, one in England, viz. Vandenhuten and Hunsden, gave us each a word of advice as to the sort of investment to be chosen. The suggestion made was judicious; and, being promptly acted on, the result proved gainful –

I need not say how gainful; I communicated details to Messrs Vandenhuten and Hunsden; nobody else can be interested in hearing them.

Accounts being wound up, and our professional connection disposed of, we both agreed that, as mammon was not our master, nor his service that in which we desired to spend our lives; as our desires were temperate, and our habits unostentatious, we now had abundance to live on – abundance to leave our boy; and should, besides, always have a balance on hand, which, properly managed by right sympathy and unselfish activity, might help philanthropy in her enterprises, and put solace into the hand of charity.

To England we now resolved to take wing; we arrived there safely; Frances realized the dream of her lifetime. We spent a whole summer and autumn in travelling from end to end of the British islands, and afterwards passed a winter in London. Then we thought it high time to fix our residence. My heart yearned towards my native county of —shire; and it is in —shire I now live; it is in the library of my own home I am now writing. That home lies amid a sequestered and rather hilly region, thirty miles removed from X—; a region whose verdure the smoke of mills has not yet sullied, whose waters still run pure, whose swells of moorland preserve in some ferny glens that lie between them the very primal wildness of nature, her moss, her bracken, her blue-bells, her scents of reed and heather, her free and fresh breezes. My house is a picturesque and not too spacious dwelling, with low and long windows, a trellised and leaf-veiled porch over the front door, just now, on this summer evening, looking like an arch of roses and ivy. The garden is chiefly laid out in lawn, formed of the sod of the hills, with herbage short and soft as moss, full of its own peculiar flowers, tiny and star-like, imbedded in the minute embroidery of their fine foliage. At the bottom of the sloping garden there is a wicket, which opens upon a lane as green as the lawn, very long, shady, and little frequented; on the turf of this lane

generally appear the first daisies of spring – whence its name –
Daisy Lane; serving also as a distinction to the house.

It terminates (the lane I mean) in a valley of wood; which
wood – chiefly oak and beech – spreads shadowy about the
vicinage of a very old mansion, one of the Elizabethan struc-
tures, much larger, as well as more antique than Daisy Lane,
the property and residence of an individual familiar both to
me and to the reader. Yes, in Hunsden Wood – for so are those
glades and that grey building, with many gables and more
chimneys, named – abides Yorke Hunsden, still unmarried;
never, I suppose, having yet found his ideal, though I know at
least a score of young ladies, within a circuit of forty miles,
who would be willing to assist him in the search.

The estate fell to him by the death of his father, five years
since; he has given up trade, after having made by it sufficient
to pay off some incumbrances by which the family heritage was
burdened. I say he abides here, but I do not think he is resident
about five months out of the twelve; he wanders from land
to land, and spends some part of each winter in town: he
frequently brings visitors with him when he comes to —shire,
and these visitors are often foreigners; sometimes he has a
German metaphysician, sometimes a French savant; he had
once a dissatisfied and savage-looking Italian, who neither sang
nor played, and of whom Frances affirmed that he had 'tout
l'air d'un conspirateur'.

What English guests Hunsden invites, are all either men of
Birmingham or Manchester – hard men, seemingly knit up in
one thought, whose talk is of free trade. The foreign visitors,
too, are politicians; they take a wider theme – European progress
– the spread of liberal sentiments over the Continent; on their
mental tablets, the names of Russia, Austria, and the Pope are
inscribed in red ink. I have heard some of them talk vigorous
sense – yea, I have been present at polyglot discussions in the
old, oak-lined dining-room at Hunsden Wood, where a singular
insight was given of the sentiments entertained by resolute

minds respecting old northern despotisms, and old southern superstitions; also, I have heard much twaddle, enounced chiefly in French and Deutsch, but let that pass. Hunsden himself tolerated the drivelling theorists; with the practical men he seemed leagued hand and heart.

When Hunsden is staying alone at the Wood (which seldom happens) he generally finds his way two or three times a week to Daisy Lane. He has a philanthropic motive for coming to smoke his cigar in our porch on summer evenings; he says he does it to kill the earwigs amongst the roses, with which insects, but for his benevolent fumigations, he intimates we should certainly be overrun. On wet days, too, we are almost sure to see him; according to him, it gets on time to work me into lunacy by treading on my mental corns, or to force from Mrs Crimsworth revelations of the dragon within her, by insulting the memory of Hofer and Tell.

We also go frequently to Hunsden Wood, and both I and Frances relish a visit there highly. If there are other guests, their characters are an interesting study; their conversation is exciting and strange; the absence of all local narrowness both in the host and his chosen society gives a metropolitan, almost a cosmopolitan freedom and largeness to the talk. Hunsden himself is a polite man in his own house: he has, when he chooses to employ it, an inexhaustible power of entertaining guests; his very mansion too is interesting, the rooms look storied, the passages legendary, the low-ceiled chambers, with their long rows of diamond-paned lattices, have an old-world, haunted air: in his travels he has collected stores of articles of *vertu*, which are well and tastefully disposed in his panelled or tap-estried rooms: I have seen there one or two pictures, and one or two pieces of statuary which many an aristocratic connoisseur might have envied.

When I and Frances have dined and spent an evening with Hunsden, he often walks home with us. His wood is large, and some of the timber is old and of huge growth. There are winding ways in it which, pursued through glade and brake, make the walk back to Daisy Lane a somewhat long one. Many a time, when we have had the benefit of a full moon, and when the night has been mild and balmy, when, moreover, a certain nightingale has been singing, and a certain stream, hid in alders, has lent the song a soft accompaniment, the remote church-bell of the one hamlet in a district of ten miles, has tolled midnight ere the lord of the wood left us at our porch. Free-flowing was his talk at such hours, and far more quiet and gentle than in the daytime and before numbers. He would then forget politics and discussion, and would dwell on the past times of his house, on his family history, on himself and his own feelings – subjects each and all invested with a peculiar zest, for they were each and all unique. One glorious night in June, after I had been taunting him about his ideal bride and asking him when she would come and graft her foreign beauty on the old Hunsden oak, he answered suddenly –

'You call her ideal; but see, here is her shadow; and there cannot be a shadow without a substance.'

He had led us from the depth of the 'winding way' into a glade from whence the beeches withdrew, leaving it open to the sky; an unclouded moon poured her light into this glade, and Hunsden held out under her beam an ivory miniature.

Frances, with eagerness, examined it first; then she gave it to me – still, however, pushing her little face close to mine, and seeking in my eyes what I thought of the portrait. I thought it represented a very handsome and very individual-looking female face, with, as he had once said, 'straight and harmonious features'. It was dark; the hair, raven-black, swept not only from the brow, but from the temples – seemed thrust away carelessly, as if such beauty dispensed with, nay, despised arrangement. The Italian eye looked straight into you, and an independent, determined eye it was; the mouth was as firm as fine; the chin ditto. On the back of the miniature was gilded 'Lucia'.

'That is a real head,' was my conclusion.

Hunsden smiled.

'I think so,' he replied. 'All was real in Lucia.'

'And she was somebody you would have liked to marry – but could not?'

'I should certainly have liked to marry her, and that I *have* not done so is a proof that I *could* not.'

He repossessed himself of the miniature, now again in Frances' hand, and put it away.

'What do *you* think of it?' he asked of my wife, as he buttoned his coat over it.

'I am sure Lucia once wore chains and broke them,' was the strange answer. 'I do not mean matrimonial chains,' she added, correcting herself, as if she feared misinterpretation, 'but social chains of some sort. The face is that of one who has made an effort, and a successful and triumphant effort, to wrest some vigorous and valued faculty from insupportable constraint; and when Lucia's faculty got free, I am certain it spread wide pinions and carried her higher than –' she hesitated.

'Than what?' demanded Hunsden.

'Than "les convenances" permitted you to follow.'

'I think you grow spiteful – impertinent.'

'Lucia has trodden the stage,' continued Frances. 'You never seriously thought of marrying her; you admired her originality, her fearlessness, her energy of body and mind; you delighted in her talent, whatever that was, whether song, dance, or dramatic representation; you worshipped her beauty, which was of the sort after your own heart: but I am sure she filled a sphere from whence you would never have thought of taking a wife.'

'Ingenious,' remarked Hunsden; 'whether true or not is another question. Meantime, don't you feel your little lamp of a spirit wax very pale, beside such a girandole as Lucia's?'

'Yes.'

'Candid, at least; and the Professor will soon be dissatisfied with the dim light you give?'

'Will you, monsieur?'

'My sight was always too weak to endure a blaze, Frances,' and we had now reached the wicket.

I said, a few pages back, that this is a sweet summer evening; it is – there has been a series of lovely days, and this is the loveliest; the hay is just carried from my fields, its perfume still lingers in the air. Frances proposed to me, an hour or two since, to take tea out on the lawn; I see the round table, loaded with china, placed under a certain beech; Hunsden is expected – nay, I hear he is come – there is his voice, laying down the law on some point with authority; that of Frances replies; she opposes him, of course. They are disputing about Victor, of whom Hunsden affirms that his mother is making a milksop. Mrs Crimsworth retaliates:–

'Better a thousand times he should be a milksop than what he, Hunsden, calls "a fine lad"; and, moreover, she says that if Hunsden were to become a fixture in the neighbourhood, and were not a mere comet, coming and going, no one knows how, when, where, or why, she should be quite uneasy till she had got Victor away to a school at least a hundred miles off; for that with his mutinous maxims and unpractical dogmas, he would ruin a score of children.'

I have a word to say of Victor ere I shut this manuscript in my desk – but it must be a brief one, for I hear the tinkle of silver on porcelain.

Victor is as little of a pretty child as I am of a handsome man, or his mother of a fine woman; he is pale and spare, with large eyes, as dark as those of Frances, and as deeply set as mine. His shape is symmetrical enough, but slight; his health is good. I never saw a child smile less than he does, nor one who knits such a formidable brow when sitting over a book that interests him, or while listening to tales of adventure, peril, or wonder, narrated by his mother, Hunsden, or myself. But though still, he is not unhappy – though serious, not morose; he has a suscept-ibility to pleasurable sensations almost too keen, for it amounts to enthusiasm. He learned to read in the old-fashioned way out of a spelling-book at his mother's knee and as he got on without driving by that method, she thought it unnecessary to buy him ivory letters, or to try any of the other inducements to learning now deemed indispensable. When he could read, he became a glutton of books, and is so still. His toys have been few, and he has never wanted more. For those he possesses, he seems to have contracted a partiality amounting to affection; this feeling, directed towards one or two living animals of the house, strengthens almost to a passion.

Mr Hunsden gave him a mastiff cub, which he called Yorke, after the donor; it grew to a superb dog, whose fierceness, however, was much modified by the companionship and caresses of its young master. He would go nowhere, do nothing without Yorke; Yorke lay at his feet while he learned his lessons, played with him in the garden, walked with him in the lane and wood, sat near his chair at meals, was fed always by his own hand, was the first thing he sought in the morning, the last he left at night. Yorke accompanied Mr Hunsden one day to X—, and was bitten in the street by a dog in a rabid state. As soon as Hunsden had brought him home, and had informed me of the circumstance, I went into the yard and shot him where he lay licking his wound: he was dead in an instant; he had not seen me level the gun; I stood behind him. I had scarcely been ten minutes in the house, when my ear was struck with sounds of anguish: I repaired to the yard once more, for they proceeded thence. Victor was kneeling beside his dead mastiff, bent over it, embracing its bull-like neck, and lost in a passion of the wildest woe: he saw me.

'Oh, papa, I'll never forgive you! I'll never forgive you!' was his exclamation. 'You shot Yorke – I saw it from the window. I never believed you could be so cruel – I can love you no more!'

I had much ado to explain to him, with a steady voice, the stern necessity of the deed; he still, with that inconsolable and bitter accent which I cannot render, but which pierced my heart, repeated –

'He might have been cured – you should have tried – you should have burnt the wound with a hot iron, or covered it with caustic. You gave no time; and now it is too late – he is dead!'

He sank fairly down on the senseless carcase; I waited patiently a long while, till his grief had somewhat exhausted him; and then I lifted him in my arms and carried him to his mother, sure that she would comfort him best. She had witnessed the whole scene from a window; she would not come out for fear of increasing my difficulties by her emotion, but she was ready now to receive him. She took him to her kind heart, and on to her gentle lap; consoled him but with her lips, her eyes, her soft embrace, for some time; and then, when his sobs diminished, told him that Yorke had felt no pain in dying, and that if he had been left to expire naturally, his end would have been most horrible; above all, she told him that I was not cruel (for that idea seemed to give exquisite pain to poor Victor), that it was my affection for Yorke and him which had made me act so, and that I was now almost heartbroken to see him weep thus bitterly.

Victor would have been no true son of his father had these considerations, these reasons, breathed in so low, so sweet a tone – married to caresses so benign, so tender – to looks so inspired with pitying sympathy – produced no effect on him. They did produce an effect: he grew calmer, rested his face on her shoulder, and lay still in her arms. Looking up, shortly, he asked his mother to tell him over again what she had said about Yorke having suffered no pain, and my not being cruel; the balmy words being repeated, he again pillowed his cheek on her breast, and was again tranquil.

Some hours after, he came to me in my library, asked if I forgave him, and desired to be reconciled. I drew the lad to my side, and there I kept him a good while, and had much talk with him, in the course of which he disclosed many points of feeling and thought I approved of in my son. I found, it is true, few elements of the 'good fellow' or the 'fine fellow' in him; scant sparkles of the spirit which loves to flash over the wine cup, or which kindles the passions to a destroying fire; but I saw in the soil of his heart healthy and swelling germs of compassion, affection, fidelity. I discovered in the garden of his intellect a rich growth of wholesome principles – reason, justice, moral courage, promised, if not blighted, a fertile bearing. So I bestowed on his large forehead, and on his cheek – still pale with tears – a proud and contented kiss, and sent him away comforted. Yet I saw him the next day laid on the mound under which Yorke had been buried, his face covered with his hands; he was melancholy for some weeks, and more than a year elapsed before he would listen to any proposal of having another dog.

Victor learns fast. He must soon go to Eton, where, I suspect, his first year or two will be utter wretchedness: to leave me, his mother, and his home, will give his heart an agonized wrench; then, the fagging will not suit him – but emulation, thirst after knowledge, the glory of success, will stir and reward him in time. Meantime, I feel in myself a strong repugnance to fix the hour which will uproot my sole olive branch, and transplant it far from me; and, when I speak to Frances on the subject, I am heard with a kind of patient pain, as though I alluded to some fearful operation, at which her nature shudders, but from which her fortitude will not permit her to recoil. The step must, however, be taken, and it *shall* be; for, though Frances will not make a milksop of her son, she will accustom him to a style of treatment, a forbearance, a congenial tenderness, he will meet with from none else. She sees, as I also see, a something in Victor's temper – a kind of electrical ardour and power – which emits, now and then, ominous sparks; Hunsden calls it his spirit, and says it should not be curbed. I call it the leaven of the offending Adam, and consider that it should be, if not *whipped* out of him, at least soundly disciplined; and that he will be cheap of any amount of either bodily or mental suffering which will ground him radically in the art of self-control. Frances gives this *something* in her son's marked character no name; but when it appears in the grinding of his teeth, in the glittering of his eye, in the fierce revolt of feeling against disappointment, mischance, sudden sorrow, or supposed injustice, she folds him to her breast, or takes him to walk with her alone in the wood; then she reasons with him like any philosopher, and to reason Victor is ever accessible; then she looks at him with eyes of love, and by love Victor can be infallibly subjugated; but will reason or love be the weapons with which in future the world will meet his violence? Oh, no! for that flash in his black eye – for that cloud on his bony brow – for that compression of his statuesque lips, the lad will some day get blows instead of blandishments – kicks instead of kisses; then for the fit of mute fury which will sicken his body and madden his soul; then for the ordeal of merited and salutary suffering, out of which he will come (I trust) a wiser and a better man.

I see him now; he stands by Hunsden, who is seated on the lawn under the beech; Hunsden's hand rests on the boy's collar, and he is instilling God knows what principles into his ear. Victor looks well just now, for he listens with a sort of smiling interest; he never looks so like his mother as when he smiles – pity the sunshine breaks out so rarely! Victor has a preference for Hunsden, full as strong as I deem desirable, being considerably more potent, decided, and indiscriminating than any I ever entertained for that personage myself. Frances, too, regards it with a sort of unexpressed anxiety; while her son leans on Hunsden's knee, or rests against his shoulder, she roves with restless movement round, like a dove guarding its young from a hovering hawk; she says she wishes Hunsden had children of his own, for then he would better know the danger of inciting their pride and indulging their foibles.

Frances approaches my library window; puts aside the honeysuckle which half covers it, and tells me tea is ready; seeing that

I continue busy she enters the room, comes near me quietly, and puts her hand on my shoulder.

'Monsieur est trop appliqué.'

'I shall soon have done.'

She draws a chair near, and sits down to wait till I have finished; her presence is as pleasant to my mind as the perfume of the fresh hay and spicy flowers, as the glow of the westering sun, as the repose of the midsummer eve are to my senses.

But Hunsden comes; I hear his step, and there he is, bending through the lattice, from which he has thrust away the woodbine with unsparing hand, disturbing two bees and a butterfly.

'Crimsworth! I say, Crimsworth! take that pen out of his hand, mistress, and make him lift up his head.'

'Well, Hunsden? I hear you.'

'I was at X— yesterday! your brother Ned is getting richer than Crœsus by railway speculations; they call him in the Piece Hall a stag of ten, and I have heard from Brown. M. and Madame Vandenhuten and Jean Baptiste talk of coming to see you next month. He mentions the Pelets too; he says their domestic harmony is not the finest in the world, but in business they are doing "on ne peut mieux", which circumstance, he concludes, will be a sufficient consolation to both for any little crosses in the affections. Why don't you invite the Pelets to —shire, Crimsworth? I should so like to see your first flame, Zoraïde. Mistress, don't be jealous, but he loved that lady to distraction; I know it for a fact. Brown says she weighs twelve stones now; you see what you've lost, Mr Professor. Now, Monsieur and Madame, if you don't come to tea, Victor and I will begin without you.'

'Papa, come!'

THE END